—THE—
RAILWAY
HERITAGE
—OF—
BRITAIN

THE
RAILWAY

HERITAGE
· OF ·
BRITAIN

150 YEARS OF RAILWAY ARCHITECTURE
AND ENGINEERING

GORDON BIDDLE AND O.S. NOCK

WITH OTHER CONTRIBUTORS

MICHAEL JOSEPH
LONDON

First published in Great Britain by
Michael Joseph Ltd.,
44 Bedford Square,
London WC1B 3DU,
1983.

© Copyright 1983 Sheldrake Press Ltd.
Designed and produced in association with the
British Railways Board by Sheldrake
Press Ltd., 188 Cavendish Road, London
SW12 0DA.

Editor: Simon Rigge

Picture Editors: Karin Hills, Eleanor Lines

Art Direction and Book Design:
Ivor Claydon, Bob Hook

Deputy Editor: Jane Havell

Assistant Editors: Mike Brown,
Diana Dubens

Picture Researcher: Deirdre McGarry

Editorial Assistants: Annabel Lloyd,
Christine Radula-Scott, Sally Weatherill

Production Manager: Bob Christie

Typesetting by SX Composing Ltd.
Colour origination by Lithospeed Ltd.

Printed and bound in Spain by
Printer Industria Grafica,
Barcelona.
DLB 11708 - 1983

ISBN 07181 2355 7

AUTHORS AND CONTRIBUTORS

GORDON BIDDLE is the author of six books on British railway architecture, canals and waterways. In this book he wrote most of the Eastern, London Midland and Western Regions as well as the biographical profiles and other text, and acted as editorial adviser.

O. S. NOCK was formerly Chief Mechanical Engineer of the Westinghouse Brake and Signal Company. He is the author of more than 100 books on railways in Britain and overseas. In this book he was responsible for the regional introductions, railway company profiles and other text on railway operation.

MARTIN ROBERTSON is a Principal Inspector of Ancient Monuments and Historic Buildings for the Department of the Environment which is responsible for listing in England. He wrote many of the entries on bridges and viaducts in England and Wales, and some of those on stations in the Southern Region.

JOHN R. HUME is Senior Lecturer in Economic History at the University of Strathclyde and author of several books on Scottish history and industrial archaeology. In this book he wrote most of the Scottish Region.

JEOFFRY SPENCE was for 25 years Editor of the *Journal of the Railway and Canal Historical Society* and is the author of several books on steam railways. In this book he wrote most of the Southern Region.

HISTORICAL ADVISER

JACK SIMMONS is Emeritus Professor of History at the University of Leicester and author of numerous books on British railway history. He gave invaluable help in selecting the contents of this book and commenting on individual entries.

THE RAILWAY HERITAGE OF BRITAIN is an official publication of the British Railways Board. The authors and editors wish to offer their thanks to the Board, in particular to Bernard Kaukas, Director – Environment, without whose support the book could not have been published.

The Board's positive policy on conservation and environmental improvement dates back to 1977 when Sir Peter Parker appointed Bernard Kaukas to the specially created post of Director – Environment. At the same time a panel was set up with the following eminent advisers as its members:

David McKenna (Chairman), former General Manager, Southern Region and Board Member;
The Viscount Esher, former Rector, Royal College of Art;
The Lord Reilly, former Director, Design Council;
Sir Hugh Casson, President, Royal Academy;
Michael Middleton, Director, Civic Trust;
George Stewart, former Chief Commissioner, Land and Forests, Scotland;
Elizabeth Chesterton, town planner.

They are supported by the present members of the British Railways Board and heads of departments.

As the book illustrates, the Board's efforts have already produced noticeable improvements to many historic railway buildings. The background to this programme and the policy for the next phase of conservation are discussed by Bernard Kaukas on pages 25-28.

First endpaper: Eastern approaches to Newcastle Central station, 1890s.
Last endpaper: Bridge over River Amber, Ambergate, 1849.
Frontispiece: Western trainshed of Liverpool Street station, c.1905.
This page: Ribblehead Viaduct on the Settle & Carlisle Railway, 1975.

FOREWORD

In 1981 the Secretary of State for the Environment decided that the record of the rich heritage of historic buildings in the care of his own department should be available in published form, and the first volume has been completed and issued by the Property Services Agency.

The Secretary of State suggested that others might follow this example and, conscious of the interest and variety of British Rail's heritage in this field, we were delighted to respond.

Here then is the unique architectural record of British achievement embodying the confident and pioneering spirit of the Railway Age which, a century and more later, still forms the environment for a busy, working, modern railway.

SIR PETER PARKER

CONTENTS

HOW TO USE THIS BOOK
page 6

INTRODUCTION
page 7

EASTERN REGION
page 11

SPLENDOURS AND MISERIES OF
BRITISH RAIL'S
ARCHITECTURAL HERITAGE
page 25

LONDON MIDLAND REGION
page 57

SCOTTISH REGION
page 121

SOUTHERN REGION
page 175

WESTERN REGION
page 211

GLOSSARY OF TERMS
page 246

APPENDIX
BRITISH RAIL'S LISTED
BUILDINGS
page 249

PICTURE CREDITS
page 253

ACKNOWLEDGEMENTS
page 254

INDEX
page 255

HOW TO USE THIS BOOK

There are two ways to use this illustrated guide. If you know the name of the place you want to find, consult the index. If not, use the locator map on this page and select the area you are interested in.

Counties and Scottish local government regions are grouped geographically into areas such as South Midlands or Eastern Counties and keyed with page numbers to the sections of the book in which they are covered.

The gazetteer, which takes up most of the book, is divided into five sections representing the operating regions of British Rail: Eastern, London Midland, Scottish, Southern and Western. In keeping with the practice adopted for office circulars when the railways were nationalised in 1948, the regions are organised alphabetically. The region title appears in the running headline of each left-hand page, the name of the group of counties at the head of each right-hand page.

All regions except Scottish start with London and work outwards. As a result London is divided into four sections. You will find Liverpool Street, Kings Cross and Fenchurch Street stations at the beginning of Eastern Region; Euston, St. Pancras and Marylebone at the beginning of London Midland; Cannon Street, Charing Cross, Victoria and Waterloo in Southern, and Paddington in Western Region.

Reflecting the history of railway operation, North Wales appears in London Midland and South Wales in Western Region. Regional divisions occasionally cut across counties, in which case there is an entry for the county in both the appropriate regions. Northern Ireland's railways do not form part of the British railway system and are therefore excluded.

A detailed map is provided at the beginning of each region. It is marked with the locations of all sites for which entries are provided in the book, except where they fall in big cities, in which case the city name only is given.

All major Inter-City lines are shown on the detailed maps with such other lines as are required to mark items in the book. Defunct routes are shown by broken lines.

Contents lists at the beginning of each region give page references for the relevant counties. Entries are arranged alphabetically within counties, which are themselves organised geographically according to their distance from London or the Scottish border.

Each entry begins with italic text giving the date the building was erected or the line opened, the name of the original operating or construction company, the architect or engineer where known, and information about listing, operation and location.

Buildings in England and Wales which have been listed by the Department of the Environment as being of Special Architectural or Historic Interest are graded I, II* and II in order of the official assessment of their importance. In Scotland they are graded A, B and C(S) – the (S) stands for statutory and indicates those C-grade buildings which are protected by law. Some items are scheduled as Ancient Monuments by the Historic Monuments Commission.

The legend 'closed' indicates that a line or building is no longer in British Rail use; 'sold' that it has passed out of British Rail ownership. A station described as sold but not closed is one

where the platforms are used by trains but the station building is privately occupied. A building may also be let for private occupation yet remain in British Rail ownership.

Where a building's location is not immediately obvious, the italic text states which line it is on or which stations it falls between. In the most obscure cases, an Ordnance Survey grid reference or a street name is provided.

All the sites described in the book have been visited and recorded at different times, but the authors and editors cannot guarantee that every entry precisely describes the features of

the building as it is today. Because the photographs provide an important record, they have been labelled with the date or approximate date on which they were taken.

The fact that a building has been included in the book does not necessarily mean it can be visited; it may be on private property.

Technical terms have been kept to a minimum. Those that are used are defined in the illustrated glossary on pages 246-48.

For ease of reference, the full list of British Rail's listed buildings is given in the Appendix on pages 249-53.

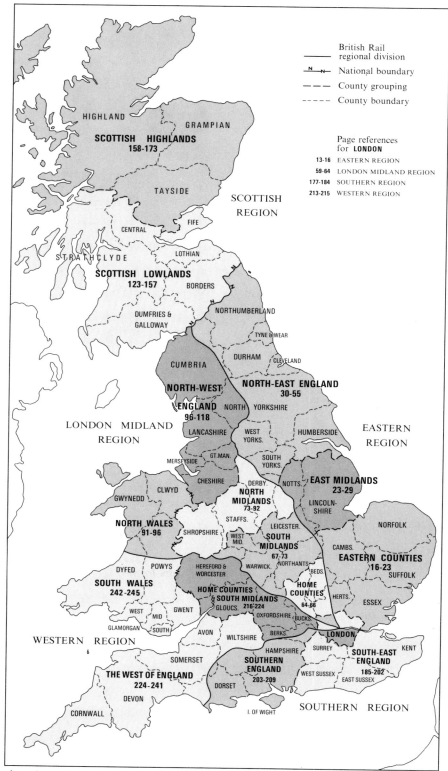

British Rail regional division
National boundary
County grouping
County boundary

Page references for LONDON
13-16 EASTERN REGION
59-64 LONDON MIDLAND REGION
177-184 SOUTHERN REGION
213-215 WESTERN REGION

INTRODUCTION

In July 1850 a grand banquet was held on the platform of Newcastle Central station to celebrate the completion of the East Coast route from London to Edinburgh. The guest of honour was Robert Stephenson. Beneath the high vaulted glass and iron roof of the trainshed he rose to congratulate the men who under his direction had built the final engineering works: the High Level Bridge over the Tyne, the Royal Border Bridge across the Tweed and the trainshed of the station itself, shortly to be opened by Queen Victoria.

These were pioneering structures built with what was then the latest technology and an unlimited supply of cheap labour, men prepared to live on the job in appalling conditions and yet capable of producing generally high standards of workmanship. This quality has been proved over more than a century by the relatively small amount of rebuilding found necessary, and some of the earliest bridges now carry far heavier loads than their designers ever envisaged.

Those across the Tyne and Tweed are only two notable examples. Throughout the British Isles scores of similar monuments survive from the same period, the age of the Crystal Palace and the Great Exhibition of 1851 in Hyde Park. There, too, Queen Victoria performed the opening ceremony and a great banquet was held beneath a soaring iron and glass roof. More than six million people came to marvel at the arts and manufactures of all the nations. At least 160,000 of them travelled to London on special rail excursions organised by Thomas Cook – a powerful demonstration of the possibilities of mass travel on the new network.

The Great Exhibition is history now, but much of the infrastructure of the railways is still in use for its original purpose, an open-air exhibition which is there to be admired if we only know what we are seeing.

To many people a station is a place to catch a train, a bridge or viaduct no more than a means of crossing a valley, a tunnel an unwelcome interruption to the scenery. We hope this book will demonstrate that railway buildings are much more than that.

Major stations such as Bristol Temple Meads, Paddington, St. Pancras or Huddersfield can be ranked with the great country houses, cathedrals and public buildings of Britain. The architects who designed them belonged to some of the great practices of the day. Charing Cross Hotel, for example, was the work of Edward M. Barry, younger son of Sir Charles Barry who built the Houses of Parliament. The hotel at St. Pancras was the creation of Sir George Gilbert Scott, known also for the Albert Memorial in Hyde Park.

Civil engineering breakthroughs such as Isambard Kingdom Brunel's Royal Albert Bridge over the Tamar at Saltash, Robert Stephenson's Britannia tubular bridge over the Menai Strait or the later Forth Railway Bridge can be compared with such landmarks of mechanical engineering as James Watt's separate condenser for the steam engine, the first large iron ship, Brunel's *Great Britain*, or Charles Parsons' steam turbine. Making the attendant tunnels, cuttings, embankments and trackside buildings formed one of the greatest construction projects ever undertaken in Britain, changing the face of the country faster and more completely than anything before.

John Ruskin was prompted to castigate this revolutionary upheaval in a famous passage directed against the new breed of railway promoters: 'There was a rocky valley between Buxton and Bakewell, once upon a time, divine as the Vale of Tempe; you might have seen the Gods there morning and evening – Apollo and all the sweet Muses of the light – walking in fair procession on the lawns of it, and to and fro among the pinnacles of its crags. You cared neither for Gods nor grass, but for cash (which you did not know the way to get); you thought you could get it by what *The Times* calls "Railroad Enterprise". You Enterprised a Railroad through the valley – you blasted its rocks away, heaped thousands of tons of shale into its lovely stream. The valley is gone, and the Gods with it; and now, every fool in Buxton can be at Bakewell in half-an-hour, and every fool in Bakewell at Buxton; which you think a lucrative process of exchange – you Fools Everywhere.'

Although landowners and, sometimes, the railways themselves could and did insist on architectural embellishments to stations, bridges and

A 1901 lithograph captures the bustle of Charing Cross station when it was still the gateway to the Continent.

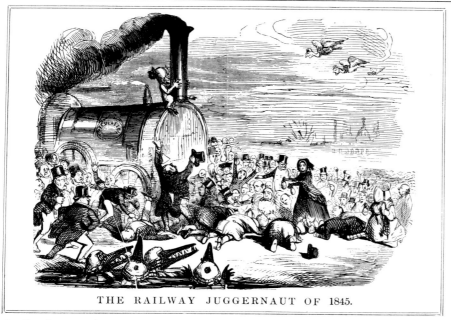

THE RAILWAY JUGGERNAUT OF 1845.

In a Punch *cartoon, the citizens of England surrender their savings to the Juggernaut of railway speculation.*

tunnel portals to minimise the damage to the environment – to the ultimate benefit of all of us – the process of railway building was unstoppable. By the end of the 19th century the British network had some 19,000 miles of track, 9,000 stations, 60,000 bridges, 1,000 tunnels, hundreds of viaducts, and trackside buildings ranging from warehouses and engine sheds to signal boxes and crossing keepers' cottages. By far the largest proportion of what remains, now an accepted and even valued part of the landscape, is still in the ownership of British Rail. The intention of this book, published on the initiative and with the full backing of the British Railways Board, is to describe and illustrate a broad selection.

The most prolific architects and engineers are introduced in the text. So, too, are the railway companies which commissioned them and thereby established distinctive styles in building that complemented the liveries of their engines and trains and emphasised their competitive individuality.

Britain was exceptional in Europe for its *laissez-faire* approach to railway building. Between the years 1844 and 1847, often known as the period of Railway Mania, scores of speculative companies sprang up to build lines over short and long distances. Many collapsed without completing a yard of track. Those that survived sometimes wastefully duplicated routes and services in efforts to outdo their rivals. As late as 1922, the railways of

Britain were still owned by well over 100 different companies. The Grouping imposed by the government in 1923 brought all of them (except the London underground railways and a few very small lines) into four companies – the London Midland & Scottish, the London & North Eastern, the Great Western and the Southern Railways – and a quarter of a century later they were reduced to one: the nationalised British Railways, set up under the 1947 Transport Act which came into effect on 1st January, 1948. The name British Rail was introduced in 1962.

Today's rail traveller may be forgiven if he is unaware that the lines he traverses were built not by British Rail but by numerous individual companies. Many distinguishing features of the original railway companies such as signboards, furniture and canopies have gone from the stations; engine sheds, coaling plants, distinctive signals and signal boxes have gone from the lineside. Similarly, the main trunk road from London to Glasgow (the M1 and M6 motorways and the A74 north of Carlisle) was built between 1958 and 1974 in a number of different sections (still distinguishable to an observant eye by the different styles of bridges and landscaping). Yet the motorist has already long forgotten how he once drove between one section and the next and thinks of it now as a single route.

Standardization has settled on the railways. And yet, has it? Not quite.

It is still possible to recognise the work of the different architects and engineers. You can tell where one contract changed to another, even on an electrified line such as the West Coast route to Scotland where many of the overbridges have been rebuilt, the underbridges disfigured by power gantries, the stations rebuilt or altered for high-speed running, their canopies cut back or removed to keep the metalwork a safe distance from the overhead wires.

The West Coast route originally consisted of the nine lines shown in the table (*opposite page*). Of these, seven were envisaged as trunk lines from the outset, while the two short lines between Warrington and Wigan were built by small local companies that were quickly swallowed up by their larger neighbours, although their lines remained bottlenecks for many years afterwards.

Some of the features to look out for are the heavy cornices used by Robert Stephenson on his bridges and tunnels, and the elaborately rusticated voussoirs (or wedge-shaped stones) on Locke's arches. Vignoles on his part of the line gave a very different kind of treatment to the stonework of the retaining walls of bridges and cuttings, building with carefully squared stones of different sizes. The Jacobean treatment of the few surviving buildings on the Trent Valley line, designed by J. W. Livock, is in marked contrast with Sir William Tite's more robust Tudor north of Lancaster and his Scottish baronial on the Caledonian Railway. In many places local stone is used, much of it quarried from cuttings and tunnels along the way.

In the choice of routes, too, there are clues. The most striking contrast is between the work of the great engineers Robert Stephenson and Joseph Locke. Stephenson on his line decided to go straight and level, tunnelling through the hills; Locke, on the other hand, avoided tunnels, believing that the locomotives of the 1840s were powerful enough to master steep gradients. As a result, the southern part of the route in the much gentler terrain between London and Stafford has eight tunnels while Locke's part north of Lancaster, incorporating Shap and Beattock summits, has none and is by no means straight.

A book called *The Railway Heritage of Britain* should strictly speaking present the railway system as it is today with both modern and traditional equipment suitably balanced. A heritage after all is what is handed down from one generation to another and so the new stations at Euston and Birmingham New Street are as much a part of it as the rebuilt Waterloo of 1921 or anything earlier.

But just as we take for granted the concrete bridges, flyovers and sophisticated interchanges which are part of the motorway heritage, so we pay scant attention to the stations, signalling centres and other fixed railway equipment designed in the modern idiom. Time is needed before anyone can make a proper appreciation of what has been built. We have therefore selected 1939 as the concluding date for the book, and have made no attempt to assess the work of railway architects and engineers in the post-war years.

For many reasons the book deals mainly with the 19th century: first, because that is when most railways were built; and second, because the official listing of Buildings of Special Architectural or Historic Interest is very selective in the 20th century.

The book's main aim is to describe British Rail's 600-odd listed buildings, which include not only stations, viaducts and bridges but also hotels, memorials, gateways and ancient monuments ranging from a Roman governor's palace to tank traps and pill boxes from the Second World War. Listing began in 1947 under the 1945 Town and Country Planning Act, and is carried out by the Department of the Environment using selection criteria laid down by the Historic Buildings Council. It confers strong protection against demolition and alteration. One of the principal criteria used to decide whether to list a building is its age: more recent buildings are thus in a minority. Until 1982 listing was restricted to the period before 1914; it now ends, like the book, at 1939.

In order to provide a fair cross-section of building types throughout the country we have added a number of non-listed buildings (many of which happen to be protected in Conservation Areas) and a number that are listed but no longer owned by British Rail. Some of these additions are comparable in architectural quality and historical importance with buildings already listed, others such as viaducts and tunnels have been included for their unusual technical or engineering interest.

We have, on the other hand, excluded certain topics from our scope. We have, for example, made no attempt to guide or influence conservation policy. Our inclusion of non-listed items does not imply that we think they should be listed: that is a decision which rests with the Department of the Environment and the Scottish and Welsh Offices. Equally we have not tried to give a systematic survey of preserved locomotives and rolling stock, an aspect of the railway heritage that has been very well covered by other publications. Nor have we provided more than incidental coverage of topographical features such as cuttings or embankments or the design of the track, confining ourselves to what might, for want of a better word, be termed structures.

Our goal has been historical: to present the story of the British railway system as it can still be seen and appreciated through its engineering and architectural heritage.

No one who travels by rail can fail to notice that he is using an old form of land transport, the first in fact to offer an advance on horse power. The trains may be modern or relatively so, but neon signs, petrol stations and all the clutter and ribbon development associated with the ubiquitous motor car are comparatively absent along the railway lines. The countryside very often comes up to the tracks, the scene is more pastoral, still recognisably the world portrayed by the early railway artists such as J. C. Bourne, A. F. Tait and many others, in which sheep grazed beneath the viaducts and the carriage-borne gentry travelled out to admire the ornamental tunnel portals and the steam horses of the iron roads.

Even in the cities the railways usually approach the stations against a backdrop of old mills and warehouses, some still bearing enamel or wooden advertising signs, all mixed up with Victorian terraces displaying their backyards and too often awaiting the demolition contractor. Here we scent the Victorian underworld of Doré, Mayhew and Dickens.

If this is a form of antiquarianism we make no apology for it. It is part of an interest in history, a continuous process that on the railways goes back beyond the opening of the first all-steam passenger and freight line, the Liverpool & Manchester in 1830, to the horse-drawn colliery tramways of the 18th century, and comes up to date with the inauguration of the Inter-City 125s, the battle for traffic with the lorry, bus and car, and the rising tide of interest in our industrial heritage.

Station	Railway Company	Date	Engineer
London Euston	London & Birmingham	1838	R. Stephenson
Rugby	Trent Valley	1847	R. Stephenson & G. P. Bidder
Stafford	Grand Junction	1838	J. Locke
Warrington	Warrington & Newton	1831	R. Stephenson
Newton	Wigan Branch	1832	C. B. Vignoles
Wigan	North Union	1838	C. B. Vignoles
Preston	Lancaster & Preston Junction	1840	J. Locke & J. E. Errington
Lancaster	Lancaster & Carlisle	1846	J. Locke & J. E. Errington
Carlisle	Caledonian Railway	1848	J. Locke & J. E. Errington
Glasgow			

Each railway company in this table built the line northwards from the station beside which it is listed.

EASTERN REGION

CONTENTS

LONDON: PAGE 13   **EASTERN COUNTIES:** ESSEX PAGE 16   CAMBRIDGESHIRE PAGE 18

HERTFORDSHIRE (PART) PAGE 19   SUFFOLK PAGE 20   NORFOLK PAGE 22

EAST MIDLANDS: NOTTINGHAMSHIRE (PART) PAGE 23

LINCOLNSHIRE PAGE 23   **NORTH-EAST ENGLAND:** HUMBERSIDE PAGE 30   SOUTH YORKSHIRE PAGE 32

WEST YORKSHIRE PAGE 32   NORTH YORKSHIRE (PART) PAGE 37   CLEVELAND PAGE 41   DURHAM PAGE 42

TYNE & WEAR PAGE 44   NORTHUMBERLAND PAGE 51

Behind the burning remains of a partly demolished wool mill, the Paddock Viaduct carries the Penistone branch 70 feet above the Colne Valley in Huddersfield.

The Eastern Region of British Rail runs from London to the Scottish border, taking in the Eastern Counties, parts of the East Midlands and the whole of North-East England. In keeping with the history of the railways, which grew first in the north country and later put out tentacles to London, the regional headquarters is at York, the old power centre of the 'Railway King' George Hudson (*p.38*), whose slogan was 'Mak' all t'railways cum t'York'.

The region was formerly operated by the London & North Eastern Railway, one of the Big Four companies created at the Grouping of 1923 (*p.8*) and itself an amalgamation of five earlier companies. The Southern Area of the LNER incorporated the 'Three Greats': the Great Eastern Railway, the Great Northern Railway and the Great Central Railway.

The great curving trainshed at York in the 1890s, still with its original glass lanterns, offers a vista uninterrupted by the footbridge built later to join the platforms. The design of the roof is based on that of Newcastle-upon-Tyne, built 27 years earlier.

The North Eastern Area included the North Eastern Railway and the Hull & Barnsley Railway.

Significant parts of all these old lines remain, with the exception of the Great Central which has virtually disappeared. Formerly the Manchester Sheffield & Lincolnshire Railway, the Great Central was set up in 1897 to construct the London Extension line between Nottingham and Quainton Road Junction in Buckinghamshire, with access to London via the Metropolitan Railway. This superfluous and expensive line so weakened the company that it never paid a dividend on its ordinary shares. Since nationalisation, once-competitive routes have been closed and in the Eastern Region the only major remnant of the company's network is the eastern part of the line between Sheffield and Grimsby.

In the south, the whole of East Anglia was served by the Great Eastern Railway from its terminus at Liverpool Street, while on the Great Northern Kings Cross was the start-ing point for the fast East Coast route to Scotland. Both lines once carried large tonnages of coal from South Yorkshire and Nottinghamshire to London and the Eastern Counties; the Great Northern specialised in conveying bricks from Peterborough to London for the building trade.

In addition, both companies, along with the Great Central, had a large seasonal traffic in fish, particularly from Hull, Grimsby and Yarmouth. Grimsby, originally developed by the Manchester Sheffield & Lincolnshire Railway, became the greatest fishing port in Europe. The Great Eastern was similarly responsible for creating Lowestoft as a railway port.

Among the old companies the Great Eastern probably had the most diverse traffic. It handled so much farm produce that at railway centres used by several companies the Great Eastern's trains were always nick-named 'Sweedy'. In the expanding suburbs of East London, its organi-sation and handling of commuter traffic from about 1915 onwards was

11

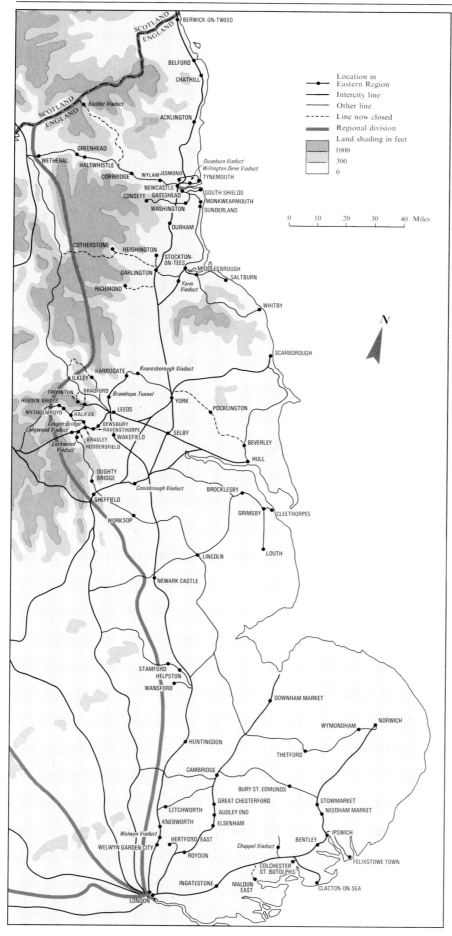

Location in Eastern Region
Intercity line
Other line
Line now closed
Regional division
Land shading in feet
1000
300
0

0   10   20   30   40 Miles

N

masterly. An imaginative idea was the painting of carriage doors in bright colours to distinguish first, second and third-class compartments, giving rise to the affectionate nickname 'Jazz trains'. Passengers came to know exactly where their class of carriage would arrive at the platforms, so that station stops were counted in seconds. The Great Eastern also ran sumptuously appointed Continental Boat Expresses to Parkestone Quay at Harwich.

The Great Northern secured a permanent place in the public's affections with its passenger expresses from Kings Cross to Scotland. Later they became the named trains *Queen of Scots,* the all-Pullman express via Leeds and Harrogate, and the night trains *Aberdonian, Highlandman* and *Night Scotsman.* To the famous *Flying Scotsman* were added in the 1930s the high-speed streamlined trains *Silver Jubilee, Coronation* and *West Riding Limited.*

The North Eastern Railway was by far the largest of the pre-Grouping companies, with an annual turnover of some £10 million before 1914. It had the most historic associations: from 1860 it incorporated the oldest line in the country, the Stockton & Darlington, opened in 1825. By 1863 it also included the first railway built across England, the Newcastle & Carlisle, opened in 1835-39.

Although it participated in the East Coast traffic to Scotland and had fine stations at York, Darlington and Newcastle, the North Eastern was primarily a mineral line: in the last 20 years of its life it owned 2,000 locomotives, of which fewer than 150 could be regarded as top-line expresses for the passenger class. While some of this mineral traffic involved long hauls of coal from Co. Durham to London, by far the greater proportion consisted of short runs from collieries to ports on the north-east coast, from which coal was exported or conveyed to London by ship.

The development of the North Eastern in its most prosperous years was symbolized by the relocation of the headquarters of the locomotive department from Gateshead to a more spacious site on the outskirts of Darlington and the building of the fine new headquarters at York opposite the old station. The new office building was on so magnificent a scale that it was known locally as Buckingham Palace.

LONDON

BISHOPSGATE GOODS STATION

Built 1848-49 for Eastern Counties Railway. Architect Sancton Wood. Forecourt wall and gates listed Grade II. Shoreditch High Street, E.1.

Before the opening of Liverpool Street station, main-line trains from the eastern counties ran into a terminus at Shoreditch. Built in 1840 and later named

BISHOPSGATE IRON ENTRANCE GATE, 1980

Bishopsgate to make it seem closer to the City, it was rebuilt in 1848-49 by Sancton Wood and in the early 1860s was handling nearly four million passengers a year. When Liverpool Street opened in 1874-75, Bishopsgate became a goods station, but a disastrous fire in 1964 destroyed all but a fragment of the forecourt wall and the magnificent iron entrance gates.

CHADWELL HEATH COAL DUES OBELISK

Erected 1851. Listed Grade II. Alongside London-Ipswich-Norwich main line ten miles from Liverpool Street on boundary of Havering and Barking boroughs. Map ref. TQ 489878.

To make good the devastation of the Great Fire of 1666 the City of London

1981

ENGRAVING OF BISHOPSGATE STATION FROM A DRAWING BY DUNCAN, 1850

Corporation was empowered to levy a duty on coal and wine carried to any point within a 20-mile radius of the General Post Office in St. Martin's-le-Grand. Under an Act of 1851, when London and its transport had grown and multiplied many times over, boundary markers bearing the City arms and a citation of the Act were erected alongside roads, railways and waterways. In 1861 the boundaries were altered to coincide with the Metropolitan Police area and where necessary the markers were moved. The duty was abolished in 1889, but about 30 markers are still maintained by the City Corporation as historical monuments. There are four main types, of which one is this 14-foot-high obelisk.

FENCHURCH STREET

STATION. Built 1854 for London & Blackwall Railway. Engineer/architect George Berkeley. Front portion listed Grade II.

Fenchurch Street was the first station to be built in the City. Tucked away in a side street called Railway Place, it is nowadays the most modest and least known of the London termini.

The present building is the second, replacing the smaller original terminus which stood in the Minories, and was built to accommodate the trains of the London Tilbury & Southend Railway as well as those of the London & Blackwall. The London & Blackwall line ran trains from the west side of the station in competition with river traffic on the Thames, but it was never a great success. The guest company soon became far bigger than the host, and eventually under the successor companies set up in 1923 the thriving Tilbury and Southend service provided the bulk of the traffic. This disproportion grew until Fenchurch Street became unique as a terminus belonging to one

company (by then the LNER) but used by another (the LMS).

George Berkeley, Engineer of the London & Blackwall, erected a short segmental arched roof 110 feet wide which he carried forward to form a giant curved pediment over the facade – a technique popular on the Continent but rare in

1981

Great Britain. The tall serried windows interposed between pilasters in grey stock brick with stone embellishments lend the front a certain quiet dignity, and the standard zig-zag saw-toothed awning with which the Great Eastern replaced the original flat canopy adds an element of charm.

The trainshed stands on arches at first-floor level and passengers ascend to the platforms from the gloomy ground-floor ticket office by an ornate iron balustraded staircase.

WAREHOUSE. Built mid-19th century. Listed Grade II. 43-44 Crutched Friars.

Crutched Friars is a street passing diagonally beneath the station, where space was found for a three-storey warehouse in pink brick with yellow dressings. The top floor was used as railway offices.

KINGS CROSS

*Built 1852 for Great Northern Railway.
Architect Lewis Cubitt. Listed Grade I.*

The building of Kings Cross could be called a family affair. Lewis was the nephew of Sir William Cubitt, consulting engineer to the Great Northern, whose son Joseph, Lewis's cousin, was Chief Engineer. Lewis's design is at once simple and functional. Like Fenchurch Street, the facade reflects the profile of the train-shed behind it, but in a quite different way, for here it is merely a brick screen framing the ends of the twin-span roof. The only flourish is the Italianate clock tower between them.

The trainshed arches are semi-circular, 105 feet wide and 71 feet high, springing from stone corbels in the side walls and an elliptical arched arcade down the centre of the station. The ribs of the roof were originally of laminated timber, replaced later by wrought iron. Kings Cross has been called an engineer's station; all its elements are visible, whereas St. Pancras next door is all towers and spires. Sir John Betjeman described the two stations as the 'romance of Gothic and the romance of engineering . . . side by side'.

Kings Cross is a one-sided station with the main offices ranged along the original departure platform on the west side. When built, the front screen wall overlooked a pair of segmental arched arcades

LEWIS CUBITT, ARCHITECT

The Cubitts, who stemmed from Norfolk farming stock, were an engineering family of all the talents. Thomas and William founded the famous firm of contractors, and were joined by their brother Lewis (born in 1799) who had trained as an architect under H. E. Kendall. Their uncle William (later Sir William, *p.193*) and his son Joseph were engineers, both heavily involved with the construction of the Great Northern Railway, for which Lewis designed Kings Cross station and hotel. He was also the architect of Bricklayers Arms station, the original London terminus of the South Eastern and London & Croydon Railways of 1844. Another uncle, Benjamin, was the first locomotive superintendent of the Great Northern.

Lewis designed many of the non-railway buildings built by his brothers, notably those in Eaton Square and Lowndes Square in London.

on each side of the clock tower, to which a glass-and-iron *porte cochère* was later added. Later still there accumulated in front of the station a conglomeration of untidy wooden huts, kiosks and the Underground station entrance (long known to railwaymen as 'the native village'), which completely ruined the aspect. Thankfully, they have now gone, replaced by a new entrance and travel centre.

c.1853

Over the years the original two platforms separated by carriage sidings have increased to eight, while to the west outside the main building there are two **suburban platforms** (formerly six) lying partly beneath a separate glass roof. Until recently this suburban section included a connection from the Underground's Circle Line which climbed up through a sharply curved tunnel on a 1-in-35 gradient beneath Cubitt's Great Northern Hotel (built facing the west side of the station in 1854) and was known as the Hotel Curve. The line in the opposite

PACIFICS PREPARING TO LEAVE KINGS CROSS WITH HOLIDAY EXPRESSES, AUGUST 1934

direction descended through a separate tunnel on the east side from a detached platform named York Road. Through them suburban trains ran to Moorgate.

In steam days the Hotel Curve was notorious for its foul and difficult conditions. On one occasion an engine slipped so severely on the greasy rails that it came to a standstill and then started sliding backwards. So dense was the smoke that the crew were unaware of what was happening until they collided with another train behind. Since electrification and diversion of the Moorgate trains via Drayton Park, the tunnels are no longer in use.

Tunnels and gradients bedevilled the main line approaches too. Immediately after leaving the platforms, trains enter the 528-yard Gas Works Tunnels which dip down under the Regent's Canal and then climb at 1 in 105, closely followed by the longer Copenhagen Tunnels. With constant shunting operations in and out, the tunnels were always full of smoke. The approaches also formed a notorious bottleneck which even modern track improvements have not entirely eliminated. Lifting a heavy train like *The Flying Scotsman* or one of the LNER Pullmans out of Kings Cross with a steam locomotive on a wet day was a highly skilled job which the advent of diesels only partly helped. Not until the arrival of the Inter-City 125s, with their two driving cars, were the problems significantly reduced.

LIVERPOOL STREET

Built 1874-75 for Great Eastern Railway. Designer Edward Wilson. Gothic-style offices flanking west ramp and two western bays of trainshed listed Grade II.

Liverpool Street spells out thoughts of East Anglia, Harwich boat trains and – twice a day – commuting multitudes streaming in and out of one of London's busiest termini.

The frontage is L-shaped, typically mid-Victorian Gothic in white Suffolk brick with pointed arches and plate tracery. Dormers line a roof that is subdued now that the elaborate iron cresting has gone. The squat clock tower lost its spire in the bombing of 1941.

The building was designed by the GER's Chief Engineer, Edward Wilson, a man little known to the general public or even to other engineers. He was also responsible for the western trainshed over platforms 1-10, built at the same time as the frontage. The station was a byword for dirt in steam days, but in this cleaner electric age the delicacy of the lofty roof can at last be fully appreciated. The four pitched iron spans 76 feet high are of unequal width. The effect of the curved ties, double rows of slender columns with deep filigree brackets and the airy, pointed aisles and transepts is like some great

LIVERPOOL STREET, 1929

Gothic iron-and-glass cathedral. Such spaciousness is perfectly countered at the outer end by spiky valancing instead of the more common glass screen, and at the inner by a charming domestic touch provided by two little elevated Edwardian bow-windowed tea-rooms. One is now an office and the other a bistro. The eastern trainshed over platforms 11-18 was added by W. N. Ashbee in 1894, again in four spans but lower.

In 1884 the Great Eastern Hotel was opened – the only one in the City now that Cannon Street has gone. It was designed by Charles Barry and his son Charles Edward. (Charles was the son of Sir Charles of Houses of Parliament fame.) It fronts on to Liverpool Street itself, in a vaguely Dutch Renaissance style. Its greater merit is the magnificent interior, particularly the main staircase and the glass-domed restaurant.

Colonel Robert Edis, who also designed the Hotel Great Central at Marylebone, added an extension in 1901. Named the Abercorn Rooms and entered from Bishopsgate, this block contains richly decorated Georgian and Baroque-styled assembly rooms. The rococo plasterwork in the Hamilton Hall (named after Lord Claud Hamilton, Chairman of the GER from 1893 to the 1923 Grouping) is even more sumptuous, while away from the public eye are two Masonic temples, one Grecian and the other Egyptian.

The station has its unique fascinations. Before the alterations of 1962-64 the lines between platforms 9 and 10 mysteriously disappeared into a gloomy area of sidings known as 'the backs' which ran into the basement of the hotel and were crossed by a footbridge. A much larger footbridge performs a zig-zag across the full width of the station, giving access to the old tea-rooms on the way. To reach platforms 11-18 from the main entrance one still has to use this footbridge or face a long walk around the ends of Nos. 9 and 10 behind the hotel. At the eastern end, in the brick-

EDWARD WILSON, ENGINEER, AND W. N. ASHBEE, ARCHITECT

The names of Wilson and Ashbee are linked with Liverpool Street station. Wilson was an engineer who had worked in Scotland, Yorkshire and Ireland (where he was engineer to the Midland Great Western Railway) before his appointment in 1858 as locomotive and permanent-way engineer to the Oxford Worcester & Wolverhampton Railway. There he conducted experiments on firebox design, continuing under West Midland and then Great Western owners until 1864 when he set up in London as a consulting engineer.

One of Wilson's first jobs was to design the Metropolitan Railway's extension from Moorgate to Liverpool Street under Sir John Fowler. In 1868 Robert Sinclair retired as Locomotive Superintendent and Engineer to the Great Eastern Railway. The positions were split, and Wilson was appointed engineer to the company at the age of 48, with the task of designing a new terminus. The result, after several boardroom arguments over costs, was Liverpool Street. So far as is known he was solely responsible for the engineering and architectural designs, although Sir William Fairbairn, head of the celebrated Fairbairn Engineering Company of Manchester (who supplied the ironwork) may have helped. The station was opened in 1875, but unfortunately Wilson did not live long to see it in operation, as he died in 1877. By all accounts a modest and retiring man, he was one of the last non-specialists, covering a range of engineering and architectural work which in future tended to be divided between the different professions.

In 1874 W. N. Ashbee joined Wilson's office, although by this late stage he could have done little other than work on the final touches to Liverpool Street. From 1883 to 1916 he was head of the Great Eastern's architectural department and was responsible for much of the work in enlarging the station in 1890-94 under Edward Wilson's nephew John, who was Chief Engineer from 1883 to 1910. Ashbee's other notable designs were Norwich (*p.22*), Hertford East (*p.19*), Felixstowe (*p.21*) and the royal station for Sandringham at Wolferton.

work above the Bishopsgate booking office, lunettes display moulded cherubs acting as driver, fireman, porter and signalman, while in the main booking hall the Great Eastern war memorial is a reminder of the assassination of Sir Henry Wilson, Chief of Imperial General Staff, in 1922. He was shot by IRA gunmen on his way home from the unveiling. Outside, the letters GER can still be seen high on the Barrys' frontage; inside they remain entwined in the plasterwork of the Hamilton Hall.

NORTH WOOLWICH

Built 1847 for Eastern Counties Railway. Architect possibly Sancton Wood. Listed Grade II. End of branch from Stratford.

An ancient ferry crossed the Thames between a marshy area on the north bank and Woolwich with its Royal Arsenal, Artillery Barracks and Military Academy on the south. The railway took over the ferry service, buying two steamers for the purpose, and opened a branch line to it through East London, naming the terminus North Woolwich in order to attract

1968

passengers for Woolwich proper.

It was not until the opening of the Royal Docks and the growth of Silvertown on the north bank that rail traffic started to flourish on this line. The terminus is surprisingly large and handsome for such a desolate spot – Italianate, in brick with stone trimmings, regular fenestration and a nice balustrade.

STEPNEY EAST VIADUCT

Built 1840 for London & Blackwall Railway. Engineers Robert Stephenson and G. P. Bidder. Listed Grade II. Stepney East to Limehouse line. Closed.

The brick viaduct between the London & Blackwall's original London terminus in the Minories and West India Dock Road was 4,020 yards long on 285 arches. It crosses part of the Regent's Canal Dock and the entrance locks to the Regent's Canal, where three extra wide arches were erected, each of 87-foot span with elegant iron arcaded parapets intended to reduce noise echoing back into the trains.

VIADUCT OVER REGENT'S CANAL, 1981

ESSEX

AUDLEY END

Built 1845 for Eastern Counties Railway. Architect Francis Thompson. Main building listed Grade II. Between Bishops Stortford and Cambridge.

This handsome station was originally called Wendon after the nearby village but was later renamed after the well known 17th-century mansion it served, latterly the home of Lord Braybrooke, the last private owner, and now in public ownership. Thompson designed it in his

1977

characteristic style with a two-storey yellow brick main block placed symmetrically between single-storey side blocks supporting flat verandahs, features which distinguished his work on other railways. Here the main outline is square offset by round-headed windows. Antici-

pating the station's use by the big house, Thompson added a fine single-arched *porte cochère* on the front in rusticated stone, for the carriages of Victorian aristocracy.

CHAPPEL VIADUCT

Built 1849 for Stour Valley Railway. Engineer Peter Bruff. Listed Grade II. Marks Tey to Sudbury branch.

Chappel Viaduct carries the railway over the River Colne on 32 arches each of 35-foot span. At 355 yards it was the longest viaduct on the Great Eastern Railway, which by the 1860s controlled virtually the whole of East Anglia, and was built at a cost of £32,000 using seven million bricks.

When the line to Sudbury was opened for all traffic on 2nd July, 1849, the triumphal arch that had been put up at Marks Tey was dislodged by the engine and remained festooned around the chimney and dome during the ceremonial first journey – a nice touch.

The line was single track throughout, but the contractor, Jackson, had left space for a second track to be added later.

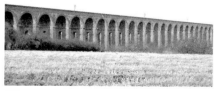

1954

CLACTON-ON-SEA

Built 1929 by London & North Eastern Railway.

Of the 'big four' railways established at Grouping in 1923 (*p.8*), the LNER was least noted for the quality of its building

1954

work. With a few exceptions such as the rebuilt stations between York and Northallerton and on north Tyneside, new LNER stations were mainly derivations from pre-Grouping styles. Clacton on the other hand was built in a heavy pseudo-Georgian style, using brick with stone window casings and a prominent stone centrepiece. It looks like many a post office or labour exchange of the period.

COLCHESTER ST. BOTOLPHS

Built 1866 by Stour Valley Railway. House early 19th-century, listed Grade II.

The station is a typical Great Eastern building with a characteristic awning which is repeated on the road frontage. Despite its plainness, it forms a pleasant group with the modestly late Georgian house next door. This building, with its little Tuscan porch, pre-dates the railway and was acquired when the line was built. St. Botolphs is on a short terminal spur, so trains have to reverse in and out.

1981

ELSENHAM

Built by Great Eastern Railway. Timber station building and canopy on up platform listed Grade II. Between Bishops Stortford and Cambridge.

The small building on the up platform is a typical example of a late-19th-century Great Eastern Railway standardised

ELSENHAM UP-PLATFORM BUILDING, 1980

ORIGINAL DOWN-PLATFORM BUILDING, 1845

structure. The broad awning, slender iron columns, intricately cast brackets and the deep, frilly valancing also bear strong Great Eastern characteristics which could be found from the East London suburbs to Norfolk. Small stations like Elsenham gave them added charm.

GREAT CHESTERFORD

Built 1845 for Eastern Counties Railway. Architect Francis Thompson. Main station building listed Grade II. Between Bishops Stortford and Cambridge.

This station's likeness to Audley End is obvious; only the details differ. Here we see square-headed windows instead of round, emphasised to match a more pro-

nounced cornice, and the same flat awning but supported by angled wooden brackets carefully articulated with the door and window openings to break up the strong horizontals and verticals. The whole composition shows Thompson's skilful symmetry at its best. The main building is now used as a restaurant.

1980

INGATESTONE

Built 1846 by Eastern Counties Railway. Listed Grade II. Between Shenfield and Chelmsford.

Sir Niklaus Pevsner in his series *The Buildings of England* describes the main building as 'friendly neo-Tudor', which it is, with its tall gables and angled chimney stacks. It was reputedly designed at the insistence of Lord Petre to match Ingatestone Hall, which now houses Essex County Record Office. The smaller building on the other platform is a typical late 19th-century Great Eastern structure in Domestic Revival style with patterned tile-hung gables and a standard flat wooden awning with 'ripsaw' valances.

MALDON EAST

Built 1848 by Eastern Counties Railway. End of branch from Witham. Closed.

Occasionally a minor branch line would be provided with a splendid terminus far larger than the potential traffic warranted, possibly for a reason quite uncon-

INGATESTONE, 1971

MALDON EAST, 1977

nected with the railway. This magnificent Jacobean mansion of a station had only one platform. Its size is attributable to the Eastern Counties deputy chairman who was parliamentary candidate for Maldon and thought that by prolonging construction until the election he could swell the number of his supporters among the workmen. It worked, and he was elected.

ROYDON

Built 1841 by Eastern Counties Railway. Listed Grade II. Between Broxbourne and Bishops Stortford.

The bow-fronted verandah, coupled columns and deep-cut valance make this early wooden station unusually elaborate. The platform side has round-headed windows and a canted awning.

1975

CAMBRIDGESHIRE

CAMBRIDGE

Built 1845 for Eastern Counties Railway. Architect Francis Thompson. Listed Grade II.

Sancton Wood may have had a hand in the design here as well as at Bury St. Edmunds (*p.20*), although a contemporary engraving clearly designates Thompson as 'archt', and the long single-platform layout is certainly typical of him. The facade is almost entirely composed of a striking fifteen-arched *porte cochère*, now bricked up at the ends, beneath a deep, rich cornice. The arms of the Cambridge colleges are decoratively incorporated in the spandrels.

On the platform side the style of the facade was repeated by a narrow trainshed in the form of an elegantly arched colonnade. Later it was replaced by a conventional wooden awning, but the long single platform remains and it can still be used by two full-length trains at the same time. Until recent years this arrangement was unique for a large station, but now

CAMBRIDGE, 1976

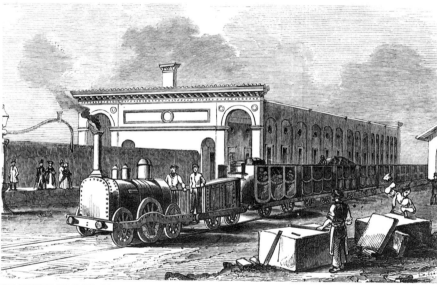

CAMBRIDGE, NEARING COMPLETION, 1845

British Rail have re-introduced the layout as an economy measure at some of their remodelled stations.

Thompson gave the main public rooms at Cambridge decorative cornices and friezes, some of which can still be seen.

HELPSTON GOODS SHED

Built by Midland Railway. Listed Grade II. Leicester to Peterborough line. Closed.

1957

For five miles north of Peterborough the Midland line from Leicester ran alongside the Great Northern portion of the East Coast main line. The GN had only a signal box at Helpston, but the Midland had a small, low passenger station of considerable rural charm. Like the Midland line itself, the station has gone, but the handsome red brick grain warehouse still stands in the old goods yard.

Though elaborate in appearance, it is in fact a strictly functional building. The overhanging eaves on their sturdy iron brackets gave weather protection to road and rail wagons during loading and unloading. Above each broad doorway, matching brackets support dainty balconies which housed the hoists for lifting loaded sacks. The small windows were designed and spaced to maintain the overall symmetry. Inside, sacked grain was stored on the ground floor, with bulk storage in large wooden bins above.

HUNTINGDON, 1969

HUNTINGDON

*Built 1850 for Great Northern Railway.
Architect Henry Goddard. Listed Grade II.*

Intermediate stations on the Great Northern were all of a pattern. Huntingdon, although partly demolished, is one of the few remaining examples. These stations were an early form of standardization with only minor variations, comprising a two-storey house and adjoining single-storey offices in buff stock brick.

WANSFORD

*Built 1845 for London & Birmingham
Railway. Architect J. W. Livock. Northampton
to Peterborough line.*

The Tudor stations on this branch made up one of the finest series anywhere (in striking contrast with those on the main line) culminating in Jacobean Wansford which perhaps was the most perfect.

The front is built of finely dressed local ashlar stone to match the village; the sides and rear are somewhat coarser. The exquisitely proportioned gables, spiky finials and oriel window are offset by a diamond-patterned roof, but what a pity the original chimneys have gone! A plain

WANSFORD, 1968

wooden awning with scrolled brackets on the platform side has also long since been removed. It acted as a perfect foil to the elaboration of the building.

The station is now the home of the preserved Nene Valley Railway and (somewhat incongruously to some) a collection of foreign steam locomotives.

HERTFORDSHIRE

HERTFORD EAST

*Built 1888 for Great Eastern Railway.
Architect W. N. Ashbee. Listed Grade II.*

In many ways Hertford East is a smaller edition of Norwich (*p.22*) and a good

19

HERTFORD EAST, 1981

example of the so-called 'Free Renaissance' style of architecture popular in the last decades of the 19th century. Its chief feature is the chunky red brick *porte cochère* which almost overshadows the main building.

The elliptical arches with stone trimmings project from an otherwise very freely treated Tudoresque building enhanced by delicately latticed stone parapets, Jacobean gables and tall, panelled chimney stacks. Doors and windows are equally well-proportioned and decorated in moulded terracotta brick and stone, complete with wooden panelling and 'Booking Hall' etched in the glass. The booking hall interior has a decorated coffered ceiling.

The platforms have ridge-and-furrow awnings with plain valances forming strikingly shallow ellipses, setting off the filigree iron brackets and patterned columns. Delicately tapered and fluted iron stalks carrying the buffer-stop lamps complete a design which is entirely in keeping with this part of the county town.

KNEBWORTH

DEARDS END BRIDGE. Built 1849-50 for Great Northern Railway. Engineer Joseph Cubitt. Ancient Monument. Map ref. TL247208.

This fine bridge carries a minor road over the four tracks of the East Coast main line with a single arch of about 96-foot span. A particularly good example of a larger-than-average overbridge on this line, it is finished in blue engineering bricks with pilasters and abutments of red brick and a stone cornice and coping. The blue bricks were added during re-facing, which affected a number of other structures on the line (*see Welwyn Viaduct*).

LETCHWORTH

Built 1913 by Great Northern Railway. Station, including booking hall, public rooms, offices and footbridge listed Grade II. Between Hitchin and Cambridge.

The first garden city, based on the ideas of the social reformer Ebenezer Howard, was started at Letchworth in 1903. The Great Northern provided a wooden halt, and it was not until 1913 that the company built a station designed to reflect its surroundings. Despite its strong GN

characteristics, the entrance building was given an 'Arts and Crafts' flavour by the use of rustic bricks, herringbone nogging in the gables, leaded lights and bottle glass windows. The matching but plainer platform buildings had standard flat GN wooden awnings.

1981

WELWYN GARDEN CITY

Built 1926 by London & North Eastern Railway. Between Hatfield and Hitchin.

Like Letchworth, this station matches the character of its garden city surroundings, in this case neo-Georgian. Again, rustic brick was used and dormer windows peep over the flat Doric-styled portico which matches the parade of shops opposite. The platforms originally had nameboards on matching concrete pedestals. The station was opened by the future Prime Minister Neville Chamberlain, at that time Minister of Health.

1926

WELWYN OR DIGSWELL VIADUCT

Built 1850 for Great Northern Railway. Engineers Sir William and Joseph Cubitt. Listed Grade II. Between Welwyn Garden City and Welwyn North.

The great size and severely plain appearance of this viaduct make it a most striking contribution to the landscape of the Mimram valley and a fine memorial to the work of the Cubitts and the contractor, Thomas Brassey. Forty entirely unornamented arches give a total length of 519 yards and required the use of 13 million bricks. The viaduct's height of up to 100 feet is surprisingly difficult to appreciate from the train and really has to be seen from the valley.

SUFFOLK

BURY ST. EDMUNDS

Built 1846 for Ipswich & Bury Railway. Architect Frederick Barnes. Listed Grade II.

The design of this station has been attributed to Barnes, an Ipswich architect who built the other original stations on this line, and also to Sancton Wood. But whilst the flamboyantly 'Free Renaissance' towers and other touches could

1948

well be by Wood, the generally Jacobean styling of the 'house' portion and the positioning of the station on an embankment are hallmarks of Barnes, who seems to have been an expert in the handling of awkward sites.

The twin towers and matching brick screen walls with their blind arcading formerly flanked an overall roof spanning four tracks. Long ago the Great Eastern Railway replaced the roof with one of their typical flat wooden awnings, and more recently the tracks have been reduced to two; but the main structure remains a remarkable essay in mixed yet harmonious design.

WELWYN OR DIGSWELL VIADUCT, 1850

FELIXSTOWE TOWN

*Built 1898 for Great Eastern Railway.
Architect W. N. Ashbee. Listed Grade II. Sold.*

Felixstowe Town is one of the best examples of the GER Architect's Department's flirtation with end-of-century 'Domestic' styling, with echoes of Norman Shaw in the combination of striped and plain Dutch gables, stone string courses in the neat red brickwork and six-light window sashes – all quite homely and sober, but given a light touch of whimsy by an elaborate octagonal cupola and even more elaborate iron verandah brackets which were repeated under the side platform awnings. The concourse roof was a miniature repeat of the one at Norwich (*p.22*).

IPSWICH

*Built 1860 for Great Eastern Railway.
Designed by Robert Sinclair.*

Sinclair was one of those versatile mid-Victorian engineers who could turn their hands to designing anything from locomotives to stations, and much else besides. Ipswich was a long single-platform station like Cambridge, hence the long, symmetrical building that Sinclair designed to front it.

In many ways the station represents the peak of much Great Eastern Italian-

FELIXSTOWE TOWN, 1976

ate styling. White Suffolk brick is enlivened with vividly contrasting string courses, window arches and a pair of heavily pedimented 'wings' to the main entrance block which look rather like outsize sentry-boxes. Chimneys and three curious belfries (without bells) punctuate the roof line.

THE GREAT NORTHERN RAILWAY

'In matters of speed and smartness the Great Northern has worked like an inspiriting leaven on everything it has touched,' wrote Professor Foxwell in his famous work of 1889, *Express Trains – English and Foreign*.

It was essentially a main-line company deriving its traffic from the extremities. In the splendidly straight line engineered by William Cubitt by tunnel and viaduct through the northern heights of London and across the chalk ridges beyond, and in the great terminus of Kings Cross built by his nephew, Lewis, the Great Northern has a heritage of fine works. But it was often said that its business really began at Doncaster, whence it provided a route to London for so many other railways.

At the Doncaster locomotive works – always known as 'The Plant' – a succession of distinguished engineers including Archibald Sturrock, Patrick Stirling, H. A. Ivatt and Sir Nigel Gresley produced high-speed locomotives of lasting fame. It was Gresley who carried the Doncaster tradition into the Grouping era and, in the Silver Jubilee year of 1935 was knighted, as *The Times* happily expressed it, for his work as 'Engineer and speeder-up to the LNER'.

From 1935 onwards the Doncaster Plant built for the LNER the famous 'A4' streamlined Pacifics, of which *Mallard*, preserved at York, holds the world record for the highest speed ever attained with steam, 126 miles per hour.

Above: GNR No. 1, the original 8-footer built by Patrick Stirling in 1870, is now preserved at York. These famous 4-2-2s worked the main-line expresses between London and York.
Left: Ticket from Doncaster, where the GNR connected with numerous other lines.

NEEDHAM MARKET, PEDIMENTED DOORWAY INSET, 1976

NEEDHAM MARKET

Built 1846 for Ipswich & Bury Railway.
Architect Frederick Barnes. Listed Grade II.
Between Ipswich and Bury St. Edmunds.

The Illustrated London News of 1849 called
Needham 'a pleasing structure', which is
an understatement for Barnes' somewhat
free Elizabethan station built in brick
with Caen stone trim. The joining of
embattled corner-towers to higher gabled
bays was an odd but effective ploy, nicely
balanced by wing walls and pedimented
doorways. The rusticated and diamond
patterned brickwork and the clustered
hexagonal chimneys provide a superb
finish to the composition.

STOWMARKET

Built 1849 for Ipswich & Bury Railway.
Architect Frederick Barnes. Listed Grade II.
Between Ipswich and Bury St. Edmunds.

Here we see the same beautifully executed
brickwork as at Needham, with similar
door and window treatment but hardly
any stone, and massive Jacobean gables
which give a quite different effect. On
either side of the central entrance building the architect has provided a pair of
two-storey blocks with octagonal corner
towers that do not relate quite so successfully to the rest of the building as
Needham's. The platforms originally had
screen walls and matching flat, simple
awnings of equal length, creating a pleasant symmetry to match the frontage.

c.1950

22

NORFOLK

DOWNHAM MARKET

Built 1846 by Lynn & Ely Railway. Listed
Grade II. Between Ely and Kings Lynn.

1976

This cosy little country station exhibits
the use of local material and styles:
carstone with brick quoins and angled,
coupled chimney stacks. The tall
Jacobean gables and lozenge-patterned
windows add a touch of distinction.

NORWICH, c.1950

NORWICH

Rebuilt 1886 for Great Eastern Railway.
Designed by John Wilson and W. N. Ashbee.
Conservation Area.

On the Great Eastern Railway, Norwich
was second only to Liverpool Street in the
volume of its traffic and for years people
had been agitating for something better
than the original station built in mid-
century by the Eastern Counties Railway.

John Wilson, who succeeded his uncle
Edward as Chief Engineer of the GER,
and W. N. Ashbee, head of the company's
architectural department, finally built a
replacement in a handsome 'Free Renaissance' style that took full advantage of the
commanding site overlooking the River
Wensum. The old station was now relegated to a goods depot.

Behind the elliptical-arched *porte cochère*
rises a prominent French-style zinc dome
topped by a cupola and surrounded by a
parapet set with moulded urns and a
pedimented clock. The rest of the frontage, in the same deep red brick with Bath
stone dressings, tends towards the classical. The spacious booking hall interior
has a decorated coffered ceiling. The
equally spacious concourse has a lofty
glass roof on iron columns carrying elliptical-arched trusses and cross girders.
The individual awnings which shelter the
platforms have elliptical-shaped valances
similar to those at Hertford East.

THETFORD

Built 1845 by Norfolk Railway. Original
station building listed Grade II. Norwich to
Ely line.

Flint is a building material much used in
Norfolk and is the chief characteristic of
the original station, a single-storey build-

1972

NOTTINGHAMSHIRE

NEWARK CASTLE

Built 1846 by Midland Railway. Main station buildings listed Grade II. Nottingham to Lincoln line.

The naming of stations is a study in itself. Several bore the suffix 'Castle', to differentiate them from another, often rival, company's station at the same place. (The other station at Newark is Northgate, on the Great Northern line.)

1973

Newark Castle station quietly follows a classical style in buff brick. It has an unusual rounded end, stone window casings and hoods with moulded brackets and square pilasters on the projecting entrance bay, repeated on the platform side.

WORKSOP

Built 1849 by Manchester Sheffield & Lincolnshire Railway. Listed Grade II. Sheffield to Lincoln line.

'The most architecturally elegant station on the railway,' wrote George Dow, describing Worksop in his definitive history of the Great Central (the later name of the Manchester Sheffield & Lincolnshire). It is built of locally quarried grey Steetley stone, a very long and irregular station with a remarkably elaborate display of

Jacobean motifs: gables, pilasters, medallions, strapwork and even a broken pediment over a small projecting window.

What was the reason for such an imposing appearance? Perhaps it was the proximity of Clumber Park, seat of the Duke of Newcastle, for which it was the nearest station.

LINCOLNSHIRE

LINCOLN

ST. MARKS STATION. Built 1846 by Midland Railway. Listed Grade II.

Lincoln has two stations, equally meritorious but completely different. St. Marks is the older of the two and was built as a terminus covered by a pitched overall roof with slatted gable-ends. It became a through station when the Manchester Sheffield & Lincolnshire Railway started using it in 1849.

ST. MARKS, 1903

The main building is classical, with fluted Ionic columns on the portico and flanking square Doric pilasters which produce a subdued Grecian effect. The windows are similar to those at Newark Castle, set symmetrically in the brick walls. There was a handsome stone cornice and parapet to complete it but it was replaced by the present dull brick parapet which hides the low pitched roof.

CENTRAL STATION. Built 1848 for Great Northern Railway. Architect possibly Lewis Cubitt. Listed Grade II.

The Battle of the Styles that raged so furiously in architectural circles in the first half of the 19th century is nowhere illustrated so vividly in its effect on railways as at Lincoln, for if St. Marks is uncompromisingly classical, Central displays Tudor to the full. The medieval-looking tower is the dominating feature,

THETFORD STATION.

1845

ing with brick dressings and enormous pointed Jacobean gables on all four sides. A later brick addition declares itself with the words 'Thetford Station 1889' incised in the curved pediment over the door, which is flanked by large ball finials.

The platforms have Great Eastern style awnings on decorative iron brackets and columns, deep saw-tooth valances and rear screen walls.

WYMONDHAM

Built 1845 by Norfolk Railway. Station and warehouse listed Grade II. Between Norwich and Thetford.

This unassuming railway station is built, like Thetford, of local flint, offset by prominently rusticated brick quoins, elegant sash windows, and a steeply gabled centrepiece. The platform canopies have rounded saw-tooth valances on one side and pointed on the other, both supported on ornamental iron brackets.

The goods shed, on the other hand, is a far from unassuming red brick building with giant four-centred arch openings, those along the side (now bricked up) alternating with prominent buttresses.

WYMONDHAM GOODS SHED, 1981

THE GREAT EASTERN RAILWAY

This line was formed in 1862 by an amalgamation of the Eastern Counties, Eastern Union and Norfolk Railways. Traversing a relatively flat countryside it needed no great engineering works but included a high proportion of fine station buildings.

The GER had some great men in its locomotive department at Stratford. Having had four superintendents in the space of 19 years, in 1885 the company appointed James Holden, who carried through a very thorough modernisation. Best known were his handsome express passenger 4-4-0s of the Claud Hamilton class.

In its earlier years the Great Eastern had had a reputation for lack of punctuality, and Holden's new engines were part of a thorough overhaul of services. When his chief draughtsman, F. V. Russell, was transferred to the operating department he became the principal architect of the famous 'Jazz' suburban service from Liverpool Street, which in precision of timing, close headway between trains and punctuality became a model of successful commuter traffic working. Comfort, however, was not provided. The four-wheeled third-class carriages were moving slums. They had bare-boarded seats, no partitions and back rests only shoulder high.

Above: A GER Claud Hamilton heads a passenger express, displaying the fine proportions for which these 4-4-0s, inaugurated in 1900, were much admired. **Inset:** A third-class ticket issued to a theatrical party.

complete with crenellations and, amazingly, a sham rose window. The symmetrical centrepiece has the full Tudor range of mullioned windows, steep gables and on one side an oriel. Tall, slender chimney shafts complete the arrangement. Hardly less elaborate is the platform side, which at one time had separate iron overall roofs for up and down trains, the through lines passing between them in the open.

Joseph Cubitt, the GN's engineer, has been suggested as the designer but his cousin Lewis would seem more likely, although neither they nor anyone else did anything quite like this for the Great Northern, a company noted for stern functionalism. Someone must have put pressure on the company to provide a station suitable for the ancient city of Lincoln.

LOUTH, 1962

LOUTH

Built 1848 for East Lincolnshire Railway. Architects Weightman & Hadfield. Part of main station buildings listed Grade II. Boston to Grimsby line. Closed.

After Kings Cross and Lincoln Central, the only imposing stations on the Great Northern were those inherited from smaller railways it absorbed. Three on the East Lincolnshire Railway were built to the same plan but given different stylistic finishes. Both Alford and Firsby were in Italianate; Louth is Jacobean, its fine detail making it the most handsome station on the GN.

The red brick gables and balustraded roof balance the light stone arcade in a delightful manner. Originally the platforms were covered by light twin-span iron overall roofs supported on arcaded columns between the tracks.

STAMFORD

TOWN STATION. Built 1846-48. Original operating company Midland Railway. Architect Sancton Wood. Listed Grade II. Leicester to Peterborough line.

The grey limestone town of Stamford is one of the most beautiful and unspoiled in England, and Stamford Town station, built in manor house Tudor with a promi-

nent bell-tower type of turret, is entirely in keeping with it.

The station preserves a characteristic snippet of British railway history. It was built for the Syston & Peterborough Railway, a company created by George Hudson (*p.38*) in order to increase his hold over the East Midlands, and was taken over by the Midland – another Hudson line – before opening. However, the short-lived smaller company has left its initials in the weathervane on the turret.

EAST STATION. Built 1856 for Stamford & Essendine Railway. Architect William Hurst. Branch from Great Northern main line at Essendine. Closed and sold.

(*Continued on page 29*)

THE SPLENDOURS AND MISERIES OF BRITISH RAIL'S ARCHITECTURAL HERITAGE

BY BERNARD KAUKAS
DIRECTOR – ENVIRONMENT BRITISH RAILWAYS BOARD

The Victorians built too well. In spite of the sharp practices prevalent in the building and contracting industry of that age they had the advantage of working with well-tried materials which had been proved to stand the test of time. Stone, clay products, timber and iron were their basic materials, to which lead, copper and slate were added as coverings; and stucco, plaster and paint as finishes. Victorian architects practised in a climate of almost overwhelming confidence, retained by clients and patrons who set no bounds to their ambition. Their building works were accomplished with virtually an inexhaustible supply of cheap labour – both in the manufacturing and the building process. The result was workmanship of permanence, if not always of quality.

Since there was no such thing as a single national style of architecture between 1840 and, possibly, 1920, all architecture was of necessity eclectic. Playing variations on old styles was not only perfectly acceptable, it was almost mandatory and the only real passion arose over which of the two camps claimed the architect's allegiance, Classic or Gothic. In practice Gothic was predominant in the major railway buildings, local domestic styles in the far greater number of small stations.

Because the steam train was so revolutionary an innovation, there was an obvious desire on the part of the early railway entrepreneurs to mitigate the novelty – and calm travellers' fears – by providing a passenger environment which was as ordinary and familiar as possible in the rural environment and as impressive as possible in the large towns and cities. Hence the variety of styles from small cottages to modest manor houses and on to ducal palaces.

The Effects of Old Age

But over the span of a hundred years or so, which is pretty average for the life of a railway station, one remarkable fact is often overlooked. Over that long period the station building was open for use by traffic, staff and passengers for 24 hours a day for 364 days in the year. There is no other building type or category which has had to take such severe wear and tear – not even the domestic house. And because of the obvious robustness of the building fabric, maintenance was more honoured in the breach than the observance. But a building cannot take neglect of this kind for ever; while it is in use it remains alive; it is heated and lighted and lived in. But when it is no longer occupied the decay and the rot appear almost immediately, and grow insidiously until the point of no return is reached and the building is fit for nothing but demolition.

Many railway buildings which are still in busy daily use are also suffering from the effects of old age. The term often used in connection with railway buildings – crumbling infrastructure – is only too accurate. A walk along the roof of St. Pancras Chambers will produce

Beneath the Italianate clock tower at Ulverston in Cumbria, the vast expanse of disintegrating iron and glass station canopies, built in 1873, await costly restoration to their former, always exceptional grandeur.

25

Edge Hill station in Liverpool is stripped during restoration for the 150th anniversary of the Rainhill Trials and the Liverpool & Manchester Railway.

Cleaning has revealed the colour of the local sandstone, the prominent rustication of the lower storey and the dentilled cornice of the station, built in 1836.

The grimy facade of Manchester Victoria (above), designed by William Dawes in 1909, has been returned to its original splendour, right down to the new gold leaf on the stone letters of its name (left).

literally handfuls of evidence. The oolite limestone cappings and bases to the forest of chimney stacks have weathered to the consistency and appearance of cod's roe. Short of protecting every such exposed area with lead flashings – which was never envisaged by the architect – it is difficult to see how the process of further erosion can be altogether prevented. The brickwork also is spalling and crumbling.

Of course, the Clean Air Act has proved to be of real benefit in checking the damage caused by acid rain, and proper cleaning and some judicious renovation and repointing will go a long way to conserving the fabric; indeed the deterioration has been arrested in the parts already treated. But the cost of even partial restoration is astronomically high, and projects of this kind compete for money which is urgently required for British Rail's primary aim of modernising the railway.

In the heyday of the railway, stations were designed and built to accommodate the staff as well as the passengers, and the staff were organised on quasi-military lines, which meant that the various grades and occupations each had their own accommodation. The run down in staff over the last two decades has been dramatic. Stations which once required 17 or 20 staff now manage with five or six. Thus significant areas of accommodation, particularly in large stations, are no longer in use and are boarded up. Their life support mechanisms are switched off.

The dilemma is two-fold: firstly it is quite impossible to demolish parts of integral buildings – especially those supporting double cantilever glass and iron canopies. Secondly, many such buildings are listed, which means that they cannot be demolished without statutory consent. There is a third negative factor: such redundant parts of stations are hardly, if ever, suitable for commercial lettings to outside parties, either on the grounds of safety (mostly because they are close to the running lines or overhead electrification) or on the grounds that because of their location they are not attractive to the potential lessee.

So the concerned conservationist gazes with dismay at an obviously deteriorating building fabric, and a concerned railway management declares that it has no option but to put its limited funds into working buildings rather than redundant ones, which produce no betterment or return to the business.

A Costly Heritage

British Rail's inheritance includes a legacy of engineering masterpieces without parallel anywhere in the world. The two names Brunel and Stephenson alone are sufficient to justify such a sweeping statement. How well they built in that thrusting pioneering age! The sections of the Menai tubular bridge, when put in their final positions by hydraulic jacks, settled to within three-eighths of an inch of their calculated deflection. The Royal Albert Bridge at Saltash has a timeless quality in its design which is the true hallmark of genius. Brunel was literally carried out on his deathbed to see its completion. By the very fact that such structures are subject to dynamic daily stress their maintenance is a matter of continual and close attention. Following the disaster to the Menai bridge, partially destroyed by fire in 1970, it was possible not only to provide new support to the tracks but to build a road bridge above. What is this but further testimony to the inherent rightness of the original design?

Bridges and viaducts which look so solid and permanent nevertheless need extensive maintenance. The massive and noble Ribblehead Viaduct on the Settle & Carlisle Railway has been exposed to extremes of climate for more than a hundred years, and the vertical cracking in the outer freestone of the great piers is plainly visible. Similarly, the wooden Barmouth Viaduct has been so badly attacked by the Teredo worm that the bottoms of the main timbers have been completely eaten away and have needed expensive replacement. The repairs to Cannon Street Bridge alone have cost £6 million.

The great trainsheds, with their mixture of cast iron, wrought iron and steel, have suffered from a degree of corrosion over the years; not sufficient to become dangerous, but enough to require formidable sums of money – running into millions of pounds – merely to repair them. The £4 million repair bill for the western trainshed at Liverpool Street is an example, and the two splendid towers of Cannon Street station, which are such an important part of the Thames riverscape, though no longer of use to British Rail, will need at least half a million pounds spent on them merely to stabilise their foundations.

Looked at another way, it is remarkable how cheap today's repairs to Victorian structures are compared to the enormous remedial costs of repairing just small sections of motorway flyovers built within the last 20 years.

Legal Restraints

The designated architectural heritage of Britain is protected by the simple statutory process of listing a building or structure as being of Special Architectural or Historic Interest. Once such a notice has been served on the building owner no works can be carried out to that building which may alter its character, without formal statutory consent through the process of a planning application.

There would appear to be a deliberate air of vagueness in the wording used on a notice to describe the premises listed. It has become

Imaginative painting has transformed the trainshed at Brighton, one place where the cast-iron work which proliferates throughout the railway has begun its escape from the ubiquitous battleship grey of latter years.

Cleaning and painting of decorative Midland Railway canopies has created a holiday atmosphere at Skipton.

common practice therefore to regard everything within the curtilage (boundaries) of the land on which the building is situated as being covered by the notice.

In addition to protecting individual buildings, the law provides a blanket coverage by designating Conservation Areas, in which no building or structure of any kind may be demolished without consent.

There appears to be a growing tendency on the part of those people responsible for listing to select buildings which have been disused and scheduled for demolition by British Rail for a number of years. Prior to demolition such buildings have had their life support systems switched off and have been allowed to fall into complete disrepair. Halifax and Hellifield are just two examples of such buildings which have been listed. Who then is to pay for their grossly expensive renovation, and for what purpose? No one is prepared to answer this question.

A Balanced View

Two polarised schools of thought about listed building legislation are now current. The preservationists and conservationists (they adopt different viewpoints) are wholly in favour of and in support of such legislation; and, it is to be expected, the developers (of whom there are many varieties from the good through the indifferent to the bad) regard it as a positive inhibition on their activities which they consider are essential to the economic wellbeing of the community.

It is possible – but rare – to find the combination of a thoughtful conservationist and an enlightened developer. Such a pair can come up with a happy solution to what seemed at first to be an intractable problem. But the preservationist is uncompromising. He believes that a building must be preserved at all costs regardless of whether or not it is more than second- or third-rate and whether any use can be found for it. He will use any device to pursue his ends, even if it leads to the eventual ruin of the building by the process of decay. The conservationist, on the other hand, is aware of the imperative need to find a beneficial use for a building he wishes to see kept. His outlook fits in with a judicious definition of conservation as 'the creative synthesis of preservation and change'.

There are problems which make the finding of uses for listed but redundant railway buildings especially difficult. In the case of listed buildings which cannot be let or sold because they have no commercial attraction, the ideal solution is to give them away to outside bodies which have a stable and permanent role, such as local authorities or charitable trusts. Such buildings, however, are nearly always in a desperate state, since they are almost always over a hundred years old and extremely run down. So it is normally necessary to hand over a financial contribution, in addition to the building, in order to help with the cost of repairs. In the case of some important listed buildings, such as Liverpool Road station in Manchester (the oldest railway station in the world) and the Curzon Street Arch in Birmingham by Philip Hardwick, this has proved to be the formula for success.

Since the late 1970s British Rail has made a positive effort in conservation, but the work has highlighted the need for more effective building maintenance – there is a large backlog to be made up and funds are insufficient. More effective grant aid is needed; the amount which is obtainable from central government is so small as to be derisory when compared to the size of the obligation. This is not in any way an implied criticism of the Historic Buildings Council which is as generous as it can be with such a small national budget.

It is greatly to the credit of the Railways

27

The western tower of Sir George Gilbert Scott's masterpiece at St. Pancras has a freshly washed face, but comes up against a tidemark where the money ran out. At least another £1 million is needed to finish cleaning the exterior.

The limestone base of this chimney stack on the roof of St. Pancras station is crumbling inexorably.

Inside Hellifield station, listed while awaiting demolition, decay had already taken a firm hold.

Board that, during a period of hard teeth-gritting slog to come to terms with all the problems faced by and imposed upon the railways, it has had the courage – and the foresight – to earmark funds, however modest, to conserve a significant number of its most important historic buildings. The decision to use such funding to clean the building fabric was made by the Director – Environment in 1978 and is an essential part of any maintenance and repair work.

Meeting the Challenge

The results of British Rail's conservation efforts have been fully justified by the public reaction. Although the cost of proper conservation is high, the cost of cleaning (as opposed to fully restoring) the building fabric is surprisingly modest, and the visual improvement makes such a small investment a bargain in conservation terms. Such work encourages other building owners to follow suit and engenders a growing confidence in our decaying city centres.

Victoria station in Manchester is an example of such an exercise. Rather than wait for money that might never be available for a thorough restoration of this building, British Rail agreed in 1977 on a joint partnership venture with the Greater Manchester Council to clean the station facade and clear away the decaying buildings that stood in front. The results far exceeded expectations. For an expenditure of only £150,000, Victoria re-emerged in its original golden sandstone. But just as important, in front of it a new civic square was created to the benefit of the railways, the inner city and the travelling public.

At the same time in the Salford area a number of rail bridges crossing local roads were painted in two or three colours rather than the orthodox battleship grey. The results were so dramatic as to attract the attention of numerous local authorities which requested similar treatment. In Merseyside, the Metropolitan Authority has willingly and generously co-operated with British Rail in the thrust to improve the railway environment, with a particular interest in providing work for the young unemployed.

It is important that conservation should be attempted in phases. To try and do all the restoration needed to any one building or structure at one time invariably makes the cost submission unacceptable to management. The experience gained in cleaning and partial restoration work makes its application to other buildings more realistic and economic. Certainly the most important lesson learned is the obvious, but unglamorous, necessity of making a building wind- and water-tight. It is a fact that one important building had to be demolished in past years as a result of rot caused by blocked gutters and downpipes. To attempt major conservation work to any building before such elementary remedial works are carried out is folly.

Following the undoubted success of the Manchester Victoria project, British Rail offered to enter into joint partnership with any local authority or other properly constituted body to improve the environment of its land and buildings, and that offer remains open. The railway station belongs to the local community – it has their name on it. British Rail are merely appointed as agents to run a transport undertaking; the destiny of the historic railway station is, to some extent at least, in the hands of the local people.

STAMFORD TOWN, 1958

(*Continued from page 24*)

The Marquis of Exeter was principal shareholder in the Stamford & Essendine Railway, so not surprisingly the influence of nearby Burleigh House showed in its station at Stamford East. It is one of England's best Tudor town stations. Like the rival Town station it fits perfectly into the Stamford scene and has particularly delicate detail work.

Inside the lofty booking hall, well lit by a lantern roof, a delightful gallery with a wrought-iron balustrade runs round all four walls, giving access to what were formerly the company's offices.

STAMFORD EAST FACADE, c.1950   STAMFORD EAST BOOKING HALL, c.1950

BROCKLESBY, 1977

HUMBERSIDE

BEVERLEY

Built 1846 for York & North Midland Railway. Architect G. T. Andrews. Hull to Bridlington line. Conservation Area.

A typical Andrews station in buff brick from the Wolds, Beverley retains its hipped overall trainshed roof. The frontage is plain, but enlivened by sparse Italianate features, stone dressings and a small awning on delicate iron scrollwork.

BEVERLEY, 1974

BROCKLESBY

Built 1848 for Manchester Sheffield & Lincolnshire Railway. Engineer Sir John Fowler. Scunthorpe to Grimsby line.

The Chairman of the Manchester Sheffield & Lincolnshire was the Earl of Yarborough, so what was more natural than that the nearest station to his country seat should reflect the style of the big house?

Just along the road from the station is the massive Tudor-Gothic north gateway of Brocklesby Park, whose grounds were laid out by Capability Brown, and the station's neo-Jacobean matches it well. Gabled end and side walls, mullioned windows, patterned roof tiles, cresting and tall octagonal chimneys provide a fine array of detail.

Prince Albert used the station when he stayed at Brocklesby on his way to lay the foundation stone of Grimsby's first dock in 1849.

CLEETHORPES

Built 1863 by Manchester Sheffield & Lincolnshire Railway; extended 1880-81. Former refreshment room (between platform 3 and the promenade), clock tower, station buffet and buildings alongside Station Road listed Grade II.

Many seaside resorts owe their origin to a railway company eager to promote excursion traffic. Cleethorpes went further; the seaside attractions were actually built and owned by the railway, which in the 20 years up to 1900 spent more than £100,000 in developing the resort.

When the railway arrived in 1863, the only station buildings were those alongside platform 1: a loose assemblage of two-storey blocks built of brick and given but little cohesion by coupled round-headed windows within giant blind arches.

Encouraged by its thrusting chairman Sir Edward Watkin, the M S & L in 1880 extended the station towards the pier and the following year the company built a promenade (complete with colonnade), a substantial sea wall, baths, kiosks, even a grotto, and in 1885 Prince Albert Victor performed the grand opening ceremony. Further attractions included the pavilion

OLD REFRESHMENT ROOM, 1981

30

and gardens, and in 1904 the railway bought out the pier company.

Hand-in-hand with this development went progressive enlargement of the station alongside the promenade, including the clock tower and refreshment room, both in appropriately ornate seaside iron-and-glass style. British Rail replaced the 1880 entrance with a sympathetically designed ridge-and-furrow arcade in 1961-62.

GRIMSBY

CUSTOMS HOUSE. Built 1874. Listed Grade II. Cleethorpes Road.

A small red brick building with stone trim and hipped roof was erected by the Office of Works for housing the customs at this Manchester Sheffield & Lincolnshire Railway port.

HULL

Original building completed 1848 for York & North Midland Railway; hotel 1851. Architect G. T. Andrews. Trainshed and booking hall built 1904-05 for North Eastern Railway. Architect William Bell. All listed Grade II.

The long golden-grey ashlar stone building along the south side of the station shows Andrews at his best, and clearly indicates that Hull was originally a one-sided station. It remains virtually as he built it, except for the classical *porte cochère* whose arched openings between coupled Doric columns were filled in many years ago with matching stone and glazing to form offices.

The flat roof of the *porte cochère* has a handsome balustrade forming a terrace in front of the first-floor windows of the central two-storey block, which is Italianate with strong classical motifs. Flanking single-storey wings lead to less elaborate end-blocks, one of two storeys and the other of three. A small balustraded doorway with porch intervenes in the eastern wing.

The present main entrance is through Paragon House, an office block built in 1962 on the site of a huge iron *porte cochère* added by Bell during the 1904-05 reconstruction of the station. Inside is Paragon's chief glory, the lofty booking hall 80 feet long and 70 feet wide, lit from above by four large lantern lights in a decorated ceiling. The walls are tiled in cream and brown above a bottle-green glazed brick dado, broken by deep arched arcaded windows giving on to offices on one side and the hotel on the other.

In the centre is a magnificent booking office in carved oak, with a clock on each corner and no less than 12 booking windows. Their original designations offer interesting clues to the travelling habits of 80 years ago and reflect Hull's importance as a provincial town which served

ORIGINAL STATION BUILDINGS, CLEETHORPES, 1981

HULL BOOKING HALL, 1972

as a metropolis of a small regional system: 1 Goole, Cudworth and Intermediate Stations; 2 Thorne, Doncaster and beyond; 3 Selby, Leeds, York and beyond; 4 Local; 5 Hornsea and Withernsea; 6 1,000-mile Tickets; 7 Advance Booking, Luggage, etc.; 8 General; 9 Enquiries; 10 York and beyond, via Market Weighton; 11 Bridlington and Scarborough; 12 Season Tickets, Pleasure Parties, etc.

Through the booking hall is a light and airy concourse covered by two transverse arched roof bays, and beyond a five-bay trainshed. The roof is typical of Bell's work; its steel ribs rest on latticed cross-girders and plain iron columns, and it is finished off by deep glazed end-screens. There were nine main platforms, and five shorter ones outside, but with reduced traffic some of the platforms on the west side have been filled in to make a car park.

The concourse is enlivened by a series

of charming little wooden art nouveau structures behind the buffer-stops, also dating from 1905, complete with 'Queen Anne' porches. They were used as a hairdressing salon, refreshment room (with a fine elliptical glass dome), 'temperance room', tea-room and lavatories.

A 1908 account describes the tea-room interior as having white woodwork, green walls, mahogany counters and tables, and French wicker chairs and settees. Potted palms and a tastefully tiled fireplace completed this relaxing scene.

The Royal Station Hotel occupies the south-east corner of the complex between Paragon House and Andrews' station, and was extended by Bell in the 1904-05 alterations. It is in Italian Cinquecento style, with 13 bays, and the main staircase and restaurant decorations are particularly fine. A rear entrance leads in direct from the concourse.

CONISBROUGH VIADUCT, 1980

SOUTH YORKSHIRE

CONISBROUGH VIADUCT

*Completed 1907 for Dearne Valley Railway.
Engineer Stanley R. Kay.*

The Dearne Valley was a coal line controlled by the Lancashire & Yorkshire
Railway, running between Brierley and
Shafton Junctions south of Wakefield to a
complicated series of junctions at Black
Carr and Bessacarr south-east of Doncaster. Conisbrough Viaduct over the
River Don is the last major work of its size
built in Britain. It is 508 yards long with
21 arches faced in finely detailed blue
brick. The river span is latticed steel, 150
feet long and 113 feet high.

OUGHTY BRIDGE

*Built 1845 by Sheffield Ashton-under-Lyne &
Manchester Railway. Original station building
listed Grade II. Closed.*

The original station at Oughty Bridge is
on the down side leading to Sheffield. It
bears a family likeness to Hadfield, nearer
Manchester on the same line, a low neo-
Tudor building with prominent gables
and narrow mullioned windows, all in
Pennine gritstone.

1965

SHEFFIELD

*MIDLAND STATION. Rebuilt 1904 for
Midland Railway. Architect Charles
Trubshaw. Frontage block and offices fronting
platform 1 (including refreshment rooms and
former 1st-class dining room) listed Grade II.*

Arriving to catch a train, you enter Sheffield Midland through a grand arcade
and a large covered cab drive. This is the
principal constituent of the new frontage
block added when the station was extended at the turn of the century. The
additions made it the largest on the
Midland Railway after St. Pancras.

AERIAL VIEW OF SHEFFIELD, 1968

The cab drive is roofed with glass and
iron in 12 bays carried on open elliptical
trusses which are filled with scrolled ironwork and supported by a stone arcade on
each side. The outer one through which
you pass first has elliptical arches and a
ridge-and-furrow parapet; the inner
arcade has coupled round-headed arches
with fan-shaped iron grilles. Decorative
stonework liberally incorporates a wheel
motif, the Wyvern emblem of the Midland and the monogram 'MR'. At the
left-hand end of the frontage is a matching
two-storey building sporting a pair of
pediments and prominent chimneys,
originally the station master's house.

A contemporary comment in *The Railway Magazine* called the new station
'pleasing and chaste', but the editor of the
Sheffield Telegraph was not so happy. He
thought it 'depressing-looking' and 'un-

worthy of a great and wealthy body like
the Midland Railway Company'.

Between the cab drive and platforms is
a broad passenger concourse with a deep
coved ceiling and three large glass lantern
lights. Two new platforms added in 1904
were given broad cantilevered awnings of
the latest Midland pattern. The old two-
bay arched overall roof was left in position
over the earlier portion of the station and
lasted until the late 1950s. The original
Italianate frontage block still stands on
the central island platform.

*WICKER BRIDGE. Built 1848 for
Manchester Sheffield & Lincolnshire Railway.
Engineer Sir John Fowler. Listed Grade II.
Crosses The Wicker.*

WICKER BRIDGE, 1890s

On extension of the M S & L line east-
ward from the original Sheffield station at
Bridgehouses, it was necessary to construct a 330-yard viaduct across the Don
valley. Known as the Wicker Arches, it
was built by a native of Sheffield, Sir John
Fowler (*p.185*). Across The Wicker (a
main street) he provided a handsome
elliptical ashlar stone arch of 72-foot
span, with two small side arches for
pedestrians. It is embellished with coats
of arms, pilasters, much rustication and a
deep cornice.

*BRIDGEHOUSES OR SPITAL HILL
TUNNEL. Built 1847 for Midland Railway.
Engineer Frederick Swanwick. West portal
listed Grade II. Near Brunswick Road. Closed.*

This 300-yard tunnel was constructed to
connect the M S & L Railway near its
Bridgehouses station to the Sheffield &
Rotherham Railway at its Wicker station;
the latter company became part of the
Midland shortly before the line opened. It
was steeply graded at 1 in 36, and was
used only for the exchange of freight traffic. It is an early example of cut-and-cover
construction and part collapsed in 1861,
killing six men.

WEST YORKSHIRE

BRADFORD FORSTER SQUARE

*Rebuilt 1890 for Midland Railway. Architect
probably Charles Trubshaw. Conservation
Area.*

BRADFORD FORSTER SQUARE, 1973

As at Sheffield Midland (*p.32*), you enter Bradford Forster Square through an arcaded stone screen wall, embellished in this case with coats of arms and nice iron gates, and pass into an open cab area formerly roofed with glass.

The main facade, overshadowed by the Midland Hotel (formerly railway-owned), has a low balustrade punctuated by tall chimneys and, at one end, a stumpy octagonal turret crowned with a minaret-like top.

Originally the station had a light iron trainshed of two bays supported on tall stone side walls that still remain, dwarfing the modern platform awnings. Only two platforms are now in regular use for passengers.

BRAMHOPE TUNNEL

Built 1849 for Leeds & Thirsk Railway. Engineer Thomas Grainger. Leeds to Harrogate line.

Bramhope north portal is one of England's most impressive tunnel mouths, crenellated with twin flanking towers, one larger than the other, and forming at the end of a deep cutting an

1975

excellent example of the early Victorian interest in 'medievalism'.

The tunnel runs for 2 miles 241 yards through the ridge between Leeds and Wharfedale and is a maximum of 280 feet below ground level. It gave a great deal of trouble during construction. More than 1,500 million gallons of water had to be pumped away to prevent the workings from flooding, and 23 men died in accidents. A miniature replica of the north portal stands as a monument to their memory in nearby Otley churchyard.

INSCRIPTION ON BRAMHOPE MEMORIAL

BRAMHOPE MEMORIAL, OTLEY CHURCHYARD, 1961

COOPER BRIDGE

Built 1840 for Manchester & Leeds Railway. Engineer Thomas L. Gooch. Listed Grade II. Between Brighouse and Mirfield.

Two segmental stone skew arches carry this bridge over the River Calder at Bradley, and a modillioned cornice provides pleasant decoration. When the line was widened in 1900-02, a second bridge was built on the south side.

1982

DEWSBURY

Built 1849 by Huddersfield & Dewsbury Railway. Extended 1889. South entrance building, platform buildings and canopies, footbridge and south-west block listed Grade II.

The original Dewsbury station is an asymmetrical assemblage of Tudor features in the style beloved of the early Victorians: ogee gables, pointed arches, mullioned windows and slender hexagonal chimney stacks.

1971

The London & North Western Railway after they took over added a somewhat less ebullient entrance block in matching stone and, later still, glass and iron platform canopies ridged on one side and hipped ridge-and-furrow on the other. An LNWR standard iron-latticed covered footbridge was constructed to join the platforms.

HALIFAX

Built 1855 for Lancashire & Yorkshire Railway. Architect Thomas Butterworth. Original station building, including east platform and island platform, listed Grade II.

For decades the main building of Halifax station was hidden by a century's hotchpotch of awnings, additions and other accretions, not to mention a thick layer of

1912

soot. Probably few townsfolk and even fewer travellers realised that in the midst of it all stood a late classical building of considerable dignity.

Reduction of the station's facilities and cleaning of the stonework has now returned the building to something like its original appearance, revealing the elaborately dentilled cornice and pedimental centrepiece over the former frontage.

The remaining platforms have glass awnings and deep saw-tooth valances of typical LYR design, the moulded cast-iron work picked out in contrasting colours.

HEBDEN BRIDGE

Rebuilt c. 1909 by Lancashire & Yorkshire Railway. Passenger station buildings including signs and canopies listed Grade II. Todmorden to Halifax line.

Here is a remarkable survivor. The mansard roof at Hebden Bridge is unusual in a station – the LYR had only one other of this kind, at Nelson. More unusually the staggered platforms beneath their standard glass-and-iron awnings are connected by a subway which has a sloping ramp on one side and stone stairs on the other. An hydraulic lift, intact but no

1962

longer working, was provided to take the luggage barrows to it.

The structure has survived with very little alteration. So, most remarkably, have the old wooden sign boards with their large, screwed cast-iron letters, including one over a subway entrance that displays a pointing hand beside the words 'To the Up Trains'.

Once a small woollen town, Hebden Bridge has become 'The Pennine Centre' with emphasis on arts and crafts and the Yorkshire Pennine heritage. The station, which has been most carefully restored, forms a fitting part of this rejuvenated community.

HUDDERSFIELD

STATION. Built 1847 for Huddersfield & Manchester Railway. Architect James Pigott Pritchett. Station listed Grade I; railings on north side of St. George's Square listed Grade II.

J. P. Pritchett was architect to Earl Fitzwilliam at Wentworth Woodhouse near Barnsley, and had a practice in York. At Huddersfield he built what was undoubtedly the foremost classical station frontage of its type in the country after Euston. Like Euston, too, it was a monumental expression of the triumph of the early railway promoters. Unlike Euston, it has been retained and restored.

The frontage is 416 feet long. At its centre is a giant Corinthian portico flanked by colonnades ending in small matching pavilions, each carrying a coat of arms. The arms are not those one might expect to see. Shortly before completion the station was taken over jointly by the Lancashire & Yorkshire and London & North Western Railways. One pavilion displays the LYR's arms while the other, oddly, bears not the LNWR arms but those of the original owner, the Huddersfield & Manchester Railway & Canal Company (to give it its full title as carved in the stonework).

The central section was for a time an hotel, but is now leased by the local authority as well as serving as a station.

In 1884 work began on replacing the original trainshed roof with a new one of LNWR 'Euston' type. It was partly complete when it collapsed a few minutes after a train had left the station, killing three workmen. Work started again and the roof, which is still there today, was completed in 1886.

GOODS YARD BUILDINGS. Built 1878-83. Stone warehouse and tower adjoining former pumphouse, listed Grade II. Entered from Fitzwilliam Street.

Overlooking the station is the former Goods & Wool Warehouse, a multi-storey red-brick building and an excellent example of a north-of-England railway warehouse erected for the textile trade. There are numerous iron-framed win-

HUDDERSFIELD, 1971

ILKLEY

Built 1865 for Otley & Ilkley Joint Railway. Architect J. H. Sanders. Listed Grade II.

When the Ilkley – Skipton line closed in 1965, Ilkley station became once again a terminus, as it had been a century earlier. It is a single-storey Italianate building of local ashlar stone with a raised centre section. Corbels under the eaves and pilaster strips to the main windows give a touch of distinction, while delicate lean-to glass verandahs flank the entrance.

The light glass-and-iron roof and awnings date from the enlargement of the station for the Skipton trains in 1888, and are typical Midland work of that period.

1976

dows and the heavy wooden-trussed roof has a line of brick dentils under the eaves. The first floor is of 'fireproof' construction on brick arches, but those above are timber on rolled iron joists and stanchions.

At one side is an elevated brick structure on giant iron columns which contained a wagon hoist for raising railway wagons to the second floor. There they were conveyed to loading docks by an electric traverser which picked up its current from an overhead wire alongside its track, rather like an electric tramcar. Capstans hauled the wagons along rails to

WAGON-HOIST BUILDING, 1983

the final positions required. These and numerous hoists (known as 'jiggers') were worked hydraulically.

At the entrance to the yard is the red-brick former hydraulic pumphouse. An adjoining tower of vaguely Italianate design contained the hydraulic accumulator that powered the machinery.

Across the yard stands a two-storey stone-built warehouse with a parapet and semi-circular lunettes in the gable ends. Judging by its appearance it may be contemporary with the station.

HUDDERSFIELD'S TUNNELS AND VIADUCTS

Huddersfield stands at the junction of three deep, narrow valleys. As a consequence the railway builders had to construct numerous masonry viaducts and tunnels which are of dramatic quality. Most date from the 1840s and are listed (*see below for details*).

North of the station is Huddersfield (or Hillhouse) Viaduct, 663 yards long with

Huddersfield Viaduct, 1983

two iron and 45 stone spans reaching a maximum height of 53 feet. As built in 1847 the viaduct had two tracks which widened to four part-way across, but in 1883 the whole structure was widened on the west side to take five lines of rails.

At the south end of the station the railway immediately enters the two parallel Huddersfield Tunnels, curving westwards for 685 yards. The original tunnel is the western one with the rock-faced portal; the second tunnel alongside was cut in 1886.

Sandwiched between these two tunnels and the twin-bore Paddock (or Gledholt) Tunnels which come next lies Springwood Junction. The main line of the Leeds Dewsbury & Manchester Railway goes on towards Manchester, through the Paddock Tunnels and then over Longwood Viaduct, with its 20 round arches, while the branch to Penistone diverges to the left.

This line, opened in 1850 by the Man-

chester & Leeds Railway with Sir John Hawkshaw as engineer, immediately crosses the Paddock (or Gledholt) Viaduct over the Colne Valley. The viaduct stands 70 feet high on a sharp curve and has 11 stone arches (2 blocked), 4 iron latticed spans (renewed in 1882) and one flat iron span over a road.

Beyond, the railway passes through the short Lockwood Tunnel and immediately after Lockwood station crosses the Holme valley over the Lockwood Viaduct, 476 yards long, 122 feet high and one of the most spectacular in the North of England (*see photograph, p.37*).

Hawkshaw constructed it of stone with snecked rubble facings, the stone being taken from the deep cuttings at the south end. It has 32 semi-circular-topped arches of 30-foot span and two skew arches of 70-foot and 42-foot span respectively.

HUDDERSFIELD TUNNEL. Completed 1849 for Leeds Dewsbury & Manchester Railway. Engineer Alfred S. Jee. West portal listed Grade II.

HUDDERSFIELD (OR HILLHOUSE) VIADUCT. Completed 1847 for L D & M R. Engineer A. S. Jee. Listed Grade II.

LOCKWOOD VIADUCT. Completed 1848 for Manchester & Leeds Railway. Engineer Sir John Hawkshaw. Listed Grade II.

LONGWOOD VIADUCT. Completed 1849 for L D & M R. Engineer A. S. Jee. Listed Grade II.

PADDOCK (OR GLEDHOLT) TUNNELS. Completed 1849 for L D & M R. Engineer A. S. Jee. Both portals listed Grade II.

PADDOCK (OR GLEDHOLT) VIADUCT. Completed 1850 for Manchester & Leeds Railway. Engineer Sir John Hawkshaw. Listed Grade II.

QUEENS HOTEL, LEEDS, 1969

MYTHOLMROYD FRONTAGE, 1972

MYTHOLMROYD PLATFORM, 1979

LEEDS

QUEENS HOTEL. Opened 1937 by London Midland & Scottish Railway. Chief Architect William H. Hamlyn, Associate Architect W. Curtis Green. Listed Grade II.

The Queens replaced an earlier hotel of 1867 and was part of a large scheme to amalgamate the adjacent Wellington and New stations of the LMS and LNER respectively, the new combined station being renamed Leeds City. The 115-foot-high hotel has been variously described as Art Deco and Classical but the most accurate description of its style perhaps is the one included in the contemporary LMS advertising brochure: ' "cosmopolitan classic" with a decided transatlantic base'.

Its broad, flat Portland stone front is broken only on the ground and top floors by pavilions of classical appearance which show the influence of Sir Edwin Lutyens. Between the first-floor windows the original lead window boxes are still in position. The roofline is broken by a taller central pavilion containing the lift motors and ventilating plant.

The Queens was the first air-conditioned hotel in England and with double glazing and sound insulation provided a high standard of comfort. Leeds Corporation was even persuaded to move its tramlines 30 feet further away and fit specially insulated points in order to reduce the noise level. All 206 bedrooms in the hotel had a bath.

The interior still retains much of its 1930s sumptuousness, particularly in the restaurant and the Italian Classical ballroom with its cool columns, Roman arches, and Art Deco balcony. Even though modern tower blocks surround it, The Queens still predominates in City Square.

Behind is the concourse that was built,

also by Hamlyn, to connect the two former stations. It is well known for its early use of the Portal-type frame and concrete. The uncluttered floor area and deep coffered ceiling with original 1937 lighting pendants present a dignified scene, but since the closure of the former LMS side of the station part has been screened off as a car park.

KIRKSTALL ROAD VIADUCT. Built 1849 for Leeds & Thirsk Railway. Engineer Thomas Grainger. Listed Grade II.

This long curving stone viaduct brings the railway down from the heights of Horsforth to the Aire Valley, its 22 arches forming a prominent feature in this part of Leeds.

1976

MYTHOLMROYD

Built c. 1847 by Manchester & Leeds Railway. Between Todmorden and Halifax.

The curious design of this station is dictated by the geography of the narrow valley in which the village stands. The stone building is taller than it is wide, with three storeys stretching up the side of the viaduct on which the platforms are partly built.

Inside there are five flights of stone stairs, and part way up a wooden subway

to the up platform leads off, slung beneath one of the arches. The platform canopy is a smaller repeat of the main hipped and slated roof, on plain iron columns.

RAVENSTHORPE

Built 1891 by London & North Western Railway. Listed Grade II. Huddersfield to Dewsbury line.

Most of the large railways developed standardized wooden station buildings towards the end of the 19th century. Among the most prolific was the LNWR who assembled them from partly-made

1964

sections manufactured at their Crewe works.

Despite this high degree of uniformity, individual touches could still be found. Ravensthorpe has two of these modular buildings. Most of the features are standard: the hipped slated roofs, horizontal boarding, deep sash windows and flat

LOCKWOOD VIADUCT, HUDDERSFIELD, c.1850

awnings on floral iron brackets with lantern roof lights and serrated valances. But at the ends are 'Gents' where the boarding has been taken up only halfway, leaving the upper portion open.

WAKEFIELD KIRKGATE

Rebuilt 1857 by Lancashire & Yorkshire and Great Northern Railways jointly. Entrance block listed Grade II.

The frontage of this station is severe but dignified. A tall pedimented centrepiece containing a clock rises above low, short wings terminating in small pavilions with broken parapets. The window hoods are alternately flat and curved. Originally the interior had an overall roof.

1977

NORTH YORKSHIRE

COTHERSTONE

BALDER VIADUCT. Built 1868 by Tees Valley Railway. Barnard Castle to Middleton-in-Teesdale line.

The viaduct carrying the branch line up Teesdale occupies a spectacular location across the deep, narrow valley of the River Balder at the village of Cotherstone. It has nine lofty arches in stone, with a cast-iron parapet.

HARROGATE

CRIMPLE VIADUCT. Built 1848 for York & North Midland Railway. Engineer John C.

Birkinshaw. Listed Grade II. Church Fenton to Harrogate branch.

Crimple is a magnificent structure by any standards. Its 31 slender arches, the highest rising to 110 feet, look particularly graceful from the distant valley approaches. Built of grey stone, the viaduct is 624 yards long and each arch is of 50-foot span. It crosses Crimple Beck and an abandoned portion of the Leeds & Thirsk Railway.

CRIMPLE VIADUCT, 1847

KNARESBOROUGH VIADUCT

Built 1848 for Leeds & Thirsk Railway. Engineer Thomas Grainger. Listed Grade II. Between Harrogate and York.

Knaresborough Viaduct is one of the best-known landmarks in North Yorkshire, having been featured on innumerable picture postcards of the gorge of the River Nidd which it spans by four broad arches. Weathered rock-faced stone and a castellated parapet add to the impression that it has always been part of the scene, which no doubt is what its builders had intended.

KNARESBOROUGH VIADUCT, 1976

POCKLINGTON

Built 1847 for York & North Midland Railway. Architect G. T. Andrews. Listed Grade II. Market Weighton to York line. Closed and sold.

Pocklington is the best of Andrews' smaller shed-type stations. It has his customary hipped roof and brick side walls, enlivened with stone window casings and rusticated quoins which were also applied to the station master's house at one end. The entrance is through a delightful five-arched colonnade beneath a dentilled cornice.

The station has been converted into a sports hall, but still retains its basic characteristics.

RICHMOND

Built 1846 for Great North of England Railway. Architect G. T. Andrews. Station bridge listed Grade II. Station closed and sold.

For an ancient town Andrews chose an ancient style: Gothic, almost medieval in concept and execution. This building was the terminus of the Richmond branch. It is an astonishing place, with a cloister-like entrance arcade, heavy buttresses, mullioned windows and tall chimneys, all of

1966

local freestone. The gable ends of the trainshed have herringbone-patterned close-boarding, delicately shaped openings and decorated bargeboards.

Since closure the station has been a garden centre. The station bridge, built by the railway in matching style to gain access to the station across the river, is still in use.

SCARBOROUGH

Built 1845 for York & North Midland Railway. Architect G. T. Andrews. Station, including roof, retaining walls and railings along Valley Bridge Road, listed Grade II.

The terminus at Scarborough is a particularly interesting example of adaptation. To keep pace with the development of the resort and its traffic, the station was extended several times using the existing buildings.

The frontage block is original, a low and symmetrical building of grey ashlar stone with projecting pavilions and matching pediments, one at each end and a third in the centre. Doors and windows are carefully treated, as one would expect from Andrews. Behind is the original trainshed over platforms 3, 4 and 5, again a typical Andrews structure with stone walls, round-headed windows and a hipped, slated roof on light iron trusses. The outer end rests on iron bowstrings tied between two horizontal members by vertical struts.

Beyond the far wall lie platforms 6 and 7 in a second, narrower shed with a similar roof but crossed bowstrings. This was a goods shed extension which was converted for passenger use. The further wall is brick with semi-circular windows, on the other side of which is the original goods shed with a lower, timber-trussed roof. Platform 8 lies along the outer wall, brick again and pierced by round-headed arches leading out on to platform 9 in the open.

1910

Scarborough's most memorable feature is the huge, ungainly Baroque clock tower balanced on top of the central pavilion. It was added in 1884. The railway company agreed to provide an illuminated clock (at the cost of an extra £15) if Scarborough Corporation supplied free gas to light it.

SELBY, 1974

SELBY OLD STATION, 1966

SELBY

STATION. Built 1891 for North Eastern Railway. Architect probably William Bell. Buildings on up platform, canopies on both platforms, footbridge and benches listed Grade II.

The main station building at Selby is a plain brick structure. Its character comes from the broad platform awnings, which are slated and glazed and rest on elaborate iron trusses decorated with ornamental cusps, curved open brackets and slender iron columns. The valancing was attractively scalloped, with moulded corbels to support the gutters at intervals.

OLD STATION. Built 1834 by Leeds & Selby Railway. Listed Grade II.

Though later used as a goods shed, this barn-like building is the original Leeds & Selby terminus. Early passenger stations were little different from goods sheds and in some cases doubled up as both. Here at Selby goods traffic used one side and passenger trains the other.

The walls are red brick, the outer gables timber-clad and the inner ends hipped but partly concealed by a low parapet facing the road. Over the doorways are simply decorated cast-iron beams, one bearing the date 1841. Possibly it records an alteration to the original building.

Francis Whishaw writing in 1842 noted that although the building was spacious and well-proportioned, passengers suffered through the lack of platforms. It could accommodate 98 carriages (short

four-wheelers of course) and wagons, and also contained an engine turntable. The booking office was in the superintendent's house.

Until 1840 passengers for Hull continued their journeys by steamer from a jetty on the river bank, but that year the Hull & Selby Railway arrived by an iron bascule bridge over the river, completing a through route between Leeds and Hull.

WHITBY

STATION. Built 1847 for York & North Midland Railway. Architect G. T. Andrews. Listed Grade II.

When the Y & NM acquired the horse-operated Whitby to Pickering Railway in 1845 they immediately set about improving it for steam locomotive working, and G. T. Andrews was called upon to provide stations. At Whitby and Pickering he built characteristic stone trainsheds with hipped overall roofs (both roofs have now been removed), and Whitby station was enhanced by the addition of a five-arched

porte cochère, moulded cornice and five Georgian-styled windows.

George Hudson, chairman of the Y & NM, was interested in developing the town as a resort, hence all these added embellishments.

1956

When West Cliff station was opened, the older station became known as Whitby Town.

ESK VALLEY or LARPOOL VIADUCT. Erected 1885 for Scarborough & Whitby Railway. Engineers Sir Douglas Fox & Partners. Listed Grade II*. Closed.

This disused viaduct, 305 yards long and 125 feet high above the river bed, is esti-

ESK VALLEY OR LARPOOL VIADUCT, 1962

mated to contain five million bricks. It has 13 arches spanning on average 60 feet, the three over the river being built on the skew so as not to deflect the flow of the water.

The viaduct also crosses two railway routes: the line to Whitby Town from Pickering and Middlesbrough, and the trackbed of the sharply curved horseshoe which ran down from West Cliff Station just to the north. Trains coming up from Scarborough crossed the viaduct, stopped at West Cliff and then reversed steeply down, this time beneath the viaduct, into Whitby Town.

YORK

STATION. Designed by Thomas Prosser for North Eastern Railway; completed 1877 by William Peachey. Listed Grade II.

York provides one of England's most dramatic iron station vistas. The effect of its arched roof curving away into the distance is best seen on a day when shafts of sunlight slant down through the glass.

The roof has four spans of varying height, the widest 81 feet and the tallest 48 feet high. The ribs are five-centred arches tied by iron rods so slender as to make them barely perceptible. Quatrefoil holes add decoration and help for lightness as the ribs taper down to and project below deep open-pattern cross-girders – originally with pendant finials. Sturdy, foliated Corinthian columns support every third rib and the elliptically-curved brackets have spandrel decoration, some with the NER monogram and others with the company's coat of arms picked out in heraldic colours.

WEST COUNTRY PACIFIC *CITY OF WELLS* AND INTER-CITY 125 IN YORK STATION, 1982

One of the most familiar and appealing features is the series of end-screens, each made up of curved transoms and radial glazing bars to form three crescent-shaped areas of glass. They exactly complement the profile of the roof. Additional platforms with individual awnings were later added outside. In 1906 William Bell built a charming art nouveau tea-room on the concourse, complete with curved bay windows, coloured glass and, inside, oriental-style filigree arches.

Contrasting with the splendours of the trainshed the nine-bay balustraded *porte cochère* on the frontage is very dull, quite overshadowed by Peachey's contemporary Royal Station Hotel alongside. Among the interior features of the hotel is a set of iron galleries on three levels, bridging the main staircase.

Before the 1923 Grouping of the railways (*p.8*), a wide selection of different company liveries could be seen at York. The Great Northern, North Eastern, Midland, Lancashire & Yorkshire and Great Central Railways all worked trains into the station with their own locomotives; in addition they brought in through coaches from other systems, providing a great variety of colours and styles.

OLD STATION. Built 1841 for York & North Midland Railway. Architect G. T. Andrews. Hotel added by Andrews, 1853. Station, railings of forecourt on south and east front, main gates and wicket gates to forecourt of former York Old Station Hotel (now West Offices) listed Grade II. Closed.

YORK FRONTAGE AND HOTEL, 1961

In order to enter York the railway had to pass through the city walls, which Andrews accomplished by cutting a pointed arch. Inside he constructed the first U-shaped terminus to have continuous buildings on all three sides (although all were not completed at once).

On the departure side facing Tanner Row he built a three-storey Italianate block in grey brick with generous stone dressings. It has a five-bay centrepiece with round-headed windows and radial glazing bars which are repeated in the end blocks, and it is flanked by recessed wings with Tuscan columns between the ground-floor windows.

A plainer building was added on the arrival side shortly afterwards, followed in 1853 by a hotel across the head of the station. The hotel has a three-storey central block with a deep dentilled cornice beneath the attic windows, and lower wings curving round the corners to link up with the side blocks.

As traffic grew the station became increasingly difficult to work, particularly as all trains to and from the north had to reverse to get in and out. It closed when the present station (*see p.40*) was completed in 1877. A modern railway office block, Hudson House, has been built on the site of Andrews' trainshed.

RAILWAY HEADQUARTERS OFFICES.
Built 1906 for North Eastern Railway.
Architects Horace Field and William Bell.

Pevsner in his *Buildings of England* describes this design as 'Grand Edwardian William-and-Mary'. It won its designers a silver medal at the Paris Exposition of 1905 and contains most of the architectural devices of the period, from giant Dutch gables and a lofty arched entrance to giant pilasters, banded chimney stacks and as many as three rows of dormers in the tall, steep roof. It also has a corner turret with a locomotive weathervane.

NORTH EASTERN RAILWAY WAR MEMORIAL. Unveiled 1924. Architect Sir Edwin Lutyens. Listed Grade II. Leeman Road.

This memorial with its 54-foot cross commemorates the 2,236 NER employees

MIDDLESBROUGH, 1968

MIDDLESBROUGH, 1952

who died in the 1914-18 war. When the design was first shown it caused a controversy because local people thought the screen walls containing the names of the dead would spoil the view of the city wall, so the screens were reduced in size.

CLEVELAND

MIDDLESBROUGH

Built 1877 for North Eastern Railway.
Frontage block designed by William Peachey, trainshed by W. J. Cudworth. Listed Grade II.

Middlesbrough is a good example of later Victorian Gothic, a subdued building in dark grey stone. The main block sits back on a terrace approached by a road ramp

carried on a series of pointed arches used as shops and finished off with a pierced parapet. A second parapet acts as a counterpart around the roof, broken by two large dormers containing a form of plate tracery.

Originally a ridge-and-furrow awning sheltered the front, articulated with round-headed windows. Later it was replaced by a glass lean-to awning, which in turn has now gone.

Inside the booking hall a hammerbeam roof is supported on decorated stone corbels beneath a cornice, and there is a tiled frieze. The fine decorative ironwork, including twisted downpipes and a bridge parapet, is by Handysides of Derby.

Complementing the Gothic frontage was a lofty pointed-arched trainshed on latticed ribs, in two bays. The larger was 60 feet high but only 74 feet wide, giving it a dramatic lancet-like profile that was much admired. W. W. Tomlinson in his *History of the North Eastern Railway* called it 'an architectural tribute to the greatness of Middlesbrough'. Unfortunately it suffered severe bomb damage during the Second World War and was dismantled shortly afterwards, to be replaced by concrete awnings.

SALTBURN

Built 1861 for Stockton & Darlington Railway.
Architect probably Thomas Prosser. Listed Grade II. End of branch from Middlesbrough.

The Stockton & Darlington became much more than a well-known pioneer railway serving the towns in its name; by the time it amalgamated with the North Eastern Railway in 1863 it possessed a network of lines stretching from Saltburn and Guisborough in the east to Tebay and Penrith in Cumbria. The two companies started working in liaison in 1861, which may explain why the NER architect Prosser appears to have been associated with Saltburn station.

SALTBURN, 1976

A great Quaker family of north-east industrialists, the Peases, was closely involved in the S & D, and Alfred Pease was Chairman of the Saltburn Improvement Company which built most of the town including the Zetland Hotel (by William Peachey). So Saltburn can be considered to be a railway-inspired seaside resort.

The station is built of buff brick (probably from the Peases' brickworks) in harmony with the buildings in the square outside, and has an Andrews-type hipped roof. The frontage has a large three-bay *porte cochère* with round arches, Doric pilasters and a bold entablature, in dark freestone.

Originally the main platform ran right up to the rear entrance of the hotel, which stands next door, and a pretty little glass roof provided shelter for the alighting passengers. But the trainshed is now trackless and trains use the former excursion platforms outside.

STOCKTON-ON-TEES

48-56 BRIDGE ROAD. Early Stockton & Darlington Railway building. Listed Grade II.

People claim that No.48 Bridge Road is the original Stockton & Darlington Railway booking office, but it is known that in the first few years inns were used for that purpose, so there may be no truth in it. Nevertheless, the building certainly has early S & D associations and the local authority has made it into an interesting museum.

The ground floor is set up as an early railway booking office and waiting room, and the upper floor contains a number of small exhibits. A plaque outside records the centenary celebrations of the Stockton & Darlington in 1925, and, on the wall opposite, another commemorating the laying of the first rail.

YARM VIADUCT

Opened 1852 for Leeds Northern Railway. Engineers Thomas Grainger and John Bourne. Listed Grade II. Between Northallerton and Stockton-on-Tees.

1975

This long, straight viaduct crosses the valley of the Tees on 43 arches, all brick except for two broad spans over the river, which are of stone. Above the central river

DURHAM VIADUCT UNDER CONSTRUCTION, 1855

pier is the inscription: 'Engineers: Thomas Grainger & John Bourne. Superintendent: Joseph Dixon. Contractors: Trowsdale, Jackson and Garbutt 1849.'

DURHAM

CONSETT

HOWNES GILL VIADUCT. Built 1858 for Stockton and Darlington Railway. Engineer Sir Thomas Bouch.

Built to replace inclines on either side of a steep valley, this viaduct was seen until recently in dramatic conjunction with the Consett steelworks; a vision of great beauty according to the architectural writer Ian Nairn, or possibly not if your idea of the sublime lies elsewhere.

It is 243 yards long and has 12 grey brick semi-circular arches on slim piers up to 150 feet in height which give a very fine appearance; but it also has historic interest, for the buttresses on the piers, which have done nothing to damage the design, were added as a precaution after Bouch's Tay Bridge collapsed in 1879. An immediate and understandable panic led to the strengthening of many of his other bridges which continued to be used successfully, but his reputation was irreversibly ruined.

DARLINGTON

NORTH ROAD STATION. Built 1842 by Stockton & Darlington Railway. Listed Grade II. Ancient Monument. Darlington Bank Top to Bishop Auckland line.

The Stockton & Darlington was the world's first public railway to use steam locomotives and, as on other early lines, passengers boarded and alighted from trains at convenient points rather like bus-stops along the line.

From 1825 to 1833 passenger trains were operated by contractors using horse-drawn coaches; only the freight was hauled by steam. But after the railway

company took the traffic into its own hands and started using steam engines for all trains it became evident that proper stations were needed.

At first Darlington was served by a warehouse on the eastern side of North Road. In 1842 the present North Road station was opened on the west side. The long colonnaded late Georgian frontage has changed little since it was built, and stands attractively at the head of a curving, tree-lined drive.

DARLINGTON NORTH ROAD, 1977

The station now houses the North Road Station Museum, containing a fascinating collection of S & D and North Eastern Railway exhibits, including the historic engines *Locomotion* of 1825 and *Derwent* of 1845 as well as rolling stock, a period booking office and a wealth of other relics.

After passing through the booking office passengers arrived on a wooden platform separated from the track by iron railings. To reach the island platform where the trains were boarded, they crossed a wooden bridge under the roof, a heavy wooden-trussed structure of two bays, of which the outer was formerly a carriage shed. To form the museum the ends of the shed have been enclosed but the footbridge and a spiral staircase to the first-floor offices have been retained. Large exhibits are housed here; smaller ones in the main building. An outside platform is still used by paytrains running to Bishop Auckland.

SKERNE BRIDGE. Built 1825 for Stockton & Darlington Railway. Architect Ignatius Bonomi. Ancient Monument. East of Northgate, Darlington.

This historic bridge over the River Skerne is the one depicted in John Dobbins' well known painting of the opening of the S & D. It is an elegant stone structure with a broad arch flanked by two narrow ones and by gracefully curved wing walls, and was the largest masonry structure on the original line.

It is probably the first work ever commissioned by a railway company from a professional architect. Bonomi had a practice in Durham where he was also County Surveyor, and designed a number of buildings in the North East. He was the elder son of the better-known Joseph Bonomi, an Italian expatriate who built many English country houses and mansions and was also honorary architect to St. Peters Basilica, Rome.

Today, surrounded by more than 150 years of industrial development, the Skerne Bridge is difficult to reach; both sides are partly obscured – one by a widening of the bridge with a concrete arch and the other by gas pipes – but it can be seen from Albert Road and John Street.

BANK TOP STATION. Built 1887 by North Eastern Railway. Architect William Bell. Listed Grade II.

The semi-circular arched roof of Darlington Bank Top is characteristic of a number of the North Eastern Railway's principal stations – we have already seen its final development at Hull (*p.31*). The three spans cover a broad island platform

of the type that became popular in the 1880s; similar large examples can be seen at Rugby and Dundee. This arrangement made it possible to provide a single block of offices and amenities for the whole station and avoided the need for internal bridges or subways. Here the roof spans are carried on brick outer screen walls and intermediate Corinthian columns of iron. The whole aspect is one of airy spaciousness, in direct contrast to the heavy gloom of North Road in the days of steam. A subway leads from the equally spacious low-level covered entrance-way and cab drive.

The red brick Dutch gables and lofty clock tower of Bank Top Station make it a well-known Darlington landmark.

1966

DURHAM

STATION. Built 1857 for North Eastern Railway. Architect possibly G. T. Andrews. Conservation Area.

Durham station sits high above the town at the end of the viaduct (*see p.42*), looking across the Wear gorge to the castle and the cathedral. Although Thomas Prosser was architect to the North Eastern by this time, the Tudor of the main building smacks so strongly of Andrews, and is particularly reminiscent of Richmond (*p.38*), that one wonders whether it was based on a design of his which was laid aside when George Hudson's downfall

delayed completion of this line, and was brought out and dusted down later.

The grey stone fits in well with the old city, as does the castellated portico with its five Perpendicular pointed arches, its heavy buttresses and mullioned windows.

The large, matching station master's house is linked to the entrance building by a screen wall, and the platforms have box-style ironwork supporting the awnings, similar to, but wider than, those at Selby.

VIADUCT. Built 1856 for North Eastern Railway. Engineer probably T. E. Harrison. Listed Grade II.

Immediately south of the station is Durham viaduct, which crosses a side valley of the River Wear on ten stone arches and dominates the east of the city.

DARLINGTON BANK TOP TRAINSHED, 1979

ARCHITECTS OF THE NORTH EASTERN RAILWAY

The North Eastern was one of the few 19th-century railways to employ professional architects continuously for a significant period, in this case almost 60 years. The first office-holder, from 1857 to 1874, was Thomas Prosser, who is chiefly remembered for his three large works: the modification and completion of Dobson's portico at Newcastle; the construction of Leeds New station in 1869, now replaced, where he employed an interesting mansard-shaped roof; and above all, York.

Prosser was followed in quick succession by Benjamin Burleigh (1874-76) and William Peachey (1876-77). It fell to Burleigh to complete York, which he did with minor modifications, but Peachey managed to cram several stations into his short period of office, the most noteworthy of which was Middlesbrough.

William Bell followed and stayed with the NER until the 1923 Grouping, a period of 46 years. He left distinctive marks, in particular his majestic overall roof design which could be seen in successive stages of development at Sunderland, Darlington Bank Top, Alnwick, Stockton-on-Tees and Hull. While much of his work on smaller stations was standardized and dull, many of his iron platform awnings were full of intricate detail.

HEIGHINGTON

*Opened by Stockton & Darlington Railway.
Darlington to Bishop Auckland line.*

Heighington is one of the very few stations
to have survived unaltered from the 1820s
and 1830s. Although the line is part of the
Stockton & Darlington of 1825, it is not
known when the station was constructed.
Originally it was a stopping-place called
Aycliffe Lane Crossing, and it was here
that George Stephenson's pioneer engine
Locomotion (now in North Road Station
Museum, Darlington – *see p.42*) was
placed on the rails 11 days before the
official opening.

HEIGHINGTON, 1966

The station has two interesting early
features. The 'platform' is nothing more
than a small cobbled area at rail level in
front of the small stone cottage-type
building which from this side appears to
be single-storeyed. From the road side,
however, it can be seen that it is in fact
two storeys high. The ground floor containing the dwelling quarters is at the foot
of a low embankment, with the booking
office in effect upstairs. This arrangement
was later copied here and there by other
railways.

The separate staggered platforms used
by present-day trains were added later
and extended during the 1939-45 war for
use by a local munitions factory.

NEWCASTLE HIGH LEVEL BRIDGE, 1849

WASHINGTON

*VICTORIA BRIDGE. Built 1838 for
Durham Junction Railway. Engineer T. E.
Harrison. Washington to Penshaw line.*

At the time of construction the 160-foot
central span of this viaduct was reputed to
be the widest masonry arch in the world,
although it was soon exceeded. There are
two other wide spans, one of 144 feet and
two of 100 feet, together with three narrow ones on either side, each of 20 feet.

The viaduct stands an impressive 135
feet above the River Wear and is one of
most graceful railway viaducts in
England. The final stone was laid on
Queen Victoria's coronation day, hence
its name.

Victoria Bridge, over River Wear.

c.1910

TYNE & WEAR

GATESHEAD

*DUNSTON COAL STAITHES. Built 1890
by the North Eastern Railway. Listed Grade II.
On south bank of Tyne east of Redheugh Bridge.*

Braced timber jetties were a feature of the
North East coal trade for loading sea-
going colliers from railway wagons. Dunston Staithes were the last to operate on
the Tyne and can accommodate three
ships. Extending more than 567 yards
into the river to form a basin, they are of
traditional 'double-decker' construction,
capable of handling wagons on two levels,
and symbolize the trade which brought
prosperity to Tyneside.

*RAILWAY WORKSHOPS. Built by North
Eastern Railway. Listed Grade II. Rabbit
Bank Road, Gateshead.*

The NER had two main locomotive
works; Gateshead was the principal one
until the locomotive department headquarters was moved to Darlington in
1908. The works were a landmark from
the riverside, standing at the top of the
steep bank between the High Level and
King Edward Bridges. The listed building is the former boiler shop, a two-storey
stone structure with round-arched windows. The ground floor has a barrel-
vaulted ceiling on heavy stone piers.

*GREENESFIELD STATION HOTEL.
Built 1844 for Brandling Junction Railway.
Architect G. T. Andrews. Listed Grade II.*

This was one of the first hotels and
stations to be designed as a complete unit,

(Continued on page 49)

MACHINERY
OF MOVEMENT

The mechanical engineering heritage of the railways is largely defunct. Unlike the stations, bridges and tunnels through which they once ran, locomotives and rolling stock of any age now survive only in museums or are privately preserved.

Most of this book describes and illustrates the fixed equipment of the railways, the buildings and civil engineering works which are dispersed all over Britain from Cornwall to the Far North of Scotland. These four pages by contrast portray the very different state of the mechanical heritage, which has a much shorter working life. Steam locomotives, rolling stock and smaller items of moving equipment such as luggage barrows or milk drays were mostly scrapped when they became obsolete.

The remaining examples are now gathered in relatively few places, on the lines of privately run steam railways or in the major transport museums. The most comprehensive collection

At Sheffield Park on the Bluebell Railway (top), *the 4-6-2* Blackmore Vale (left) *and partly restored 0-6-0 and 2-10-0 locomotives flank an 0-4-4 tank engine, while at Loughborough a restored tank wagon is included in a preserved Great Central Railway train* (above). *Commercial sponsors often pay for restoration in return for advertising.*

is at the National Railway Museum in York.

The first museum at York was created by the LNER in 1925-26, initially open to visitors by appointment only. The large exhibits were housed in part of the old Queen Street Works and the small ones in the former first-class refreshment room at the Old Station.

After the Second World War a national collection was set up at Clapham in South London, although the York museum remained open as well; and in 1975 both collections were removed to the present museum in York, run as a branch of the Science Museum.

The National Railway Museum contains the largest collection of locomotives and rolling stock to be found in a single museum anywhere in Europe. More than 20 locomotives dating from 1829 to our own time and a notable assortment of passenger carriages fill the whole of the main hall, itself a railway building. Two of the roundhouse locomotive sheds north of the station have been knocked into one, according to a design by Bernard Kaukas, Chief Architect for the National Railway Museum. The turntables and radiating stalls (which still connect with British Rail) are ideal for display. The convenience of a rail connection was one of the prime reasons for choosing York as the site of the national museum. The facility to change the exhibits by rail was infinitely preferable to the cripplingly expensive transfers by heavy road vehicles when the collection was at Clapham.

Few visitors, however little they may care about the technology of railways, can remain untouched by this great spectacle of colour – for the machines are painted in green and black, blue and crimson and brown – and of bright metalwork in iron and steel, picked out in copper and brass, all immaculately polished and maintained.

The diversity of colour and design reflects the history of the British railways themselves, still owned and run by more than 100 companies in 1922. This book illustrates how the companies followed different practices in station building and engineering works, whether to emphasize difference from a competitor or for some commercial or technical reason. Here these variations are expressed in their machines, arising largely from the particular demands the companies made for economy, greater power or higher speed.

In addition to the machinery of movement, the museum also displays a very broad range of the railways' fixed equipment. At one end stands a prime piece in the history of British civil engineering: the Gaunless bridge of 1825, designed for the Stockton & Darlington Railway by George Stephenson (probably helped by the contractors John and Isaac Burrell). It was the first railway bridge of substantial size constructed of metal anywhere. At the other end there is a display showing the evolution of the track, the most essential element of the 'rail way' itself.

The museum has much to show of the small things the railways used in their work (clocks and watches for example: the railways played a leading part in establishing one standard time throughout the country and in making ordinary people time-conscious) and the methods they chose to describe and publicise it, their notices and warnings, their alluring and sometimes brilliant posters.

In short, this is a place where the railway heritage can be seen and appreciated in summary, as a microcosm of the whole.

At the National Railway Museum is the saloon built for Queen Victoria by the LNWR. Its body dates back to 1869.

This clock formerly stood among Ionic columns at the south end of Philip Hardwick's Great Hall at Euston station.

Now-fragile silks provide the upholstery in Queen Victoria's saloon. It was said to be her favourite railway vehicle and was not replaced until after her death in 1901.

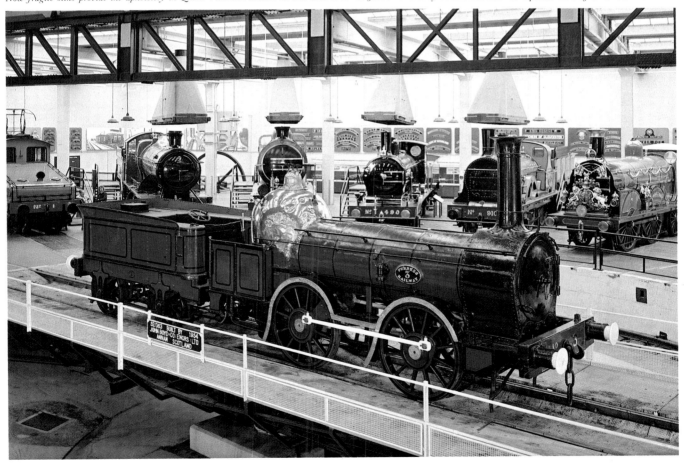

On a turntable stands 'Old Coppernob', the Furness Railway's 0-4-0 No. 3 built in 1846, surrounded by later locomotives including an LBSCR 0-4-2 in royal regalia.

At Didcot Railway Centre, the cab and boiler of Bonnie Prince Charlie, a privately-owned 0-4-0 industrial saddle tank built in 1949, await reassembly.

Drays like this were used to transport milk from the railheads to the many local distributors until they were replaced by so-called mechanical horses in the 1920s.

The GWR 'Dukedog' 4-4-0 Earl of Berkeley, which was built in 1938, incorporates parts of two older 4-4-0s: the boiler of a 'Duke' mounted on the frame of a 'Bulldog'.

(*Continued from page 44*)

and formed the Gateshead terminus of the Brandling Junction Railway. Only the hotel building remains. It is part of the Gateshead Works complex and lies in Hudson Street amidst the triangle of lines at the south end of the High Level Bridge. A three-storey building in stone with a prominent cornice and a classical main doorway, it is still used as railway offices.

NEWCASTLE-UPON-TYNE

CENTRAL STATION. Built 1850 for York Newcastle & Berwick Railway. Architect John Dobson. Engineer Robert Stephenson. Part listed Grade II.*

Writing about John Dobson, Christian Barman in his *Introduction to Railway Architecture* called him 'an architect of the finest and most developed type – planner, engineer and man of affairs as well as a sensitive designer'. His output was immense: country houses, bridges, churches, docks, public buildings. He was

c.1909

also a notable landscape gardener and town planner, and in collaboration with Richard Grainger he laid out Newcastle's fine new city centre of the 1830s and 1840s. Central station is his greatest work, and by some considered to be the finest in the country.

The trainshed, built by Dobson in collaboration with Robert Stephenson, was the first of the great arched roofs and

represented a bold step forward which was copied by others. It has three spans 60 feet wide, the central one higher than the other two. Sited on a curve the shed has the same dramatic quality as that at York, and represented the first use of malleable rolled iron ribs, to produce which Dobson himself invented bevelled rollers. He also devised the system – used later at Paddington and York – of supporting only every third rib on columns; the intermediate ribs are joined by two tiers of cross girders on shallow brackets. The tiers are braced by Gothic-shaped struts but he decided to cover them with rectangular wooden panels in order to match his classical frontage.

Dobson's large buildings were in the grand classical tradition of Vanbrugh, and his design for Central station's frontage block is generally acknowledged as his best. Undoubtedly it would have been one of the finest 19th-century classical buildings in Europe had it been completed, but unfortunately when the walls were half finished the railway directors decided to move their headquarters to Newcastle from York and demanded both more office accommodation and also a smaller building to save expense. Modifications had to be hastily devised and the result, by comparison with the plans, was a disappointment. Dobson's immense portico was omitted and it was left to Thomas Prosser to complete it in a similar style, though without Dobson's detail.

Even so, Newcastle Central today is magnificent, inside for its spectacular combination of curves and outside for its sheer size and length.

It has little-noticed secrets, too, such as the ingeniously contrived curve of the rear wall of the main block, designed to match the curve of the roof, and the elaborate walls and ceiling in the refreshment room (now obscured but not entirely hidden by dark paint). Above the entrance to the refreshment room on the platform side are the heads of Queen Victoria and Prince Albert who opened the station in 1850.

The date, 28th September 1849, is wrong; that was the day the Queen opened the High Level Bridge (*see below*).

In 1893 two more spans were added to Dobson's roof by William Bell, and the number of platforms finally reached 15.

Alongside the station is the Royal Station Hotel, built in 1854 as an integral part of the frontage; it was extended in 1892. The entrance hall has pedimented doorways and a decorated iron balustrade on the staircase and landings which run around a central well; there is much terracotta work in the corridors and a grand coffered ceiling and columns in the restaurant. At the opposite (west) end of the station frontage there is a smaller but matching domed building, formerly the accounts office.

HIGH LEVEL BRIDGE. Built 1849 for York Newcastle & Berwick Railway. Engineer Robert Stephenson. Listed Grade I.

It was decided that the new bridge across the Tyne to Newcastle Central should be on two levels carrying both road and rail. For this purpose Stephenson chose to employ the bowstring girder principle. The cast-iron 'bows' carrying the three-track railway deck 120 feet above the river are tied by horizontal wrought iron 'strings'

1968

below which support the 20-foot roadway and two 6-foot footways. Vertical struts tie the two decks.

The bridge has six spans carried on tall sandstone piers, the highest 146 feet above the river bed. The piers rest on timber piles which were driven into the bed by a specially adapted version of James Nasmyth's newly-invented steam hammer, the first occasion power was used for pile-driving on a major bridge job. Stephenson himself supervised the driving of the first pile.

The bridge had an important social effect, for the new road crossing (about which there had been discussion but no action for years) joined Newcastle and Gateshead far more effectively and conveniently than the old road bridge 100 feet below, with its steep, winding approaches. The High Level Bridge thus marked the beginning of Tyneside as a single urban entity.

Queen Victoria performed the opening ceremony. A year later, just before she opened Central station and the Royal Border Bridge at Berwick (*p.53*), a banquet was held to celebrate the completion

NEWCASTLE CENTRAL. c.1909

of the railway from London to Edinburgh. Robert Stephenson was guest of honour. Appropriately the dinner was held in the station beneath Dobson's great iron roof and within a stone's throw of Stephenson's bridge, both pioneer structures and still in use under far more arduous conditions than their creators could possibly have envisaged.

JESMOND STATION. Built 1864 by Blyth & Tyne Railway. Listed Grade II. Newcastle to Whitley Bay line. Closed.

The original Jesmond station on the Blyth & Tyne is a red brick building with stone

1978

trim. It has Tudor features such as numerous gables, eaves, kneelers and octagonal chimneys, but is spoiled by typical mid-Victorian sash windows. The station has been replaced by a new Jesmond station on the Tyne & Wear Metro nearby.

RAILWAY ARCH IN DEAN STREET. Built 1848 by York Newcastle & Berwick Railway. Listed Grade II. Part of viaduct between Central and Manors stations.

c.1860

The railway here runs above the roof tops as they slope steeply down to the Tyne. It is in part of old Newcastle, and the high bridge over Dean Street is in two stages, and is notable for its superb masonry.

OUSEBURN AND WILLINGTON DENE VIADUCTS. Built 1839 for Newcastle & North Shields Railway. Engineers John & Benjamin Green. Newcastle to North Shields line.

These two viaducts across deep valleys running down to the Tyne are unusual for having been built originally with laminated timber and radial struts (a section of the timber is in the National Railway

OUSEBURN VIADUCT, 1869

Museum at York) and then respectively replaced in 1860 and 1880 with iron to a similar design, so that outwardly they retain their initial appearance.

Ouseburn, which is near Byker station on the Metro, has seven spans on stone piers. It is 306 yards long and 108 feet high and is disused. The line of the Tyne & Wear Metro now runs alongside on a new concrete viaduct, equally revolutionary in being the first major bridge in the United Kingdom to be built by cantilevered construction from counter-cast, pre-cast segments joined with epoxy resin and stressed together.

The similar Willington Dene viaduct, near Hadrian station on the Metro, is 347 yards long and 82 feet high, also with seven arches.

SOUTH SHIELDS

Built 1879 for North Eastern Railway. Architect probably William Peachey. East wall of trainshed and tile map listed Grade II.

The tiled wall map of the NER system was once a common feature at many principal stations, and contained locations of cathedrals, abbeys, castles, parks and battlefields; even insets showing the

1975

layout of the company's various docks were included. A number still exist at other stations in the region.

SUNDERLAND

WEAR BRIDGE. Built 1879 for North Eastern Railway. Engineer W. G. Laws. Listed Grade II.

The railway bridge spans the River Wear alongside the road bridge. It has a segmental iron arch with openings, and was built to connect Monkwearmouth and Sunderland, so providing a direct route from Sunderland via Monkwearmouth to Newcastle. Laws was assistant to the company's Chief Engineer T. E. Harrison, who would also have been involved in the design.

MONKWEARMOUTH. Built 1848 for Brandling Junction Railway. Architect Thomas Moore. Listed Grade II. Closed and sold.

When George Hudson, the 'Railway King', was elected MP for Sunderland in 1845 he had a grand terminus built just across the river at Monkwearmouth to celebrate the event. The Brandling Junction Railway running from Gateshead was one of his lines, but until the Wear Bridge was built 30 years later, Monkwearmouth was the closest it could come to Sunderland. When the bridge was built Monkwearmouth became a suburban station.

Few stations express power and prestige in such small compass. Indeed, one of the fascinations of Monkwearmouth is that in railway terms it is quite a small station, which makes its huge Ionic portico seem all the more important. Curved lower wings with pilasters and fluted Doric columns link the portico to arcaded side walls which back the platform and complete this superbly noble folly.

MONKWEARMOUTH, 1975

After closure the local authority restored the interior and converted it into a museum which includes a most realistic replica period booking office.

QUEEN ALEXANDRA BRIDGE. Built 1909 for North Eastern Railway. Engineer Sir William Arrol in conjunction with Charles A. Hewison. Closed.

At the turn of the century Sunderland exported six million tons of coal annually, most of which had to cross this bridge by train. The bridge, built to carry two decks with railway tracks above and a roadway

1975

below, was therefore made immensely strong.

When it was first tested with a dozen locomotives weighing 1,190 tons, the bridge deflected less than an inch.

TYNEMOUTH

OLD STATION. Built 1847 for Newcastle & North Shields Railway. Main passenger building listed Grade II. Closed.

This former terminus is a stone Tudor building, two-storeys high with a large projecting gabled centrepiece featuring a mullioned oriel window above a three-bay portico with shallow pointed arches and shield motifs. Gabled dormers on

1975

either side make a symmetrical composition broken by a single-storey wing with a wooden ventilator. The station became a goods depot in 1882 when it was replaced by the present through station by William Bell. Notable as an extravaganza of NER decorative ironwork, the second one is now a Tyne & Wear Metro station.

NORTHUMBERLAND

ACKLINGTON

Built 1847 for Newcastle & Berwick Railway. Architect Benjamin Green. Station, including single-storey extension at right angles to the south, and goods shed listed Grade II. Morpeth to Alnmouth line.

Acklington is one of the attractive family of neo-Tudor stations designed by Green for this railway, the final link in the East Coast route in Scotland. With its strong lines, finely detailed yet sparingly embellished, the grey stonework blends well into the Northumbrian landscape. The stone goods shed was built to match. Together they form a unity of composition not widely found elsewhere.

BELFORD

Built 1847 for Newcastle & Berwick Railway. Architect Benjamin Green. Station house listed Grade II. Alnmouth to Berwick line. Closed.

This is another of Green's precisely proportioned neo-Tudor stations, more

1976

elaborate than Acklington and possessing, perhaps, the finest frontage in the series with its almost lancet arches and buttresses, again built in the cool grey ashlar stone of the district.

The concept is manorial both in size and use of the typically Tudor E-shaped plan, whose recesses Green used for a waiting shelter on the platform side. The building is now used as a private house.

ACKLINGTON, 1972

ROYAL BORDER BRIDGE, 1976

BERWICK, 1963

BERWICK-ON-TWEED

ROYAL BORDER BRIDGE. Built 1850 for York Newcastle & Berwick Railway. Engineer Robert Stephenson. Listed Grade I.

The rail link between England and Scotland at first was made across a temporary wooden bridge over the Tweed while Stephenson's superb viaduct of 28 red stone-faced brick arches on tall stone piers was being completed. The viaduct was formally opened in September 1850 by Queen Victoria on her way to her palace of Holyrood. It was on this occasion that Stephenson was offered, but declined, a knighthood.

Standing 126 feet above high water, the sweeping curve above the roofs of Berwick at the south end, set magnificently against Hallidon Hill, makes it in the words of Stephenson's biographer L. T. C. Rolt the most 'romantic and evocative railway structure in the world'. The best way to appreciate it is to cross the bridge by train and then walk along the north bank of the Tweed and savour it from below.

STATION. Built 1927 by London & North Eastern Railway. Listed Grade II.

The first station at Berwick was built by the North British Railway in 1843 on the site of the 12th-century castle. This was

THE NORTH EASTERN RAILWAY

Before the 1930s the North Eastern was the most preservation-minded of all the British railway companies. As the proud heir of the Stockton & Darlington Railway, its management saw that the railway diamond jubilee of 1875 was fittingly celebrated by a display of locomotives and rolling stock; and when the centenary year came in 1925, a fine collection of historic locomotives was available for the pageantry. None of these was subsequently scrapped, and the collection formed the nucleus of the Railway Museum set up at York by the successor company the LNER and now part of the National Railway Museum (*p.46*).

The NER was the wealthiest constituent of the LNER. It operated a vast freight traffic and was the largest dock-owning railway company in the world. It had docks at Hull, Middlesbrough, Hartlepool, and Tyne Dock (near Jarrow) complete with graving docks, slipways, numerous steam tugs, coal discharging staiths, foreign cattle depots, cold storage, fish and fruit markets, and every modern type of electric, hydraulic and steam crane.

The North Eastern was a pioneer in the use of the electro-pneumatic system of signal and point operation in 1906 and was also at the forefront in railway electrification. It electrified its North Tyne suburban lines on the third-rail system in 1904, and the busy, steeply graded mineral line between Shildon and Newport near Middlesbrough was converted to overhead electric traction in 1915.

A Class 'R' 4-4-0 crosses King Edward Bridge, Newcastle, with the 12.20pm train for Sheffield, 1908.

CHATHILL, 1972

an historic piece of railway vandalism. The remains of the great hall of the castle, in which Baliol did homage to Edward I for the crown of Scotland, were all swept away, and the line cut straight through the outer walls. Some of the stone went into the building of the station, and only a fragment of the castle now remains, including part of the old station wall and some vaults which are listed as ancient monuments. In true early Victorian fashion the railway tried to make amends by building a station in keeping with the site, with crenellated towers, pointed arches and a 'watch-tower' on each corner of the stone-walled trainshed.

In 1927 the LNER built a new island-platform station with a detached frontage block joined to the platform by a covered footbridge. The facade is in Dumfries-shire red ashlar sandstone, two storeys high with a central clock and a Union Flag patterned iron railing forming a parapet. When built, the name of the station was displayed on the front canopy in rather nice art nouveau lettering.

CHATHILL

Built 1845 for Newcastle & Berwick Railway. Architect Benjamin Green. House and offices, including west wing and one-storey extension, waiting shed on up platform and lamp posts on both platforms listed Grade II. Alnmouth to Berwick line.

This, another of Green's stations, bears a family likeness to Acklington and Belford, although the similarity stops after the Tudor styling for here the designer chose a two-storey projecting bay as his dominant feature.

The roof at one side is ingeniously carried forward to make a charmingly bracketed platform shelter, while the gable and chimney details are as much a delight as at the other stations on the Newcastle and Berwick Railway.

KIELDER VIADUCT

Built 1862 for Border Counties Railway. Engineer Peter Nicholson. Ancient Monument. Between Reedsmouth and Riccarton Junction. Map ref. NY 632924. Closed.

Built in stone with a castellated parapet this most attractive viaduct crosses the Kielder Burn, a tributary of the North Tyne. Its appearance is well suited to its historic border surroundings, but its real importance and the reason for its preservation is that it was built to a skew arch design developed by Nicholson, who was a Newcastle mathematician, and here used for the first time.

By means of a particular geometrical technique each block of masonry was individually shaped for its place in the structure. It was a far more accurate and economical method than that used at Rainhill (*p.104*) and elsewhere, which dated back to William Jessop and the building of the Rochdale canal.

LAMBLEY VIADUCT, 1980, ON THE NEWCASTLE & CARLISLE RAILWAY (*see overleaf*)

NEWCASTLE &   CARLISLE RAILWAY

Opened 1838. Engineer Francis Giles.

The Newcastle & Carlisle was a very early main line and the first to cross the country. Perhaps because it is now a secondary route, albeit an important one, it has retained more of its original character than any other 60 miles of railway.

The line has notable engineering works, particularly the deep Cowran Hills cutting near How Mill and three viaducts between Brampton and Wetheral. The three arches of the Gelt Viaduct were at the time the largest skew arches in Britain, while further west Corby has seven arches across the Corby Burn 70 feet high. Only a quarter of a mile beyond, Wetheral Viaduct starts right at the eastern end of the Wetheral station platforms, crossing the River Eden by five 80-foot spans 95 feet high. They are all constructed in Eden Valley sandstone. Gelt and Wetheral have inscriptions, the former recording the names of Francis Giles, civil engineer, and John McKay, builder, dated 1832-35. Wetheral has a Latin inscription on the inside of one parapet at the station end – which can be easily seen – with an English translation on the opposite side:

'In testimony of respect for their late colleague Henry Howard of Corby Esq. who on the 25 March 1830 laid the foundation stone of this bridge the directors of the railway lay this tablet.'

No less important are the numerous stations, again probably the oldest series retaining most of their original features that now exist in close proximity. There is evidence to suggest that Benjamin Green of Newcastle was the architect of these stations – two-storey stone Tudorish buildings incorporating living quarters and each embellished with a small but distinctive cross-gabled upper window projecting on stone corbels over the platform. Wylam is one example; Haltwhistle is a larger edition.

Some of the original buildings can easily be identified by their position set back from the tracks (for which they were criticised at the time), with detached platforms added later in the conventional position. Corbridge, the odd man out, probably dates from about 1848, built like (or adapted from?) a private house. It has a long narrow passageway containing the booking window which leads from the front door to the platform, emerging beneath a glass verandah on Tuscan columns – a surprising touch on an otherwise vernacular-styled building.

The Alston branch of 1852 passes over two splendid viaducts designed by Sir George Barclay-Bruce. Lambley is very narrow (only single line width) and slender as it curves over the deep valley of the South Tyne on nine arches 110 feet high, while Burnstones, near Slaggyford, is another early example of a skew viaduct, made up of five arches skewed in one direction and one in the other with a blind arch between.

The cast-iron water tank at Haltwhistle, dated 1861, is an example of the care which railway companies could take with even small structures. Its bolted sections are nicely panelled, and sit on a stone base arcaded with arched doors and windows.

HALTWHISTLE STATION WATER TOWER and WATER CRANES. Listed Grade II. Hexham to Carlisle section.

WYLAM STATION. Listed Grade II*. Newcastle to Hexham section.

CORBRIDGE STATION. Listed Grade II. Newcastle to Hexham section.

LAMBLEY and BURNSTONES VIADUCTS. Listed Grade II. Alston branch. Closed.

MIDDLE GELT and CORBY VIADUCTS. Listed Grade II. Hexham to Carlisle section.

Haltwhistle, 1978

Corbridge, 1978

Wylam, 1978

Wetheral Viaduct, 1970s

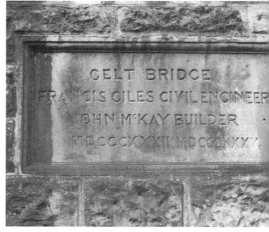

Inscription on Gelt Viaduct

...by Bridge, c.1840

...ltwhistle Tower, 1978

Water Crane, Haltwhistle, 1978

LONDON MIDLAND REGION

CONTENTS

LONDON: PAGE 59   **HOME COUNTIES:** HERTFORDSHIRE (PART) PAGE 64   BEDFORDSHIRE PAGE 64

BUCKINGHAMSHIRE PAGE 65   **SOUTH MIDLANDS:** WARWICKSHIRE PAGE 66   NORTHAMPTONSHIRE PAGE 68

LEICESTERSHIRE PAGE 70   WEST MIDLANDS PAGE 72   **NORTH MIDLANDS:** NOTTINGHAMSHIRE (PART) PAGE 73

DERBYSHIRE PAGE 75   STAFFORDSHIRE PAGE 86   SHROPSHIRE PAGE 90   **NORTH WALES:** POWYS PAGE 91

DYFED (PART) PAGE 92   CLWYD PAGE 94   GWYNEDD PAGE 96   **NORTH-WEST ENGLAND:** CHESHIRE PAGE 96

GREATER MANCHESTER PAGE 98   MERSEYSIDE PAGE 103   LANCASHIRE PAGE 107

NORTH YORKSHIRE (PART) PAGE 113   CUMBRIA PAGE 114

The London Midland Region has a greater route mileage than any other in the British Rail network. Like Eastern Region, it extends from London to the Scottish border, serving the entire western half of England north of Hereford, Worcester and Oxfordshire, as well as North Wales. It thus takes in some of the densest conurbations in the country, including Manchester, Liverpool and Birmingham, as well as some of the highest mountains, notably the western Pennines along the divide with Eastern Region, the northern half of the Welsh mountains and the Lake District.

The independent companies which built the railway network in the 19th century formed relationships with lines across the Scottish border. These connections were maintained at the Grouping of 1923 with the establishment of the London Midland & Scottish Railway, which incorporated the Caledonian, Glasgow & South Western and Highland Railways as well as its English lines. On nationalisation in 1948, however, Scotland was made into a separate region.

The English companies swallowed up by the LMS were the old London & North Western, which went north from Euston; the Midland, based in Derby with its London station at St. Pancras; the Lancashire & Yorkshire, whose headquarters were at Manchester; and a number of smaller lines including the North Staffordshire, Furness and Maryport & Carlisle Railways.

With its main line running from London up the west coast of England to Carlisle, the London & North Western was always in the forefront of fierce competition to run the fastest trains to Scotland. Competition with

Inside Robert Stephenson's cavernous Kilsby Tunnel, 28 feet high and 25 wide, men and horses gather in the light of a working shaft. The scene was drawn by J. C. Bourne in 1837, a year before the tunnel's completion.

the rival East Coast route reached its peak in the last decades of the 19th century with the famous Races to the North; and even after Grouping rivalry continued. Indeed, a friendly and unofficial competition between the two routes remains to this day.

The region incorporates the oldest main-line passenger and goods service in the world, the Liverpool & Manchester Railway. Opened in 1830, it includes such early structures as the Sankey Viaduct and the fine skew bridge at Rainhill, both by George Stephenson. His son Robert achieved even greater fame with numerous works in the region, including Kilsby Tunnel south of Rugby, and the two remarkable tubular bridges at Conwy and Menai. The second has been rebuilt following a disastrous fire, incorporating the majestic piers of the original bridge.

Also included in the region are parts of the Great Central and several former joint railways from post-Grouping days, the largest of which were the LMS and GWR lines from Chester to Warrington and Birkenhead and the LNER and LMS Cheshire Lines Committee which operated a network in North Cheshire and South Lancashire. At Derby and Crewe are British Rail's two most important workshops, the latter including the railway's technical and research establishment.

Many of the region's most outstanding engineering achievements arose from the determination of the railway companies to put lines over hitherto unconquered terrain. There is the dramatically engineered line over the Cumbrian fells, for example. Further east, the Settle & Carlisle line, opened in 1876 by the Midland Railway, stands as a monument to its engineer-in-chief, John Crossley. Its combination of bold planning, resolute building in the country's most extreme climatic conditions and a

wild magnificence of scenery give it an unequalled status in the British railway heritage. Four of its largest viaducts are scheduled as Ancient Monuments.

The western parts of the four railway routes which cross the Pennines are in the London Midland Region, with numerous notable viaducts and the impressive Summit, Woodhead and Standedge Tunnels. Standedge had the distinction of containing the only water-troughs ever laid in a tunnel – simply because it was the only stretch of line between Manchester and Huddersfield that was level.

These mountainous lines contrast strongly with the coastal routes such as the Cumbrian coast line which winds its way gently around the edges of the Lake District, with long viaducts over the Kent and Leven estuaries. And on Lake Windermere the region operates the only inland Sealink shipping service, although the steamers no longer connect, as they once did, with scheduled British Rail trains.

The region is no less rich in its architectural heritage. The Midland was especially noted for the high standard of its stations, from the majestic St. Pancras to the matching wayside stations of the Settle & Carlisle line.

The London & North Western, not itself noted for elegance of lineside architecture, nonetheless inherited some delightful structures from earlier lines. Those designed by Francis Thompson for the Chester & Holyhead Railway were especially fine, and include the notable station at Chester itself. J. W. Livock was responsible for some charming Tudor-Jacobean buildings on the Trent Valley Railway, and the prolific Sir William Tite produced one of his masterpieces at Carlisle. The smaller lines had some attractive buildings, especially the North Staffordshire and the Furness Railways.

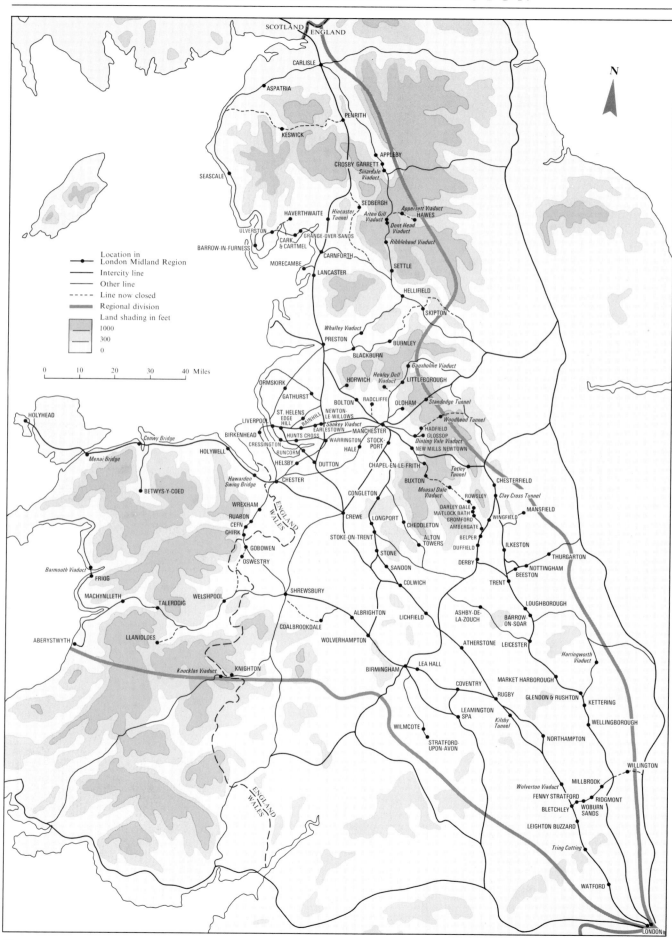

SCOTLAND / ENGLAND

N

CARLISLE

ASPATRIA

PENRITH

KESWICK

APPLEBY

CROSBY GARRETT
Smardale Viaduct

SEASCALE

SEDBERGH
Appersett Viaduct
HAWES

HAVERTHWAITE
Hincaster Tunnel
Arten Gill Viaduct

ULVERSTON
Dent Head Viaduct
GRANGE-OVER-SANDS

CARK & CARTMEL
Ribblehead Viaduct

BARROW-IN-FURNESS

CARNFORTH

MORECAMBE
SETTLE

LANCASTER

HELLIFIELD

SKIPTON

Whalley Viaduct

PRESTON
BURNLEY

BLACKBURN

Gauxholme Viaduct

Healey Dell Viaduct
ORMSKIRK
HORWICH
LITTLEBOROUGH

GATHURST

BOLTON
RADCLIFFE
OLDHAM
Standedge Tunnel

ST. HELENS
EDGE HILL
NEWTON-LE-WILLOWS
Woodhead Tunnel

LIVERPOOL
RAINHILL
EARLESTOWN
MANCHESTER
HADFIELD
GLOSSOP

BIRKENHEAD
Sankey Viaduct
HUNTS CROSS
WARRINGTON
STOCK-PORT
Dinting Vale Viaduct

CRESSINGTON
RUNCORN
HALE
NEW MILLS NEWTOWN

HOLYHEAD

HOLYWELL
HELSBY
DUTTON

Conwy Bridge

Menai Bridge
CHAPEL-EN-LE-FRITH
Totley Tunnel

CHESTER
BUXTON
CHESTERFIELD

BETWYS-Y-COED
Hawarden Swing Bridge
CONGLETON
Moosal Dale Viaduct
ROWSLEY
Clay Cross Tunnel

WREXHAM
CREWE
MANSFIELD

RUABON
CEFN
LONGPORT
DARLEY DALE
MATLOCK BATH
WINGFIELD

CHIRK
CHEDDLETON
CROMFORD

GOBOWEN
STOKE-ON-TRENT
ALTON TOWERS
AMBERGATE
ILKESTON

OSWESTRY
BELPER

Barmouth Viaduct
STONE
DUFFIELD
THURGARTON

FRIOG
SANDON
DERBY
NOTTINGHAM
BEESTON

MACHYNLLETH
WELSHPOOL
COLWICH
TRENT

TALERDDIG
SHREWSBURY

LLANIDLOES
LOUGHBOROUGH

ABERYSTWYTH
ALBRIGHTON
LICHFIELD
ASHBY-DE-LA-ZOUCH
BARROW-ON-SOAR

COALBROOKDALE
ATHERSTONE
LEICESTER

WOLVERHAMPTON
Harringworth Viaduct

Knucklas Viaduct
KNIGHTON
LEA HALL

BIRMINGHAM
MARKET HARBOROUGH

COVENTRY
KETTERING

RUGBY
GLENDON & RUSHTON

LEAMINGTON SPA
WELLINGBOROUGH

WILMCOTE
Kilsby Tunnel

STRATFORD-UPON-AVON
NORTHAMPTON

WILLINGTON

MILLBROOK

Wolverton Viaduct
FENNY STRATFORD
RIDGMONT

BLETCHLEY
WOBURN SANDS

LEIGHTON BUZZARD

Tring Cutting

WATFORD

LONDON

ENGLAND / WALES

Legend

● Location in London Midland Region
━━ Intercity line
── Other line
- - - Line now closed
━━ Regional division
Land shading in feet
1000
300
0

0 10 20 30 40 Miles

LONDON

CAMDEN

THE ROUNDHOUSE. Built 1847 for London & North Western Railway. Designed by Robert Stephenson and R. B. Dockray. Listed Grade II. Closed and sold.

Now a well-known theatre, the Roundhouse, close by Primrose Hill station, can be seen on the left of the railway just before the Euston-bound train starts the final run down Camden Bank to the terminus. It was built as a locomotive shed and, as its name implies, is circular with a diameter of 160 feet.

It contained a turntable in the centre, with radiating tracks over pits for stabling the engines. The roof is near pyramidal with a central louvre for letting out smoke, and its ironwork is slender, resting on 24 columns.

It did not last long as an engine shed: by the 1860s the engines had become too long to be turned and stored there. For a while it was used as a goods shed and in 1869 was sold for other purposes.

EUSTON

Robert Stephenson's statue on forecourt, two entrance lodges, railings around Euston Square gardens and Eversholt House listed Grade II.

Right from the beginning in 1837 Euston station was regarded as the gateway to the north. The London & Birmingham Railway certainly had no doubts, proclaiming the fact with the great Doric arch at the entrance. Since then Euston has seen many changes, the greatest being the complete rebuilding carried out in 1969, but a glance at the destinations on the new departure indicator shows that its function remains the same.

Several significant parts of the old station have been kept. Robert Stephenson still stands out in front, at the head of the railway he built. At Euston itself he designed the original iron trainshed that served as a pattern for LNWR overall roofs for well over half a century. The bronze statue by Carlo Marochetti was presented to the LNWR by the Institution of Civil Engineers in 1870, and formerly stood between the two entrance lodges in Euston Road that were opened at the same time.

The lodges, designed c.1869 by the company's architect, J. B. Stansby, are in Portland stone with heavily rusticated Romanesque arches and quoins, and decorated pediments. Engraved in the quoins are impressive lists of destinations once reached by the LNWR. Now long out of date, they include such unlikely places as Swansea, Cork, Cambridge and Newark, reminding us of the fierce competition between the old railway companies. Of the 72 stations listed, only 37 were on reasonably direct routes.

Between and slightly behind the lodges is the LNWR war memorial. The waiting room just off the concourse contains a sculpture of Britannia by John Thomas. It once adorned the doorway into the old shareholders' room, which led from the Great Hall of 1849 (now demolished), perfectly symbolising the company's claim to be Britain's 'Premier Line'.

EVERSHOLT HOUSE. Built 1934 for London, Midland & Scottish Railway. Architects W. H. Hamlyn and A. V. Heal. Listed Grade II. 163-203, Eversholt Street, London NW1.

Around the corner from Euston station, Eversholt House is a three-storey brick office block built as the headquarters of the LMS. Square-cut with some Georgian features, it is a typical example of the more restrained office architecture of the 1930s. It functioned for many years as the Railway Clearing House, apportioning receipts from joint running to the appropriate railway companies.

CAMDEN ROUNDHOUSE. 1959

EUSTON, c.1838

THE *ROYAL SCOT* EXPRESS AT EUSTON. 1932

ENTRANCE LODGE, EUSTON, 1976

HARROW & WEALDSTONE

Rebuilt 1910 for London & North Western Railway. Architect Gerald Horsley. Between Wembley and Watford.

Horsley, a pupil of Richard Norman Shaw (one of whose best-known works is New Scotland Yard), was engaged by the LNWR to design new stations for the widening and suburban electrification work from Euston to Watford. The influence of Shaw is readily apparent, particularly here and at Hatch End.

In dark red brick, there is much rustication, and a broken pediment and decorated blank shield surmount a Venetian window in the lofty portico. A stone parapet bears the letters LNWR in circular openings, all overshadowed by a startlingly red and white banded clock tower-cum-chimney stack. The down-side building is the original in yellow brick Italianate style with stone dressings.

1913

HATCH END

Built 1911 for London & North Western Railway. Architect Gerald Horsley. Station entrance block listed Grade II. Between Wembley and Watford.

This little gem of a station shows Horsley at his best. Built in contrasting brick and stone, it has a Romanesque arched door and window framed by broad rusticated quoins and a delicately part-dentilled cornice beneath a near-pyramidal roof,

topped by a stylish cupola and weather-vane.

A broad vertical stone band dividing the arches contains a lavish arrangement of festooned fruit and foliage ('swag'), the date and the railway's initials; while in the background are more of Horsley's banded chimney stacks.

1963

MARYLEBONE

Built 1899 by Great Central Railway.

No single designer seems to have been responsible for Marylebone. The engineers for the London end of the line were Sir Douglas and Francis Fox, and 'architectural' details were drawn out by H. W. Braddock of the GCR Engineer's staff.

The last main line into London set off from north of Nottingham with a fine flourish, but by the time it got to Marylebone there was barely enough money left for even a modest terminus. Space was left

for additional platforms which were never built (the site is now occupied by a modern office block, Melbury House), so that from the concourse the platform area has a curious lop-sided appearance. A glass roof covers the concourse on light steelwork at right angles to the trainshed over the four platforms.

The frontage is red brick, with terracotta dressings, in a rather retiring Flemish style with a low turret that is no higher than the gables. Inside is more terracotta work and a dark oak booking office, and at the west end a wonderfully preserved Edwardian bar, all mahogany and brass with a real fireplace. The air of quiet dignity is not dispelled until one emerges under the glass-and-iron *porte cochère* which with its mass of elaboration seems designed to draw attention away from the station itself. To left and right were the iron gates, emblazoned 'GCR', which closed off the forecourt and, through the covered way in front, the vast Hotel Great Central, boasting 700 bedrooms.

Now occupied by the British Railways Board, it was built by a separate company to a flamboyant design by Col. Robert Edis who did part of the Great Eastern Hotel (*p.15*). Most of the exterior is in gold-brown terracotta with a tower to the main Marylebone Road frontage, in an Edwardian version of Flemish Renaissance. It was not a commercial success and the LNER bought it for offices in 1945. But a number of its interior appointments have been retained, most notably the spacious marble entrance lobby and broad stone staircase.

MARYLEBONE, 1980

PRIMROSE HILL TUNNELS

First built 1837 for London & Birmingham Railway. Engineer Robert Stephenson. Designer of south portal W. H. Budden. Second built 1879. Portals to both tunnels listed Grade II. Between Camden and South Hampstead.

There are four tunnels at Primrose Hill. The original is the one to the right of the most recent pair, 1,164 yards long and easily distinguished by the massive architecture at its south end. The tunnel mouth is set in wide curved wing walls, each broken by four large rusticated square pillars with curved pediment tops and modillions. The portal itself is flanked by a pair of similar but much larger pillars, linked by a deep cornice, and the arch is in two stages.

To the left is the second, matching, tunnel, cut in 1879 to improve the bottle-neck. By comparison the northern tunnel mouths are plain.

Further to the right are the two single line tunnels opened in 1922 for the Watford electrified lines, in connection with the system of junctions at Chalk Farm immediately to the south.

PRIMROSE HILL TUNNEL, SOUTH PORTAL, c.1837

GREAT CENTRAL 4-4-2 LOCOMOTIVE AT MARYLEBONE, 1912

THE GREAT CENTRAL RAILWAY

Today this enterprising and energetically run railway is little more than a memory, but in the late 19th century it seemed to possess grand possibilities. Then known as the Manchester Sheffield & Lincolnshire, it had as its chairman that unscrupulous railway tycoon Sir Edward Watkin, who was simultaneously chairman of the South Eastern and the Metropolitan Railway. Watkin aimed to link all three by building a London Extension of the M S & L.

The new line would run from Annesley, north of Nottingham, to join the Metropolitan at Quainton Road, north of Aylesbury, thus providing access to London and the south-east. Watkin was also chairman of the first Channel Tunnel Company, and his greater ambition was to control a through route from Manchester to the Continent.

The London Extension was completed in 1899, providing a fitting occasion for the M S & L to change its name to Great Central. The work was superbly done and the new trains and locomotives were second to none. Under its general manager Sam Fay the company's enterprise was abounding and from its central position it established cross-country services in conjunction with many existing lines – excepting of course its deadly rivals the Midland and the London & North Western. But passenger traffic came slowly and the new Marylebone terminus acquired a reputation as the quietest of the London stations, where pigeons cooed unruffled from the light and airy roof. The company, always one of the least prosperous of the leading English railways, found the cost of the London Extension crippling.

Then, to exploit its strong northern position in the coalfields, it embarked on the remarkable project of creating an entirely new port on waste land at Immingham, some six miles north of Grimsby.

Immingham was conceived primarily for the export of coal across the North Sea, and from virgin ground all the facilities were laid out on the most lavish scale. It was a venturesome thing to embark on. The railway was already heavily encumbered by the cost of a new line, yet it launched out on a project eventually costing nearly £3 million. But it was completed in 1912 and opened by King George V. Fay received a knighthood.

Unfortunately the intended results of this great enterprise were never realised. The war of 1914-18 cut off the company's trade across the North Sea, which did not recover afterwards.

The Great Central locomotives designed by John G. Robinson became great favourites for their handsome proportions, efficient working and always immaculate turn-out. While it was naturally the passenger classes that attracted most attention, Robinson's large 2-8-0 mineral engine brought him his greatest honour when it was chosen to be manufactured in bulk for service with the British Army in France during the First World War. A beautiful example of his express passenger 4-4-0, *Butler Henderson*, is preserved at Lough-borough.

ST. PANCRAS

Trainshed built 1868 for Midland Railway, engineer W. H. Barlow; frontage block (former hotel) built 1873, architect Sir George Gilbert Scott; both listed Grade I. Water tower at outer end listed Grade II.

Ever since it was built, St. Pancras has been controversial: arguments raged and continue to rage over the extremes of its Gothic styling, its ostentation, its cost. But on one point there cannot be any disagreement: it is sensational.

From wherever one sees it, its outline is unmistakeable – whether it is the brief glimpse from the train entering Kings Cross, the slow unfolding as it curves into view when walking down the north side of Euston Road, or the hazy half-silhouette on a misty day captured in John O'Connor's sunset picture of 1884 from Pentonville Road (*pp.154-55*). Today there is probably the least argument about it, since the hotel is now recognised as the greatest example of Victorian monumental commercial Gothic in the country,

while the trainshed, though no longer the largest single-span roof in the world, remains the finest. St. Pancras has a further distinction – it is the first single station to have had an entire book written about it, by Professor Jack Simmons (*St. Pancras Station*, 1968).

Barlow's trainshed is 100 feet high to the point of the arch, 689 feet long and 240 feet wide and completely uncluttered by struts and ties. The new overhead catenary is suspended directly from the roof by the most unobtrusive of cables so that the trainshed's broad sweep remains virtually uninterrupted – a great improvement on the arrangements adopted at Liverpool Street and Kings Cross.

The roof ribs spring directly from and are tied by the platform floor, which is at first floor level and constructed of iron plates on a grid of girders supported by 688 iron columns on brick piers. The unit adapted for the column spacing was the length of a beer barrel, for the ground floor was designed as a vast store for Burton beer brought into the capital by

the Midland Railway. Wagons entered it by a hoist at the outer end of the station. The latticed ribs of the roof provide a link with the earliest days of railways: they were made by the Butterley Company of Derbyshire, founded in 1791-92 by the canal engineers William Jessop and Benjamin Outram, which provided rails for some canal feeder tramways. Barlow received considerable assistance and advice in his design from R. M. Ordish, an engineer of wide experience in cast ironwork who had worked on the Crystal Palace.

The opening of the station in 1868 symbolised the Midland Railway's entry into London. Based in Derby, it had hitherto relied on rival companies for access to the capital. Now it had its own independent route, and St. Pancras station was the means of advertising it. The great trainshed was not enough; an impressive frontage was needed as well, preferably one that would outdo its competitors. The hotel block designed by Gilbert Scott certainly fulfilled its pur-

1906

ERECTION OF IRON COLUMNS, c.1866

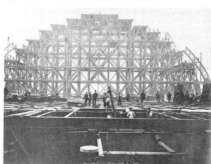

CONSTRUCTION OF TRAINSHED, c.1867

BOOKING HALL INTERIOR, c.1880

pose. To quote Simmons, it made 'Euston appear the old-fashioned muddle it was and Kings Cross a very ordinary piece of austere engineer's building'.

Gilbert Scott was the foremost British architect of his day and he nursed a thwarted ambition to design a really large commercial or public building. The Midland wanted a big name for their hotel, so they held a competition and Scott's design won. Thus the railway got its man and Scott got his prestige job.

Inside, the hotel is as spectacular as its exterior. In fact, Scott had to give way over some of the external details – there are no statues in the niches he designed for them, for instance – but within, only the best would do. He supervised much of the work personally, and entrusted the rest – from gas lighting to china and glass – only to those with the highest reputations. There were around 500 rooms, hydraulic lifts, broad corridors, an incredible amount of decoration, furniture by Gillows, and ten walnut-cased pianos.

An elaborate iron balustrade and stone staircase wind up through the 80-foot high vault within the western tower. Much of the original decoration and Minton tiling are still there, together with the decorated iron chandeliers and radiators. It has to be seen to be believed. Not for nothing was it declared to be 'the most sumptuous and best-conducted hotel in the Empire'. And just to make quite sure that there should be no mistaking its purpose, the railway named it The Midland Grand Hotel.

Above all St. Pancras is a place to look at. The great iron ribs in the trainshed bear plates cast with the name of The Butterley Company – not in some obscure position but at platform level, where everyone could see. Along the top of the side walls is a frieze of coloured tiles in diamond patterns. The great vault of the roof is a masterpiece of visually exciting structural engineering and, incidentally, used to provide the best acoustic effects of any station in London in the days of steam, particularly when an engine gave a 'push' to an out-going train.

The booking hall interior, also designed by Scott, retains its linen-fold panelled ticket office and its sculpted figures of railwaymen on stone corbels. Outside, one can always marvel at the forest of spires and pinnacles, the great clock tower, the 'west window' alongside Midland Road and the intricate brick and stone vaulting over the carriage entrance.

Not quite everything was grand, however. Down beneath the platforms were the beer cellars, where men worked all day by gaslight, and further down still was St. Pancras Tunnel which connected the Midland with the Metropolitan Railway in the same way as the tunnels under Kings Cross (p.14). Like them, the St. Pancras tunnel was steeply graded, sharply curved and – inevitably – rarely clear of smoke. Halfway through, a signal box was built into the wall, reached only by a spiral staircase from the station 46 feet above. Eight hours duty alone in that box must have been one of the worst jobs at St. Pancras.

Above MIDLAND 4-4-0 AT ST. PANCRAS, 1926; *left* WATER TOWER, 1980

TRING CUTTING, A MAJOR WORK ON THE LONDON & BIRMINGHAM RAILWAY. LITHOGRAPH BY J. C. BOURNE, 1839

STONEBRIDGE PARK

BRENT VIADUCT. Built 1837 for London & Birmingham Railway. Engineer Robert Stephenson. Listed Grade II. Between Willesden and Wembley.

Now crossing the North Circular Road (A406) instead of the River Brent, this stock-brick viaduct remains largely unaltered though only the west face can now be seen. It should not be confused with the longer Brent viaduct on the Midland line north of Cricklewood.

The large central arch is framed by pilasters with modillioned capitals supporting a continuous parapet cornice. There are a further series of smaller side arches. The survival of the viaduct in so good a condition is remarkable considering the amount of engineering work that has gone on in the neighbourhood.

HERTFORDSHIRE

WATFORD

OLD STATION. Built c.1837 for London & Birmingham Railway. Architect G. Aitchison Snr. Listed Grade II.

This modest single-storey brick building, without embellishments, stands at the top of a retaining wall on the north side of St. Albans Road bridge. The only surviving London & Birmingham intermediate station, it probably had steps (perhaps also an intervening terrace) leading down to the line, as at Tring and Coventry.

BEDFORDSHIRE

LEIGHTON BUZZARD

LINSLADE TUNNEL. Built 1838 for London & Birmingham Railway. Engineer Robert Stephenson. Entrances listed Grade II.

Three tunnels start north of Leighton Buzzard station. The central tunnel is the original and is double-tracked. When the line was progressively quadrupled, two more single-line tunnels were added, one on each side: the east side was opened in 1859 and the west side in 1876.

The tracks were then rearranged so that the down fast line used the western tunnel, up fast and down slow the original tunnel and the up slow the eastern tunnel. The southern portals are castellated.

WATFORD OLD STATION, 1981

LINSLADE TUNNEL, NORTH PORTAL OF ONE OF THE SINGLE-TRACKED TUNNELS, 1979

LINSLADE TUNNEL, SOUTH PORTAL, 1976

BUCKINGHAMSHIRE

BLETCHLEY

*DENBIGH HALL BRIDGE. Built 1838
for London & Birmingham Railway. Engineer
Robert Stephenson. North of Bletchley station.*

From April to September 1839 this point
served as a temporary terminus while
Kilsby Tunnel (*p.69*) was being completed. The bridge, which takes its name
from an inn, crosses Watling Street,
making it a convenient place from which
stage coaches could take passengers to
and from Rugby or Coventry, whence the
railway was open to Birmingham.

The railway crosses the road at an
acute angle, although the stone arch is
rectangular in plan, and bears a plaque
commemorating its historic association.
The west face is original and its iron
balustrade has the same pattern as that
on the boundary wall on the west side of
the track opposite the Roundhouse at
Primrose Hill (*p.61*).

DENBIGH HALL BRIDGE PLAQUE, 1976

CHARLES BLACKER
VIGNOLES, ENGINEER

Vignoles was an unfortunate engineer,
partly through circumstance and partly
through his over-enthusiasm which on
occasion could overcome his judgement
when he ventured into other affairs. Born in
Ireland in 1793, Vignoles saw service in the
Army in the Napoleonic Wars before entering the engineering profession. He worked
for John and George Rennie on the Liverpool & Manchester Railway and was
largely responsible for the skilful piloting of
the plans through Parliament. When construction commenced, he worked for
George Stephenson who replaced the
Rennies as engineer, but the relationship
was uneasy and Vignoles resigned when he
felt he had been made a scapegoat over
errors in the Wapping Tunnel.

He was engineer for a number of subsequent lines, including the Midland
Counties, North Union and Dublin &
Kingstown Railways, and was briefly
Engineer-in-Chief to the Sheffield Ashton
& Manchester. He invested heavily and
imprudently in the line and lost a great deal
of money. He resigned in 1840 and was
succeeded by Locke.

Despite this and other setbacks he was in
considerable demand, particularly overseas where he acted as consultant on railways in France, Germany, Switzerland,
Brazil, Spain and Poland. In Russia he
built the Dnieper suspension road bridge at
Kiev, then the largest in the world.
Vignoles was also an inventor. He patented
a device for assisting the ascent of steep
inclines (with John Ericsson) and introduced the flat-bottomed Vignoles rail
which, although it was not used in Britain
until recent years, became the standard
nearly everywhere else.

In his later years he became something of
a grand old man of engineering, having
outlived most of his contemporaries. He
was the first professor of civil engineering at
University College, London, and later
President of the Institution of Civil
Engineers. His scientific interests were reflected in his election to a fellowship of the
Royal Astronomical Society. He lived to be
82, dying in 1875.

CREATING THE PICTURESQUE

Between Bletchley and Bedford, a remarkable quartet of stations was built in the style known as *cottage orné*, derived from the picturesque movement of the 18th century which produced so many of the ornamental gate lodges to country estates.

The station buildings at *FENNY STRATFORD*, *WOBURN SANDS*, *RIDGMONT* and *MILLBROOK* (all listed Grade II) could have been taken straight from the pages of an architect's design book, such as J. C. Loudon's *Encyclopaedia of Cottage, Farm and Villa Architecture and Furniture* of 1833. They were opened in 1846 for the Bedford Railway (and shortly afterwards taken over by the LNWR) and their style was intended to tone in with the Duke of Bedford's estate at Woburn.

All are half-timbered, with projecting gables, dormers, fretted bargeboards and other trimmings felt necessary for a proper rural atmosphere. Of the many small country stations with the same theme, these four are among the very best.

Ridgmont, 1967

Millbrook, 1982

Fenny Stratford, 1976

Woburn Sands, 1976

WOLVERTON VIADUCT

Built 1838 for London & Birmingham Railway. Engineer Robert Stephenson. North of Wolverton station.

The 1½-mile long embankment across the Ouse valley is 48 feet high, the highest on the LBR. Near its centre is Wolverton viaduct, six graceful elliptical brick arches of 60-foot span, with pilasters and two narrow side arches at each end. The heavy stone cornice, running the whole length of 220 yards, gives horizontal emphasis to the design and is characteristic of Stephenson's work.

This and other mammoth early 19th-century structures were the largest of their kind since Roman times and certainly conveyed the sense of awe and achievement desired by the railway companies.

WARWICKSHIRE

ATHERSTONE

Built 1847 for Trent Valley Railway. Architect J. W. Livock. Listed Grade II. Between Nuneaton and Tamworth.

The Trent Valley Railway is now that part of the West Coast main line between Rugby and Stafford, and as the train slows for the curve at Atherstone there is a chance to see the station building on the east side.

Of Livock's complete sets of buildings – stations, lineside houses, level crossing gate lodges and other small structures – on this particular line, only the station at Atherstone survives with most of its original features intact.

1958

Although the station is open to passengers, the station building itself is not used by the railway. It is Tudor in style, constructed of red brick with lavish stone dressings to the gables, dormers, windows and porch. The station master's dwelling portion had the distinction of a shallow oriel over the front door; handsome coupled chimneys and patterned roof slates completed the effect. For an example of Livock's Jacobean styling see Wansford (*p.19*).

LEAMINGTON SPA

Rebuilt 1938 by Great Western Railway.

This is a good example of Great Western between-the-wars architecture, chunky

and solid in white stone and resembling
something built from a child's building
blocks. It is largely unaltered, complete
with stainless steel window frames and
walnut veneer in the waiting and refreshment rooms. The platform canopies are
also typical 1930s GWR.

RUGBY

STATION. Rebuilt 1886 by London & North Western Railway.

Charles Dickens gave a picture of the
conditions at the old Rugby station in his
sketch 'Mugby Junction', in 1866. Despite a number of so-called improvements
it could barely keep pace with the rapid
growth of traffic; by the time a firm decision was made to replace it, it was a
wretched place indeed.

The new station had a broad island
platform with bays at both ends, very
spacious, with a large block of very dull
two-storey red brick buildings in the
middle. Its main feature is the vast roof
covering platforms and running lines,
with lateral spans at each end and a lofty
transverse ridge-and-furrow central section extending out over the fast lines as
well, carried on deep rolled girders to
massive brick side walls. The characteristic LNWR end- and side-screens and
the iron *porte cochère* have gone, but otherwise the station is little altered.

LEAMINGTON SPA, 1957

AVON VIADUCT. Built 1839 for Midland Counties Railway. Engineers Charles Vignoles and Thomas Jackson Woodhouse. Closed.

The Midland Counties line to Leicester
crosses the Avon on this brick viaduct
almost immediately after leaving Rugby.
It has eleven 50-foot semi-elliptical arches
carried on triple piers with large stone
springers, while a touch of horizontality is
added by a continuous heavy parapet
cornice.

The whole structure is extremely like
Robert Stephenson's at Wolverton on the
London & Birmingham line, but in a far
more original condition. It is one of the
first large railway structures to have been
faced in blue engineering brick.

1976

RUGBY, c.1890

STRATFORD-UPON-AVON

STATION. Built 1864-65 by Great Western Railway.

Almost buried among later additions, the original frontage at Stratford is Italianate with a hipped, overhanging roof in the style of the earlier work of Brunel, featured at so many GWR stations built in the 20 years or so after 1840 (see Mortimer, *p.216*). Later-style awnings were added over the platform, probably in 1899 when the station was enlarged and the footbridge erected with the extension of the line to Cheltenham. The station became a terminus in 1976.

1974

WELCOMBE HOTEL. Built 1867. Architect Henry Clutton. Listed Grade II. Two miles north of Stratford off the Warwick road (A46).

This large neo-Tudor-Jacobean mansion, built originally for a Manchester magnate, was acquired by the London Midland & Scottish Railway and opened as a hotel in 1931. The symmetrical garden front has three tall bays with mullioned windows topped by curly gables.

1976

The hotel was the subject of an interesting experiment by the LMS in 1932. A single-deck bus was fitted with additional flanged wheels which enabled it to run on road or rail. Called the 'Ro-Railer', it connected at Blisworth with main line trains from Euston and ran along the former Stratford & Midland Junction line to Stratford. Here, on a special section of track in the goods yard, the rail wheels were lifted and the road wheels lowered for the vehicle to run along the roads to the Welcombe Hotel. This innovative idea was not, however, a success, and the 'Ro-Railer' was withdrawn after only a few months.

WILMCOTE

Rebuilt c.1899 by Great Western Railway. Between Stratford and Henley-in-Arden.

Wilmcote, the next station to Stratford, typifies the GWR's late 19th-century style. It is very dull in red brick but has

1964

nice little shallow awnings and a typically elaborate Great Western covered footbridge, complete with monogram and date. The valancing on the awnings and footbridge roof is also characteristic.

NORTHAMPTONSHIRE

GLENDON & RUSHTON

Built 1857 for Midland Railway. Architect C. H. Driver. Station and station master's house listed Grade II. Between Kettering and Market Harborough. Closed.

The smaller stations on the Leicester to Hitchin section of the Midland were marked by two notable features: standardised structures and the use of local materials. Buildings of similar design could thus be seen in red brick, white brick, ironstone and, at Glendon – the least altered of the closed stations on the line – pale grey limestone.

A two-storey house adjoins a single-storey office building with a ridge-and-furrow roofed waiting shelter on the platform side, finished off with coupled round-headed windows and the delicate wavy bargeboards and iron lozenge-pattern windows so beloved of the Midland. The same style spread to other parts of the company's system and could be seen in Derbyshire, Nottinghamshire and Yorkshire.

HARRINGWORTH VIADUCT

Built 1879 for Midland Railway. Engineer probably John Underwood. Between Kettering and Melton Mowbray.

The broad, flat valley of the River Welland necessitated the longest viaduct on the British railway system, discounting those on the various suburban lines into London. On a misty day, this truly impressive series of red brick arches can easily look endless: in fact, the viaduct is 1,275 yards long and 60 feet high. Its 82 arches, each of 40-foot span, were given

GOODS YARD OFFICE, GLENDON & RUSHTON, 1980

GLENDON & RUSHTON, 1980

c.1964

variety by making every sixth pier slightly wider than the others and adding a pilaster.

KETTERING

Rebuilt c.1890 for Midland Railway. Island platform awnings designed by C. Biddle 1857; main buildings and canopy probably designed by Charles Trubshaw c.1890; wooden building on island platform and platform 4 canopy listed Grade II.

Kettering is an excellent example of the Midland's end-of-century style; fashionable terracotta in an orange-pink shade contrasting with dark red brick. Ball finials surmount the end gables and two tall, well-proportioned chimney stacks spring surprisingly from a pair of smaller curved gables decorated with a sunflower motif, popular at the time.

The front and platform awnings are cantilevered ridge-and-furrow structures, glazed with hipped ends, and represent the final stage of this familiar Midland feature. The island platform awnings, however, with their delicately scrolled ironwork, date from the earlier station.

KILSBY TUNNEL

Built 1838 for London & Birmingham Railway. Engineer Robert Stephenson. Between Bletchley and Rugby.

Kilsby Tunnel is a stupendous civil engineering work, by the standards of any era. It is 1 mile 682 yards long and at the time it was constructed nothing of such length had ever been built for steam trains. Naturally there were fears that passengers would be suffocated, so Stephenson designed it 28 feet high and 25 feet wide with two huge ventilation shafts of 60-foot diameter, one 120 feet and the other 90 feet deep. Their crenellated tops can be seen from roads above the tunnel, alongside the mounds created by soil dumped from the workings.

The building of the tunnel met so much unforeseen trouble that it delayed the opening of the railway. Quicksand and water were encountered in far greater quantities than anticipated; the workings were flooded; the contractor gave up in despair (he died soon afterwards). Stephenson took over, using direct labour. It took 13 steam pumping engines, extracting 1,800 gallons a minute

for 19 months, to conquer the water before the tunnel could be finished. There were 1,250 men on the site, aided by 200 horses; and instead of the estimated £99,000, the tunnel cost £300,000. Shortly before it was completed, a special dinner was held at the Dun Cow, Dunchurch, at which Robert Stephenson's staff presented him with a silver soup tureen; his father George was present to celebrate.

KETTERING, 1981

THE MIDLAND RAILWAY

The Midland Railway, based on Derby, was a provincial company and proud of it. Even so, it was determined to enter London, and did so in 1868 with a great flourish, marked by the building of St. Pancras Station. Later it made a bid for the Scottish traffic, reaching Carlisle in 1876, and other lines spread right down to the south coast and as far west as Swansea.

The Midland was renowned for the superiority of its stations and its rolling stock, which was distinguished by the splendid 'Crimson Lake' livery. Moreover, it was known for the genuine concern it showed its passengers. The first railway to offer third-class travel on every train, it was also the first by many years to upgrade third class and abolish second.

By the end of the 19th century the Midland was handling an enormous amount of mineral traffic, but not with any great efficiency. Its trains to St. Pancras were frequently unpunctual and freight bottlenecks sometimes amounted to total blockages.

In the early 1900s, its management structure underwent a complete and radical change. Hitherto, general managers had always risen from the ranks of the traffic departments, but in 1905 Guy Granet, a barrister who had been Secretary to the Railway Companies Association, was appointed Assistant General Manager. He became General Manager the following year. A shrewd judge of personalities, he brought to the task a deep perception of railway affairs which was soon evident in the imaginative and efficient way he reorganised the company.

In 1907 he created an entirely new post, that of General Superintendent, and to fill it he appointed Cecil Paget, a locomotive engineer by profession. Under Paget the whole philosophy of train operation was revitalised. He arranged the timetables for both goods and mineral traffic to provide frequent services with light trains pulled by small locomotives. When unusually heavy loads were being transported, two were used instead of one.

In 1909 Henry Fowler was appointed Chief Mechanical Engineer. His work in the remaining 14 years of the company's independent existence lay mainly in making detailed improvements to existing stock, such as adding superheaters to the three-cylinder compound 4-4-0s. Some beautiful examples of 19th-century Midland locomotives are preserved at The Midland Railway Centre near Ripley in Derbyshire.

Midland Railway express, 1905

NORTHAMPTON

CASTLE. Ancient Monument. Now part of Northampton station goods yard.

Northampton Castle, extremely important in the early Middle Ages, was largely destroyed during the Civil War. What remains today is the north-east part of the courtyard bounded by a bank which may conceal the ruins of a stone curtain wall dating probably from the 12th century.

WELLINGBOROUGH

Built 1857 for Midland Railway. Architect C. H. Driver. Station, goods shed and hand cranes all listed Grade II. Between Kettering and Bedford.

Larger and more elaborate than the typical Leicester to Hitchin line stations, Wellingborough bears all the same characteristics. Built in cottage style in the local red brick, it has coloured brick dressings, slated roofs and a five-bay blind arcade: each bay has a two-light arched window with lozenge glazing.

1982

GOODS SHED HAND CRANE. 1982

The object of the saw-tooth roof over the platform waiting shelter can be seen here – it articulates with the glass-and-iron awning with which the larger stations were provided.

The goods shed is an interesting example of a matching building designed to form a single entity with the station. It has a six-bay arcade with a single cast-iron lozenge in each bay. The two hand cranes surviving inside are part of the structure: the main roof trusses rest on them.

70

LEICESTERSHIRE

ASHBY-DE-LA-ZOUCH

Built 1849 by Midland Railway. Listed Grade II. Leicester to Burton-on-Trent line. Closed and sold.

This charming Grecian building of great delicacy was intended to match the Royal Hotel and one-time Ivanhoe Baths opposite. (Ashby had hopes of becoming a spa, but the prospects failed to develop.) The centrepiece has two Doric columns

1966

flanked by matching pavilions which are linked by two little bow-fronted bays, one containing a window and the other a door. The stonework has been cleaned, and the building renovated for use as offices.

Outside the station is a length of tramline, the only remains of the Burton & Ashby Light Railway, an electric tramway that lasted from 1906 to 1927.

BARROW-ON-SOAR

NORTH STREET BRIDGE. Built c.1875 for Midland Railway. Engineer J. S. Crossley. Listed Grade II. Between Leicester and Loughborough.

This bridge, part of the widening of the line between Trent Junction and Leicester, is an unusual one for the Midland. It has two spans carried on a central brick pier. The construction is of wrought-iron girders and cast-iron face girders with decorative pierced spandrels and solid cast-iron parapets above. All

the other bridges on the line are of brick so this one may include older components.

LEICESTER LONDON ROAD

Rebuilt 1892 for Midland Railway. Architect Charles Trubshaw. Frontage screen listed Grade II.

Trubshaw chose orange-brown terracotta for his frontage screen when he reconstructed the station (see Kettering, p.69). Rather florid in appearance, it comprises a very long arcade of massive arches giving on to a split-level *porte cochère*, one level being for arrivals and the other for departures, each with separate entrances and exits. The frontage terminates in a tall, hexagonal clock turret, and decoration is profuse and ornate, particularly the line of urns along the parapet.

The entire station is spacious, from the ample booking hall down the paired wide staircases to the two broad island platforms, well designed to handle large crowds of passengers. Originally it had a three-bay light overall roof, with individual ridge-and-furrow awnings over the outside platform faces, representing the very latest in large through-station layout at the time. The platforms have been reconstructed with buildings in local brick.

1981

LEICESTER LONDON ROAD. 1981

LOUGHBOROUGH. 1981

LOUGHBOROUGH

Built 1871 by Midland Railway. Station building, platform canopies and ticket hall fittings listed Grade II.

The symmetrical yellow brick building at Loughborough has well executed round-arched stone-cased openings and dentils, but is otherwise of no particular merit. The distinction of the station lies in the hipped ridge-and-furrow platform awnings, the climax of this Midland Railway feature.

The slender columns are finely fluted and decorated, the filigree brackets are even more delicate, while immediately under the glazing there are the lightest of scrolled iron inserts. The outer ends of the ridges have been cut short.

The entrance to the platform from the booking hall, which still has its original fittings, is screened by glass and iron tracery to match. Richards of Leicester made the ironwork and produced a similar design at Melton Mowbray.

MARKET HARBOROUGH

Built 1884 jointly by Midland and London & North Western Railways. Listed Grade II.

Market Harborough contains much Georgian architecture, so the two railways for whom the station was reconstructed made a happy choice in selecting that style, then coming back into fashion.

The frontage could be called Queen Anne, a term used somewhat loosely at the time, very pleasant and symmetrical in red brick with stone pilaster strips, curved and moulded door and window casings, a charming little dormer and some elegant chimney stacks. The rear elevation in the angle between the diverg-ing lines is equally in keeping. Not many stations of this date could boast such quiet distinction. In 1978 the President of the Royal Academy, Sir Hugh Casson, planted a tree to commemorate the restoration of the station to its original appearance.

Above REAR, 1976; *right* FRONT, 1966

WEST MIDLANDS

BIRMINGHAM CURZON STREET

Built 1837 for London & Birmingham Railway. Architect Philip Hardwick. Listed Grade I. Sold. Grand Junction Viaduct listed Grade II.

Curzon Street frontage was built as the northern counterpart to the Arch at Euston and like it was intended to express the triumph of the railway. Euston was Doric; the smaller Curzon Street is Ionic with four great columns supporting a massive entablature. There was also a classical hotel which is now demolished.

It was at Birmingham that the lines from London and from the north met. The Grand Junction Railway from Liverpool and Manchester was there first, with a station alongside the London & Birmingham's, soon to be joined by a third, the Birmingham & Derby Junction Railway's station at Lawley Street not far away. But the interchange was obviously inconvenient and in 1854 a new through station was opened at New Street, with Curzon Street being relegated to goods traffic. Lawley Street had already gone the same way three years previously.

The original arches of the Grand Junction Railway now carry a newer viaduct on top, which was built when the approaches to New Street were remodelled in 1896.

LITHOGRAPH OF BIRMINGHAM CURZON STREET BY J. C. BOURNE, c.1839

COVENTRY

COAT OF ARMS BRIDGE, STIVICHALL. Built 1844 by London & Birmingham Railway. Listed Grade II. Leamington branch.

This elliptical arch over the road in rock-faced sandstone, flanked by a pair of blind arches, bears in the centre the arms of the Gregory family, Lords of the Manor of Stivichall. Widened when the line was doubled in 1916, the bridge retains its original form.

LEA HALL

Built 1939 for London Midland & Scottish Railway. Architect W. H. Hamlyn. Between Coventry and Birmingham.

Between 1936 and 1939 the LMS opened a number of new or rebuilt stations in

1956

COVENTRY, COAT OF ARMS BRIDGE, 1981

brick and ferro-concrete, notable for their cantilevered concrete awnings. Apsley, near Watford, and several on the Wirral are good examples of this functional style.

Lea Hall was built to serve new housing estates and is in the same mould, with its entrance on an overbridge. Standardised components were widely used, including concrete lamp-posts, although those at Lea Hall carried gas lamps – a strange anachronism on what was considered to be the ultimate in modern station design.

WOLVERHAMPTON

Built by Shrewsbury & Birmingham Railway but opened 1852 by London & North Western Railway. Former entrance listed Grade II. Closed. Horseley Fields.

ROBERT STEPHENSON, ENGINEER

Robert Stephenson was one of the giants of the early days of railways. The famous son of a famous father, he was born near Newcastle in 1803. He was apprenticed to the mining and early railway engineer Nicholas Wood and assisted his father George on the Stockton & Darlington surveys. After six months at Edinburgh University to broaden his education, he managed the new firm of Robert Stephenson & Co., locomotive builders, set up with his father at Newcastle.

Robert made his name in his own right on the construction of the London & Birmingham Railway, opened in 1838, accomplishing a major engineering feat with the boring of Kilsby Tunnel (*p.69*), and was a staunch supporter of the standard 4 feet 8½ inch (Stephenson) gauge in the battles over Brunel's 7 feet broad gauge. He worked on the principle of maintaining as level a route as possible, and his main lines are noted for the heavy engineering works necessary to achieve that end.

Best known for his bridges, Stephenson was nearly ruined when his iron bridge over the Dee at Chester collapsed in 1847. However, his reputation was soon regained with the Newcastle High Level Bridge, opened in 1849 (*p.49*) and the Royal Border Bridge at Berwick (*p.52*). His best known work is probably the Britannia Tubular Bridge over the Menai Strait (*pp.95, 128*). Brunel, who remained a firm personal friend despite the battle of the gauges, gave him encouragement during the raising of the spans. Stephenson returned the compliment at Saltash (*pp.192, 241*).

M.P. for Whitby for 12 years, he declined a knighthood, and died in 1859 from ill health resulting from overwork within four days of his 56th birthday. He is buried in Westminster Abbey alongside his fellow engineer Thomas Telford, and there is a statue of him outside Euston Station (*p.59*).

Contrary to popular belief, this impressive building is not the original station at all, but the carriage entrance at the beginning of the approach road from the town, and in its day it must have been very handsome.

In yellow brick with stone Romanesque arches (the two for vehicles are now bricked up) and Tuscan pilasters, the prominent cornice has a low, flat-topped turret at each end. There were offices on the first floor and the ground floor is thought to have contained the ticket office, although this is doubtful. The long drive to the station was necessary in order to cross the intervening canal, but it is not clear why such a commanding structure was built at the entrance.

NOTTINGHAMSHIRE

BEESTON

Built 1847 by Midland Railway. Nottingham to Derby line.

The Midland Railway evolved a particular basic style for small stations which was retained for over 60 years. The three distinguishing features were a single-storey building comprising a pair of gabled pavilions linked by a short central section parallel to the platform; iron lattice windows in diamond or lozenge patterns; and open-work bargeboards and finials.

Beeston station was one of the first to display all these characteristics, and its bargeboards are particularly intricate.

The gables bear shields containing the company's initials and the date. The ridge-and-furrow awning sheltering the platform is a much later addition.

MANSFIELD

DRURY DAM VIADUCT. Built 1871 by Midland Railway. Listed Grade II. Between Mansfield South Junction and Rufford Colliery.

This ten-arched viaduct consists of a central span of four cast-iron arched girders flanked by brick-faced arches. The piers and abutments are made of stone. The line is now relegated to goods traffic and serves Rufford Colliery.

KINGS MILL VIADUCT. Built 1819 for Mansfield & Pinxton Railway. Engineer Josias Jessop. Listed Grade II. Closed and sold. On south side of A38 west of Mansfield.

Built of local Mansfield stone, this five-arched bridge carried the tramroad of the MPR: wagons were pulled at first by bullocks and later by horses. In 1847 the line was bought by the Midland Railway and converted for use by locomotives.

DRURY DAM VIADUCT, 1977

BEESTON, 1977

c.1960

NOTTINGHAM

LONDON ROAD LOW LEVEL STATION. Built 1857 for Ambergate Nottingham & Boston & Eastern Junction Railway. Architect Thomas Hine. Listed Grade II. Closed.

The owning company, with one of the longest titles adopted by a railway, was leased by the Great Northern in 1854, but continued to use London Road station as its nominal headquarters until 1923. Despite its important-sounding name, it reached neither Ambergate nor Boston, but its continued existence is marked by this station, which is far more elaborate than anything the Great Northern would have built (see Huntingdon, *p.19*).

1964

It is a grand place, a mixture of conflicting styles including a French-inspired gable and turret, a variety of windows including Venetian, a large T-shaped arched *porte cochère* and diamond-patterned parapets and balustrades in Tudor style. It retains its iron trainshed, which has later additions by the Great Northern including some nice valancing. The station saw its last passenger trains in

NOTTINGHAM MIDLAND BOOKING HALL, 1904

1944, but is still used for goods and parcels traffic. London Road High Level was a separate station opposite, opened in 1900, closed in 1967 and now demolished.

MIDLAND STATION. Built 1904 for Midland Railway. Architect A. E. Lambert. Listed Grade II.

The first Nottingham station in 1839 was a terminus, which was replaced in 1848 by a through station on the site of the present one but entered from the side in Station Street. This was quite a handsome place, with a light iron trainshed in three spans and a dignified classical frontage incorporating a projecting five-

bay arcade of columns. Despite enlargements it steadily became inadequate, and in 1900 a new and direct competitor, the Great Central Railway, arrived in Nottingham with a spacious new station named Victoria. The Midland had to look to its laurels. It rebuilt its station with broad platforms, although not before a derailment had demolished part of the old trainshed, thus precipitating action.

A new entrance was erected in London Road on the bridge at the western end, in the Midland's favourite orange-brown terracotta with sandstone trim. Victoria station had a tall clock tower, so the Midland had to have one too – it erected a huge central turret with protruding angled corner blocks. The facade, in effect, is a vast screen in front of a covered cab drive, similar to those at Leicester and Sheffield; ostentatious and proudly Edwardian. The airy booking hall is largely unaltered, retaining numerous windows set in bottle-green glazed tiles and lit by an arched lantern. At platform level the concept of the overall roof was discarded in favour of individual standard Midland awnings.

THURGARTON

Built 1846 by Midland Railway. Listed Grade II. Nottingham to Newark line.

Traditional styling was a hallmark of the stations of the Midland in its early years, and was nowhere displayed with greater effect than in the exuberant series of Tudoresque stations between Nottingham and Newark. Thurgarton is the best and least altered, in brick with stone dressings. Only one of the two bay win-

1846

dows to the platform elevation survives, but the main building displays two of those most endearing Midland characteristics, beautifully scalloped bargeboards and diamond-pattern latticed iron window frames. There can be no doubt that when it was built it succeeded in imparting to the untutored local inhabitants a feeling of the homely and familiar to reassure them about this new mode of travel. It is now used as a residence.

TRENT

REDHILL TUNNELS. West tunnel built 1840 for Midland Counties Railway. Engineers Thomas Jackson Woodhouse and Charles Vignoles. East tunnel built 1875 for Midland Railway. Engineers J. S. Crossley and J. A. McDonald. North portals listed Grade II. Just south of Trent railway bridge.

Two tunnels side by side which cut through the small eminence of Redhill have grand castle-style entrances at the north end. The original bowstring girder bridge over the Trent, long since gone, was a source of company pride and no doubt bridge and tunnel entrance were supposed to be seen together from the river bank.

The later of the two tunnels, on the eastern side, was made necessary by the widening of the Midland line between Trent and Leicester in 1875. Its entrance, though not identical to the other, is de-

1963

signed as a piece. Both are constructed in rock-faced stone with a castellated and machicolated parapet flanked by small octagonal turrets of different heights.

DERBYSHIRE

AMBERGATE

Built 1840 for North Midland Railway. Engineer George Stephenson. Goods shed, Newbridge Road bridge and Toad Moor tunnel all listed Grade II. Between Derby and Chesterfield.

The pretty Jacobean-style station at Ambergate, one of Thompson's best, has unfortunately gone, but three original structures still remain. The goods shed is a charming survival. It is built of sandstone ashlar with a hipped slate roof and has two arched entrances with elliptical heads. The Newbridge Road bridge, of brick faced with sandstone with a roll cornice to the parapet, is typical of the single arched bridges on this line. The very short and shallow Toad Moor tunnel can, unusually, be seen as a whole. It is elliptical in section with the track set below the median, and is lined with fine ashlar in winding courses which give an impressive effect when you stand at the north end and look through at the sunshine – the whole tunnel appears to be rifled. The stonework on the two identical portals is exceptionally good; each bears a roll cornice which is Stephenson's trademark on the North Midland.

BELPER

Built 1840 for North Midland Railway. Engineer George Stephenson. Retaining walls; bridges over railway at Field Lane, George Street, Gibfield Lane, Joseph Street, Long Row, Pingle Lane and William Street; Milford Tunnel portals and ventilation shaft all listed Grade II. Between Derby and Chesterfield.

Belper, standing on sloping ground running down to the River Derwent, had no space for the railway: the only possibilities were to tunnel beneath the town, which would have been expensive and inconvenient, or to cut through it. Stephenson chose the latter alternative, and the railway passes right through the centre in a handsome stone-walled narrow cutting which kept demolition of property to a minimum, but required ten overbridges in a mile to accommodate the existing streets.

1840

South of Belper is the Milford Tunnel, 836 yards long, with heavily rusticated stonework and a roll cornice at the south portal, ring arches in the Norman manner at the north, and a ventilation shaft in the style of a tower.

ENGRAVING OF AMBERGATE, c.1840

AMBERGATE, ORIGINAL STATION, 1911

BUXTON

Built 1863 for London & North Western Railway. Design associated with Sir Joseph Paxton. Listed Grade II.

Rivalry between the London & North Western and the Midland Railways dated from the early days of the companies, when Capt. Mark Huish and George Hudson waged almost open warfare. So it was unusual, to say the least, to find them collaborating when it came to designing stations. Both companies had branches to Buxton opened within a few days of each other, for which each designed a terminus in its own styling, complete with overall roofs. As the stations were side-by-side with a common approach road between them, identical gabled screen walls were built across the ends, each having a giant fan window with the name of the company in gold letters around the edge. This remarkable co-operative effort was brought about by the Duke of Devonshire who owned most of the town. He was busy developing it as a spa, and had no intention of allowing the railways to build anything that might be considered inappropriate. Conveniently, his agent, Sir Joseph Paxton, designer of the Crystal Palace, was also on the boards of both the Midland Railway and the Stockport Disley & Whaley Bridge Railway (the nominee of the LNWR), giving the Duke a directorial foot in both camps. Both companies held official opening dinners on the same day. The Duke chose to attend the Midland's dinner; Paxton was apparently gastronomically robust enough to go to both. The Midland's station is now gone, but on the LNWR side the screen wall and window remain.

BUXTON c.1965

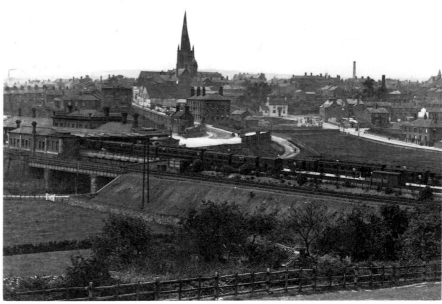

CHESTERFIELD, 1888

CHAPEL-EN-LE-FRITH

CHAPEL MILTON VIADUCTS. Built 1866 and 1893 for Midland Railway. Engineers J. S. Crossley (1866) and J. A. McDonald (1893). Between Chapel-en-le-Frith and Chinley.

High above Chapel Milton two great curving stone viaducts form a V at the south end of the triangular junction, truly dominating the village. The south-to-north viaduct was opened in 1866 as part of the last stage of the Midland's line from Derby to Manchester. The south-to-east viaduct came later, in 1893, when junctions were made for the new Hope Valley line to Sheffield.

CHESTERFIELD

Engineer's office in goods yard, built c.1840 for North Midland Railway. Architect probably Francis Thompson. Listed Grade II.

This little stone structure near the passenger station is probably part of Thomp-

son's original station buildings, and if so is the only survivor. It bears a striking resemblance to the style of the main building as illustrated in a contemporary engraving by Sam Russell, with its pointed Tudor gable, coupled chimneys and decorated medallion (possibly for a coat of arms) over the door. It may well have been an entrance lodge at the foot of the station approach.

CLAY CROSS TUNNEL

Built 1840 for North Midland Railway. Engineer George Stephenson. North portal listed Grade II. Between Derby and Chesterfield.

The Clay Cross Tunnel, which is 1 mile 26 yards long and brick-lined throughout, has a grand sandstone front in the castle style at the north end. The entrance is flanked by octagonal turrets with arrow slits, castellated tops and a castellated

parapet between them. Its quality is hard to appreciate because it lies in a deep cutting which can only be approached through a factory car park. The south portal for some reason is just a plain arch built of brick.

1977

MIDLAND 4-4-0, CROMFORD, c.1910

CROMFORD

Built c.1860 for Midland Railway. Architect probably G. H. Stokes. Main building, building on east platform, footbridge and station master's house all listed Grade II. Derby to Matlock line.

Cromford is French, but French with a Midland touch. On the up platform stands a little waiting room in stone with diamond-lattice windows, steep-pitched roof and a gabled steeple of a turret over the door. There is nothing else quite like it on a British railway station. The main building opposite is much more re-strained, while overlooking the station from the hill behind is a large station master's house like a mini-chateau. On all three buildings the delicate iron finials are superb.

The platforms are linked by a standard Midland latticed iron footbridge, and at the northern end a tunnel gives an appro-priately dramatic setting. G. H. Stokes, thought to be the architect, was assistant to Sir Joseph Paxton, agent to the Duke of Devonshire whose Chatsworth estates covered a large part of Derbyshire (see Buxton, *p.76*).

CROMFORD, 1976

DARLEY DALE

Built 1849 by Manchester Buxton Matlock & Midlands Junction Railway. Station and building on north platform both listed Grade II. Matlock to Buxton line. Closed.

Darley Dale was Gothic, in a debased style common in mid-19th century build-ing, with very prominent chimneys, tall gables and cresting. The main building on the west side has gone but the smaller, matching building on the opposite plat-form remains.

LMS CLASS '8F' 2-8-0, DARLEY DALE, 1963

DERBY

STATION AND MIDLAND HOTEL. Built 1839-41 for Midland Counties, Birmingham & Derby Junction and North Midland Railways. Architect Francis Thompson; subsequently much altered. Hotel and war memorial listed Grade II. Part of Derby Midland Railway Conservation Area.

STATION AND HOTEL. c.1925

Derby was one of the major railway towns of the 19th century, though unlike Crewe and Swindon it was not created by the railways. For centuries it had been a county and market town, and by the 18th century already possessed a number of important industries.

In one sense it was more of a railway town than any other in the world. As the capital city of the Midland Railway empire it not only built locomotives, rolling stock, signalling and other equipment, but also served as the headquarters of the railway administration. The Midland's London terminus at St. Pancras was never, like Euston or Paddington, the seat of company power.

The station is an appropriately dominant building. Built originally by Francis Thompson for three railways, and known therefore as the 'Tri-junct' station, it had an immensely long brick facade of 1,050 feet leading through to a long single platform under a light iron trainshed built by

STATION FRONTAGE. 1979

Robert Stephenson. The shed had three bays covering nine sets of tracks connected by transverse rails and turnplates, a common feature at large early stations.

Thompson and others subsequently built long single platforms at Chester *(p.96)*, Cambridge *(p.18)* and elsewhere, but at Derby the scheme was quickly found to be impractical so further platforms were added. Stephenson's shed remained intact until 1941 when a bomb demolished 100 yards of it. The rest was

LOCOMOTIVE WORKS AND CLOCK TOWER WITH LMS CLASS '2F' 2-6-0, 1959

pulled down in 1952.

Major changes were made to Thompson's frontage block in 1856 and 1872, when more offices, the present facade and the large glass-roofed *porte cochère* were added. A pair of three-storey pedimented office blocks now stand at each end of the front, and between them is a balustraded two-storey block with three pediments, a central clock and three wyverns, the mythical two-legged dragon with barbed tail which the Midland adopted as its symbol.

Only vague traces of Thompson's facade remain, although the old western wall of the trainshed with arched windows can still be well appreciated from the platforms.

Thompson's hotel still faces the station, extended but otherwise hardly altered. The oldest purpose-built station hotel in the world, it is a plain brick structure with stone quoins and dressings and regular fenestration. For some years a glass covered way joined it to the station. Along the side of the hotel in Midland Road is the railway company's war memorial, standing in a small garden.

LOCOMOTIVE WORKS. Original engine shed, built c.1840 for North Midland Railway; locomotive works offices built probably c.1851 for Midland Railway. Engine shed and clock tower listed Grade II. In Railway Terrace.

Each of the three companies using the Tri-junct station had its own engine shed on the north-east side of the station. The North Midland's roundhouse was later incorporated in the locomotive works which were established at Derby in 1851 by Matthew Kirtley, Locomotive Superintendent of the Midland Railway. It is a 16-sided red-brick building with a heavy wooden-trussed conical roof, and had a turntable in the centre with radiating tracks which could accommodate up to 30 locomotives.

The clock tower is attached to the three-storey office block next to the shed, but probably was originally free-standing and may be of earlier date. The tower is brick, with embellishments, and supports a wooden clock turret with a weathervane shaped to represent an early locomotive. The works expanded to include the nearby carriage and wagon works in Litchurch Lane, and by about 1900 some 12,000 men were in railway employment in Derby. The railway is still a major employer in the town.

FRIARGATE BRIDGE. Built 1878 by Great Northern Railway. Listed Grade II. Closed.

The GNR could not hope to be other than second fiddle to the Midland in Derby, but nevertheless marked its presence by a handsome and intricately decorated iron arched bridge in Friargate adjacent to its own station. Friargate is one of Derby's

DERBY ROUNDHOUSE, 1927

c.1970

few gracious Georgian streets and the Great Northern made an effort to provide a handsome bridge. Now trackless, it has been nicely painted in contrasting colours to pick out its features, including stags from Derby's coat of arms.

DUFFIELD

MAKENY ROAD BRIDGE, DUFFIELD and ALFRETON ROAD BRIDGE, BREADSALL. Built 1839 for North Midland Railway. Engineer George Stephenson. Listed Grade II. Between Derby and Ambergate.

Two excellent and unaltered examples of George Stephenson's larger bridges on the North Midland survive at Duffield and at nearby Breadsall. Both are of brick faced with sandstone and have a continuous roll cornice, Stephenson's special trademark. The Breadsall bridge has three elliptical arches built on the skew, and the Duffield one five similar arches that are straight.

The exceptional quality of the stonework and design on this line may be due in some degree to Francis Thompson, who built many of the stations. Interestingly, all these structures appear on the first edition of the Ordnance Survey which was published in 1839, before the railway was open.

GLOSSOP

Built privately 1845, worked by Sheffield Ashton-under-Lyne & Manchester Railway. Listed Grade II. End of branch from Manchester to Hadfield line at Dinting.

This 1½-mile length of line, built privately by the Duke of Norfolk, was taken over by the SAMR in 1846. The station is a plain grey stone structure incorporating a screen wall across the inner end surmounted by the Howard family's emblem, a stone lion.

1980

1978

79

ILKESTON

BENNERLEY VIADUCT. Built 1878 for Great Northern Railway. Engineer Richard Johnson. Listed Grade II. Closed.

Lacking the dramatic scenery of the similarly constructed Meldon viaduct (*p.239*), Bennerley viaduct makes a valuable contribution to the landscape of the Erewash valley. Indeed, it has little competition other than the dramatic profile of Ilkeston

1977

on a nearby spur. The viaduct has 16 spans of crossed lattice girders in wrought iron on cast- and wrought-iron piers. It is 500 yards long and 60 feet high with brick abutments at both ends. Each pier consists of ten iron columns tied together with diagonal and horizontal struts, producing a light and decorative effect. It is of great importance as one of the only two major all-metal viaducts to survive.

MATLOCK BATH

Built 1880s by Midland Railway. Listed Grade II. Derby to Matlock line. Closed.

Early Victorian writers were fond of comparing the romantic scenery of the Lake District and Derbyshire with the Alps, so

MATLOCK BATH, 1976

it is not surprising that a 'Swiss Chalet' style of architecture became popular there. In some places even the railways followed the trend and when it came to building a station at the growing spa of Matlock Bath the Midland forsook its traditional styling in favour of something considered more in keeping with 'Little Switzerland'.

Three separate chalet-style buildings were erected on the northbound platform and two on the other, with exposed timber frames, herringbone brick nogging, deep bracketed eaves projecting out to form verandahs and – that irresistible Midland touch – diamond window panes. Some

have now gone but enough remains to convey the station's special character.

MONSAL DALE VIADUCT

Built 1863 for Midland Railway. Engineer William Barlow. Listed Grade II. Matlock to Buxton line. Closed and sold.

This five-arched viaduct crosses Ruskin's 'Vale of Tempe' to which it brought what he called the railway's 'close clinging damnation'. But despite his passionate denunciation, the viaduct is regarded

(Continued on page 85)

MONSAL DALE VIADUCT, 1963

The decorative faience, or multi-coloured glazed tiles, on this room at Worcester Shrub Hill is enhanced by blue paint on columns, cornices and on the round-arched windows.

RAILWAYS AND LANDSCAPE

If you climb the Howgill Fells in Cumbria and look down into the Lune Gorge, you will hardly notice the railway climbing towards Shap. Here and elsewhere, sympathetic design and the use of local materials made the railways part of the landscape. Even iron bridges could have grace. Gauxholme Viaduct at Todmorden, shown here, has Gothic-shaped ironwork and crenellated abutments which epitomise the early Victorian concept of embellishing structures to fit into – and even improve – a romantic landscape.

The Big Water of Fleet Viaduct strides across the bare landscape at Gatehouse of Fleet on 20 masonry arches. The piers have been strengthened by brick casings.

A London-bound High Speed Train passes alongside the retaining wall and under one of the two bridges in Sydney Gardens, Bath, built by I. K. Brunel in 1840.

The towers of the 13th-century castle on the west bank of the River Conwy (far left) inspired the medieval abutments of Robert Stephenson's tubular bridge of 1849.

ROWSLEY OLD STATION, 1963

FRANCIS THOMPSON, ARCHITECT

Little is known about Thompson's background other than that he may have been a fashionable London tailor with artistic flair who, during the railway boom of the 1840s, found it more profitable to design railway stations instead of clothes. We are fortunate that he did, for he left to posterity buildings of superb quality.

Although many have gone, sufficient remain in East Anglia, the North Midlands and North Wales for us to be able to appreciate his skill. On the North Midland Railway he designed the termini at Derby (*p.78*) and Leeds and a delightful series of small intermediate stations of which only Wingfield (*right*) and a fragment at Chesterfield (*p.76*) remain. They were his first and without doubt his finest work, all different and with particularly delicate proportions.

It seems that he next went to the Eastern Counties Railway Cambridge line where he may have worked under or alongside Sancton Wood with whom his name has often been associated (Sancton is Wood's Christian name). At all events, a style adopted there was used by Thompson on the Chester & Holyhead Railway and some of its later branch lines, where Holywell (*p.95*) is particularly notable, and stations in his manner were also found in the East Midlands and East Anglia. His largest surviving station, and possibly his best, is Chester (*p.96*).

(Continued from page 80)

today as virtually part of the rocky landscape into which it blends so well. A railway preservation society plans to put the lines back so perhaps before long we shall once more be able to emerge from Headstone Tunnel by train and look straight down into the River Wye 72 feet below.

ROWSLEY

Built 1849 for Manchester Buxton Matlock & Midlands Junction Railway. Architect Sir Joseph Paxton. Listed Grade II. Matlock to Buxton line. Closed.

This company was closely supervised by the Midland as part of its drive northwards to Manchester, and Rowsley was the station for the Duke of Devonshire's seat at Chatsworth, hence the involvement of Paxton (see Buxton, *p.76*, and Cromford, *p.77*).

The old station, which remained a terminus for 18 years, lies east of the main road in the former goods yard. The gable ends of the roof form hollow pediments and attractive projecting eaves are supported by curved brackets matching the round-topped windows. The station was superseded by a second one when the line was extended, but has outlived its successor which closed in 1967. The original portion of Matlock station is very similar.

WINGFIELD

Built 1840 for North Midland Railway. Architect Francis Thompson. Listed Grade II. Between Derby and Chesterfield. Closed and sold.

Wingfield has been rated the most perfect of Thompson's North Midland stations, not for its perfection of detail, although it possesses that, but for the strict classical symmetry of its execution. The shallow roofed central pavilion is flanked by recessed smaller and lower wings, in dark ashlar stone including a side wall with ball finials. The station name in gold lettering divided itself on either side of an elaborately decorated clock facing the platform.

ENGRAVING BY S. RUSSELL, c.1840

85

STAFFORDSHIRE

ALTON TOWERS

Built 1849 by North Staffordshire Railway. Listed Grade II. Leek to Uttoxeter line. Closed and sold.

The Florentine station of Alton Towers is perhaps most remarkable for being so thoroughly out of keeping with the two great houses which dominate the landscape around it. The River Churnet here runs through a deep ravine overlooked on one side by Alton Towers and on the other by Alton Castle, built by the 15th and

1974

16th Earls of Shrewsbury respectively, and perched in romantic Bavarian fashion on the top of a cliff. The 16th Earl, a remarkable eccentric with a passion for everything medieval, had as his architect

A. W. N. Pugin, a kindred spirit and a leading gothic revivalist. Pugin made additions to Alton Towers and in 1847 set about building Alton Castle. Then the North Staffordshire Railway arrived.

Not far away was Trentham Hall, designed by Sir Charles Barry in Italianate style for the Duke of Sutherland. Trentham Station, with its strong Florentine flavour, was not unlike part of the Duke's stable-block and is in fact thought to have been designed by Barry as well. Barry and Pugin had collaborated in the building of the Houses of Parliament during which they had violently disagreed. The architect of Alton Towers station is unknown, but can it be an accident that, like Trentham, it is also in the Florentine manner? Since neither the Earl of Shrewsbury nor Pugin was likely to have welcomed the railway, the erection of so nongothic a station must have added insult to injury. Was Barry in some way involved, and did he settle old scores with Pugin by deliberately erecting a strongly Italianate station on his doorstep?

Trentham Hall and Trentham station have now both gone; so has the Churnet Valley Railway. Only the incongruous neighbours of Alton Towers, Alton Castle and Alton Towers station remain, as reminders of a minor architectural mystery.

CHEDDLETON

Built 1849 for North Staffordshire Railway. Architect William Sugden. Leek to Uttoxeter line.

Further up the Churnet Valley from Alton Towers the NSR built a series of finely detailed Tudor stations in grey stone, some with unusual little hipped and tiled platform awnings and others, like Cheddleton, with one of their standardised flat awnings. Cheddleton has been restored and is now used by the (new) North Staffordshire Railway, a preservation group aiming to reopen part of this picturesque line. Nearby, James Brindley's restored Cheddleton Flint Mill and the Caldon Canal complete a trio of interesting industrial archaeological sites.

COLWICH

Built 1847 for Trent Valley Railway. Architect J. W. Livock. Engineers Robert Stephenson and G. P. Bidder. Lichfield Drive bridge and tunnel entrances in Shugborough Park listed Grade II. Between Rugeley and Stafford.

In return for the Earl of Lichfield's agreement to allow the line to cross Shugborough Park, the railway company undertook to erect an ornamental bridge

CHEDDLETON, 1963

COLWICH, 1974

across the Lichfield Drive and appropriate portals to Shugborough Park tunnel. The results form some of the most remarkable decorative features on any railway. Lichfield Drive bridge comprises a low stone arch flanked by pairs of Ionic columns and a curved balustraded wing wall on each side. The parapets are enormous, each carrying three plinths; the outer ones bear a seahorse and a lion representing the supporters of the Lichfield arms which are emblazoned on a shield on the centre one, backed by the robe of state and surmounted by a coronet.

The nearby tunnel is 774 yards long and its entrances are nicknamed 'The Gates of Jerusalem'. The western portal is in Norman style, with battlements, gargoyle-like corbels and a pair of turrets decorated with crenellations. The eastern end is less elaborate – more in the Egyptian style than anything else – with a moulded cornice, battered side walls and the Lichfield shield above the arch. Shugborough Hall now belongs to the National Trust and houses the Staffordshire County Museum.

The presence within the park of the noted Shugborough 'follies' – the Arch of Hadrian (a dramatic sight from the approach to the eastern portal) and the Tower of the Winds – doubtless influenced the designs of the bridge and the tunnel. It is not known whether Livock was responsible for them, but he certainly designed all the other buildings along the line (see Atherstone, *p.66*), including the little stone Jacobean house at Colwich itself, which is all that remains of the station.

LICHFIELD DRIVE BRIDGE, 1970

GREAT HAYWOOD

TRENT LANE and MILL LANE BRIDGES. Built 1849 for North Staffordshire Railway. Listed Grade II. Between Rugeley and Stoke.

These nicely proportioned bridges are both built in grey ashlar stone. Trent Lane has an elliptical arch balanced by a small pedestrian arch on each side, and Mill Lane has a segmental arch with rusticated voussoirs.

SHUGBOROUGH PARK TUNNEL, WESTERN PORTAL, 1981

MILL LANE BRIDGE, 1982

LONGPORT, 1977

LICHFIELD

Bridge over Upper St. John Street built 1849 for South Staffordshire Railway. Architect Thomas Johnson. Abutments listed Grade II.

Johnson was a local architect who designed the original iron bridge which was fitted with stone battlement parapets and side towers, complete with arrow slits and pointed side arches for pedestrians. Reconstruction has left only the abutments, although the heraldic shields – the Royal and four bishops' arms – designed by Richard Greene, a Lichfield banker, have been retained.

LONGPORT

Built 1848 by North Staffordshire Railway. Listed Grade II. Stoke to Crewe line.

The North Stafford was noted for its neat neo-Tudor and Jacobean stations, mostly constructed of brick. Longport is Jacobean, the curly gables on both buildings, now shorn of their awnings, enclosing patterned red and blue brickwork.

SANDON

Built 1849 by North Staffordshire Railway. Listed Grade II. Between Rugeley and Stoke. Closed and sold.

Only the main building remains of this charming station, built primarily for the Earl of Harrowby of Sandon Hall, but it is sufficient to convey the atmosphere of the place. Now a private house, it is T-shaped

SANDON, c.1962

in plan and has a projecting arched *porte cochère* for the earl's carriage with a room above. Again the NSR's favourite Jacobean features predominate.

STOKE-ON-TRENT

WINTON SQUARE. Station built 1848 for North Staffordshire Railway, architect H. A. Hunt; houses and North Stafford Hotel built 1849, architect probably also H. A. Hunt; statue of Josiah Wedgwood 1863 by Edward Davis; all listed Grade II. Hotel not in British Rail ownership.

One of the few pieces of deliberate civic planning by a railway company, Winton Square is undoubtedly the best in the country. Perhaps the decision to use the railway to enhance the town is hardly surprising, since the North Staffordshire Railway was firmly Potteries-controlled: John L. Ricardo, M.P. for Stoke, was its first chairman, and most of the influential local people sat on the board.

The station frontage is Jacobean, remarked on at the time for its purity of design, two- and three-storeyed with a projecting Tuscan collonaded *porte cochère* with radial glazing to some of the arches. Above it, forming a centrepiece, is a large square bay-window with numerous mullions, said to be modelled on the one at Charlton House, Wiltshire, which it closely resembles. It is surmounted by a moulded parapet and the company coat of arms, and gives on to the oak-panelled former NSR boardroom, which retains its atmosphere of grandeur. The rest of the upper floor was company offices.

The interior is no less unaltered. The entrance to the platforms now comprises a broad elliptical arch erected by the NSR as a 1914-18 war memorial to its employees, while the platforms are covered by a low ridge-and-furrow glass roof which replaced separate arcaded iron trainsheds in 1893. In front of the station, the square is made up of a row of modestly

NORTH STAFFORD HOTEL, 1974

STOKE-ON-TRENT, 1967

JOSIAH WEDGWOOD STATUE, c.1980

matching houses on each side, originally for railway employees. Facing it is the North Stafford Hotel, three storeys high with attic dormers, matching gables and diaper brickwork, with an entrance in the middle of three projecting bays. The entire composition, finished off with a bronze statue of Josiah Wedgwood in the centre of the square, is a unique piece of careful railway planning.

STONE

Station built 1848 for North Staffordshire Railway, architect H. A. Hunt; crossing keeper's cottage, Whitebridge Lane; both listed Grade II. Stafford to Stoke line.

This example of North Stafford Jacobean is placed awkwardly in the angle of V-shaped platforms at a junction, but is strongly assertive for all that. The three spiked gables, with a lower one in the centre over the three-arched entrance, are faithfully repeated at the back. The small keeper's cottage at the level crossing in Whitebridge Lane, designed in keeping with the station, is similar to a number of others on the early NSR lines.

c.1965

SHROPSHIRE

ALBRIGHTON

Main building probably built 1849 by Shrewsbury & Birmingham Railway. Other buildings and canopies built later by Great Western Railway. Between Wolverhampton and Wellington.

This is an interesting example of an early two-storey building in the style of a house, containing offices and dwelling rooms. It is Italianate in character, and a fairly typical GWR awning was later added.

On the up side, the building is a standard GWR brick structure of the 1880s, again with a typical awning but of a later period, while the diamond patterned blue-brick platform and the ornate latticed iron footbridge are also characteristic. An underbridge with cast-iron parapets adjoins the platform end.

ALBRIGHTON. 1978

ALBERT EDWARD BRIDGE, c.1976

90

COALBROOKDALE

ALBERT EDWARD BRIDGE. Built 1862 for Great Western Railway. Engineer Sir John Fowler. Listed Grade II. Between Coalbrookdale and Ironbridge.

This is a fine bridge for its period, crossing the River Severn with a single graceful cast-iron span of 200 feet. It was manufactured by the nearby Coalbrookdale Iron Company and is named after the Prince of Wales, born in 1841, whose 21st birthday coincided with the opening.

Now used only for the coal deliveries to Ironbridge power station, it belongs to a group of four historically significant bridges over the Severn: Ironbridge (1779), the first large iron bridge in the world, then the slightly younger Coalport Bridge (1818), followed by Albert Edward itself, and finally an early and reasonably attractive reinforced concrete road bridge of 1909.

GOBOWEN

Built 1846 by Shrewsbury & Chester Railway. Listed Grade II. Between Shrewsbury and Wrexham.

The Shrewsbury & Chester built a remarkable variety of small stations: half-timbered at Leaton and Whittington; Tudor at Chirk (*p.94*), Rossett and Ruabon; *cottage orné* at Baschurch with gables and turret; and strangest of all, this perfect little essay in Florentine at Gobowen, a village with little else of any interest.

1963

Faced with stucco, with coupled round-headed windows on the first floor, a gracefully curved end-bay, discreet window mouldings and a tall turret, the place has great charm and once more illustrates the wide diversity of English station building in the first decades of the railways. The attractive platform awnings and footbridge were added by the Great Western in later years.

SHREWSBURY

Built 1848 jointly for Shrewsbury & Birmingham, Shrewsbury & Chester, Shrewsbury & Hereford and Shropshire Union Railways. Architect T. K. Penson. Frontage block listed Grade II.

Shrewsbury was a joint station from the start and is an interesting mixture. The ownership quickly resolved itself into that of two companies, the Great Western and the London & North Western. The GWR lines converged from Chester and the Severn Valley, the LNWR from Crewe, and the jointly owned lines from Wellington, Hereford and Welshpool. The station fittings, the north end awnings and most of the signalling were of LNWR pattern, including the huge signal box in the triangular junction which must have been one of the largest on the North Western. For a time after nationalisation the station was in the Western Region, and even more interesting combinations could be seen, like signals from Swindon on wooden posts from Crewe.

The two-storey collegiate Tudor facade was well suited to Shrewsbury, in grey stone with a prominent pepper-pot shaft breaking up the embattled parapet and a lofty clock tower containing a two-storey oriel window. In 1903-04 the whole build-

SHREWSBURY AFTER REMODELLING IN 1904

ing was underpinned and an additional storey added below, for which the courtyard had to be lowered. The resultant three-storey structure is even more imposing than the original. Part of the station is on a bridge over the Severn, and from 1904 until recently the platforms in this section had a massively cumbersome transverse roof of low latticed girders spanning the entire width between side walls in order to avoid intermediate supports. It was a complex and unusual design, and the signal box beneath it had a special flat roof to fit.

REFECTORY PULPIT. Listed Grade I and Ancient Monument. At goods yard, south of the station.

A surviving part of the monastic buildings of Shrewsbury Abbey, this 14th-century oriel-like structure is shaped like three sides of an octagon with lancet windows, carved figures and a vaulted ceiling (*see photograph, p.137*).

POWYS

KNIGHTON

Built 1861 by Knighton Railway. Central Wales line, between Shrewsbury and Llandrindod Wells.

The Knighton Railway was one of a string of small railways that became part of the Central Wales line, an outpost of the

1957

London & North Western system. It was the means by which through coaches ran from Euston to Swansea via Stafford and Shrewsbury – a delightful journey for those with time to spare.

Many of the stations are standard LNWR wooden structures of varying types but Knighton, together with its neighbour Bucknell, stands out in sturdy stone. The steep gables and dormers, a turret-like roof at one end, narrow pointed windows, patterned roof slates and fretted bargeboards over the porch put the frontage almost into the realms of romantic Gothick. By contrast the platform side is quite plain.

KNUCKLAS VIADUCT

Built 1864 for Central Wales Railway. Engineer Henry Robertson. Between Shrewsbury and Llandrindod Wells.

The viaduct is in the attractive setting of the Heyhope Valley, which it crosses by

13 arches up to 75 feet high, its total length being 190 yards. The use of undressed freestone gives it a rugged appearance enhanced by a prominently corbelled parapet with crenellations and, at each end, a pair of semi-circular castellated turrets complete with mock cross-shaped arrow-slits.

1977

THREE RAILWAY HEADQUARTERS

Oswestry, Shropshire (Cambrian Railways, c.1866, closed); Welshpool, Powys (Oswestry & Newtown Railway, 1860), listed Grade II; Llanidloes, Powys (Mid-Wales Railway, 1864, closed). Architect probably Benjamin Piercy.

The Oswestry & Newtown and the Mid-Wales united with two other companies to form the Cambrian Railways with its headquarters at *OSWESTRY*. The offices were in the large two-storey Italianate main station building, constructed of brick with stone dressings and attractive bay windows. A slightly smaller block occupied the opposite platform. The company's works (no longer in railway occupation) are close by, marked by a little cupola with a locomotive weathervane.

LLANIDLOES is similar to Oswestry but not quite so large. Again, its size in relation to the place it served is explained by its housing the headquarters' offices.

WELSHPOOL, equally large for the same reason, is quite different and the most remarkable building of the three – a powerful French Renaissance composition with pavilion-roofed end-turrets, dormers and plentiful iron cresting. Oddly enough, it only housed the Oswestry & Newtown's headquarters for little over a year before they were moved to Oswestry. A typical Cambrian lean-to awning shelters the main platform.

The narrow-gauge Welshpool & Llanfair Railway used to run from the station yard, but it now starts at Raven Square on the outskirts of the town and is operated by a preservation society.

Together these three stations constitute a most interesting group with a common background. There was also a fourth – Ellesmere in Shropshire, a similar but smaller edition of Oswestry and one-time headquarters of the Oswestry, Ellesmere & Whitchurch Railway.

The GWR 4-6-0 Foxcote Manor *at Oswestry, 1965*

Welshpool: **above** *1963;* **right** *1976*

ABERYSTWYTH

Rebuilt 1924 for Great Western Railway. Listed Grade II.

For years Aberystwyth station had been inadequate to cope with the resort's holiday traffic, but reconstruction was put off until the GWR acquired the Cambrian Railways in the 1923 grouping, when it received top priority. Platforms were extended, passenger facilities were improved and modernised, and the old Cambrian awnings were lengthened in GWR style although they retained their earlier gothic ironwork.

A lofty glass-roofed concourse was incorporated, but most immediately

1926

apparent was the new frontage block of white stone, two storeys high in a post-Edwardian Georgian style. The roofline has a curious, unfinished look. The parapet is low with some half-hearted decoration at one end; at the other a stumpy clock tower with a flat top looks as though it is waiting to be finished with a dome or spire.

FRIOG ROCKS

Line opened 1865 for Aberystwyth & Welsh Coast Railway. Engineer Benjamin Piercy. Between Llwyngwril and Fairbourne.

The line follows the coast on a shelf cut in the near-vertical cliffs 86 feet above the shore, and ever since it was built it has been subject to the threat of falling rocks. From the opening a speed limit of 4 m.p.h.

1960

was imposed, and regular inspections were made. Even so, on New Year's Day 1883 a landslide hit a train, killing the driver and fireman. The engine was hauled back up from the beach, repaired and went on running for 30 more years. A permanent watchman was installed, but after the Great Western carried out further improvements in the 1920s the speed limit was raised to 15 m.p.h. and from 1930 the watchman was only used in bad weather. Then in the spring of 1933 disaster struck again. The rocks were loose following bad winter weather and the sound-waves from an engine's exhaust as it laboured up the gradient started a landslide which threw it on to the beach. Once more the crew were killed but there were no other casualties. After this the GWR built the concrete avalanche shelter, still there today.

MACHYNLLETH

Built 1863 by Newtown & Machynlleth Railway. Between Newtown and Aberystwyth.

MACHYNLLETH, 1976

Less than a year after opening, this line became part of the Cambrian Railways. It has a set of noteworthy *cottage orné* stations, of which Machynlleth is the largest. Constructed in local stone, it is two storeys high with three prominent gables, decorative bargeboards and finials, and finished off with a standard Cambrian lean-to awning.

TALERDDIG CUTTING

Built 1863 for Newtown & Machynlleth Railway. Engineers Benjamin and Robert Piercy.

The original plan was for a tunnel here, but a cutting was decided on instead in order to provide stone for bridges on the line. At 120 feet, it was at the time the deepest cutting in the world, and some gold was found during its construction. Built for a single line it is very narrow and spectacular: 'From the footplate it seems as if the razor-sharp rocks will shave off the cab sides' (Christiansen & Miller, *The Cambrian Railways*).

CHURCHWARD 2-6-0 BLASTING THROUGH TALERDDIG CUTTING, c.1963

CHIRK, 1976

CLWYD

CHIRK and CEFN

Line opened 1848 by Shrewsbury & Chester Railway. Engineer Henry Robertson. Between Shrewsbury and Wrexham.

CHIRK STATION, close to the drive to the 13th-century Chirk Castle which is one of the most interesting feudal buildings in the country, is built in a symmetrical Tudor style. Carefully composed in ashlar stone, it has three central gables, well proportioned mullioned windows and coupled chimneys.

CHIRK VIADUCT AND AQUEDUCT, 1848

DEE VIADUCT, 1952

CHIRK VIADUCT runs right next to the older Llangollen Canal aqueduct, built by William Jessop and Thomas Telford in 1800, which is 300 yards long with ten arches 70 feet high and is actually an iron trough encased in stone. The railway viaduct, built of stone, is 100 feet high and 283 yards long. Originally it had ten stone arches with a broad laminated timber arch at each end, but these were replaced by masonry arches in 1858-59. Together with Chirk canal tunnel at the north end of the aqueduct, the valley of the River Ceiriog here presents an important triumvirate of civil engineering achievements.

Little more than two miles north of Chirk the even greater *DEE VIADUCT* crosses the River Dee at Cefn. Similar in style to Chirk, it is 510 yards long and 148 feet high with nineteen 60-foot arches – at its completion it was said to be the largest in the country. Like Chirk, it has a companion canal structure, further away but easily visible upstream, in the shape of Jessop and Telford's famous Pontcysyllte aqueduct of 1805 – a bare iron trough this time, supported 121 feet high above the river on stone piers and one of the greatest achievements in canal engineering.

HAWARDEN SWING BRIDGE

Built 1887-89 for Chester & Connahs Quay Railway (promoted by Manchester Sheffield & Lincolnshire Railway). Engineer Francis Fox. Between Wrexham and the Wirral.

Hawarden Bridge was built to serve two purposes, one economic and the other political. It would provide a much-needed link across the Dee estuary between North Wales and the Wirral, so that, among other things, North Wales slack coal could reach the Cheshire salt works; and it was the key to a scheme by the MSLR chairman Sir Edward Watkin (the second 'Railway King') simultaneously to penetrate Wales and reach Birkenhead, both areas that were dominated by the London & North Western and

Great Western companies.

The bridge was designed on the bowstring girder principle with two 120-foot fixed spans and an opening span of 287 feet, then the longest ever constructed. Operated hydraulically, it could open in 40 seconds, giving a clear navigable width of 140 feet. The spans stand on cylindrical iron piers.

Typically Watkin made the most of the publicity potential. In 1887 he arranged for W. E. Gladstone, then leader of the Opposition, and his wife ceremonially to lower the first cylinder. To start the operation Mrs. Gladstone gave a blast on an inscribed gold whistle and W. E. himself waved a specially embroidered silk pennon on an ebony staff, also inscribed and mounted. The crowds cheered, craft on the river sounded their hooters, and the guests – all 500 of them – repaired to a marquee for lunch.

Two years later the Gladstones were back to perform an opening ceremony which if anything was arranged with even more ballyhoo. Mrs. Gladstone rang an electric bell and the bridge swung open to the strains of 'Men of Harlech'.

The bridge did its job, too. Watkin reached Wrexham and Birkenhead, and North Wales coal and iron flowed to the salt works and the docks.

RUABON

Opened 1846 by Shrewsbury & Chester Railway. Engineer Henry Robertson. Listed Grade II. Between Wrexham and Shrewsbury.

The station building here possibly dates from a few years after the station opening. It is a Tudor-style single-storey structure built of sandstone with two gabled pavilions, mullioned windows and finials. A ridge-and-furrow glass-and-iron canopy covers the platform, supported on iron columns with simple brackets. The canopy has vertical outer gables, but is hipped where it joins the building. The opposite platform, an island, had a later-type glass ridge-and-furrow umbrella awning, now removed.

As the junction for the line to Llangollen, Barmouth and Pwllheli, Ruabon was a station of some importance until the Pwllheli service was withdrawn in 1965, although it still serves as a railhead for the Vale of Dee.

1976

THE TUBULAR BRIDGES

*Conwy built 1849, Britannia (Menai) built 1850
for Chester & Holyhead Railway. Engineer
Robert Stephenson. Conwy bridge listed Grade II.*

For the crossing of the Menai Strait the
Admiralty demanded a clear headroom of
100 feet, and Stephenson decided to construct a wrought-iron box-section tube
through which the rails would pass. Such a
revolutionary principle (at first it was
thought necessary to have suspension
chains as well) required trial, and fortunately the bridging of the River Conwy
provided the opportunity. Two 400-foot
tubes were fabricated, floated out on pon-
toons and hydraulically hoisted into position 18 feet above the water. The bridge,
alongside Telford's suspension road bridge
and its modern companion, has crenellated
piers skilfully designed to blend with
Conwy Castle on the west bank, the outer
defences of which had to be pierced.

The Menai bridge was altogether much
more spectacular. It was a stupendous
undertaking, the twin tubes each comprising two 230-foot and two 460-foot spans
supported on three piers, the central one
being 221 feet high to the top of the tower.
The tubes were made from iron plates
riveted together on the Caernarvon shore,

then floated out and lifted into place with
the tackle that had been used for Conwy
which was towed round the coast. Stephenson's friend Brunel was there to watch it.
The towers, Egyptian in concept, are
thought to be designed by Francis Thompson. At the entrances to the tubes the sculptor John Thomas set up four huge couchant
lions to symbolize the strength of the
bridge. It was intended to add a huge figure
of Britannia atop the centre tower, but expense precluded it; in any case, the clean,
strong proportions of the bridge itself were
a sufficient monument.

Disaster befell the Britannia bridge in
May 1970. The timber linings caught fire
and flames spread through the bridge with
a flue-like effect, weakening the ironwork.
Stephenson's tubes were taken down and
replaced by steel arched spans between the
existing towers; the bridge was reopened
for rail traffic in 1972. A roadway above the
rail deck was completed in 1980, to act as a
relief for Telford's Menai suspension
bridge. Although regrettably Stephenson's
tubular bridge is no more, passengers have
gained. They can now look out at the strait
and its mountain backcloth, whereas from
inside the tubes they saw nothing.

Above *Conwy, c.1920;* **inset** *Menai under construction, 1849*

HOLYWELL JUNCTION

*Built 1848 for Chester & Holyhead Railway.
Architect Francis Thompson. Listed Grade II.
Between Chester and Rhyl. Closed.*

After working on the North Midland
Railway, Thompson designed stations for
the line between Chester and Holyhead.
A number still exist, having had varying
degrees of modification and alteration
over the years. Holywell Junction was his
best and, apart from losing its platforms,

is the least altered. It is in dark red,
almost purple, brick with stone jambs,
frieze and classical window casings
(round-headed on the ground floor and
flat on the first), decorated with prominent rose-motifs. A contemporary print
shows corner pavilions linked on all four
sides by a flat verandah, but if they
existed at the front they were removed
many years ago. The platform pavilions
have survived, and the verandah and
shallow pitched roof were clad with
Roman pantiles.

1930s

HOLYHEAD

*Salt Island, George IV arch, customs house,
harbour office, pier and lighthouse all listed
Grade II.*

For a number of years at the end of the 18th
century the government had been seeking
an improvement in communications between London and Dublin, and Holyhead
offered the shortest crossing. In the early
1800s, therefore, Thomas Telford was empowered to improve the Holyhead road,
and John Rennie was entrusted with the
construction of a new harbour, which was
started in 1810. He built a pier 360 feet long
and, as with much of his work, designed a
complete set of ancillary buildings, including a lighthouse at the end of the pier and,
at the landward end of the harbour, a
customs house and harbour office with a
clock turret. In 1821 he designed a large
Doric arch to commemorate the visit of
George IV to Holyhead on his way to
Ireland. Built of Mona marble, 20 feet high,
it has inscriptions in Welsh and English
marking the event. The arch, customs
house and office form a pleasing and harmonious group.

With the opening of the Chester & Holyhead Railway in 1848, rapid expansion
commenced. In his *Railway Companion from
Chester to Holyhead* (published in 1848),
Edward Parry expressed the opinion that
Holyhead would make 'one of the most
splendid refuge harbours and packet
stations in the universe'. The government
started work on a harbour of refuge, designed successively by James M. Rendel
and Sir John Hawkshaw, culminating in
the 1870s in the Great Breakwater, over a
mile long, that encloses the New Harbour.
A 7-foot gauge railway along it, built to
carry stone from Holyhead Mountain, is
still used for maintenance work.

The company and its successor the
London & North Western played a leading
part in developing the commercial activities of the port, by contributing to the cost
of the works and starting their own steamer
service to Dublin in competition with the
City of Dublin Steam Packet Company,
which for many years held the Irish mail
contract. The LNWR steamers ran to
Dublin North Wall, and then in 1873 the
company sponsored the Dundalk Newry &
Greenore Railway in Ireland and ran a
service from Holyhead to Greenore. In
addition to the popular passenger services,
a heavy traffic developed in Irish cattle, for
which a large lairage was specially constructed at Holyhead.

The Chester & Holyhead owned the
Royal Hotel and in 1851 opened a new
station at the south end of the inner harbour; both were replaced in 1880 by the
present station and hotel (closed in 1951).
The station is in two halves, with separate
platforms on either side of the hotel building that extend alongside the quays beyond
so that trains can draw up beside the
steamers. Each platform has its own
Euston-style overall roof. The former hotel,
a grim four-storey block in red brick
characteristic of the LNWR's uncompromising architecture of the period, is somewhat relieved by an intricately decorated
iron canopy along the front.

GWYNEDD

BETWS-Y-COED

CETHYN'S BRIDGE. Built 1879 for London & North Western Railway. Engineer Williams Smith. Listed Grade II. Between Betws-y-Coed and Ffestiniog.

This short line had much heavy engineering work including five tunnels and 18 bridges, but Cethyn's Bridge is the only large one. Also known as the Lledr Viaduct, it is 357 yards long. It has seven

c.1975

stone arches, one of which crosses the Afon Lledr and another the road, and is massively constructed and ornamented with battlements and semi-circular bastions containing refuges for men working on the track.

The stonework in particular attracted the attention of Colonel Rich, the Board of Trade Inspector who checked the bridge before its opening. He noted that it was constructed of large undressed local stone with apparently unmortared joints. 'I am informed', he wrote in his report, 'that it was adopted to please the frequenters of the valley, who thought the beauty of the scenery would be affected by the construction of a Railway, but good rustic rubble work, with fitted joints filled with mortar, toned to a proper colour, would have been more in accordance with old building, pleasanter to the eye, and more secure.'

BARMOUTH or MAWDDACH VIADUCT

Built 1867 for Cambrian Coast Railway. Engineer Benjamin Piercy. Between Dovey Junction and Pwllheli.

Timber viaducts were once fairly common on the British railway system (see Brunel's Timber Viaducts, *p.240*), but this is now the only large one still in use and consequently of great interest.

It carries the railway across the Barmouth estuary on 113 narrow spans of heavy timbers with two steel bow-string girders of 1906 at the north end, one of which used to swing open for shipping. Many of the timbers have been replaced over the years, particularly those in the sea which have been attacked by wave action and marine worms, but the original form has been retained. There is a similar but smaller bridge further north on the same line at Penrhyndeudraeth.

CHESTER, 1840

CHESHIRE

CHESTER

Built 1848 jointly for Chester & Holyhead and Shrewsbury & Chester Railways. Architect Francis Thompson. Listed Grade II*.

Like Derby and Shrewsbury, Chester was a true joint station, although collaboration often did not extend far behind the scenes – in this case no further than the booking office. The owning companies were backed, and later owned, by the LNWR and GWR respectively, between whom there was long-standing rivalry for access to Birkenhead. Chester station was managed by a joint committee in which the LNWR had a majority and, after one particular quarrel over the routeing of

CHESTER, 1977

passengers, the LNWR had the Shrewsbury & Chester booking clerk forcibly ejected from his office. Connections with S & C trains were deliberately timed to create maximum inconvenience, and when the S & C replied by running horse buses to Birkenhead they found LNWR employees barring them from Chester station yard and defacing their timetables. These tactics, typical examples of what went on at various places during the 1840s and 1850s, were only stopped by a court injunction.

Thompson chose a strong Italianate style for his station, with the one-sided layout used at Derby (*p.78*) and a very long frontage block (over 1,000 feet) in buff brick with liberal stone dressings and sculptured decoration by John Thomas. Considered to be his best large station, it is symmetrical, two storeys high, the central section flanked by arcaded projections with Venetian windows, pierced parapet and a pair of low campanile-like turrets. In each direction beyond them stretch immensely long arcaded walls which terminate in two further turreted projections. The roof has a low profile, covered with pantiles.

The interior appointments were in keeping, particularly the wood and plasterwork in the principal passenger accommodation. The long through platform was supplemented by three bay platforms at each end, which had to suffice until the early 1890s when a long island platform was added, connected by a broad footbridge with brick stairs designed to harmonise with the character of the station. The original iron trainshed was designed by C. H. Wild with Robert Stephenson involved in his capacity as C & H engineer. Further roofing, added

WEAVER VIADUCT, 1890

with the platform extensions, is all now very fragmented.

CONGLETON

DANE and CONGLETON VIADUCTS. Built 1849 for North Staffordshire Railway. Engineer J. C. Forsyth. Listed Grade II. Between Congleton and Macclesfield.

The Dane Viaduct takes its name from the river which it crosses by twenty arches built from blue brick. Congleton Viaduct, on the same line a little to the south, has ten arches 130 feet high and crosses the course of the NSR's Biddulph branch, from which a steep curve connected with the main line.

DUTTON

WEAVER VIADUCT. Built 1837 for Grand Junction Railway. Engineer Joseph Locke. Between Crewe and Warrington.

This fine structure built of red sandstone is more than 440 yards long, 30 feet wide and 60 feet high. It consists of twenty arches each with a 60-foot span, with heavily rusticated voussoirs so characteristic of Joseph Locke's work on the Grand Junction and other railways.

HELSBY

Built c.1863 for Birkenhead Joint Railway (LNWR & GWR). Engineer R. E. Johnston. Warrington to Chester line.

Helsby, a junction with four platforms, lies in the angle formed by the diverging lines to Chester and to Birkenhead. On the Birkenhead line there is a set of pleasant stations in rock-faced sandstone at Ince, Little Sutton and Ellesmere Port, the first two Tudor and Ellesmere Port strikingly Jacobean. Helsby, also Jacobean, is particularly interesting in that the curved gables of the main building were repeated in miniature in the two smaller buildings, one of which is now

HELSBY, 1964

demolished. The stonework has recently been cleaned, with startlingly refreshing results, including the rather ugly later LNWR-style booking office which, surprisingly, was built of matching stone instead of the more customary brick.

RUNCORN BRIDGE

Built 1869 for London & North Western Railway. Engineer William Baker. Between Runcorn and Liverpool.

The best place from which to appreciate the grandeur of Runcorn Bridge is the Mersey shore at Widnes; but for a close-up of its detail either drive across the adjacent road bridge or, better still, walk along the footway attached to the bridge itself. The bridge shortened the distance between Crewe and Liverpool by over eight miles, avoiding the severe Earlestown curve and the congestion around Warrington. It consists of three large latticed girder spans, each 305 feet long and 75 feet high, supported by stone piers. The trains run inside the girders, and on the prominent tower at each end is a plaque recording Baker's name. At the north end the line rises to the bridge over the Ditton Viaduct – 59 arches on a gradient of 1 in 114.

JOSEPH LOCKE, ENGINEER

Locke stands next to the Stephensons and Brunel as Britain's leading railway engineer, although unlike them he kept major works like tunnels and viaducts to the minimum. Consequently his lines are more circuitous and steeply graded; they were cheaper to construct but more expensive to operate.

Locke was born near Sheffield in 1805, and his Yorkshire background never left him. He was educated at Barnsley Grammar School and is commemorated by Locke Park, which he presented to the town. After serving his articles under George Stephenson he assisted in the construction of the Liverpool & Manchester Railway. He rapidly established himself as a leading civil engineer and successively built the Grand Junction (Birmingham to Warrington) and London & Southampton Railways. He took over the construction of the Sheffield Ashton & Manchester from Charles Vignoles, including Woodhead Tunnel, and in partnership with J. E. Errington built the Lancaster & Carlisle and Caledonian Railways which completed the first trunk route from London to Scotland. Although passing through mountainous country, they have no tunnels and few major viaducts; before electrification the two steep inclines at Shap and Beattock were a severe test for locomotives.

Locke engineered numerous other lines, both in Britain and in Europe, and died comparatively young after an arduous life – in 1860 at the age of 55.

WARRINGTON

CENTRAL STATION. Built 1873 by Cheshire Lines Committee. Horsefair Street. Goods warehouse, Winwick Street, listed Grade II.

Most passengers use the staircase entrance in Horsefair Street and therefore do not see the impressive original frontage block along the north side. Built in yellow brick with generous stone dressings, it forms a long single-storey facade broken by numerous round-headed windows boldly rusticated, some in pairs. The parapet is broken in the centre by a projecting entrance block with a prominent pediment and flanking balustrades. The west end terminates with a pyramidal roofed pavilion; curiously, there is no counterpart at the east end, which upsets the symmetry of the whole.

BOLTON, 1976

1976

WAREHOUSE, 1977

The warehouse, a typical Cheshire Lines building, is in brick with segmental arched fenestration and pilasters to the upper floor. The ground floor has large door openings for loading and unloading, with a canopy on iron columns.

GREATER MANCHESTER

BOLTON

Rebuilt 1903 for Lancashire & Yorkshire Railway. Chief engineer William Hunt.

Bolton station represents an excellent example of early 20th-century railway 'modernisation'. It has two long, broad island platforms beneath generous awnings, giving spacious passenger accommodation. A full range of refreshment and waiting rooms runs down each side, nowadays mostly used for other purposes

although in some cases retaining their original uses etched in the window glass. Separate tracks for through trains and goods traffic pass clear of the platforms.

The entrance block, on the road bridge at one end, is a two-storey building in bright red Accrington brick, of typical LYR design of the time, topped by a pair of cupolas and a domed clock tower. The iron *porte cochère* has been removed. Inside the booking hall, wooden panelling on the booking office screen, now painted in contrasting colours, preserves a 'period' atmosphere.

GATHURST

Built 1855 by Lancashire & Yorkshire Railway. Between Wigan and Southport.

Gathurst is representative of a string of Tudor stations built on this line in local stone, all neat and well fitted to their localities. It is remarkable for being quite different from, not to mention superior to, most small stations the company was building elsewhere at the time.

HADFIELD

Built 1845 by Sheffield Ashton-under-Lyne & Manchester Railway. Between Manchester and Sheffield.

With the closure of the Great Central Railway's Woodhead route across the Pennines, Hadfield is now a terminus. In nicely detailed Tudor, it is similar to Oughty Bridge on the Yorkshire side (*p.32*) but larger.

1973

GATHURST, 1976

HALE

Rebuilt c.1890 by Cheshire Lines Committee. Between Altrincham and Northwich.

A typical late CLC station, Hale station has been renovated and restored to something very close to its original condition. It is built in red brick with shallow-pointed door and window openings and elaborate glass-and-iron awnings on both platforms. The fabric has been cleaned to reveal its original colouring and the ironwork attractively painted and picked out, notably the decorative capitals on the footbridge columns. Residual etched glass in the waiting room windows and the characteristic Cheshire Lines herringbone-panelled doors have been retained.

1976

HEALEY DELL VIADUCT

Built 1870 for Lancashire & Yorkshire Railway. Engineer Sir John Hawkshaw. Rochdale to Bacup line. Closed.

The wooded ravine of Healey Dell is crossed by this very slender single-line viaduct 105 feet high. Constructed from local stone, it has eight arches, three being skewed, and an iron span over a road.

HORWICH

MECHANICS' INSTITUTE. Built 1888 for Lancashire & Yorkshire Railway. Architect Henry Shelmerdine. Extended 1892.

Like all railway towns, Horwich was provided by the company with a Mechanics' Institute for the improvement of its employees' education. A vast, rather ugly, red brick building, it has a twin-arched entrance with a brick balustrade beneath a plain Dutch gable. At right angles behind stands the main block containing a lofty hall on the upper floor that seats 900; a library, reading rooms and classrooms were also provided.

LITTLEBOROUGH

STATION. Built 1839 by Manchester & Leeds Railway. In Conservation Area. Between Rochdale and Todmorden.

The present station buildings are not original, being in plain Lancashire & Yorkshire Railway style and of no great interest, but they bear a plaque commemorating the opening of the line from Manchester to this point in 1839 and throughout in 1841.

WESTERN PORTAL. ENGRAVING BY F. TAIT. 1845

SUMMIT TUNNEL. Built 1841 for Manchester & Leeds Railway. Engineer George Stephenson. East of Littleborough station.

'Taking it as a whole, I don't think there is such another piece of work in the world. It is the greatest work that has yet been done of this kind.' George Stephenson's words

HEALEY DELL VIADUCT. c.1905

remain true. Even though his tunnel, which at 1 mile 1,125 yards was then the world's longest railway tunnel, was soon eclipsed by much longer ones, it still ranks among the triumphs of early railway engineering. At each end there are curves and subsidiary tunnels: Summit East, 41 yards long, is separated from the main one by a broad oval shaft and clearly shows the invert at that end; Summit West, 55 yards long, is further away and forms a good vantage point from which to see the heavily rusticated western portal in its craggy cutting as the line disappears beneath a pyramid of rock.

MANCHESTER and SALFORD

CENTRAL STATION. Built 1880 for Cheshire Lines Committee. Consultant engineer possibly Sir John Fowler. Listed Grade II. Closed and sold.

Manchester Central and, to a lesser degree, Liverpool Central were the northern counterparts to St. Pancras (*p.62*). Both had single-span arched roofs, Manchester's only 30 feet narrower than St. Pancras', and although they were owned by the CLC Midland trains from London ran into both. Several writers have attributed its design to Sir John Fowler, although strangely the actual drawings bear only the names of the engineers of the three companies that formed the Cheshire Lines Committee: the Midland, the Manchester Sheffield & Lincolnshire (later the Great Central) and the Great Northern. The station was erected on the same principle as St. Pancras, with the 90-foot high roof ribs tied by the platform floor at what is effectively first floor level. The ironwork was made by Andrew Handyside & Co. of Derby. Differences lie in the profile, which is segmental not pointed, and the undercroft which is brick-vaulted instead of having iron joists. Unlike St. Pancras, Central station never had a proper front-

age. Wooden offices along the front were only intended as a stop-gap until a hotel could be built; but instead the Midland Hotel was put up across the street, and the temporary frontage remained as a permanent debasement of the great roof rising above it. After closure in 1969 Central lay for years crumbling and disused, apart from a car park, but in 1982 restoration and conversion into an exhibition centre was at last commenced.

DEANSGATE GOODS STATION. Built 1898 by Great Northern Railway. Listed Grade II. Closed and sold.

Next to Central station was the CLC goods warehouse, now demolished, and beyond that the vast complex of the Great Northern's goods station bounded by Watson Street, Peter Street and the length of Deansgate down to Great Bridgewater Street: it amounted to nearly a quarter of a mile of frontaging, comprising offices and screen wall with shops beneath. Behind lies the great five-storey brick warehouse, considered fireproof by virtue of its brick-arched floors on a grid of steel beams on riveted box-girder columns. Rails ran into the ground and first floors via sloping ramps from the extensive yard. Giant letters in white brick proclaim on all four sides 'Great Northern Railway Company's Goods Warehouse'. The last word in warehousing in 1898, it is reputed to have cost £1 million.

The Deansgate frontage block is a little more up-to-date, with lettering referring to the Great Northern's successor, the LNER. In 1981 cleaning and refurbishing of the whole site commenced.

MIDLAND HOTEL. Built 1898 for Midland Railway. Architect Charles Trubshaw. Listed Grade II. St. Peters Square.

Trubshaw's massive hotel opposite Central station has received a fair degree of vilification: it still represents the vulgar, ostentatious aspect of late Victorian commercial architecture and, as such, has a place in the history of our cities. Its vast brown terracotta bulk sits between the square and the station, bulbous and uncompromising. The interior is considerably more restrained, and to some it is still the most comfortable hotel in Manchester. At one time a glass-covered way connected it to the station, crossing the tramlines in Windmill Street.

VICTORIA STATION. Main frontage block built 1909 for Lancashire & Yorkshire Railway. Architect William Dawes. Canopy listed Grade II. Hunts Bank approach in Cathedral Conservation Area.

Manchester Victoria is something of a conglomeration, although with the closure of the adjacent Exchange station to which it was connected by a common platform (the longest in the country), it has become slightly less complicated.

The station, really in two parts, has a long subway leading to the high-level platforms beneath an unusual overall roof completed in 1881. The massive transverse bays comprise deep girders perforated in floral patterns, supporting curved ribs with pitched glazing laid tangentially and providing a flat top on which rests narrow ridge-and-furrow work. Part was removed in the 1930s and more was demolished by wartime bombing. The low-level terminal section of the station has more conventional pitched

CENTRAL, 1965

VICTORIA, 1960

100

trainsheds on columns, including the concourse where in one corner there is a charming Edwardian buffet with art nouveau detailing, marble columns and a decorated glass dome. It has recently been refurbished and restored to something approaching 1909 style. On the outside and on the adjacent bookstall, coloured mosaic lettering displays 'LYR'. The large wooden Victorian booking office is still in use and alongside the main entrance a large black and white wall-map shows the Lancashire & Yorkshire system.

William Dawes' four-storey frontage block is very long, broken up by pilasters and heavy rustication. A balustrade above the cornice is interrupted by two giant curved false gables with radial rustication and over the acute corner in Long Millgate is a shell-shaped pediment and clock. 'Lancashire and Yorkshire Railway Victoria Station' appears in gilt lettering twice on the lofty facade. Down below, the delicate glass-and-iron canopy displays an impressive list of one-time destinations in art nouveau lettering on the glass valancing, among which Hull, Belgium and Liverpool appear cheerfully side by side.

At right angles to this block stands a more self-effacing section at the head of the Hunts Bank slope. The lower storey is all that remains of the original building of 1844; when an upper floor was built on top, the original parapet and clock space were left as evidence.

In 1980 an imaginative restoration scheme was completed in conjunction with Greater Manchester Council, as part of the Cathedral Conservation Area project. The old offices opposite the station were pulled down, the entire frontage was cleaned and restored to its original buff colour and the newly opened area land-scaped. It has given an entirely new dimension to this formerly seedy part of central Manchester, and for the first time the impressive station frontage can be seen in its entirety.

SALFORD STATION BRIDGES. South bridge built 1844 for Liverpool & Manchester Railway; engineer Sir John Hawkshaw. Middle bridge built 1865 for Lancashire & Yorkshire Railway; engineer Sturges Meek. North bridge built 1894 for Lancashire & Yorkshire Railway; engineer William Hunt. All listed Grade II.

Three iron bridges which cross New Bailey Street outside Salford Station were built to carry the lines between Liverpool, Manchester, Bolton and Leeds. The decks have been renewed in steel but still rest on the original cast-iron columns.

All three possess decorated plate girderwork of considerable detail. Repainting in bright, contrasting colours has brought out the moulded panelling and floral decorative effects. Similar treatment has been given to other iron bridges in the twin cities, notably to those at the foot of Deansgate, in Liverpool Road (*p.104*) and over Great Ducie Street.

NEW MILLS NEWTOWN

Built c.1890 by London & North Western Railway. Footbridge listed Grade II. Stockport to Buxton line.

This latticed iron footbridge is of a broadly characteristic type used by many railways, although in this case it is a standard pattern of the LNWR built from wrought-iron components on cast-iron columns. The curved wind braces and the decorative stair balusters incorporating a wheel motif are typical features.

NEW MILLS FOOTBRIDGE. 1971

THE LANCASHIRE & YORKSHIRE RAILWAY

Local both in name and in geographical extent, the LYR operated heavy goods traffic and intensive passenger services in a dense network over lines that were frequently very difficult to operate because of their steep gradients and frequent junctions. The company had a monopoly of services from Manchester to north-east Lancashire and the holiday resorts on the Fylde coast; it was also in keen competition for the Liverpool to Manchester traffic and the route from Manchester to the West Riding of Yorkshire.

For much of its early history, however, it was something of a byword for poor trains and unpunctuality. This poor reputation changed dramatically when J. A. F. Aspinall was appointed Chief Mechanical Engineer in 1886. He had the rare distinction of going on from this position to be made General Manager in 1899. As well as being a first-rate engine designer – he opened the fine new locomotive works at Horwich in 1886 – he was a born manager. Under his control the railway began to prosper.

First he set about achieving a real improvement in passenger services on the railway's busiest lines. He pioneered the provision of lavish accommodation for first-class passengers on the residential trains to Blackpool, in the form of special 'club' carriages for patrons who were prepared to pay extra. This innovation was copied by the Midland on the Bradford to Morecambe run´ and by the LNWR between Manchester and Llandudno.

Under Aspinall's direction the LYR became an early user of electro-pneumatic signalling. It inaugurated electric traction for suburban trains as early as 1904 between Liverpool and Southport, and also between Manchester and Bury, which brought a large increase in commuter business.

In the locomotive field the company's record was not entirely successful after Aspinall's promotion. The legacies from his period were the splendid 'Highflyer' 4-4-2s, which did dashing work with lightly-loaded passenger trains, and the 2-4-2 tank engines built for local work and upgraded with superheaters by George Hughes who became Chief Mechanical Engineer in 1904.

Hughes continued Aspinall's use of the 0-8-0 type for heavy freight work, but his large four-cylinder 4-6-0s of 1908 were as near to complete failures as one likes to say. In 1921 they were entirely rebuilt and became reliable if not very economical engines.

LYR 'Highflyer' 4-4-2, c.1914

OLDHAM

CLEGG ST. GOODS WAREHOUSE.
Built by London & North Western Railway.
Listed Grade II. Corner of Park Road and
Woodstock Street.

Oldham was served by three railways, each with one or more large goods stations. The LNWR warehouse is a large four-storey red brick edifice with a curved front. Each of the six loading doors has an individual canopy, and the hipped roof is partly hidden by a prominent cornice and low parapet.

CLEGG ST. GOODS WAREHOUSE, 1970

RADCLIFFE

OUTWOOD VIADUCT. Rebuilt c.1880 for
Lancashire & Yorkshire Railway. Engineer
Sturges Meek. Listed Grade II. Between
Radcliffe and Clifton Junction. Closed.

This viaduct is a very late example of a major cast-iron bridge, built just after the infamous collapse of the Tay Bridge in Scotland. That disaster (*p.157*) made engineers think twice about using cast iron for railway bridges, but of course arches cast by an experienced and reputable company such as Handyside of Derby, who undertook this contract, were very different from the work of Hopkins Gilkes of Middlesbrough, the builders of the Tay Bridge. Outwood Viaduct has been used successfully by heavy traffic for many years.

The bridge consists of five cast-iron arches carried across the River Irwell on tall brick piers with stone caps, the two in the river bed having stone bases and cutwaters. The arches are made of six ribs so spread as to carry rails directly, a strong and economical structure requiring only light wooden decking.

STOCKPORT

VIADUCT. Built 1842 for Manchester &
Birmingham Railway. Engineer G. W. Buck.
Listed Grade II.*

This immense structure in red brick has 27 arches spanning some 600 yards and up to 110 feet high. A completely plain viaduct, huge in scale, it has an overpowering presence in the Stockport town centre. Despite widening on the west side in 1888-89, and the addition of electrification gantries in 1966, it remains 'one of the most imposing works of the kind whether viewed as to its general design or exquisite workmanship.' (Francis Whishaw, *Railways of Britain*, 1842.)

HEATON NORRIS GOODS
WAREHOUSE. Built 1877 by London &
North Western Railway. Listed Grade II.
Wellington Road North.

This large four-storey warehouse typifies the railway's response to the needs of the cotton industry. In outline it resembles the later one at Huddersfield (*p.35*), with which it should be compared. Broad, vertical slots in the walls, with an opening on each floor, had a hoist at the top. As usual the railway company's name was displayed in large white brick letters below the roofline. Inside, the wooden floors are carried on cast-iron columns, for this warehouse was built without 'fire-proofing' (see Manchester, Deansgate,

STOCKPORT VIADUCT, ENGRAVING BY F. TAIT, 1848

p.99). The complex also includes the accumulator tower which provided hydraulic power for the capstans and cranes.

MERSEYSIDE

BIRKENHEAD

HAMILTON SQUARE STATION. Built 1886 for Mersey Railway. Architect G. E. Grayson.

The primary aim of the Mersey Railway was to link Liverpool and Birkenhead by a tunnel beneath the river. Since it was steam operated, it is hardly surprising that most commuters preferred the fresh air of the ferries, which continued to prosper at the expense of the railway until it was electrified in 1903. The lofty brick tower at Hamilton Square, which completely dwarfs the entrance building, was built to house the water tanks that powered the hydraulic lifts to the underground station. In the style of an Italian crenellated campanile, it had a counterpart at James Street station, Liverpool (now demolished).

1976

EARLESTOWN

Built c.1840 by Liverpool and Manchester Railway. Listed Grade II. Between St. Helens Junction and Newton-le-Willows.

This curious little building in the angle of the junction platforms, built of golden stone, is basically Tudor in style but carries an amazing variety of decoration.

TRANS-PENNINE TUNNELS

WOODHEAD. Build 1845 for Sheffield Ashton-under-Lyne & Manchester Railway. Engineers Charles Vignoles and Joseph Locke. Between Hadfield and Penistone. Closed.
STANDEDGE. Built 1849 for Huddersfield & Manchester Railway. Engineer Alfred S. Jee. Between Stalybridge and Huddersfield.
TOTLEY. Built 1894 for Midland Railway. Chief engineer J. A. McDonald. Sheffield to Manchester line.
DINTING VALE. Built 1844 for Sheffield Ashton-under-Lyne & Manchester Railway. Engineer Joseph Locke. Between Broadbottom and Hadfield.

After the Severn Tunnel, Woodhead, Standedge and Totley are the next three longest in Britain. The diabolical conditions in which the *WOODHEAD* navvies lived and worked is graphically told by Terry Coleman in *The Railway Navvies* (1965). The tunnel is 3 miles 22 yards long, took six years to construct, and provides a good illustration of how quickly the public accepted rail travel. There was no longer that need to reassure timid passengers felt by Robert Stephenson at the building of the Kilsby Tunnel only seven years earlier (*p.69*). Woodhead was a narrow single line bore, the crown of the arches being semi-elliptical, with castellated portals. A second single line tunnel was opened in 1852; both of them were notoriously foul. On the opening of a third double line tunnel in connection with electrification in 1954, the old tunnels were closed; later they were to carry electric power cables. More recently the new tunnel has also been closed.

STANDEDGE is slightly longer, 3 miles 66 yards, and was equally difficult to construct. Jee had worked under Locke at Woodhead, and here too there was at first only a single-line tunnel, followed by a

second in 1871 and a third (double line) bore in 1894. The two older ones are no longer used. A fourth tunnel, older than all the others, runs parallel and below, carrying the Huddersfield Canal. It was used by the railway engineers for carrying materials and is connected to the rail tunnels by adits.

TOTLEY, much younger and the longest at 3 miles 950 yards, is a double line tunnel constructed to give the Midland a competitive route between Manchester and Sheffield.

Totley tunnel, western portal, 1965

On the climb up to Woodhead Tunnel there are two lofty viaducts of special merit, Etherow and *DINTING VALE*. Both were built with laminated wooden arches, replaced some 20 years later by wrought-iron girders. Dinting is the larger, 484 yards long and 125 feet high. It forms a notable landmark as it curves between the steep sides of the Vale, and has seven brick approach arches on one side and four on the other. The five iron spans had to be strengthened in 1918-19 by the insertion of seven extra piers.

There are three sets of different octagonal chimneys, three large saw-tooth crenellations over blank shields on a frieze, deep mullioned windows and a slated lean-to awning on wooden posts and curved brackets. In 1903 a very steep-pitched roof was replaced by the present one, and the chimneys were carefully altered to retain the overall design. The interior comprises a large room with heavily carved exposed beams and a superior stone fireplace.

EARLESTOWN, 1970

LIVERPOOL & MANCHESTER   RAILWAY

Opened 1830. Engineer George Stephenson.
MANCHESTER LIVERPOOL ROAD
STATION listed Grade I; agent's house and 1830
warehouse, listed Grade II. All closed and sold.

Manchester's Liverpool Road station is the most important large-scale early railway site in the world to retain so many of its original features. It shared with the Liverpool terminus in Crown Street the distinction of being the world's first purpose-built station and since Crown Street has long since gone, it can truly be called the world's oldest. Restoration work was started in

Manchester Liverpool Road, 1956

1981 by Greater Manchester Council in conjunction with British Rail, the Historic Buildings Council and the Department of the Environment, with the aim of forming a new home for the North West Museum of Science and Industry.

The Liverpool & Manchester Railway terminated in Manchester on a viaduct alongside Liverpool Road, which gradually rose to rail level at the Lower Byrom Street end of the station. The viaduct was flanked on one side by the passenger station and on the other by the goods warehouse. Starting from the Water Street end, the first building is the two-storey brick station agent's house on the corner, dating from before 1822 and taken over by the railway. Next to it stands the passenger building of 1830-31, retaining its original rusticated facade. The first and second class booking offices had separate entrances: over the first-class one a small stone plinth once carried a brass sundial. Separate staircases led up to the waiting rooms on the first floor at rail level, of which only the first-class staircase survives. There was no platform on the viaduct, and not even a shelter for passengers until 1834, when a shed was erected.

Continuing up Liverpool Road, the facade, now in red brick, resembles a row of

two-storey terraced houses. These were offices, with the ground floor once let off as shops, and they front the site of the carriage shed. At the far end, continuing round the corner into Lower Byrom Street, is the shipping or transit shed, a London & North Western Railway building dating from c.1860 when it replaced an earlier one of 1831.

On the other side of the viaduct, facing the passenger station across the tracks, stands the magnificent 1830 warehouse, built to hold 10,000 bales of cotton. Constructed in brick with stone quoins and dressings, it has a slightly curved rail frontage and is 320 feet long and 70 feet wide. The four levels – cellar, road or yard level, rail level and upper floor – are all timber on wooden posts, except for the cellar which has iron columns. There are ten bays, marked on the frontage by pilaster strips and ridge-and-furrow roof gables. Rails entered at right angles to the viaduct by means of turnplates, and barrel-winch cranes loaded and unloaded carts below. In 1831 the three bays at the western end had an intermediate floor inserted between rail and yard levels, and a steam engine was installed to work the cranes and hoists.

NEWTON-LE-WILLOWS, HUSKISSON
MEMORIAL. Listed Grade II.

Alongside the line, where it passes beneath the A573 road, stands a marble memorial to William Huskisson, M.P. for Liverpool and President of the Board of Trade. Alighting from one of the trains on the ceremonial opening day, at which he accompanied the Duke of Wellington, he was run down and killed by another train hauled by the *Rocket*. His train had stopped at Parkside station, which stood at this spot.

Huskisson Memorial, 1976

RAINHILL SKEW BRIDGE. Engineer
probably Jesse Hartley.

The bridge west of Rainhill station is the most acute of the fifteen skew bridges on the LMR, at 34 degrees to the line. In heavily rusticated sandstone, it was described as being 'of a very curious and beautiful construction'.

Rainhill bridge, 1831

LIVERPOOL.

Compared with Manchester, few buildings remain. East of Edge Hill station, trains still run through the chasm of Stephenson's Olive Mount Cutting, while to the west are fragments of the Moorish Arch. The tunnels, now disused, to the original Crown Street station and to Wapping goods station survive. Of Crown Street itself nothing is left and the area around the tunnel mouth has been landscaped. The tunnels were operated by cable haulage from engine houses at Edge Hill, as was the 1836 tunnel down to the second Liverpool station at Lime Street (*p.105*) which was later opened out. A fourth tunnel on the north side of the main line, constructed in 1849 down to Waterloo Dock, was also operated by rope.

SANKEY VIADUCT. Listed Grade II. West of
Earlestown Station.

Sankey viaduct, the earliest large railway viaduct, excited great admiration when it was built and features in several contemporary engravings. Nine semi-circular arches of 50-foot span, in brick faced with stone and 60 feet high at the loftiest point, cross the valley of the Sankey Brook and the course of the St. Helens Canal, now filled in at this point. The piers have a pronounced batter, giving an appearance of great strength.

Earlestown station, Edge Hill station: see
separate entries.

EDGE HILL

Built 1836 by Liverpool & Manchester
Railway. Listed Grade II. Between Liverpool
Lime Street and Broad Green.

Edge Hill station is one of the most historic spots at the Liverpool end of the Liverpool & Manchester Railway, close to the site of the famous Moorish Arch and the tunnels to Crown Street and Wapping. Two equal-sized near identical blocks of two-storey buildings face one another from the platforms, with prominent rustication, dentils and parapets, all

in pink sandstone probably taken from the deep Olive Mount Cutting lying just west of the tunnel. The tunnel portals, retaining walls and station approach walls are also in the same stone, but behind the building on the up platform is a larger red brick building – a former engine house built in 1848 for winding goods trains up through the Waterloo tunnel, and a reminder of the days when trains were also hauled to Crown Street, and from Wapping and Lime Street by cable to Edge Hill. The building was restored for the commemoration of the

Rainhill Trials in 1980.

1979

HUNTS CROSS

Built 1879 by Cheshire Lines Committee. Listed Grade II. Between Liverpool and Widnes.

Typical of the Cheshire Lines in its details, this station, beside the road bridge, is a surprising four storeys high. A row of

1976

peaked dormers is interspersed with a frilly valance beneath the eaves gutter. Entry to the platforms is by stairs from a first floor balcony that has a highly decorative iron balustrade, bracketed out from the walls.

LIVERPOOL

LIME STREET STATION. Rebuilt from 1867 for London & North Western Railway.

Trainsheds 1867-1874, engineers William Baker and Francis Stevenson; hotel 1871, architect Alfred Waterhouse: all listed Grade II.

Now cleaned, the former North Western Hotel fronting Lime Street Station once more makes a fitting companion to the group of handsome civic buildings facing St. George's Hall. It has a strong vertical emphasis in a facade which otherwise is a fairly quiet composition up to the fifth floor. There, above the cornice, it suddenly erupts into a profusion of dormers, chimney stacks and pyramidal turrets, the two in the centre having corner spirelets in addition and the whole creating one of Liverpool's best known skylines. Above the central entrance at third-floor level, tapered columns are surmounted by the figures of a king and queen.

Originally the interior, with over 200 bedrooms, was decorated in French Renaissance style to match the frontage; inside the arched entrance, a handsome staircase with an elaborate iron balustrade rises through the full height of the building. The plumbing, lavish for its time, included 37 water closets and eight baths. The station is the third on this site, its predecessor fronting Lord Nelson Street (part of which still remains), being an Italianate structure of 1849 designed by Sir William Tite. The handsome

Georgian stone entrance screen that adjoined, however, was demolished to make way for the hotel. It faced Lime Street and had been retained from the first station of 1836, designed by John Foster Jnr.

The northernmost span of the crescent-trussed glass-and-iron trainshed, carried on cast-iron Doric columns, is 219 feet wide and was erected in 1867, its 186-foot wide neighbour being added in 1874. The gentle vertical and horizontal curves of the roof and complementary gable screens at the outer end (now partly masked by overhead wires) combine to give it a striking visual quality against the dark rock cutting beyond.

EXCHANGE STATION. Former frontage and hotel block built 1884-86 for Lancashire & Yorkshire Railway. Architect Henry Shelmerdine. Listed Grade II. Closed and sold.

When Exchange station was closed in 1977, its main line services were diverted to Lime Street and its suburban ones to the new Merseyrail system. The station proper has been demolished but the former hotel remains. A station was first opened on the site in 1850; it was jointly owned by the Lancashire & Yorkshire and East Lancashire Railways who, as with most things, were unable to agree on the sharing arrangements. So they pro-

LIME STREET, c.1900

vided two of everything – booking offices, waiting rooms, refreshment rooms, iron roofs, even names: the LYR called the station Exchange, but to the ELR it was Tithebarn Street. The problem ended when the companies amalgamated in

1953

1859. The hotel frontage is in free Renaissance style with columns dividing the windows, an intricately decorated iron *porte cochère* and a matching projecting clock. John Pearson, one-time chairman of the LYR, mayor of Liverpool and High Sheriff of Lancashire, is commemorated by a bust in bas-relief.

ADELPHI HOTEL. Built 1912 for Midland Railway. Architect F. Atkinson. Listed Grade II.

ST. MICHAEL'S, 1980

The Midland reached Liverpool through its part-ownership of the Cheshire Lines' Central station across the street. Pevsner calls its white exterior 'big, stone-faced and stodgy' but it contains interesting features inside and out that marked a prelude to the art deco styles of the next decade, and remains something of a Liverpool institution, particularly on Grand National night.

AIGBURTH and ST. MICHAEL'S STATIONS. Built 1864 by Garston & Liverpool Railway. Became part of Cheshire Lines Committee in 1865. Listed Grade II.

Both of these suburban stations bore similar CLC characteristics, notably the platform awnings – a lean-to on one side and a much larger glazed awning on the other with sawtooth valancing – and the intricately scrolled bargeboards on the

AIGBURTH, 1980

AIGBURTH, 1980

entrance buildings. The entrances are at the top of the cuttings and each has a two-storey house adjoining, one on an overbridge and the other alongside the railway.

CRESSINGTON. Built 1873 by Cheshire Lines Committee. Listed Grade II. Between Liverpool Central and Garston.

This restored station, now served by the electric trains of Merseyrail, was built to serve the once-private Cressington Park Estate and is still reached through a pair of ornamental stone gate pillars on Aigburth Road. The entrance building at the top of a cutting has a half-hipped gabled roof with decorative eaves valancing, while the platform buildings are similar with short glass awnings. The style is debased Gothic with various trimmings typical of the CLC. Wooden station nameboards and iron platform lamps complete the period atmosphere.

ADELPHI HOTEL, 1975

ST. HELENS

Marshalls Cross Road and New Street bridges over the St. Helens & Runcorn Gap Railway built c.1832. Engineer C. B. Vignoles. Both listed Grade II.

The line was built to carry coal from pits at St. Helens to the Mersey at Runcorn Gap (now Widnes) to break the monopoly of the St. Helens Canal. It crossed the Liverpool and Manchester line by a bridge near what is now St. Helens Junction, where there was a connection with the LMR. That bridge is the subject of a well-known print, and the casual conveyance of passengers on the line was graphically described by Sir George Head in 1835. He travelled in a horse-drawn coach and as a result of the experience wrote, 'It behoves not those people to whom time is of value to travel by the branch railroad from St. Helens to Runcorn.'

The two bridges over the line are in rusticated sandstone, with segmental arches flanked by pilaster-strips. The section from St. Helens to St. Helens Junction is still used for freight, but the remainder to Widnes has been closed.

LANCASHIRE

BLACKBURN

Built 1888 by Lancashire & Yorkshire Railway on the site of an earlier station.

The Italianate style of the new Blackburn station was almost old-fashioned by the

BLACKBURN, c.1900

time it was complete. It has two storeys, in red brick with substantial stone dressings, and a central clock that sits among a variety of carved stone foliage and the letters LYR. The booking hall has been modernised without detracting from the period frontage. The main point of interest is the retention of the lofty two-bay overall roof, which covers the large one- and two-storeyed yellow brick platform buildings. Some of the windows in them still have etched glass designations such as 'First Class Ladies Room'.

BURNLEY

ASHFIELD ROAD VIADUCT. Built 1848 for East Lancashire Railway. Listed Grade II. Between Burnley Barracks and Central Station.

The valley in the centre of Burnley is dominated by this masonry viaduct striding across the rooftops, providing train passengers with a fine view over the town. The earlier Leeds and Liverpool Canal crosses the same valley by a lofty embankment, affording an interesting contrast in engineering techniques.

ASHFIELD ROAD VIADUCT, 1970

CARNFORTH

*Built 1846 for Lancaster & Carlisle Railway.
Architect Sir William Tite. Later extensions
formed London & North Western and Furness
Railways Joint station. Between Lancaster and
Kendal.*

Carnforth is a railway crossroads. The
original low buildings, stone-built in
Tudor style, occupy the main northbound
platform; extensions were added in 1857
when the platform for what later became
the Furness Railway was built, curving
sharply away to the west. The main
southbound platform building that forms
the present entrance was added later.
North of the station, crossing the electrified West Coast main line and connecting
with the Furness line by a triangular
junction, is the Furness & Midland Joint
Line. This completes Carnforth's rather
complicated layout by which LNWR
trains from Lancaster and Carlisle, Midland trains from Leeds and Furness trains
from Barrow provided connecting services. The joint ownership was apparent
in the platform awnings, those on the
main line being clearly of LNWR design,
while the Barrow platform had a quite
different type with FR cast into the
brackets. The single platform and bay for
the Barrow and Leeds trains had to suffice
until 1938, when the LMS added a second
platform on the Furness curve. In recent
years the main line platforms have been
taken out of use. Passengers to and from
Barrow now change at Lancaster, so
Carnforth is no longer the important
junction it was, although Leeds and Barrow trains still use it. It has recently come
into prominence in another way: Steamtown, a centre for preserved locomotives,
is sited at the nearby engine shed, with its
mechanical coaling plant, the only remaining operational one in the country.
Steamtown is the operating base for many
steam-hauled excursions.

1945

GAUXHOLME VIADUCT

*Built 1841 for Manchester & Leeds Railway.
Engineer George Stephenson. Between
Littleborough and Todmorden.*

The Manchester & Leeds Railway stands

as one of the great feats of early railway
engineering, particularly Summit Tunnel
(*p.99*) and the 15 miles from there to
Sowerby Bridge as it threads its way
down the narrow, winding gorge of the
Calder, competing for space not only with
the river but also with the road and the
canal which it constantly criss-crosses. At
Gauxholme, just above Todmorden, the
canal is crossed twice within a few hundred yards, by a stone viaduct of 18 arches
and by a very fine 101-foot wide iron skew
bridge of bowstring construction with two
stone approach arches and crenellated
turrets. The ironwork is from Butlers'
Stanningley Foundry near Leeds and
dated 1840; it was strengthened in 1905
by inserting plate girders underneath.
Stephenson's assistant, Thomas L.
Gooch, was responsible for most of the
construction work on the line.

LANCASTER

*OLD STATION. Built 1840 by Lancaster &
Preston Junction Railway. Listed Grade II.
Penny Street, Lancaster. Closed and sold.*

The building looking down Penny Street
which is now part of the hospital nurses'
home was the frontage to the original railway terminus. Its grey dressed stone,
heavy cornice, pedimented porch and
generally Georgian aspect put it completely at ease with the local town houses
– an example of the good architectural
manners of many of the earlier railways.

*CASTLE STATION. Built 1846 for
Lancaster & Carlisle Railway. Architect Sir
William Tite. Extended 1858 and 1900-06.*

When the West Coast main line was ex-

CARLISLE BRIDGE, 1976

tended north of Lancaster, the old Penny
Street station was bypassed and this new
one opened close to the castle. Tite's
symmetrical arcaded portion is at the
north end on the west side. With the
stonework cleaned, the 1858 extension
can be clearly defined, terminating in a
low keep-like tower and turret as befits its
location and forming a good example of
early railway companies' concern to fit
harmoniously into their surroundings.
The 20th-century extensions on the east
side, also in harmony with the older
buildings, are now used as the main
entrance.

*CARLISLE BRIDGE. Built 1840 for
Lancaster & Carlisle Railway. Engineer
Joseph Locke. Listed Grade II.*

The bridge carries the railway across the
River Lune immediately north of Lancaster station. Only the stone piers remain from the original bridge, which had
three laminated timber arches; the
springing can still be seen just above the
cutwaters. In 1868 the timber was replaced by wrought-iron plate girders; in
1962-63 they were replaced by reinforced
concrete spans in preparation for electrification of the West Coast main line.

LANCASTER CASTLE, 1975

TOWN AND COUNTRY STYLES

Rebuilt 'West Country' Class 34025 Whimple *steams out of Cannon Street with a train for Ramsgate in 1958. Dismantling of the bomb-damaged trainshed had just begun.*

Brunel's wrought-iron and glass trainshed at Paddington was strongly influenced by the Crystal Palace, which was built three years earlier for the Great Exhibition of 1851.

The station and promenade at Grange-over-Sands, looking out over Morecambe Bay, were built as part of the Furness Railway's development of the resort in the 1870s.

Local slate was used by the Cockermouth Keswick & Penrith Railway for the station at Keswick in the Lake District. The line is now closed and the building has been sold.

MORECAMBE

Built 1907 for Midland Railway. Architect Thomas Wheatley. Listed Grade II.

Morecambe as a resort was created by the 'Little' North Western Railway (so called to distinguish it from the London & North Western), and for some years steamers ran across Morecambe Bay to Piel Pier, near Barrow, and to Belfast in conjunction with the trains. The Midland absorbed the smaller company and re-built the station in Northumberland Street, later replacing it by the present station. The London & North Western also had a station, in Euston Road on their branch line to Morecambe, so the Midland station was called Promenade to distinguish it.

It is built in warm honey-coloured stone in a mild form of gothic. There are attractive quatrefoil embellishments in the gables, a dormer clock and a large iron *porte cochère* with nicely scalloped valancing. A spacious glass-roofed concourse leads out to the platforms which had standard Midland ridge-and-furrow hipped awnings.

The line to Morecambe and Heysham from Lancaster was electrified in 1908 by pioneer use of overhead wires at 25 cycles, 6,600 V A/C; services were withdrawn in 1966 in favour of the former LNWR route, but Promenade station is still used via a connecting link.

MORECAMBE PROMENADE, 1907

MORECAMBE PROMENADE, 1965

UNLOADING HORSES AT ORMSKIRK DURING THE FIRST WORLD WAR

ORMSKIRK

Built 1848 by Liverpool, Ormskirk & Preston Railway. Station and drinking fountain on corner of bridge in Derby Street listed Grade II. Between Liverpool and Preston.

Ormskirk is now the terminus of the electrified Merseyrail line from Liverpool. The stone building on the northbound platform probably dates from the opening of the station, but the larger red brick building on the opposite side and the deep, generous platform awnings are additions built by the Lancashire & Yorkshire. The station saw busier times when it was on the direct line from Preston and East Lancashire to Liverpool. After those services were withdrawn in 1969, the line to Preston was singled and it now has only a shuttle diesel service. The actual track has been severed, with a pair of buffer stops back-to-back, and only a siding connection between them.

PRESTON

RIBBLE BRIDGE. Built 1850 for East Lancashire Railway. Engineer Sturges Meek. Northernmost arch listed Grade II. Closed.

This line, forming a cut-off between Preston and Bamber Bridge on the Blackburn line, necessitated a 53-arch stone

PRESTON LYR ENTRANCE, 1980

112

viaduct across meadows south of the Ribble, two cast-iron spans over the river and a final stone arch on the north bank. The viaduct was converted to an embankment in 1884-86 and the river spans were replaced by steel girders in 1930, so that only the northernmost arch now remains from the original structure. It can be seen from the parallel Ribble Bridge used by trains on the West Coast main line.

STATION. Built 1880 jointly for London & North Western and Lancashire & Yorkshire Railways. Engineer William Baker.

For some years there were three stations in the centre of Preston, none of whose owners could come to agreement. By 1844 most trains were concentrated on one station and it soon proved hopelessly inadequate; nonetheless, despite frequent representations, the owning companies delayed reconstruction until 1880.

The present station comprises four bays of Euston-style roofing with a central entrance building at the north end approached by a ramp from Fishergate Bridge. This was the jointly-owned portion of the station and it survives largely intact, apart from the removal of the westernmost roof bay (the platforms beneath are still used for parcels traffic). It is the only station to retain so much of this type of roof, which at one time was common at many large LNWR stations. The Lancashire & Yorkshire had its own entrance at one side in Butler Street.

In 1903 the LYR built a new entrance in Butler Street, together with its own bay platforms around the curve of the East Lancashire line that led from the west side of the main station, with separate umbrella awnings. These were quite distinct in appearance denoting the LYR's sole ownership compared with the joint portion of the station. These East Lancashire platforms have now been demolished but the characteristic entrance building in Butler Street remains.

One of the oddities of Preston was the means of taking a southbound train from, say, Blackpool to the north without its having to reverse in the station, a most useful facility when dealing with heavy bank holiday and excursion traffic. It was done by traversing a series of curves and junctions to the south enabling a train to

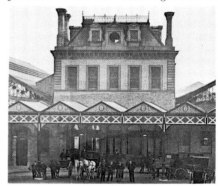

PRESTON LNWR ENTRANCE, c.1880

pass through in the southerly direction and, after a 5½ mile journey, return through the station in the opposite direction some 10 minutes later.

PARK HOTEL. Built 1882 jointly for London & North Western and Lancashire & Yorkshire Railways. Architect Arnold Mitchell.

Situated on the top of a bluff, the former Park Hotel has one of the best locations of any railway-built hotel in England, overlooking Avenham Park and the Ribble

1896

with an extensive view southward. In red brick, it has overtones of Norman Shaw with its prominent gables and tall banded chimneys, while a tall, offset tower with strong vertical lines gives a sense of impregnability. A little Scottish baronial turret sits snugly on the south-west corner.

WHALLEY VIADUCT

Built 1850 for Bolton, Blackburn, Clitheroe & West Yorkshire Railway. Engineer Terence Flanagan. Between Blackburn and Clitheroe.

This brick viaduct, with 28 arches of a completely plain profile, crosses the valley of the River Calder next to the village of Whalley like a long straight wall protecting the site from the open valley on the west. It has a most curious central feature in which the spans flanking the road have been filled to form a blind Gothic arch,

CLASS '5' 4-6-0 HEADING NORTH OUT OF SKIPTON, 1964

presumably to tone in with the adjacent gateway to the medieval Whalley Abbey. This concern to try to blend the new structure with it surroundings may well have stemmed from a certain consciousness that bright red brick was hardly the most appropriate material in what was otherwise predominantly stone country. Its use was determined by the fortuitous discovery of a bed of suitable clay in a nearby field: a temporary brickworks was promptly set up on the spot to take advantage of it.

NORTH YORKSHIRE

HELLIFIELD

Built 1880 by Midland Railway. Listed Grade II. Between Skipton and Settle.

Hellifield became a junction in 1880 when the Lancashire & Yorkshire line from Blackburn was extended to meet the Midland. Over it the Midland ran Pullman car expresses from Manchester and Liverpool via the Settle & Carlisle line to Scotland, in competition with the LNWR. Hellifield, which hitherto had been a small village, became a railway colony, both companies providing engine sheds and railwaymen's houses.

The station comprises a broad island platform with bays, and a block of stone buildings in the centre surrounded by an uncharacteristically profiled sloping awning. Midland features reassert themselves beneath the glazing, with MR and the wyvern emblem cast in the iron brackets.

Withdrawal of the Blackburn passenger trains and severe reductions on the Settle & Carlisle line have changed Hellifield. The engine sheds and many of the sidings have gone, and the station itself is now an unstaffed halt. After a brief interruption, the rural calm of the Yorkshire Dales has returned.

SKIPTON

Built 1876 by Midland Railway. Between Keighley and Settle.

Skipton is an excellent example of the typical well-built Midland station. It has good stone buildings and a very well preserved set of glass-and-iron awnings on both platforms. These are in ridge-and-furrow style with hipped ends complete with iron finials, elaborate brackets and decorated columns. The frontage has a projecting entrance with flanking arched porches and a wyvern, the emblem of the Midland Railway, on a stone panel.

LMS 'JUBILEE' CLASS *HARDY* AT HELLIFIELD, 1964

113

SETTLE & CARLISLE LINE

Opened 1875 by the Midland Railway. Engineer J. S. Crossley. Smardale, Arten Gill, Dent Head and Ribblehead (Batty Moss) viaducts all Ancient Monuments. Appersett viaduct (Hawes branch) listed Grade II.

'There is a railway line in England which fights its way over the gaunt Pennine uplands to make a vital communication between South and North. A line which tested to the utmost the peerless constructional skill of British railway engineers. A line which braves the rugged contours of wild fell and striding dale, and which defies the freakish, unpredictable weather of its chosen path.' (F. W. Houghton & W. Hubert Foster, *The Story of the Settle & Carlisle Line*).

Crossley worked for the Midland continuously from 1852 to 1875, after which he was retained as consulting engineer until he died four years later. Of all his many works the Settle & Carlisle is his greatest achievement, crossing 72 miles of some of the most difficult and isolated country in England. Including the Hawes branch there are 23 viaducts and 15 tunnels, and Ais Gill summit is 1,169 feet above sea level.

The Settle & Carlisle was built to give the Midland its own route to Scotland, in competition with the LNWR and, to a lesser extent, with the east coast companies. It cost nearly £3.5 million to build and, with maintenance charges, it is doubt-ful if it ever paid for itself financially in direct returns. It was the last major line to be built by traditional pick and shovel methods (by the time the Great Central was built in the 1890s steam shovels were available) causing thousands of labourers to descend on remote Pennine settlements where they were housed in shanty towns erected by the company. Many died.

The longest and highest viaduct is Ribblehead, 440 yards long with 24 arches, the highest 165 feet. A short distance from the north end is the longest and deepest tunnel, Blea Moor, 1 mile 869 yards long and 500 feet below the surface. Smardale viaduct, 130 feet high, is the site of the final act of construction where Crossley's wife Agnes laid the last stone in June 1875.

Settle & Carlisle stations were an exercise in standardisation, but with subtle differences. Their design stemmed from a style Crossley had evolved extensively on the Midland, basically comprising a single-storey building with two gabled pavilions linked by a central section that housed a recessed waiting area enclosed by a wooden or iron-latticed screen. All the S & C stations except Garsdale, Crosby Garrett and Culgaith were in this form, but varied to suit local requirements. Settle and Appleby had three pavilions, as befitted their importance. As the line progressed materials changed, reflecting the locality.

Appleby, 1976

Dent Head viaduct, 1980

Arten Gill viaduct, 1964

ASPATRIA

Built 1841 by Maryport & Carlisle Railway. Between Carlisle and Maryport.

Most of the Maryport & Carlisle's first stations were small single-storey stone buildings. Aspatria, however, received more careful detailing, giving it a Tudor touch: it represented extremely good work for such a small local railway. The main buildings comprised a symmetrical

1975

row of three, the centre one T-shaped in plan with dormer windows and hexagonal chimneys, flanked by a smaller rectangular building on each side, all with stone mullions. A small matching building occupied the opposite platform.

BARROW-IN-FURNESS

FORMER STATION. Built 1863 for Furness Railway. Design attributed to Job Bintley. Listed Grade II. St. George's Square. Closed.

The Furness Railway was Sir James Ramsden, and Ramsden was Barrow-in-Furness. The railway arrived at a small wooden terminus in 1845, and a year later Ramsden was appointed locomotive superintendent, from which positon he rapidly rose to be managing director. Under his direction, the company developed Barrow as a railway town: it built the town hall, market hall, Royal Hotel, shops, offices, school and reading room. It owned the sea front and harbour, built the docks and supplied the new town with gas and water. By 1875, investments held by the industrial syndicate that was dominated by the railway amounted to £6.5 million and the town was nicknamed 'the British Chicago'. Behind all this was Ramsden, who was also director of the town's main industries, including the steel works, shipyard and corn mill.

Surprisingly during these boom years, no move was made to build a proper terminus. It was not until 1863 that the red brick station was opened in St. George's Square, in a subdued Italianate style like the other railway-owned buildings in the area, with a two-arched entrance. Behind it stands the old ridge-and-furrow roofed trainshed. Across the square in 1864 the company built a headquarters in red sandstone: it had two storeys with a prominent campanile clock tower from which the top has now gone. An imposing

FORMER BARROW STATION, 1983

drive led through a shrubbery from handsome iron gates.

The station closed in 1882 when a new through station, Barrow Central, was opened. An amazing mixture of Swiss chalet, red brick gothic and half-timbering with a huge lofty roof, this was damaged during air raids in the war and has now been replaced by the present station.

CARK & CARTMEL

Built 1857 by Ulverstone (sic) & Lancaster Railway. Between Carnforth and Ulverston.

The Ulverstone & Lancaster stations have neat little grey limestone buildings, two storeys with lean-to platform shelters on wooden posts, and well in keeping with the local vernacular.

Cark was fairly important, being the station for Holker Hall, one of the seats of the Duke of Devonshire (now open to the public in the summer). The station also housed the little company's workshops, and developed a lively trade in cockles from the nearby sands which were put on a nightly fish train to the northern industrial districts.

When the Furness Railway took over they put up a long stone and timber building on the up platform opposite the original, in their favourite Swiss chalet style, complete with a short ridge-and-furrow glass awning which has now been removed. There are Minton tiled floors in the waiting rooms, and superior fittings were provided suitable for the Duke of Devonshire's guests.

JOHN SIDNEY CROSSLEY, ENGINEER

An orphan by the age of two, Crossley was brought up by his guardian who was a Leicester architect. He was articled to the engineer of the Leicester Navigation Company, whom he succeeded in 1832, and assisted in the surveys for the Leicester & Swannington Railway, the first railway in Leicestershire. From there he went on to work for C. B. Vignoles and later Charles Liddell who was Chief Engineer of the Midland Railway.

With the exception of a brief interlude with the Leicester Waterworks Company in 1851-52, he worked on Midland Railway projects for the rest of his life, acting as engineer for the Leicester-Hitchin, Erewash Valley, Bath and Shipley-Guiseley lines. In 1852 he suffered a paralytic stroke but recovered and succeeded Liddell as Chief Engineer in 1858. His monument is the great Settle & Carlisle line (*p.114*), opened in 1876. Although he resigned before it was fully completed, he was retained as consultant.

Crossley resumed his early relationship with waterways as joint consulting engineer for the Leeds & Liverpool Canal. His interests were not restricted to pure engineering, as he was a Fellow of the Geological Society and Member of the Society of Arts. He died in his native Leicestershire in 1879 at the age of 66.

CARK & CARTMEL, c.1979

CARLISLE

CITADEL STATION. Built 1847 jointly for Lancaster & Carlisle and Caledonian Railways. Architect Sir William Tite. Listed Grade II.

Before 1923 Carlisle surpassed even York in the colourful variety of the trains that entered the station. Seven companies used it: the London & North Western and the Caledonian, who were joint owners; the Midland, North Eastern, North British, Glasgow & South Western and Maryport & Carlisle. Above all, as be-fitted a station in the border area, Carlisle

1977

'JUBILEE' CLASS 4-6-0 *SEAHORSE*, CARLISLE, 1963

Citadel was where English and Scottish companies met, exchanged traffic or changed engines. With so many railways interested, the early history of the station is a long series of inter-company quarrels, agreements, renunciations and even, at one stage, a court order restraining the Maryport & Carlisle from obstructing the Lancaster & Carlisle's approach lines and empowering the L&C to take possession of M&C land. This they quickly did, and not only removed the rails but demolished the M&C's Crown Street station in the process. Order was not achieved until 1861, when the Citadel Station Joint committee was formed by Act of Parliament.

The station takes its name from the nearby law courts, completed in 1810-11 by Sir Robert Smirke in the form of two large towers based on Henry VIII's citadel. Tite, architect to both the Lancaster & Carlisle and the Caledonian, was asked to design the station on the opposite side of the square. He produced a strong Tudor composition and quite the best large English station in this style. The frontage is asymmetrical in grey ashlar,

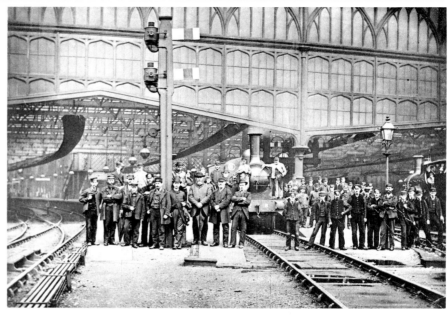

CARLISLE CITADEL, 1890

with a heavily buttressed entrance arcade bearing above it the Royal arms, those of the L&C and Caledonian Railways and two blank shields. Tradition has it that these were provided for the arms of the Newcastle & Carlisle and Maryport & Carlisle companies in the hope that they would join the partnership, but they never did. The main two-storey portion is in nine bays between buttresses, with a row of small dormers on one side of a lantern-style clock tower and crenellated shafts on the other. Behind the Italianate County Hotel – built by A. Salvin in 1856-57 – are two gabled projections. The window of one gives on to the former re-freshment room which is in splendid Tudor, with a pair of stone fireplaces complete with carved Latin inscriptions.

The interior of the station has been altered several times. The last major ex-tension was in 1878-80 and done so well that the buildings on the island platform look original. They include a two-storey decorated bay window overlooking the platforms, which until a few years ago was a signal box controlling the crossovers in the middle of the station. The roof was rebuilt at the same time with transverse ridge-and-furrow bays that admit plenty of light but are out of keeping with the station's general character. Deep end-screens with heavy gothic glazing bars were added in an attempt to make amends, but have now been removed.

VICTORIA VIADUCT. Built 1877.

North of the station a blue-brick road viaduct was built to span the railway lines which before had tended to cut the city off from its western suburbs. It is an un-common example of collaboration be-tween railway and municipality, par-ticularly unusual in a town which, apart from employment, did not derive much direct benefit from the railways.

GRANGE-OVER-SANDS

Rebuilt c.1877 for Furness Railway. Architect E. G. Paley. Listed Grade II. Between Carnforth and Ulverston.

In 1866 the Grange Hotel was opened as one of Sir James Ramsden's promotions (see Barrow, *p.115*). The result was that the village, magnificently located on Morecambe Bay, became a select railway resort and, in the words of J. D. Marshall (*Old Lakeland*), 'full of quiet self-assurance

c.1910

. . . not quite, perhaps, as a silk hat on a Bradford millionaire, but rather as a good serge suit on its comfortable Bradford owner'. The railway company laid out gardens near the old station and in 1877 built a new one in the local grey limestone to match the restrained Italianate of the hotel, with pleasant hipped roofs, a modest wooden porch and a pair of slender glass-and-iron platform awnings. All have been excellently restored and conserve the atmosphere of quiet Vic-torian dignity.

HAVERTHWAITE

Built 1869 by Furness Railway on its Ulverston to Lakeside branch; now operated by Lakeside and Haverthwaite Railway.

Like most railways the Furness developed standard station designs, one of which is

HAVERTHWAITE, c.1958

represented by Haverthwaite. Similar stations were built at Drigg, Bootle and Ravenglass in harmonious local stone, but at Sellafield, Greenodd and Haverthwaite a vivid yellow brick with red bands was used, quite out of keeping with the Lake District. The station comprises a two-storey house with adjoining one-storey offices; here is a bay window from which the station master could observe the activity on his station. Haverthwaite served the ironworks at Backbarrow and the local gunpowder works, from which a narrow gauge tramway ran in to the station yard for the powder to be loaded into special gunpowder vans. The Lakeside & Haverthwaite Railway now operates steam trains over 3½ miles of line to the foot of Windermere.

HINCASTER TUNNEL

Towpath, railway underbridge and retaining walls south of east portal listed Grade II. South of Kendal.

This disused tunnel, 378 yards long, took the Lancaster Canal beneath Hincaster Hill. When the Lancaster & Carlisle Railway was opened to Kendal in 1846 it passed over the top of the tunnel, and it was necessary to lower and bridge the towpath south of the tunnel. The path was rebuilt between low stone retaining walls; in addition to the railway arch, two miniature stone canal bridges were erected to give access to and from the land on each side. The canal passed into railway ownership in 1885, and became British Waterways Board property on nationalisation in 1947. The towpath, however, is in railway ownership.

KESWICK

Built 1865 by Cockermouth, Keswick & Penrith Railway. Listed Grade II. Closed.

The CK&P Railway was controlled by the London & North Western but never-

theless had a character quite different from its large neighbour. The station has a large two-storey building in uncoursed stone, with a recessed entrance and porch; over the remaining platform is a ridge-and-furrow verandah. Next to it is the Keswick Hotel, built in 1869, with an iron first-floor balcony at one end and a Roman porch. It was once connected to the station by a passageway.

c.1960

PENRITH

Built 1846 for Lancaster & Carlisle Railway. Architect Sir William Tite. Listed Grade II.

Just as Lancaster station was designed with its proximity to Lancaster Castle in mind, so Tite remembered the ruins of Penrith Castle when he came to build the station opposite. He used the same dark red sandstone from which the town is built, and gave the station a baronial Tudor look with a prominent central mullioned and latticed window, gables and tall, square chimneys to the frontage. The northbound platform has an interest-

1963

Tite was one of those Victorian architects who was successful both as a designer and as a businessman. He had a very large London practice and followed a distinguished career in many fields: bank and railway company director, M.P. for Bath from 1855 to 1873, Royal Gold Medallist, Master of the Spectacle Makers' Company, twice President of the R.I.B.A., Governor of Dulwich College and St. Thomas's Hospital, and much else. He was also an expert land valuer, and did a great deal of that work for several railway companies. It was the foundation of his position in the railway world.

Born in London in 1798, he was articled to David Laing and set up his own practice in 1824, working for many years with a partner called Edward N. Clifton. His best known stations were the London & Southampton Railway termini at Nine Elms and Southampton (*p.205*), which were classical compositions; the second Liverpool Lime Street (*p.105*), which was more Italianate; and Carlisle (*p.116*) and Perth (*p.162*), built in a Tudor collegiate style. He also prepared a design for Edinburgh Princes Street station, but money was never found to build it and the station eventually took a quite different form.

The wayside stations on the Lancaster & Carlisle, Caledonian and the London & South Western Railway as far as Salisbury were also his and probably more besides. His railway work took him to France where he designed stations between Paris and Le Havre.

Tite's non-railway work was even more prolific, including numerous churches, several cemeteries (including Brookwood, with Sidney Smirke) and, perhaps best known of all, the Royal Exchange in the City of London. He was knighted in 1869, became a Companion of the Order of the Bath and was a Fellow of the Royal Society. He died in 1873, aged 75.

ing awning supported on shallow iron brackets and columns that present an arcaded appearance. They are derived directly from the designs of Robert Stephenson at Euston, which were used in conjunction with the Euston-style roof at many LNWR stations; here they are unusual in that they are under a canopy. On the far side, part of the overall roof that covered lines once used for the Kirkby Stephen and Workington trains remains, although those services have long since disappeared.

ULVERSTON, c.1895

THE LONDON &
NORTH WESTERN RAILWAY

The London & North Western Railway was often styled the 'Premier Line' of Great Britain. At its height it ran from London to Carlisle, throwing off lines to Birmingham, Holyhead, Liverpool, Manchester and Leeds; it even extended down to South Wales from Shrewsbury.

It came into existence in 1846 as an amalgamation of some of the most historic railways in the world. Indeed, one of its succession of distinguished General Managers claimed that it was the oldest firm in the business, since it included the Liverpool & Manchester Railway, which when opened in 1830 was the first railway in the world to operate freight and passenger services with locomotives.

The LNWR had an annual revenue greater than any other British railway before the 1923 Grouping and maintained a consistently high level of profitability, never paying less than 5½ per cent on its ordinary shares and often as much as 7½ per cent.

At its two great terminals in London and Birmingham, the company had lavish architectural adornments, but elsewhere it did not spend much on lineside buildings. Its money went in the magnificent permanent way, superb in alignment and grading, and in the great excavations for cuttings and tunnels.

Its viaducts and bridges were notable, especially on the Chester & Holyhead Railway opened in 1850 to carry the Irish Mail. Robert Stephenson's route included some tremendously impressive engineering, such as the tubular bridges at Conwy and the Menai Strait and the harbour works at Holyhead (p.95). The Lancaster and Carlisle line, completed in 1846 by Joseph Locke, was also a remarkable engineering achievement.

At Crewe the LNWR had what was regarded in the early 1900s as the most famous locomotive works in the world. Its intense activity and high productivity were monuments to 19th-century industry. Nearly two new locomotives a week was the general average. The 5,000th engine, the *Coronation* of 1911, was of the well known and successful 'George the Fifth' 4-4-0 type, introduced in the previous year, while the 'Prince of Wales' 4-6-0 class, eventually consisting of 245 locomotives, was one of the most numerous of any British passenger design in pre-Grouping days.

SEASCALE

Water tower built for Furness Railway. Listed Grade II. Closed. In former goods yard. Between Barrow and Whitehaven.

This circular stone tower has a conical top and forms a distinctive landmark. Seascale had wooden station buildings in a substantial, exposed-frame style built after the company bought a tract of land and planned a new seaside resort. But unlike Grange-over-Sands (*p.116*) the

1976

scheme misfired, due to the collapse of the Furness iron industry; despite inducements by the railway, Seascale as a watering place never really got off the ground.

SEDBERGH

WATERSIDE VIADUCT. Built 1861 for London & North Western Railway. Engineer John E. Errington. Low Gill to Ingleton line. Closed.

Of the several fine viaducts on this line, Waterside is the highest at 100 feet and also the most spectacular with its wide latticed iron central arch over the River Lune. The three flanking arches on each side are of Penrith sandstone. The viaduct is 177 yards long and when completed was tested in the customary manner by having three engines put on it at once.

ULVERSTON

Rebuilt 1873 for Furness Railway. Architects Paley and Austin. Listed Grade II. Between Carnforth and Barrow-in-Furness.

For a small market town, albeit an ancient regional centre, Ulverston station is a remarkably large and elaborate place. The third station to serve the town, its long frontage with prominent two-storey block and tall clock tower indicates its importance to the Furness Railway. In dark red sandstone with strong Italianate features – particularly the tall ground floor windows, iron cresting around the pavilion roof and large ball finials on each corner of the tower parapet – it is by far the most imposing building in the town. Delicate glass-and-iron awnings to the platforms, complete with FR-monogrammed brackets, are repeated in a similar verandah on the front. Restoration has retained the period atmosphere.

LNWR Express near Bushey, c.1907

ACQUIRED PROPERTIES

36 Craven Street, listed Grade I.

Newlay Lane iron bridge, Horsforth, West Yorkshire.

62 and 66 Grove Park Terrace W4 with level crossing where No. 64 used to stand.

British Rail has inherited a surprising number of properties that have no direct connection with the railways. Many were acquired together with land for possible track deviations or for expansion which then never took place. Some, including those illustrated here, are now listed buildings. Just outside Leeds, an iron toll bridge over the River Aire at Horsforth, built in 1819, was acquired to give access to Newlay station. Alongside Charing Cross station 36 Craven Street, built in c.1730, was the home of Benjamin Franklin from 1757 to 1772 while he was posted to England as agent for the American colonies. Three early 19th-century brick terrace houses in West London were purchased by the London & South Western Railway, and one demolished, so that the line could cross the street between Chiswick and Kew Bridge.

THOMAS BRASSEY, CONTRACTOR

No brief appreciation can possibly do justice to the greatest of all the railway contractors. Some measure of his immense achievements can be gained by considering that in the 1840s he employed 75,000 men whom he paid a total of £15,000 to £20,000 a week for working on a range of projects capitalised at some £36 million. Between 1848 and 1861 he won contracts to construct 2,374 miles of railway at a cost of £28 million. By 1847 he had built one mile in three in Britain, three out of every four in France, and by his death in 1870 was responsible for the construction of a substantial proportion of the world's railways.

Brassey's great talent which raised him head-and-shoulders above other contractors was a flair for organisation, coupled with integrity and reliability. When the Barentin Viaduct in France collapsed, although not through his fault, he rebuilt it at his own expense. He lost £1 million on the Grand Trunk Railway of Canada at the age of 55, yet stayed in business and re-established his position when he could have retired. He was a quiet, gently spoken man, and his men literally followed him to the ends of the earth.

He was born in 1805 and went into partnership with the surveyor to whom he had been articled. His contract for the Grand Junction Railway (from Birmingham to Warrington) quickly earned him the friendship of Locke (*p.97*), with whom he retained a close personal and business acquaintanceship for 25 years. The Grand Trunk contract was taken in partnership with two other great contractors, Sir Samuel Morton Peto and Edward Betts.

Brassey's name was synonymous with sound workmanship. His recent biographer, Charles Walker, says he was 'a man with a mission, and he believed firmly in the rightness of what he was doing. He believed he was conferring a benefit on mankind and he gloried in doing so. He gloried, too, in the hard work inseparable from his life and business'. (*Thomas Brassey, Railway Builder.*) He died aged 65, a remarkable yet simple man, unchanged by his prosperity.

SCOTTISH REGION

CONTENTS

SCOTTISH LOWLANDS: BORDERS PAGE 123   DUMFRIES & GALLOWAY PAGE 124   STRATHCLYDE PAGE 125
LOTHIAN PAGE 143   CENTRAL PAGE 149   FIFE PAGE 151   **SCOTTISH HIGHLANDS:** TAYSIDE PAGE 158
GRAMPIAN PAGE 164   HIGHLAND PAGE 166

Two striking Scottish viaducts are the Barncluith at Hamilton (left) and the Avon at Linlithgow (above), built in 1842 by the prolific engineers Grainger and Miller.

Few railways have had more romance woven into them by enthusiastic writers than Scotland's, yet for much of this century they have been the despair of economists. Lengthy mileages in the Highlands, condemned as unprofitable by the business-minded, have been kept open purely on grounds of social need. In the Lowlands, the inter-city routes from England and between Edinburgh and Glasgow, a world centre of the locomotive industry, were the scene of some of the most cut-throat railway rivalry ever seen in Britain.

The Scottish Region has more listed viaducts than any other region of British Rail – 65 in all. It incorporates all the railways in the country

and, unlike any other part of British Rail, is an amalgamation of systems that were previously operated quite separately. Before Grouping in 1923, three rival associations of Scottish and English companies operated the cross-border routes. The Caledonian ran the West Coast Joint service via Carlisle in partnership with the London & North Western, while the North British allied itself with the Great Northern and North Eastern Railways to provide the East Coast Joint route via Berwick-upon-Tweed. From 1890 the eastern route offered a through service from London to Aberdeen over the Forth and Tay bridges. The third route, opened by the Midland Railway from Settle to

Carlisle in 1876, enabled both the North British and the Glasgow & South Western to team up with the most aggressively competitive of the English companies.

The Scottish Highlands remained largely the preserve of two other railways. At Perth the Highland picked up through traffic for Inverness and the Far North from both East and West Coast routes, while beyond Aberdeen the Great North of Scotland, rather grander in name than its extent and activities justified, had the north-east of the country to itself.

Because the wild, sparsely populated country of the Highlands presented engineering difficulties and promised only modest returns to in-

121

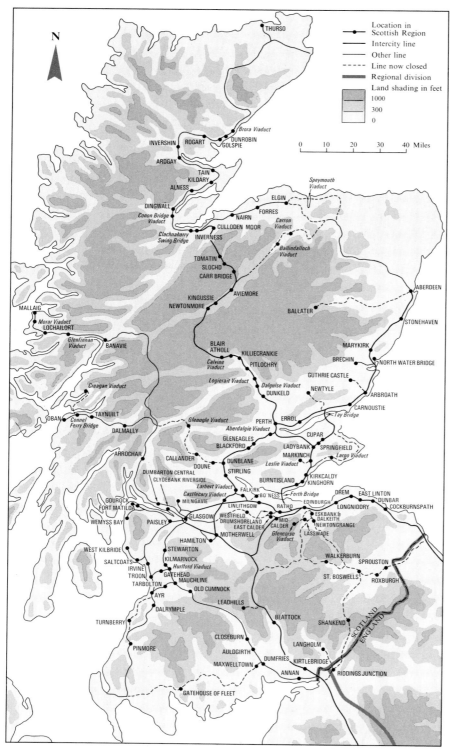

North British Railway's West High-land line to Fort William and the Caledonian-worked line from Callander to Oban for the splendour of its mountain scenery and for its romantic associations. These lines weaving through the mountains to the west coast are not, and perhaps never have been, profitable. Indeed, the West Highland Extension to Mallaig, built to serve the Western Isles, was made possible only by a massive government subsidy in 1897.

Grouping, which was intended to rationalize the railways, divided the Scottish system into two. The North British and the Great North of Scotland became part of the LNER while the Caledonian, Glasgow & South Western and Highland were incorporated into the LMS because it was felt that the Scottish railways on their own did not form a viable group. This amalgamation only increased the competition between the East and West Coast routes from England, and from 1932 there were notable developments in both service facilities and speed. The two post-Grouping lines also continued to compete for the combined rail and steamer traffic on the Clyde, and further north the LNER and the LMS fought for the traffic to western Scotland.

The Scottish system survived the Grouping period with its main lines intact, though many branch lines and a few long-distance routes were closed in the 1930s. Further closures were implemented during the 1950s. The Beeching axe struck sharply in the 1960s, although its full effects were mitigated as far as the Highland lines were concerned. Major closures included the Edinburgh-Carlisle 'Waverley' route and the connecting border lines, the old Caledonian line from Perth to Montrose, the Dumfries-Stranraer route and most of the lines in north-east Scotland.

Scotland has been left with a basic skeleton of railways, most of them maintained by subsidy. They offer a remarkable range of experience: from the ultra-modernity of Glasgow's Argyle Line suburban services to the lonely Far North and Kyle of Lochalsh lines; and from the 'Electric Scots' on the West Coast route to the high-speed trains on the East Coast main line. With the surviving relics of closed lines and preserved rolling stock, they make up some of the finest railway inheritances in Britain.

vestors, it was the last part of Britain to complete its network. The railway did not reach the northern outposts of Wick and Thurso until 1874. On the west coast Oban had to wait for a line until 1880, Mallaig until 1901.

Among the Scottish companies the Highland Railway was exceptional for its splendid engineering works and for the circumstances of its inception. It was an enterprise conceived in Inverness, engineered entirely by a native of that town, Joseph Mitchell, and carried through without any wealthy English sponsors. Highland chieftains and other landowners, anxious to see their remote country opened up, gave their wholehearted backing to the project.

The Highland's 'Dingwall & Skye' line, with its rock-bound extension to the Kyle of Lochalsh, vies with the

BORDERS

SPROUSTON

Built 1851 by York Newcastle & Berwick Railway. Closed.

This handsome station is the only surviving Scottish station built for an English company. Under George Hudson's management the York Newcastle & Berwick was an aggressive line, and during the late Railway Mania promoted a branch from Tweedmouth, which linked with the North British Railway's line from St. Boswells at Kelso. The house and offices are in sandstone-rubble, with finely-dressed door and window surrounds and mullions; there is a notable bay window on the platform side. The line was closed in 1968 and the rails have been removed.

1974

THE BORDER VIADUCTS

Of the great network of railways that once traversed the Borders, only the Caledonian and North British main lines now survive. In this generally sparse landscape, the viaducts are features as distinctive as the castles and fortified houses. Although many are disused they have mostly avoided demolition and they continue to occupy a place deep in the heart of the Borderers. They date mainly from the 1860s and several are listed *(see below)*.

The oldest of the bridges, and the only original one still in use in the region, is Dunglass Viaduct at Cockburnspath, a magnificent structure with a splendid 135-foot central span, flanked by two smaller arches on one side and three on the other. With its fine ashlar masonry, good proportions and the delicacy of its incised linear ornament, it belies the early reputation of the North British for building on the cheap. The 14-arched Teviot Viaduct at Roxburgh is in the same style; instead of a large central arch, it has six central spans which are curved and skewed. Again, its ashlar masonry is of a very high quality. It incorporates an early wrought-iron footbridge at the base of the three northern piers – a most unusual feature.

On the scenically spectacular Border Union Railway, opened in 1862, stands Shankend, a structure lacking the grandeur of the pioneers of 20 years earlier but thoroughly workmanlike all the same. To the north-west, spanning the Tweed on the line that connected the fashionable resort of Peebles with the Waverley route north are the five-span Horsburgh Viaduct near Innerleithen (opened in 1864) and the Haugh Head Viaduct near Walkerburn (opened in 1866). These bridges are notable very early examples of plate-girder construction in iron, their slightly bowed girders blending admirably with the low rolling hills of the Tweed valley.

On the western route to Peebles, operated by the rival Caledonian Railway and opened in 1864, are two skew bridges in matching style. That at Lyne is modest in scale, with three river arches and a plate-girder span over a minor road; the Neidpath Viaduct has eight spans and is on a curve over the Manor Water. Both have cast-iron railings, rock-faced ashlar spandrels and voussoirs, with pilasters, decorated with cruciform arrow slits, that extend from the rounded cutwaters.

The most striking of all the Border viaducts is undoubtedly Drygrange, commonly called Leaderfoot. Its 19 tall semi-circular arches on tapering piers of masonry and brick span the magnificently wooded valley of the Tweed. The arch rings, of light-coloured brick, make a pleasing contrast with the rich red of the sandstone piers and spandrels. The viaduct forms a fine group with the 18th-century Drygrange road bridge and its modern concrete successor.

DUNGLASS VIADUCT, COCKBURNS-PATH. Built 1846 for North British Railway. Designed by Grainger & Miller. Listed Grade B.

TEVIOT VIADUCT, ROXBURGH. Built 1850 for North British Railway. Designed by Grainger & Miller. Listed Grade B. Closed.

DRYGRANGE VIADUCT, ST. BOSWELLS. Built 1865 by Berwickshire Railway. Listed Grade B. Closed.

SHANKEND VIADUCT. Built 1862 by Border Union Railway. Listed Grade B. Closed.

Drygrange Viaduct, 1970s

Teviot Viaduct, 1974

DUMFRIES AND GALLOWAY

ANNAN

STATION. Built 1848 by Glasgow Dumfries & Carlisle Railway.

On the beautiful Nithsdale route from Carlisle to Glasgow completed in 1850 stands the best surviving early station in south-west Scotland. Two storeys in height, it is very well constructed in red sandstone ashlar, with a bay window and colonnaded entrance on the street side. The roof has the projecting eaves characteristic of much railway architecture of the 1840s. On the platform side is a late Victorian glazed awning, supported on cast-iron columns.

ANNAN, 1974

RIVER ANNAN VIADUCT, 1974

PORT STREET and RIVER ANNAN VIADUCTS. Built 1848 by Glasgow Dumfries & Carlisle Railway. Designed by Grainger & Miller. Both listed Grade B.

The viaducts on the Glasgow & South Western's route, all designed by the partnership of Grainger & Miller, are solidly constructed, though there were few opportunities for the grand gesture. The Port Street Viaduct has four segment-headed arches, one large and three small, in fine ashlar masonry with rustication. The River Annan Viaduct is similar to Port Street in style, but has five large spans and one small.

THE CALEDONIAN RAILWAY

The Caledonian originated in 1845 when Parliament authorized a continuation northwards of the Lancaster & Carlisle line, part of what was to become the London & North Western Railway. With the great Joseph Locke (*p.97*) as engineer, the route was carried to Perth and later, by the construction of several lines that all eventually became part of the Caledonian, to Aberdeen.

In its business results the Caledonian shared with the North British the premier position in Scotland, dominating the industrial lowland belt with its coal, iron and ship-building industries and running efficient services to the Clyde coast resorts. The company's main station was Glasgow Central which between 1900 and 1905 was enlarged, developed and fitted with the most sophisticated equipment to handle its enormous traffic.

The Caledonian was in many ways a most attractive railway. At tourist resorts and country stations the airy, glass-covered concourses were gay with hanging baskets of flowers – a tradition repeated at the large stations and still continued today at Stirling. Another particularly fine example was at Wemyss Bay where floral decorations greeted passengers for the Rothesay ferry.

But to many enthusiasts the company's abiding joy was the bright blue livery of the Caledonian locomotives, introduced about 1906. The colour had till then – officially at least – been a rich Prussian blue, finely set off by purple under-frames. But at one repair works the contract painters discovered that the blue paint could be made to go further if a little white was mixed with it. The result was such a beautiful sky blue that it was eventually made the official colour.

Passenger locomotives built at the St. Rollox Works in Glasgow achieved fame out of all proportion to their relatively small numbers. The 'Dunalastair' 4-4-0s, introduced by John F. McIntosh, were chosen by the Belgian State Railways as a standard locomotive, while the very large and impressive 'Cardean' class of 4-6-0s attained an almost legendary reputation for their work both north and south of Glasgow. The later 4-4-0s, built from 1916 onwards to designs by William Pickersgill, were so massively constructed that many of them lasted to the end of steam, attaining ages of nearly 50 years.

Three Caledonian locomotives are preserved, among them the famous 4-2-2 No. 123 built for the Edinburgh Exhibition of 1886.

Bench with Caledonian Railway monogram, 1978

CR 4-4-0 Dunalastair III, near Beattock, c.1914

AULDGIRTH

BRIDGE OVER BALLOCHAN LINN.
Built 1850 for Glasgow Dumfries & Carlisle
Railway. Designed by Grainger & Miller.
Listed Grade B.

This tall four-span bridge, situated in a wooded valley, is built of fine rusticated ashlar masonry. Unlike the other bridges on this line, it has semi-circular, rather than segmental arches.

BEATTOCK

Built 1848 for Caledonian Railway. Architect
Sir William Tite. Closed.

Beattock station, now closed, is situated at the foot of the famous Beattock bank which, with its gradient of 1 in 70, was a formidable obstacle for steam locomotives. Though the platforms have been cut back, the offices and house survive. The L-plan building has one storey and an attic and is built of snecked rubble with ashlar dressings which give it a very distinctive character, similar to that of Lockerbie.

1971

The main block has a symmetrical front with a central gable on the platform side, while on the street side is a handsome porch. The prominent gables are crow-stepped in the traditional Scottish style. The original timber-framed, lead-roofed awning has now gone.

CLOSEBURN

CAMPLE WATER VIADUCT. Built 1850
for Glasgow Dumfries & Carlisle Railway.
Designed by Grainger & Miller. Listed
Grade B.

This skewed viaduct in fine ashlar masonry with segmental arches is set in relatively flat country, close to Cample Mill, a water-powered grain mill.

DUMFRIES

Built 1859 by Glasgow & South Western
Railway. Listed Grade B.

Like Annan, Dumfries station is superbly built, but with less style. The red sandstone main buildings consist of a central two-storey block with single-storey wings. An elaborate ridge-and-furrow glazed awning extends to form a trainshed for the

bay platforms which served the lines to Stranraer and Moniaive. Judging by its style, the awning was probably added towards the end of the 19th century.

GATEHOUSE OF FLEET

BIG WATER OF FLEET VIADUCT.
Built 1861 by Portpatrick Railway. Listed
Grade B. Closed.

Situated in a mossy wilderness, this viaduct is a spectacular feature of the landscape. Originally a masonry structure with 20 segmental arches, it developed weaknesses that were remedied by encasing the piers in brickwork and bracing the spandrels with old rails. The Portpatrick Railway was worked as a joint line from 1885 to 1923 by the Glasgow & South Western, Caledonian and Midland Railways (*pp.135, 124 and 69 respectively*).

KIRTLEBRIDGE

KIRTLEWATER VIADUCT. Built 1848
for Caledonian Railway. Engineer Joseph
Locke. Listed Grade B.

Since the Caledonian Railway's Annandale route was cheaply built with temporary bridges in many places, few of the original viaducts survive. Of these, the largest is Kirtlewater with five segmental arches over a small stream. It is constructed in rock-faced ashlar.

KIRTLEWATER VIADUCT, 1976

CREAG AN ARNAIN VIADUCT, 1976

DUMFRIES, 1970

MAXWELLTOWN

GOLDILEA and GARROCH VIADUCTS.
Built 1859 by Castle Douglas & Dumfries
Railway. Listed Grade B. Closed.

The Castle Douglas & Dumfries was the first part of the line from Dumfries to Stranraer and Portpatrick. These two viaducts are near the beginning of the route and both span shallow valleys. Goldilea is the more spectacular, with ten semi-circular masonry spans in a pleasant wooded setting. Garroch, with eight modest segmental spans, appears to have been more cheaply constructed. The line was closed in 1965.

RIDDINGS JUNCTION

RIDDINGS JUNCTION VIADUCT
and TARRASFOOT VIADUCT,
LANGHOLM. Built 1864 by North British
Railway. Riddings Junction Viaduct listed
Grade B. Both closed.

Riddings Junction is a very attractive nine-span masonry viaduct with elliptical arches which carries the Langholm branch line over the Liddel Water, which marks the border between Scotland and England. Further north on the same branch is Tarrasfoot Viaduct, a 12-span bridge over a wooded valley with brick arch rings and spandrels patched with brick and strengthened with old rails. The Langholm branch closed in 1967.

STRATHCLYDE

ARROCHAR

CREAG AN ARNAIN VIADUCT. Built
1894 by West Highland Railway. Listed
Grade B. Between Arrochar and Ardlin.

The only conventional masonry viaduct on the West Highland Railway (*see box on p.172*), Creag an Arnain is built on a curve on the hillside above Loch Lomond and has nine arches with craggy spandrels. Although difficult to see through the surrounding trees, it is a handsome, well sited structure and has battlemented parapets.

AYR

Rebuilt 1886 by Glasgow & South Western
Railway. Listed Grade B.

Ayr station has both through platforms serving the line to Girvan and Stranraer and bay platforms at the north end. The cast-iron and steel-framed low overall roof is similar in design to the awnings at Irvine and Kilmarnock (*p.135*) and at one time was much more extensive.

The main offices, on the up platform, are on the ground floor of the massive four-storey red sandstone Station Hotel, built in 1886 in a plain French Renaissance style popular in the West of Scotland at that time and finished with a corner turret. On the down platform is a long single-storey red sandstone building with a small central pediment.

AYR STATION HOTEL, 1969

GRAINGER AND MILLER, ENGINEERS

Thomas Grainger and John Miller exerted a decisive influence on early railway development in Scotland. Beginning with the pioneer Monkland & Kirkintilloch Railway of 1823, the pioneer line in Scotland, the partnership went on to design the Edinburgh & Glasgow and the North British Railways and a number of other lines in the southern half of Scotland.

Grainger also laid out the harbours at Broughty Ferry and Ferryport on the Tay, for which he designed a steam vessel to take wagons across the river. A Scot from Midlothian, where he was born in 1794, he built two railways in Yorkshire, where he was responsible for the Bramhope Tunnel (p.33). He died in a collision on the Leeds Northern Railway in 1852, aged 57.

Grainger seems to have concentrated on English lines after about 1840, and the corollary of this is that Miller should take credit for the bulk of the Scottish work, including more than half the four main lines through Scotland to England. Born in Ayr in 1805, Miller settled in Edinburgh and attended the University there. His competence as an architect, expressed in his Bridge Street station, Glasgow (now demolished) and the Haymarket station, Edinburgh, suggests that the refined character of major works such as Ballochmyle Viaduct at Mauchline (p.136), on the Kilmarnock to Dumfries line, is attributable to him.

Miller retired from practice in 1849 and purchased an estate at Innerleithen, Peeblesshire. From 1868 to 1874 he represented Edinburgh in Parliament. He died in 1883, leaving an estate valued at £37,475.

CALLANDER & OBAN RAILWAY

This line, engineered by B. & E. Blyth, was promoted as an extension of the Dunblane & Callander Railway and became part of the Caledonian. It proved difficult to attract enough capital to complete it, and from 1873 it terminated at a temporary station at Tyndrum. The section from Tyndrum to Oban was opened in 1880. The connection with the main Callander to Oban line at Dunblane was closed during the Beeching cuts, and the metal bridges were removed, but the viaducts on the hillside in Glenogle survive (p.150). The remaining structures of importance are on the Tyndrum to Oban section, and on the branch from Connel to Ballachulish, built by the Caledonian Railway in 1903 and also a victim of the Beeching cuts.

DALMALLY. Between Tyndrum and Taynuilt.

This is a two-platform station, with single-storey offices and a two-storey station house on the up side built of red sandstone with crow-stepped gables. The glazed, pitched awning has ornamental brackets on iron columns and neat, square serrations along the valancing, with a V-shaped section in the gable ends to match the brackets.

OBAN.

At the end of the line, Oban terminus is a delightful feature of this handsome town. It was built to connect with steamers running from the new railway pier, and accordingly has something of a seaside air. It consists of a wooden-framed trainshed with timber cladding and a transverse ridged glazed roof. The offices are grouped around an attractive glass-roofed concourse, and the exterior has exposed timber framing with rendering and exposed gable framework in the form of brackets, like a Swiss chalet. The wooden clock tower with its steep-pointed top is a prominent landmark.

TAYNUILT. Between Dalmally and Oban.

Taynuilt has two platforms with the offices on the down side in a lofty single-storey wooden building, which has exposed framing and herring-bone boarding painted in contrasting colours. The awning continues the slope of the roof over the platform on decorated iron brackets. The detailing of the valancing is particularly ornate. The station is superbly situated, with a fine view of Ben Cruachan and of the hills on the north side of Loch Etive.

CONNEL FERRY BRIDGE. Engineer H. M. Brunel. Ballachulish branch. Closed.

A splendid steel cantilever bridge in a commanding position on Loch Etive, this is the second largest bridge of its type in Britain. It spans the Falls of Lora where the rush of water through a narrow gap in the sea loch at ebb and flood tides creates the effect of a waterfall. It was used by both road and rail traffic but since closure of the branch has been converted, with minimal alteration, entirely for road use. (*Photograph p.129.*)

CREAGAN VIADUCT. Ballachulish branch. Closed.

This bridge occupies a position comparable with that of the Connel Ferry bridge. It consists of two steel trusses with castellated masonry abutments pierced by pointed arches at each end. The one at the south end is used by a road. Both the abutments and central pier are constructed of rock-faced granite ashlar.

The Callander & Oban Railway includes two notably picturesque stations, Oban (top) and Taynuilt (above). The CR 'Oban Bogie' (left) was a light but powerful class of engine designed to run on this line.

The LNER brought out this poster in the 1930s to advertise their East Coast route to Scotland.

OVER THE FORTH ⟨LNER⟩ TO THE NOR[TH]

POSTERS AND POSTCARDS

Early railway posters were designed to convey the greatest amount of information with the largest variety of typefaces in the smallest space. Not until the 1890s did pictorial posters begin to appear. Perhaps the most famous was John Hassall's jolly fisherman proclaiming, on behalf of the Great Northern Railway, 'Skegness is so bracing'.

In the 1930s Frank Pick of the London Underground pioneered the use of posters by well-known artists. The main-line companies followed suit, led by the LNER which commissioned avant-garde posters to advertise their new streamlined trains.

Picture postcards were another form of advertising, adopted by the railways from the turn of the century (*see overleaf*). The LNWR claimed by 1914 to have sold more than 11 million cards.

"THE CORONATION"
CROSSING THE ROYAL BORDER BRIDGE BERWICK-UPON-TWEED
IT'S QUICKER BY RAIL
FULL INFORMATION FROM ANY L·N·E·R OFFICE OR AGENCY

ROYAL BORDER BRIDGE

TOM PURVIS

A view of the LNER's 1937 Coronation *express emphasises the modern profile of Gresley's A4 Pacifics, which ran from London to Edinburgh in six hours.*

An LNWR Irish Boat Express from Euston to Holyhead steams north from the Britannia Tubular Bridge in this 'Tuck oilette' – a trade name for the coloured postcards published by Raphael Tuck. It was Number 9 in a series of Famous Expresses.

An Ivatt 4-4-2 (right) and 4-4-0 (left) feature in this F. Moore postcard issued in about 1907.

This hand-tinted photograph of the LBSCR trainshed and platforms at Queens Road was published by the Pictorial Centre, Brighton.

CLYDEBANK RIVERSIDE

Built c. 1896 for Lanarkshire &
Dunbartonshire Railway. Architect probably
Sir J. J. Burnet. Closed.

The Lanarkshire & Dunbartonshire Railway was built by the Caledonian to link Central Glasgow with Dumbarton, and to serve the riverside industries and docks on the north bank of the Clyde. Clydebank was, in 1896, a prosperous town with the largest sewing machine factory in the world (Singer's) and one of the biggest shipyards (becoming John Brown's after an 1899 takeover).

The station was built in a style befitting the importance of its site and though it was closed in 1964, the main up platform building survives. It is a red sandstone and brick structure, richly textured in a manner that was very fashionable in the 1890s.

CLYDEBANK RIVERSIDE, 1978

CONNEL FERRY BRIDGE, c.1977

DUMBARTON CENTRAL

Rebuilt 1896 by Dumbarton & Balloch Joint Line Committee.

Rebuilt to accommodate both the North British and the new Caledonian services from the Lanarkshire & Dunbartonshire Railway, Dumbarton Central has two island platforms on a viaduct. The book-

STAIRWAYS TO STREET LEVEL, 1970

ing office is at ground level and the platforms are approached by richly tiled stairways. The brick platform buildings are completed by steel-framed awnings. Though not particularly refined in design, this large urban station is a handsome example from a period not now well represented in Scotland. Dumbarton East, on the Lanarkshire & Dunbartonshire line, is similar in style, but smaller in scale with only a single-island platform.

FORT MATILDA

Built 1889 for Caledonian Railway. Designed by James Miller. Listed Grade B.

Serving an upper-middle-class suburb of Greenock, this station was opened as part of the Caledonian's new line from Greenock to Gourock Pier. It is mainly of brick, with timbered gables, Tudor chim-

1978

DUMBARTON CENTRAL, SOUTHERN PLATFORM, 1970

LAIGH MILTON MILL VIADUCT, 1967

ney stacks in moulded brick and a steeply-pitched roof, which overhangs the platform to provide shelter. Though it lacks the refinement of the station at West Kilbride (*p.142*), it is a satisfying building, well suited in its solid construction to its exposed position above Gourock Bay.

GATEHEAD

LAIGH MILTON MILL VIADUCT. Built 1812. Closed to railway traffic but still used as a footbridge. Listed Grade B.

This is the oldest railway viaduct in Scotland, built on the route of a horse-haul plateway. When the Kilmarnock and Troon Railway converted the route to locomotive working in 1847 the viaduct was bypassed. It is a four-span masonry bridge with segmental arches and rounded cutwaters; these were later extended to form semi-circular buttresses.

GLASGOW

As the country's largest urban centre, Glasgow was the focal point of railway development in Scotland in the 19th century. Rationalization and urban renewal have resulted in the obliteration of some fine structures – notably Bridge Street and St. Enoch stations; the 1855 part of Queen Street station; most of the superb stations on the Glasgow Central Railway; the original Glasgow Central bridge; and the classical Cowlairs incline engine house. But enough survives to give an indication of the scale and quality of Victorian and Edwardian railway building in the city.

As well as major stations and hotels, the smaller scale Crookston and Kelvinside stations survive on lines built during the expansion of suburban services in the 1880s and 1890s, in addition to warehouses, offices and other railway buildings.

Above GLASGOW CENTRAL, c.1906; *inset* GLASGOW CENTRAL, 1980; *below* CENTRAL STATION HOTEL, POSTER c.1885

CENTRAL STATION. First phase completed 1879 for Caledonian Railway, architect Sir R. Rowand Anderson; extended 1899-1905, architect James Miller, engineer Donald Mathieson. Listed Grade B.

OFFICES. Built 1901 for Caledonian Railway. Architect James Miller. Listed Grade B. 75-95 Union Street.

By far the most important railway building in the city is the Caledonian's terminus, Central station. The pioneering steel trussed roof and the heavy 'Queen Anne' main frontage on Gordon Street survive from the late 1870s. There is a delightfully ornate iron *porte cochère* with the station's name in elaborate iron lettering, and highly decorated wrought-iron gates. In later remodelling, the number of platforms was increased to 13, some extending out on to the bridge over the Clyde. To overcome the restrictions of space, platform ends were staggered, and curved ends for the indicator screen, concourse offices and bookstalls were introduced to ease passenger flow, forming a well-known feature of the station.

The architect, James Miller, also designed the great screen wall in Hope Street with its tall, round-headed windows and fine glazing; an extension to the hotel in 1907; and the massive seven-storey office block at 75-95 Union Street.

Central is still one of the busiest

stations in Britain, and Mathieson's foresight is shown by the admirable way in which it still copes with heavy mainline and suburban traffic. Its most notable feature is the roof, which has massive deep horizontal trusses supporting lofty ridge-and-furrow glazing over the concourse and inner ends of the main platforms, thus avoiding the need for supporting columns. Beyond there are lower, light-section trusses with elliptically curved ribs for longitudinal ridge-and-furrow glazing. The unique destination indicator uses linen blinds printed with station names which are inserted by hand into windows overlooking the concourse. Unlike many modern indicators, the type is clearly legible and since the screen is parallel to the flow of passengers it may be easily read in passing.

The concourse is broad and uncluttered and contains 'The Shell', a First World War collecting box which for many years was a popular meeting place for Glaswegians (equivalent to 'under the clock' at St. Pancras) which has recently been restored to its long-established position.

The low level station, on the erstwhile Glasgow Central Railway and running at right angles beneath the main station, has two platforms. Modernization for the electric 'blue trains' has transformed it from its once notoriously smoky and dirty condition.

CENTRAL STATION HOTEL. Built 1883 for Caledonian Railway, architect Sir R. Rowand Anderson; extended 1907, architect James Miller. Listed Grade B.

Above the booking office of the main station rises the five-storey hotel; it was originally conceived as offices, but was hastily converted after the success of the Glasgow & South Western's St. Enoch Hotel in 1879. It retains much of its Victorian interior, giving a general impression of solid comfort rather than of grandeur; but the staircase contrived in the angle between Hope Street and Gordon Street is very fine. External detail, effectively disguising the great bulk of the building, contrasts with the simplicity of the upper stages of the pyramidal clock tower, a notable city landmark.

131

GLASGOW CENTRAL UNDER CONSTRUCTION, 1870s

QUEEN STREET STATION. Rebuilt 1877 for North British Railway. Engineer James Carswell. Trainshed listed Grade B.

An 1842 guide book described Queen Street station as 'an almost fairy palace'. After passing through the 1 mile 33 yards of the Queen Street Tunnel passengers no doubt saw it like that. But for those responsible for the smooth running and efficiency of the railway, the station has always been an operational nightmare.

The North British was seldom a company for the grand gesture and Queen Street was allowed to grow piecemeal from the opening of the Edinburgh and Glasgow Railway in 1842 until, in the face of public criticism, it was substantially rebuilt in the 1870s.

The lofty segmental arched glass-and-iron trainshed built by Carswell in the 1870s preserves the bright and airy atmosphere of the original. Inspired by the larger and grander roof at St. Enoch, now demolished, it is the only remaining arched trainshed north of the border. It has a single span of 250 feet and is 78 feet high, with prominent radially glazed gables. The frontage is provided by the North British Hotel, which was there before the station. The concourse buildings were reconstructed and modernized in the 1950s.

The chief problem with Queen Street is the approach tunnel, which has always been a notorious bottleneck and cramps the platforms, which even now are too short for many of the trains.

Descending from Cowlairs on a gradient of 1 in 42, the tunnel was too steep to be operated by locomotives under their own power. Instead a rope was used to haul trains (complete with locomotives) up out of the station by means of a stationary winding engine at the top,

QUEEN STREET, 1980

NORTH BRITISH HOTEL, 1870s

where the hook was dropped off as the train gathered speed.

Incoming trains stopped at Cowlairs to have the locomotive replaced by special brake vehicles which controlled the descent into the station. For 66 years, therefore, no train entered Queen Street behind a locomotive (though locomotives were coupled on for departure). When ropes and brake vehicles were abolished the situation did not greatly improve, since ascending trains then needed a banking engine, so that the tunnel became permanently smoke-logged. Only the advent of diesels brought some relief, but the inconvenience inherent in the arrangement of the station still remains.

The low level station, like that at Central station, runs at right angles beneath the main station. It has two tracks, now served by the Trans-Clyde electric suburban trains.

NORTH BRITISH HOTEL. Built c. 1780. Listed Grade B.

The hotel is the last of the original buildings in George Square. The North British Railway took it over during the remodelling of the station in the 1870s, and added an extra storey and attic in the 1890s, attracting criticism from conservationists.

Its frontage is patently pre-Victorian, lacking the florid ostentation of many of its later brethren. The walls are stuccoed in grey and cream, setting off well the pilasters and generally restrained Georgian appearance. The interior has been divided up over the years, but the restaurant has its original deep panelled ceiling, pilasters and columns.

COLLEGE STATION. Built 1871 for North British Railway. Closed. Off High Street.

Terminus of the North British Railway's services to Coatbridge and points east, this station was built on part of the site of the magnificent 17th-century Old College of Glasgow. For a time, the original front building of the college served as the booking office for the station. The station was closed to passengers in 1886, when the Glasgow City & District Railway was opened, giving direct access to Queen Street, but survived as a goods shed. The trainshed remains, its massive cast-iron columns supporting broad, shallow brackets, the angular openings of which form an arcade spanned by wrought-iron roof trusses – a classic structure.

The price paid for the site by the North British and by the Glasgow & South Western, who built a goods station to the south, enabled the University to establish itself on Gilmorehill in a new Gothic building designed by Sir Gilbert Scott, which is thus a memorial to 19th-century railway development and also the core of the present campus.

CROOKSTON STATION. Built 1885 for Glasgow & South Western Railway. Listed Grade B. Closed and sold.

The Glasgow & South Western had inherited an unusual asset when it was formed in 1850: the Glasgow Paisley & Johnstone Canal. In the early 1880s the company drained the canal and built over it a new line bypassing the Glasgow & Paisley Joint Railway, so gaining access to land suitable for development as residential suburbs.

Crookston, the best of the stations on this line, is a two-platform through station, with a single-storey station house and offices on the up side. Distinctive features are round-headed openings and a particularly fine glazed screen in the waiting area, with Georgian fanlights and delicate eaves brackets.

KELVINSIDE STATION. Built 1896 for Glasgow Central Railway, worked by Caledonian Railway. Architect Sir J. J. Burnet. Listed Grade B. Closed. 1051 Great Western Rd.

The last complete example of the fine stations designed for the Glasgow Central (a subsidiary of the Caledonian), Kelvinside closed in 1942, and after a period as a private house was converted into a restaurant.

Designed to blend with the nearby mansions of Glasgow magnates, the offices and houses are in a distinguished two-storey cream sandstone block with a handsome curved projection carrying a terrace fronted by a balustrade and two large stone urns. The building is mounted over the mouth of a tunnel with stairs leading down to the platform, which is in a cutting. The style is Italian Renaissance with balustraded screen walls and prominent chimneys.

WAREHOUSE AND OFFICE. Built c.1880 for Glasgow & South Western Railway. Listed Grade B. 175-191 Bell Street.

This two-storey warehouse and office block with round-headed openings is of a sandstone ashlar. It is most interesting for its floors, which are flat mass-concrete arches between cast-iron beams – probably the earliest use of mass concrete in a Glasgow building.

CUSTOMS & EXCISE WAREHOUSE. Built 1882-83 by Glasgow & South Western Railway. Listed Grade B. 105-169 Bell Street.

Built as bonded stores for the booming trade in blended Scotch whisky, this massive six-storey structure cost £100,000. It has 31 bays along one side and four along the other.

The main frontages are of rusticated ashlar on the ground floor with segmental-arched doorways, and rock-faced masonry on the upper floors with polished ashlar pilasters dividing the frontage into

CROOKSTON, 1971

KELVINSIDE, c.1970

BELL ST. WAREHOUSE, BACKED BY CUSTOMS & EXCISE WAREHOUSE, c.1970

three sections. A string course below the first floor and a heavily moulded cornice also help break up what would otherwise be a forbidding structure.

Internally there is a cast-iron frame, with mass-concrete arches; on the ground floor the columns are 12 inches in diameter and 18 feet high. At the rear there was access from the goods shed of the now demolished College station, and nine hoist bays are still visible.

STABLE BLOCK. Built c.1900 by Glasgow & South Western Railway. Listed Grade B. Closed. 174 Bell Street.

This L-plan terracotta brick building, three storeys high with a 17-bay frontage, was built as stables for the cartage department and is now the only surviving railway stable block in the city. The ground floor was used for cart storage, the first floor for stabling and the top floor for storing grain and hay. Access to the upper floors was by ramps and balconies at the rear. The frontage is broken up by a moulded string course between the ground and first floors, and by low relief arches over the top floor windows. Most of these spring from corbels just below the windows but some have pilasters extending from ground floor level.

GOUROCK PIER

Built 1889 for Caledonian Railway. Architect James Miller.

Designed as a major railway-steamer interchange, Gourock is the most advanced of the railway piers built in the 1880s and 1890s, with the trains drawing up parallel to the steamers. The station itself is a long, single-storey structure, with brick walls and a glass roof. Facing the river it has 20 small timbered gables which made a bolder impact before they were painted over in a single colour. Gourock is superbly situated in a sheltered bay but is now, with the decline of steamer services, past its heyday.

HAMILTON

BARNCLUITH VIADUCT. Built 1857 by Caledonian Railway. Listed Grade B. Between Hamilton and Motherwell.

This four-span viaduct over the river Avon, with segmental arches constructed of rock-faced masonry, is picturesquely situated in a well-wooded valley. Downstream are a 17th-century ribbed-arch bridge, and Telford's 1820 Avon Bridge.

TUNNEL MOUTH. Built 1857 by Caledonian Railway. Listed Grade B. Between Hamilton and Motherwell.

Immediately to the east of Barncluith Viaduct a double-track tunnel begins. The entrance, built of rusticated ashlar masonry, consists of a semi-circular arch flanked by piers and surmounted by a moulded string course and a parapet with pedimented terminals.

When the Hamilton Circle was electrified in the early 1970s the line through the tunnel was reduced to single track to give adequate clearance for the overhead wires. In an area that was badly affected by mining in the late-19th and early-20th centuries, the tunnel mouth completes a remarkably picturesque scene.

HURLFORD VIADUCT

Built 1848 for Glasgow Paisley Kilmarnock & Ayr Railway. Designed by Grainger & Miller.

At Hurlford a relatively modest seven-span viaduct crosses the valley of the Irvine Water. With its semi-circular arches and superb ashlar masonry, it is in the best Grainger & Miller style.

IRVINE

STATION. Built 1839 for Glasgow Paisley Kilmarnock & Ayr Railway.

This two-platform through station stands on a walled embankment. The two-storey main offices on the down platform side are finely constructed in sandstone ashlar, while the subsidiary offices on the other side are of snecked rubble sandstone. Both platforms are sheltered by awnings of good late-Victorian design with cast iron columns and brackets.

QUEEN'S BRIDGE. Built 1839 for Glasgow Paisley Kilmarnock & Ayr Railway. Designed by Grainger & Miller. Listed Grade B. North of Irvine station.

Across the River Garnock stretches a low six-span viaduct designed in typical Grainger & Miller style, with flat segmental arches, good ashlar masonry and the incised ornament also found at Dunglass, Ratho and Ballochmyle (*p.136*). Unusually for a viaduct by these engineers, brick patching has been necessary.

QUEEN'S BRIDGE, 1978

IRVINE, 1971

HURLFORD VIADUCT, 1966

KILMARNOCK

Original station built 1843 by Glasgow Paisley Kilmarnock & Ayr Railway; extended 1878. Original station (now goods department); extensions (now station); subway to Garden Street, all listed Grade B.

This station developed in the course of the 19th century into a major communications centre, but is now served only by through trains from Glasgow to Carlisle via Dumfries and a daily boat-train to Stranraer. The down platform buildings, however, survive virtually intact. They

1979

OLD STATION. c.1975

incorporate the two-storey cream sandstone building of the original station as well as the later red sandstone ashlar buildings, dominated by a neat tower with circular windows and small pediments at its top. On the platform side are the reduced remains of iron-and-glass ridge-and-furrow awnings, with hipped ends and intricate ironwork, including monogrammed brackets. At street level there is a small Tudor-style crenellated entrance to the subway.

VIADUCT. Built 1848 for Glasgow Paisley Kilmarnock & Ayr Railway. Designed by Grainger & Miller. Listed Grade B.

At the south end of the station a 23-span viaduct carries the railway across the town centre and the Kilmarnock Water. The fifth span from the north is a wide elliptical arch spanning a main road; the others are smaller and segmented. The masonry has stood up well both to heavy traffic and atmospheric pollution. Since the clearance of older buildings, this viaduct has become a dominant feature of the rebuilt central area of Kilmarnock.

THE GLASGOW & SOUTH WESTERN RAILWAY

Dominated throughout the 73 years of its existence by fierce rivalry with the Caledonian, the Glasgow & South Western inspired in everyone – from its most senior manager to its humblest line-worker – a spirit of loyalty and pride that carried it through many difficulties. Furthermore, it paid its shareholders better dividends than either the Caledonian or the North British.

Its main area of operation was accurately described by its name: it served the rich coal and iron-producing districts of Ayrshire as well as having important agricultural traffic. But with the Midland Railway it also ran expresses direct to London via Kilmarnock, Dumfries, Carlisle and Leeds. Between Portpatrick and Castle Douglas these Anglo-Scottish trains passed over a 62-mile section of line that was jointly owned by no fewer than four railways, two English and two Scottish. Both this stretch and the line southwards from Girvan had single track throughout, contained severe gradients and were very difficult to work.

The GSWR operated services to Northern Ireland via Stranraer – the only route over which it had no competition from other companies. On the Clyde Coast route, for which it was in cut-throat rivalry with the Caledonian, its services were especially notable for smartness and sophistication. Its steamers were arguably the most beautiful of all those running from British ports.

In locomotive practice as in all else the GSWR had proud traditions. In the interests of fuel economy, drivers were encouraged to run easily uphill and to make up their time with speeds of more than 85 mph downhill, which were made possible by the excellent track alignment.

Sound locomotives were built by James Manson, who was in charge at the Kilmarnock Works from 1890 to 1912 and had previously been with the Great North of Scotland. His 4-4-0s were still performing admirably 40 years later. His outside-cylindered 4-6-0s, though powerful and efficient, were not so sound structurally and were extensively rebuilt.

Manson's successor in 1912 was Peter Drummond, previously of the Highland Railway. After a somewhat shaky start he introduced some very fine 2-6-0s for express goods work. He was succeeded six years later by Robert Whitelegg who built some large and imposing 4-6-4 tank engines to serve on the fast Clyde Coast lines.

G&SW Manson 4-4-0, c.1925

KILMARNOCK VIADUCT, 1966

Forman was a partner in Forman & McCall of Glasgow. He was born and apprenticed in the city, and he started his career on dock works on the Clyde. He went on to work on several Scottish railways. His best known line is the West Highland, for which he was largely responsible in getting parliamentary approval.

The line is nearly 100 miles long, from Helensburgh on the Clyde to Fort William in the Western Highlands and is one of the most dramatic and scenic routes in Britain. In January 1889 with six companions Forman tramped 40 miles across the largely trackless Rannoch Moor, gathering information about the route. The expedition took two days during which they squelched through miles of bog, climbed up to 1,300 feet, faced driving rain and sleet, not surprisingly got lost, and nearly forfeited the life of one of the party. None seem to have been adequately clad for the venture (two actually carried umbrellas) yet they somehow survived. However foolhardy it seems in retrospect it speaks much for their determination, particularly Forman's. He was not over strong and died of consumption in 1901 at the comparatively young age of 48.

His other major work was the underground line across the centre of Glasgow, the Glasgow Central Railway of 1890-96. Like the Metropolitan in London, it was built on the cut-and-cover system and involved complicated work beneath the streets. At the time of his death Forman was also involved with other lines in the Glasgow area and the Highlands.

LEADHILLS

WANLOCKHEAD VIADUCT. Built 1902 for Leadhills & Wanlockhead Light Railway; worked by Caledonian Railway. Designed by Sir Robert McAlpine & Sons. Listed Grade B. Closed. Between Leadhills and Wanlockhead.

This late and unusual structure is on the section that served the highest village in Scotland, reaching on the way the highest point on any public railway worked by normal locomotives in Britain. The nicely-proportioned eight-span curved bridge has brick spandrels and piers and concrete arch rings characteristic of the designing firm. Sir Robert McAlpine & Sons pioneered the use of concrete for railway building in the 1890s, earning McAlpine the nickname 'Concrete Bob'.

MAUCHLINE

BALLOCHMYLE VIADUCT. Built 1846-48 for Glasgow Paisley Kilmarnock & Ayr Railway. Designed by Grainger & Miller. Listed Grade B. South of Mauchline.

By any standards a most distinguished bridge, Ballochmyle is the apogee of early Scottish railway engineering. Its long semi-circular central arch of 181 feet is

WANLOCKHEAD VIADUCT, 1974

flanked on each side by three 50-foot semi-circular approach spans. The bridge is 163 feet above the river. As befits such a technically advanced structure, the detailing is sophisticated, with moulded voussoirs and tapering piers on either side of the main arch.

BALLOCHMYLE VIADUCT, 1970

Grainger & Miller's characteristic incised ornament extended to include inset panels in the spandrels of the main arch. The bridge spans the thickly wooded gorge of the Water of Ayr, and is best seen in winter.

MILNGAVIE

Opened 1863 by North British Railway. Listed Grade B.

The station offices of this three-platform terminus are on the up platform. The original single-storey stone building was extended in the late 19th century by the addition of attractive slated and glazed awnings. They are supported on cast-iron columns and lattice girders.

MILNGAVIE, 1971

MOTHERWELL

BRAIDHURST VIADUCT. Built 1849 for Clydesdale Junction Railway. Engineers Locke & Errington. Listed Grade B. About a mile north of Motherwell station.

The Clydesdale Junction line gave the Caledonian a shorter route to Glasgow than the original line via Coatbridge. It ran from Motherwell to Rutherglen, where it linked with the Polloc & Govan Railway which gave access to South Side station in Glasgow, long demolished.

1976

This viaduct is of rock-faced masonry, with nine semi-circular spans of unusually slender appearance. It bridges the North Calder Water where it runs through a wooded valley – now part of Strathclyde Park, a large local authority recreation area formed in the 1970s out of derelict and under-used land.

OLD CUMNOCK

TEMPLAND VIADUCT. Built 1848 for Glasgow Paisley Kilmarnock & Ayr Railway. Designed by Grainger & Miller. Listed Grade B. North of Cumnock station.

Though not as spectacular as Ballochmyle, Templand is a very fine example of Grainger & Miller's work. It has 14 spans, all with semi-circular arches, and is 145 feet above the Lugar Water. The thickly wooded slopes of the valley tend to disguise the remarkable scale of this viaduct.

PAISLEY

GILMOUR STREET STATION. Built 1839 by Glasgow & Paisley Joint Railway. Extended early 1890s. Architect for extension probably James Miller. Conservation Area.

This station marked the limit of the Glasgow & Paisley Joint Railway, and was originally a two-platform through station on a viaduct, with the entrance in a two-storey castellated building, designed to match the nearby Renfrew County Offices and Jail. The original entrance survives, together with an extension in the same style, as does the large, segmental-arched viaduct over the River Cart. The rest of the station was obliterated when the joint line was quadrupled in the early 1890s. It now consists of four platforms, two each for the Ayr and Greenock lines, with attractive light steel-framed glazed awnings and wood and red sandstone screen walls at platform level. The wooden parts are notable for exactly matching the moulded stonework.

Of interest as a group are the surviving road underbridges of the Glasgow Paisley & Greenock Railway. The most striking is the sharply skewed Underwood Road bridge. The railway bridge at Blackhall was built as an aqueduct for the Glasgow Paisley & Ardrossan Canal in c.1810 and converted for rail use in 1885. Its engineer was John Rennie.

GILMOUR STREET, 1966

FORMER AQUEDUCT AT BLACKHALL, 1966

ANCIENT MONUMENTS ON RAILWAY LAND

The railways built many fine structures which are now of historic interest, as this book describes, but in the days of their expansion, especially in the 1830s and 1840s, they also destroyed.

They ran right through prehistoric and Roman sites, including for example a stone circle at Shap and a fort at Ravenglass; cut across the town of Flint, destroying the 13th-century grid pattern of its streets; partly demolished castles at Berwick and Newcastle, Huntingdon, Clare and later Northampton; and at Shrewsbury left intact nothing of the 14th-century abbey except the refectory pulpit (*see p.91*).

Many of the remnants of these early buildings are still in railway ownership, reminders of Victorian vandalism now officially preserved as Ancient Monuments. A few later constructions on railway land, including Second World War tank traps at Christchurch, are similarly protected.

Railways also posed a much more extensive threat to urban amenities and the rural landscape. Perth narrowly escaped having a line across the South Inch, and in London the bridge over Ludgate Hill was allowed to impair the great view of St. Paul's from the west (prompting *Punch's* suggestion in 1863 of turning the cathedral into a station).

But people had begun to recognize long before that the railways might have to be curbed. In 1833 the London & Birmingham Railway had to accept a statutory protection accorded to Berkhamsted Castle. Maumbury Rings at Dorchester was saved in 1846 by vigorous local protest.

By the 1880s the tide was turning. Plans for putting railways across the Lower Close at Norwich, through the Avenue at Stonehenge and high above Aysgarth Force in Wensleydale were all defeated. The Central London tube railway in the 1890s was refused permission to have the Mansion House removed to the Embankment and to demolish Hawksmoor's church of St. Mary Woolnoth.

The policies of protection which apply to so many railway buildings today owe their formulation in large measure to this series of challenges which took place during the building of the early network a century and more ago.

Refectory Pulpit, Shrewsbury

Tank traps, Christchurch

PINMORE

KINCLAIR VIADUCT. Built 1877 for Girvan & Portpatrick Railway. Listed Grade B. Between Pinmore and Pinwherry.

Set in lovely wooded countryside, this handsome ten-span viaduct built on a curve with semi-circular arches is of masonry construction with dressed stone arch rings, coursed rubble piers and random rubble spandrels. The Glasgow & South Western Railway intended that this branch line, which is still in use, should connect Girvan with Portpatrick for sailings to Ireland.

SALTCOATS

Built 1894 by Glasgow & South Western Railway. Listed Grade B.

Saltcoats is quite different in style from other Glasgow & South Western stations of the same period. The main offices and station house are on the down platform in a dignified two-storey red sandstone block, vaguely Renaissance in style, with round-headed openings on the ground floor and pedimented doorways. There is a single-storey extension housing a wait-

1974

ing room – a treatment that is repeated on the up platform, where there is a fine bracketed glazed awning. The solid, settled appearance of the station was probably designed to suit a resort which was at the same time conscious of its civic status and of its dignity as a port.

STEWARTON

ANNICK WATER VIADUCT. Built 1873 by Glasgow Barrhead & Kilmarnock Joint Railway. Listed Grade B. South of Stewarton station between Neilston and Kilmarnock.

This sturdy, ten-span masonry viaduct is constructed of rock-faced ashlar with a moulded string course, and carries the line on a curve over a small stream. The Glasgow Barrhead & Kilmarnock Joint Railway was promoted jointly by the Caledonian and the Glasgow & South Western Railway, whose original route to

PINMORE, 1976

ANNICK WATER VIADUCT, 1967

Kilmarnock via Dalry was rather indirect. The new line ran from Neilston to Kilmarnock via Stewarton and Kilmaurs, and immediately became the Glasgow & South Western's main route to the south, enabling it to develop such effective links with the Midland Railway in England that a new Glasgow terminus, St. Enoch, was built later in the 1870s to handle the extra traffic.

TARBOLTON

BRIDGE NEAR MONTGOMERIE POLICIES. Built 1870 by Glasgow & South Western Railway. Listed Grade B. Between Ayr and Mauchline.

This handsome bridge over a main road consists of a single elliptical arch, a form rare in railway bridges north of the border. The voussoirs are bordered by a

MONTGOMERIE POLICIES BRIDGE, 1976

TROON

Rebuilt 1892 for Glasgow & South Western Railway. Designed by James Miller.

This fine early example of the architect's 'seaside' style has single-storey 'Domestic Revival' buildings on both platforms in timber framing with external rendering. Elegant steel-framed awnings and a covered footbridge complete the station. The treatment is most appropriate to what was at the time a developing middle-class holiday resort and residential town with several fine golf courses. Prestwick, built perhaps a little later, is a more modest example of a similar type.

TURNBERRY

HOTEL. Built 1905 for Glasgow & South Western Railway. Architect James Miller. Listed Grade B. On the coast south-west of Ayr.

The hotel was built as a golfing centre and the Maidens & Dunure Light Railway was opened at the same time with a station close by. The northern part of the line finally closed in 1933 but the section from Girvan to Turnberry remained open until 1942 mainly for the hotel.

The hotel has restrained Queen Anne features in the gables and fenestration. The projecting main entrance is formed by a striking pavilion with columns.

TROON, 1976

moulded course, and there are inset panels in the spandrels and in the parapet, which has a moulded coping. The wing walls are of rusticated ashlar. The bridge was presumably designed to grace the proportions of a fine late 18th-century house, now demolished.

FAILFORD VIADUCT. Built 1870 by Glasgow & South Western Railway. Listed Grade B. Between Ayr and Mauchline.

On the Glasgow & South Western's 'Ayrshire Lines' stands a rock-faced masonry viaduct with nine semi-circular arches, crossing a wooded valley. Most unusually, the piers are built with alternate broad and narrow bands of masonry. Parts of the spandrels of four of the arches have been renewed in brick.

TROON, 1976

FAILFORD VIADUCT, 1976

RAILWAY HOTELS

The railway hotel was an institution long renowned for a high standard of comfort and service. The earliest, completed at Derby in 1841, was the first purpose-built hotel in the world, and that at York was the first to form part of station buildings.

In the 1850s the great luxury railway hotels began to open, starting with the Great Western at Paddington and setting a pattern for hotel development at home and overseas. The opening of the remodelled Great Eastern Hotel at Liverpool Street was sufficiently newsworthy to fill 39 pages of a leather-bound volume with press cuttings and drawings. Probably the finest railway hotel in its day was the Midland Grand at St. Pancras. Many are still in operation, displaying the opulence which was an essential part of railway travel in the grand manner.

Diners inaugurate the grill room of the Great Eastern Hotel, reopened after modernisation on 7th December, 1901.

Lawns with urns and statuary surround the Park Hotel at Preston in 1896.

MR PERCY LINDLEY

The curved façade of the Great Northern Hotel at Kings Cross, designed by Lewis Cubitt, has hardly altered since this photograph was taken in the 1890s.

In the Great Eastern Hotel, white tie and cigars complement the sumptuous interior of the Dining Room designed by Colonel Robert Edis at the turn of the century and still in use today.

Guests converse in front of the Tregenna Castle Hotel, St. Ives, in 1896, a year after this Georgian country house was acquired by the Great Western Railway.

This advertisement by the North Eastern Railway appeared in about 1910. The company also ran the Station Hotel at Newcastle-on-Tyne, the Zetland in Saltburn and the Grand at West Hartlepool.

Antimacassars, reading desks and gas chandeliers complete the spectacular magnificence of the coffee lounge at the Midland Grand Hotel, St. Pancras, soon after its opening in 1873. The hotel, designed by Sir George Gilbert Scott, was one of the first to have lifts; they were worked by hydraulic power and were known as 'ascending rooms'.

141

WEMYSS BAY

*Rebuilt 1903 for Caledonian Railway.
Designed by James Miller and Donald
Mathieson. Listed Grade B.*

Wemyss Bay has been described as
Scotland's most beautiful station. It
acquires its special character from the
curving lines of the platforms, covered
walkway, concourse and booking office.
The designers were working at the same
time on the rebuilding of Glasgow
Central, and Mathieson's views on passenger flow, influenced by a visit to the
United States, conditioned both designs.

In each case straight lines were avoided,
and extensive use was made of light steel
construction and roof glazing.

Externally the station is treated in
Miller's developed 'Domestic Revival'
rustic style, with sandstone footings,
rendered and pseudo-half-timbered
upper walls and steep gables.

The complex is dominated by a tall
clock tower of Italianate design. The
wooden covered way to the steamers ends
in an arch flanked by a pair of stumpy
'Glasgow Movement' Japanese-style
towers.

Perhaps the best feature of this outstanding station is the concourse with its
circular booking office and strikingly
curved fan-like roof glazing. When the
station is decorated with hanging flower
baskets in the summer, no finer introduction to a seaside holiday can be imagined.

WEST KILBRIDE

*Rebuilt c. 1900 for Glasgow & South Western
Railway. Designed probably by James Miller.*

Another rebuild, this is a mature example
of the Arts and Crafts style as applied to
station building. The main offices on the

1974

down platform have inward-sloping
rustic rubble walls up to a height of about
four feet, then white rendering, with discreet timbering in the gables. There are
tapering, rendered chimney stacks.
Though modest in scale, and to some extent modernized on the platform side, this
is a wholly delightful building, designed
for a select 'suburb by the sea'.

WEMYSS BAY, 1971

WEMYSS BAY, c.1903

142

THE NORTH BRITISH RAILWAY

A railway with such a fine station as Edinburgh Waverley for its headquarters and containing within its network such tremendous constructions as the Forth and Tay bridges could be considered outstanding on these counts alone. The North British was also the largest of the Scottish systems with a monopoly of most of eastern Scotland, including the whole of Fife, and its coal traffic was particularly important.

But from the passengers' point of view, during the 19th century at least, it was not a very good railway. Its trains were notoriously unpunctual. Much of its trouble arose from the piecemeal construction of Waverley station. The site, in the ravine between the old and new towns, was constrained by a narrow-arched bridge, and the interlinking between the North British and the original Edinburgh & Glasgow stations was unsatisfactory. Complete rebuilding took place at the turn of the century.

Ferry crossings caused delays before the building of the bridges over the Forth and Tay. The second Tay Bridge, opened in 1887 to replace the poorly designed and badly constructed original one that collapsed in December 1879 (*p.157*), was notable at the time as the longest railway bridge in the world. It represented one part of the company's ambitious scheme for shortening the journey from Edinburgh to Dundee and Aberdeen.

Another was the expedient of bypassing the Forth ferry. In the 1880s through trains made a long diversion to the west, for which they had special running powers over tracks belonging to the Caledonian. Finally, in 1890, came the building of the gigantic cantilever Forth Bridge, undertaken in conjunction with three other railways. One of them, surprisingly, was the Midland Railway, which was keen to develop an Anglo-Scottish service to places north of Edinburgh; it accepted the highest proportion of liability in the Forth Bridge

Company: 32½ per cent. The North British Railway accepted 30 per cent liability; the Great Northern and North Eastern Railways each 18¾ per cent.

In the 20th century, North British passenger locomotives were distinguished by their attractive names. The standard express 4-4-0s were named after characters in Sir Walter Scott's 'Waverley' novels, and the smaller wheeled 4-4-0s, designed for the West Highland line, after glens lying on or near the route.

The large and powerful 'Atlantic' engines, used on the Midland trains between Edinburgh and Carlisle and on the East Coast main line north of Edinburgh, had a miscellany of fine names appropriate to their routes – such as *Aberdonian*, *Thane of Fife*, *Liddesdale* and *Borderer*. One of the 4-4-0s, *Glen Douglas*, has been preserved, as has the goods locomotive *Maude* which served in France during the First World War.

North British 4-4-0 Glen Douglas

LOTHIAN

DALKEITH

GLENESK VIADUCT. Built 1847 for North British Railway. Engineer John Miller of Grainger & Miller. Listed Grade B. Closed.

A single large semi-circular arch carries the Hawick branch line of the North British Railway over the River North Esk. The masonry is of the good quality generally associated with the firm of Grainger & Miller, but owing to subsequent mining subsidence it has been strengthened with steel centering. The line was closed to passengers in 1969 during the Beeching era and the track has been removed.

GLENESK VIADUCT, 1974

FORTH BRIDGE

Built 1882-90 for Forth Bridge Railway Company, a consortium of the North British, Great Northern, North Eastern and Midland Railways. Engineers Sir John Fowler and Sir Benjamin Baker. Listed Grade A. DALMENY Platform buildings and station office listed Grade B.

Probably the best known bridge in Britain, the Forth Bridge owes its striking appearance to an Admiralty requirement that under any railway crossing of the firth there should be adequate headroom and manoeuvring space for warships. Crossing by bridge at first seemed impracticable; but by the 1870s greater experience with large wrought-iron bridges led the railway companies to consider a number of designs and investigated several sites.

The point chosen was that of the medieval ferry between Lothian and Fife, known as the Queen's Ferry after the 11th century Saint Margaret, consort of King Malcolm III. Work was actually started on a suspension bridge of unparalleled size designed by Sir Thomas Bouch in 1873, but the collapse of his Tay Bridge (*p.157*) undermined his reputation and work stopped in 1880. The stump of one pier survives and still carries a small lighthouse.

A new design was prepared by Sir John Fowler. Consisting of three giant double cantilevers with truss approach spans, it was constructed of steel – the first large bridge built of this material. Preparing the cantilever bases took a long time, but the erection of the steelwork took only three years. The material was prepared at Dalmeny with the use of many specialised machines.

Opened in 1890, the bridge is of massive proportions. The two main spans are 567 yards long. The height to the top of the towers is 361 feet, and the headroom at the centre of each span is 150 feet. The bridge's total length is 1 mile 1,005 yards; 51,000 tons of steel were used in its construction. Even the approach viaducts are vast. On the south there are ten spans of 168 feet, four arches of 66 feet and abutments 34 feet wide, while on the north there are five 168-foot spans and three arches. The steel truss spans stand on solid granite piers. The cost was about £3,000,000.

New approach lines for the bridge were built from both north and south. The southern approach lines converge at Dalmeny station, where the single-storey stone office of the Forth Bridge Railway Company, now disused, still stands nearby. On the north side, the main line runs through Inverkeithing and skirts the Firth of Forth to join the old Edinburgh & Northern route at Burntisland.

Dalmeny station is an attractive wooden structure with delicate awning decoration.

Forth Bridge under construction, c.1888

Forth Bridge, c.1900

LNER Class D29 4-4-0 Ivanhoe *crossing Forth Bridge with Stirling to Edinburgh train*

DREM, 1976

RIVER ALMOND VIADUCT, 1983

DREM

Built 1846 by North British Railway. Station footbridge and road overbridge listed Grade B. Edinburgh to Berwick line.

This wayside station has the single storey and U-plan design, with flanking wings, typical of the original North British main line. It became the junction for North Berwick when that branch was opened in 1849-50. A characteristic lattice girder footbridge and a masonry road overbridge were added later in the century. The station is remarkable for having survived in such an unspoilt condition.

DRUMSHORELAND

BIRDSMILL VIADUCT. Built 1849 for Edinburgh & Bathgate Railway. Engineer probably John Miller. Listed Grade B. Between Ratho and Bathgate.

This viaduct, which spans the valley of the Almond, consists of eight segmental arches, constructed of rock-faced ashlar with a moulded string course below the

1983

parapet. The masonry has been patched quite extensively in blue brick. From 1870 the line it carries was part of an alternative route from Edinburgh to Glasgow. It closed to passengers in 1955, but is still used for freight.

DUNBAR

Built 1846 by North British Railway. Between Edinburgh and Berwick.

A two-platform through station on a curve, Dunbar has its main offices and station house on the up side. The two-storey red sandstone building is in the Scottish Tudor style favoured by the North British Railway. The offices have been modernized, but the general character of the building has been little affected, and is enhanced by flower displays in summer.

EAST CALDER

VIADUCT OVER RIVER ALMOND. Built 1885 by North British Railway. Listed Grade B. On branch mineral railway from Uphall to Camps. Closed.

Picturesquely sited in the wooded valley of the Almond, now part of Almondell Country Park, stands a nine-arched via-

DUNBAR, 1973

DUNBAR, 1976

duct on tall snecked rubble piers with brick arch rings six courses thick. The low masonry parapets are surmounted by iron railings. The viaduct spans both the river and the main feeder to the Union Canal, owned from the 1840s to 1948 by the Edinburgh & Glasgow Railway and its successors.

EAST LINTON

Built 1846 by North British Railway. Edinburgh to Berwick line. Closed.

The station's main offices were originally in the handsome two-storey, five-bay ashlar building on the up platform. It has a castellated feature in the centre and a Georgian doorway with a glazed fanlight and pilasters, an unusual design which suggests that the station might have been a conversion of an existing house. There are also two small stone pavilions on the down platform, which were later connected by a wooden shelter. The building is now an occupied house once again.

EDINBURGH

Edinburgh was at one time well served by both long-distance and suburban train services, justifying two major stations, the Caledonian's Princes Street and the North British's Waverley. Attrition has removed all but one suburban service, and the main-line services are now concentrated at Waverley. Princes Street is closed, leaving the Caledonian Hotel stranded, as it were. But a number of other fine railway buildings survive.

WAVERLEY STATION. *Rebuilt 1892-1902 for North British Railway. Engineers Blyth & Westland.*

Waverley has 19 platforms laid out as a broad, spacious island (the widest in the country) with through lines on the outside long enough to take two full-length trains, and numerous bays at both ends. A subsidiary island platform for suburban trains lies outside the main station wall on the south side. When it was built Waverley had more platform accommodation than any other British station after Waterloo. The overall roof is of transverse ridge-and-furrow type, looking from above like a vast array of greenhouses, with steel girders supported on delicately decorated Corinthian iron columns. The elliptically curved end-screens are a familiar sight to travellers, and the ashlar stone side walls have blind arcading. The offices are in a large two-storey block in the centre of the complex, with a spacious booking hall which originally had a superb wooden booking office. The strikingly decorated glazed dome, ceiling and finely detailed sandstone features survive as a reminder of past glories. The North British war memorial faces platform 10.

WAVERLEY WITH NORTH BRITISH HOTEL, 1970s

In size Waverley is a great station, relatively modern in its concept, but with no real frontage. The sensitive site in the valley between Edinburgh's Old and New Towns, under the shadow of the castle on its rock, militated against a more spectacular structure. Previously the station had been a byword for congestion, made even worse by the increased traffic following the opening of the Tay and Forth Bridges, so that it was commonplace for through expresses to be an hour or more late; its notoriety even led to a leader in *The Times*.

The old station was really a combination of two earlier terminal stations back-to-back, the Edinburgh & Glasgow's and the North British's. The site was narrow and cramped, and among other factors the city authorities' opposition to further invasions in the valley and the Bank of Scotland's insistence on height restrictions under the law of servitude and ancient lights gave the railway no en-

couragement to rebuild. When they eventually decided there was no other solution, public clamour for improvements turned to protest when it was realised that a strip of Princes Street Gardens and additional tunnels under The Mound and Calton Hill would be required. Consequently the station was kept as low and unobtrusive as possible. The most attractive feature, in fact, is the three-span iron and steel North Bridge, which was built in 1896-97 by Blyth & Westland to replace the old, narrow arches and allow the new station to be completed.

NORTH BRITISH HOTEL. *Built 1902 for North British Railway. Architects Hamilton and George Beattie.*

After the Scott monument, the North British Hotel is probably the best known landmark in Princes Street and one of the most impressive turn-of-the-century buildings in Edinburgh. A very large cream sandstone block on a roughly square plan, it is built in a typically florid Edwardian French Renaissance style, with a huge, bulky clock tower. The hotel is five storeys high with attics and three basements, with frontages to Princes Street and to South Bridge overlooking Waverley Steps, the latter carrying most of the architectural embellishments including a bewildering array of Dutch dormers, pediments, and corner turrets piled one above the other.

Known generally as 'The NB', it is renowned for its solid comfort, to ensure which the North British board sent a committee on a grand tour of European hotels (they tried at least a dozen) to get ideas. They were most impressed by the Royal at Budapest but thought little of continental kitchens. Everything was done in the grand manner, including commissioning Professor Barr of Glasgow University to design the electrical equipment. He was told to ensure that no matter how many switches he installed in the bedrooms, only one light should be turned on. A special NB whisky was blended in the basement and sold at 6*d.* and 9*d.* a glass.

A lift goes down to the sub-basement from which a long corridor leads to a footbridge and second lift to the station platforms.

HAYMARKET STATION. *Built 1842 for Edinburgh & Glasgow Railway. Engineer John Miller.*

The original trainshed of 1842, which had a cast- and wrought-iron-framed roof on cast-iron columns linked by arches, was dismantled in 1982-83 and removed to the Scottish Railway Preservation Society's Bo'ness site for re-erection. This leaves the original frontage block, a handsome stone two-storey classical building in the Georgian manner of Edinburgh's New Town, with a four-column Doric portico

c.1980

and a central clock above the cornice, as the only part of note, standing above the railway and facing up Atholl Place. Apart from Cupar (*p.151*) this, the headquarters of Scotland's most significant early railway, is probably the most important early station building in the country. It was the first proper station in Edinburgh.

CALEDONIAN HOTEL. *Built 1903 for Caledonian Railway. Architects J.M. Peddie and G. Washington Browne.*

Sir William Tite designed a classical Edinburgh station for the Caledonian Railway and the foundation stone was laid with full masonic honours by the Duke of Atholl in 1847. That was as far as it got. When the line from Carstairs and the south was opened in 1848 a 'temporary' station was opened, followed by a second wooden station (also 'temporary') nearer Princes Street in 1870. Sir William Acworth in *The Railways of Scotland* called it 'a wooden shanty'. Fortunately it was burned down in 1890 while a proper

1983

station was being built, completed as Princes Street station in 1894. It was a terminus, with a high, curving ridge-and-furrow roof and its main entrance under the Caledonian Hotel on the corner of Lothian Road and Rutland Street. The station closed in 1965, leaving the hotel as the only reminder of the Caledonian Railway in central Edinburgh.

It is a massive red sandstone block, of four storeys plus an attic, on a triangular

LEITH CENTRAL, 1970

site and was designed to compete with the rival North British Hotel at the other end of Princes Street. Despite its bulk, the Caledonian is not an unpleasant building. The main frontage, with a large Dutch gable and some fair sculpture, provides a prominent feature at the apex of the site. Numerous matching gables and dormers overlook the streets along the sides, but otherwise it is plainer than the North British although its interior appointments were no less lavish. At the west end of the Rutland Street facade there is a good cast-iron double gateway, with wrought-iron gates which once led into Princes Street station.

LEITH CENTRAL STATION. Built 1903 by North British Railway. At the foot of Leith Walk. Closed.

Built in competition with the Caledonian Railway for Leith's suburban traffic, Leith Central is a massive structure, with a very heavy four-bay steel-framed, ridged roof with a deep end-screen, panelled ashlar walls, and a two-storey frontage with shops on the ground floor, round-headed windows at first floor level, and a fine clock tower. When the North British asked Leith Council to pay for the electricity to light the clock on the grounds that the general public benefited, the council agreed. It was a terminus from which trains ran to Waverley station, bringing passengers to the foot of long flights of steps up to Princes Street. Because of this inconvenient climb the branch succumbed first to the trams and then to the buses which deposited their patrons in Princes Street itself. Leith Central closed in 1952 and has been disused since the early 1970s.

SLATEFORD VIADUCT. Built 1848 for Caledonian Railway. Engineer Joseph Locke. Inglis Green Road.

This is a fine fourteen-span masonry viaduct across the Water of Leith, with

SLATEFORD VIADUCT, c.1975

segmental arches in rock-faced ashlar, which has been patched in brick. Apart from its interest as an early Caledonian Railway structure, the viaduct is notable for its proximity to the Edinburgh & Glasgow Union Canal's Slateford Aqueduct alongside, a juxtaposition unique north of the border which enables the constructional details to be easily seen.

WARRISTON ROAD BRIDGE. Built 1841-42 for Edinburgh Leith & Granton Railway. Designed by Grainger & Miller. Listed Grade B.

A very fine three-span bridge on the skew, with curved wingwalls, Warriston Road Bridge has ashlar masonry, and is of the high quality associated with Grainger & Miller. The detailing is particularly good, with pilasters separating the spans, a string course and rusticated voussoirs.

WARRISTON ROAD BRIDGE, 1970

ESKBANK & DALKEITH

Built 1847 for North British Railway. Designed by Grainger & Miller. Closed.

Originally known as Eskbank, the station was renamed when the short Dalkeith branch was closed to passengers in 1942. Until its closure in 1969, it was a two-platform through station, with the platforms in a cutting. The offices and station house were at ground level in a fine two-storey ashlar building in the Tudor style. This is a highly developed example: it has a double roof, moulded drip courses above the windows, most of which are mullioned, and a handsome porch with a doorway in Perpendicular Gothic style.

GLENCORSE VIADUCT

Built 1872 by Penicuick Railway. Listed Grade B. On branch line from Millerhill. Closed.

Spanning the broad, shallow valley of the River North Esk close to Glencorse Bar-

1983

racks is a viaduct with 16 semi-circular arches. Built, unusually for a Scottish viaduct, of brick, it is a pleasing feature in the landscape.

LASSWADE

VIADUCT OVER BILSTON BURN. Built 1872 by Penicuick Railway. Listed Grade B. On branch to Polton. Closed.

In a thickly wooded valley, overshadowed on the west by the massive waste-heaps of Bilston Glen Colliery, stands a bridge unique in Scotland and extraordinary by any standards. It consists of a single deep

1983

wrought-iron truss, supported on low abutments and carrying the line along the top. A second pair of massive abutments support the line at high level on either side of the truss.

LINLITHGOW

STATION. Built 1842 by Edinburgh & Glasgow Railway.

The main offices of this two-platform through station are in a two-storey sandstone building. The station is built on a walled embankment, with the entrance at the lower level and the waiting rooms in an extension at the upper level. The plat-

1966

forms are linked by a vaulted subway. Despite alterations to the interiors and to the platform facade in the late Victorian period and again in 1964-65, Linlithgow remains the best preserved original through station built by the Edinburgh & Glasgow Railway.

AVON VIADUCT. Built 1842 for Edinburgh & Glasgow Railway. Engineers Grainger & Miller. Listed Grade A and Ancient Monument.

1974

This handsome 26-span viaduct over the Avon valley has 20 segmental arches with three semi-circular arches at each end. Made of ashlar throughout, it was originally built with hollow spandrels, but the voids were filled with lightweight concrete when the line was upgraded in the 1960s. In addition, the arch centres are now radially braced with old rails.

WALL AT HEAD OF LION WELL WYND. Built 1842 for Edinburgh & Glasgow Railway. Engineers Grainger & Miller. Listed Grade C(S). West of Linlithgow station.

This retaining wall carries the main line of the railway, with ramps leading to a delightful original cast-iron footbridge of slightly arched form. It forms a picturesque contribution to the medieval town.

LONGNIDDRY

ST. GERMAINS LEVEL CROSSING HOUSE. Built 1846 by North British Railway. Listed Grade B. Between Longniddry and Drem.

1974

The crossing keeper at St. Germains was provided with a neat little single-storey stone cottage with prominent low-pitched roofs in the Italian manner. The snecked rubble masonry is of high quality. It is built on an L-plan and in the angle of the L there is a little wooden office. The crossing, a minor one used mainly by pedestrians, was superseded by a footbridge in the late 1970s.

MIDCALDER

VIADUCTS OVER LINHOUSE WATER. Built 1848 and 1869 for Caledonian Railway. Earlier viaduct: engineer Joseph Locke, listed Grade A.

These two six-span masonry viaducts are situated about a mile apart. The earlier, southern one, is on the main line of the Caledonian Railway from Carstairs to Edinburgh, while the other is on that railway's route from Edinburgh to Glas-

EARLIER VIADUCT AT MIDCALDER, 1983

gow via Shotts, opened for inter-city traffic to compete with the Edinburgh & Glasgow Railway. The earlier viaduct is beautifully situated in open country in which it forms a notable feature. As with other Locke viaducts, the masonry is all rock-faced. The later bridge, in a narrow wooded gorge and more difficult to see, is similar in character. Both have semi-circular arches and are still in sound and original condition.

NEWTONGRANGE

LOTHIAN BRIDGE. Built 1847 for North British Railway. Engineer John Miller of Grainger & Miller. Listed Grade B. Closed and sold. Near Lady Victoria Colliery.

This 23-span viaduct was built to carry the Hawick branch of the North British over the River South Esk. The semi-circular arch rings of all but one of the spans are of brick, but the skewed road arch at the south end has a polished ashlar arch ring, and is flanked by battered pilasters. The spandrels are rock-faced and the piers – which have all been braced with old rails – are of ashlar.

RATHO

ALMOND VIADUCT. Built 1842 for Edinburgh & Glasgow Railway. Engineers Grainger & Miller. Listed Grade A.

1976

The longest bridge on the Edinburgh & Glasgow line, this superb curved masonry viaduct is similar in construction and later strengthening to the Avon Viaduct at Linlithgow (p.148). Its 36 arches span the valley of the River Almond, which is at this point wide and shallow.

VIADUCT OVER NEWBRIDGE TO BROXBURN ROAD (A89). Built 1842 for Edinburgh & Glasgow Railway. Engineer John Miller. Listed Grade A.

When first opened, this must have been one of the most striking viaducts in Scotland. Unlike the other Edinburgh & Glasgow bridges it has a wide central arch flanked by three standard arches on each side, with abutments decorated with incised ornament in typical Miller style. The central span has for long showed signs of settlement, which has been cured

1983

by the effective if unsightly expedient of casing the piers in blue engineering brick and inserting steel centering and tie-rods. These modifications have considerable technical interest.

WESTFIELD

AVON VIADUCT. Built c.1850 by Monkland Railways. Listed Grade B.

This 12-span masonry viaduct is a handsome structure for a single line, made of rock-faced ashlar, with brick arch rings behind ashlar voussoirs. It has a polished ashlar double string course and cast-iron radial bracing plates at the arch heads.

CENTRAL

BO'NESS

BIRCHILL VIADUCT. Built 1851 by Slamannan & Bo'ness Railway. Listed Grade B. On former Bo'ness branch from Manuel Junction. Closed.

Birchill is a six-span curved masonry viaduct with semi-circular arches. The arch rings are of polished ashlar and the piers and abutments of rock-faced masonry. The low parapet, above a moulded

1976

string course, is surmounted by an iron railing. The viaduct crosses the River Avon at a point where it runs in a deep wooded gorge. It has been leased with three miles of track and the trackbed of the rest of the branch by the Scottish Railway Preservation Society for operation as a steam-worked line.

CASTLECARY VIADUCT

Built 1842 for Edinburgh & Glasgow Railway. Engineers Grainger & Miller. Listed Grade B. Between Croy and Falkirk.

1974

This eight-span viaduct in rusticated ashlar, with a moulded string course, is in the same style as other viaducts on the Edinburgh & Glasgow. Like them it is also strengthened with concrete and iron braces. Originally over the Red Burn and a turnpike road, this viaduct now spans the main A80 road from Glasgow to Stirling.

DOUNE

Built 1858 by Dunblane Doune & Callander Railway. Station house listed Grade C (S).

The Dunblane Doune & Callander Railway was built to link the growing tourist resort of Callander with the Scottish Central Railway at Dunblane. The principal intermediate station was at Doune, whose castle was the seat of the Earls of Moray, famed in Scottish traditional song.

The station house is a picturesque single-storey building constructed of snecked rubble with rock-faced dressings. It has a gabled entrance and prominent eaves with barge boards.

1981

DUNBLANE

STATION. Built 1848 for Scottish Central Railway. Architect probably Andrew Heiton of Perth. Between Stirling and Perth.

Dunblane was an important three-platform station on the Scottish Central Railway, which functioned as an extension of the Caledonian Railway from just outside Coatbridge to Perth.

Like Larbert on the same line, it has a brick station house and offices with sandstone features, including crow-stepped gables, and is similar in style to the all-stone stations in Tayside, notably Greenloaning, Auchterarder and Forteviot, all now closed.

VIADUCT OVER ALLAN WATER (No. 4). Built 1848 for Scottish Central Railway. Engineer Joseph Locke. Listed Grade B. North of Bridge of Allan.

This fairly modest four-span bridge of rock-faced masonry crosses the broad, slow-flowing Allan Water in a pleasant, lightly wooded setting. It has segmental arches and stepped voussoirs of polished ashlar. The spandrels have been strengthened with tie-rods and plates.

TUNNEL MOUTH, OLD MILL OF KEIR. Built 1848 for Scottish Central Railway. Engineer Joseph Locke. Listed Grade B. North of Bridge of Allan.

This is a striking piece of railway architecture, with broad abutments flanking a vertical elliptical arch, heavily rusticated. There is a moulded string course, with a low parapet above. It is similar in character to the tunnel mouth at Glasgow Buchanan Street which has now been obscured by infilling.

VIADUCT OVER ALLAN WATER

(No. 7). Built 1848 for Scottish Central Railway. Engineer Joseph Locke. Listed Grade B. South of Kippenross House.

The plate girder central span of this three-span bridge is presumably a late 19th-century replacement of an original wrought-iron or wooden structure. On either side there are masonry abutments pierced by small elliptical arches which have modestly castellated parapets. The voussoirs are rusticated, and the rest of the stonework rock-faced. The viaduct is in a pleasantly wooded location.

FALKIRK GRAHAMSTON

Built c.1848 by Stirlingshire Midland Junction Railway. Between Carmuirs Junction and Polmont.

1980

The original offices and station house of this two-platform station are in a two-storey brick building in Italianate style, with prominent eaves and ornamental bargeboards. Cast-iron and wood-framed awnings were added in the late 19th century, when a single-storey block of offices with a similar awning was constructed on the up (Edinburgh) platform.

GLENOGLE VIADUCT

Built by Callander & Oban Railway. North of Callander. Closed.

This 12-span masonry viaduct, spanning a depression in the side of the glen, is parallel to the lie of the land – a most unusual design feature. It is complemented by a similar three-span bridge

1978

just to the south. At this point the railway climbs up the glen to cross the pass leading west to Crianlarich. It was a difficult and dangerous stretch of line to construct, constantly threatened by avalanches of stones.

LARBERT VIADUCT, c.1971

LARBERT VIADUCT

Built 1848 for Scottish Central Railway. Engineer Joseph Locke. Listed Grade B. About half a mile south of Larbert station.

Locke constructed this 23-span masonry viaduct with brick arch rings faced in ashlar, rock-faced ashlar piers and spandrels, and a moulded string course. It crosses the valley of the Carron river, with a fine view to the north of Larbert's early Gothic Revival parish church. The spandrels have now been strengthened by bracing.

STIRLING

Rebuilt 1912 for Caledonian Railway. Architect James Miller. Listed Grade B. Glasgow to Perth line.

In a conscious reference to the original 1848 station of the Scottish Central Railway, designed by Perth architect Andrew Heiton, the new structure, a single-storey building of dressed stone, was given crow-stepped gables and crenellated wall heads; one gable bears the Scottish lion, others the date and initials. Inside there is a circular booking office in a matching concourse with a glass roof, similar to though smaller than Wemyss Bay (*p.142*).

STIRLING CONCOURSE, 1975

STIRLING BRIDGES, 1981

For years the station has been noted for its magnificent floral displays – flowers and potted plants adorn every flat space.

About half a mile north of Stirling station over the River Forth are two striking bridges. One (*on the left, above*) was built for the Caledonian Railway in c.1905 to replace an earlier bridge of 1848; the other was built for the North British Railway in c.1870.

Stirling was formerly served by the North British routes to Balloch, Dunfermline and Kinross, as well as by through and branch Caledonian trains.

STIRLING, 1975

FIFE

BURNTISLAND

*OLD STATION. Built 1847 for Edinburgh &
Northern Railway. Architect probably David
Bell. Ancient Monument. Closed.*

On the south side of the rather non-
descript station built to align with the
Forth Bridge approach line stands the
original southern terminal building of the
Edinburgh & Northern. This railway was
built to link Edinburgh with Dundee and
points north via ferries over the Forth and
Tay. The ferries, inaugurated in 1849 on
the initiative of Thomas Bouch, were the
first to carry railway vehicles in Europe
and, some say, in the world.

Burntisland was thus a transfer point,
and the building is classically handsome,
with a colonnade flanked by pedimented
porches. The upper floor is surmounted
by a prominent dentilled cornice. After
long use as railway offices, the station has
been disused since the late 1960s.

CUPAR

*Built 1847 for Edinburgh & Northern
Railway. Architect probably David Bell.
Station and road bridge listed Grade B.
Queensferry to Dundee line.*

Perhaps the most important surviving
early railway station in Scotland in terms
of architectural distinction and com-
pleteness is Cupar, a two-platform station
with the offices and house on the down
platform. The most attractive Italianate
buildings take the form of a two-storey
central block, with an oriel window above
a pair of elliptical arches, linked to two-
storey end pavilions by single-storey
wings. All are executed in sandstone
ashlar of high quality. On the platform
side is a wooden awning, running the full
length of the buildings, supported on cast-
iron columns with lotus capitals.

At the south end of the station the
tracks are crossed by a three-span road
bridge constructed of ashlar, with rusticated voussoirs, a moulded dentilled
string course and castellated end features.
North of the passenger station are the
goods facilities, which include a four-
storey sandstone rubble warehouse with
arched stores underneath, and a range of
compartments below the track for the coal
that came from West Fife, also executed
in masonry. These staithes into which
coal was dropped from bottom-opening
wagons were fairly common on early
Scottish and north-east English railways.

KINGHORN

*Built 1847 for Edinburgh & Northern
Railway. Architect probably David Bell.
Queensferry to Dundee line.*

CUPAR, 1967

CUPAR GOODS WAREHOUSE, 1967

A modest example of an Edinburgh &
Northern station, this one has the house
and offices on the down platform in a
two-storey sandstone ashlar building
with a street frontage in the Tudor style.
On the platform side is a wooden awning
which has been boxed in to form a shelter.

KIRKCALDY

*INVERTIEL VIADUCT. Built 1847 for
Edinburgh & Northern Railway. Engineers*
*Bouch & Grainger. Listed Grade B. About a
mile west of Kirkcaldy station.*

Crossing the highly industrialized valley
of the Tiel Burn, this nine-span masonry
viaduct is on the E&N's main line. It has
seven large segmental arches, flanked by
single smaller spans, all executed in rock-
faced masonry. Kirkcaldy used to be
notorious for the smell of linseed oil from
its linoleum factories, but this end of the
town was more notable for its linen mills,
ropeworks and brewery.

KINGHORN, 1977

LADYBANK, 1971

LADYBANK SHED AND OFFICES, 1971

LADYBANK

Built 1847 for Edinburgh & Northern Railway. Architect probably David Bell. Main west block of station listed Grade A. East block, former lodge & ticket office on east platform and workshop all listed Grade B.

Ladybank is an important intermediate station on the Edinburgh & Northern, where the line to Perth diverges from the main route to the north. The office and station house are on the down platform in a two- and three-storey ashlar block, with the platform at first-floor level. There is a wooden awning supported on cast-iron columns. Though the design is basically simple Italianate, the massing of the building is most effective. On the up platform there is a wood and brick waiting room of typical late North British design, with an awning on cast-iron brackets.

In the angle between the Perth and Dundee lines stand a four-track shed in sandstone rubble with arched doors and a two-storey office block in snecked rubble, latterly used as a signal and telegraph works, but originally probably a carriage shed. Both offices and shed have cast-iron diamond-paned window frames. They are unique examples of early railway workshops in Scotland.

LARGO VIADUCT

Built 1857 by East of Fife Railway. In the centre of Lower Largo village. Conservation area. Closed.

A handsome viaduct for a single line, this four-span structure is built of finely

dressed ashlar. The line formed part of the North British Railway's Fife coast route to St. Andrews, opened in stages in the 1850s and 1860s. The line was closed in 1964, but the viaduct survives, dominating the attractive village where Alexander Selkirk, the inspiration for Defoe's Robinson Crusoe, was born.

LARGO VIADUCT, 1977

LESLIE VIADUCT

Built 1861 for Leslie Railway. Engineer Thomas Bouch. About half a mile south of Leslie village. Closed.

This very attractive single-line viaduct carried a goods-only line. Now used as a footbridge, it has remarkably slender piers and, unusually in Scotland, elliptical arches.

LESLIE VIADUCT, 1977

MARKINCH

Built 1847 for Edinburgh & Northern Railway. Architect David Bell. Station and viaduct listed Grade B. Between Ladybank and Kirkcaldy.

A two-platform through station in a cut-

ting, Markinch has its main offices and house on the down side. The one- and two-storey ashlar building, Italianate in style, is most unusually elevated above the railway. There is even a wooden awning supported on cast-iron columns at the upper level, as well as a similar structure at platform level, which has been glazed to provide a waiting room.

South of the station is the Markinch Viaduct, with eight large central spans flanked by single smaller ones, all semi-circular, executed in rustic ashlar and strengthened with iron tie rods.

MARKINCH, c.1974

MARKINCH VIADUCT, 1965

BALBIRNIE VIADUCT. Built 1861 for Leslie Railway. Engineer Thomas Bouch. Listed Grade B. About a mile from Markinch station on the Leslie branch. Closed.

This ten-span viaduct passes over the river Leven with semi-circular arches made of rubble. The railway was promoted to serve the paper and linen mills of the small central Fife town of Leslie. For such a short line (only 6¼ miles in length) the engineering works were heavy.

SPRINGFIELD

Built 1847 for Edinburgh & Northern Railway. Architect probably David Bell.

Remarkably unspoiled for a small through station, the house and offices on the up platform are in a two-storey L-plan ashlar building in Tudor style. There is a timber awning on cast-iron columns. In

(*Continued on page 157*)

RAILWAY ART

Railways have attracted artists of many kinds, including Romantics and Impressionists among whom Turner and Monet were pre-eminent. J. C. Bourne's early lithographs are now valued as accurate pictorial records from the days before photography, while the highly detailed narrative painting so popular in the mid-19th century cannot be better exemplified than by William Frith's famous scene at Paddington station in 1862.

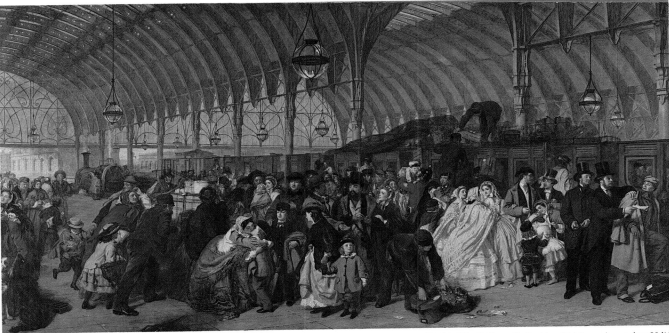

A view of Knaresborough Viaduct by R. D. Hodgson, engraved by J. C. Bourne in c.1846, makes a contrast to Frith's 'The Railway Station' in which he used more than 80 life models including members of his own family (his wife and son are kissing in the foreground) and a train with an engine modelled on the 1847 locomotive Sultan.

153

In his evocative sunset painting of St. Pancras from Pentonville Road in 1884, John O'Connor has exaggerated the height of Scott's soaring Gothic spires.

154

Commissioned to celebrate the centenary of Waterloo station in 1948, Helen McKie depicted the same scene during and after the Second World War. In war-time the roof is partly blacked out, the Guards are in khaki, and the green of the Southern Railway locomotives ('Merchant Navy' Class 4-6-2 in the foreground) is painted over.

(*Continued from page 152*)

the abandoned goods yard is a block of six coal staithes, similar in style to those at Cupar, but with the arches bricked in.

SPRINGFIELD, 1971

SIR THOMAS BOUCH, ENGINEER

Bouch was born in Cumberland in 1822, son of a sea-captain, and learned civil engineering on the Lancaster & Carlisle Railway under Locke and Errington, and on the Stockton & Darlington under Dixon. He left to become manager and engineer of the Edinburgh Perth & Dundee Railway where he devised wagon ferries for crossing the Forth and the Tay. He worked extensively in the north and south of England and in Scotland where he was responsible for over 260 miles of railway, including two very fine lofty iron trestle viaducts at Belah and Deepdale on the South Durham & Lancashire Union Railway (now demolished) and the Hownes Gill viaduct at Consett, Co. Durham (*p.42*) which is his chief surviving work.

His greatest achievement brought him fame, obloquy and death: the Tay Bridge, completed in 1877. In 1879, six months after he received a knighthood from Queen Victoria, the centre spans blew down in a gale while a train was crossing, with the loss of 75 lives. The shock was too much for him and he died the following year aged 58. A recent re-appraisal of the Tay Bridge disaster suggests that he may not have been so much at fault as people have thought.

TAY BRIDGE

Built 1870-78 for North British Railway. Engineer Sir Thomas Bouch. Partly destroyed 1879; rebuilt on a new site 1882-87. Engineers W. H. Barlow & Crawford Barlow.

The first Tay bridge was constructed to designs by Sir Thomas Bouch, who had been successfully constructing railways in Scotland since the 1850s, and whose large iron truss viaducts on the South Durham & Lancashire Union Railway had been both economical and stable. He was almost certainly chosen as engineer for the Tay Bridge because of his reputation for cheapness.

The bridge he designed had wrought-iron trusses which were to be carried on brick piers. In the event, the foundations proved inadequate for brick and so braced cast-iron columns were substituted in some instances. These were indifferently made on a narrow base, since the bridge was single track only. In the centre, in order to give the navigational clearance required by the Admiralty, the spans were higher – 79 feet above water level – and became known as the high girders.

The Firth of Tay is noted for its funnel-like effect on winds, and no previous bridge had been built to withstand the wind-forces that could be experienced there.

The night of 28th December 1879 a gust – estimated to be of hurricane proportions – struck the high girders just as a train was crossing them. They collapsed. The train fell into the river beneath, and all 75 people on board were killed.

The Tay Bridge collapse was one of the worst disasters in British railway history. All sorts of explanations for it have been put forward. In addition to insufficient allowance for wind-pressure, the subsequent enquiry established, among other things, that supervision of the work had been slack and faults in the iron columns concealed. The impression remains of poor design, slipshod construction and extraordinary weather conditions, all of which combined to create tragedy.

Bouch was held to blame, which cost him his reputation and led to his early death. The immediate repercussions were considerable. In Scotland, Bouch's contract for the Forth Bridge was cancelled, and two bridges at Montrose on a line designed to connect with the Tay Bridge were redesigned – one in brick and the other on riveted iron piers. Cast-iron work elsewhere was also critically examined.

A replacement bridge was essential and an Act obtained to go ahead in 1880. The new bridge was constructed on entirely new piers, on brick foundations. Many of the old girders were re-used, but the high girders were completely replaced by massive 245-foot and 227-foot trusses. The bridge consists of 74 spans – 13 over the central channel, 24 to the north shore and 37 to the south shore. With a length of 2 miles and 50 yards, it is still the longest bridge in Britain. Not unnaturally, its construction was much more substantial than the original, to counter public fears. After its completion, the piers of the old bridge were cut down to just above high water, where they are still visible downstream of the new.

TAY BRIDGE DISASTER, ENGRAVING, 1880; *inset* SECOND TAY BRIDGE FROM SOUTH, c.1912

TAYSIDE

ABERDALGIE VIADUCT

Rebuilt probably late 1860s for Caledonian Railway. Engineer probably George Graham. Between Perth and Auchterarder.

This is a good example of the first generation of wrought-iron truss bridges in Scotland. The three central spans are of bowed form supported on cylindrical cast-iron piers in rows of three. The only other surviving bridge of this kind is at Carstairs on the Caledonian main line.

Aberdalgie Viaduct was built originally by the Scottish Central Railway, opened in 1848 to link Castlecary and Perth on the west coast route to Aberdeen. Like its partners, the Caledonian, Scottish Midland Junction and Aberdeen railways, this company built its viaducts on the cheap. Hence when the Caledonian absorbed these northern lines it began a long programme of replacement and this bridge was one of the first to be renewed.

ARBROATH

Rebuilt 1911 for North British Railway. Engineer probably J. Carsewell.

Though lacking the style of contemporary stations on the Caledonian and Glasgow & South Western Railways, Arbroath is a well planned, solid station of its period, in character with its location.

It is a three-platform through station; the booking office is in a single-storey sandstone ashlar building on a bridge, and the single-storey stone and wood platform buildings have steel-framed awnings. The platforms are on a curve.

The station was originally the terminus of the Dundee & Arbroath Joint line opened in 1839, which became joint with the Caledonian when the North British Railway completed the first Tay Bridge in 1878. In the adjacent goods yard is a large stone shed which may well have been the original Arbroath & Forfar Railway engine shed.

BLACKFORD

KINCARDINE GLEN VIADUCT. Built 1848 for Scottish Central Railway. Engineers Locke & Errington. Listed Grade B. About half a mile south-west of Auchterarder station.

A handsome seven-span rock-faced masonry structure, this viaduct spans Ruthven Water and its wooded valley. It is difficult to see, as the only access is through a private estate. The six main arches are semi-circular on tapering piers, and there is a small driveway arch at the west end.

ABERDALGIE VIADUCT, 1978

BLAIR ATHOLL

STATION. Built 1869 for Highland Railway. Listed Grade B. Perth to Inverness line.

The Inverness & Perth Junction Railway, absorbed into the Highland Railway in 1865, was designed to link the branch from Perth to Dunkeld with the Inverness & Aberdeen Junction Railway at Forres, forming a new main line to Inverness. The line was constructed as economically as possible, and the original station buildings were probably just temporary structures. Blair Atholl, a three-platform through station, appears to be the oldest surviving replacement.

It has a random stone central two-storey block flanked by single-storey wings with projecting end pavilions and a lean-to awning between them on plain iron columns. The southern wing was demolished in the early 1970s.

Blair Atholl retains its engine shed which was used to house engines to assist north-bound trains to reach Druimuachdar Summit, at 1,484 feet the highest altitude reached on a main line in Britain.

TILT VIADUCT. Built 1863 for Inverness & Perth Junction Railway. Engineer Joseph Mitchell. Listed Grade B. South of Blair Atholl station.

Mitchell pioneered the use of lattice truss bridges in Scotland, and this is a relatively modest example with a single span of 150 feet, now strengthened by triangular welded steel braces outside the original girders. It has castellated arches at each end, indicating its proximity to Blair Castle, seat of the Dukes of Atholl.

BLAIR ATHOLL, 1974

TILT VIADUCT, 1974

BRECHIN

Built 1847-48 for Aberdeen Railway; extended 1894-95 for Caledonian Railway. Architect for extension Thomas Barr. Listed Grade B. Closed.

At the end of a branch from Montrose which closed to passengers in 1951, Brechin is an attractive example of a Scottish branch line terminus. It has single-storey ashlar offices with wood and cast-iron awnings on street and platform sides. There is a central clock surmounted by a ball finial. The station house is a two-storey structure at the side.

BRECHIN, 1974

The building has been leased to the Brechin Railway Society for restoration as part of a project to develop a steam tourist railway.

CALVINE VIADUCT

Built 1863 for Inverness & Perth Junction Railway. Engineer Joseph Mitchell. North of Blair Atholl.

Mitchell took the opportunity to construct this bridge over an existing road bridge. It has a central 80-foot span flanked by two 40-foot spans, all semi-circular, and is built of rock-faced masonry, ashlar for the piers and rubble for the spandrels, with polished ashlar arch wings. The cut-waters are carried up to form battlemented features. A steel girder bridge was added on the east side in 1898.

CALVINE VIADUCT, 1974

DALGUISE VIADUCT, 1974

DALGUISE VIADUCT

Built 1863 for Inverness & Perth Junction Railway. Engineer Joseph Mitchell. Listed Grade B. Between Dunkeld and Pitlochry.

This monumental structure is superbly situated in the wooded valley of the Tay. The biggest of Mitchell's lattice-girder bridges, it has two spans, 210 feet and 141 feet long, and the piers are carried up to form castellated towers.

DUNKELD

DUNKELD & BIRNAM STATION. Built 1856 for Perth & Dunkeld Railway. Architect Andrew Heiton. Listed Grade B.

Originally the terminus of a branch from the Scottish North Eastern Railway at Stanley, Dunkeld became a through station when the Inverness & Perth Junction Railway was opened in 1863. The original building survives, though its

DUNKELD FRONTAGE, 1974

DUNKELD PLATFORM, 1974

HERMITAGE ROAD BRIDGE, 1976

trainshed has been replaced by a simple awning. In style it is Tudor, of a magnificence unique in Scotland. Particularly impressive are the carved bargeboards, arched porch, mullioned windows and stone chimneys.

INVER VIADUCT HERMITAGE ROAD BRIDGE and TUNNEL ENTRANCE. Built 1863 for Inverness & Perth Junction Railway. Engineer Joseph Mitchell. All listed Grade B. Between Dunkeld and Ballinluig.

Relatively modest in scale, these works were designed to harmonize with the wooded gorge of the river Braan, a tributary of the Tay, which was developed by the Dukes of Atholl from the late 18th century as a picturesque, romantic pleasure garden known as the Hermitage.

The viaduct is a single-span structure with flat segmental ashlar arch rings, rubble spandrels, and a low parapet with a raised central portion featuring a

INVER VIADUCT AND TUNNEL, 1971

decorative plaque. It leads north to the little semi-circular road arch, with rusticated voussoirs, rubble spandrels and a 'truncated pedimented parapet'. Immediately beyond is the tunnel mouth, again semi-circular, with curved rubble wing walls.

The Hermitage is now in the care of the National Trust for Scotland, so that the bridge and viaduct may readily be viewed.

ERROL

Built 1847 by Dundee & Perth Railway. Listed Grade B. Between Dundee and Perth.

The Dundee & Perth was planned as a branch connecting the Scottish Central at Perth with the thriving manufacturing town of Dundee. After 1848 it provided a through rail route to the south that was on the whole more convenient than the more direct line through Fife, with its ferries over the Forth and Tay estuaries.

1973

The route from Perth to Dundee did not call for any major engineering works, except the Tay viaduct at Perth. The stations were simple structures in the Italianate style. Errol, the best surviving example, has stylistic similarities to stations on the Edinburgh & Northern Railway. It is a two-platform station, with the offices and house in a one-storey-and-attic block on the down side, built of snecked rubble and completed by a wood and cast-iron awning.

GLENEAGLES

STATION. Rebuilt 1919 for Caledonian Railway. Architect James Miller. Station, footbridge, entrance block and car park wall all listed Grade B. Between Stirling and Perth.

The original station here was called Crieff Junction and was rebuilt to serve the new hotel to which it is connected by a beech-lined avenue. The station is in a restrained Edwardian domestic style with good

1976

woodwork, much rendering and unusual bow windows on the footbridge towers. The detached booking office has crow-stepped gables containing 'CR' and date monograms and, inside, a charming little Queen Anne booking window.

HOTEL. Built 1924 for Caledonian Railway.

Architect Matthew Adam. Opened by London Midland & Scottish Railway. Sold.

Gleneagles Hotel can be directly attributed to the vision of Donald Mathieson, general manager of the Caledonian, who played a leading part in the reconstruction of Glasgow Central station (*p.131*). Mathieson was so impressed with the beauty of Glen Eagles during a holiday in 1910 that he decided the railway ought to build a hotel there that would equal the fashionable spas of Europe. The result was Gleneagles Hotel. He interested himself in every detail of the planning, from the broad corridors, intimate little Georgian-styled shopping arcade and the magnificently elegant Edwardian banqueting room to the formal gardens. The finely panelled entrance lobby gives an immediate impression of quiet, restrained opulence, which is repeated in the spacious lounge with its panelled ceiling, marble columns and sweeping bay window looking out over Strathallan and up Glen Eagles itself.

The interior is to some extent belied by the rather plain, vaguely Queen Anne-styled exterior of this very rambling four-storey grey stone building, with a low square turret, dormer windows and a small curved pediment on the south front as almost its only embellishments.

Mathieson was also responsible for making Gleneagles one of the world's greatest golfing centres. He hired a famous golfer, James Braid, to lay out two courses. Since his time two more have been added. Owing to the intervention of the First World War, the hotel and its grounds were not completed until after the Caledonian became part of the LMS Railway in 1923.

GUTHRIE CASTLE

RAILWAY UNDERBRIDGE. Built 1839 by Arbroath & Forfar Railway. Listed Grade B. Between Arbroath and Forfar. Sold.

1974

This extraordinary bridge, convincingly disguised as a castellated entry to the castle's main drive, consists of a Perpendicular Gothic archway flanked by octagonal towers with castellated tops and lancet windows. Above the arch is a low-relief sculpture of a coat of arms and at the angles of the turrets at two levels there are corbels carved as faces.

The Arbroath & Forfar Railway, designed to link the textile town of Forfar with the existing Dundee & Arbroath line, was originally built to the 5 feet 6 inch gauge, but was converted to standard gauge when the Scottish Midland Junction Railway reached Forfar in 1848.

KILLIECRANKIE

VIADUCT and TUNNEL MOUTH. Built 1863 for Inverness & Perth Junction Railway. Engineer Joseph Mitchell. Both listed Grade B. Between Pitlochry and Blair Atholl.

KILLIECRANKIE VIADUCT, 1976

KILLIECRANKIE TUNNEL, 1976

The viaduct at the Pass of Killiecrankie stands on a slight curve with ten semi-circular arches, each of 35-foot span. The masonry is all rock-faced, semi-circular castellated projections decorate both the ends and the middle, and a dentilled string course runs below the parapet – details which Mitchell carefully designed to create a structure that would blend with the striking and historic scenery of the pass. On the whole he succeeded. The same treatment is carried into the mouth of the 128-yard tunnel adjoining the north end of the viaduct, quite an elaborate treatment for so short a tunnel.

LOGIERAIT VIADUCT

Built 1865 for Highland Railway. Engineer Joseph Mitchell. About a mile west of Ballinluig between Perth and Inverness. Closed.

1974

Carrying the former Aberfeldy branch over the Tay, this viaduct has two 137-foot iron lattice truss spans supported on cast-iron columns with short plate-girder side spans. A similar but shorter bridge over the Tummel about half a mile to the east was demolished in 1981; this one now carries a private road.

NEWTYLE

OLD STATION. Rebuilt c.1836 by Dundee & Newtyle Railway. Closed. North-west of Dundee.

A rubble-walled trainshed with a wood-framed overall roof and elliptical-arched entrances stands just north of the line of the Hatton incline, one of a series of rope-

1974

worked inclines that carried the Dundee & Newtyle over the Sidlaw Hills. After the line was acquired by the Caledonian, the route was altered to allow it to be worked by locomotives throughout. This station with its single-storey office wing then became a goods depot. Since closure in 1951, the shed has been a store.

NORTH WATER BRIDGE

VIADUCT. Built 1865 by Montrose & Bervie Railway. Listed Grade B. Near Hillside, just north of Montrose. Closed.

A striking masonry viaduct, this structure forms an interesting contrast to the splendid road bridge immediately upstream, built in 1770-75. It has five large slightly skewed arches over the River North Esk and six narrower arches, five at the north and one at the south end. The arch rings are of polished ashlar, and the piers and spandrels of rock-faced coursed rubble.

PERTH, EARLY 1900s

PERTH

STATION. Built 1847. Architect Sir William Tite. Extended 1865; from 1866 owned jointly by Caledonian, North British and Highland Railways.

Perth is a remarkable station in several respects, and is well named 'the Gateway to the Highlands'; before the Grouping of 1923 (*p.8*) it was here that enormous volumes of summer traffic were exchanged with the Highland Railway.

In the summer of 1923, for instance, 25 major long-distance expresses containing sleeping cars, Pullmans and through coaches to and from a wide variety of destinations were re-marshalled at Perth each day for the south-bound direction.

For its design Tite clearly copied many features from his station at Carlisle, particularly the generally Tudor styling and the turret. The main footbridge (added later) is virtually a replica of the Carlisle

PERTH GOODS, c.1980

footbridge.

The fine two-storey buildings have had several extensions over the years, and at one time housed three separate booking offices, for the Highland, the Caledonian and the North British. The old refreshment room still retains its Corinthian columns, deep panelled ceiling and marble fireplace, relics of more prosperous times.

VIADUCT AT NORTH WATER BRIDGE, 1974

THE HIGHLAND RAILWAY

This dramatic and finely constructed line was born at Inverness, with the object both of serving the far north and making connection with Perth to the south via the Pass of Druimuachdar, 1,462 feet high.

The plan of going over the pass, worked out by Joseph Mitchell, the engineer, was at first ridiculed on account of the steep gradients required, so the original section of the line, dating from the mid-1850s, was built over level country eastwards to Forres. Later, when he had overcome the opposition, Mitchell went due south and built his splendid line right over the mountains. Forty years later, the Highland built a new line from Aviemore directly to Inverness to shorten the route. The Forres line was closed in the 1960s.

By contrast, the line northwards from

Highland Railway Coat of Arms

Inverness followed the east coast and was therefore more easily graded. One exception is the inland detour north of Invershin, which necessitated some stiff climbing. In this area the Highland had two stations, Culrain and Invershin, which were only 1½ miles apart across the Kyle of Sutherland at each end of the Oykel Viaduct. But they are nearly 10 miles apart by the alternative route. When the basic third-class fare was a penny a mile, travelling over the viaduct made a good deal of difference to the cost: the only snag was that there were only three trains a day in each direction.

The route northwards from Inverness came into prominence during the First World War when the Grand Fleet was based at Scapa Flow and all supplies and personnel had to be hauled over this lonely single-tracked line. Loads were often very heavy, requiring two engines per train and straining the Highland's resources almost to breaking point.

Although the company did not possess a very large stud of locomotives, the ones they had were of robust design and very well maintained. For many years the traffic was worked largely by small 4-4-0s until in 1894 the Highland broke new ground with the 4-6-0 type, designed by David Jones. One of these famous 'Jones Goods' engines is still preserved in the Glasgow Museum. They and their successors of the 'Castle' class did a tremendous job with the heavy war-time traffic.

The Highland's final engine design was the 'Clan' class, introduced in 1919 and named after the clans Campbell, Fraser, Munro, Stewart, Chattan, MacKinnon, Mackenzie and Cameron. Superheated outside-cylindered 4-6-0s, they were ideal for hard slogging on severe gradients.

HR Clan Class 4-6-0 Clan Campbell, c.1920

with a bay window looking out on to the platform.

On the east side of the station two external platforms curve sharply away, covered by separate ridge-and-furrow awnings. They are used by the Dundee trains and today see more traffic than the main part of the station. In the angle between these platforms and the older part is the present main entrance (recently rebuilt) and the Station Hotel. This mildly Scottish Baronial-style building, built by the joint railways at the same time as the station, was at one time linked to the platforms by a private covered way.

GOODS STATION. Built by Caledonian Railway. North of passenger station.

The best surviving example of a large Victorian goods station in Scotland, rivalled only by Dundee West, this complex has as its most striking feature a two-storey red and white brick building housing the offices and transit shed. The openings are all segmental-arched, with chamfered edges. The little two by five bay weighhouse is in the same style.

PITLOCHRY

Built 1863 by Inverness & Perth Junction Railway; rebuilt c.1890 by Highland Railway. Between Perth and Blair Atholl.

Pitlochry is a two-platform station, with the main offices in a long single-storey range in the Highland Railway's developed Scottish Tudor style. As with other examples of the type (Nairn is the closest parallel) this takes the form of a U-plan building with ornamental gables and an awning filling the recess. Details

1974

include terracotta roof ridging, a variety of finials and tall ornamental chimney stacks. The down platform is similar to that at Nairn, constructed of wood with a bellcast roof and ornate iron cresting. On the up platform is a cast-iron drinking fountain surmounted by a figure of a heron, brought from Strathyre on the Callander & Oban Railway when that line closed in the late 1960s.

The main north-south platform is a broad island with a series of north and south-facing bays on the west side. It was converted from the original single platform in 1885, when Tite's frontage became partly hidden from the outside world by the present overall roof which originally extended right across the station to stone screen walls, but now only covers part of platforms 3 and 4. These screens are also similar to Carlisle's; the westernmost one contains filled-in windows and doors of the Scottish Central Railway offices which stood on

the other side.

The main concourse was on the west side, where the overall roof has been replaced by light Caledonian-style awnings, and here is a memorial to members of the Perth General Station Joint Staff who fell in the First World War.

In the east side screen wall an opening leads out to the carriage sheds beyond, and above it at one time there was an elevated signal box, Up Centre box, which was notoriously dirty as engines tended to stand beneath it. The Down Centre box was in part of the main block

GRAMPIAN

ABERDEEN

*STATION. Rebuilt 1913-16 by Caledonian
and Great North of Scotland Railways.
Engineer J. A. Parker.*

The early history of railways in Aberdeen
was stormy. There were two stations:
Guild Street, owned by the Aberdeen
Railway and opened in 1852; and the
Waterloo station of the Great North of
Scotland Railway opened in 1856. They
were about half a mile apart and connected only by a horse-operated line
along the quay for exchanging goods
traffic.

Passengers and mails were conveyed by
horse buses and vans. Delays were notorious, particularly as the Great North at
one period deliberately kept a particularly tight margin between arrival of
trains for the south and its departures for
the north which allowed only the bare
minimum of time for transit between the
stations. They refused to hold their trains
for late arrivals, and E. L. Ahrons writing
in *The Railway Magazine* in 1922 recalled
that the Great North staff would wait
until they could see passengers hurry
from Waterloo and then slam the gates
and give the 'right away' to the train.

Sense eventually prevailed and a new
Joint Station was opened in 1867, built by

ABERDEEN, 1970s

EAST GREEN VAULTS, 1981

ABERDEEN STATION HOTEL, 1983

the Caledonian (who had succeeded to
the Aberdeen Railway) and the Great
North, and to which the North British
was also admitted on sufferance by virtue
of its running powers from Kinnaber
Junction 36 miles to the south. By the turn
of the century the station had long out-
grown its capacity so the joint owners set
about rebuilding it. The result was the
present structure.

It is a very long station with a facade
comprising a chunky, lofty centrepiece in
cream sandstone having three large,
heavily rusticated semi-circular openings

between coupled pilasters, broad diamond-paned windows above, a dentilled
cornice and a solid parapet. Lower
flanking buildings are in granite and a
verandah runs the length of the frontage.
The former booking office is now a travel
centre, but the passageway to the concourse retains its nice elliptical domed
rooflight and panelled woodwork. The
spacious concourse has elliptical trusses
supporting a light glazed and ridged roof
with attractively glazed end-gables, and
the ladies' waiting room still has some
Edwardian panelling. The platforms
have ridged and glazed umbrella awnings
on trussed steelwork, in typical late-
Caledonian style.

There are two interesting signal boxes.
The Centre box on platforms 7 to 8 has an
awning column and brackets 'growing'
out of it, and is in Caledonian style, while
the North box is a Great North structure
with deep overhanging eaves.

*STATION HOTEL. Acquired by the Great
North of Scotland Railway in 1910. Listed
Grade B.*

The Great North had two hotels in
Aberdeen, the Station and the Palace
(burned down in 1941). The Station was
considered to be the commercial and
family hotel and stands opposite the railway station, as its name implies.

EAST GREEN VAULTS. Listed Grade B.

This remarkable series of masonry
vaulted chambers underneath Market

Street is one of the few instances where the
arches have been used to form a large
storage area. It is now used as a private
car park.

BALLATER

*Built 1866 by Aboyne & Braemar Railway;
subsequently extended. Closed.*

A single-storey wooden structure, with a
steel-framed glazed platform awning on
square panelled columns, the station at
Ballater originally housed a royal waiting
room, the *porte cochère* of which still
survives. It was the nearest station to
the royal family's Highland home at

1974

Balmoral, and the royal train regularly
stopped there.

Closed since 1965, the station buildings
are now used in part by a tourist information office and restaurant.

BALLINDALLOCH VIADUCT

*Built 1863 by Strathspey Railway. Closed.
Between Aviemore and Craigellachie.*

A fine lattice truss bridge over the river
Spey with a small plate-girder approach
span at each end, this is comparable in
scale and construction to Mitchell's Inverness & Perth Junction bridges but,
unlike them, Scottish built – by G.
McFarlane of Dundee. The approach
spans have most attractive interlaced
cast-iron railings. The Strathspey Rail-

BALLINDALLOCH VIADUCT, 1974

way met the Highland at Boat of Garten, but was operated by the Great North of Scotland Railway. It was closed in the Beeching era.

CARRON VIADUCT

Built 1863 by Strathspey Railway. Between Aviemore and Craigellachie.

A complete contrast to the technically advanced bridge at Ballindalloch, this is a combined road and rail bridge over the Spey, built in cast iron with three bridge ribs. The road is separated from the railway by a fence made of unusually thin cast-iron plates. On each side of the main span there are segmentally arched flood-relief spans. These and the abutments are of rock-faced ashlar.

ELGIN

OLD STATION. Rebuilt 1902 by Great North of Scotland Railway. Listed Grade B. Closed.

A conical-roofed corner turret, crow-stepped gables and oriel windows give this elaborate single-platform station a Scottish Baronial character. The main offices, still in railway use but closed to passengers since the 1960s, are in a remarkably large two-storey grey granite building, laid out on an H-plan with wings at both ends. On the platform side is a substantial glazed ridge-and-furrow awning.

The fine interior of the booking hall survives intact, its walls decorated with plaster pilasters and a dentilled cornice above a wooden panelled dado. Over the doors there are moulded pediments and the deeply coved ceiling has a large lantern-style light. The booking windows are similarly panelled and decorated, and in front of them the once-familiar short barriers have twisted barley-sugar struts.

ELGIN OLD STATION, 1971

ENGINE SHED. Built 1858 for Inverness & Aberdeen Junction Railway. Engineer Joseph Mitchell. Listed Grade C (S). On the eastern outskirts of Elgin.

A medium-sized two-track engine shed, one of the few surviving examples of the type in Scotland, this building is constructed of random rubble, with round-headed windows and doors and a circular ventilator in the front gable. At the rear there is a single-storey lean-to office block. Very typical of early engine sheds on what became the Highland Railway system, this structure is comparable with the engine sheds at Aviemore and Blair Atholl and with the Lochgorm Works at Inverness.

ELGIN ENGINE SHED, 1973

FORRES

FINDHORN VIADUCT. Built 1858 for Inverness & Aberdeen Junction Railway. Engineer Joseph Mitchell. West of Forres.

This three-span box girder bridge crosses the River Findhorn near Forres by the coast of Moray Firth. The 150-foot

1974

girders are made of wrought-iron plates, butt jointed and supported on stone abutments and piers of solid ashlar. Owing its inspiration to Robert Stephenson's Chester & Holyhead tubular bridges, this is a remarkable survival from more than a century ago.

MARYKIRK

NORTH WATER VIADUCT. Built c.1849 for Aberdeen Railway. Engineer Joseph Locke. Rebuilt late 1880s by Caledonian Railway. Between Montrose and Stonehaven.

The Aberdeen Railway's bridges were mostly built with timber arches and converted to steel or wrought-iron trusses or

1976

plate girders from the late 1870s on. This 13-span viaduct on a curve is one example. Its original massive stone piers now support steel trusses, but the cast-iron shoes for carrying the wooden arches can still be seen.

SPEYMOUTH VIADUCT

Built 1886 for Great North of Scotland Railway. Engineers Blyth & Westland. Closed. Just east of Garmouth village.

This remarkable bridge has a 350-foot bowed central truss and six 100-foot plain truss approach spans, all carried on

SPEYMOUTH VIADUCT, 1974

INVERNESS & ABERDEEN JUNCTION RAILWAY OPERATING ACROSS THE SPEY, c.1860

STONEHAVEN, 1976

cylindrical masonry piers. The need for a wide central span was dictated by the meandering course of the Spey near its mouth. The steelwork was executed by Blaikie Brothers of Aberdeen.

The bridge was on the Great North's Moray Coast line, designed to serve the fishing ports on the Banffshire coast and also to provide a basis for an independent line to Inverness. After long disuse the bridge is now open as a footbridge.

STONEHAVEN

Built c.1850 by Aberdeen Railway. Original stone-built station and platform verandah listed Grade B. Between Aberdeen and Montrose.

A two-platform through station on an embankment, this is the only surviving original station on the main line of the

Aberdeen Railway. The house and offices are in a two-storey building on the up side, built of sandstone ashlar in Italianate style, with round-headed openings. Subsequently a single-storey wing was added to the north, in a similar style; a light steel-framed awning was built on to the frontage, and a canted awning on scrolly iron brackets was constructed on the platform side.

HIGHLAND

ALNESS

STATION. Built 1863 by Inverness & Aberdeen Junction Railway. Between Dingwall and Invergordon.

Formerly a two-platform through station, Alness is now a single-platform station using only the former down platform. The house and offices are in a two-storey ashlar block in Italianate style with single-storey wings, one end pavilion and

1974

a flat awning on columns, similar to Blair Atholl (*p.158*).

Other stations in Easter Ross built in the same style but differing in detail were Ardgay (formerly Bonar Bridge), Fearn and Kildary (closed). The section of line to Invergordon was planned as the Inverness & Ross-shire Railway, which became part of the Highland Railway in 1865, as a link in the 'Far North' line to Wick and Thurso. Promoted by the Inverness & Aberdeen Junction Railway, the line from Invergordon to Bonar Bridge was opened in 1864.

1974

VIADUCT. Built 1863 for Inverness & Aberdeen Junction Railway. Engineer Joseph Mitchell. Listed Grade B. South of Alness.

This handsome sandstone ashlar bridge over the River Alness has two large segmental arches; at the south end a smaller semi-circular arch passes over a minor road. The central piers and the abutments are carried up to castellated terminals in the manner commonly adopted by Mitchell.

ARDGAY

BRIDGE OVER RIVER CARRON. Built 1864 for Inverness & Aberdeen Junction Railway. Engineer Joseph Mitchell. Listed Grade B. Between Tain and Invershin.

This is an elegant two-span masonry bridge over the shallow river Carron, constructed of ashlar with segmental arches. The central pier has a rounded cutwater. The style of building is reminiscent of Thomas Telford's work, which abounds in this area.

AVIEMORE

Originally built 1863 for Inverness & Perth Junction Railway; rebuilt 1892 for Highland Railway. Engineer Murdoch Paterson. Between Newtonmore and Inverness.

1978

This is a four-platform junction station, with the main offices in a single-storey building, mostly of wood, on the down side. There is a capacious wood and cast-iron awning sheltering the platform with finely detailed valances and end-gable decorations. On the island platform there

AVIEMORE, 1974

is a large waiting room block with awnings of similar character.

Aviemore, rebuilt for the opening of the Inverness Direct Line, was the largest through station on the Highland Railway. It is now also served by the preserved Strathspey Railway, which has its own platform to the east of the British Rail station. It runs steam-hauled trains to Boat of Garten, and uses the four-track stone engine shed dating from the original station of 1863.

BANAVIE

SWING BRIDGE OVER CALEDONIAN CANAL. Built 1901 for West Highland Extension Railway (North British). Engineers Simpson & Wilson. North-west of Fort William.

1974

This massive steel bowed-truss swing bridge passes over Thomas Telford's Caledonian Canal which opened in 1822. It has its own wooden signal box, with a hipped roof and overhanging eaves, and is magnificently situated. Ben Nevis, Britain's highest mountain, dominates the view to the east, and 'Neptune's Staircase', a series of eight locks on the canal, lies immediately to the north.

BRORA

BRIDGE. Built 1871 by Duke of Sutherland's Railway. Listed Grade C (S). About a quarter of a mile south of Brora station.

A large single segmental masonry arch, this simple but dignified structure spans

BRORA, 1974

the gorge of the River Brora in the centre of the village. It has rusticated voussoirs and spandrels of coursed rubble. Unusually there is no string course decorating the parapet. Its severely functional character is no doubt due to the economical construction of the Duke of Sutherland's Railway, intended to encourage the development of Brora as an industrial centre.

CARR BRIDGE

Built 1892 by Highland Railway. Between Aviemore and Inverness.

The Highland Railway developed a fine wooden station style, of which this is one of the larger examples, similar to Plockton

1981

and various closed stations. At Carr Bridge there is a main building with projecting gabled wings, the space between being filled by an awning supported on cast-iron columns with wooden brackets. A projecting glazed office contains the signalling instruments.

CLACHNAHARRY SWING BRIDGE

Opened 1862 by Inverness & Ross-shire Railway; replaced 1909 by a similar structure for Highland Railway. Engineer of original bridge Joseph Mitchell. North of Inverness.

This massive bowed steel box-girder structure, 42 yards long, crosses the Caledonian Canal on a 65 degree skew, and is protected by signals controlled

1974

from a small signal box of standard Highland Railway pattern on the north side of the bridge. It was built to the same design as the original structure of 40 years earlier. It has always been painted white to reduce expansion of the metal in hot weather.

CONON BRIDGE

VIADUCT. Built 1862 for Inverness & Ross-shire Railway. Engineer Joseph Mitchell. Listed Grade B. Between Inverness and Dingwall.

1976

A five-span masonry viaduct with segmental arches, handsomely built of sandstone ashlar, carries the railway over the River Conon. The bridge is skewed but, unusually, each 73-foot span consists of four staggered ribs. At the time of construction, Mitchell believed it was the biggest bridge of its type. It originally ran parallel to Telford's Conon Bridge, dating from 1809, but only the distinctive octagonal tollhouse of the earlier structure now survives.

CULLODEN MOOR

NAIRN VIADUCT. Built 1898 for Highland Railway. Engineer Murdoch Paterson. Listed Grade A. Between Daviot and Inverness.

The largest engineering work on the Inverness Direct line, this 28-span red sandstone viaduct is the longest masonry

NAIRN VIADUCT, 1976

viaduct in Scotland. Its overall length is 600 yards and all but one of its semi-circular spans are 50 feet in length. The span over the river is 100 feet long. The viaduct can be seen to advantage as it is situated in a rather bare valley, not far from the famous battlefield which saw the end of the Jacobite rising of 1745-46.

DINGWALL

Rebuilt 1886 for Highland Railway. Architect probably William Roberts. Between Inverness and Invergordon.

The junction for the Dingwall and Skye Railway which goes to Kyle of Lochalsh is at this three-platform through station. The main building is on the up platform and consists of a single storey in stone, with crow-stepped gables, similar to those at Pitlochry (*p.163*). The station's most

DINGWALL, 1974

notable feature is a fine awning with fan-like glazing bars in the gables, supported on cast-iron columns and brackets. It gives a light and airy feeling that is reflected in the neat single-storey wooden range of offices on the opposite platform.

DUNROBIN

Built 1870 by Duke of Sutherland's Railway; rebuilt for the Duke in 1902. Architect L. Bisset. Between Golspie and Brora.

DUNROBIN, 1974

GLENFINNAN VIADUCT, 1976

This delightful little half-timbered building, with its three-bay awning, was a private station for the Duke of Sutherland who, until nationalization, retained the right to run his private train on the Far North line and to use his large saloon for journeys to London. The shed which housed his engine stands nearby. The Duke's railway ran from Golspie to Helmsdale and thus formed a significant link in the route to Wick and Thurso.

GLENFINNAN VIADUCT

Built 1901 for West Highland Extension Railway. Engineers Simpson & Wilson. Listed Grade A. Between Fort William and Mallaig.

Glenfinnan is one of the most magnificent viaducts in Britain, situated on a sharp curve in splendidly remote surroundings at the head of Loch Shiel. It is 416 yards long with 21 spans, and is notable for its early use of mass concrete in such a large structure: it is the longest concrete railway bridge in Scotland. It overlooks the monument to the raising of Bonnie Prince Charlie's standard at the start of the 1745 Jacobite rising.

GOLSPIE

Built 1868 by Sutherland Railway. Between Rogart and Brora.

At the terminus of the Sutherland Railway which ran from Bonar Bridge, this was originally a two-platform station, but is now reduced to one platform on which stands a delightful L-plan building of snecked sandstone rubble with mullioned

windows. The gable and dormers in the low roof are extended on short wooden posts to form an awning in the angle of the L. The overbridge at the north end of the station bears a plaque commemorating the second Duke of Sutherland's involvement with the extension to the north. Helmsdale station on the Duke of Sutherland's Railway is similar in outline but larger and lacks Golspie's charm.

GOLSPIE, 1974

169

JOSEPH MITCHELL, ENGINEER

Here is a little-known engineer whose achievements lie almost entirely in his native Scottish Highlands. Born in Forres in 1803, he died in Inverness at the age of 80, having spent a lifetime improving communications north of Perth.

He worked for Telford on the Caledonian Canal and then succeeded his father John Mitchell in the charge of Highland roads and bridges for 18 years, during which time he also built 40 churches for the Church of Scotland. His first railway work was to survey a route for the Edinburgh & Glasgow Railway via Bathgate in 1837, followed by a route for the Scottish Central Railway. His scheme for a line from Perth to Inverness in 1846 was thought to be impracticable, but was eventually followed when the lines forming the Highland Railway were built. Mitchell was also responsible with his partners William and Murdoch Paterson for other lines including the Far North route from Inverness to Wick and Thurso.

Mitchell's bridges and viaducts are particularly notable for their fine proportions. He retired through ill health in 1867 but lived for another 16 years during which he was active in many public works around Inverness. His *Reminiscences of my Life in the Highlands*, published in 1884, are among the most interesting works of the sort left by any engineer.

INVERNESS

STATION. Opened in 1855 by Inverness & Nairn Railway.

Inverness was the hub of the Highland Railway, containing its head offices, locomotive works and largest station. The station was, and still is, unique in its layout. It takes the form of an inverted triangle with the platforms at the apex, curving around the two sides. The third side of the triangle is formed by a connecting line. Most of the incoming trains run along the connecting line and reverse into the station; the engine thus remains at the outer end and can quickly be released.

A short four-bay overall roof covers the inner ends of the seven platforms and the spacious concourse, but otherwise the platforms are open and always have been. Considering the amount of changing of trains that takes place, not to mention the Highland weather, it is surprising that awnings have never been erected. The

INVERNESS STATION HOTEL, 1970s

concourse contains plaques displaying the Inverness & Aberdeen Junction Railway coat-of-arms and the names of the directors and engineer, brought from the Spey Viaduct at Dalvey, alongside the old station bell inscribed 'I & A J R, 1858, Wilson Christie, Bellfounders, Glasgow'. The I & A J R monogram can also be seen on a corbel on the wall.

STATION HOTEL. Built 1855 for Highland Railway; extended 1858-59. Architect for original probably Joseph Mitchell; for extensions Matthews & Lawrie. Listed Grade B.

A handsome three-storey building in a French-Italianate style, the hotel is constructed of cream sandstone and originally possessed a low tower with a convex roof and cupola in the French style. Internally the entrance hall with its grand T-shaped staircase is particularly fine, lit by a lantern light above two tiers of galleries. The dining room, with prominent pilasters, retains much of its Victorian dignity.

OFFICES. Built 1873-75 for Highland Railway. Architects Matthews & Lawrie. Listed Grade A. 28-34 Academy Street.

Opposite the Station Hotel, and with the station forming the third side of an open square, stands this three-storey Italianate block which was the headquarters of the Highland Railway Company. The interior is now broken up into smaller offices, some in private occupation, but the former boardroom remains with its lofty, highly decorated coffered ceiling and elaborate bosses. The staircase is similar to the one in the hotel. On the outside wall a plaque commemorates the employees of the Highland Railway who died in the First World War.

VIADUCT. Built 1862 for Inverness & Ross-shire Railway. Engineer Joseph Mitchell. Listed Grade B. North of Inverness station.

1976

This is a beautifully-proportioned bridge over the River Ness, and overlooking Inverness Harbour. It has five flat segmental arches, each 73 feet long, and is decorated with a moulded string course and pilasters rising from rounded cut-waters. On the north side there is a single plate-girder approach span, and on the south are four short segmental arches and a plate-girder span. The sandstone ashlar masonry is of the highest quality.

INVERSHIN

OYKEL VIADUCT. Built 1867 for Sutherland Railway. Engineers Joseph Mitchell and Murdoch Paterson. Listed Grade B. Between Culrain and Invershin.

This fine example of Mitchell's favourite wrought-iron lattice truss design is, at 230 feet, equal in span to his box girder bridge over the Spey at Boat o'Brig, but unusually for Mitchell the deck is on the top of the truss. The main span is approached

1976

from the south by two tall semi-circular spans and from the north by three. The masonry, apart from the arch rings, is of coursed rubble. The viaduct spans the boundary between the old counties of Ross & Cromarty and Sutherland, and is the only bridge across the River Oykel for some distance. Culrain station, on the south side of the river, was built to serve local people wanting to avoid the long way round: as the crow flies, it is only a quarter of a mile away from Invershin on the other bank.

KILDARY BRIDGE, 1976

KILDARY

BRIDGE OVER RIVER BALNAGOWAN. Built 1864 for Inverness & Perth Junction Railway. Engineer Joseph Mitchell. Listed Grade B. Close to Kildary station.

THE GREAT NORTH OF SCOTLAND RAILWAY

This company, with its high-sounding name, set out in the 1840s with the intention of building a railway from Aberdeen to Inverness. It was the earliest company to operate so far north, issuing its first prospectus in 1844 before the Caledonian's line entering Aberdeen from the south had even been promoted. But despite several attempts it did not manage to get further than Elgin – and if all the stories of its internal strife and warfare with other companies are to be believed it is surprising that it built any railway at all.

But by the 1880s the GNS had become an efficient railway, and in 1906 it began a fruitful co-operation with the Highland Railway between Aberdeen and Inverness. There were four trains in each direction, each company providing locomotives for two – a pleasant *entente* after earlier rivalry.

The Great North lacked the grandeur of scenery characteristic of so much of the Highland Railway but it still included some beautiful stretches. The most spectacular was on the inland route to Elgin, where the line ran through the dramatic Glen Fiddich between Dufftown and Craigellachie. And on a clear day, the coastal route passing through Cullen, Buckie and Spey Bay afforded some of the finest distant prospects to be seen from a train anywhere in Britain, with a view extending northwards across the Moray Firth to the mountains of Sutherland and Caithness 50 miles away. Of the original network, only the stretch from Aberdeen to Keith now remains open.

The Buchan lines were very important, carrying the fish traffic from the east-coast ports of Peterhead and Fraserburgh. And in LNER days, the longest through-carriage service in Britain used GNS lines: carrying sleeping cars, it ran from Kings Cross to Lossiemouth, a distance of 610 miles.

In locomotive practice, the Great North at first did not show any particular distinction, but after the appointment of James Manson as Locomotive Superintendent in 1883 some excellent new engines of moderate proportions were introduced. The company was unique among the railways of Britain in using the 4-4-0 type on both main-line passenger and goods trains to the exclusion of all others. The freight traffic was mainly fish and not heavy, and 4-4-0s were well suited to it.

The 4-4-0s designed by William Pickersgill in 1899 were among the most handsome of their type ever to run, distinguished by commodious cabs with side windows and clerestory roofs. One of them, *Gordon Highlander*, was restored in 1958 to its original state and after several years running enthusiasts' specials is now preserved in the Glasgow Museum.

Restored GNS 4-4-0 Gordon Highlander, *c.1960*

This ornamented bridge of a single masonry span is buttressed on either side. There is a raised central panel bearing the Cromartie family arms and the date 1864; at the side is a small approach arch over an estate drive. The lush scenery at this point is typical of Easter Ross, with views right across the Cromarty Firth.

KINGUSSIE

Built 1863 for Inverness & Perth Junction Railway; rebuilt 1891 for Highland Railway. Architect William Roberts. Listed Grade B. Between Newtonmore and Aviemore.

This two-platform through station serves a prosperous Highland town. The main offices are in a single-storey range on the down platform, with crow-stepped gables and mullioned windows, linked to a two-

KINGUSSIE, 1974

storey station house in simpler style. On the platform side there is a glazed awning, supported on cast-iron columns with decorated brackets not commonly found on the Highland Railway.

LOCHAILORT

LOCH NAN UAMH VIADUCT. Built 1901 for West Highland Extension Railway. Engineers Simpson & Wilson. Listed Grade B. Between Fort William and Mallaig.

With eight spans in two groups of four, this viaduct has the semi-circular arches of 50-foot span that were adopted as standard on the West Highland Extension. Like most of the structures on this

1976

line, it is built of reinforced concrete. It stands in an extraordinarily beautiful situation, by the sea loch where Bonnie Prince Charlie landed in 1745.

BORRODALE VIADUCT. Built 1901 for West Highland Extension Railway. Engineers Simpson & Wilson. Listed Grade B. Between Fort William and Mallaig.

The concrete viaduct here is unusual for the West Highland Extension in that it consists of one large span, 127 feet wide and 86 feet above river level, flanked by single 20-foot arches. The whole structure

1976

is cased in rubble masonry and has a castellated parapet – a condition laid down by the landowner. The engineers and the contractors, Sir Robert McAlpine & Sons, adopted the large central span because it was cheaper to clad than a series of shorter arches. At the time of building the bridge was the longest concrete railway arch in the world.

MORAR VIADUCT

Built 1901 for West Highland Extension Railway. Engineers Simpson & Wilson. Listed Grade B. Between Fort William and Mallaig.

This 90-foot mass concrete bridge, with a single large span and two smaller arches on the north side, spans the River Morar just below the spectacular Falls of Morar.

NAIRN

STATION. Built 1855 for Inverness & Nairn Railway; rebuilt 1885 for Highland Railway. Architect probably William Roberts. Listed Grade B. Between Inverness and Elgin.

Nairn is one of the most striking of the Highland's late Victorian stations, its style and scale being commensurate with the town's rising reputation as a holiday resort. The main stone building is on the down side, and is in Scottish Tudor style similar to Pitlochry, but larger (*p.163*).

1974

On the platform side there is a long wooden awning supported on cast-iron columns in the recess between the two end-pavilions, which have crow-stepped gables surmounted by finials in the form of a thistle and a rose. One pavilion also has a bay-window for the station master. On the up platform there is a single-storey wooden shelter with a bellcast roof. The general effect is distinctly pleasing.

VIADUCT. Built 1857 for Inverness & Aberdeen Junction Railway. Engineer Joseph Mitchell. Listed Grade B. East of station.

The well proportioned four-span masonry viaduct over the River Nairn has segmental arches and pointed cutwaters carried up to terminate in corbelled refuges. As with all the bridges on the Inverness & Nairn and Aberdeen Junction lines, there are no parapets.

NEWTONMORE

STATION. Built 1863 for Inverness & Perth Junction Railway; rebuilt 1893 for Highland Railway. Architect probably William Roberts. Listed Grade C (S). Between Blair Atholl and Aviemore.

Basically a smaller, simpler version of what had become the Highland's typical later stations, Newtonmore has two platforms with the offices on the down side in

1974

172

THE WEST HIGHLAND RAILWAY

The West Highland Railway, which was opened by the North British company in 1894, runs from Craigendoran to Fort William through some of the most spectacular scenery in the British Isles.

The surviving stations of original design can conveniently be divided into two types: island-platform stations, with double-sided buildings; and two-platform stations, with single-sided buildings.

The former were more numerous, and are now represented by Arrochar & Tarbet, Bridge of Orchy, Garelochhead, Helensburgh Upper, Rannoch and Tyndrum Upper. All these are single-storey buildings with brick bases and timber upper works. The concave roofs overhang the walls to provide awnings and glazed end-screens afford some protection from the Highland climate.

At the time of their completion, these stations were considered to be in the Swiss style, and indeed the upper part of the walls, where not glazed, is hung with wooden shingles imported from Switzerland. Rannoch is notable for its low-relief sculpture of J. H. Renton, who helped to finance the building of the railway. It was carved by navvies working on the line.

The two-platform stations are Spean Bridge and Tulloch. The platform side of these buildings is similar to the frontage of the island-platform types, but the road side is plainer and built of brick.

All the major bridges on the West Highland, except the conventional masonry viaduct at Creag an Arnain (*p.125*), are steel truss structures on masonry piers. The engineers for the line, Formans & McCall, followed Joseph Mitchell (*p.170*) in preferring metal bridges, so that a large number of parts could be made in advance.

The largest viaduct crosses a depression in the Moor of Rannoch and has nine spans of 70 feet 6 inches; the largest single span is that over Glen Falloch, 118 feet long and 144 feet above the stream. The Lochy Viaduct at Fort William has four 80-foot trusses, but the most spectacular structures are the pair of steel viaducts on the horseshoe curve north of Tyndrum, where the line crosses two valleys as it follows the contours of the hillsides.

WEST HIGHLAND EXTENSION RAILWAY

At Banavie (*p.167*) you enter the West Highland Extension Railway. Opened in 1901, it contains some rare examples of concrete railway viaducts with fine landscape qualities. (Those at Glenfinnan, Lochailort and Morar are listed and have separate entries.) The only notable building is at Mallaig, where the station is a rugged random rubble two-storey block with prominent eaves.

The West Highland Extension gains its special attraction from its views. The route follows the north shore of Loch Eil, then crosses to Glenfinnan where the viaduct affords vistas across Loch Sheil. Past picturesque Loch Eilt the line emerges at Lochailort on the west coast of Scotland, providing spectacular views westwards to the islands of Eigg, Rhum and Muck, and north to Skye. At the end of the line Mallaig generally has a strong smell of fish from the railway's quay and the adjoining smoking houses.

Horseshoe Bend, Tyndrum, 1974

a single-storey coursed rubble building with gabled end-pavilions and a wooden awning in the recess, supported by a pair of ornate wooden brackets on iron columns. Ornaments such as mullioned and transomed windows and decorated gables are less detailed than those at more elaborate stations such as Nairn and Pitlochry (*p.163*), while the hood mouldings over the main windows are delightfully different – one square and the other rounded.

SPEY VIADUCT. Built 1863 for Inverness & Perth Junction Railway. Architect William Roberts. Engineer Joseph Mitchell. Listed Category C (S). About half a mile south-west of Newtonmore station.

This two-span iron truss bridge is the most upstream railway crossing of the Spey (the furthest downstream is Speymouth Viaduct, *p.166*). To the north, Monadhliath Mountains rise to over 3,000 feet.

ROGART

Built c.1868 by Sutherland Railway. Between Lairg and Golspie.

Rogart, Lairg and Invershin stations on the Sutherland Railway are all similar. They have twin railway houses with dormer windows linked to a simple booking office and waiting room and are con-

1974

structed of very large, roughly-squared stone blocks. All served small communities, and their strong vernacular styling gives the impression of their having been converted from private dwellings; in fact, their identical styles prove that this cannot be the case. There are also simple domestic-style stations further north – on the Sutherland & Caithness Railway, for example, at Forsinard and Scotscalder – but they lack the modest sophistication of stations such as Rogart.

SLOCHD

VIADUCT OVER ALLT SLOCHD MHUIC. Built 1897 for Highland Railway. Engineer Murdoch Paterson. Listed Grade B. Between Aviemore and Inverness.

1974

Slochd Summit is the second highest summit on the Highland main line and this attractive eight-span masonry viaduct with semi-circular arches and tapering piers is situated near it in wild, remote country.

TAIN

Built 1864 by Inverness & Aberdeen Junction Railway. Listed Grade B. Between Invergordon and Ardgay.

Tain's two-platform station has its main offices in a single-storey range on the down platform. This is on an H-plan with an elongated central section between end-pavilions, nicely constructed in coursed rubble. The entrance is through a porch

1974

flanked by stone pilasters and supported by two cast-iron columns, while the platform side has a simple awning on identical columns in the space between the wings. At first sight rather an ordinary Highland station, this building engages the attention because of its excellent proportions and good detail, particularly the ashlar window casings.

Tain is known to many travellers to the Far North as the station where the buffet car is detached from the north-bound train and attached to the south-bound one.

THURSO

Built 1874 by Sutherland & Caithness Railway.

The Sutherland & Caithness Railway completed the 'Far North' line from Helmsdale to Wick and Thurso, creating in Thurso the most northerly railway station in Britain. Its unusual style is very similar to that at Wick; the single-storey building has low, round-headed windows and a projecting gable with a trefoil opening. This fronts a deep-roofed trainshed with wooden trusses on low, almost dwarf, walls with a limited amount of roof lighting. A solid wooden outer gable has

THURSO TRAINSHED, 1974

THURSO, 1974

an elliptical lower edge. Thurso is built of snecked sandstone rubble, unlike Wick which is of Caithness flagstone and bears a plaque with the date of construction.

TOMATIN

VIADUCT OVER RIVER FINDHORN. Built 1897 for Highland Railway. Engineer Murdoch Paterson. Listed Grade B. Between Aviemore and Inverness.

This striking viaduct is very unusual for the Highland: it consists of nine light steel trusses supported on slender, tapering masonry piers approached by abutments pierced by small semi-circular arches. Like most of the Highland's bridges, it is exceedingly well proportioned and admirably fits its situation across the broad, lightly wooded valley of the Findhorn.

TOMATIN VIADUCT. Built 1897 for Highland Railway. Engineer Murdoch Paterson. Listed Grade B.

This handsome nine-span masonry viaduct is constructed of rock-faced ashlar with semi-circular arches and slightly tapering piers. The supports for the wooden arch centering can still be seen. The voussoirs are of brick with stone on the outside faces.

AULTNASLANASH VIADUCT. Built 1897 for Highland Railway. Engineer Murdoch Paterson. North of Tomatin village.

This five-span trestle bridge, the only wooden bridge on a main-line railway in Scotland, was built to cross a stream at a point where firm foundations could not be sunk. Wooden bridge-building enjoyed a vogue in Inverness-shire at the turn of the century, which is probably why such an expedient was adopted.

AULTNASLANASH VIADUCT, 1974

SOUTHERN REGION

CONTENTS

LONDON: PAGE 177   **SOUTH-EAST ENGLAND:** KENT PAGE 185   EAST SUSSEX PAGE 194   WEST SUSSEX PAGE 197

SURREY PAGE 199   **SOUTHERN ENGLAND:** HAMPSHIRE PAGE 203   ISLE OF WIGHT PAGE 206

BERKSHIRE (PART) PAGE 207   WILTSHIRE (PART) PAGE 208   DORSET (PART) PAGE 208

In a cartoon entitled the 'Pursuit of Pleasure under Difficulties', crowds on a fête day pour homewards down one of the vast staircases of Crystal Palace Low Level station.

Occupying a neat and compact area south of the Thames, Southern Region is geographically the smallest of British Rail's five regions. But it has always operated very densely trafficked lines and has no fewer than seven London termini. Its major concerns have always been with London commuter traffic and with passengers bound for Channel crossings to the Continent.

The region comprises the former Southern Railway, which at the Grouping of 1923 incorporated three major and highly competitive lines: the London & South Western, the London Brighton & South Coast and the South Eastern & Chatham. The region also acquired the Great Western's line to Weymouth.

As part of its London & South Western inheritance the Southern Railway ran trains from Waterloo to Plymouth, North Devon and North

Standing underneath the Ouse Viaduct at Balcombe in West Sussex, you can look down a corridor of pierced piers supporting the 37 brick arches. The viaduct was built by the London & Brighton Railway, predecessor of the LBSCR (p.207), in 1840.

Cornwall, which as far as Exeter were in direct competition with the Great Western. The *Atlantic Coast Express* to resorts like Ilfracombe, Bude and Padstow was one of its most famous trains. But such rivalry is over: expresses for Exeter and beyond now leave London from Paddington and are exclusively Western Region's concern. Beyond Salisbury, the former Southern Railway lines, at first in Southern Region, are now operated by Western Region.

In Waterloo, extensively rebuilt by 1922, the London & South Western had one of the most efficient passenger stations in the country; its business included both heavy short-distance traffic to commuter suburbs in the Thames Valley and longer distance services to the 'stockbroker belt' in Surrey and Sussex.

The London Brighton & South Coast Railway built up a complex network of passenger lines from London Bridge and Victoria serving the south coast between Hastings and Portsmouth. Although its longest through run was a little under 88

miles, it had an extraordinary profusion of alternative routes and branch lines within its small area.

There was a proliferation of routes between London and the Channel ports which arose out of the 19th-century competition between the London Chatham & Dover and the South Eastern Railways. They eventually put an end to their bickering by establishing a working agreement in 1899 that in future the two companies would be managed, maintained and improved as one undertaking by a joint committee, known as the South Eastern and Chatham Railway Managing Committee. For all practical purposes the words Managing Committee were omitted and the distinctive lettering S.E. & C.R. was used generally on rolling stock and other equipment.

Nevertheless, the legacy of conflict between the two companies proved invaluable between the wars. By this time, holiday travel to the Continent had increased dramatically. The many alternative routes available could be used to the full, ensuring

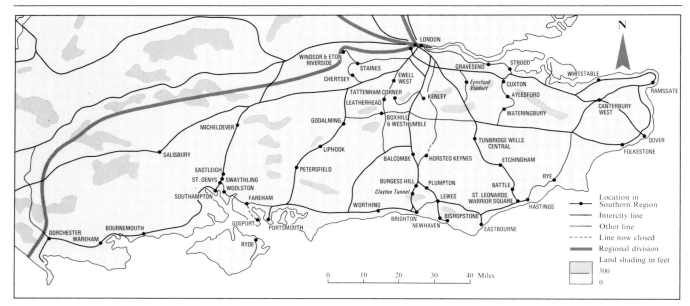

that boat-trains did not interfere too much with the timetabling of regular internal traffic.

Now with the increase in car and air travel, the importance of the boat-trains has considerably diminished: no longer can one see the all-Pullman *Golden Arrow* or the *Night Ferry* with its sleeper service to Paris and Brussels setting off from Victoria, with wagons-lits and French coaches.

The requirements of dealing with heavy passenger traffic concentrated in periods of peak activity put the pre-Grouping companies of southern England in the forefront of modernisation. Electrification of the inner suburban area around London began at the turn of the century. Later the Southern Railway assiduously promoted its 'Southern Electric' image and was the first of the 'Big Four' companies created at Grouping to establish a distinctive corporate style, accompanied by a programme of station modernisation and reconstruction. Electrification spread rapidly in the inter-war years and now covers virtually the whole of the region east of a line from London to Bournemouth.

Innovative traction was not limited to electrification, however, for in 1941 the Southern's last Chief Mechanical Engineer, O. V. Bulleid, produced a series of 4-6-2 express passenger locomotives with a number of revolutionary features including a unique streamlined casing, chain-driven valve gear, patent disc wheels and electric lighting. Called the 'Merchant Navy' class, they were followed by the similar but lighter 'West Country' class. The valve gear was

not a success and was replaced, and some of the engines had their streamlining removed, but they carried out excellent service on the Bournemouth and West of England trains.

Programmes of modernisation were also generated by the cross-Channel traffic at Dover and Folkestone, and the railway improvements to Southampton docks have substantially contributed to the decline of Liverpool as a premier British port.

Although some of the region's historic structures disappeared in the modernisation programme, many are still in use. J. U. Rastrick's great viaduct across the Ouse valley, built in 1840, remains without alteration, as does his later London Road viaduct at Brighton, successfully repaired after an almost direct hit in a wartime air raid.

Further east, the former South Eastern lines contain a number of architecturally interesting stations

while Sir William Cubitt's magnificently engineered line along the coast between Folkestone and Dover includes the Foord Viaduct at Folkestone, and a series of tunnels and deep cuttings which culminate in the twin-bore tunnel beneath Shakespeare's Cliff at Dover.

It is often asserted that streamlining and modernisation – particularly the introduction of electric traction – is in itself enough to generate additional passenger traffic. Known as the 'sparks effect', this creates its own problems the nearer one approaches to London. To carry vast numbers of passengers swiftly and safely requires not only the most sophisticated control systems but also a large fleet of rolling stock, for which there is a much lower demand during off-peak hours. The resulting under-use of expensive capital equipment remains one of Southern Region's greatest financial problems.

A D-Class Wainright 4-4-0 emerges from Shakespeare Tunnel with a Continental boat train in c.1902.

LONDON

ANERLEY

Built 1839 by London & Croydon Railway.
Between New Cross Gate and Norwood
Junction.

William Sanderson, a Scot, built a house
here and called it 'Anerley' from the Scots
word for 'lonely'. He offered the London

1980

& Croydon Railway part of his property
free of charge on condition that they built
a station and called it by the same name.

Early on the London & Croydon was
an atmospheric railway like the South
Devon *(see Starcross p.239)*. It seems that
when a new Croydon up line was being
built in the 1840s the original up platform
had to be demolished, and a new platform
and buildings were provided. Nevertheless what appears to be the crenellated
dwelling-house shown in contemporary
prints still survives.

BARNES

Built 1846 for London & South Western
Railway. Architect Sir William Tite.
Northernmost end Conservation Area. Between
Clapham Junction and Richmond.

Many of Tite's stations were Tudor, and
Barnes, the only survivor of a series in
brick on the Richmond branch, could be
regarded as a precedent for the finest of
the type, his royal station at Windsor &
Eton Riverside *(p.207)*. It has tall roofs,
twisted chimney stacks, mullions and
lozenge patterns in the brickwork. The
station has retained its character despite
considerable alterations in about 1880.

1983

BATTERSEA PARK, 1979

BATTERSEA PARK

STATION. Built 1867 by London Brighton &
South Coast Railway. Listed Grade II. Between
Victoria and Clapham Junction.

Battersea Park is an interesting three-
storey station, squeezed between two
bridges over the road. It is built in brick
decorated with string courses. The
ground and top-floor openings are round-
headed set in polychrome brickwork, and
make an unusual contrast with those in
the middle floor, which are shallower and
stone-set, with flower motifs adorning the
keystones.

The lofty booking hall is the most unusual feature, combining blind arcading
with a row of slender coupled columns
supporting arched arcading down the
centre. The spandrels are decorated with
extraordinary roundels displaying
classical female heads.

EASTERNMOST BRIDGE. Built 1865 for
London, Brighton & South Coast Railway.
Engineer probably F. Dale Banister.

The chief interest of the bridge is provided
by the decoration of the cast-iron parapets and facings, or screens. (The
wrought-iron girders which carried the
track have long since been replaced.) The
spandrels of the single arch contain the
date, the coat of arms of the railway and a
quantity of oak foliage, for which there
was a vogue in the late 19th century. (*See*
Worcester Foregate Street, p.223, and *Derby*
Friargate, p.79.)

BLACKFRIARS

THE BLACKFRIAR PUBLIC HOUSE.
Built late-19th century, remodelled 1905 by H.
Fuller Clark with decorations by Henry Poole.
Acquired by London Chatham & Dover
Railway. Listed Grade II. 174 Queen Victoria
Street, EC4.

Built on a narrow corner site beside, and
indeed under, the arches of the Queen
Victoria Street railway viaduct, this is one
of the most amazing public houses in
London. Standing on the site of a
Dominican Priory, where Cardinal
Wolsey heard the case for Henry VIII's
divorce from Catherine of Aragon, it is
built of yellow brick with stone dressings;
but its real quality results from the 1905
remodelling of the ground and first floors
and the interior.

A profusion of coloured granite, carved
stone, mosaic and metal work (particularly beaten copper) covers the exterior and
is seen also in the saloon bar and the
carvery, where, in mosaic pictures,
beaten copper and mixtures of the two,
black friars busy themselves at their daily
tasks of farming, brewing, apple-picking,
etc. All this was designed and made by
Henry Poole in his fruity Arts & Crafts
manner, and should not be missed on any
account.

1982

178

BLACKFRIARS RAILWAY BRIDGE.
Built 1863 for London Chatham & Dover
Railway. Engineer Joseph Cubitt.

This is really two bridges, the original
upstream one now being the oldest across
the Thames below Battersea Bridge. It
has five lattice spans on piers made up of
quadrupled cast-iron cluster columns
with foliated capitals. At track level each

c.1960

pier is topped by a decorative cast-iron
capital, while the piers nearest the banks
carry the arms of the railway. The downstream bridge was added in 1889 and is
typical of the period. It has five wrought-
iron arches with cast-iron lozenge infill set
on stone-faced brick piers.

BLACKHEATH

Built 1849 for South Eastern Railway.
Architect George Smith. Listed Grade II.
Between London and Charlton.

Instead of the usual weatherboarded
building so favoured by the South Eastern, Blackheath was built of brick, a two-
storey Italianate structure with round-
headed windows on the ground floor and
segmental heads on the first.

1979

In 1864 a new entrance building was
built on the road bridge, superseding the
older one which still survives behind a
platform. It, too, is Italianate, with
attractively dentilled wings; it may have
been thought 'proper' to blend it with the
Georgian architecture of Blackheath
Village.

The station buildings, yard, and line to
the west of the station form part of a
Conservation Area.

QUOIN STONES FROM THE OLD BLACKFRIARS
STATION, NOW PRESERVED IN THE NEW

CANNON STREET

Built 1864 for South Eastern Railway.
Engineer Sir John Hawkshaw. Towers listed
Grade II.

Cannon Street was the terminus of the
City branch of the Charing Cross Railway
(worked from the beginning by the South
Eastern), although it was often consider-
ed as an intermediate station because so
many trains, on arriving from London
Bridge, reversed out again and ran on to
Charing Cross.

The pair of tall, baroque, yellow-brick
towers at the ends of the side walls are all
that remain of Hawkshaw's station and

CANNON STREET TOWERS, 1970s

form a familiar landmark on the Thames
river bank. Topped by square domed
roofs with squat lanterns and spires, the
towers were more than decoration: they
contained water tanks to provide hydraulic power for the station lifts. Hawkshaw's crescent-trussed roof, 190 feet
wide and 106 feet high, was dismantled
after war-time bomb damage.

The hotel which stood at the head of
Cannon Street station was designed in

French Renaissance style by E. M. Barry. Opened in 1866, it was almost a replica of his hotel at Charing Cross. On the night of 10th-11th May, 1941, probably the worst of the London blitzes, the hotel caught fire and was gutted. It was replaced by the present office block in 1965.

A Roman Governor's Palace once stood on a site that includes part of the station. Its remains are scheduled as an Ancient Monument.

RAILWAY BRIDGE. Built 1863 for South Eastern Railway. Engineer Sir John Hawkshaw.

The functional design of Cannon Street bridge can hardly be considered very attractive, but it is typical of the larger river crossings by this notable railway engineer (*p.234*). It has five spans of iron girders, the three centre ones being 167 feet long and the side spans 135 feet. The enormous cast-iron cylinders which carry the girders were originally arranged in pairs; they were added to when the bridge was widened in 1889.

When the station was bombed in May 1941 all the trains were pulled out on to the bridge – a tempting target that proved beyond the bomb-aimers' skill.

CHARING CROSS

STATION. Built 1864-65 for South Eastern Railway. Engineer Sir John Hawkshaw.

The Charing Cross Railway was inspired by, and worked by, the South Eastern Railway, whose aim was to acquire a station in the West End. It was opened from London Bridge in 1864, an expensive and difficult line to construct. St. Thomas's Hospital had to be bought and moved out of the way at a cost of over a quarter of a million pounds; and from the College Burial Ground, which was also in the way, 7,950 bodies had to be disinterred and 5,000 cubic yards of earth removed to a depth of 16 feet.

The station was the work of Sir John Hawkshaw. His original crescent-trussed roof rested on arcaded side walls and was 98 feet high with a 164-foot span. In December 1905 a tie-rod broke and a large portion of the roof collapsed, killing six men and pushing part of the western wall down on to the Avenue Theatre alongside. The 3.50 pm train to Hastings was buried in rubble. A new transverse ridge-and-furrow roof on steel girders was erected in place of the old one. The station has only six platforms, but even so it carries heavy commuter traffic and is the terminus for the Folkestone and Dover trains via Tonbridge.

HOTEL. Built 1864. Architect Edward Middleton Barry.

Barry's hotel, which made such an excellent and grand frontage, was designed in

HUNGERFORD BRIDGE, WITH ORIGINAL CHARING CROSS STATION ROOF BEHIND, BEFORE 1900

the French Renaissance style, with pavilion roofs and rows of dormer windows high above ground level in a fashion he repeated in his Cannon Street Hotel two years later. It is thought to be one of the first buildings in England to make extensive use of artificial stone. After wartime damage the top storey was reconstructed in much plainer fashion, but the Italian Renaissance interior remains intact. The grand corridors and staircase lead to over 350 bedrooms, and the magnificent restaurant with its richly decorated walls and domed ceiling is one of the finest mid-Victorian rooms in London. Many royal personages have stayed at the hotel, but after Continental rail traffic was transferred to Victoria in 1920 the clientele became less glamorous.

ELEANOR CROSS. Built 1865 for Charing Cross Hotel Company. Architect E. M. Barry. Listed Grade II.

When Eleanor of Castile, Queen of Edward I, died in 1290 her body was taken from Lincoln to Westminster for burial, a journey lasting several days. The King ordained that a cross be erected at each point where her body had rested; there were originally 12 such crosses, of which only three remain: at Geddington, Northampton and Waltham.

The original Charing Cross stood in Whitehall on the site now occupied by Le Sueur's statue of Charles I. It was demolished in 1647 and only the name survived until 1865 when the Charing Cross Hotel Company built a replica in the forecourt of their new railway hotel.

Since there was little evidence to establish the appearance of the original, Edward Middleton Barry based the design on the surviving Eleanor Crosses.

CHARING CROSS HOTEL, c.1867

The Portland stone figures and pinnacles and red Mansfield stone panels were carved by the firm of Thomas Earp.

HUNGERFORD BRIDGE. Built 1866 for South Eastern Railway. Engineer Sir John Hawkshaw.

Charing Cross station was built on the site of Hungerford Market, and when building the railway bridge Hawkshaw made use of parts of Brunel's 1845 suspension bridge across which the people of South London had been able to reach the market. Two brick piers from the old bridge stand somewhat incongruously among their cast-iron successors.

Hawkshaw's bridge is an iron lattice girder structure with six river spans each of 154 feet.

The bridge will always be remembered through Claude Monet's evocative paintings, but how many visitors to the South Bank know that the Metropolitan Board of Works paid £98,450 for the provision of the permanent footway on the east side?

CLAPHAM

Built 1867. Listed Grade II. Between Victoria and London Bridge. Voltaire Road, SW4.

Clapham station is something of an enigma. It was the property of the London Chatham & Dover Railway, but the London Brighton & South Coast Railway used two of the four tracks, and both companies had their own platforms. (The Chatham's part was closed in 1915.)

Not surprisingly, perhaps, the station has been called many names. The Brighton's side was sometimes referred to as 'Clapham Road', occasionally with the addition of '& North Stockwell'. The LSWR issued tickets to it labelled 'Clapham Town'. Whatever the name – and it is not Clapham Junction, which lies a mile and a half to the west – it was and is useful for commuters, being only a short ride from Victoria.

The main building, now disused, is a square, two-storey structure with a pyramidal slated roof and a moulded wooden cornice. The chief interest of the building is its structural polychromy: the stock brick background is enlivened with a black-and-white plinth and a dado of pale terracotta with a darker rail. The windows rise to a shallow-pointed arch and are decorated with attractive three-leaf-clover motifs.

CRYSTAL PALACE LOW LEVEL

Built 1875 by London Brighton & South Coast Railway. Listed Grade II. End of branch from Sydenham.

The Low Level station (as opposed to the London Chatham & Dover Railway's High Level station, now demolished) was originally opened in 1854 after the Crystal Palace had been moved from Hyde Park to Sydenham Hill. The grander building which replaced it in 1875 has a French Renaissance flavour and contains a booking hall with a fine clerestory roof There was a five-bay iron *porte cochère* which has since been removed.

A trainshed below had a twin-span, crescent-shaped roof between massive brick walls with blind arcading and heavy buttresses; everything was in the best solid Victorian tradition. The trainshed was shortened following the collapse of the similar roof at Charing Cross in 1905, and now only the walls remain.

Three grand staircases built for the Crystal Palace crowds lead up from the platforms to the booking hall, their masonry balustrades punctuated by massive newel posts. On a cold day it was as well to be in a crowd, for the station was notorious for its bitter gusting winds.

In 1857 a line was opened to Norwood Junction, for which separate platforms were built outside the trainshed. They are very much the poor relation of the main station, but today they deal with almost all the Crystal Palace traffic.

CLAPHAM, 1983

JOHN URPETH RASTRICK, ENGINEER

Rastrick's greatest monument is the Ouse valley viaduct on the London Brighton & South Coast Railway (*p.197*). He came from Northumberland, where he was born in 1780 the son of an engineer, and his early working life was spent in iron manufacture in Shropshire and Worcestershire.

Rastrick experimented with steam locomotion, and his unusual engine *Agenoria*, which has three boiler-flues, is in the National Railway Museum at York. He was one of the judges at the Rainhill locomotive trials on the Liverpool & Manchester Railway in 1829 and was in demand as a parliamentary witness in favour of steam locomotives during the passage of many early railway Bills.

Rastrick was engineer not only for the London & Brighton but for a number of other lines in the south of England, the East Midlands and Lancashire. He also built the iron road bridge over the Wye at Chepstow. He lived to be 76, and died at Chertsey, Surrey in 1856.

CRYSTAL PALACE, 1954

one of three (the other two were at London Bridge and Greenwich) and was the first constructed; it is an evocative relic of London's first passenger railway.

DENMARK HILL, 1959; *inset* PLATFORM TICKET, 1942

DENMARK HILL

Built 1866 by London Brighton & South Coast Railway. Conservation Area. Between Peckham Rye and Brixton.

Denmark Hill appears very palatial for a South London railway station, reflecting an era when it served a prosperous suburban community. Built right on the edge of the road in the Italianate manner, it established a style that was to mark LBSCR stations for the next 20 years.

The most eye-catching part of the station was the central pavilion with its hipped roof, cornices and round-headed windows balanced by French convex roofs. Damaged by fire in 1980, it was adopted for restoration by a specially established preservation society with British Rail meeting half the cost and voluntary contributions and grant aid making up the remainder.

The rear has tall, glazed arcading and a covered staircase to the platforms.

DEPTFORD

LONDON & GREENWICH RAILWAY RAMP. Built 1836 for London & Greenwich Railway. Engineer Col. George Thomas Landmann, R.E. Listed Grade II.

The London & Greenwich Railway ran entirely on a viaduct – a four-mile stretch of 878 stock brick arches. Landmann's

idea was that the company would earn a substantial revenue from letting off the arches, some as private houses. Not surprisingly, people did not relish the thought of trains rumbling over their heads, and tenants were unforthcoming.

To link street and track levels required considerable engineering. Deptford, at first the only intermediate station on the line, also housed the company's repair workshop in the arches beneath. A dog-leg ramp was designed for moving both rolling stock and passengers' carriages up and down from the station. Formed of a series of brick arches rising up from Deptford High Street, it is the only surviving

GREENWICH

Built 1878 by South Eastern Railway. Listed Grade II. Between London Bridge and Dartford.

The London & Greenwich Railway reached Greenwich on Christmas Eve 1838, and a permanent station was opened there in 1840. George Smith was the architect, and a very handsome job he made of it, fitting it in well with the local Georgian surroundings.

GREENWICH AFTER ENEMY ACTION, 1944

When the line was extended to Maze Hill in 1878 a new Greenwich station was required. It has been said that the old one was taken down and rebuilt on the new site but this is not true, though the 1840 and 1878 buildings were conspicuously alike, and some of the materials from the old were used in the new.

The station today is a rectangular, two-storey building with a grand central entrance and Tuscan columns. The three windows on either side nicely balance those on the second storey, and all the windows have flat window hoods and prominent scrolled brackets. There is a low-hipped roof with a deep dentilled cornice and a booking hall designed in Grecian-Doric style.

DEPTFORD RAMP, 1982

181

HAMPTON COURT

Built 1849 for London & South Western Railway. Architect Sir William Tite. Terminus of branch from Surbiton.

Tite's particular brand of Tudor could nowhere be more suitable than at Hampton Court, itself the grandest example of Tudor architecture in the country. Though altered in 1896 and 1933, the building has the correct plan, with a central entry and flanking cross-wings. It is topped by Flemish gables, and built of a mellow red brick with stone dressings.

Now almost entirely a commuter station, Hampton Court used to be very busy with excursion traffic in the days of Jerome K. Jerome's *Three Men in a Boat*, the platforms thronged with boaters, blazers and white flannels.

1962

HERNE HILL

ROSENDALE ROAD BRIDGE. Built 1869 for London Chatham & Dover Railway. Engineer probably F. T. Turner. Listed Grade II. Just north of Guernsey Grove, over Rosendale Road, SE24.

The principal quality of this bridge lies in the use of colourful building materials which enliven an otherwise plain structure. The elliptical road arch is flanked by round-headed arches over the footways,

1982

each framed by wide rusticated pilasters carrying an entablature with modillions and a stone cornice. The greyish yellow brickwork is decorated with red brick and stone dressings, and panels in moulded red brick add interest to the side arches and spandrels. A red and yellow brick parapet completes the effect.

KEW RAILWAY BRIDGE

Built 1869 for London & South Western Railway. Engineer W. R. Galbraith.

This standard iron lattice girder bridge of the 1860s has some unusual decorative details. The iron piers which support the four spans have three stages: a cylindrical base, a drum with four engaged columns and then, above track level, a tabernacle with an arched roof carried on paired columns, framing an elaborate cast-iron screen. It is similar in design to the original Blackfriars Bridge (*p.178*) and carries trains on the North London line and London Transport's District Line.

LONDON BRIDGE

ABBEY STREET BRIDGE SE1, SPA ROAD BRIDGE SE16. Built 1836 for London & Greenwich Railway. Engineer Col. Thomas Landmann. Both listed Grade II.

These two similar bridges each consist of a brick arch carried on cast-iron Doric columns which separate the carriageway from smaller arches over the footways on either side. Although now incorporated in much larger bridges, they survive as relics of London's first passenger railway. The Spa Road bridge, built first, is London's oldest operational railway bridge.

KEW RAILWAY BRIDGE, 1983

1979

MITCHAM

Built 1855 by Wimbledon & Croydon Railway.
Entrance building c.1830. Listed Grade II.
Between Wimbledon and Mitcham Junction.

This building is one of a select number that pre-date the railways and were taken over and adapted for railway use.

The Surrey Iron Railway, the world's first public railway, passed immediately by it, but it was the Wimbledon & Croydon line that converted the building into a station. (The WCR used part of the Surrey's route.)

Mitcham station could have been a pair of cottages between which the railway built an arch, or a small merchant's house with offices on the ground floor and an arch leading to the yard behind. At all events it is an interesting survivor and dates from around 1830. It is in brick, with a nice pedimented gable facing the street, and the elliptical arch is well proportioned. The platforms are in a cutting below.

NORTH DULWICH

Built 1868 for London Brighton & South Coast Railway. Architect Charles Barry. Between Peckham Rye and Sutton.

The station was designed by Charles Barry the younger, architect to nearby Dulwich College which was being built at the same time; but here he chose a rather different architectural style.

1953

The station appears to be seen as the lodge to a large Jacobean mansion, one perhaps with some Renaissance detailing like Cobham Hall in Kent. Built of brick with stone dressings, it has the characteristic Jacobean features of rather slight pilasters, large mullioned windows, an elegant pierced parapet and tall clustered chimney stacks – no fewer than 26 of them, presumably many more than such a small building demanded.

RICHMOND BRIDGE

Built 1906-08 for London & South Western Railway. Engineer J. W. Jacomb-Hood.

The Richmond to Windsor line was opened in 1849. This wrought-iron bridge, however, dates from after the collapse of the cast-iron Portland Road bridge at Norwood Junction in May 1891 – a major scare which led to the renewal of all cast-iron beam railway bridges. One of four interesting bridges over the Thames at Richmond, it has five wrought-iron arches on stone piers.

SURBITON

Built 1937 by Southern Railway.
Between Waterloo and Woking.

Under Sir Herbert Walker the Southern Railway carried out a massive programme of electrification in the 1930s. To promote it the company created the 'Southern Electric' image and reconstructed numerous stations in the current fashion of straight lines and green and black decor. At the time they were unkindly known as 'Odeon Cinema style' or even more unkindly as 'Super Wireless Sets'.

Nevertheless, Surbiton station has been described by Pevsner and Nairn (*Buildings of England, Surrey*) as 'one of the first in England to acknowledge the existence of a modern style'.

The original station at Surbiton was known as Kingston (then the nearest built-up area) and the settlement that grew around the station became known as Kingston-on-Railway to differentiate it from Kingston-on-Thames. It was renamed Surbiton when Kingston acquired its own station in 1863.

SURBITON. c.1939

RICHMOND BRIDGE, 1850s

VICTORIA

STATION. East side built 1860 for Victoria Station & Pimlico Railway and used by London Chatham & Dover Railway. Roof completed 1862 by Sir John Fowler; frontage built 1909 for South Eastern & Chatham Railway by A. W. Blomfield. Listed Grade II. West side built 1860 for London Brighton & South Coast Railway. Roof and frontage by Sir Charles L. Morgan, 1908.

Victoria is really two stations in one. There was no access between the two parts until after the 1923 Grouping when the Southern Railway knocked a hole in the party wall and made them into a single station.

The original station is unique in having been built by a 'terminal company', common enough in the United States but not in Britain; it was called the Victoria Station & Pimlico Railway Company. Completed in 1862, the station was leased to the London Chatham & Dover Railway. It now forms the eastern part of the terminus and still has its original two-bay arched roof with striking radial struts.

The upper-class inhabitants of Pimlico prevented Victoria from being built at viaduct height, which accounts for the steep 1 in 64 gradient from the station up to the bridge over the Thames.

The London Brighton & South Coast Railway, who had a majority holding in the Pimlico Company, had originally agreed to use the same station, but instead they built one of their own alongside, to the west.

In the 1890s they decided to rebuild their station. Private property in Buckingham Palace Road had first to be acquired at great cost, and it was 1908 before the new station was opened, with an entrance in Buckingham Palace Road that was used for most royal occasions.

The new frontage – replacing the temporary wooden structure that had stood since 1860 – was designed by the Brighton's chief engineer, Sir Charles Morgan. It was built of red brick and Portland stone in Edwardian Baroque

1910

style, much rusticated and topped by a large clock set in a scroll; in effect forming an extension of the neighbouring Grosvenor Hotel, it was all a little pompous.

At the same time the old roof was replaced by the present broad ridge-and-furrow one, and the platforms were lengthened to take two trains each, with ingenious cross-over arrangements half way along.

Meanwhile in 1899 the London Chatham & Dover had amalgamated with

the South Eastern to become the South Eastern & Chatham Railway. The directors were aware that the appearance of their own property was not above criticism: the great overall roof had bits missing, and in front it had a rickety canopy and vast hoardings (proclaiming that this was the shortest route to Paris, Brussels, Cologne, Switzerland, Italy and India). It was not a pretty sight.

A. W. Blomfield designed a new station frontage block in a style slightly more restrained than the Brighton's Edwardian Baroque alongside. It had similarities but was in white Portland stone, and sufficiently distinct to indicate that there was no connection with the firm next door.

There was a profusion of pediments and pilasters, and four remarkable Amazonian caryatids. Above the broad, elliptically-arched cab entrance there was not only the SECR's name but for very many years that of the Great Western Railway. As the Great Western ran one or two trains into Victoria via Clapham Junction from time to time, and had helped finance the station, it was entitled to advertise itself.

GROSVENOR HOTEL. Built 1860-61. Architect J. T. Knowles. Listed Grade II. Buckingham Palace Road, SW1.

The Grosvenor Hotel occupied the north-western side of the Brighton company's station, but was independently owned. In the 1890s when the new station was being planned, the hotel had to be bought out for £100,000; in 1899 it was leased to Gordon Hotels. It is tall and hefty in the Italianate style but with a French Renaissance roof. It retains some good interiors, including the dining-room and the Roman stair hall.

WATERLOO

Rebuilt 1922 for London & South Western Railway. Architect J. R. Scott. Engineers J. W. Jacomb-Hood and A. W. Szlumper.

The original London & Southampton Railway station was opened in 1839 at Nine Elms, an inconvenient point for a London terminus. Then the line was extended two miles downriver to a three-quarter acre site of Thames-soaked marshy ground, and here the first Waterloo station was built in 1848.

Its three platforms soon became inadequate, and by 1860 an extension for Windsor trains, known as the 'North Station', was opened. It was also confusingly called the 'Windsor Station'.

Further piecemeal enlargement took place in 1878 and 1885, resulting in the most confusing of all the London termini. There was even a single line from the main station to the South Eastern's station on the other side of Waterloo Road; it crossed the concourse on the level and went out through a hole in the wall on

to a bridge over the street.

In 1899 powers were sought for rebuilding. Six and a half acres were required, involving the closing of seven streets, the removal of 1,750 people and

1980

the demolition of All Saints Church. The task of reconstruction was exceedingly complex as the site was awkward and train services had to be maintained whilst the work progressed. Platforms 1-5 were opened in 1909, but (partly due to the intervention of the First World War) the station was not completed until 1922, when it was opened by Queen Mary.

The most striking feature of Waterloo is its spaciousness. The row of platforms terminating at the broad, gently curving concourse under a vast acreage of glazed transverse ridge-and-furrow roof is not inspiring in the Paddington or St. Pancras sense, but nevertheless produces an air of order which suggests that it would be difficult to catch a wrong train at Waterloo. One hardly notices that the roof bays over platforms 16-21 run in the opposite direction; they are all that remain of the old 'North Station', extended in 1885.

The curved frontage block is designed in the best grand Edwardian style, sometimes called Imperial baroque, but its giant columns and sculptures are sadly obscured by the former South Eastern Railway viaduct opposite so that from no point can one view the entire building. The main entrance is formed by the huge Victory Arch which represents the London & South Western war memorial. In Portland stone and bronze, it carries sculptures depicting War and Peace. High above on the cornice sits Britannia.

The new Waterloo was provided with some very gracious internal appointments. The main booking hall, now no longer used as such, had a plain curved ceiling and marble columns. Upstairs the spacious Surrey Dining Room had Georgian-style panelled walls. The Windsor Bar and the Long Bar were stylishly Edwardian, the first having Ionic columns, pilasters and two delightful little pay-boxes with fluted domes. The Long Bar was richly baroque in its decorations and dates from 1913, when a five-course *table d'hôte* dinner cost 3s. 6d.

KENT

Fowler is best known for designing the Forth Bridge in partnership with Benjamin Baker, which marked the apex of his career.

Born in Sheffield in 1817, he received his engineering training under the Leeds engineer J. T. Leather and then on the London & Brighton Railway under J. U. Rastrick. Like his contemporaries he did not restrict himself to civil engineering, becoming engineer, general manager and locomotive superintendent on the Stockton & Hartlepool Railway in 1841, where he stayed three years before commencing practice as a consultant in London.

Fowler built the Manchester Sheffield & Lincolnshire Railway east of Sheffield, the first railway bridge over the Thames, to Victoria station (1860), and the same year became engineer of the Metropolitan Railway, constructing in stages what now forms the greater part of London Transport's Circle Line. Fowler, one of the most grasping of Victorian engineers, charged the vast fee of £309,000 for this work. An unsuccessful experiment was his fireless locomotive for use on underground lines. Nicknamed 'Fowler's Ghost', it was charged with steam from stationary boilers but ran short of steam too quickly.

Fowler's handsome segmental arched roofs still grace the eastern side of Victoria station. Fowler worked in Egypt and India, and with Baker was joint consulting engineer for the first tube railway, the City & South London. He was made a baronet in 1890, and died in 1898 aged 81.

AYLESFORD

Built 1856 by South Eastern Railway. Between Strood and Maidstone.

Aylesford is an excellent, if late, example of the sympathetic use of local materials by a railway company: the heyday of this sort of enlightened thinking was already over by 1856.

The popular Tudor style was chosen, and the building has such similarities with the earlier, larger Wateringbury (*p.188*) that one is tempted to think it was by the same architect, or else a copy.

1979

It could hardly have been done better. The traditional Kentish ragstone is set off by ample dressed Caen stone quoins and mullions, although all this is somewhat spoiled by the angled chimneys in red brick which may be later replacements. Could the presence of the 14th-15th century Aylesford Friary have been a factor in choosing the design?

CANTERBURY WEST

Built 1846 for South Eastern Railway. Architect probably Samuel Beazley. Listed Grade II. Between Ashford and Margate.

The station is a low, one-storey building in stucco, with a shallow hipped roof behind a low parapet and broad cornice. A centrally recessed entrance has a pair of fluted columns and side pilasters, flanked by three well-proportioned sash windows on either side with slender glazing bars, to form a quietly balanced classical composition.

1970s

Nearby was the terminus of the Canterbury & Whitstable Railway, opened in 1830, the first steam-hauled railway in the south of England.

CUXTON

Built 1856 by South Eastern Railway. Between Strood and Maidstone.

This little station is built of brick in a Tudor style with steeply pitched roofs and characteristic tall chimney stacks. It is

1970s

really 'minimum Tudor' and looks rather like a tiny village school with its single-storey hall and gabled outline. It seems to have survived well, no doubt because it is still able to provide the basic necessary amenities of a country station.

THE SOUTH EASTERN & CHATHAM RAILWAY

The Act of 1899 that united the South Eastern and the London Chatham & Dover Railways marked the end of a business conflict unequalled in British railway history. The two companies had been bitterly hostile rivals for almost 50 years.

The South Eastern, opened in 1842, had a fine main line that ran straight and level from its junction with the LBSCR at Redhill to Ashford in Kent. The London Chatham & Dover, incorporated 13 years later, had to cope with cramped conditions in London and some steep hills at the country end. The merger enabled a link to be made between the two companies' lines where they crossed at Chislehurst.

Neither company's locomotives had been notably picturesque in the 19th century, though at the South Eastern's Ashford Works James Stirling had built a series of locomotives that were sound in construction and excellent in performance. For the Chatham William Kirtley was responsible for a tradition of fine engineering at the Longhedge Works, Battersea.

After the merger, both men retired. H. S. Wainwright, hitherto a carriage man on the South Eastern, was appointed Locomotive Carriage and Wagon Superintendent. R. Surtees of the Chatham became Chief Locomotive Draughtsman and designed some splendid new engines. One of them is now preserved in the National Railway Museum at York. The work of Wainwright's successor, R. E. L. Maunsell, was also highly successful.

SECR 'D' class 4-4-0 leaving Rye, 1920s

DOVER

SOUTHERN HOUSE. Built 1853 for South Eastern Railway. Architect Samuel Beazley. Listed Grade II.

Originally the Lord Warden Hotel, this Italianate four-storey building was converted to offices by the Southern Railway.

SHAKESPEARE TUNNEL. Built 1844 by South Eastern Railway. Engineer William Cubitt.

The Gothic portals of this 1,387-yard twin-bore tunnel embellish the final stage of the cliff-side line from Folkestone to Dover.

DOVER SOUTHERN HOUSE, 1970s

EYNSFORD VIADUCT, 1960s

SHAKESPEARE TUNNEL, 1840s

FOORD VIADUCT, 1844

EYNSFORD VIADUCT

Built 1862 by Sevenoaks Railway (later South Eastern Railway). Listed Grade II.

This most attractive and dramatic viaduct crosses the Darenth valley on nine red-brick, semi-circular arches rising from tall slim brick piers. The fine effect is greatly accentuated by the flat valley bottom which means, unusually, that all the piers are the same height. This feature gives the bridge a strong likeness to a Roman aqueduct, an apt enough comparison since Lullingstone Roman Villa lies in its shadow.

Lullingstone Castle is also nearby and its mellow Tudor brickwork is matched by that of the viaduct. The contrasting stone parapet is the finishing touch to what is a valuable contribution to the landscape.

FOLKESTONE

FOORD VIADUCT. Built 1843 for South Eastern Railway. Designed by Sir William Cubitt. Listed Grade II. In Bradstone Road.

The section of the South Eastern line between Folkestone and Dover, opened in 1844, required massive engineering works which included this viaduct, the largest on the South Eastern railway. It strides across the village of Foord on 19 yellow-brick arches supported on slim piers up to 100 feet in height. It still provides a fine spectacle despite being described by a contemporary as a 'gigantic and ponderous mass of manual labour and ingenuity'. It is rather more encroached upon, nowadays, by Folkestone than its quality deserves.

GRAVESEND

STATION. Built 1849 for South Eastern Railway. Architect Samuel Beazley. Listed Grade II. Between London and Chatham.

In its general plan, and in details such as the low roof, balustraded parapet and windows with fine glazing bars, Beazley's main building at Gravesend is similar to Canterbury West; but it has two-storeyed side-blocks and is a far superior building. Built of stock brick with stuccoed dressings, the station has a central recess with a fine colonnade.

TOWN PIER. Built 1834. Listed Grade II.

In 1884 the London Tilbury & Southend Railway obtained an Act to run passenger steamers from Tilbury to Gravesend Town Pier. This river connection enabled them to offer cheap through tickets to Gravesend from Fenchurch Street, in competition with the South Eastern Railway's direct train service on the other side of the river from London Bridge via the North Kent line to Gravesend Central (now Gravesend).

The Tilbury company purchased the Town Pier in 1895. It is an iron structure

GRAVESEND AFTER RENOVATION, 1978

on tubular columns with a wood-covered superstructure, embellished with pilasters and other classical features. The entrance to the pier is a wooden building with a typical railway-style verandah, its roof supported on thin columns and finished with serrated valancing.

SAMUEL BEAZLEY, ARCHITECT

The series of pleasantly dignified stations on the South Eastern Railway's North Kent line was the work of Samuel Beazley. His best undoubtedly was Gravesend, designed in classical style, and probably he was also responsible for the similar station at Canterbury West (*p.185*). Dartford and Erith were Italianate, and New Cross Gate may also be his work.

Born in 1786 he trained under his uncle Charles Beazley, but architecture was only one of his talents. He fought in the Peninsular War, wrote two novels and was a prolific playwright and theatrical producer, an interest he carried through to his architectural work when he designed the colonnade at Drury Lane Theatre and the St. James Theatre in London. Several country mansions and the Lord Warden Hotel at Dover were among his other works, as well as the original South Eastern Railway terminus at London Bridge. He died in 1851.

GRAVESEND TOWN PIER, 1982

RAMSGATE

Built 1926 for Southern Railway. Engineer A. W. Szlumper. Between Canterbury and Margate.

In 1926 the Southern Railway lines in Thanet underwent an upheaval. Two stations, Margate Sands and Ramsgate Town, were closed, as was the branch of the South Eastern section that ran between them. Also, the old Chatham &

OPENING OF NEW LINE TO BROADSTAIRS, 1926

Dover line running through Margate West station and Broadstairs was diverted from Ramsgate Harbour to a new inland station. It was built in brick, in strictly plain 1920s style, with attention given to a very lofty, airy booking hall with three huge, round-headed windows on both the frontage and platform sides – a very dominant building which has the appearance more of a power station than a railway station.

STROOD

HIGHAM TUNNEL. Opened 1824 for Thames & Medway Canal. Engineer William Tierney Clark. Converted 1844-47 for rail use by Thames & Medway Canal, later South Eastern Railway.

In 1824 the Thames & Medway Canal completed a tunnel from Higham to Frindsbury, near Strood. At 2 miles 389 yards, it was the second longest canal tunnel in Britain. The waterway did not prosper, however, and in 1844 the company decided to run a single line of railway through the tunnel on the tow-path; when the path proved too narrow to take even one pair of rails, the outer rails were laid on a wooden viaduct cantilevered out above the water, and railway traffic began to run on this improvised track in February 1845.

The company was then bought up by the South Eastern Railway, the canal was closed and a double line of rails laid along its bed, to form part of the extension of the North Kent Railway running from Gravesend to Rochester. It was opened in 1847.

The passage through the tunnel by train is made memorable by the circular opening towards the middle, which was cut to provide light for canal barges passing one another. It forms an enormous well of skylight between two long stretches of pitch darkness.

TUNBRIDGE WELLS CENTRAL, LITHOGRAPH c.1846 BY J. C. BOURNE

TUNBRIDGE WELLS CENTRAL

Up (west) side built 1845-46 for South Eastern Railway. Designed by R. B. Gardener. Listed Grade II. Down (east) side built 1911 for South Eastern & Chatham Railway. Designed by Sir Reginald Blomfield.

The South Eastern Railway's main line from Reigate Junction (now Redhill) to Tonbridge was opened in 1842, and a branch to Tunbridge Wells opened in 1845. Here there was a temporary terminus pending the completion of the tunnel leading into the new main station in the following year. This station remained a terminus until the line was extended to Robertsbridge in 1851.

The up side plainly contains the original Italianate building depicted in J. C. Bourne's print, with its divided chimney stacks, prominently bracketed eaves, cornice and small rectangular openings on the end walls. There have, of course, been numerous modifications over the years. The old building is now overpowered by the much taller building on the down side, designed by Sir Reginald Blomfield in 1911. It has two large, heavily rusticated arched openings in brick beneath a Portland stone cornice, and an elaborate false gable hiding the lower part of a tall clock turret.

The London Brighton & South Coast Railway also had a station in the town, further west with no differentiation in the name, so that it was possible in earlier times to buy an LBSC ticket at their station bearing the idiotic legend: 'Tunbridge Wells to Tunbridge via Tunbridge Wells'. (Tonbridge was spelt with a 'u' until the 1890s.) In 1923 the newly formed Southern Railway sensibly added 'Central' and 'West' to the respective names.

Tunbridge Wells was not an easy place to reach by railway; the line required severe up-gradients immediately after leaving Tonbridge. This 4¾-mile stretch has two tunnels, heavy earthworks and the listed Southborough Viaduct (*p.193*).

WATERINGBURY

Opened 1844 by South Eastern Railway; additions 1886-99. Listed Grade II. Between Paddock Wood and Maidstone.

1978

(*Continued on page 193*)

This rare view from a rafter supporting the deck of the Forth Bridge reveals in detail the rivetted steel tubes and latticed cross girders of one of the three central towers.

LONG-LIVED SIGNAL BOXES

The individuality of the old railway companies has survived notably in many of the early signal boxes still in service on British Rail. While most of the Inter-City network has now been modernised with new panel signal boxes providing thumb-switch control of vast areas, on many of the feeder routes and surviving branches, signal boxes with mechanical apparatus remain.

The longevity of much of this equipment is remarkable: it dates back to pre-Grouping days and reflects the preferences of the different companies for particular manufacturers.

In the Eastern Region today there are still examples of the Great Northern style on the East Lincolnshire lines, as at Boston, while on the Newcastle & Carlisle line (formerly operated by the North Eastern Railway) there are interesting examples of boxes built on gantries spanning the tracks so as to give signalmen a good view up and down the line. One survives at Wylam, and a very lofty box with delicately curved brackets is still in use at Haltwhistle.

An excellent example of a preserved Great Eastern box may be seen in the Science Museum at South Kensington. It was originally at Haddiscoe Junction, Norfolk, where the main line from London to Yarmouth intersected a cross-country line from Norwich to Lowestoft. Dismantled when that part of the main line between Beccles and Yarmouth was closed, it has been rebuilt as a working exhibit. Visitors may go right into it and study all the various items of equipment.

On the London Midland Region the distinctive building styles of the Midland and London & North Western Railways are still evident, despite much modernisation. On the Midland line there are, in addition to the listed boxes at Bedford, Kettering and Kilby Bridge, some fine examples on the historic Settle & Carlisle line at Settle Junction, Blea Moor and Culgaith. In former LNWR territory at Shrewsbury, there is the very large box in the fork between the Birmingham and the Hereford lines, and a variety of styles large and small on the Chester to Holyhead main line. The LNWR mechanical interlocking frame was unique; it had a stirrup type of catch handle, designed at Crewe to circumvent other manufacturers' patents.

In the Scottish Region Caledonian-style boxes exist at Stirling and on the Oban line; North British types on the West Highland line between Helensburgh, Fort William and Mallaig; and there is a good Highland Railway box at Welsh's Bridge, Inverness.

On the Southern Region most of the network has been electrified and equipped with colour light signalling. But some of the old boxes have been retained to house the new equipment, including examples at Chichester (LBSCR style) and Haslemere (LSWR style).

The Western Region, although much modernised for 125-mph trains, still retains many fine examples of the standardised Great Western design in operation up to 1948, with large boxes at Taunton, Exeter and Newton Abbot as well as many smaller but excellent examples in Cornwall. The little wooden box at Instow on the London & South Western branch from Barnstaple to Torrington, now open only for freight, is a listed building.

The box at Ayot in Hertfordshire is a type that was common on Great Northern Railway branch lines.

At Sandown, once a junction, the box was built tall to give views of both main and branch lines.

This Midland box at Armathwaite, now with automatic barriers, serves the Settle & Carlisle line.

A railwayman operates signals in the old way at Desford Junction (Leicester to Burton line, 1960s).

Framed by the arch of a pier, a forest of hangers and chains suspends the deck of Brunel's Royal Albert Bridge from one of the two giant overhead wrought-iron tubes.

SOUTHBOROUGH VIADUCT, 1978

Sir William was the uncle of Lewis Cubitt (*p.14*), Thomas and William Cubitt the contractors. All of them worked on the construction of the Great Northern Railway. By that time he already had a varied career behind him.

Sir William was inventive. He patented self-regulating windmill sails in 1807 and in 1817 invented the treadmill, one of his less attractive devices; it was quickly adopted in British gaols. Between 1812 and 1826 he worked for Ransomes, the well known agricultural engineers of Ipswich, becoming a partner.

In 1825 he set up an engineering practice in London and worked on several canals, and then in 1836-46 he built the South Eastern Railway where one of his most difficult jobs was removing the face of Round Down Cliff near Folkestone, for which task he used 18,000 lb. of gunpowder in a single explosion detonated electrically. The nearby Shakespeare Cliff Tunnel was part of the same line. Towards the end of his Great Northern Railway work Cubitt superintended the erection of the Crystal Palace, for which he gained his knighthood. He was born in 1785 and died in 1861.

(*Continued from page 188*)

Wateringbury is a particularly attractive example of railway Tudor: a red brick, two-storey building with stone quoins, tiled roofs and all the decorative paraphernalia of gables, mullioned windows with lozenge glazing and tall diagonally set chimneys.

The station was opened to traffic in 1844, but all the other South Eastern stations of the 1840s appear to be Classical or Italianate; it is more likely that the station building was put up in 1855, a date that coincides with similar designs by William Tress and the almost identical Tudor of Aylesford (*p.185*).

WHITSTABLE

Built 1915 by South Eastern & Chatham Railway. Between Faversham and Margate.

This station replaced the old Whitstable Town station to the west, which had been opened in 1860. It is a heavily classical composition in brick, with four sets of coupled brick pilasters in the front and two pairs on each end wall, beneath an overpowering stone cornice and low parapet. The windows are set in moulded stone casings and have Georgian glazing. The unusual platform awnings are supported on ungainly riveted steel brackets which 'grow' out of the stanchions, looking as though they spring directly from the platforms. But the awning profiles are pleasing, and the valances deeply serrated.

1970s

EAST SUSSEX

BATTLE

Opened 1852 by South Eastern Railway. Architect William Tress. Between Tunbridge Wells and Hastings.

1930s

Battle is the pearl among the stations on this line, which are built to a very high quality in several different styles. Here the choice is medieval, intended no doubt to tone in with the nearby Battle Abbey. (Perhaps surprisingly no attempt was made to use Norman in deference to William the Conqueror, whose battle it was.)

The building is in roughly coursed rubble with a decorative tiled roof; it is laid out on a medieval plan with a central hall and cross wings. Lancet windows light the station master's house and two grand traceried ones are provided for the waiting room. The interior of the booking hall has exposed beams, and the design is completed with a belfry.

WAITING ROOM, 1970s

BISHOPSTONE

Built 1938 by Southern Railway. Between Lewes and Seaford.

The original Bishopstone station was opened in 1864; it was reduced in status to an unstaffed halt in 1922, closed in 1938 and reopened as Bishopstone Beach Halt a year later.

A new Bishopstone station was opened nearer Seaford and is a typical example of the functional, red brick and concrete architecture employed by the Southern Railway at the time of its vast electrifica-

tion and modernization programme between the wars.

The frontage is long and low with single-light steel-framed windows and, above the booking hall, an octagonal brick lantern with a concrete top looking not unlike a gun emplacement. On the platform side are canted glass awnings on unadorned steelwork, and a somewhat stark footbridge. The contemporary work of Charles Holden on the London Underground clearly inspired Bishopstone, but Holden's flair is lacking.

c.1980

BRIGHTON

STATION. Frontage block built 1840-41 for London & Brighton Railway. Architect David Mocatta. Trainshed built 1883 for London Brighton & South Coast Railway. Architect H. E. Wallis. Original portion and trainsheds on covered platforms to the north listed Grade II.

Long before the railway arrived, Brighton had been a fashionable resort among royalty, the aristocracy and the elegant – and with them, or very shortly after, the social climbers, the sycophants and the rogues. It all made Brighton a very obvious target for a railway.

The first portion of the London & Brighton was opened between Brighton and Shoreham in 1840. Whether the entire station was completed by then is not certain, but illustrations show the trainshed in place and the board minutes of the company record complaints about draughts in the summer of 1840. David Mocatta designed the handsome stuccoed entrance building which is still in existence. In its early days the station looked out over the town to the sea, but in 1882 a glass-and-iron *porte cochère* was added, which spoiled the elegance.

There is a nine-arched arcade along the central part of the ground floor with columned arcades on either side, and a parapet fronting a terrace above. Fifteen windows look out from the first floor with alternate segmental and triangular pediments. A second floor at each end is joined by another parapet, with a central curved false gable containing a clock. A deeply dentilled cornice runs between the first and second floors and also above the nine-arched arcade. Above the booking hall, with its coffered ceiling and iron columns, were the board-room and administrative offices.

The original timber-trussed pitched trainshed was designed by the London & Brighton's engineer J. U. Rastrick (*p.180*) and replaced in 1883 by one to the design of H. E. Wallis. He ingeniously erected the new roof on arched ribs over the old, which was then removed. The side walls are brick-arcaded and the iron columns supporting the roof bear the arms of the London Brighton & South Coast Railway. Lines curve out from the terminus in two directions so that the roof's dramatic qualities are accentuated. There is a particularly fine narrow bay along the eastern side. Brighton, like so many of the bigger stations, has its famous clock, and here the one hanging over the concourse has especially delicate wrought-ironwork.

For many years two renowned train services operated between London and Brighton. The *Southern Belle*, which started in 1908, was renamed *Brighton Belle* in 1934, and was withdrawn in April 1972; its distinguished passengers enjoyed its equally famous breakfast kippers. Then there was the *City Limited*, 8.45 a.m. up and 5.00 p.m. down from London Bridge; it was a named train from 1921 to 1939, but had been running since 1844.

FRONTAGE BLOCK, 1841

NEW ROOF REPLACING OLD, BRIGHTON, 1883

LEWES ROAD VIADUCT. Built 1869 for London Brighton & South Coast Railway. Engineer Frederick Dale Banister. Listed Grade II.

This is a rather uneven red-brick viaduct with the largest arch, over Lewes Road, by no means in the centre. It is segmented with smaller round-headed pedestrian arches on either side, and the three are framed by projecting pilasters. There are nine further arches to the west, and on the east two more and a later plain steel span. The whole design is given a uniform appearance by the balustraded parapet.

LONDON ROAD VIADUCT. Built 1845-46 for Brighton Lewes & Hastings Railway. Engineer J. U. Rastrick; architect David Mocatta. Listed Grade II.

This is the main engineering work on the line from Brighton to Lewes and was built in a wide curve from the main London line round to London Road station. Built of red and yellow brick with stone dressings it is 400 yards long and up to 67 feet high where it crosses London Road on an elliptical arch of 50-foot span. There are a further 26 round-headed arches of 30-foot span, and the whole is brought together by a modillioned cornice and balustraded parapet. Each of the piers is pierced by an arched opening, like the same designer's

c.1950

Ouse Viaduct (*p.197*), achieving a great saving in weight and material.

Originally a magnificent sight, the viaduct has been largely obscured by later housing. The London Road arch was demolished by a bomb in the war but was quickly rebuilt, and the structure is otherwise unaltered.

EASTBOURNE

Opened 1866 by London Brighton & South Coast Railway. Extended 1886. Engineer F. Dale Banister. Extended again c.1930 by Southern Railway. Listed Grade II.

In 1800 East Bourne (as it was then spelt) was still a small country village about a mile from the sea, connected with the outside world by a thrice-weekly coach to London. The opening of the railway from Lewes to a point near Hastings brought its inhabitants a station at Polegate, only a few miles distant, and in 1849 a branch was opened from that station.

Eastbourne now grew rapidly, becom-

1976

ing something of a resort for gentlefolk, many of whom came to visit and stayed on. Unlike Brighton, which was nearer London with a better train service, it did not attract the more lively and dissolute type of visitor. The population of the area had increased enough by 1866 to warrant the opening of a new station to the east of the old one. Improvements were made in 1872 and a further enlargement in 1886.

It is a double-fronted station in a mixture of Brighton-style Italianate and French Renaissance. A corner clock tower has dentilled cornices and a conical top. To the left is a semi-domed French pavilion roof with fish-scale tiles and iron cresting, and to the right, above the large concourse, a rectangular arcaded upper storey with hipped roof, surmounted by the characteristic LBSC wooden lantern surrounded by a trellis of ornamental ironwork and finials. The Southern Railway added an extension in contemporary style in the 1930s.

From 1890 traffic had risen enough to create a demand for an 8.30 a.m. non-stop train to London Bridge with slip-coaches for Victoria detached at East Croydon. Yet Eastbourne remained gently respectable: for it, no clanking trams (or ankles displayed while boarding them). It was one of the first English towns to go straight to motor-buses, the resort's first form of mass public transport.

ETCHINGHAM

Built 1851 for South Eastern Railway. Architect William Tress. Between Tunbridge Wells and Hastings.

This is a pleasant Tudor station in two shades of stone, with the later addition of a typical deep South Eastern awning

whose end-valances follow the curve of the brackets. Most of Tress's stations on this line are in Italianate style and bear strong similarities to one another, but Etchingham, like Battle and Frant, was singled out for different treatment. It is an agreeable example of Victorian antiquarianism, though somewhat haphazard and from the front lacking the cohesion usual in Tress's work. His treatment of the platform elevation is much more satisfactory.

1978

Etchingham appears to be the first station in the world to have had an authentic 'slip' carriage, detached from a train without stopping – later a common feature on British railways. It has always been held, even officially, that the first 'slip' was at Haywards Heath in February 1858, but the South Eastern timetable for January 1858 has a note for the 4.25 p.m. fast train from London Bridge to Hastings: 'Leaves London Passengers at Penshurst, Etchingham and Battle. The Train does not stop at Etchingham.' Good publicity may have stilled the fears of passengers who might otherwise have been alarmed by this sinister sentence.

HASTINGS

Rebuilt 1931 for Southern Railway. Architect J. R. Scott.

Hastings was originally a South Eastern Railway station. By 1851 the London Brighton & South Coast Railway had driven eastwards from Lewes and claimed the right to use a quarter of a mile of South Eastern line from Bo-peep Junction (named after a pub frequented by shepherds). The South Eastern removed the track at the junction, marooning LBSC trains that had been taken to the station for the next day's traffic, not to mention the Brighton clerk in his office. They also turned off the gas. The LBSC promptly hired a bus, so the South Eastern erected a barricade across the station forecourt, and it took an injunction to persuade the SER to accept the situation.

The station, opened in 1851, was rebuilt 80 years later. The main station building is in Wealden multi-red brick with cream stone dressings, a flat roof and terracotta capping. The booking hall is octagonal, with a matching roof-light, tall round-headed glazed openings and glass-panelled doors. The exit to the platforms is through a square hall lit by a lantern light, and flanking sections contain offices and refreshment rooms. Until the early 1960s the white-tiled booking hall had an interesting and slightly Spanish-American Art Deco frieze, depicting children with buckets and spades, a beach, a cricket match, a promenade and a 'Southern Electric' train, among numerous other scenes.

The station, built without interrupting rail traffic, was opened on 6th July, 1931.

QUEENS ROAD BRIDGE. Built 1851 for South Eastern Railway. Engineer probably Peter Barlow. Listed Grade II.

This wrought-iron girder bridge is carried on two pairs of large cast-iron Doric columns with thick fluting but no other embellishment. These piers, combining compressive strength with a certain importance in appearance, are typical of the

1982

earliest railway bridges (*see also London Bridge p.182*) although by 1851 they were already rather old-fashioned. The collapse of Robert Stephenson's Dee Bridge at Chester (*p.73*) in 1847 had done much to discredit the use of cast iron in bridges.

HORSTED KEYNES

Built 1882 for London Brighton & South Coast Railway. Architect T. W. Myres. Between East Grinstead and Haywards Heath. Sold.

Myres designed a number of stations for the Brighton company in the 1880s, all based on a typical late-Victorian idea of 'Old English' comprising modern half-timbering with stylized 'pot-plant' pargeting in the stucco-work, quatrefoil designs, moulded chimney stacks and tinted glass. At Horsted Keynes the half-timbering and decoration was later covered with patterned tile-hanging, Sussex fashion.

When the station was closed in 1955 a

1882

local resident pointed out that there was a legal obligation to run a minimum of four trains each way daily. The station was therefore reopened until parliamentary sanction was obtained in 1958 to close it legally. It is now the northern terminus of the Bluebell Railway, the country's first standard-gauge preservation scheme.

LEWES

Built 1889 by London Brighton & South Coast Railway.

This is the third station to have been built at Lewes, which is in an area of bulging hills that are of no help to an engineer wanting to plan a straight and level line. The first station, built in 1846, was on the line from Brighton. It could not cope with all the traffic that poured in when lines were opened from Hastings, Haywards Heath and Newhaven, so a second station was opened a short way off in 1857. But the following year the Uckfield line

opened and in 1889 it was necessary to build a third station.

The clapboard of the 1857 station was replaced by something in the more solid LBSC tradition by now in vogue; it was topped by a hipped roof with a characteristic Brighton pagoda-like lantern above, behind a parapet with huge 'acorn and spike' urns.

PLUMPTON

Built 1863 by London Brighton & South Coast Railway. Main building on north side of line, subsidiary building on south of line and connecting footbridge and signal box all listed Grade II. Between Lewes and Haywards Heath.

Plumpton is a good example of the better kind of mid-Victorian wooden station. It is single-storeyed with a hipped roof, broad overhanging eaves and finely glazed Georgian sash windows. The external cladding is in the Sussex clapboard tradition, and the subsidiary shelter on the up platform has alternately pointed and rounded saw-teeth on the valancing.

The station belongs to that period between the good vernacular building of the 1840s and early 1850s on the one hand, and late-Victorian solidity on the other. It was a time of intense competition and generally low dividends when railway companies in the south of England, lacking the lucrative heavy-goods traffic of their northern counterparts, were struggling to make ends meet. Station-building suffered accordingly, though to modern eyes the expedient of building in wood created quite pleasing results.

PLUMPTON, 1982

LEWES, c.1906

RYE

Built 1851 for South Eastern Railway. Architect William Tress. Station building on south east side of line listed Grade II. Between Ashford and Hastings.

Tress's design for the stations on this line culminates here in one of the most sophisticated of all small stations. Despite the historic nature of this Cinque Port, Tress made no attempt to provide a medieval building as at Battle (*p.194*); instead he indulged in a rather more determined

c.1970

Italianate than elsewhere.

Built of brick with stucco quoins and dressings and very shallow hipped roofs, the station has a five-bay front, the three centre ones with an entrance loggia from the Florentine Renaissance.

On the platform side the plain arches leading to the booking hall are recessed between side wings, and a neat canopy on brackets covers the front with no further projection; it is a post-1877 addition but adds to the perfect quality of the station.

ST. LEONARDS WARRIOR SQUARE

Built 1852 for South Eastern Railway. Architect William Tress. Between Battle and Hastings.

All the stations on the South Eastern between Tonbridge and Hastings are supposed to be the work of Tress but they come in two definite styles; medieval or classical. St. Leonards is close to exemplifying the latter; it is the largest version of a design which appears in small form at Robertsbridge and Stonegate, and in medium-sized form at Wadhurst.

Four central bays are framed by plain pilasters with a broken pediment above the centre pair. Flanking bays are set back, but a projecting house on the right, also pedimented, breaks the symmetry. The platform side is a repeat, and the whole structure is in brick with stucco dressings and shallow pitched slate roofs. A distinct effort was made to fit in with the town but not to the extent of adopting a self-consciously special design. The building carries on the contemporary tradition of public buildings, workhouses, barracks, hospitals and the like.

ST. LEONARDS WARRIOR SQUARE, 1960s

BALCOMBE

OUSE VIADUCT. Built 1840 for London & Brighton Railway. Engineer J. U. Rastrick. Listed Grade II. Between Three Bridges and Haywards Heath.

This is considered by many to be the most elegant of all the country's railway viaducts. It crosses the Ouse valley on 37 brick arches 92 feet high and of 30-foot span, and it is crowned by a stone balustrade and flanked at either end by Italianate pavilions. (These architectural features may well be a contribution by David Mocatta – *see Burgess Hill p.198.*) The structure is an immensely satisfying man-made contribution to the landscape, successful from all distances and angles. The vista through the pierced piers is a famous one. The viaduct has the advantage of standing unaltered.

OUSE VIADUCT, c.1970

BURGESS HILL

*Original station built 1841 by London &
Brighton Railway. Present building built 1877
by London Brighton & South Coast Railway.
Between Haywards Heath and Brighton.*

There are two buildings of interest here.
At the southern end of the north-bound
platform stands a small house in white
stucco, with plain moulded window
hoods; it has all the appearance of being
an early railway building, possibly the
station master's house.

BURGESS HILL OLD STATION, 1981

Backing on to the opposite platform, in
what is now the goods yard, is a carefully
detailed, single-storey red brick building
with a slate roof – the original station of
1841, but now used as a coal office. It has
an Italianate flavour with coupled,
round-headed windows arranged symmetrically. A recessed central area contains the entrance doorway; the roof here
is supported by two nicely moulded
brackets.

This second building smacks strongly
of David Mocatta, the London & Brighton company architect who designed
original stations using a standard ground-
plan but with different external styling to
produce harmonious variations. Burgess
Hill is not among the many drawings by
Mocatta still in existence, nor was red
brick a material he chose elsewhere; yet
this was one of the original stations on the
line and Mocatta favoured Classical and
Italianate styles. Moreover there are
strong similarities between Burgess Hill
and the existing part of the old stuccoed
station at Hassocks known to be by
Mocatta.

The replacement station of 1877 is in a
style sympathetic to the earlier building;
it is a single-storey pavilion having gabled
bays at either end and a central entrance,
with a flat canopy added in 1897.

CLAYTON TUNNEL

*Built 1841 for London & Brighton Railway.
Engineer J. U. Rastrick. Between Hassocks and
Brighton.*

The portal at the north end of the tunnel is
castellated, with a tower on each side and
a cottage in between. This seems an unlikely place to perch a cottage as a whim,
and one explanation is that it may have
been for the use of whoever was in charge
of the gas with which the tunnel was lit in
early days. The site of the gas works is

CLAYTON TUNNEL, c.1900

uncertain, but is thought to have been on
the down, or east, side between Hassocks
station and the tunnel.

WORTHING

*OLD STATION. Built 1845 by London &
Brighton Railway. Listed Grade II. Between
Brighton and Chichester.*

Worthing was originally a station built to
serve what *Lewis's Topographical Survey* of
1835 considered to be a reasonably important market town and bathing resort,
with libraries and other public buildings.
A new station was built on the other side
of the road in 1870, and this in its turn was
replaced in 1907-09 – but the original
two-storey building of 1845 still stands. It
looks more like a private house (which it
now is), domestic in character without
architectural pretension. There is a
single-storey wing on each side, and the
building is attractively faced with panels
of coursed cobbles between heavily
rusticated red brick quoins and door and
window openings. Without this local style
of finish it would be extremely plain.

WORTHING OLD STATION, c.1870

SURREY

BOXHILL & WESTHUMBLE

Built 1867 for London Brighton & South Coast Railway. Architect Charles H. Driver. Listed Grade II. Between Leatherhead and Dorking.

When the LBSCR bought the land on which this station stands, it accepted a condition imposed by the landowner, Thomas Grissell of nearby Norbury Park, that 'The station at West Humble Lane shall be of an ornamental character'. The result was a charmingly ornate French-style building.

A crested pyramidal turret projects above tall, steeply gabled roofs clad with patterned tiles and exposed timber framing. A cosy little porch leads into a booking hall with a miniature hammerbeam roof. The porch itself is on short stone columns with capitals and brackets intricately decorated with floral work, and all different. No better evidence of the company's good faith could be required.

CHERTSEY

Built 1866 by London & South Western Railway. Between Weybridge and Virginia Water.

Chertsey station was originally opened in 1848 as the terminus of a branch from Weybridge, but after many complaints about the service the line was extended to Virginia Water and the station was rebuilt.

1980

The new station is an almost exact twin of Netley, which opened earlier in 1866; it is a brick building in the Italianate style, with bay wings on either side of the recessed centre. The entrance has semicircular arches that are repeated on the platform. Carved eaves-brackets and hipped slate roofs complete the design.

EWELL WEST

Built 1859 by London & South Western Railway. Station, platform and shelter on west side of line listed Grade II. Between Epsom & Raynes Park.

BOXHILL & WESTHUMBLE, 1980

Ewell follows a plan used at several of the contemporary stations on the Portsmouth Direct line (*see Petersfield, p.204*). The brick building is in a Palladian style with a two-storey centrepiece and single-storey wings; in 1892 the right-hand wing was raised and given a barge-boarded gable and an oriel window, spoiling the symmetry although no doubt improving the station master's accommodation.

GODALMING

Built 1859 for London & South Western Railway. Architects probably Sir William Tite and Edward N. Clifton. Between Guildford and Portsmouth.

The original terminus at Godalming was a larger version of Tite's London & Southampton Railway stations such as Micheldever (*p.204*), but in 1859, when the Portsmouth Direct line was opened, the company provided a new building in golden-brown rubble with ashlar trimmings.

The station house is of three storeys with a steeply gabled roof and Tudor-style windows, and has a single-storey office adjoining. The building bears such a strong resemblance to Tite and Clifton's larger stations between Salisbury and Exeter, and to Petersfield further down the line, that it seems likely they were the architects.

EWELL WEST, 1982

GODALMING, 1970s

LEATHERHEAD, 1974

KENLEY

Built 1856 for Caterham Railway. Architect Richard Whittall. Between Purley and Caterham.

Originally named Coulsdon, the station was designed by Richard Whittall in what was then referred to as 'Old English style of Domestic Architecture' – really *cottage orné*, with a very tall steeply pitched gable, half-timbering on the upper portion, and quoined masonry rubble walls. It is the last station of Whittall's still extant.

1951

The 4½-mile Caterham Railway led a delightfully independent and rather wicked life for three years, pointedly snubbing its powerful neighbours, the Brighton and the South Eastern (on whom it had to rely); it played one off against the other in turn, until, totally impoverished but stiff-upper-lipped, it was taken over by the South Eastern in 1859.

LEATHERHEAD

Built 1867 for London Brighton & South Coast Railway. Architect Charles H. Driver. Listed Grade II. Between Epsom and Dorking.

The first station at Leatherhead, inconveniently situated about a quarter of a mile north of the present one, was opened by the Epsom & Leatherhead Railway in 1859, and transferred in 1860 to joint ownership of the London & South Western and the London Brighton & South Coast Railways. It was replaced by a separate station for each company in 1867. The South Western station was closed in 1927 and traffic diverted to the former Brighton station, which is far superior.

As at Box Hill (*p.199*), the former landowner Mr. Grissell had a hand in ensuring that the 1867 station was built to suit his taste, in this case in a Lombardic style. The frontage has elaborately decorated round-headed openings, with coupled windows on central shafts with foliated capitals, and a colourful, herringbone brick frieze adorns the low French-style turret. The canopies on the front and platform sides are carried on the slenderest of columns, with small, intricately decorated brackets. The valancing originally carried applied decorative vertical strips.

TATTENHAM CORNER

Built 1901 by South Eastern & Chatham Railway. End of branch from Purley.

The Chipstead Valley line, which left the Caterham line immediately south of Purley, had reached Tadworth & Walton-on-the-Hill by 1900 and was extended to Tattenham Corner on the eve of Derby Day the following year. It was the most convenient station for the racecourse, even if it was a little further from London than the Brighton company's station at Epsom Downs.

1975

The station was erected in the familiar and parsimonious wooden style that the South Eastern had been using ever since 1842, with a hipped roof slightly enhanced by a central gable. It is rather larger than usual as it was intended to deal with race crowds and the company also hoped to encourage visitors to the Downs. Its regular traffic was only a few trains running in the summer months, and even they were stopped short at Tadworth in 1914 as a war-time economy; the station was not fully reopened until electrification in 1928.

DECORATION AND DETAIL

The decoration of railway buildings faithfully followed the development of Victorian architecture and art from classical and the picturesque through to Gothic. The urge to embellish the surfaces of buildings grew almost obsessive. Decoration in iron became not only more intricate but, aided by mass-production methods, also cheaper and more general, spreading from station roofs and canopies to the structural elements of bridges. Only recently have designers realised the possibilities of brightening city streets by painting ironwork in contrasting colours, while the cleaning of stone on a wide scale has revealed much hidden richness in carving and moulded terracotta.

The imaginative painting of iron bridges spanning Water Street in Manchester is one of many improvements funded by British Rail and local councils in partnership.

The facade of London Road station, Leicester, is rich in moulded terracotta work such as this exit sign.

A canopy bracket at Abbotsbury carries the shield of the Abbotsbury Railway which promoted this Dorset branch. The increasing skill of the foundryman made possible ever more intricate decoration in the later 19th century.

In the booking hall at Norwich station, pilasters with Ionic capitals lead the eye up to the delicate plasterwork cornice with its swags and dentils. The blue and white painted ceiling has more swags set around a central rose.

Delicate carving in stone round one of the windows at Norwich perfectly matches the elaborate interior.

Oak leaves and acorns (above), picked out in the original colours, decorate the capital of an awning column at Great Malvern. The station has more than 40 such columns, each with a different design of capital. The tradition of decorative ironwork is reiterated at Dorking by a floral bracket (right) designed in 1867 by Charles H. Driver, who also did the decoration at Boxhill & Westhumble.

HAMPSHIRE

EASTLEIGH

Opened 1839 by London & Southampton Railway. Architect Sir William Tite. Extended c.1895 by London & South Western Railway. Between Winchester and Southampton.

Known as Bishopstoke until 1889, this station was important in its early days as the junction for the line to Gosport and Portsmouth, which opened in 1842 but carried a declining traffic after 1859 when the Portsmouth Direct line was built.

Eastleigh subsequently developed as a railway town, containing from 1909 the locomotive works of the London & South Western, and at the end of the century the station was substantially enlarged.

The original building, which was incorporated in the development, is an example of the Micheldever style (*p.204*), a small two-storey classical block typical of Tite's work. Its stucco finish and finely detailed chimney stacks help it escape the grimness of later stations of this type such as Farnham and Andover.

It now stands on an island platform, reached by a footbridge from the new entrance building. This was designed in LSWR 1880s style with 'Board School' windows and a stone pediment and pilaster strips over the entrance arch. Luggage was carried across the intervening line on a swivel bridge.

FAREHAM

PORTCHESTER ROAD and QUAY STREET VIADUCTS. Built 1848 for London & South Western Railway. Engineer Joseph Locke. Both listed Grade II.

The Fareham to Cosham section of the LSWR was opened in 1848; at Cosham it was joined by the LBSCR to form a joint line into Portsmouth and Southsea. Hampshire is remarkably free of viaducts (a consequence partly of geography and partly of Locke's liking for level lines); these two are among the most important. They are both of red brick, with white brick string courses and stone copings, and each has one skewed arch flanked by pilasters, the other arches being segmented. Portchester Road Viaduct has 18 arches in all, two of which are blocked, while Quay Street has 11.

PORTCHESTER ROAD VIADUCT, 1982

GOSPORT

Built 1841 for London & South Western Railway. Architect Sir William Tite. Closed.

The line from Bishopstoke (now Eastleigh) to Gosport was the original route to Portsmouth, reached by means of a ferry across the harbour. The military demanded that the station building be kept to a low height so that it would not interfere with the fortifications, and this probably accounts for the fact that the chimneys were no higher than the train-shed roof.

The line had to be closed after four days in operation owing to the instability of the tunnel near Fareham and to a wet cutting which slid down on to the track. It was reopened two months later, in February 1842.

1965

The station was badly damaged by fire some years ago and is closed, but its noble frontage survives as an example of some of Tite's best work. Classical in concept, it has a very long Tuscan colonnade of 14 bays in Portland stone, terminating in large pavilions with round-headed rusticated openings and parapets featuring miniature segmental pediments. Queen Victoria used it for her journeys to Osborne House on the Isle of Wight, which may have been when the matching gate pillars and iron railings were added. Later a private station was opened for the Queen at Clarence Yard on a short extension from Gosport.

THE LONDON & SOUTH WESTERN RAILWAY

The London & South Western, with its coastal lines to Bournemouth, the Isle of Wight, Devon and north Cornwall, claimed to be the 'holiday line', advertising that it ran 'in the path of the sun, for health and pleasure'. It also provided short-distance commuter services to the dormitory suburbs along the Thames and, slightly further afield, to Surrey's 'stockbroker belt'. Its coastal connections inevitably brought it to the forefront of troop movements, especially at Southampton during the First World War.

In passenger business the LSWR strove to develop a year-round rather than a seasonal service to the coast. It had special associations with Queen Victoria, of whom memories abide in the royal waiting room at Windsor & Eton Riverside and in the colonnade at Gosport where she used to break her journeys to the Isle of Wight.

The South Western was one of the earliest railways to use automatic signalling with semaphore arms activated by low-pressure compressed air. The main line between Woking and Basingstoke was completely equipped with this apparatus from 1901, and it gave excellent service for 50 years. The enormous 'A' signal box that at one time spanned all the outgoing tracks at Waterloo was regarded as one of the signalling wonders of the world.

The LSWR had a distinguished succession of locomotive engineers. W. Adams's beautiful outside-cylinder 4-4-0 design is represented in the National Railway Museum, while Dugald Drummond brought the Scottish tradition of massive engines to the south; it was continued, with simpler layout, by his successor, R. W. Urie. Urie was the first British exponent of having all the working parts of a locomotive outside the frames so that they would be readily accessible for maintenance. His N15 class 4-6-0 of 1918 was later developed into the famous King Arthur class of the Southern Railway.

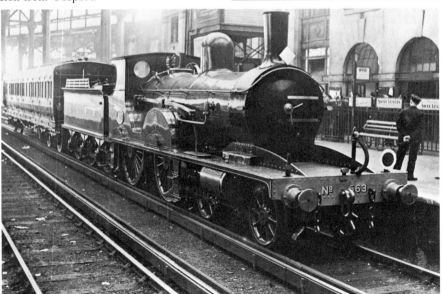

LSWR ADAMS 4-4-0 AT WATERLOO, c.1916

LIPHOOK, 1979

LIPHOOK

Built January 1859 for London & South Western Railway. Architect possibly Sir William Tite. Between Guildford and Portsmouth.

Liphook is a perfect example of the stations designed by Tite for the Portsmouth Direct line, and probably his most successful small station. Built in brick with a slate roof, it has single-storey wings flanking a gabled two-storey centre – a Palladian villa with gently Italianate details. It is a welcoming building, domestic in scale but at the same time clearly not a private house. The design is repeated at Witley and at Rowland's Castle, and survives in altered form at Ewell West (*p.199*), also built in 1859.

MICHELDEVER

Built 1840 for London & South Western Railway. Architect Sir William Tite. Listed Grade II. Between Basingstoke and Winchester.

This lonely station three miles from the village of its name was opened as Andover Road; Andover itself was 11 miles away and had no station until 1854. It is situated on that superbly engineered stretch of line between Basingstoke and Winchester which sweeps over the western foothills of the Hampshire Downs, negotiating three tunnels, heavy cuttings and embankments; the ruling gradient between the summit at Litchfield Tunnel and Eastleigh (with a few minor variations near Winchester) is only 1 in 252.

As Micheldever was on the last section of the London & Southampton line to be completed, it was the scene of the customary opening-day 'cold collation' at the

invitation of Thomas Brassey, the contractor. Guests sat 'in marquees amply set forth with delicate viands and rare wines'; the labourers had roast ox and strong beer.

Sir William Tite designed many of the London & Southampton stations 'with utility and desirability at the smallest possible cost'. Micheldever is severe and practical: a two-storey building, flint-faced with yellow brick dressings, a low hipped roof and a flat canopy carried round all four sides on thin iron columns.

PETERSFIELD

Built 1859 for London & South Western Railway. Architect probably Sir William Tite. Between Guildford and Portsmouth.

Petersfield is a well preserved example of the medium-sized station on the Portsmouth Direct line, which was engineered by Locke and Errington to reduce by 20 miles the 95-mile London-to-Portsmouth route via either Eastleigh or Brighton. It is the twin of Godalming (*p.199*), opened in the same year, and there exists a mutilated example of the same design at

1978

Milford, also situated on the Portsmouth Direct line.

Like Godalming, Petersfield is probably by Sir William Tite. His Tudor style has here been simplified for economy's sake; there is a three-storey house on the left, a central entrance with booking office window beside, and a gabled waiting room to the right. The windows are mullioned, with moulded hoods, and the gables have the usual scalloped barge-boards. A short flat awning on the platform side rests on very long, shallow brackets.

MICHELDEVER, 1970

SOUTHAMPTON

TERMINUS STATION. Built 1839-40 for London & Southampton Railway. Architect Sir William Tite. Listed Grade II. Closed.

Sir William Tite's station, now closed, was designed as a 'head station', with the main building behind the buffer stops. It is a handsome classical building with a heavily rusticated five-bay arcade forming the entrance. Above is an open balustrade with a clock. The first-floor windows have angled pediments and the low hipped roof hides behind a deep, dentilled cornice. The station was complementary to the London terminus at Nine Elms.

SOUTHAMPTON TERMINUS, 1890s

SOUTH WESTERN HOUSE. Built 1872 for London & South Western Railway. Architect John Norton. Listed Grade II. Canute Road.

This was originally the South Western hotel, putting the station rather in the shade by its size. It is four storeys high with two attics, in red brick with numerous stone and terracotta embellishments in a somewhat heavy French Renaissance style, although the little iron window balconies are quite delicate. The mansard roof has upper attic dormer windows, with circular panes. A vast French pavilion roof with the inevitable iron cresting dominates the front; over the entrance is a rounded pediment containing a portrait of Queen Victoria surrounded by winged figures and nautical and railway emblems.

It was a magnificent place in its day and in 1939 still offered bed-and-breakfast for ten shillings. Its hospitable doors were closed after bombing in 1940, and when it was repaired it was converted into railway offices.

SWAYTHLING

Built 1883 by London & South Western Railway. Main building (including ticket hall) on down side listed Grade II. Between Eastleigh and Southampton.

Built some 20 years after the end of the Tite period, Swaythling represented the latest LSWR station style with its prominent Dutch gable, and its minute dormer ventilators (since removed) looking as though they have been taken from a doll's house. The 'Board School' windows, dark brick, and nicely bracketed porch are typical of the so-called Domestic Revival style. The main building is connected to the platform by a curious short covered way.

1982

In January 1941 a bomb crashed through the booking office roof and floor without exploding, but scattering the office fire. When the resultant blaze was put out the authorities declared that the bomb must have exploded, so the office staff calmly went back to work. The following day the landlord of the nearby pub insisted that the bomb had not exploded; digging was started, and nearly three weeks later the live bomb was found.

REAR ENTRANCE TO SOUTH WESTERN HOUSE, SOUTHAMPTON, 1890s

ISLE OF WIGHT

ST. DENYS, 1982

WOOLSTON and ST. DENYS

WOOLSTON STATION. Built 1866 by London & South Western Railway. Main building including ticket hall on down side listed Grade II. Between St. Denys and Portsmouth.

ST. DENYS STATION. Built c.1866-68 by London & South Western Railway. Main building including ticket hall on up side listed Grade II. Between Eastleigh and Southampton.

These two stations are in the same area and in almost identical Italianate villa style. St. Denys originated as Portswood in 1861 and was rebuilt when the Netley branch line opened in 1866, sweeping in over a long curve and viaduct across the Itchen; it was renamed St. Denys in 1876. It is in brick with stone dressings, rusticated quoins, and curly wooden brackets under the eaves. Two storeys high, it has a shallow projection at one end, repeated on both front and platform sides.

Woolston is the same but in stucco, and

although built to a stock design these stations, and others like them, clearly derive from Tite's original London &

ST. DENYS TICKET OFFICE ENTRANCE, 1983

Southampton company stations some 20 years earlier (*see Micheldever p.204 and Chertsey p.199*).

RYDE

PROMENADE PIER. Built 1813-14 by Ryde Pier Company. Listed Grade II. ESPLANADE STATION AND PIER. Built 1880 by London Brighton & South Coast and London & South Western Railways. Conservation Area.

Ryde's first pier, the Promenade Pier, was extended and altered over the years until it reached a length of half a mile and became the easiest approach to the Isle of Wight. When the first section of the Isle of Wight Railway was opened in 1864 from Ryde St. John's Road to Shanklin, the Ryde Pier Company opened a horse tramway along the pier, so that passengers

ESPLANADE STATION AND PIER, 1880s

arriving by boat from the mainland could be transported to St. John's Road station.

In 1880 the London Brighton & South Coast and London & South Western Railways opened a joint line and a new pier alongside the existing one, with a station at its head. They constructed a tunnel to take the line to St. John's Road, with an intermediate station called Esplanade. Owing to the high cost of construction parliament sanctioned special fares – 7d. from Pier Head to Esplanade station, and 7d. from Esplanade to St. John's Road – which were said to be the highest fares in the world for the distance. After the Southern Railway took over, these fares were reduced to 1½d. and 2½d. respectively.

The Pier is a cast-iron structure, with a planked deck; the cast-iron balustrade has panels decorated with scrolls, ovals and linked circles, and dates from 1880. Shelters project outward at intervals, with turned-wood columns topped by

PROMENADE PIER, 1982

dragon and gryphon cast-iron brackets and fretted eaves.

It was at Ryde Pier that the Empress Eugenie, wife of Napoleon III, landed after her flight from Paris when the Third Republic was proclaimed in 1870.

RYDE ST. JOHN'S ROAD, c.1865

BERKSHIRE

WINDSOR & ETON RIVERSIDE

Built 1849 for London & South Western Railway. Architect Sir William Tite. Station and royal waiting room listed Grade II.

The London & South Western arrived in Windsor in the same year as the Great Western, after ten years' resistance from those bodies (particularly Eton College) which considered the railway a danger to morals. Both companies were made to pay for the privilege: the Commissioners of Woods and Forests – i.e. the Crown – demanded new bridges and streets, a rebuilt access to Windsor Castle, and a station befitting the Castle.

Built of mellow red brick with stone dressings, Windsor & Eton Riverside is certainly one of the most delightful of all Tudor-style railway buildings. Behind a very large oriel window is a booking hall

meant to put one in mind of a great hall. To the left there is a large carriage entrance, and to the right a three-bay loggia for passengers arriving on foot.

TRAINSHED WALL, 1982

Round the corner, on Datchet Road, are two more large mullioned windows and the long buttressed wall of the trainshed. The wall has 12 pointed-arch openings fitted with double doors for the entrainment of cavalry and throughout its length it is decorated with an amazing series of black brick patterns forming lozenge shapes and a series of large

monogrammed initials: VR and PA under crowns, for the Queen and her consort; WC for the railway's chairman, William Chaplin; WT for Tite himself; and several others including LSWR and the date, 1851.

Like the Great Western's Central station up the hill, Windsor & Eton

1979

Riverside has a royal waiting room. It is in a separate building at the outer end of the trainshed wall, its porch flanked by the VR and PA monograms. The building is crowned by a bell turret which is said to have been used as a look-out from which the station staff could be warned of the approach of the Queen's carriage.

THE LONDON BRIGHTON & SOUTH COAST RAILWAY

The London Brighton & South Coast Railway – or the 'Brighton' as it was known – served a triangle of lines with the base along the south coast from Portsmouth to Hastings and the apex in London. Within this area, the profusion of alternative routes and branch lines was immense.

The Brighton, sometimes sarcastically referred to as a glorified suburban railway, was not, in the 19th century, noted for treating its passengers well: its services were slow and unreliable. Most of its energies seemed to be taken up in bickering with its arch-rival, the South Eastern (*p.185*).

It had no corridor carriages on its express trains, though it is true that journeys were short – the longest through run, from Victoria to Portsmouth, was not quite 88 miles. Pullman cars were carried on many trains, for those prepared to pay extra. A very high proportion of first-class accommodation was provided on the commuter

lines from the south coast, notably on such famous trains as the *Brighton Belle* and the *City Limited*, the latter nicknamed the 'Stockbrokers' Express'.

Early in the 20th century the inner suburban area was electrified. The main line to the coast was so lavishly provided with fast, punctual trains and good facilities for all classes that no longer was it only stockbrokers who could afford to travel daily into London to work.

The express trains from Brighton had a splendidly engineered line to run on. It crossed the lengthy Ouse Viaduct (*p.197*) and passed through three notable tunnels under the North and South Downs. Despite the hilly country in between, the gradient was even and the journey fast and smooth.

The LBSCR was not only a passenger line. At Keymer Junction, south of Haywards Heath, the line diverged to Lewes and Eastbourne with a branch to Newhaven Harbour, over which the company ran services to Europe via Dieppe. The

company justifiably took pride in its *grande vitesse* express goods trains on this route, for which special engines were built at the Brighton Locomotive Works.

The Brighton Works will always be held in reverence by engineers and enthusiasts alike for its production of the famous range of engines designed by William Stroudley, once described as 'an artist in metal'. They had striking yellow livery – fortunately preserved on the 0-4-2 engine *Gladstone* in the National Railway Museum – and were in every sense the work of a perfectionist. No great output of power was required of them, so they could always be kept clean.

A successor to Stroudley, Douglas Earle Marsh, made locomotive history in the early 20th century, but in a different way. He was one of the earliest exponents in Britain of super-heating: his '13' class of 4-4-2 tank engines were notably economical in fuel consumption despite carrying much heavier loads than their 19th-century predecessors.

Above LBSCR 0-4-2 Gladstone; *inset LBSCR Share Certificate, 1847*

WILTSHIRE

SALISBURY

STATION. Opened 1859 by Salisbury &
Yeovil Railway. Original building by
Sir William Tite.

Salisbury's first railway, opened in 1847, was a branch from Eastleigh (then called Bishopstoke) to Milford in the south-east of the city. When the London & South Western reached Salisbury with their main line they at first used Milford station; after the Salisbury & Yeovil opened their station in 1859 the LSWR adopted that.

Tite designed the building in a re-strained Italianate style. It is built of brick and the windows have stone casings bracketed below the sills. The frontage is asymmetrical, with round-headed door and window openings, and along the roof a dentilled cornice and parapet.

For some years the station had only one platform, and when a second platform was built for London-bound trains it was nearly a quarter of a mile away because the Great Western's station (*see below*) was in the way; a long subway had to be built to give access.

Complete reconstruction took place in 1900 when new platforms were built and a new red brick frontage block added next to the old.

GOODS SHED. Built 1856 for Wilts
Somerset & Weymouth Railway. Architect I. K.
Brunel. Listed Grade II. Fisherton Street.

The Salisbury terminus of the Wilts Somerset & Weymouth (a company inspired by the Great Western and quickly taken over by it) was built alongside the LSWR station. Now part of the goods station, it is a typical Brunel wooden trainshed. Gables with vertical glazing project above the low brick frontage;

GOODS SHED, FORMERLY GWR STATION, 1925

doors and windows have stone dressings, and a flat wooden canopy is decorated with the familiar lion's heads (*see Heyford, p.221*). Inside, the roof is cantilevered from wooden cross-braced horizontal timbers with moulded brackets and square wooden posts.

Brunel's station was closed to passenger traffic in 1932 when SR trains began using the former LSWR station.

SALISBURY LSWR STATION, 1972

DORSET

BOURNEMOUTH

Built 1885 by London & South Western
Railway. Listed Grade II.

Until the middle of the 19th century Bournemouth was an insignificant village. In only a few years, however, it became a fashionable watering-place, considered health-giving for its sea and sand and the scent of its pine forests. In 1870 the Ringwood Christchurch & Bournemouth Railway (operated by the London & South Western) reached the town, and in 1885 a magnificent new terminus was opened, replacing the original station which was a short distance to the east. The new building became a through station in 1888 when the line from Brockenhurst was opened.

Central station, as it was known from 1899, is basically a huge trainshed. The high brick walls on either side form the

1970s

facades, to which are attached the offices and other facilities.

The massive overall roof, now lacking its central section, was designed as a series of lateral ridge-and-furrow clerestories carried on deep latticed girders.

The girders are tied to the side-walls by unusual diagonal braces and huge, elaborate brackets curving down to supporting buttresses, which are repeated on the outside, capped by miniature stone pediments. Between them open narrow lancet windows.

DORCHESTER

WEST STATION. Built 1857 in Brunel style
for Great Western Railway. Station, excluding
building on west platform, and Wareham
Bridge, Alington Road, listed Grade II.
Between Yeovil and Weymouth.

Dorchester West is in the Chippenham and Mortimer style (*p.225 and p.216*) but larger than both, and has the characteristic overhanging hipped roof, here supported on the frontage by large curved wooden brackets with round bosses. The Italianate window openings are in threes, and the two doorways (one now converted into a window) have scrolled hood brackets. The appearance is considerably enhanced by rendering.

The platform side has been altered and extended out to the eaves, and a standard Great Western ridged canopy added.

1968

WAREHAM

STATION. Completed 1886 by London & South Western Railway. Station, including platform shelter and lamp standards, listed Grade II. Between Bournemouth and Dorchester.

The present station replaced a Tudor-style Southampton & Dorchester Railway building of 1847 on the other side of the level crossing; it was built to serve the new Wareham-Swanage branch engineered by W. Galbraith and opened in 1885. Designed in the Flemish-Queen Anne style inspired by the work of Richard Norman Shaw and J. J. Stevenson, it is similar to Swaythling (*p.205*) and other LSWR stations but much more elaborate.

The gables are particularly exuberant, with ball finials, decorative stone panels and the company's coat of arms blossoming in profusion; there are assorted windows (one with an elegant pediment) and dormers, and a well shaped cupola with a weathervane. After several decades of dull uniformity, such enthusiasm was a welcome awakening.

OLD GOODS SHED. Listed Grade II. Sandford Lane.

The original goods shed is built in red brick with round-headed blind arches on the ends and segmental-headed openings along one side, now altered. It has a hipped roof on heavy timber trusses, like many of its kind.

WAREHAM, 1976

OLD GOODS SHED, 1976

RAILWAY BRIDGE OVER RIVER PIDDLE, WAREHAM COMMON. Opened 1847 by Southampton & Dorchester Railway. Engineer Capt. William S. Moorsom. Listed Grade II.

The Hamworthy Junction to Dorchester section of the Southampton & Dorchester Railway was opened in 1847 and shortly afterwards became part of the London & South Western. This largely original bridge is one of the chief remaining civil engineering features of the line. In addition to the flat iron span in the centre there are two red brick arches on the skew (that on the north-east side has been mainly renewed), and brick quadrant retaining walls at either end.

RAILWAY BRIDGE OVER RIVER PIDDLE, 1976

WESTERN REGION

CONTENTS

LONDON: PAGE 213 **HOME COUNTIES & SOUTH MIDLANDS:** BERKSHIRE (PART) PAGE 216

OXFORDSHIRE PAGE 218   HEREFORD & WORCESTER PAGE 222   GLOUCESTERSHIRE PAGE 224

THE WEST OF ENGLAND: WILTSHIRE (PART) PAGE 224   AVON PAGE 227   SOMERSET PAGE 235

DORSET (PART) PAGE 237   DEVON PAGE 237   CORNWALL PAGE 240   **SOUTH WALES:** GWENT PAGE 242

SOUTH GLAMORGAN PAGE 243   MID GLAMORGAN PAGE 243   DYFED (PART) PAGE 244

The royal waiting room at Windsor & Eton Central in 1900 (left) offers luxury to compare with the engineering brilliance of Brunel's Maidenhead bridge (above).

The Great Western Railway was the only company to keep its old name at the 1923 Grouping. Instead of becoming part of a larger group, it was itself enlarged by the addition of the Welsh railways whose separate identities were soon lost in the 'greater Great Western'. On nationalisation it became the Western Region of British Railways, at first retaining its old boundaries and remaining recognizably its old self in many details of style and operation.

During the 1920s and 1930s the distinguished locomotive work that had marked the company's performance at the turn of the century continued without a break. Churchward's successful 4-cylinder 4-6-0 design of 1907 was developed, first into the famous 'Castle' class of 1923, of which a number are preserved, and then in 1927 to the 'Kings' which for power and economy were among the world's most outstanding steam locomotives. All the GWR main lines were equipped with a system of automatic train control, an invaluable safety device which was a forerunner of the present-day system on British Rail whereby the brakes are auto-matically applied if a driver overruns a warning signal.

The GWR's famous chocolate-and-cream carriage livery was continued through the post-Grouping period when the other three major companies adopted single-colour liveries, and was even revived for a while after nationalisation. Perhaps because of this sense of uniqueness, the railway (and the region) clung to the lower-quadrant semaphore signal at a time when the other railways adopted the standard upper-quadrant type. Western Region secondary lines still have many of them.

The Great Western was in many ways a country railway. It specialised in the speedy conveyance of early spring flowers and Cornish broccoli for the London markets, and gave close consideration to country pursuits, including a special instruction to drivers to avoid running down packs of hounds that might be crossing the line. Many trains were deliberately scheduled at moderate speeds to enable horse-boxes to be conveyed, and time was allowed for attaching and detaching them at intermediate stations.

Despite its attachment to old traditions, however, the GWR changed in many significant ways during the 25 years between Grouping and nationalisation, carrying through a much-needed reorganisation of its operations and launching a vigorous marketing campaign accompanied by improved and accelerated passenger services. The company advertised itself as 'The Holiday Line'. Trading on the mild winter climate of the south west, it made a strong bid to develop year-round traffic to the coast it skilfully named the 'Cornish Riviera', a name it also gave to its most famous train.

After the Second World War the popularity of the West Country resorts led to the development of a highly complex organisation to ensure punctuality of the intense summer weekend holiday traffic. The Great Western was one of the first British railways to introduce advance seat reservations, a system which not only ensured that passengers would have seats but provided a forecast of the numbers to be catered for.

The inter-war policy of building large numbers of mixed traffic loco-

211

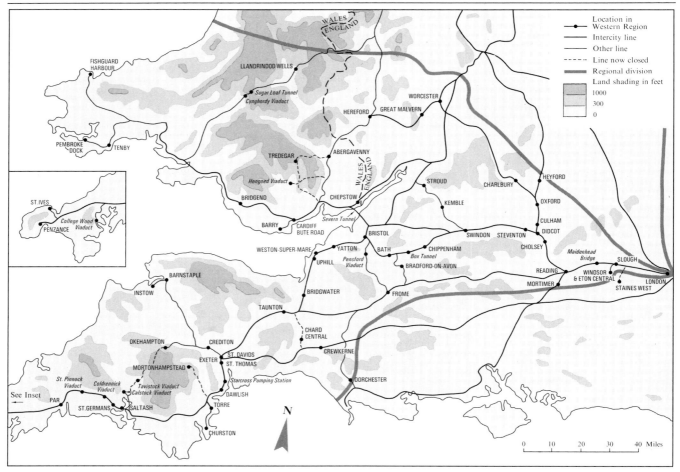

Location in
Western Region
Intercity line
Other line
Line now closed
Regional division
Land shading in feet
1000
300
0

WALES
ENGLAND

FISHGUARD
HARBOUR

LLANDRINDOD WELLS

Sugar Loaf Tunnel
Cynghordy Viaduct

WORCESTER

HEREFORD   GREAT MALVERN

PEMBROKE
DOCK   TENBY

TREDEGAR   ABERGAVENNY

Hengoed Viaduct

WALES
ENGLAND

STROUD   CHARLBURY   HEYFORD

ST.IVES

College Wood
Viaduct

PENZANCE

CHEPSTOW   OXFORD

BRIDGEND   KEMBLE   CULHAM

BARRY   CARDIFF   Severn Tunnel   SWINDON   STEVENTON   DIDCOT
BUTE ROAD   BRISTOL   CHOLSEY
WESTON-SUPER-MARE   YATTON   CHIPPENHAM   Maidenhead
UPHILL   Pensford   BATH   Box Tunnel   Bridge   SLOUGH
Viaduct   BRADFORD-ON-AVON   READING   WINDSOR   LONDON
BARNSTAPLE   MORTIMER   & ETON CENTRAL
INSTOW   BRIDGWATER   FROME   STAINES WEST

TAUNTON

CHARD
CENTRAL

OKEHAMPTON   CREDITON   CREWKERNE

ST.DAVIDS
EXETER   ST.THOMAS
MORTONHAMPSTEAD   DORCHESTER
St. Pinnock   Coldrennick   Starcross Pumping Station
Viaduct   Viaduct   Tavistock Viaduct
See Inset   Calstock Viaduct   DAWLISH
PAR   SALTASH   TORRE
ST.GERMANS   N

CHURSTON

0   10   20   30   40 Miles

motives of the 4-6-0 type enabled many engines normally employed in freight service to be used for the extra passenger trains on summer Saturdays. The incorporation of the Cambrian Railways into the Great Western also made possible some integration of services to Central and North Wales resorts: Aberystwyth, Barmouth, Criccieth and Pwllheli. The many special Saturday services included one from Pontypridd in South Wales to the holiday camp at Penychain, near Pwllheli.

Although the campaign to increase holiday traffic succeeded, the GWR carried its heaviest and most profitable passenger traffic between South Wales and London, a route for which there was no competition.

In other respects, South Wales became a problem after the First World War. The staple coal traffic of lines like the Taff Vale, the Rhymney and the Barry Railways was decimated by the depression of the 1920s, never to recover anything approaching its pre-war volume, and it was only inclusion in the Great Western that saved those lines from closure.

The Great Western was a leading participant in a number of cross-country services operated in conjunction with other railways, particularly the south-west to north-east through trains (including daily through coaches from Aberdeen to Penzance), and the services between Birkenhead and the south coast which brought green Southern Railway coaches to Shrewsbury and Chester and the chocolate-and-cream of the GWR to Dover and Folkestone. Some of these through services are still to be found in the present-day BR timetable, and new ones have been introduced from Paddington to Liverpool, Manchester and Glasgow, fulfilling old dreams that must make many an ex-Great Western man sigh with satisfaction.

Today the Western Region of British Rail stops short at a line roughly between Banbury, Worcester, Craven Arms (between Shrewsbury and Hereford) and Aberystwyth. All routes north of it are now in the London Midland Region, while in the south west the former Southern Railway lines west of Salisbury have been taken into the region. These changes have brought about a level of integration that would have been impossible in the days of company ownership.

The region is rich in monuments of earlier days, particularly the work of Isambard Kingdom Brunel: Paddington station, the viaducts at Hanwell and Maidenhead, the deep excavation of Sonning cutting, Box Tunnel and, above all, the Royal Albert Bridge over the Tamar at Saltash. It also possesses Britain's longest tunnel, driven under the Severn to form a shorter route to South Wales at the end of the 19th century.

At Swindon, where the Great Western created a railway town with its own church, baths, lecture rooms and Mechanics' Institute, the remaining station buildings still contain the celebrated (though now modernised) refreshment rooms whose lessees exercised for nearly half a century the profitable right to make all trains stop for 10 minutes. The locomotive works, birthplace of so many famous steam locomotives, still survives in much reduced form. To Swindon works fell the job of building British Railways' last steam locomotive, a 2-10-0 freight engine aptly named *Evening Star* and, in the Swindon tradition, provided with a copper-capped chimney.

LONDON

HANWELL

STATION. Built 1877 by Great Western Railway. Main up-side building and down-side island-platform building listed Grade II. Between Paddington and Slough.

Hanwell is a second-generation station which replaced a Brunel structure. Built on an embankment, it has a three-storey brick entrance building reaching up from the road.

Externally it is in the lifeless red and yellow brick style found at numerous Great Western stations of this period, with wooden platform buildings. However, the centre island platform has a delightful canopy that completely transforms it, again standardized but decorated with a saw-tooth valance that extends across the ends around a deep Gothic cut-out gable. The flat awning on the side platform has matching valances and rests on foliated iron brackets which are repeated on the island platform columns, so that the station at rail level presents a cheerful, balanced appearance.

WHARNCLIFFE VIADUCT. Built 1837 for Great Western Railway. Engineer I. K. Brunel. Listed Grade I.

The viaduct is the first major engineering work after Paddington, crossing the River Brent on eight elliptical brick arches, each resting on elegantly tapered divided piers. A prominent stone cornice runs beneath the parapet.

The bridge is 65 feet high and 300 yards long, and in the 1870s was widened in similar style, to take four tracks. It was named after Lord Wharncliffe who chaired the House of Lords Committee considering the Bill for the incorporation of the GWR, enacted in 1835, and bears his arms over the centre pier.

PADDINGTON

STATION. Erected 1854 for Great Western Railway. Designers I. K. Brunel and Sir Matthew Digby Wyatt. Listed Grade I. HOTEL. Opened 1854. Architect P. C. Hardwick. Listed Grade II.

The first Paddington station was a temporary building, opened in 1838 with the offices in some of the arches of Bishop's Road bridge, but like so many other temporary measures it lasted for longer than was intended.

To construct the present station the line was extended a short distance to terminate below ground level in the angle of Eastbourne Terrace and Praed Street.

For his great three-bay arched roof, Brunel followed the principles pioneered by Dobson at Newcastle (*p.49*), bringing the wrought-iron ribs down to 'clasp' the diagonally-braced cross-girders, with a column under every third rib. The ribs themselves are highly decorated in their lower sections, with bolted-on iron trellis-work, and are pierced by decorative holes to give lightness.

An innovation was the construction of two transepts running across the station, ending at elaborate oriel windows on the Eastbourne Terrace side through which the directors of the Great Western could overlook the platforms. These transepts were originally intended to provide space for a set of large traversers for moving railway vehicles from one line to another. The equipment was never used, but the transepts fortunately remain as a splendid architectural feature. Henry-Russell Hitchcock in his *Early Victorian Architecture in Britain* says 'they provide a richness of space composition and a wealth of effective diagonal vistas almost unique in Victorian railway stations'.

The intricate patterns, mouldings and filigree work along the Eastbourne Terrace wall are in cement, very hard so that it looks – and feels – like cast iron. That it has withstood time so well is a tribute to the care that was taken in its mixing and application.

The end-screens at the Praed Street end of the roof are decorated by slender wrought-iron arabesques. All the decorative work was carried out by Brunel's architect friend Digby Wyatt, including the Moorish decoration on the columns and balconies, but Hitchcock considers that the integrated handling of the spaces and structural elements suggests much greater collaboration between the two men than has been stated. For his glazing Brunel followed Paxton's ridge-and-furrow principle developed for the Crystal Palace (now all replaced).

A fourth roof bay was added in 1916, matching Brunel's originals, and during the next few years the iron columns were progressively replaced by hexagonal riveted steel stanchions. Tie rods have also been added to strengthen the roof.

The main offices are on the Eastbourne Terrace side flanking platform 1. The upper storeys are externally very plain, but the ground floor has a series of arcaded windows which are nicely detailed though difficult to appreciate because of their location below street level.

The head of the station is occupied by the Great Western Royal Hotel, by P. C.

ENGRAVING OF WHARNCLIFFE VIADUCT BY J. C. BOURNE. 1837

Hardwick. He designed the Great Hall at Euston and his father built the Doric Arch (*p.59*). Hardwick's facade has been both criticised and praised. Hitchcock calls it 'dreary' and 'tawdry', but when it was opened it was much acclaimed, and Pevsner in his *Buildings of England* describes it as 'one of the earliest buildings, if not the earliest building in England with marked influence from the French Re-

'KING' CLASS 4-6-0 *KING JOHN*, PADDINGTON, 1962

naissance and Baroque'. Before the frontage was 'modernised' in 1933-36 it had numerous ornate iron balconies, a *porte cochère* and a row of giant urns beneath the central pediment, all of which were removed together with other decorative touches. The pediment contains sculpted figures by John Thomas representing the

Victorian aspirations of Peace, Plenty, Industry and Science, and he also modelled a series of giant caryatids which held up a balcony, also removed in the 1930s purge.

With its 165 rooms the Great Western was the largest hotel in the country at the time and began the movement for the erection of large purpose-built hotels in London, as well as setting the pattern for 19th-century luxury hotel building in the country as a whole.

When it was opened Paddington station had only two platforms, one for arrivals alongside the offices and the other for departures, with ten tracks and two auxiliary or lamp platforms (from which staff could attend to the lighting of trains) between them. There was no connection for passengers between the platforms (station staff had a narrow subway) so Brunel devised movable bridges which could be hydraulically retracted beneath the platform surfaces when the running lines had to be cleared. One remained in use right up to 1920.

Over the years the intermediate tracks were removed in order to provide more platforms, and in 1863 a separate station called Bishop's Road was opened on the

connecting curve from the Great Western to the Metropolitan Railway, enabling the GWR to run trains through to the City. When Paddington was remodelled in 1933, Bishop's Road was incorporated in the main station.

Paddington, like most large termini, has its oddities. The present concourse is known as 'The Lawn', a name said to derive from a grassy area that once existed between the original temporary station and Praed Street. For nearly a century it was an unpleasant place, cluttered with barrows, horse-drays and numerous cast-iron columns supporting short-span roofs. But in 1933, when large new offices were built and the hotel extended, it was re-roofed and cleared for passengers. A statue of Brunel by John Doubleday now stands in the middle.

Alongside platform 1 is the former royal waiting room, distinguished by a crown over the external doorway and the royal and GWR arms on the doorway to the platform. The room was appropriately decorated and furnished for the use of Queen Victoria when she travelled to Windsor. (She had made her first railway journey from the original Paddington station.) Further along the platform, be-

PADDINGTON, 1963

neath the former GWR headquarters' offices and boardroom, stands the GWR war memorial sculpted by C. S. Jagger, a good example of its kind.

The oriel windows of the boardroom overlook a station no longer filled with

HOTEL FACADE, 1976

chocolate and cream coachwork, brass safety valves and copper-capped chimneys yet still, as the amplified West Country destinations echo back from Brunel's roof, unmistakably Great Western.

SOUTHALL

WINDMILL BRIDGE. Built 1859 for Great Western & Brentford Railway. Engineer I. K. Brunel. Ancient Monument. Branch from Southall to Brentford.

The Great Western's wish to have direct access to the River Thames led to the construction of this branch from the main line at Southall to their own Brentford Dock. The track had to cross the Grand Junction (later Grand Union) Canal and the place chosen was where Windmill Lane already crossed the canal at the head of the Hanwell flight of locks.

To carry three transport systems at different levels, Brunel created a unique structure completed in the year of his death, a bridge complex where road, rail and canal cross at the same spot – road over canal over rail.

The road bridge goes high over the top on brick piers and the railway passes underneath in a cutting with the cast-iron trough of the canal sliding between. The bridge has the name of the iron founders cast on to the side plate girders: Matthew T. Shaw, 64 Cannon Street. And just to the east the canal is supported by arches across the railway cutting

HORSEBOAT CROSSING RAILWAY UNDER WINDMILL BRIDGE, c.1910

GREAT WESTERN ROYAL HOTEL, 1962

BERKSHIRE

MAIDENHEAD BRIDGE

Built 1839 for Great Western Railway.
Engineer I. K. Brunel. Listed Grade II*.

Brunel had a triple problem when faced by the River Thames at Maidenhead. The arch had to be of a height and width to provide for navigation; anything higher than the absolute minimum would create havoc with the gradients on the line; and only yellow stock brick was available to build it. He solved it daringly by designing two very shallow elliptical arches – the 'flattest' brick arches in the world – which cross the river in two leaps of 128 feet, yet are only 24 feet high to the crowns.

His detractors confidently predicted that the bridge would collapse, particularly when the eastern arch showed signs of movement (the young John Fowler said its outline became 'perfectly Gothic'). The contractor then admitted that he had eased the wooden centering before the mortar had set. After repairs, the centres were again eased a few inches, this time

1971

on Brunel's orders, although this was not made public. He wanted them to remain in position until the bridge had withstood another winter. However, in the autumn of 1839 a storm blew them down and the bridge was seen to be standing perfectly, in confirmation of its designer's calculations. Brunel must have appreciated the joke: while his opponents supposed that the bridge was being held up by centering, it had in fact been free-standing for the previous nine months.

Still in use a century and a half later, Maidenhead is one of the most graceful of our railway bridges. On each side of the main spans it has four semi-circular arches and the river piers have broad brick pilasters rising to a stone cap beneath a broad cornice carrying the parapet. In 1890-93 Sir John Fowler widened the bridge on each side using red bricks.

MORTIMER

Built 1848 for Berks & Hants Railway.
Designer I. K. Brunel. Station, including buildings and shelter on west side, listed Grade II. Between Reading and Basingstoke.

For his small stations Brunel originally designed a Tudor building with a flat verandah which projected on all four

sides, so precluding the need for glazed awnings (*see Culham, p.218*). After the first few years it evolved into an Italianate style with a broad hipped roof also extending on all four sides, and for a considerable time both types continued to be built on Great Western lines and others within the company's sphere of influence.

The Basingstoke line was an important link in the GWR's plan to reach the south coast with their broad gauge and pre-empt the rival standard-gauge London & South Western Railway before it could push northward. Mortimer was built only after considerable discussion with the Duke of Wellington who had the right, written into the Act authorizing the line, to forbid the construction of any station within five miles of his house, Stratfield Saye. His neighbours persuaded him to allow this one to be built only three miles off, and the GWR agreed that it should be 'as commodious as His Grace may think fit to require'.

The station is in Brunel's Italianate style. It is built of brick and has been restored almost unaltered, down to the small matching shelter on the down platform and the fittings in the ticket office. Among others Charlbury (*p.218*) and Bridgend (*p.243*) are similar in style.

Although all its associations are with the Western Region, Mortimer is now operated by Southern Region.

READING

Built 1840 for Great Western Railway.
Designer I. K. Brunel. Present frontage block built c. 1870, remodelling of station completed 1899. Listed Grade II.

Brunel was an advocate of the one-sided station, (*see Cambridge, p.18*). At Reading he went further than the then conventional long single platform and built what in effect were two separate stations, one for up trains and the other for down, both

on the same side of the line.

Brunel argued that with this arrangement passengers were less likely to board a train going in the wrong direction and, moreover, did not have to cross the line; at a time before footbridges and subways became general, this was quite a point. Nevertheless, it seems odd that so prac-

1976

tical a designer ignored the overriding inconvenience, not to mention dangers, of the criss-crossing train movements dictated by this layout, all controlled by individually operated points and hand signals, and the fact that such stations required at least two of everything. Even odder is the attitude of the GWR in allowing so busy a station as Reading to remain thus, basically unaltered, for 56 years, during the greater part of which it produced operating chaos.

Real improvements started about 1870 when the present frontage block was built; at least the administration and passenger facilities could now be concentrated in one place. Stylistically the new building was something of an anachronism, a two-storey Italianate block of a type popular earlier, built of grey brick with stone dressings and given interest by flat, segmental and triangular window hoods and a nicely proportioned, not too elaborate pantiled clock turret rising above the parapet. But it has dignity, and certainly in 1870 was a cut well above the average GWR station of the time.

MORTIMER, c.1910

SLOUGH

Opened 1838 by Great Western Railway. Rebuilt 1886. Architect/Engineer J. Danks.

Slough was another one-sided double station like Reading, with a pair of pitched overall roofs and a hotel opposite. Until the Windsor branch was opened it was the station used by the Queen when she travelled to Windsor Castle. The one-sided station lasted at least until 1879 and may have continued in use until the present station was built in 1886.

The lower portion of the main frontage (on the down side) is based on the fairly ordinary style adopted by the Great Western in the 1870s. Then above the cornice it suddenly springs into life with three remarkable curved French pavilion roofs, a large one in the centre and smaller ones at each end. The GWR built a number of stations in this manner, but elsewhere they had straight-sided roofs and none was as elaborate as Slough.

The roofs have nice bulls-eye windows between trefoil pilaster-caps and are clad

1979

with what look like fish-scale tiles but are in fact metal, with gingerbread-spiral capping down the corner angles. Each pavilion is topped by most delicate French-style iron railings with spiky corner-finials, and the central one carries a clock surmounted by a curved pediment. The up-side building is a shorter edition of the same thing.

STAINES WEST

Opened by Great Western Railway 1855. Listed Grade II. Closed. Station building sold.

Although this station now falls in the Southern Region it was at the end of a Great Western branch and has therefore been included with other GWR structures.

The station building is a good example of an existing house put to railway use. It is a typical late-Georgian villa, and when it was operated by the railway the former entrance hall with its staircase remained clearly domestic in character.

WINDSOR & ETON CENTRAL

STATION. Opened 1850 by Great Western Railway. Rebuilt 1897. Listed Grade II*.

The original station was apparently a Brunel timber trainshed adapted for

WINDSOR & ETON CENTRAL, c.1900

royal patronage by somewhat clumsy modifications. One could be mischievous and say that the Diamond Jubilee year rebuild was a standard Great Western station with special extras, particularly if it is compared with the London & South Western's older but purpose-built Riverside station down the hill (*p.207*).

The curved three-storey office block in cherry-red brick has French turrets, a dentilled parapet, pedimented first-floor windows and typical round-headed ground-floor openings. Beyond it the glass-roofed concourse led to platforms covered by standard umbrella awnings on riveted steel trusses and columns.

What transforms the station is the series of extras. The cab drive at the side is covered by an elliptical glass-and-iron roof, like a mini-Paddington, from which led the entrance to the booking hall. At the street end, opposite the castle, this roof is faced-up with a giant red brick 'Queen Anne' gable screen with broad white stone bands over a partly glazed elliptical arch which originally bore the company name in gold lettering.

Out of sight around the corner of the office block is a second identical roofed area for royal traffic; spacious enough to turn the royal carriage and accommodate a full military escort, mounted or on foot. Alongside is the royal waiting room, bearing two crowns with Victoria's cipher and, added later, Edward VII's. This building, too, is in standard GWR style, but faced with stone instead of brick and inside finished with a wooden panelled dado and panelled ceiling lit from above by an art nouveau glass dome.

The last monarch to use the waiting room was George VI, in 1936, and the

station is now far too large for the single-line shuttle service from Slough, but it was given a new lease of life when Madame Tussaud's opened their permanent 'Royalty and Railways' exhibition in 1983. The waiting room was restored to something like its original condition and the former booking office and concourse became an exhibition hall. The visitor is intended to assume that the royal train has just arrived with guests for the Diamond Jubilee celebrations, and sees the Queen and her retinue in the waiting room and again on the platform, accompanied by her guests, local dignitaries and a full guard of honour.

(*See also Windsor & Eton Riverside, p.207.*)

BRIDGE OVER RIVER THAMES. Built 1849 for Great Western Railway. Engineer I. K. Brunel. Listed Grade II*.

The Windsor branch crosses the Thames on the skew by a wrought-iron bowstring bridge of 203-foot span with a timber deck. It is Brunel's oldest surviving iron bridge and originally stood on six cast-

1971

iron cylinders, later replaced by brick abutments. The arch ribs are triangular in section, braced by vertical and diagonal 'strings'. Initially the approach arches on the Slough side were of timber, later replaced by brick.

OXFORDSHIRE

CHARLBURY

*Built 1853 by Oxford Worcester &
Wolverhampton Railway. Standard Brunel
design. Main station building and original
nameboard on up platform listed Grade II.
Between Oxford and Evesham.*

The OWW was originally a broad-gauge
line, engineered by Brunel and intended
to come under Great Western influence
(although it was nearly lost at one stage to
standard-gauge rivals). It was also short
of money which is why its stations were
built of wood. Two of them, Charlbury
and the original Evesham were in
Brunel's standard Italianate style like
Mortimer (*p.216*). Evesham was rebuilt in
a later brick style but Charlbury remained and has been restored to its
original condition.

CHARLBURY, 1979

CHOLSEY

*MOULSFORD VIADUCT. Built 1840 for
Great Western Railway. Engineer I. K. Brunel.
Listed Grade II. Between Reading and Didcot.*

Brunel's bridge here crosses the Thames
by three low segmental arches springing
virtually from water-level. They are constructed on the skew in red brick with
attractively rusticated stone voussoirs
and a stone coping on the parapet. When
the line was widened in 1892 a second
bridge was added on the downstream
side. It has a similar profile but is built
entirely of brick. It is linked to the older
bridge by short cross-arches and bracing
made from old rails.

CULHAM

*Built c. 1845 by Great Western Railway.
Standard Brunel design. Main passenger
building listed Grade II. Between Didcot and
Oxford.*

Culham is the only survivor from the
series of original Tudor-style stations
erected on the Great Western and illustrated in Bourne's well-known lithograph
of Pangbourne. Their materials varied
according to the locality and their proportions gave them a distinctive rural charm.

Culham is built in brick with stone
dressings. The main feature is the all-
round flat awning on scrolled iron

1971

218

brackets with jolly little fretted valances,
narrow enough to be little more than a
frill but just right for this building. Until
recent years there was a matching subsidiary building on the opposite platform
with a near-flat roof, all part of Brunel's
symmetrical composition seen at Pangbourne and the others. These stations also
once had matching Tudor goods sheds, in
Culham's case with two shallow pointed
arches.

DIDCOT

*STATION. Rebuilt 1885 by Great Western
Railway. Between Reading and Swindon.*

Didcot is the junction for the Oxford line
and has had two timber stations. The
first, opened in 1844, burned down in

1978

1885 and was replaced by a standard
GWR wooden station of the period with
exposed timber framing and vertical
boarding.

On the south side and centre island
platform the awnings are of the same
pattern as at Hanwell (*p.213*), attractively
decorated with deeply incised valancing
and pointed cut-outs in the gable ends.
The platforms on the northern side have
later but equally typical awnings with
prominent triangular beading on the
gable ends.

*BROAD-GAUGE TRANSHIPMENT
SHED. Erected in 1863. Now part of Didcot
Railway Centre.*

Through the subway from the station is

the Great Western Society's Didcot
Railway Centre where operational steam
locomotives and other GWR equipment
can be seen. One of the particularly interesting buildings is the Transhipment
Shed which the Society has dismantled
and re-erected a short distance away from
its original site.

By 1863 the Great Western had mixed
broad- and standard-gauge track from
Paddington to Birmingham, but only
broad to Bristol, so the junction between
the two routes at Didcot became an important transhipment point. Two sidings,
one broad-gauge and one standard, entered the Transhipment Shed where the
laborious task of unloading and loading
different-sized wagons could be performed under cover.

1982

The shed is thought to be the sole
survivor of its type, and is built of timber,
207 feet long with arched end doorways
for the tracks. The roof has diagonal
wooden braces reaching down to the walls
and in the reconstruction some steel
bracing has been discreetly added to give
extra strength. To give a faithful reproduction of Brunel's original permanent
way, the broad-gauge track has been constructed of old bridge rails on baulk
sleepers that were discovered in a disused
quarry in Somerset. In addition a ⅝th-
scale reproduction of an original GWR
disc-and-crossbar signal has been constructed alongside the shed.

COMPANY MEMENTOS

The railways in their heyday embraced the whole of everyday activity, and the range of equipment was accordingly immense. As much as possible bore the companies' initials, partly to advertise and partly to combat pilferage. Indeed, the 20th-century cult of using initials can be said to have been started by the 19th-century railway companies. Railway notices had a distinctive flavour: some requested, others instructed, while yet more ordered the passenger, employee and visitor what to do and not to do, whether it was crossing the line, showing tickets (always 'shewing' on the Great Western) or not emitting smoke when passing through residential areas.

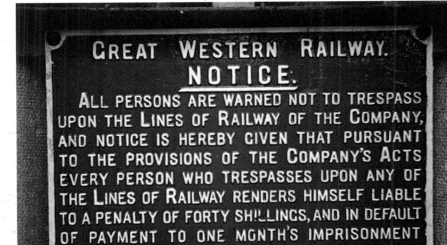

GREAT WESTERN RAILWAY.
NOTICE.
ALL PERSONS ARE WARNED NOT TO TRESPASS UPON THE LINES OF RAILWAY OF THE COMPANY, AND NOTICE IS HEREBY GIVEN THAT PURSUANT TO THE PROVISIONS OF THE COMPANY'S ACTS EVERY PERSON WHO TRESPASSES UPON ANY OF THE LINES OF RAILWAY RENDERS HIMSELF LIABLE TO A PENALTY OF FORTY SHILLINGS, AND IN DEFAULT OF PAYMENT TO ONE MONTH'S IMPRISONMENT FOR EVERY SUCH OFFENCE.
BY ORDER.

A GWR trespass notice (above) in the Keighley & Worth Valley Railway's collection at Oxenhope, and a Southern Railway notice (below) in an approach road at Cowes, Isle of Wight, exemplify the tone of company orders.

This mass-produced station clock at Liverpool Edge Hill was restored for the Rainhill exhibition in 1980.

SOUTHERN RAILWAY C?
NOTICE IS HEREBY GIVEN IN PURSUANCE OF SECTION 90 OF THE SOUTHERN RAILWAY ACT, 1924, THAT THIS ROAD IS A PRIVATE ROAD.
BY ORDER

FACING POINTS
MEN EMPLOYED BY FARMERS MUST NOT CROSS THE MAIN LINES TO FETCH MILK CANS

A museum collection of signs (above) and LMS fire buckets hanging on Midland brackets at Stamford Town recall the long-lived history of the old companies.

Brecon & Merthyr Railway.
Ticket for Bicycles, other Articles, Perambulators and Passengers.
ONE
BRECON
570

This pre-1923 ticket for '1 bike' from Brecon to Newport was priced at one shilling.

219

An elaborate coat of arms of the Lancashire & Yorkshire Railway, now in the National Railway Museum at York, incorporates the red rose of Lancaster and the white rose of York as well as lions passant gardant.

Signs like this, once familiar on British roads, have now been mostly replaced by continental patterns.

On a door handle the Metropolitan Railway promotes the land it bought up and then sold for new housing.

Rail employees collected their wages in numbered tins and carried personal identification tokens such as these.

A Bradshaw guide and a stop-watch marked with miles per hour symbolize the operation of timetables.

A selection of uniform buttons includes examples from the LNWR (second row across, left); LNER 1930s (same row, middle) and 1920s (bottom, left); GWR post-1935 (top right) and pre-1935 (bottom middle); and Midland showing the Wyvern (bottom right).

The cover of an LNWR passenger timetable of September 1886 incorporates a map of the company's system and connecting lines in Scotland and Ireland as well as scenic views along the routes.

It cost four shillings to convey an accompanied dog from Wilburton, Cambridgeshire, to Great Malvern in Worcestershire.

HEYFORD

Built 1852 by Great Western Railway. Brunel design. Between Oxford and Banbury.

After the first ten years or so the Great Western began to build rather larger country stations, although keeping the stylistic all-round flat awning. Between Oxford and Banbury there were several of these more generous stations, including Heyford which is a pleasant Cotswold stone building, faintly Tudor with a projecting entrance and a bay window in one

1978

end for the station master's office.

A smaller matching building originally occupied the opposite platform in the same manner as at the earlier stations. To add a heraldic note the awning valances on both sides of the line were decorated with unusual lions' masks in iron bas-relief, a feature of a number of other GWR stations built during this decade. Salisbury (*p.208*) had them along the frontage.

OXFORD

REWLEY ROAD STATION. Built 1851-52 for London & North Western Railway by Fox, Henderson & Partners. Part of former LNWR station listed Grade II.

On the town side of Oxford's present station stands a small timber building. Although no longer in railway use, it is significant because it was the entrance to Rewley Road station built from pre-fabricated iron sections by Fox, Henderson, who were contractors for the Crystal Palace, using principles evolved by Paxton. It is the only surviving example of the Crystal Palace type of construction.

The glazed ridge-and-furrow trainshed roof, of which a short section survives, rests on diagonally-braced girders and side columns which were clad with boarding, and they represent an important step forward in iron roof construction.

The present Oxford station is the successor to the former Great Western station, a wooden building which was a byword for inadequacy and inconvenience almost from the time it was built in 1852. In 1911 Max Beerbohm spoke of it as 'that antique station which . . . does yet whisper to the tourist the last enchantments of the Middle Age'.

REWLEY ROAD STATION, OXFORD, 1930s

SWING BRIDGE OVER ENTRANCE TO OXFORD CANAL

Built for London & North Western Railway; line opened 1851. Ancient Monument. North of Oxford Station. Map ref. SP 504066.

This steel swing bridge carries the line over an arm of the Oxford Canal to the Thames. Such a bridge would obviously have been required from the opening of the line and indeed with the waterway so much busier then it would have been constantly in use. It is evident that this is a replacement bridge dating perhaps from about 1900, although there is no maker's nameplate. The bridge is in the form of a large turntable which swings complete with several lines of track. It is still in working order as it gives rail access to the Rewley Road coal depot.

STEVENTON

FORMER SUPERINTENDENT'S HOUSE. Built c. 1839 for Great Western Railway. Architect I. K. Brunel. Between Didcot and Swindon. Sold.

By 1840 the Great Western main line from Paddington to Bristol was open as far as Steventon, which for about seven weeks was the terminus until the next section to Challow was ready. Until the opening of the branch from Didcot in 1844, Steventon served as the railhead for road coaches to Oxford.

The GWR board was composed of two committees, one meeting in London and the other in Bristol. As Steventon was half-way between London and Bristol, in 1841 it was chosen as a convenient place

1971

for full board meetings. Brunel was told to make suitable alterations to the house of the Superintendent of the Line, which accounts for its large and imposing appearance. It was the seat of power for six months – from July 1842 to January 1843; then the committees were abolished and board meetings were moved to London.

The house, now privately owned, is in the pleasant stone Tudor style beloved by Brunel with a two-storey bay window and nicely angled chimney stacks.

HEREFORD AND WORCESTER

GREAT MALVERN

Opened 1860 by Worcester & Hereford Railway. Present buildings completed 1862. Architect E. W. Elmslie. Station, road overbridge, forecourt walls and piers listed Grade II.

Malvern started developing as a spa in the late 1700s, expanding most rapidly in the 1840s, so that by the time the railway arrived it was an established inland watering place. Elmslie designed the station and its surroundings as part of a group including gardens, a landscaped approach road, the railway bridge and the Imperial Hotel (now a school).

The long single-storey frontage is built

GREAT MALVERN, 1948

random-fashion from dark, almost purplish local stone called Malvern Rag. It is a fantasy of French Gothic motifs delicately applied to doors, windows, gables, dormers and chimneys. One end is guarded by fleur-de-lis iron railings, and prominent cresting on the roof forms a

continuous line of quatrefoils. The most pleasing feature was a charmingly detailed clock turret and spirelet, or *flèche*, which has now been removed.

Quatrefoils also decorate the deep cast-iron awning brackets which give a striking arcade effect to both platforms. The cast-iron columns have extraordinary decorative mouldings in very high relief on the capitals, every one depicting differ-

GREAT MALVERN PLATFORMS, 1976

ent flowers and leaves carefully picked out in vivid colours, based on the original design, to give a most effective display. Coloured glass decorates the windows of the waiting room.

From one end of the down platform a private covered way to the former hotel

still stands, although now disused. Its corrugated iron roof is lifted from the mundane by being bell-shaped in section and capped by iron cresting.

The road bridge has a segmented arch, with embellishments on the piers and decorative parapets, while the fluted iron lamp standards along the approach road stand on conical stone bases. The whole group is a remarkably cohesive design.

HEREFORD

Built 1853 for Shrewsbury & Hereford Railway. Architect R. E. Johnston. Listed Grade II.

Here is a large two-storey building of red brick which makes an immediately striking impression with its numerous groups of lancet windows set in rusticated stone panels. Tall chimneys and gables, steep roofs and hexagonal stone finials complete the classic mid-Victorian Gothic theme.

On the platform side the long pitched awning has pointed glazing in the end gables, matching the windows, and is carried on trefoil brackets and columns with Corinthian capitals.

The island platform shows the influence of the Great Western Railway, which subsequently owned the station jointly with the London & North Western: the building matches the main one with awning brackets containing star shapes and resting on carved stone corbels, but the valances are in later GWR style.

THE GREAT WESTERN RAILWAY

Among railway enthusiasts the Great Western, based on Paddington, has always been one of the most popular railways, doubtless because it was largely unaffected by the 1923 Grouping and retained its name, character and style for another 25 years. Much of the company's individuality sprang from its association with I. K. Brunel and the adoption of his 7 foot gauge, not finally reduced to the standard 4 feet 8½ inches until 1892.

For the broad-gauge track, Sir Daniel Gooch introduced handsome single-driver locomotives, far larger than any other early engines. Later J. G. Churchward's introduction of a distinctively-shaped brass safety valve instead of a dome in the centre of the boiler, together with a copper-capped chimney, ensured that GWR engines remained visually a class apart.

In the 1860s the GWR's performance began to fade and it became a very backward railway until abolition of the broad gauge brought rejuvenation. In 1904 the engine *City of Truro* (now preserved at Swindon) achieved a speed of 100 mph with an Ocean Mail train, concurrently breaking the record for a start-to-stop run with a speed of 71 mph from Bristol to Paddington.

As part of the Great Western's development of the port of Fishguard, the Cunard

Line was induced for a time to use it to disembark passengers from the liners *Mauretania* and *Lusitania* on the New York to Liverpool run. London passengers were saved a day's sailing and conveyed to Paddington by special non-stop trains. Trains were considerably speeded up by a number of new lines, among them the last British main line, the 18-mile cut-off between Princes Risborough and Banbury.

While in many minds the Great Western was primarily associated with the West Country and South Wales, it also served a large part of the West Midlands and reached as far north as Chester on its own metals. It penetrated further by jointly-owned lines to Birkenhead and Warrington whence, at one time, it ran its own trains over the London & North Western to Manchester.

Below GWR ticket, 1897

Above City of Truro, 1957; right luggage label, pre-1948; below share certificate, 1840

HEREFORD, 1970s

WORCESTER

SHRUB HILL STATION. Built 1865 for Great Western Railway. Possibly designed by Edward Wilson, engineer. Station, including east platform, listed Grade II.

The use of blue engineering brick is not normally associated with architectural worth of even the most modest pretensions, yet if one ignores the stalky iron *porte cochère*, which must have been a later addition, the quiet two-storey facade here has a pleasant Georgian aspect.

The brickwork is relieved by stone door and window casings with projecting flat and pedimented hoods on the ground floor, rusticated quoins and a bold cornice. The building is set back on an elevated forecourt over an arcade of narrow, round-headed arches giving access to storage cellars.

Until the mid-1930s the station had a crescent-shaped overall roof with elliptical cutaways in the end-screens edged with deep valancing. It was replaced by individual awnings. Originally several small rooms and offices projected on to the platforms in a most unusual and elaborate manner. Two remain on the up

side. They have round-headed windows between very slim paired columns supporting a prominent cornice. Their most

SHRUB HILL FAIENCE WORK, 1973

notable features are the external frieze and low dado composed of intricately patterned multi-coloured glazed tiles or faience.

FOREGATE STREET BRIDGE. Rebuilt 1908 by Great Western Railway.

Looking down Foregate Street, you see a railway bridge with what appears to be a handsome segmental arch topped by a pierced balustrade. The arch has no load-bearing function but is merely a panelled cast-iron screen concealing a flat steel deck which carries the track. The large curved pedimented tops of the abutments are also iron.

1927

Each arch carries the arms of the city and the county in the spandrels, and of the GWR in the centre. The result is an interesting period effort to make an engineering structure tone with the Georgian street, and despite criticism by Pevsner in his *Buildings of England* the bridge achieves it rather more successfully than the two 1930s cinemas.

GLOUCESTERSHIRE

KEMBLE

Built 1872 by Great Western Railway. Between Swindon and Gloucester.

Kemble did not feature in the public time-tables until 1872, though the line from Swindon to Cheltenham on which it stands had been open since 1845. For nearly 30 years it remained just a wooden platform where passengers changed for the branch to Cirencester.

1964

The station serving the neighbour-hood, called Tetbury Road, was situated a mile distant, away from the land of the Kemble squire, Robert Gordon, who had originally opposed the line because it would damage his amenities. His support in Parliament for the Bill authorizing its construction had to be bought for £7,500, the promise of an unnecessary 415-yard tunnel near his house (which is still in use) and an undertaking that no station would be built on his estate.

In 1872 the GWR opened a proper station at Kemble, a pleasant Cotswold stone building designed in neo-Tudor style with generous platform awnings. Tetbury Road was closed to passengers ten years later and became the goods station for the nearby village of Coates.

Despite an objection from Gordon's daughter, a branch was opened to Tetbury in 1889, and the station became a three-way junction. Now that both the Cirencester and Tetbury branches are closed it is a simple through station, although still an important railhead for a large area of the southern Cotswolds.

STROUD

Built 1845 for Great Western Railway. Designer I. K. Brunel. Between Swindon and Gloucester.

For a Brunel station Stroud is less than satisfying. The frontage is long and low, in stone with a few sparse Tudor motifs, angled chimney stacks, a central gable and a length of frilly valancing under the eaves at one side. But it is a complete GWR station, very little altered, with both platform awnings intact on their deep quatrefoil brackets and decorated with very typical intricate valances. The Tudor-style goods shed still bears the prominent letters GWR.

Stroud was one of the stations used by the GWR's first steam railcar service (or rail motor as it was often called) in 1903.

STROUD GOODS SHED, 1975

Single carriages with built-in engines and boilers ran between Stonehouse and Chalford, and were very popular with workpeople who previously had to rely on horse-buses or go on foot. A number of intermediate halts were opened for them,

STROUD PLATFORMS, 1956

and their use grew rapidly throughout the system, later superceded by push-and-pull trains, locomotives and carriages which were kept coupled and could run equally well in either direction and which were used by the Great Western more than by any other line.

WILTSHIRE

BOX TUNNEL

Built 1841 for Great Western Railway. Engineer I. K. Brunel. Between Chippenham and Bath.

Box Tunnel was to Brunel what Kilsby (*p.69*) had been to Robert Stephenson a few years before: a venture into the un-known. At 1 mile 1,452 yards long it was the greatest railway tunnel so far built.

Like Stephenson, Brunel had trouble with flooding, and work fell behind schedule. For the last six months he put virtually his entire labour force on to the job, 4,000 men and 300 horses working round the clock by the light of candles – a ton was burned every week for two and a half years. Brunel's critics said the tunnel would never be completed, and if it were no one would venture through it. Indeed, for several years afterwards the more apprehensive travellers left their train at Corsham or Box, travelled over the hill by post-chaise and then caught the next train.

The tunnel is on a gradient of 1 in 100 dipping down towards Bath and part of the interior is unlined rock. The eastern mouth is plain, with ugly brick rings added in 1895, but the western entrance, set between curved wing walls, is a great classical portal in Bath stone. The key-stone is scroll-shaped, and carved with an acanthus leaf. The massive cornice is set on prominent curved stone corbels and surmounted by a moulded balustrade. The sun is supposed to shine through the

ENGRAVING OF BOX TUNNEL BY J. C. BOURNE, 1846

tunnel at sunrise on Brunel's birthday.

Brunel's biographer L. T. C. Rolt considers that Brunel regarded Box Tunnel as 'a triumphal gateway to the Roman city. It was for this reason that he crowned Box with that huge classic portico'.

BRADFORD-ON-AVON

Completed 1848 by the Wilts Somerset & Weymouth Railway. Opened 1857 by Great Western Railway. Brunel-style design. Between Bath and Trowbridge.

The Wilts Somerset & Weymouth was a child of the broad-gauge Great Western in its war with the standard-gauge London & South Western for supremacy in the south-west (*see also Mortimer, p.216*). But the line had progressed no further than from Chippenham to Westbury when the financial bubble of the Railway Mania burst in 1847. Money immediately ran out and work stopped in 1848.

Bradford-on-Avon station was complete and only awaiting the laying of rails from the junction near Trowbridge, less than two miles away, but nine years went by before the station came into use. It has Brunel-type 'balanced' buildings on each platform, constructed of Bath stone in Tudor style.

Formerly both buildings had all-round flat awnings, but those on the Bath platform were replaced by a GWR lean-to awning; the platform of the original survives on the Trowbridge side.

CHIPPENHAM

STATION. Built 1841 for Great Western Railway. Engineer I. K. Brunel. Main entrance building and platform canopies on down side, gateposts to station yard, weighbridge office and former British Rail Office in station car park all listed Grade II.

Chippenham station was the first that Brunel designed in his Italianate style (*see Mortimer, p.216*), which perhaps explains why it is different from those that followed. The pitched roof overhangs at front and rear but not at the ends, and the openings are square-headed instead of round.

The building is in Bath stone and a flat awning was added to the frontage on delightfully shaped wooden brackets. The platform awnings are of standard late GWR type with nice valancing.

North of the main line at the east end of the station is a large warehouse. It was originally an engineering works of Rowland Brotherhood, one of the contractors who built this part of the Great Western Railway.

Brotherhood did a variety of railway work, even building broad-gauge locomotives, and inside can still be seen, high up on each side, the rails on which the travelling overhead cranes ran.

CHIPPENHAM, 1980

BRIDGE OVER BATH ROAD. Listed Grade II.

This fine lofty bridge now presents brick faces following widening of the line, although one of the old stone side arches is still visible. The main arch is higher than its flanking pedestrian arches, and there are nicely curved abutments with a stone cornice and parapet.

VIADUCT OVER NEW ROAD. Listed Grade II*.

This viaduct is also in brick, with handsomely rusticated stone voussoirs. It is spoiled by strengthening rings added beneath, though they do taper into the piers nicely. A stone cornice and parapet give the finishing touch.

VIADUCT OVER NEW ROAD, 1971

BRADFORD-ON-AVON, 1971

225

SWINDON

THE RAILWAY VILLAGE. Built 1841-43
for Great Western Railway, with later
additions. Designers I. K. Brunel and
Sir Matthew Digby Wyatt. Whole village a
conservation area. Mechanics' Institute,
2 Emlyn Square (sold), Bristol Street wall and
London Street wall (facing village) listed
Grade II.

With Crewe and Wolverton, Swindon shares the distinction of being the first 'model' railway town planned under a policy of enlightened paternalism notably lacking among other large employers at the time, a policy that provided sanitary housing and civic amenities far in advance of contemporary standards.

The railway village stands to the east of Swindon station, of which only a few original buildings and one island platform remain. Known at the time as the New Town, it was built by the GWR for the employees of the Swindon Works, centre of GWR locomotive and rolling stock manufacture. Broad streets were laid out in a gridiron pattern with a central square, Emlyn Square. The terraced houses had narrow front gardens and rear yards, each with its own outside lavatory and washhouse (a considerable luxury at the time) giving on to a rear alleyway.

Virtually all the terraces remain intact. They are built of stone, some of it from Box Tunnel, in a number of styles including Brunel's favourite Tudor. Features include splayed window jambs, drip stones and angled chimney stacks.

Three pubs were built, and a market was held in Emlyn Square where in 1855 the company completed the Mechanics' Institute designed in Tudor style by Edward Roberts and considerably enlarged in 1892. In 1854 a hostel was built which later became the Wesleyan Chapel and is now the Great Western Railway Museum run by the local authority. Exhibits include a replica of the famous broad-gauge engine *North Star*.

St. Mark's Church was designed in the Decorated style by Gilbert Scott, later the architect of St. Pancras Hotel. It was completed in 1845 and has a 140-foot spire. Other facilities provided by the company as the town grew included a hospital, school and park.

BACKS OF COTTAGES IN RAILWAY VILLAGE, 1971

LONDON STREET WALL, 1976

MECHANICS' INSTITUTE, 1976

AVON

BATH

THE GREAT WESTERN THROUGH BATH. Railway opened from Bristol to Bath 1840, from Chippenham to Bath 1841. Designer I. K. Brunel. Listed Grade II structures, from east to west: Beckford Road bridge and retaining wall to canal; two bridges in Sydney Gardens and retaining walls; Sydney Road bridge and retaining walls; tunnel under Bathwick Terrace; St. James's Bridge; Bath Spa station; viaduct and bridge, Lower Bristol Road; Twerton Wood Tunnel entrances; Twerton (long) Tunnel entrances.

To take his railway through and above Georgian Bath Brunel built a number of bridges, tunnels and viaducts which he designed with even greater care than usual in order to ensure the greatest possible degree of harmony. He had to cross the Avon twice where it loops around the city centre and in Sydney

ST. JAMES'S BRIDGE AND BATH STATION, c.1843

Gardens he had to divert the Kennet & Avon Canal. All the work was done in Bath stone, but unsympathetic repair work by the GWR over the following century or more has resulted in unsightly patches of brick in places.

Entering Bath from London the railway runs in a cutting alongside and below the canal, requiring a sturdy retaining wall with a pronounced curved batter for a quarter mile or so. The finely dressed masonry is well up to the standards of Georgian Bath, and among the best railway work of its kind in Britain.

This section of the line is further enhanced by its bridges. Beckford Road crosses on a 29-foot 6-inch graceful elliptical arch, then in Sydney Gardens follow two ornamental bridges of 30-foot span, one elliptical on the skew with a balustraded parapet and a small side arch over a footpath, and the other a pretty little

LINE THROUGH SYDNEY GARDENS, 1976

iron bridge with pierced spandrels and an iron balustrade. Sydney Road bridge is also skewed, after which the line passes

under Bathwick Hill by two short tunnels 77 and 97 yards long, emerging on to an embankment.

So far the passenger has seen little of the approaches to Bath. Now the city suddenly spreads out on both sides of the line, set against a backcloth of steep hillsides. The train then enters a 37-arch viaduct leading to St. James's Bridge which crosses the Avon on an 88-foot elliptical span with two small side arches and prominent rustication. Still elevated, the line curves sharply through Bath Spa (formerly Bath) station.

Until 1897 Bath Spa had a smaller edition of the timber hammer-beam-style roof at Bristol Temple Meads (*p.228*), spanning four tracks. It was replaced by conventional platform awnings.

The frontage building is not one of Brunel's best compositions, but the narrow curved site beneath the railway was extremely awkward. Brunel adopted an asymmetrical design with three Jacobean-type gables and a central oriel window, and managed some enhancement with a series of nice radial fanlights over the door openings. Manvers Street, running up to the station, is of some historic interest as one of the first railway approaches laid out in accordance with legislation. Lord Manvers's directions in the GWR Act of 1835 prescribe minutely how it was to be done.

BATH STATION, c.1920

Immediately to the west the line crosses the Avon again, at an acute angle. Brunel's original bridge had laminated timber arches with cast-iron struts forming a Gothic outline in the spandrels. It has been replaced twice, most recently by a deep lattice girder bridge; but the original stone buttresses remain.

Close to Lower Bristol Road is a second viaduct of 28 segmental arches, originally stone-faced but now predominantly brick. On the north side the crenellated parapet and turreted abutments mostly remain in place.

Beyond Oldfield Park station the line rejoins Lower Bristol Road on another viaduct at Twerton, where the old Twerton station building (closed in 1917) and the steps up to it from the road can still be seen on the up side. Twerton viaduct has 28 arches, some in Gothic style, and is mostly stone faced.

6003 *KING GEORGE IV*, TWERTON TUNNEL, 1956

After the short Twerton Wood Tunnel the line enters the longer 264-yard Twerton Tunnel which has pointed arches with flanking castellated turrets at both ends. The eastern pair are of different heights with a plain parapet between them, but at the other end they are taller and of equal height, with a crenellated parapet and arrow slits.

The line through Bath remains an outstanding example of decorative railway building intended to ensure that the citizens of 1840 had the least possible cause for complaint.

GREEN PARK STATION. Built 1870 for Midland Railway. Architect J. H. Sanders. Engineer J. S. Crossley. Listed Grade II. Closed and sold.

Unlike the Great Western, the Midland crept into Bath almost unobserved. Once within the city, however, it built a station far more handsome than its rival's. Until 1951 it was known as Queen Square, although it stands some distance from John Wood's noble square of that name. It was closed in 1966, and remained without a use until 1979 when a proposal was made to convert it into a supermarket.

The Georgian classical frontage has few peers among stations of this size and design. At the public enquiry held to discuss its change of use the local authority stated: 'It is probably the best Victorian building in the City of Bath, and was clearly designed to complement the "Georgian City" on to which it opened. It is now equally clear that the trainshed itself is an important building. It is a straightforward engineering work with few irrelevant embellishments which contrasts perfectly with the elegant frontage buildings . . .'

The station, now part of the completed supermarket complex, has been restored, the decorated iron *porte cochère* has been repaired and the stone facade, including the slender Ionic columns, balustraded parapet and well proportioned windows, has been cleaned. Inside, the arched roof with its matching side arcades has been painted and re-glazed, so that Green Park again plays its role in complementing the historic buildings of Bath.

In addition to serving the Midland Railway, the station was used by trains from the north to Bournemouth via the steeply graded Somerset & Dorset Joint Railway across the Mendips, and as it was a terminus all through trains had to reverse.

BRISTOL

TEMPLE MEADS STATION. Opened 1840 by Great Western Railway, designer I. K. Brunel; extended 1865-78 jointly by Great Western, Bristol & Exeter and Midland Railways, architects Sir Matthew Digby Wyatt and probably Francis Fox; further extended 1932-35, architect P. E. Culverhouse. Listed Grade I.
BRISTOL & EXETER RAILWAY OFFICE BLOCK. Built 1852. Architect S. C. Fripp. Listed Grade II.

The station is in two distinct parts: the original GWR terminus, now a car park, on the left of the approach road, fronting Temple Gate, and ahead and to the right the through station containing the central tower and main entrance.

The Brunel station has been very little altered since Bourne illustrated it in 1846. Its castellated late-medieval-style frontage in Bath stone was intended to harmonize with the historic buildings of the city and the same style was carried along the sides in cheaper coursed rubble stone. More inventive was Brunel's trainshed, covering five broad-gauge tracks with a clear 72-foot span. The wooden roof, supported on splendid cast-iron side arcades of four-centred arches running along the platforms, looks like the great hammer-beam roof of Westminster Hall in London, and is two feet wider. In fact it is a cunningly disguised cantilever structure, but nonetheless gives a very fine effect.

BRUNEL STATION, TEMPLE GATE, c.1846

Until the end of its use as a station in 1965 Brunel's shed had only two platforms, which are still there; originally one was for arrivals and the other for departures although later each served both purposes. The whole of this part of the station is on arches and passengers arrived and departed by stairs from below. Between the platform ends and the Temple Gate facade were offices, including a boardroom, with fine Tudor fireplaces, decorated ceilings and a grand staircase. Behind are more offices built over the ends of the tracks, into which it is said smoke penetrated through the floorboard cracks when engines were standing below. The whole of the original station is undergoing long-term restoration by the Brunel Engineering Centre Trust.

At right angles to the GWR station the Bristol & Exeter Railway built their own terminus in 1845, a wooden shed of considerably less distinction designed by Brunel, who was also engineer to that

BRISTOL B&E STATION (*left*), B&E OFFICES (*centre*), AND BRUNEL TRAINSHED (*right*), c.1873

company. The obvious difficulties of trying to run through trains forced the construction of a connecting curve and platform. Meanwhile the Midland Railway had established a route into Bristol from the north, so there were now three railways using two stations. Between 1865 and 1878 they jointly carried out an extensive reconstruction, demolishing the B & E trainshed and laying out new platforms on the curve beneath a fine pointed arched roof of dramatic quality.

The old GWR terminus was retained, with an extension at the outer end connecting it to the new station, and a new frontage block was built by Sir Matthew Digby Wyatt in a flamboyant French Gothic style in variegated grey stone with the well-known central tower. It was topped at that time by an elaborate French pavilion turret and six crocketted pinnacles, all complete with battlements and twisted chimney stacks. Along the frontage there is an intricately decorated glass-and-iron canopy.

Bristol Joint Station, as it was known, stayed thus until the 1930s. Passengers were reminded of joint ownership (Great Western and Midland only from 1876, when the GWR took over the B & E) by the 'BJS' insignia displayed on the staff's uniforms, a detail which lasted until nationalisation.

Further extensions took place in 1932-35 when extra platforms were built outside the main roof, covered by standard GWR awnings and provided with buildings clad in the Great Western's current cream tiles with glazed chocolate-coloured ceramic signs and notices set in them. Large new offices were built in red brick on the site of the old B & E station.

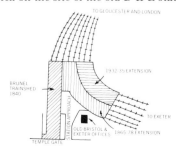

LAYOUT OF TEMPLE MEADS, 1983

At the same time the French turret was removed from the tower – some said it was an improvement – and the pinnacles were re-clad without the crocketting.

There is much to see at Temple Meads today. The lofty entrance hall has a cathedral-like atmosphere, and the 1930s Tudor-panelled booking office screen and ceiling look older than they are. Similar work distinguishes the refreshment room on platform 3, with its unusual curved mullioned windows looking out towards Brunel's trainshed. The 1930s subway and external platforms now have a period flavour too, while the Gothic of the 1878 roof exercises a particular fascination which extends to the intricate ironwork of the end-screens. Outside, the ends of alternate valleys on the ridge-and-furrow canopy carry the arms of London and Bristol, which the GWR had appropriated and made its own. On a more humble note, the rails set in the sunken roadway between the approach slope and Brunel's trainshed are said to be the last remaining tramlines in Bristol.

On the right hand side of the approach is the imposing three-storey office block

MAIN ENTRANCE, STATION APPROACH, 1955

built for the B & E in 1852 by S. C. Fripp. Jacobean in style it has two towers flanking the entrance and the initial 'F' in strapwork above it. The arched hall gives on to a broad central well with an arched gallery corbelled out around it, and the former B & E boardroom at one end overlooks the yard through a neatly curved oriel window. The ceiling, which has been restored, is beautifully decorated with geometrical panels and a large central boss, bigger even than those in the GWR offices across the forecourt.

(*Continued on page 233*)

BRUNEL'S WORKING DRAWINGS

In the building of his Great Western Railway and the other lines to which he was engineer, Brunel produced many hundreds of working drawings. Most were stored at Paddington station where they are still on file in the plan room, available to the Chief Engineers and Architects of British Rail. A selection is published here for the first time. They demonstrate Brunel's romantic perception and mastery of railway design, and the way in which he accompanied his sectional and plan drawings with pictorial representations so that no one working on the line could misunderstand his intentions.

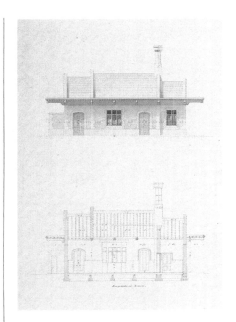

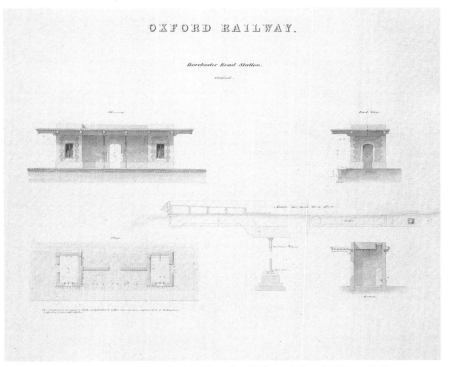

Elevation, end view, plan and sectional drawings show the subsidiary platform building at Culham station.

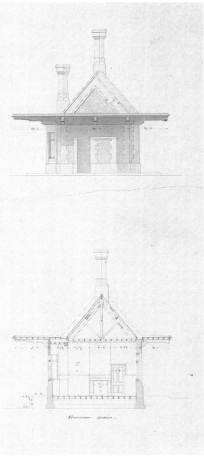

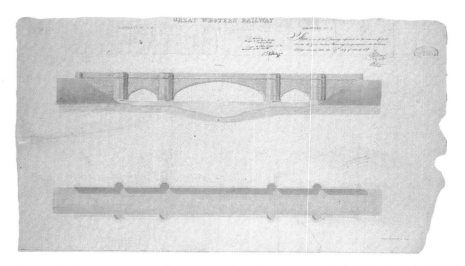

This drawing shows in elevation and plan the Avon bridge, still standing at Whitby Road, St. Anne's, in Bristol.

The drawings above and top are for the main building at Culham station in Oxfordshire, labelled by Brunel as Dorchester Road station, but opened as Abingdon Road and known as such until 1856. They illustrate the design and construction of Brunel's characteristic integral flat awning, as does the larger-scale sectional drawing for the subsidiary building (above left). The plan of the Avon bridge (left) is dated 1836 and signed in the top right corner by Brunel and W. Ranger, the contractor. All these are examples of the 600 drawings which have been stiffened with linen and bound in folios by Mr. Marian Hajwa, for 14 years controller of the plan room. They measure four or five feet by about three. The rest are still in rolls, as stored more than a century ago.

ISAMBARD KINGDOM BRUNEL, ENGINEER

A unique versatility combined with imaginative flair and ingenuity puts Brunel in the top flight of Victorian engineers; some would say at the very summit. He assisted his father Marc, a French emigré, in constructing the first Thames Tunnel between Wapping and Rotherhithe, and went on to carry out a number of dock projects on his own account, including Bristol, Plymouth and Milford Haven.

His most outstanding work was the Great Western Railway from London to Bristol, laid to the gauge of 7 feet, and extended into South Wales, the West Country and parts of the West Midlands. But although his broad gauge lasted until 1892, it came too late to overcome George Stephenson's 'narrow' gauge of 4 feet 8½ inches, which was already well established and became standard. His major bridging work was the Royal Albert Bridge at Saltash (*p.241*), which he just lived to see completed. Many of his viaducts, particularly in the West Country and South Wales, were of timber and some lasted well into the 20th century.

Brunel had his failures, too. His few locomotives were not a success and his espousal of the atmospheric system on the South Devon Railway (*see Starcross Pumping Station, p.239*) was disastrous, losing him a great deal of money.

His large steamships were really too early for their time. His first, the *Great Western*, was the largest ship afloat in 1838. It made the Atlantic crossing in 15 days. For the *Great Britain*, now preserved at Bristol, he used screw propulsion, and his largest, the *Great Eastern*, included many novel features that later became standard practice. It remained the largest ship in the world for the next half century, but suffered so many problems and mishaps during its building and trials that it broke Brunel's health and led to his death in 1859, aged 53. Nor was it a commercial success; instead of carrying passengers it was used to lay the first transatlantic cables.

It is ironic that one of Brunel's first projects, the Clifton suspension road bridge at Bristol, was the last to be finished. Started in 1836, it was delayed through lack of money until after his death, and was completed in 1864 by Hawkshaw and W. H. Barlow as a memorial to Brunel. Perhaps the most moving tribute came from his great friend and fellow engineer Daniel Gooch, who designed the locomotives that ran on Brunel's broad gauge. 'By his death the greatest of England's engineers was lost, the man with the greatest originality of thought and power of execution, bold in his plans but right. The commercial world thought him extravagant; but although he was so, great things are not done by those who sit down and count the cost of every thought and act.'

Modern statues of Brunel stand at Paddington station, in Bristol, and on the Thames embankment near Hungerford Bridge.

In this view of Bristol No. 1 Tunnel, opened out in 1888, Brunel added two figures admiring the work.

In his design for the western portal of Box Tunnel (left) Brunel added a plan of the foundations and labelled all the heights and widths in feet and inches. He separately illustrated in quarter full size details such as the entablature, balustrading and trusses, showing the keystone from both front and side (front view above). After his death his associate Sir Matthew Digby Wyatt continued the tradition of fine draughtsmanship with the design (below) for the new frontage of Bristol Temple Meads.

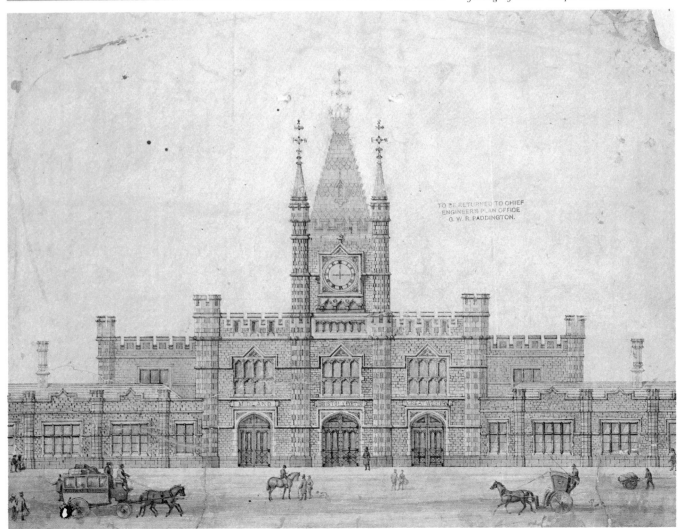

In Sir Matthew Digby Wyatt's design the main entrance of Bristol Temple Meads appears as built in 1876. The French pavilion turret was removed in the 1930s.

(Continued from page 228)

OLD GAOL ENTRANCE. Cumberland Road. Built 1816. Architect H. H. Seward. Listed Grade II.

Leading into a coal yard is a massive stone gateway, formerly part of Bristol Gaol which was sacked in the Reform Bill riots of 1831. This architectural oddment came into railway ownership after the opening in 1872-76 of the Bristol Harbour Branch, jointly owned by the Great Western and Bristol & Exeter companies.

CLIFTON DOWN STATION. Built 1874 by Clifton Extension Railway (jointly owned by Great Western & Midland). Engineer Sir James Brunlees. Between Bristol and Avonmouth.

The Clifton area of Bristol is served by a station whose spaciousness gives evidence of a busier era in railway traffic. The main building, in squared random stone with a two-storey centrepiece, is typical mid-

1950

Victorian heavy Gothic. Pointed ground-floor doorways lead into a spacious booking hall; and mullioned windows with cusps lead up to a dentilled parapet and a steep, hipped roof. The platform side had a nice glazed ridge-and-furrow awning on foliated brackets, which has now gone.

CLIFTON DOWN TUNNEL VENT. Built 1877 by Clifton Extension Railway. Engineer Sir James Brunlees. Pembroke Road, Clifton. Listed Grade II.

From Clifton Down station the line was extended in stages to Avonmouth, passing beneath the Down by a 1,738-yard tunnel on a steeply falling gradient of 1 in 64, to emerge in the Avon Gorge. Ventilation is provided through a circular vent built of squared rock-faced stone with a crenellated rim and a domed iron grille over the top.

REDLAND STATION FOOTBRIDGE. Built 1874 by Clifton Extension Railway. Listed Grade II. Between Temple Meads and Clifton Down.

IVATT 2-6-2T IN TEMPLE MEADS 1878 TRAINSHED EXTENSION, BRUNEL SHED BEHIND, 1960s

BRISTOL OLD GAOL ENTRANCE, 1980

One casualty of the building of the railway through this part of Bristol was Lovers' Walk, a shady promenade leading up to Redland Grove House; it was severed by the railway cutting. This three-span cast-iron footbridge may have been built to cross the breach for it seems older than the station, which was opened only in 1897; it must anyway have been altered then for it stands on the station platforms.

ST. ANNE'S PARK and FOX'S WOOD TUNNELS. Built 1840 for Great Western Railway. Engineer I. K. Brunel. Listed Grade II. Between Bristol and Bath.

Brunel found it necessary to cut a number of tunnels between Bristol and Bath as he followed the tortuous course of the Avon. Bristol No. 1, made famous by the Norman arch used by J. C. Bourne on the title page of his book of engravings of the GWR, was opened out in 1889.

Among those that remain is St. Anne's Park Tunnel, which is 154 yards long. The western portal was to have had a crenellated and heavily dentilled parapet, to convey the appropriate picturesque atmosphere, but when it was partly finished heavy rains brought down part of the hillside so that a retaining wall above the tunnel mouth was no longer required. Brunel decided the portal looked like a ruined medieval gateway and planted ivy on it to increase the romantic effect. It remained like that until 1900 when the GWR completed it in brick.

Fox's Wood Tunnel is 1,017 yards long and has two unequal turrets flanking the western entrance. As the rock is very hard, the tunnel is partly unlined, and Brunel left the eastern entrance in its natural state without a portal.

PENSFORD VIADUCT

Built 1873 by Bristol and North Somerset Railway. Listed Grade II. Closed.

This unadorned but finely sited viaduct has 16 semi-circular arches on tall piers, all constructed from quarry-faced stone. Built for a single track, it has a narrowness which emphasizes its great height, and on close inspection reveals a well balanced design. The spans are varied in groups of four short arches, a pierced pier, three large arches, a large solid central pier, and then the whole sequence repeated.

1976

The viaduct entirely dominates Pensford from the south, but if you approach it from the north it is so well hidden it might as well not be there.

SEVERN TUNNEL

Completed 1885 for Great Western Railway. Engineer Sir John Hawkshaw. Between Bristol and Newport.

For years the GWR was nicknamed 'The Great Way Round' but gradually it shortened the routes between London and its principal destinations by cut-off lines. The Severn remained a barrier on the approach to South Wales, which had to be reached by a roundabout route through Gloucester, until in 1873 work started on a tunnel between Pilning in Gloucestershire and Rogiet in Monmouthshire.

Under Charles Richardson as resident engineer and Hawkshaw as consultant, the first four and a half years were occupied in exploring the strata under the river and it was not until 1877 that contracts were placed for construction. By autumn 1879 pilot tunnels had been driven out from both banks and were within 130 yards of meeting when all the workings were inundated by a large spring of water which overwhelmed the pumps.

Hawkshaw now took over direct responsibility for the works with a new contractor, T. A. Walker. He decided to lower the tunnel by 15 feet under a deep channel in the river bed called the Shoots. Larger pumps were installed to cope with the Great Spring, shafts deepened and new ones dug, but it was the end of 1880 before the water was cleared. The workings were flooded by the Great Spring and by the river three more times in the next

234

SEVERN TUNNEL SHORTLY AFTER COMPLETION, c.1885

three years and Hawkshaw eventually mastered the Great Spring by intercepting it with a side tunnel and permanent pumps.

The tunnel was completed in 1885. It is 4 miles 628 yards long and cost £1.8 million. On the Welsh side it descends at a gradient of 1 in 90, and on the English side at 1 in 100 to a point 44 feet below the bed of the Shoots where there is a level section of 264 yards. The Great Spring's output of 20 million gallons a day is controlled by continuous pumping, today by electric pumps but originally by 15 steam pumping engines.

Regular passenger train services began in December 1886, and several new lines were constructed to link up with the tunnel, the most important being the 30-mile Wooton Bassett to Patchway cut-off avoiding Bristol, completed in 1903.

UPHILL

THE DEVIL'S BRIDGE. Built 1841 for Bristol & Exeter Railway. Engineer I. K. Brunel. Listed Grade II. Between Yatton and Highbridge.

Across Bleadon Hill cutting Brunel built a single-span brick 'flying' bridge, the best and tallest example of this kind of structure, supported directly on the sides of the cutting without abutments and characteristic of the Bristol & Exeter. It stands 60 feet above the line and has a clear span of 110 feet.

'The quantity of masonry in these bridges is much less than in those of the ordinary construction,' explained Brunel's biographer, 'and lofty and expensive centering is not required, as the bridge can be built before the cutting is excavated to its full dimensions.' Other advantages of this type of bridge are that building skew arches is simplified and on sharp curves there is little obstruction to the view along the line.

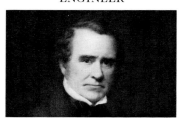

SIR JOHN HAWKSHAW, ENGINEER

Hawkshaw obtained his early training in road building in his native Yorkshire, followed by harbour works in Ireland and three years as a mining engineer in Venezuela. His first major railway appointment was as resident engineer to the Manchester & Leeds in 1845 (laid out by George Stephenson), after which he built many lines in West Yorkshire involving numerous tunnels and lofty viaducts. He was one of the first engineers to realise that the limit of adhesion for steam traction was considerably greater than supposed, and laid down lines as steep as 1 in 50.

In 1850 he set up in private practice in London and became enormously successful, adept at grappling with some of the most difficult engineering works and ultimately responsible for more major undertakings than any other 19th-century engineer. The arched station roofs and Thames bridges at Charing Cross (*p.179*) and Cannon Street (*p.178*) were his, as were many other notable bridges. He was concerned in the original Channel Tunnel scheme, and all subsequent projects have been based on his pioneering work. With William Barlow, Hawkshaw completed Brunel's Clifton suspension bridge.

Hawkshaw carried out considerable overseas work, including feasibility reports on the Suez and Panama Canals, and was very active in designing docks and harbours. His greatest work was the Severn Tunnel (*left*) which he completed in the face of tremendous difficulties. He was born in 1811 and died in London in 1891 at the end of a lifespan that covered development of almost the entire British railway system.

WESTON-SUPER-MARE

Built 1882 for Great Western Railway.
Designed 1876 by Francis Fox, engineer of
Bristol & Exeter Railway.

Weston originally stood on a branch from the Bristol & Exeter main line, but the branch was converted into a loop line and a new, elaborately designed station was erected on a sharp curve.

Built in the attractive pale grey stone of the district, the main frontage block is a long single storey with gables and, at one end, a low tower for the footbridge. A nicely bracketed verandah runs the

1978

length of the facade, and elaborate ridge-and-furrow glass-and-iron awnings cover the platforms. These are the chief glory of the place as they sweep round the sharp curve of the station supported on decorated latticed girders, intricate brackets and tapered columns embellished with a spiral design at the base and acanthus leaves on the capitals. The gable ends are partly hipped and there is delicate valancing all round.

YATTON

Built 1841 for Bristol & Exeter Railway.
Engineer I. K. Brunel. Between Bristol and
Weston-super-Mare.

Yatton, formerly the junction for the Cheddar Valley and Clevedon branches, has the most unusual distinction of possessing two different Brunel buildings in Mendip stone. On the down side is one of his Tudor buildings with a flat all-round awning, while opposite is one with his Italianate-style hipped roof but with Tudor details instead of the usual round-headed openings.

UP-SIDE PLATFORM, 1971

Both buildings have had their awnings modified, on the up side by a flat extension at one end and a curved-top umbrella awning at the other. This type of awning, of which at one time there was a second example at Yatton, was not very common on the Great Western system.

WESTON-SUPER-MARE UP-SIDE FOOTBRIDGE ENTRANCE, 1971

SOMERSET

BRIDGWATER

STATION. Built 1841 for Bristol & Exeter
Railway. Engineer I. K. Brunel. Listed Grade
II. Between Weston-super-Mare and Taunton.

In true Brunel style Bridgwater station has matching buildings on both platforms. They are of one storey with deep Georgian-style windows beneath a cor-

1976

nice and deep parapet hiding a low pitched roof. The walls are all rendered in light stucco and the platform canopies are the near-flat early-Great Western type, supported on nice ironwork and finished

with pierced sawtooth valances. The two buildings are joined by a covered footbridge.

BRIDGE OVER RIVER PARRETT.

Built 1871 by Bristol & Exeter Railway.
Ancient Monument. Map reference ST 300374.
Closed.

Built to carry a single-line branch from the Bristol and Exeter main line to the newly developed Bridgwater dock, this bridge was designed to open to let ships pass in and out. A length of track on the east bank moved to one side, making space for the main span to draw back on rollers.

Much of the machinery was dismantled in 1973 but enough remains for its workings to be understood. There are, of course, many opening bridges in British docks, but most dock bridges were reconstructed in the late 19th century and this is a particularly early survivor. It was also unusual for being converted from steam to hydraulic power almost immediately after completion.

235

CHARD CENTRAL

*Built 1866 by Bristol & Exeter and London &
South Western Railways jointly. Listed Grade
II. Closed. Between Yeovil and Taunton.*

Chard Central, or 'Joint' as it was once
known, was a meeting point for the broad-
and standard-gauge branches of the two
companies which operated it. The broad-
gauge track was not converted to
standard until 1891, a year before the
broad gauge was finally and completely
abolished, so through running was not
possible. In the eyes of the B & E (and
later the GWR, which took it over)
separation was a virtue because it prevented the LSWR from trying to gain
access via Chard to Taunton.

PRE-1962

Although it had only one through platform and a bay, the station was unique in
combining one of Brunel's extended
hipped-roofed Italianate brick buildings
with one of his wooden overall roofs, supported not by the usual timber walls but
by a brick arcade of round-topped arches
on hexagonal piers. The gable ends of the
roof were attractively glazed, using very
slender vertical glazing bars, and the
frontage was embellished with a central
pediment containing scrolled strapwork.
This remarkable combination of two
basic types was given unity by the common use of round-topped arches.

CREWKERNE

*Built 1860 for London & South Western
Railway. Architect Sir William Tite. Listed
Grade II. Between Salisbury and Exeter.*

The larger stations on the LSWR's Exeter
line featured a steeply gabled three-storey
house adjoining a single-storey office
building, both designed in Tudor style
with massive chimneys and ridge cresting. Materials varied according to
locality, Crewkerne being in a pleasant
gold-coloured ashlar stone. The shelter
on the opposite platform has small gables
matching the parent building, masking a
roof which is hipped at the back.

FROME

*Built 1850 for Wilts Somerset & Weymouth
Railway. Architect J. R. Hannaford of I. K.
Brunel's staff. Main station building listed
Grade II.*

The Wilts Somerset & Weymouth was a
protégé of the Great Western, hence
Brunel's involvement. Frome station is

S.15 CLASS 4-6-0 AT CREWKERNE, 1958

GWR 0-6-0PT (*left*) AND IVATT 2-6-2T (*right*) AT FROME, 1962

the only operational survivor of a large
group of overall-roofed wooden stations
built throughout the West Country and
South Wales. While most were of standardized design, each had at least one
individual characteristic, often in the end
gables. Frome has a cut-out immediately
below the prominent ridge ventilator,
decorated with a short length of frilly
valancing.

The roof truss has slender iron ties, and
is supported on one side by the wooden
frontage building and on the other by
wooden columns along the platform,
cantilever fashion, the overhang stretching backwards to the wooden side wall
and incorporating curly wooden brackets.
Viewed from outside, the ends of the
shed have a curiously asymmetrical appearance for this reason.

TAUNTON

*Built 1842 for Bristol & Exeter Railway.
Engineer I. K. Brunel. South block and former
Great Western Hotel listed Grade II.*

The first station at Taunton was one of
Brunel's one-sided layouts like Reading
(*p.216*) with separate up and down platforms on the same side of the track. When
the Bristol & Exeter rebuilt it in 1868 in
more orthodox fashion with an overall

roof, one of the old entrance buildings was
retained to serve the new station. It survived a further major reconstruction by
the Great Western in 1932 when standard
GWR awnings replaced the roof and
additional platforms were built.

The building is a square two-storey
brick block with a parapet and a little
stonework in the window and door
casings, which are Georgian in style and
extend along the single-storey flanking
building.

The former hotel opposite, now used as
offices, is a long two-storey block reflecting the style of the station.

1971

DORSET

DEVON

CHURSTON, 1977

DORCHESTER

POUNDBURY TUNNEL. Built 1857 for Wilts Somerset & Weymouth Railway. Engineer I. K. Brunel. Tunnel entrances listed Grade II.

This short tunnel of 264 yards was built after Brunel had been persuaded not to drive a cutting through the Iron Age hill fort of Poundbury Camp.

Brunel himself was a sensitive man with a feeling for history, but the interests of shareholders are usually paramount in conflicts of this kind, and then as now the loudness of the protests no doubt decided the issue.

TUNNEL, WITH EARTHWORKS TO RIGHT, 1963

Brunel had already built a tunnel at Kemble in 1844 to placate the local squire (*p.224*). How much more alarming was the Reverend William Barnes, rector of Winterbourne Cerne, poet in the Dorset dialect and founding light of the Dorset County Museum, who championed conservation here.

The tunnel entrances, constructed in red brick with rusticated ashlar voussoirs, have been listed to commemorate this early instance of civil engineering respecting ancient monuments.

BARNSTAPLE

CHELFHAM VIADUCT. Built 1898 for Lynton and Barnstaple Railway. Engineer Frank W. Chanter. Listed Grade II. Closed.

Chelfham viaduct has the distinction of being the largest bridge structure on a British narrow-gauge railway. It has eight yellow brick arches, 70 feet high, and extends for 133 yards on a curve.

Sir George Newnes, the publisher, was the leading promoter of the line which passed to the Southern Railway and was closed in 1935. Lynton station was inconveniently sited high above the town and by then the railway could no longer compete with buses. Had the line survived another 20 years there is little doubt that it would now be among the ranks of the restored narrow-gauge railways.

CHURSTON

Built 1861 by Dartmouth & Torbay Railway. Between Paignton and Kingswear.

The Dart Valley Railway now operates Churston station as part of their preserved line from Paignton to Kingswear and the Dartmouth ferry. Steam trains run daily during the summer.

The station has been attractively restored, the random stone walls with ashlar quoins looking well beneath the hipped roof of the single-storey main building. It has a simple flat awning, without valancing, and a small stone shelter suffices on the opposite platform.

CREDITON

Built 1851 by Exeter & Crediton Railway. Between Exeter and Barnstaple.

Down in central Devon a historical quirk resulted in a GWR-type station appearing on the line of a rival company, the London & South Western, at Crediton.

In a drawn-out battle in the 'Gauge War' of the 1840s the small Exeter & Crediton Railway was tossed to and fro between the broad-gauge Bristol & Exeter (with strings pulled from Paddington) and the standard-gauge London & South Western who saw it as a potential link to Plymouth. A double-track broad-gauge line had been more or less completed in 1847 in anticipation of a lease to the B & E, but after a boardroom row an injunction was obtained to prohibit opening on the broad gauge; so the company decided to narrow it.

Opening was again thwarted while the B & E and LSW fought over the company in Parliament. The LSW won and acquired the Exeter & Crediton, but was unable to reach it with its own trains because a section of B & E broad-gauge line stood in

1977

the way. As a temporary measure one of the tracks on the Exeter & Crediton was widened again and worked as a broad-gauge single line by the B & E, allowing the line to be opened for local traffic in 1851. When the B & E finally laid a third rail over the intervening broad section, the London & South Western was at last able to reach the little Exeter & Crediton in 1862 and convert it back to all standard-gauge line. Eventually it was incorporated into the LSW's main line to Plymouth.

Although altered, the two platform buildings at Crediton clearly show their Brunel origins; they were typical matching Tudor structures with flat all-round awnings and steep roofs. The angled chimney stacks have been replaced and the platforms widened to take up the extra track space left by the defunct broad gauge, but the family likeness is unmistakeable.

CHELFHAM VIADUCT, 1976

DAWLISH

Opened 1846 by South Devon Railway.
Engineer I. K. Brunel. Listed Grade II.
Between Exeter and Newton Abbot.

Dawlish conjures up thoughts of the railway running between the sea and red sandstone cliffs, in and out of the rock-tunnels, between stations that spelt 'holidays'. Sandwiched between the promenade and the beach, it is a two-storey white stone building prominently

1976

rusticated, with a lofty projecting booking hall which has tall segmental arched windows and prominent keystones. The platforms are at first-floor level, sheltered by ridge-and-furrow awnings on broad latticed brackets.

The original shed, described by a contemporary as 'an awkward shed Brunel sketched on the back of an envelope', was destroyed by fire on 21st August, 1873. The present station is a complete rebuild of that period. It was possibly designed by

the company engineer P. J. Margery but is very much in the Brunel idiom.

EXETER

ST. DAVIDS. Built 1844 for Bristol & Exeter Railway. Engineer I. K. Brunel. Rebuilt 1864. Architects Henry Lloyd and Francis Fox.

The first Exeter St. Davids, like Taunton and Reading (*p.216*), was another one-sided station with separate entrance buildings on the same side of the line. Lloyd and Fox replaced them with a lofty glass-and-iron roofed station between stone side walls. The wall at the front formed a facade with tall round-headed windows and Doric pilasters, a deep cornice and a broken balustrade carrying 26 large stone classical urns. Some of this survived a further rebuilding in 1911-14 when a two-storey block was built in front of it, and part of the earlier single-storey entrance building is left at one end. Subsequently the trainshed roof was replaced by standard-type awnings, but platform 1 retains a tall, elegant wooden clerestory lit by tall round-headed windows complementing those in the screen wall and forming a lofty narrow aisle. Some of the windows behind the office block have been filled in, but viewed from below they still look impressive.

ST. THOMAS. Built 1846 for South Devon Railway. Engineer I. K. Brunel. Between Exeter St. Davids and Exminster. Listed Grade II.

St. Thomas, as it was simply shown on its nameboards for many years, was built as part of Brunel's abortive atmospheric railway (*p.239*). The line here is elevated and the station has a two-storey entrance building in Italianate style, stuccoed with a delicate little frieze between the ground- and first-floor windows.

The platforms are above, but the overall roof has gone leaving only the side walls. It was one of the last Great Western main-line stations to keep its roof, which shivered and shook with the passage of trains long after its useful life was over.

ST. THOMAS, 1960

ST. DAVIDS, 1920s

MELDON VIADUCT, c.1880

MORETONHAMPSTEAD

MANOR HOUSE HOTEL. Built 1907 for Viscount Hambledon, head of W. H. Smith and Co. Became a GWR Hotel 1929. Consultant architect Detmar Blow; site architect Walter Mills. Hotel, including interior, listed Grade II*.

A magnificent Edwardian country house on the grandest scale, this is one of Detmar Blow's principal works. It is a very long, imposing building in the Jacobean style with gables, battlements, fine large mullioned windows and other characteristic features and decoration. The roof is a very important part of the design with its tall, grouped octagonal chimneys.

The interior, which is even better, helped make it one of the most agreeable of railway hotels. The main staircase is very fine and there is also a panelled dining room and a drawing room in the Adam style. The whole building was constructed using the best materials and craftsmen available and remains a credit to both client and architect.

OKEHAMPTON

MELDON VIADUCT. Built 1874 for London & South Western Railway. Widened 1879. Engineers W. R. Galbraith and R. F. Church. Ancient Monument. West of Okehampton.

Built in the beautiful wooded gorge leading down from the new Meldon reservoir, this is a classic viaduct, important in terms of railway history, technology and landscape. Over 120 feet high, it has six spans of wrought-iron Warren girders supported on open wrought-iron piers made up of clustered columns with cross-bracing. When the line was doubled a second similar but independent viaduct was built alongside.

Although long closed to passenger traffic the viaduct is still sometimes used for shunting operations from Meldon quarry, which is an important source of track ballast. This is now one of the only two large all-metal viaducts remaining (the

other is Bennerley Viaduct at Ilkeston (*p.80*) and is by far the more attractive.

STARCROSS PUMPING STATION

Built 1846 for South Devon Railway. Engineer I. K. Brunel. Between Exeter and Dawlish. Listed Grade II. Sold.

The atmospheric principle of propulsion was adopted by Brunel for the South Devon Railway because he feared that the steep gradients between Newton Abbot and Plymouth would be too much for steam locomotives. The system operated by means of a piston running in an iron pipe laid between the rails. The piston was connected to the underside of a carriage by iron plates protruding through a continuous leather flap. Pumping engines were erected at intervals along the line to exhaust the air from the pipe and create a partial vacuum, so that in effect the piston and its train were 'sucked' along the line.

Twenty-six miles were equipped between Exeter and Newton Abbot and

c.1980

during 1847-48 trains ran by this method. When the system was in good working order, 'atmospheric' trains of 28 tons reached 68 miles per hour, but the practical difficulties were so great that Brunel was forced to abandon the idea and use locomotives.

Brunel's engine houses for the steam pumps were built in Italianate style with a tall tower containing a water-tank for the boilers. Several, like the one remaining at Totnes, were built in advance and never used. Starcross also remains, built

from large blocks of roughly squared sandstone with nicely detailed doors and windows and prominently curved stone brackets under the eaves of the pantiled roof. The tower still stands, but has lost its campanile top.

TAVISTOCK VIADUCT

Built 1890 for Plymouth Devonport & South Western Junction Railway. Engineers W. R. Galbraith & J. W. Szlumper. Listed Grade II. Closed.

The Lidford to Devonport line was the last stage of the London & South Western's main line from Waterloo to Plymouth. It crossed difficult country and required heavy engineering works including three tunnels, 76 bridges and seven viaducts which are, as Major Marindin, the Inspector, said, 'remarkably handsome structures'.

The longest of these viaducts, at 483 yards, is that over the River Tavy and the highest, at 104 feet 6 inches, is Shillamill; but perhaps the most striking is that at Tavistock. Striding over a steeply rising street at the top of the town, the viaduct is built of rough-faced grey granite like most of the houses, and has an enduring quality which belies its late date, which is inscribed on the structure.

TORRE

Opened 1848 by South Devon Railway. Engineer I. K. Brunel. Listed Grade II. Between Newton Abbot and Torquay.

The main interest of this station, originally named Torquay, is that it started life as the terminus of the branch from Newton Abbot. An atmospheric pumping house was built but never used. When in 1859 the line was extended to Paignton

1973

the station was reconstructed and renamed Torre; a new station was built in Torquay proper. Torre still remained the freight depot for Torquay, however, and as a result had a fairly extensive layout.

The main building is one of Brunel's Italianate structures with overhanging eaves, larger than normal and unusual for being in timber like Charlbury (*p.218*). Substantial and spacious awnings cover the platforms in typical GWR style, and a latticed iron footbridge has a roof and glazed superstructure although, not untypically, the lower portion is open. The station is now unstaffed.

CORNWALL

CALSTOCK VIADUCT

Built 1908 for Plymouth Devonport & South Western Junction Railway. Engineers Galbraith and Church. Listed Grade II. Between Bere Alston and Gunnislake.

This very finely situated viaduct crosses between the steeply wooded banks of the River Tamar at a height of 117 feet. Of very late construction, it could be described as the last of the great viaducts and a very handsome and fitting conclusion it is.

The viaduct is built of massive concrete blocks (reputedly 11,148 of them) which were cast on the site and neatly jointed and finished to look like stone. It is 333 yards long with 12 arches and its height is

1976

emphasised by its narrow width, for it carries only a single track. Seen on an autumn morning with the trees turning to gold it is an answer to those who feel that concrete can never be a sympathetic material.

It superseded a wagon hoist alongside it on the west bank of the river, for carrying wagons to and from Calstock quay below.

PAR

ST. BLAZEY ENGINE SHED. Built by Cornwall Railway. Listed Grade II. St. Blazey Road.

This brick-built shed is laid out in an arc facing an outdoor turntable from which rails radiate to individual locomotive stables each with its own doors. It is an

1960

interesting variation on the traditional locomotive roundhouse (*see Camden, p.59, and Derby, p.78*) in which the turntable is inside the shed.

BRUNEL'S TIMBER VIADUCTS

'Mr. Brunel's timber bridges and viaducts are remarkable on account of the extensive scale on which he employed that material, and the simple and efficient type of construction which he adopted in the largest structure as in the smallest.'

With these words Brunel's son drew attention to a special feature of the West of England main line in Devon and Cornwall. Brunel built more timber viaducts than any other kind, and although none remain in existence, some of the piers on which they rested can still be seen as a reminder of a valuable engineering technique.

The principal reason for using timber was cost, for it meant that a line built by impoverished companies, such as the Cornwall and West Cornwall Railways, could be opened quickly and cheaply, leaving the viaducts to be rebuilt in more durable materials when more money was available.

On Brunel's first and most important line, the Great Western itself, there was only one timber bridge, a road bridge over Sonning Cutting. It could, however, be considered the prototype for what followed.

Brunel constructed his first timber viaducts on the Cheltenham & Great Western Union Railway (from Swindon to Gloucester), opened in 1845; there were nine made of angled timber struts tied with wrought iron. On the South Devon Railway between Newton Abbot and Plymouth, completed in 1849, there were five, all resting on masonry piers rising to rail level with diagonal timber struts tied by wrought-iron rods.

More appeared on the South Wales Railway (between Gloucester to Swansea) in 1856, including two very interesting ones at Newport and Landore which had large river spans each consisting of a four-sided truss within a five-sided one. The Newport viaduct was burned down before completion and the main span was replaced by bow-string wrought-iron girders.

In 1852-59 the West Cornwall Railway was opened with nine viaducts, mostly all-timber, but the largest number appeared on the Cornwall Railway, opened in 1859, which cut across the grain of the country and required 42 viaducts, 34 on the main

line between Saltash and Truro and eight on the Falmouth branch. Some were built on buttressed piers constructed of slate, with a fan of four timbers on each side supporting the rail deck some 35 feet above, tied with cross-struts and iron rods. Others, where estuaries had to be crossed, were entirely of timber.

Six simpler viaducts were built on the South Devon & Tavistock Railway, also opened in 1859. The Walkham Viaduct near Tavistock, 132 feet high with fifteen 66-foot spans, may be considered to have been the most mature of Brunel's designs. The timbers were bolted together, and were so designed that they could be removed individually and replaced without major works.

Yellow pine was found to be the most durable material, but it became more difficult to obtain and one by one the viaducts were rebuilt in brick or stone, the first in 1858 on the Cheltenham & Great Western Union and the last, College Wood Viaduct on the Falmouth branch, in 1934.

In Devon and Cornwall the line was originally mostly single, which meant that new stone viaducts had to be built alongside the old timber ones, usually when the line was doubled. Those on the South Devon Railway were rebuilt in 1893 and, except at Bittaford, the piers of the old viaducts can still be seen alongside the new.

On the parts of the Cornwall Railway which were double line from the outset the original piers were re-used by reconstructing one side at a time with iron spans, but on the single-line sections and the Falmouth branch new ones were built with masonry arches. Here, too, the old piers still stand, forming ivy-clad ruins. Between Saltash and St. Germans the line was diverted to a completely new route, thereby avoiding five timber viaducts.

ST. GERMANS VIADUCT. Rebuilt 1908. Listed Grade II.

ST. PINNOCK VIADUCT. Rebuilt 1882. Listed Grade II.

COLLEGE WOOD VIADUCT. Rebuilt 1934. Listed Grade II.

St. Pinnock Viaduct, 1955

Ivybridge Viaduct, 1848

St. Germans Viaduct, 1976

PENZANCE

Opened 1852 by West Cornwall Railway.
Engineer I. K. Brunel. Conservation Area.

Unlike the other West Country lines that made up the Great Western, the West Cornwall Railway started life with the standard gauge and later converted to broad. It took over the older standard-gauge Hayle Railway, and because the broad gauge was still far away it constructed its Truro to Penzance line to 4 feet 8½ inches.

The first Penzance station was a typical Brunel wooden shed with one short platform. When the broad gauge reached Truro a third rail was laid for through running, and standard and broad trains used the line from 1866. Then in 1892 it reverted to standard gauge only when the broad was abolished.

D814 LEAVING PENZANCE, 1960

The present Penzance station has a modest stone frontage and a short overall roof. It was provided initially with only two platforms, increased to four in 1937 when the layout was improved. The trainshed was kept. It has an unusual crescent-trussed roof with a large ventilator running down the middle and vertical glazing bars in the gable ends. Beneath the outer gable a deep wooden screen with a large elliptical cutaway section adds to its appearance, enhanced by triangular mouldings.

ST. GERMANS

Built 1859 for Cornwall Railway. Engineer I. K. Brunel. Between Plymouth and Liskeard. Conservation Area.

St. Germans is a charming and virtually unaltered example of one of Brunel's later-type wayside stations. Two complementary buildings face each other across

'GRANGE' CLASS 4-6-0 AT ST. GERMANS, c.1954

the rails, both with plain flat awnings. The larger of the pair has an end bay window for the station master and a smaller awning over the front entrance door. (*See also Brunel's Timber Viaducts, p.240.*)

ST. IVES

TREGENNA CASTLE HOTEL. Built 1774. Hotel and North Lodge listed Grade II.

The Tregenna Castle occupies a commanding position behind the town of St. Ives, looking out to sea. It has an imposing castellated frontage, and was built for John Stephens in 1774 by Daniel Freeman of Penryn. The architect may have been John Wood of Bath.

The GWR leased the building in 1878, long before it became popular to turn country mansions into hotels, and bought it outright in 1895. Considerable extensions have been made since and little of the original interior is left, but the house is interesting as an early example of a railway going into the country hotel business.

SALTASH

ROYAL ALBERT BRIDGE. Built 1859 for Cornwall Railway. Engineer I. K. Brunel, Assistant Engineer R. P. Brereton. Listed Grade I.

Brunel's finest and longest bridge, the Royal Albert over the Tamar at Saltash stands largely as built and now is not only a most fitting memorial to its great designer but the only main-line link with Cornwall.

Brunel's chief design considerations were economy (the bridge was completed for the amazingly low figure of £225,000) and the need to give the Royal Navy 100 feet headroom at high tide. The successful completion of the Chepstow Bridge (*p.242*) provided him with the solution to the problem. He spanned the river with two enormous wrought-iron oval tubes, each 12 feet by 16 feet and 461 feet in length, placed one after the other on immense stone piers. From these tubes, stressed into a curve for better weight bearing, the deck carrying a single track could be suspended by hangers and chains.

BRIDGE UNDER CONSTRUCTION, 1852

This design, a combination of suspension bridge and pre-stressed truss, meant that each of the 455-foot river spans could be prefabricated nearby, floated out on the high tide under the guidance of Captain Claxton, Brunel's (and Robert Stephenson's) invariable assistant in all nautical matters, and allowed to settle with the ebbing tide on to the stone piers which had been constructed to just above low water level.

Using jacks at either end the spans and the piers were raised foot by foot until the final height was reached. The first span was in place by 1857, the second in 1858. When the bridge was opened a year later by Prince Albert, Brunel was not present. He was dying and had to be taken across on a specially prepared flat car drawn slowly by a locomotive.

There are a further seven girder spans on the Devon side and ten on the Cornish side, making the bridge a total of 733 yards long. The curves of the approach spans combine with the height of the piers to produce a sense of arrogance as the bridge soars across the small town of Saltash and the river, as if to demonstrate the long-lived superiority of the railway over the puny ferry. It was 102 years before the bridge had a competitor in the road bridge alongside.

Despite improvements in design over

ROYAL ALBERT BRIDGE FROM SALTASH, 1960

the Chepstow Bridge, some of the wrought-iron members, particularly in those areas inaccessible to painting, have had to be replaced from time to time. The approach spans were renewed in steel in 1928-29, and various additional stiffeners and diagonal braces have been added to the main spans in subsequent years. The tubes and the suspension chains, however, are original and can still carry the heaviest loads. There is a 15 mph speed limit but this is largely dictated by the sharp approach curves. The Royal Albert Bridge remains a monument to the designer whose name it so proudly bears on its portal, the only railway-carrying suspension bridge in the world.

ROYAL ALBERT BRIDGE, 1983

WYE BRIDGE, 1851

GWENT

ABERGAVENNY

*Built 1854 for Newport Abergavenny &
Hereford Railway. Engineer Charles Liddell.
Listed Grade II. Between Hereford and
Newport.*

Abergavenny had three stations: this one
(originally called Monmouth Road) and
the Junction, both of which came under
Great Western ownership, and the
London & North Western's station at
Brecon Road. Now there is only one.

Liddell built good solid grey stone
stations, not particularly elegant but well
fitted to the hilly border country through
which the line passes. Abergavenny's
ashlar main building has round-headed
windows which give it a whiff of Italianate, and is not unlike other buildings in
the town.

CHEPSTOW

*STATION. Built 1850 for South Wales
Railway. Engineer I. K. Brunel. Station and
canopy to north of main building listed Grade II.
Between Newport and Gloucester.*

Although Brunel was engineer for the
line, this station was designed by W.
Lancaster Owen who presumably was on
his staff. Owen eventually succeeded his
father as Chief Engineer of the Great
Western Railway. The station is a typical

Brunel building of the Italianate variety,
constructed of ashlar stone with an overhanging pantiled roof and a matching
building opposite. The canopy extension
is a later addition.

*WYE BRIDGE. Built 1852 for South Wales
Railway. Engineer I. K. Brunel. Rebuilt 1962
for British Railways. Engineer P. S. A.
Berrige, design engineer Frank Leeming. Piers
and south-west abutments listed Grade II.*

Where the railway crosses the Wye at
Chepstow there is a cliff on one side and a
flat bank on the other. To overcome the
difficulty of the site Brunel designed a
bridge on a revolutionary principle, forming a 300-foot truss by suspending the
deck from large stressed wrought-iron
tubes, one for each line of way. He used
the method again on the much larger
Royal Albert Bridge at Saltash (*p.241*)
where his work has survived in nearly
original form.

At Chepstow, however, an almost
complete reconstruction became necessary. One of the land spans failed in 1944,
almost causing a disaster to an approaching train, which had to be prevented from
entering the bridge. The failure appears
likely to have been caused by a Royal
train, headed by two very heavy 'King'
class locomotives, which had crossed the
bridge a week earlier.

The bridge was strengthened, but by
1948 it was evident that repairs were no
longer adequate and the land spans were
reconstructed using riveted steel girders

supported on the existing Brunel cast-
iron piers.

In 1962 the river span was replaced
with a prefabricated welded steel truss,
the first use of welding on a main-line
bridge. The contractors were Fairfields of
Chepstow, the makers of the original
bridge, though they charged rather more
than the £77,000 the bridge had cost to
build in 1852. One revolutionary structure has been replaced by another and all
that now remains of the Brunel bridge are
the cast-iron piers.

DIESEL GOODS AT CHEPSTOW, 1978

TREDEGAR

*NINE ARCHES VIADUCT. Built 1864 for
Merthyr Tredegar & Abergavenny Railway.
Engineer John Gardiner. Listed Grade II.
Closed.*

The arrival of the railway at Tredegar
arises from the rivalry between the London & North Western, determined to get
a share of the lucrative coal traffic, which
attacked the valleys from the north, and
the Great Western, which was already
established at the southern end. In the
Sirhowy valley the LNWR gained entrance by acquiring the spectacular Merthyr Tredegar & Abergavenny Railway
and linking up with the existing Sirhowy
tramway which was re-engineered.

The viaduct at Tredegar is a good
example of the works on the line, built of
rock-faced masonry with round-headed
arches lined in brick and finished with a
brick parapet. It is not only handsomely
designed but has considerable landscape
value as well.

ABERGAVENNY, 1954

SOUTH GLAMORGAN

BARRY

PORTHKERRY VIADUCT. Built 1897 by Vale of Glamorgan Railway. Listed Grade II. Between Barry and Bridgend.

Now open only for freight traffic, mainly merry-go-round trains to Aberthaw power station, this line was owned by a little company which just managed to remain independent of the larger Barry Railway which operated it until they were both incorporated into the Great Western in 1923. Porthkerry Viaduct is on the first mile of line immediately west of Barry Town station; 375 yards long, it crosses Porthkerry Park on 16 stone arches 110 feet high.

Almost immediately after opening in December 1897 the viaduct partially collapsed and was closed for two years. Since the reopening in January 1900 there has been no further trouble, even under the much heavier trains of today.

PORTHKERRY VIADUCT, 1959

BRIDGEND

Built 1850 for South Wales Railway. Engineer I. K. Brunel. Down-side building listed Grade II. Between Cardiff and Neath.

For years the original station building here was barely distinguishable as one of Brunel's Italianate-type buildings with overhanging eaves, so overloaded had it become with GWR accretions. But now it has been restored its original proportions and materials can once more be appreciated. A new ticket office has been built next to it at right angles, which for all its

BRIDGEND, 1980

modernity has been carefully designed to blend with the old.

CARDIFF BUTE ROAD

Line opened 1840 by Taff Vale Railway. Engineer I. K. Brunel. Listed Grade II.

Bute Road Station, which now stands forlornly at the end of a single paytrain line, was formerly named Cardiff Docks. The stylishness and size of the two-storey white stuccoed building gives a clue to its importance as the southern terminus of the Taff Vale Railway, the first commercially important public railway in Wales.

The Taff Vale grew to handle the densest mineral traffic in the world, but despite its preoccupation with coal it ran an intensive passenger service down the

CARDIFF BUTE ROAD, 1981

valleys into Cardiff and conducted largely successful battles with neighbouring lines, such as the Rhymney Railway.

In 1900 the company gained fame – or infamy, according to one's viewpoint – when it won an important legal action, known as 'The Taff Vale Case', which made it possible to claim damages from a trade union following a strike.

MID GLAMORGAN

HENGOED VIADUCT

Built 1857 for Newport Abergavenny & Hereford Railway. Engineers and contractors Charles Liddel and R. Gordon. Listed Grade II. Closed.

This viaduct once carried much heavy coal traffic. It is one of the principal surviving structures of a line which cut across the valleys and formerly included a spectacular latticed iron viaduct at Crumlin. It crosses the village of Hengoed and the still-used line of the Rhymney Railway, and has 15 mostly very tall tapered piers of local rough-faced rubble with dramatic landscape value.

WELSH RAILWAY COMPANIES

The railways of South Wales were run by a large number of small companies which successfully resisted absorption until the 1923 Grouping when they were taken into the Great Western. The principal lines were the Barry, Taff Vale, Brecon & Merthyr, Neath & Brecon and Rhymney Railways, all of which were primarily built to carry coal.

The biggest coal hauliers were the Taff Vale, the Rhymney and the Barry, the two former converging on Cardiff docks while the Barry had its own docks at Barry itself. Passenger services were purely local except on the Barry Railway which was unique in participating with the Great Western, Great Central and North Eastern in run-

ning a through restaurant car express between Barry and Newcastle-upon-Tyne. Although the mileage over Barry metals was small, the train was hauled between Barry and Cardiff by the company's own locomotive.

The largest Welsh company, the Cambrian Railways, served North and Mid-Wales with a route mileage of nearly 300. It was more of a main-line system than the others, connecting with the Great Western at Welshpool and the London & North Western at Whitchurch and running by a long and mountainous single line across Central Wales to serve Aberystwyth, Barmouth and Pwllheli on the coast. Another long line ran south to link up with the Brecon & Merthyr Railway.

Apart from the Cambrian, which used

4-4-0 engines on its relatively long runs, the Welsh lines had as their standard type of locomotive the 0-6-2 tank. Because congestion on these lines in the boom years before the First World War resulted in much time being spent queuing up at signals, the locomotives were designed with relatively small fireboxes to minimize the amount of coal burned while waiting.

Share certificate, 1847

DYFED

CYNGHORDY VIADUCT

Built 1868 for Central Wales Railway.
Engineer Henry Robertson. Listed Grade II.
Between Llandovery and Builth Road.

This was the most heavily engineered section of the Central Wales line and was thus the last to open. Cynghordy, the largest of the viaducts, crosses the Bran valley a little below the summit at Sugar Loaf Tunnel (*p.245*). It is built on a curve, 100 feet high with 18 brick and sandstone arches finished with rough facing stone. One of the children of Richard Hattersley, the contractor, was killed during the construction of the seventh pier, which is consequently said to be haunted.

FISHGUARD HARBOUR

Built 1906 by Fishguard and Rosslare Railways and Harbour Co. Engineer J. C. Inglis.

The Great Western reached Fishguard & Goodwick (the 'town' station) in 1899, eleven days after acquiring the little North Pembrokeshire & Fishguard Railway, which was then almost complete. The GWR's aim was to develop Fishguard as a packet port for Ireland, for which purpose it had entered into partnership with the Great Southern & Western Railway in Ireland who undertook to carry out complementary developments at Rosslare.

The Harbour station at Fishguard was built in typical Great Western 1900s style. The four platforms were provided with broad umbrella awnings and an overall roof on steel trusses and stanchions – very functional and without frills, as became a busy port.

The outer platform is alongside the

1964

quay, and access from the inner platform was by a subway and by moveable bridge-platforms across the rails.

The Great Western had set its sights on more than Irish Sea traffic and from 1908 transatlantic liners started to call at Fishguard, among them the *Mauretania*. Special trains met the ships, and a tremendous effort was made to compete with Plymouth and Southampton for the North American traffic. The GWR made great play with the fact that Fishguard

offered the shortest sea route. The Atlantic trade proved to be short-lived, however, and the last liner called in 1926, leaving Fishguard once more as an Irish port, a role which it continues to play with increasing importance today.

The railway itself has declined. Only two platforms are now required at the station, the 'town' station is closed and the heavy traffic in Irish cattle is a thing of the past. In its place has come an enormous increase in 'roll-on, roll-off' ferry services to Ireland. Although road vehicles form a large part of the business, there is a considerable volume of rail-borne passenger traffic and it is still the railway which runs the port.

LLANDRINDOD WELLS

Built 1865 by Central Wales Railway. Between Shrewsbury and Swansea.

The railway turned Llandrindod Wells into a fashionable spa. When the London

& North Western acquired the line soon after completion and made it part of its Central Wales route to Swansea, the

1976

small village rapidly grew and although it never became another Cheltenham or Harrogate, a quiet late-Victorian atmosphere still pervades the town today.

The station has typical flat LNWR platform awnings with deep valancing and fine floral-patterned brackets. The buildings, however, are far from typical. Constructed in ashlar stone with vivid rustication and pointed-arch window openings, they are very much in keeping with the town.

CYNGHORDY VIADUCT, 1977

PEMBROKE DOCK

Built 1864 by Pembroke & Tenby Railway.
Listed Grade II.

Although much smaller than Fishguard, Pembroke Dock station also has seen a renaissance of cross-sea traffic to Ireland, in this case to Cork and Rosslare, for which a new ferry terminal was opened in 1979. The station building has a rather

1980

charming rustic air to it. It is built of rock-faced stone with twin half-hipped gables, and between them a matching little porch on curved wooden brackets. Decorated bargeboards, cresting and pointed windows add to the 'olde-worlde' atmosphere of the frontage.

SUGAR LOAF TUNNEL

Built 1868 by Central Wales Extension Railway. Engineer Henry Robertson.

This section was the last link in the tortuous route which gained the LNWR direct access to Swansea from Shrewsbury. It entailed heavy engineering works, including Cynghordy Viaduct (*p.244*) and the 1,000-yard Sugar Loaf Tunnel named after the distinctive mountain through which it passes.

1977

A train ascending the ledge on the broad hillside leading to the tunnel passes through dramatic scenery on gradients as steep as 1 in 60. The tunnel is very wet, caused by water dripping through the rock strata from a stream on the mountainside above.

At its northern end the lonely Sugar Loaf Summit signal box had special platforms. These were for employees and their families living in the nearby houses so that they could arrange for trains to stop on request.

TENBY

STATION. Built 1866 by Pembroke & Tenby Railway.

Stations on the Pembroke & Tenby line were all built of local stone and showed a strong local influence, Tenby itself is no exception. It is a larger edition of Pembroke Dock but instead of the main gables it has two dormers and, beneath the eaves, a line of frilly valancing.

On the platform side the main roof extends as an awning in a most unusual fashion. It is carried outwards on huge brackets decorated with lines of holes in the main members and large trefoils and

quatrefoils in the spandrels, all supported on a row of decorated iron columns. The valancing is particularly ornate, if to some extent masked by later Great Western additions: not the usual variation on the sawtooth theme, but a row of pendant rings.

VIADUCT. Built 1866 by Pembroke & Tenby Railway. Listed Grade II.

The Tenby Viaduct has seven round-headed arches built of large rusticated blocks of carboniferous limestone. It is both a prominent feature of the town and the principal viaduct on the Pembroke & Tenby Railway, which was opened in 1866 and extended to Whitland, with some help from the Great Western, in the same year.

1976

This small but proud railway had adopted the standard gauge from the outset and proved to be quite a thorn in the side of the broad-gauge Great Western. The large company hoped to take over the small, but did not succeed until 1896, long after it had been forced to change its own Welsh lines to the standard gauge. In Wales the conversion took place in 1872 twenty years before the final abandonment of the broad gauge.

TENBY, 1976

GLOSSARY OF TERMS

A

Abutment. Brick or stonework taking the lateral thrust of an arch.

Acanthus leaf. Thick fleshy scalloped leaf shapes used in moulded decoration.

Adam. Robert Adam (1728-92), an architect noted for his delicate classical style, much copied.

Adit. Passage giving access to or connection between underground mines or tunnels.

Arabesque. Flowing, interwoven decoration mainly using abstract shapes.

Arcade. Succession of arches.

—, blind. Arcade of BLIND ARCHES, usually forming a series of recesses in a wall.

Arch, blind. Arch with the opening filled in to form a recess.

—, elliptical. Arch where the head of the opening has the shape of half an ellipse.

—, four-centred. Pointed arch, slightly flattened along the top, the curves of which have four separate radii.

—, ogee. Arch with concave and convex sides that meet in a point.

—, pointed. Arch in which the curves and lines that form the head of the opening meet at a point in the centre.

—, round-headed. Arch where the head of the opening has the shape of a semi-circle.

—, segmental (or segment-headed). Arch where the head of the opening has the shape of a segment of a circle smaller than a semi-circle.

ROUND-HEADED   ELLIPTICAL

SEGMENTAL   FOUR-CENTRED

Art deco. Form of stylized decoration and design associated with the 1930s using geometrical shapes and curving lines and materials such as chromium and tiles.

Art nouveau. Style of decoration and design associated with the 1890s using rich materials, elongated figures and floral forms.

Ashlar. Smoothly finished and finely jointed squared stone blocks.

B

Balustrade. Parapet, railing or COPING held up by a succession of supports or balusters.

Bargeboard. Board following the slope of a gable, fixed to or concealing the ends of the rafters, often fretted or decorated with holes.

Baroque. Revival of a style originating in Italy in the late 16th century but previously revived in England, particularly by Sir John Vanbrugh, in the early 18th century. Design characteristics include heavy RUSTICATION, elaborate window and door surrounds with prominent VOUSSOIRS and KEYSTONES,

windows apparently small in relation to the wall surface and heavily modelled rooflines with BALUSTRADES and elaborate chimneys.

Bas-relief. Half relief work in mouldings or figures.

Bascule bridge. A form of drawbridge in which the lifting end is counterpoised by a weighted extension on the pivoted end.

Batter. The thickening of the base of a wall giving added strength and a distinctive slope.

Board School window. Type of window common in late 19th-century Board Schools which has a lintel with a SEGMENTAL ARCH and numerous lights in wooden glazing bars.

Boss. Projection concealing the intersection of ribs in a roof, often used decoratively on ceilings.

Bridge, girder. Bridge constructed with girders – either simple beams which have been rolled or cast in one piece, or beams made from many parts that are riveted or welded together.

—, bowstring. A bridge having main girders forming an arc (the 'bow') from which the deck is suspended by vertical and sometimes latticed struts.

—, box-girder. Bridge constructed with a hollow girder, box-shaped in section which may be carried on intermediate PIERS. COLUMNS may also be made in this way.

—, lattice girder. Bridge constructed of girders made from criss-cross members in the form of a lattice.

—, over-. Bridge over a railway carrying a road, etc.

—, suspension. Bridge of non-rigid construction where the deck is hung from chains or ropes that are strung between towers and allowed to curve or sag naturally.

—, Warren girder. Bridge constructed of girders made from diagonal shaped members, a design patented by Capt. James Warren in 1848.

C

Campanile. Bell-tower, usually free-standing, but the term is often used more generally to describe any ITALIANATE tower.

Cantilever. Load-bearing beam or TRUSS, fixed at one end only, and held in place by a superincumbent weight or by a greater weight on a rearward projection.

Cap. Exposed top of a COLUMN, PILASTER or PIER.

Capital. Decorative top of a COLUMN or PILASTER, used as a support. The four orders of capitals in classical architecture are:

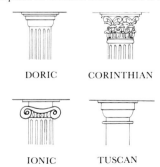

DORIC   CORINTHIAN

IONIC   TUSCAN

Caryatid. COLUMN or PILASTER, supporting an ENTABLATURE, carved in the form of a female figure.

Castellation. Battlements or crenellations of regular cut-out shape as on a castle, decorating a parapet.

Centering. A wooden frame supporting an arch during construction.

Clerestory. Row of windows in raised section of roof or upper walls of a structure that has extensions or lean-tos that prevent lighting at ground floor level.

Close-boarding. Close-fitting boards that do not overlap, usually tongued and grooved, which may be fixed vertically, horizontally or diagonally to form cladding.

Column. Free-standing pillar forming a support, usually of classical form.

—, box-girder. See BRIDGE, BOX-GIRDER.

—, engaged. Column attached to or projecting from a wall.

Coping. Sloping top course of a wall or parapet, usually made of stone or brick.

Corbel. Bracket or projection from a wall to support a beam.

Corinthian. See CAPITAL.

Cornice. Projecting ornamental moulding along the top of a wall or arch.

Cottage orné. Elaborate rustic style of the late 18th and early 19th centuries, with fancy BARGEBOARDS, FINIALS, overhanging eaves, half-timbering and other ornate decoration.

Coursed. See RUBBLE WALLING.

Cove. Curved surface between a wall and a ceiling.

Crenellation. See CASTELLATION.

Cresting. Ornamental work along the ridge of a roof or turret.

Crocket. Carved projection at regular intervals on a spire.

Cupola. Small dome, generally circular or polygonal, on the roof of a building.

Cusp. Pointed projection on window TRACERY.

Cutwater. Rounded or triangular projection on the upstream side of a bridge PIER designed to break the rush of water.

D

Dado. Lower part of an interior wall up to waist height.

Dentils. Small square blocks regularly spaced beneath a CORNICE.

DENTILS

Domestic Revival. A style popular in the late 19th and early 20th century incorporating domestic features such as low steep-pitched roofs, overhanging eaves, half-timbering, rustic brickwork, etc.

Doric. See CAPITAL.

Dormer. Window projecting from a sloping roof.

DORMER

Dressings. Smooth stone surrounding door and window openings.

Dripstone. Projecting moulding over an opening, to throw off water.

Drum foundation. Round foundation to a PIER built inside a drum or caisson which is sunk into the river so that the work can be done in the dry.

E

Entablature. Horizontal section supported by COLUMNS, composed of architrave, frieze and CORNICE.

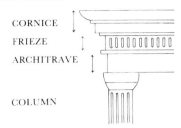

Entasis. Slight swelling in the middle of a column made to correct the optical illusion that parallel sides are concave.

F

Faience. *See* TERRACOTTA.

Fenestration. Arrangement of windows in a wall.

Filigree. Delicate cut-out work like lace.

Finial. Decorative vertical ornament on top of or sometimes pendant on a gable, parapet, turret or other vertical projection.

—, **ball.** Finial in the shape of a ball.

—, **spike.** Finial in the shape of a spike.

SPIKED   BALL

Foliation. Decoration in the likeness of foliage or leaves.

Freestone. Any locally quarried stone.

G

Gable. A triangular section of wall projecting above the eaves line with the roof forming the upper two sides of the triangle.

—, **Dutch or Flemish.** A gable with the two upper sides shaped with a curved line and sometimes with a small pediment at the apex.

—, **shaped.** The same as a Dutch gable.

—, **crow-stepped.** A gable with steps up the sides.

Gantry. Horizontal support of wood or metal, either projecting from a wall or upright, or held between two uprights in the form of a span, to support structures such as signals over tracks. In a gantry crane, the horizontal part is designed to swivel.

Gauge. The distance between the insides of the rails.

—, **standard.** 4ft. 8½in.

—, **broad.** Greater than standard; on the GWR, 7ft.

—, **narrow.** Less than standard; on the Festiniog Railway in North Wales, 1ft. 11⅜in.

Georgian. Design developed during the reigns of George I, George II and particularly George III (1760-1820). The characteristics are classical proportions with facades often divided by COLUMNS or PILASTERS, sash windows and decorative classical motifs.

Girder. *See* BRIDGE.

Gothic. Architectural style of the Middle Ages common to all Europe, characterised particularly by the POINTED ARCH and different types of vaults.

—, **decorated.** Second stage of Gothic design emanating in France and common in England chiefly in the 14th century. The principal design characteristic is very elaborate window TRACERY.

—, **French.** Gothic style which emanated from France, particularly that called High Gothic, with very boldly planned and constructed buildings featuring high vaults, flying buttresses, etc., combined with very elaborate carved decoration.

Gritstone. Hard limestone from the Pennines used for making millstones.

H

Hammerbeam. Structural device for spanning large spaces with roof TRUSSES supported on projecting brackets that carry an arched brace or strut to narrow the gap.

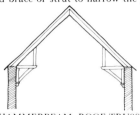

HAMMERBEAM ROOF TRUSS

Hood. Projecting moulding over an opening.

I

Ionic. *See* CAPITAL.

Italian Cinquecento. Revival of the Italian, particularly Roman, architectural style of the 16th century which became popular in the 1830s and 1840s following the gentlemen's club designs of Sir Charles Barry. Its characteristics are round-headed openings (*see* ARCH) spanned by COLUMNS and PILASTERS, and shallow HIPPED ROOFS with deep eaves on brackets. Also known as Italian Renaissance.

Italianate. ITALIAN CINQUECENTO pared down to the bare essentials for utility buildings such as railway stations. It was much used for villas in the mid-19th century.

K

Keystone. Central stone in an ARCH, sometimes prominent or decorated.

L

Lancet. Very narrow window in the shape of a pointed ARCH.

LANCET

Lattice girder. *See* BRIDGE.

Linen-fold panelling. Tudor-style wooden panelling decoratively carved to look like folds of pleated cloth.

M

Machicolation. Openings in a parapet.

Modillions. Small brackets, usually in rows, supporting a cornice.

Mullion. Vertical divider in a window.

N

Nogging. Brick panels in a timber-framed building.

O

Oriel. Bay window projecting from an upper floor.

ORIEL

P

Palladian. Roman classical style, derived from the 16th-century Italian architect Palladio.

Pantiles. Roof tiles each in the shape of an elongated S laid so that it overlaps half of the tile next to it.

Pargeting. Decorated rendering on an external surface.

Pavilion. Small building, or projecting section of a building, usually with a roof and design characteristics distinguishing it from the main building.

Pediment. Feature over a door, window or PORTICO with a horizontal base formed by an ENTABLATURE with either a curved or triangular top. A broken pediment is a triangular pediment with a gap at the top, or apex, of the triangle.

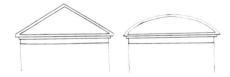

TRIANGULAR   CURVED

Perpendicular. Gothic style unique to England and used in the 15th and 16th centuries. The chief characteristics are strong vertical emphasis to buildings with panelled wall surfaces and large windows with MULLIONS and elaborate vaulting.

Pier. Support of any shape between two or more openings that carries an ARCH or beam.

Pilaster. Square, decorative projection from a wall similar to a COLUMN but usually with no structural function.

Platforms, staggered. Station platforms which are not positioned exactly opposite each other. *See also* UP PLATFORM.

Porte cochère. Large porch for entry by vehicles.

Portico. Roofed area, open-sided or enclosed and usually on COLUMNS or ARCHES, that forms the entrance and centrepiece of a facade.

Q

Quatrefoil. Similar to trefoil but with four lobes.

'Queen Anne'. Revival, c.1880s, of a style of architecture supposed to have been current in the reign of Queen Anne (1702-1714). It is a mixture of traditional English, Dutch and Flemish characteristics, commonly using red brick, white painted woodwork and shaped gables.

Quoin. Carefully finished stones or brickwork both structural and decorative at the corner of a building.

R

Renaissance, free. Loose mixture of Renaissance motifs emanating from different parts of Europe.

—, French. Revival of the 16th-century French style as shown in the great chateaux of the Loire; the term is also commonly used to describe characteristics of the later architects F. and J. H. Mansart, including elaborate wall treatment with carved decoration and particularly high 'French PAVILION' roofs with iron CRESTING. Good examples of the style's revival in England are seen around Victoria station.

Ripsaw. The same as SAW-TOOTH.

Romanesque. Round-arched or Norman style.

Rock-faced stone. Stone rough-hewn straight from the quarry or carved to simulate it.

Roof, hipped. Roof with sloping ends instead of vertical gables.

—, Mansard. Roof with two slopes on sides and/or ends, the lower slopes being steeper than the upper. Named after 17th-century French architect François Mansart.

—, pitched. Ordinary roof, triangular in section, having straight slopes meeting at the ridge.

—, ridge and furrow. Roof often with areas glazed, alternating with ridges and furrows, W-shaped in section. It was invented by Paxton for the Crystal Palace and later standardized.

RIDGE AND FURROW   HIPPED

PITCHED   MANSARD

Roundel. Small, flat, circular moulding applied to a surface as decoration.

Rubble walling. Wall made of rough undressed stones, often fragmentary. The pieces can be laid either irregularly (random rubble) or in regular courses or layers of uniform height (coursed rubble).

RANDOM RUBBLE   COURSED RUBBLE

SNECKED RUBBLE

—, snecked. Coursed rubble walling built of roughly squared stones, with the courses interrupted at intervals by deeper stones each with a small 'sneck' stone level with its upper surface.

Rustication. Large square blocks of stone with wide, deeply recessed joints giving a bold and massive appearance.

ON A QUOIN   ON AN ARCH

S

Saw-tooth. Decorative zig-zag cut-out or moulding like the teeth of a saw.

Signal, lower quadrant. Semaphore signal in which the arm falls to about 45 degrees to indicate 'line clear'.

—, upper quadrant. The opposite of lower quadrant, adopted as standard by post-Grouping railways except the Great Western which retained the lower quadrant type.

Soffit. Underside of an ARCH.

Spandrel. Roughly triangular space bounded by the curve of an ARCH, the vertical side line and the horizontal top line, or the surface area between two adjacent arches.

Stanchion. Upright iron or steel support.

Station, head. Terminus with buildings across the inner, or terminal, end.

—, high level and low level. Designations used to distinguish between two stations serving the same place and having the same name, where one is located higher than the other; the terms sometimes form official distinguishing suffixes to the station names. The same terms are also used to distinguish parts of a station which are on two different levels.

—, one-sided. Station with one long platform only, used by trains going in both directions.

—, through. Station where the tracks continue in both directions – the opposite of a terminus.

—, two-sided. Station with two or more facing platforms.

Stock brick. Brick most common to a particular district. Nowadays the term refers to the former London stock brick ('London stock') common in the south of England – it is yellow and blackens with age in towns.

Strapwork. Decoration comprising interlaced bands, or forms similar to fretwork or cut and bent leather.

String course. Decorative horizontal band of brickwork or stone along a wall surface.

Swag. Carved ornament in the form of garlands of fruit and flowers.

T

Tabernacle. Arched or canopied recess, usually decorated.

Terracotta. Very hard clay tiles or bricks used for decorative or facing work and often moulded. It was popular in the late 19th century as a cheap alternative to carved stonework. When glazed, it is known as

faience.

Tracery. Continuation of MULLIONS in a Gothic window up to decorative ribs or moulded bars that form a geometrical or flowing pattern in the upper portion.

—, plate. Tracery in which the pointed head of the window is pierced by a round or quatrefoil opening.

PLATE TRACERY

Transom. Horizontal divider in a window.

Trefoil. Three lobes formed between the cusps of a circle or ARCH.

Truss. Roof support made up of a number of pieces of timber, iron or steel, jointed or bolted together. Also, a compound girder such as a lattice or Warren girder (see BRIDGE).

Tudor. Revival of the architecture of the reign of Henry VIII (1509-47), characterised by battlements, FOUR-CENTERED ARCHES, HOOD moulds and tall, twisted chimneys.

Tuscan. See CAPITAL.

U

Undercroft. Basement or area below a main floor containing COLUMNS, ARCHES or vaults that carry the floor above.

Up platform. Generally the platform from which trains run in the direction of London, but by no means always. On lines built by the Midland Railway they mostly run up to Derby where that company had its headquarters, except on the Derby to London line. In Scotland there are peculiarities, depending on which company built the original railway. In South Wales trains run up to Swansea and Cardiff.

V

Valance. Decorative vertical edging on a canopy or awning and occasionally along the eaves of a roof.

Venetian window. Window with three lights, the central one being taller than the others and having a semi-circular head.

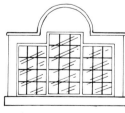

VENETIAN

Voussoirs. Wedge-shaped stones or bricks used to form an ARCH.

W

Wing walls. Walls, sometimes curved, that splay out from the buttresses of a bridge in an embankment or a tunnel mouth to act as retainers. Also, walls projecting from either side of a building to enhance its appearance.

APPENDIX

THE COMPLETE LIST OF BRITISH RAIL'S LISTED BUILDINGS

The listing of British Rail buildings of Special Architectural or Historic interest is a continuing process, carried on from year to year by the Department of the Environment. This is the official list used by British Rail architects and engineers, complete as at 31st March, 1983.

It contains all listed stations and other structures owned by British Rail, including non-railway buildings acquired for various reasons during the 150 years of the railways' existence; of the latter only a selection have been covered in the main part of the book.

The list is divided into the five operating regions of British Rail, and within each region the entries are in alphabetical order. For each entry the location is given in bold type, followed by details of what is protected (a canopy, main passenger building or trainshed, for example) and the grade of listing. All items are in railway use unless otherwise indicated.

Ancient Monuments are directly administered by the Department of the Environment and include both railway structures and a number of Roman and medieval sites (*see p.137*).

EASTERN REGION

Acklington. Station, including single-storey extension at right angles to the south and former goods shed, listed Grade II.

Audley End. Main station building on east side of line listed Grade II.

Belford. Station house listed Grade II. Let.

Bentley. Radcliffe moated site, Ancient Monument.

Berwick-upon-Tweed. Station listed Grade II. Royal Border Bridge listed Grade I. Old station wall and castle vaults beneath station, Ancient Monuments.

Bury St. Edmunds. Northgate station listed Grade II.

Cambridge. Station listed Grade II.

Chappel. Chappel Viaduct listed Grade II.

Chathill. Station house and offices including west wing and one-storey extension (let), waiting shed on up platform, and both up and down platforms with lamp-posts listed Grade II.

Chesterfield. Engineers' offices in goods yard, Corporation Street, listed Grade II.

Cleethorpes. Former refreshment room at 155 The Promenade, platform 3; station clocktower, station approach, buffet and adjacent buildings in Station Road (let) listed Grade II.

Colchester. Station house, St. Botolphs, listed Grade II.

Cooper Bridge. Bridge over River Calder, Bradley, listed Grade II.

Corbridge. Station listed Grade II.

Darlington. Northgate Viaduct, Bank Top station and North Road station (let as a museum) listed Grade II. Skerne bridge, Ancient Monument.

Dewsbury. South entrance building, platform buildings and canopies, footbridge and south-west office block listed Grade II.

Downham Market. Station listed Grade II.

Durham. Viaduct listed Grade II.

Elsenham. Timber station building (in use as waiting room) and canopy on up platform listed Grade II.

Gateshead. Dunston Coal Staithes, former hotel of Greensfield station, Hudson Street, and former boiler shop of Greensfield Works, Rabbit Bank Road, listed Grade II.

Gilsland. Hadrian's Wall, Ancient Monument.

Great Chesterford. Main station building listed Grade II.

Grimsby. Custom house, Cleethorpes Road, listed Grade II. Let.

Halifax. 1855 station building, including east platform and island platform, listed Grade II.

Haltwhistle. Station offices, water tank buildings, water columns and Lambley Viaduct (closed) listed Grade II.

Harrogate. Crimple Valley Viaduct listed Grade II.

Hawes. Appersett Viaduct listed Grade II. Closed.

Hebden Bridge. Passenger station buildings including canopies and signs listed Grade II.

Helpston. Goods shed listed Grade II. Closed.

Hertford. East station listed Grade II.

Horsforth. Newlay Lane iron bridge listed Grade II.

How Mill. Middle Gelt Bridge listed Grade II.

Huddersfield. Station listed Grade I. Railings to St. George's Square station yard, stone warehouse in goods yard off New North Parade, tower in north-west corner of Fitzwilliam Street station yard, Huddersfield Viaduct and Willow Lane East bridge listed Grade II.

Hull. Paragon station and hotel, including station roof, offices, booking hall, trainshed etc. listed Grade II.

Huntingdon. Station and Nos. 34, 35 & 36 Ermine Street listed Grade II.

Ilkley. Station listed Grade II.

Ingatestone. Station listed Grade II.

Knaresborough. Nos. 49-51 Kirkgate (let) and viaduct listed Grade II.

Knebworth. Deard's End bridge, Ancient Monument.

Leeds. Wellington Street viaduct (closed), Kirkstall Road viaduct and Queen's Hotel, City Square, listed Grade II.

Letchworth. Station, including booking hall, public rooms, offices and footbridge, listed Grade II.

Lincoln. Central station and St. Marks station listed Grade II.

Lockwood. Viaduct listed Grade II.

London

Bishopsgate. Forecourt wall and gates to old Bishopsgate goods station listed Grade II. Area let.

Chadwell Heath. Coal Dues Obelisk on embankment about 300 yards east of Whalebone Bridge listed Grade II.

Fenchurch Street. Front portion of station, and Nos. 43-44 Crutched Friars, EC3 (not in use), listed Grade II.

Kings Cross. Station listed Grade I. No. 26 Pancras Road listed Grade II. Part let.

Liverpool Street. Gothic-style offices flanking west ramp, and two western bays of trainsheds listed Grade II.

North Woolwich. Station listed Grade II.

Stepney East. Commercial Road railway bridge, and viaduct at Regent's Canal Dock partly over Commercial Road lock listed Grade II.

Longwood. Longwood viaduct, Paddock or Gledholt Viaduct, east and west portals of Gledholt Tunnel and west portal of Huddersfield Tunnel listed Grade II.

Middlesborough. Zetland Road station, premises of Winterschladen (let) and No. 4 Exchange Place (part let) listed Grade II.

Needham Market. Station listed Grade II.

Newark Castle. Main station buildings (part let) listed Grade II.

Newcastle upon Tyne. Part of Central station listed Grade II. High Level bridge listed Grade I. Jesmond main station buildings (let) and Dean Street railway arch listed Grade II.

Oughty Bridge. Original station building listed Grade II. Let.

Ravensthorpe. Station (formerly Ravensthorpe & Thornhill) listed Grade II.

Richmond. Station bridge listed Grade II. Closed.

Roydon. Station listed Grade II.

Saltburn. Station listed Grade II.

Scarborough. No. 69 Falsgrave Road (let) and station (including roof and retaining walls and railings along Valley Bridge Road) listed Grade II.

Selby. Nos. 1A, 1B, 2 & 3 Ousegate (station houses), goods shed (former station), station building on up platform, canopies on both platforms, footbridge and benches listed Grade II.

Sheffield. Front block of Sheaf Works (let), railway bridge over street in 'The Wicker', station master's house and offices of former Midland station fronting platform 1, including refreshment rooms and former first-class dining room, and west portal of Spital Hill tunnel (closed) listed Grade II.

Slaggyford. Burnstones Viaduct listed Grade II. Closed.

South Shields. East wall of station trainshed, including tile wall-map, listed Grade II.

Stamford Town. Station listed Grade II.

Stockton-on-Tees Nos. 48-56 Bridge Road listed Grade II (48 thought to be original SDR booking office). Let.

Stowmarket. Station listed Grade II.

Sunderland. Wearmouth Bridge over River Wear listed Grade II.

Thetford. Original portion of station listed Grade II.

Thirwall. Roman wall near Greenhead, Ancient Monument.

Thornton. Thornton Viaduct listed Grade II. Closed.

Tynemouth. Main passenger building of old station situated in Oxford Street listed Grade II.

Wakefield Kirkgate. Entrance block to Kirkgate station listed Grade II.

Welwyn North. Welwyn Viaduct listed Grade II.

Wetheral. Corby Bridge listed Grade II.

Whitby. Larpool Viaduct (closed) and town station listed Grade II.

Worksop. Station listed Grade II.

Wylam. Station listed Grade II.
Wymondham. Station (closed) and warehouse (let) listed Grade II.
Yarm. Viaduct listed Grade II.
York. Holgate House at No. 163 Holgate Road, war memorial and old station, including railings to forecourt of south and east front and main wicket gates to forecourt of former York old station hotel, now offices, listed Grade II. New station, Queen Street, listed Grade II*.

LONDON MIDLAND REGION

Aberystwyth. Station listed Grade II.
Ambergate. Newbridge Road bridge at station, Toad Moor Tunnel (portals and lining) and goods shed at station (closed) listed Grade II.
Anglesey. Britannia tubular bridge over Menai Strait, badly damaged by fire in 1970, listed Grade II.
Banbury. Mill Stream bridge (part of bridge deck) listed Grade II.
Barrow-in-Furness. Former station (now railwaymen's club and northern supplies warehouse) in St. George's Square listed Grade II. Ruins, water course, walls, bridge, gatehouse and boundary wall of Furness Abbey of St. Mary's, Ancient Monument.
Barrow-on-Soar. North Street bridge carrying B675 road over railway listed Grade II.
Belper. Stone wall between Nos. 53 and 58 Long Row, walls of railway cuttings from 35 yards north of Long Row to Field Lane bridge and from 45 yards north of King Street bridge to New Road bridge, northern and southern entrance portals to Milford Tunnel, bridges over railway at Field Lane, George Street, Gibfield Lane, Joseph Street, Long Row and William Street, footbridge over railway at Pingle Lane and ventilation tower over Milford Tunnel, Sunny Hill, listed Grade II.
Betws-y-coed. Lledr Viaduct (Cethyn's Bridge) listed Grade II.
Birmingham. Western portal of Ladywood Tunnel, Lawley Street viaduct, Grand Junction viaduct, Holborn Hill, and railway bridge into Curzon Street station over Digbeth Branch Canal listed Grade II.
Burnley. Ashfield Road viaduct listed Grade II.
Burton-upon-Trent. Former Midland Railway grain warehouse in Derby Street listed Grade II.
Buxton. Station listed Grade II.
Carlisle. Citadel station listed Grade II.
Cefn Newbridge Viaduct listed Grade II.
Chester. General station listed Grade II*.
Chirk. Viaduct listed Grade II.
Clay Cross. North portal of Clay Cross tunnel listed Grade II.
Coalbrookdale. Albert Edward Bridge listed Grade II.
Colwich. Lichfield Drive railway bridge and tunnel entrances in Shugborough Park listed Grade II.
Congleton. Congleton Viaduct and Dane Viaduct listed Grade II.
Conwy. Tubular bridge over River Conwy, southern arch of railway bridge over Llanrwst Road and railway embankment wall between railway bridge and west terminal pier of tubular bridge listed Grade II. Tubular bridge also Ancient Monument.
Coventry. Coat of Arms Bridge listed Grade II.

Cressington. Station listed Grade II.
Crewe. Former joiners' shop and railway workshops, Eaton Street, listed Grade II. Let.
Cromford. Main building on west platform, building on east platform (let), footbridge and station master's house listed Grade II.
Crosby Garrett. Smardale Viaduct, Ancient Monument.
Cumberland. Part of Roman wall between Glasson and Drumburgh alongside Port Carlisle branch, Ancient Monument.
Darley Dale. Station and building on north platform listed Grade II. Closed.
Dent. Arten Gill Viaduct and Dent Head Viaduct, Ancient Monuments.
Derby. Clock-tower and engine shed (closed) in Railway Terrace, Midland Railway war memorial in Midland Road, Friargate Bridge (closed) and Midland Hotel listed Grade II.
Drumburgh. Roman wall and vallum on Port Carlisle branch, Ancient Monument.
Duffield. Bridge carrying Alfreton Road over railway at Breadsall and bridge carrying Makeney Road over railway listed Grade II.
Earlestown. Original station buildings on junction platform and Sankey viaduct listed Grade II.
Edge Hill. Station listed Grade II.
Elstree. No. 1 Theobald Street, Borehamwood, listed Grade II.
Fenny Stratford. Simpson Road station buildings (part let) and Denbigh Hall railway bridge listed Grade II.
Glendon & Rushton. Main passenger building of station and station master's house listed Grade II.
Glossop. Station, Norfolk Street, listed Grade II.
Gobowen. Station listed Grade II.
Grange-over-Sands. Station, Lindale Road, listed Grade II.
Great Haywood. Mill Lane railway bridge and Trent Lane bridge listed Grade II.
Gresley. Castle Gresley motte and bailey (part), Ancient Monument.
Hale. Station listed Grade II.
Hellifield. Station listed Grade II.
Hincaster. Footpath, railway underbridge and retaining walls south of Hincaster Tunnel east portal listed Grade II.
Holyhead. Salt Island, George IV arch, custom house, harbour office, pier and lighthouse listed Grade II.
Horwich. Lower House farmhouse listed Grade II.
Hunts Cross. Station, including station master's house, listed Grade II.
Ilkeston. Bennerley Viaduct listed Grade II.
Keswick. Station buildings and platform listed Grade II. Closed.
Kettering. Main passenger building of station and attached platform canopy, wooden building and canopy on island platform, canopy on platform 4 and signal box listed Grade II.
Lancaster. Carlisle Bridge and No. 2 Castle Park (let) listed Grade II.
Leamington No. 64 Bath Street listed Grade II.
Leicester. Screen wall of London Road station listed Grade II.
Leighton Buzzard. North and south entrances to Linslade Tunnel listed Grade II.
Lichfield. Abutments to Upper St. John Street railway bridge listed Grade II.
Liverpool. Mersey Road station, St. Michael's station, Adelphi Hotel, former

North Western Hotel and trainsheds at Lime Street station and Nos. 21 & 48 Castle Street listed Grade II.
London
    Camden. No. 58 Mornington Terrace, NW1 (let), and No. 121 Parkway, NW1, listed Grade II.
    Euston. Statue of Robert Stephenson in station forecourt, Eversholt House at Nos. 163-203 Eversholt Street, two entrance lodges in Euston Square (east lodge let) and railings round square gardens listed Grade II.
    Hatch End. Entrance block to station listed Grade II.
    Primrose Hill. Portals of 1837 and 1879 tunnels and former tack-room of railway stables at Stanley sidings, Chalk Farm Road, listed Grade II.
    St. Pancras. Station (including trainshed, St. Pancras Chambers and ancillary buildings including those in forecourt) listed Grade I. Water point north of St. Pancras station (closed) and Nos. 64-66 Argyle Street listed Grade II.
    Stonebridge Park. Brent Viaduct over North Circular Road (A406) listed Grade II.
Longport. Station listed Grade II.
Loughborough. Main passenger buildings of station (including ticket hall fittings), attached platform canopy and screen wall and canopy on subsidiary platform listed Grade II.
Manchester. Midland Hotel, Peter Street, and canopy at front of Victoria station listed Grade II. Remains of eastern wall of Roman fort at Knott Mill, Ancient Monument.
Mansfield. White Hart Street viaduct, Drury Dam viaduct, and Portland Wharf warehouse (closed) listed Grade II.
Market Harborough. Rockingham Road station listed Grade II.
Matlock Bath. Northern building and main station listed Grade II. Closed.
Millbrook. Station buildings listed Grade II.
Morecambe. Station listed Grade II.
New Mills, Newtown. Station footbridge listed Grade II.
Newton-le-Willows. Huskisson Memorial listed Grade II.
Northampton. Northampton Castle (now part of goods yard), Ancient Monument.
Nottingham. London Road Low Level station and Midland station listed Grade II.
Oldham. Clegg St. railway warehouses at corner of Park and Woodstock Roads listed Grade II.
Ormskirk. Station and drinking fountain at south-west corner of railway bridge in Derby Street listed Grade II.
Preston. Bridge 100 yards south-east of Vicars Bridge, Miller Park, on Preston–Blackburn line listed Grade II.
Radcliffe. Outwood Viaduct listed Grade II. Closed.
Ravenglass. Roman port at Muncaster, Ancient Monument.
Ribblehead. Batty Moss Viaduct, Ancient Monument.
Ridgmont. Station buildings listed Grade II.
Rowsley. Old station listed Grade II. Let.
St. Albans. South signal box listed Grade II.
St. Helens. Marshalls Cross Road and New Street bridges over railway listed Grade II.
Salford. Viaducts over New Bailey Street, north-east of station, listed Grade II.
Seascale. Water tower in goods yard listed Grade II. Closed.

Shrewsbury. Station frontage block, No. 193 Abbey Foregate and adjacent sandstone remains of Abbey Mill and guest house listed Grade II. Refectory pulpit in railway yard listed Grade I and Ancient Monument.

Stockport. Railway viaduct, former LNWR goods warehouse and engine house on west side of Wellington Road North (let) and Tame Viaduct, Reddish Vale Road, listed Grade II.

Stoke-on-Trent. Main station, bronze Josiah Wedgwood statue in centre of Winton Square and Nos. 1-6 Winton Square listed Grade II.

Stone. Station and crossing keeper's cottage in Whitebridge Lane listed Grade II.

Stourbridge. Viaduct in Birmingham Street listed Grade II.

Stratford-on-Avon. Welcombe Hotel listed Grade II.

Tamworth. Bolehall Viaduct listed Grade II.

Thurgarton. Former passenger station buildings (now residential accommodation) listed Grade II.

Trent. North portals of Redhill Tunnels listed Grade II.

Ulverston. Station listed Grade II.

Warrington. Cheshire Lines warehouse in Winwick Street listed Grade II.

Watford. The Grove (M.S. Training Centre), bridge over canal and old station house at No. 147A St. Albans Road listed Grade II.

Wellingborough. Main passenger building of station and attached platform canopy and goods shed including two interior hand-cranes listed Grade II.

Welshpool. Station listed Grade II.

Wigston. Kilby Bridge signal box listed Grade II.

Woburn Sands. Station listed Grade II.

Wolverhampton. Former ticket office, Horseley Fields, listed Grade II. Closed.

Workington. Burrow Walls, part of Roman fort, Ancient Monument.

Wrexham. Wat's Dyke, south-south-west of Wrexham station, Ancient Monument.

SCOTTISH REGION

Aberdeen. East Green vaults listed Grade B.

Alness. Viaduct over River Alness listed Grade B.

Annan. Port Street viaduct and River Annan viaduct listed Grade B.

Ardgay. Bridge over River Carron listed Grade B.

Ardrossan. Nos. 63-69 Princes Street listed Grade B.

Arrochar. Creag an Arnain Viaduct listed Grade B.

Auldgirth. Bridge over Ballochan Linn listed Grade B.

Ayr. Station buildings forming part of ground floor of Ayr Station Hotel listed Grade B.

Birkhill near Bo'ness. Viaduct over River Avon listed Grade B. Closed.

Bishopton. Aqueduct over railway north-west of Bishopton, Ancient Monument.

Blackford. Kincardine Glen Viaduct over Ruthven Water listed Grade B.

Blair Atholl. Station and Tilt Viaduct listed Grade B.

Brechin. Station listed Grade B. Closed.

Brora. Viaduct over River Brora listed Grade C(S).

Burntisland. Old station, Ancient Monument. Closed.

Castlecary. Red Burn Viaduct listed Grade B.

Causewayend. Solum of old railway adjoining Union Canal and Canal Basin, Ancient Monument.

Closeburn. Cample Water Viaduct listed Grade B.

Cockburnspath. Dunglass Viaduct listed Grade B.

Conon. Viaduct listed Grade B.

Culloden. Nairn Viaduct listed Grade A.

Cupar. Station and road bridge over railway listed Grade B.

Dalguise. Viaduct over River Tay listed Grade B.

Dalkeith. Glenesk Viaduct (Glen Arch) over River North Esk listed Grade B. Closed.

Dalmeny. Forth railway bridge listed Grade A. Platform buildings and station office/store at road level listed Grade B.

Doune. Station house listed Grade B. Closed.

Drem. Road overbridge and station footbridge listed Grade B.

Drumshoreland. Birdsmill Viaduct over River Almond listed Grade B.

Dumfries. Station listed Grade B.

Dunblane. Four-span viaduct over Allan Water, tunnel mouth at Old Mill of Keir, and three-span viaduct over Allan Water south of Kippenross House listed Grade B.

Dunkeld. Station (Birnam), Inver Viaduct, Hermitage Road railway bridge and tunnel entrance listed Grade B.

East Calder. Viaduct over River Almond listed Grade B. Closed.

Edinburgh. Warriston Road bridge and Nos. 6-8 Castle Terrace listed Grade B. Nos. 12 & 13 Rutland Square and No. 28 Rutland Street listed Grade A.

Elgin. Station listed Grade B. Engine shed listed Grade C(S). Closed.

Errol. Station listed Grade B.

Fort Matilda. Station listed Grade B.

Gatehead. Laigh Milton Mill Viaduct listed Grade B. Closed.

Gatehouse of Fleet. Big Water of Fleet Viaduct listed Grade B. Closed.

Glasgow. Central station, Central Station Hotel, former Customs & Excise warehouse at Nos. 105-169 Bell Street, warehouse and office at Nos. 175-191 Bell Street, former stable block at No. 174 Bell Street, North British Hotel, Queen Street Station trainshed, former Kelvinside Station at No. 1051 Great Western Road, and Nos. 75-95 Union Street listed Grade B.

Glencorse. Old Woodhouselee Viaduct over River North Esk listed Grade B. Closed.

Gleneagles. Station, footbridge, entrance block and car park wall listed Grade B.

Glenfarg. Viaduct listed Grade C(S). Closed.

Glenfinnan. Viaduct listed Grade A.

Hamilton. Barncluith Viaduct and tunnel approach listed Grade B.

Haymarket. Station, booking office, offices and north bay platform listed Grade B.

Inverness. Station hotel and viaduct over River Ness listed Grade B. Nos. 28-34 Academy Street (Highland Railway offices) listed Grade A.

Invershin. Oykell Viaduct listed Grade B.

Irvine. Queens Bridge listed Grade B.

Kildary. Viaduct over River Balnagowan listed Grade B.

Killiecrankie. Viaduct and tunnel mouth listed Grade B.

Kilmarnock. Former station house (now goods department), station, subway to Garden Street and viaduct at Portland Street/Soulis Street listed Grade B.

Kingussie. Station listed Grade B.

Kirkcaldy. Linktown (Invertiel) Viaduct listed Grade B.

Kirtlebridge. Kirtlewater Viaduct listed Grade B.

Ladybank. Main west block of station listed Grade A. East block, former lodge and ticket office on east platform, engine shed and workshop listed Grade B.

Larbert. Larbert Viaduct listed Grade B. Lochlands Roman temporary camp, Ancient Monument.

Lasswade. Viaduct over Bilston Burn listed Grade B. Closed.

Leadhills. Viaduct over Elvan Water 3 miles east of Leadhills on closed Wanlockhead branch listed Grade B. Closed.

Linlithgow. Avon Viaduct listed Grade A. Wall at head of Lion Well Wynd listed Grade C(S). Avon Viaduct, Ancient Monument.

Lochailort. Loch Nan Uamh Viaduct and Borrodale Viaduct listed Grade B.

Longniddry. St. Germains Crossing House listed Grade B.

Markinch. Markinch Viaduct, Balbirnie Viaduct (closed) and station listed Grade B.

Mauchline. Ballochmyle Viaduct listed Grade B.

Maxwelltown. Goldilea Viaduct (closed) and Garroch Viaduct listed Grade B.

Midcalder. Viaduct over Linhouse Water listed Grade A.

Milngavie. Station listed Grade B.

Morar. Morar Viaduct listed Grade B.

Motherwell. Braidhurst Viaduct listed Grade B.

Nairn. Main station offices on north platform, shelter and ancillary buildings on south platform, footbridge and viaduct listed Grade B.

Newtongrange. Newbattle Viaduct (Lothian Bridge) listed Grade B. Closed.

Newtonmore. Station and Spey Viaduct listed Grade C(S).

North Water Bridge. North Esk Viaduct listed Grade B. Closed.

Old Cumnock. Templand Viaduct over River Lugar and Woodroad Park listed Grade B.

Paisley. Blackhall Aqueduct, Ancient Monument.

Perth. No. 53 King Street listed Grade B.

Pinmore. Kinclair Viaduct listed Grade B.

Ratho. Viaducts over Newbridge to Broxbourn Road and over Almond Valley listed Grade A.

Riddings Junction. Viaduct over Liddel Water listed Grade B. Closed.

Roughcastle (Falkirk). Section of Antonine Wall, Ancient Monument.

Roxburgh. Teviot Viaduct listed Grade B. Closed.

St. Boswells. Drygrange Viaduct listed Grade B. Closed.

Saltcoats. Station listed Grade B.

Shankend. Viaduct listed Grade B. Closed.

Slochd. Viaduct over Allt Slochd Mhuic listed Grade B.

Stewarton. Annick Water Viaduct listed Grade B.

Stirling. Station listed Grade B.

Stonehaven. Original stone-built part of station and platform verandah listed Grade B.

Tain. Station listed Grade B.

Tarbolton. Failford Viaduct and railway bridge near Montgomerie Policies listed Grade B.

Tomatin. Viaduct over River Findhorn and Tomatin Viaduct listed Grade B.

Turnberry. Turnberry Hotel listed Grade B.

Uddingston. Cast-iron arch ribs of former

viaduct listed Grade B.

Wemyss Bay. Station listed Grade B.

Westfield. Avon Viaduct listed Grade B. Closed.

SOUTHERN REGION

Ashford (Kent). Gatehouse to railway works in Newtown Road listed Grade II.

Balcombe. Ouse Valley viaduct listed Grade II.

Bournemouth. Station listed Grade II.

Boxhill & Westhumble. Up- and down-side station buildings listed Grade II.

Brighton. Original portion of station, trainsheds on covered platforms to the north, and London Road viaduct at Preston Road listed Grade II.

Canterbury West. Weighbridge Cottage, North Lane, No. 27 St. Dunstan's Street and station listed Grade II.

Christchurch. Tank traps and pill box in goods yard, Ancient Monument.

Dartford. Remains of priory walls bounding station in Victoria Road, Kingsfield Terrace and Priory Lane including doorway in Kingsfield Terrace listed Grade II.

Dorchester. West station (excluding building on west platform), tunnel entrance under Poundbury Camp, and Wareham Bridge at Alington Road listed Grade II.

Dover. Southern House, Clarence Place listed Grade II.

Eastbourne. Station, including extension c.1930, listed Grade II.

Ewell West. Station platform and shelter on west side of line listed Grade II.

Eynsford. Viaduct listed Grade II.

Fareham. Viaducts over Portchester Road and Quay Street listed Grade II.

Folkestone. Foord viaduct in Bradstone Road and Ark Café at Nos. 15-19 Beach Street listed Grade II.

Gravesend. Station and town pier listed Grade II.

Hastings. Queens Road Bridge listed Grade II.

High Brooms. Colebrook or Southborough Viaduct, Powder Mill Lane, listed Grade II.

Leatherhead. Up-and down-side station buildings listed Grade II.

London

Blackfriars. The Black Friar public house, No. 174 Queen Victoria Street, listed Grade II.

Blackheath. Station listed Grade II.

Cannon Street. Pair of station towers listed Grade II. Closed. Roman governor's palace site including part of station, Ancient Monument.

Charing Cross. Eleanor Cross listed Grade II.

Chiswick. Nos. 62 and 66 Grove Park Terrace listed Grade II.

Clapham. Station, Voltaire Road, listed Grade II.

Clapham Junction. Nos. 54-56 St. Johns Hill listed Grade II.

Craven Passage. Nos. 1, 2 & 3 listed Grade II.

Craven Street. Nos. 25-41 (excluding 36) listed Grade II. No. 36 listed Grade I.

Crystal Palace. Low level station listed Grade II.

Deptford. Ramp from railway to ground level at Deptford station listed Grade II. Closed.

Greenwich. Station listed Grade II.

Herne Hill. Railway bridge just north of Guernsey Grove, Rosendale Road, SE24, listed Grade II.

London Bridge. Railway bridge over Abbey Street, Southwark, and railway bridge over Spa Road, Southwark, listed Grade II.

Mitcham. Station (block to road) listed Grade II.

Vauxhall. Brunswick House, 30 Wandsworth Road, listed Grade II*.

Victoria. Eastern building of Victoria station, Grosvenor Hotel and British Airways Terminal Building in Buckingham Palace Road listed Grade II.

Micheldever. Station listed Grade II.

Mortimer. Station, including buildings and shelter on west side, listed Grade II.

Newhaven Harbour. Lunette Battery near West Pier lighthouse, Ancient Monument.

Plumpton. Main station building on north side of line, subsidiary station building on south of line, connecting footbridge and signal box listed Grade II.

Portsmouth (Hilsea Halt). Hilsea Lines old fortifications, Ancient Monument.

Queenborough. Castle including part of station area, Ancient Monument.

Ramsgate. Anglo-Saxon cemetery south of Ozengell Grange, on south side of line west of Ramsgate station, Ancient Monument.

Ryde. Promenade pier listed Grade II.

Rye. Station building on south-east side of line listed Grade II.

St. Denys. Main station building (including ticket hall) on up side listed Grade II.

Salisbury. Station goods shed in Fisherton Street (former Fisherton station) listed Grade II.

Sellindge. Nos. 1, 2 & 3 Railway Cottages listed Grade II.

Southampton. Terminus station (closed) and South Western House, Canute Road, listed Grade II.

Staines. Platforms and awnings of West station, previously Moor House, listed Grade II.

Swaythling. Main station building (including ticket hall) on down side listed Grade II.

Tunbridge Wells. Up side of Central station, Vale Road, listed Grade II.

Wareham. Station (including shelter and lamp-standards on platform), old goods shed in Sandford Lane and river bridge north-west of West Mill over River Piddle, Wareham Common, listed Grade II.

Weymouth. No. 10a Nothe Parade listed Grade II.

Windsor & Eton Riverside. Station, including royal waiting room, listed Grade II.

Woolston. Main station building (including ticket hall) on down side listed Grade II.

Worthing. Original station listed Grade II. Closed.

WESTERN REGION

Abergavenny. Station buildings listed Grade II.

Barry. Porthkerry Viaduct listed Grade II.

Barnstaple. Chelfham Viaduct listed Grade II. Closed.

Bath. Lower Bristol Road railway bridge and arches, two railway bridges in Sydney Gardens and retaining walls to east and west, Bath Spa station, Twerton (long) Tunnel entrances, tunnel under Bathwick Terrace, Beckford Road railway bridge and retaining wall of canal above bridge, Twerton Wood Tunnel entrances, St. James's railway bridge and Sydney Road bridge and retaining walls to east and west listed Grade II.

Bridgend. Station building on down side listed Grade II.

Bridgwater. Station listed Grade II. Moveable rail bridge over River Parrett, Ancient Monument.

Bristol. Temple Meads station listed Grade I. Entrance to old gaol wall in premises of Western Fuel Company, Cumberland Road (let), railway tunnel vent at end of Pembroke Road, Clifton Down, B & E Building, and four tunnel portals at St. Annes Park listed Grade I.

Calstock. Viaduct listed Grade II.

Cardiff. Bute Road station listed Grade II. Let.

Chard. Former Central 'Joint' station listed Grade II. Let.

Charlbury. Main station building and original nameboard on up platform listed Grade II.

Chepstow. Piers and south-west abutments of Brunel's railway bridge over River Wye, station (let) and canopy to north of main building listed Grade II. St. Peter's Cave, Ancient Monument.

Chippenham. Railway bridge over Bath Road, former gateposts to station yards, weighbridge office in station yard, main entrance buildings and platform canopies on down side, and former B.R. office in station car park listed Grade II. New Road viaduct listed Grade II*.

Cholsey. Moulsford Viaduct listed Grade II.

Crewkerne. Station listed Grade II.

Culham. Main passenger building of station listed Grade II.

Cynghordy. Viaduct listed Grade II.

Dawlish. Station listed Grade II.

Devizes. Devizes Castle (tunnel rights under part of castle grounds), Ancient Monument.

Exeter. St. Thomas station listed Grade II.

Frome. Main station building listed Grade II.

Great Malvern. Station, road overbridge at station, forecourt walls and piers to station listed Grade II.

Hengoed. Viaduct to east of Hengoed (High Level) station listed Grade II. Closed.

Hereford. Barrs Court station listed Grade II.

Instow. Signal box, including frame etc., listed Grade II.

London

Hanwell. Main up-side station building and down-side island platform building listed Grade II. Wharncliffe Viaduct listed Grade I.

Paddington. Station listed Grade I. GWR Hotel listed Grade II.

Southall. Windmill Bridge (Brentford branch), Ancient Monument.

Lostwithiel. Main station building on up platform (moved by Plym Valley Railway Company to Marsh Mills), goods shed, former carriage works and engine shed (let) listed Grade II.

Maidenhead. Thames River bridge listed Grade II.

Moretonhampstead. Manor House Hotel, including interior, listed Grade II*.

Okehampton. Meldon Viaduct and medieval homesteads south of Meldon Quarry, Ancient Monuments.

Oxford. Part of former LNWR station (Rewley Road) listed Grade II (let). Rewley Abbey (walls and gateway) and swing

bridge, Ancient Monuments.
Par. Engine sheds in St. Blazey Road listed Grade II.
Pembroke Dock. Station listed Grade II.
Pensford. Viaduct listed Grade II. Closed.
Reading. Station and No. 173 King's Road (let) listed Grade II.
Redland. Station footbridge listed Grade II.
St. Germans. Viaduct listed Grade II.

St. Ives. Tregenna Castle Hotel and North Lodge listed Grade II.
Saltash. Royal Albert Bridge listed Grade II.
Swindon. Bristol Street wall, Mechanics' Institute, and London Street wall facing 'Railway Village' listed Grade II.
Taunton. South block of station and former GWR Hotel listed Grade II.
Tenby. Viaduct listed Grade II.

Torre. Station listed Grade II.
Tredegar. Nine Arches Viaduct listed Grade II. Closed.
Windsor & Eton Central. Station listed Grade II. Railway bridge over Thames listed Grade II*.
Worcester. Shrub Hill station, including east platform, listed Grade II.

PICTURE CREDITS

Sources for pictures in this book are listed from the top of the left-hand column to the bottom of the right-hand column on every page.

Jacket designed by Bob Hook. Front cover photograph – Bernard Kaukas, Director–Environment, British Rail. Back cover photograph – R. C. Riley. First endpaper – Beamish North of England Open Air Museum. Last endpaper – Ironbridge Gorge Museum Trust: Elton Collection. Frontispiece – Royal Commission on Historical Monuments (England). Contents page – British Rail. 6 – Bob Croser and Cox Cartographic Ltd. 7 – Ironbridge Gorge Museum Trust: Elton Collection. 8 – Mansell Collection.

10 – Jeoffry Spence. 11 – British Rail. 12 – Bob Croser and Cox Cartographic Ltd. 13 – British Rail; British Rail; Illustrated London News Picture Library; British Rail. 14 – BBC Hulton Picture Library; by permission of the Trustees of the National Portrait Gallery, London; Jeoffry Spence. 15 – BBC Hulton Picture Library. 16 – Gordon Biddle; British Rail; British Rail; Philip J. Kelley. 17 – Gordon Biddle; British Rail; British Rail; BBC Hulton Picture Library; British Rail; Philip J. Kelley. 18 – Gordon Buck; British Rail; British Rail; BBC Hulton Picture Library; Gordon Biddle. 19 – British Rail; Roy Anderson. 20 – British Rail; British Rail; BBC Hulton Picture Library; Ironbridge Gorge Museum Trust: Elton Collection; Jeoffry Spence. 21 – Gordon Buck; courtesy of the National Railway Museum, York; R. C. Riley. 22 – British Rail; British Rail; Jeoffry Spence; British Rail; Jeoffry Spence. 23 – BBC Hulton Picture Library; British Rail; Gordon Buck; Gordon Buck; courtesy of the National Railway Museum, York. 24 – R. C. Riley; R. C. Riley; Gordon Biddle. 25 – British Rail. 26 – All British Rail. 27 – Both British Rail. 28 – All British Rail. 29 – R. C. Riley; Jeoffry Spence; Jeoffry Spence. 30 – Gordon Buck; Gordon Buck; British Rail. 31 – British Rail; Gordon Buck. 32 – British Rail; Gordon Biddle; British Rail; Leicestershire Museums, Art Galleries and Records Service. 33 – Gordon Buck; Gordon Buck; Peter E. Baughan; Peter E. Baughan. 34 – British Rail; British Rail; British Rail; Gordon Buck. 35 – British Rail; British Rail; British Rail; Gordon Buck. 36 – British Rail; British Rail; British Rail; British Rail; Gordon Biddle. 37 – Ironbridge Gorge Museum Trust: Elton Collection; Gordon Buck; Ironbridge Gorge Museum Trust: Elton Collection. 38 – British Rail; Gordon Biddle; K. Hoole collection. 39 – Gordon Buck; Gordon Biddle; British Rail; Gordon Biddle. 40 – Both British Rail. 41 – British Rail; British Rail; Gordon Biddle. 42 – British Rail; Iron-

bridge Gorge Museum Trust: Elton Collection; British Rail. 43 – British Rail; Gordon Biddle. 44 – Gordon Biddle; H. G. W. Household collection; Photo. Science Museum, London. 45 – Both Peter E. Baughan. 46 – Both Crown Copyright, National Railway Museum, York. 47 – Both Crown Copyright, National Railway Museum, York. 48 – All Peter E. Baughan. 49 – Beamish North of England Open Air Museum; Beamish North of England Open Air Museum; British Rail. 50 – British Rail; Ironbridge Gorge Museum: Elton Collection; Ironbridge Gorge Museum Trust: Elton Collection; Gordon Buck. 51 – Gordon Buck; Gordon Buck; British Rail; Gordon Buck; British Rail. 52 – British Rail; British Rail; O. S. Nock. 53 – Both British Rail. 54 – All British Rail. 55 – Jeoffry Spence collection; British Rail; British Rail.

56 – Ironbridge Gorge Museum Trust: Elton Collection. 58 – Bob Croser and Cox Cartographic Ltd. 59 – R. C. Riley; Jeoffry Spence; BBC Hulton Picture Library. 60 – British Rail; Roy Anderson collection; Gordon Biddle; British Rail. 61 – Jeoffry Spence; BBC Hulton Picture Library. 62 – BBC Hulton Picture Library; British Rail; British Rail; British Rail. 63 – O. S. Nock; British Rail. 64 – Ironbridge Gorge Museum Trust: Elton Collection; British Rail; British Rail. 65 – British Rail; British Rail; Mary Evans Picture Library. 66 – Roy Anderson; British Rail; British Rail; British Rail; Gordon Biddle. 67 – Jeoffry Spence; Gordon Biddle; Gordon Buck. 68 – Gordon Buck; British Rail; Peter E. Baughan; British Rail; British Rail. 69 – Dr. Ian C. Allen; British Rail; R. C. Riley. 70 – British Rail; British Rail; R. C. Riley; British Rail; British Rail. 71 – British Rail; British Rail; Gordon Biddle. 72 – Gordon Biddle; Ironbridge Gorge Museum Trust: Elton Collection; British Rail; British Rail. 73 – Photo. Science Museum, London; British Rail; Gordon Buck. 74 – British Rail; Gordon Biddle; Gordon Biddle. 75 – Ironbridge Gorge Museum Trust: Elton Collection; Peter E. Baughan; R. C. Riley; Ironbridge Gorge Museum Trust: Elton Collection; R. C. Riley. 76 – Peter E. Baughan; courtesy of the National Railway Museum, York; Gordon Buck. 77 – O. S. Nock; British Rail; Peter E. Baughan. 78 – R. C. Riley; British Rail; British Rail. 79 – R. C. Riley collection; H. G. W. Household, courtesy R. C. Riley; British Rail; British Rail. 80 – British Rail; Peter E. Baughan; British Rail. 81 – British Rail. 82-83 – Gordon Buck. 84 – John R. Hume; Gordon Buck; R. C. Riley. 85 – Peter E. Baughan; R. C. Riley collection. 86 – Gordon Buck; Peter E. Baughan. 87 – Gordon Buck; British Rail; British Rail. 88 – British Rail; Peter E. Baughan; Gordon Buck. 89 – British Rail;

Gordon Buck; H. B. Oliver collection, National Railway Museum, York; H. B. Oliver collection, National Railway Museum, York. 90 – Gordon Buck; British Rail; Peter E. Baughan. 91 – R. C. Riley collection; Gordon Biddle; Peter E. Baughan. 92 – Peter E. Baughan; Peter E. Baughan; British Rail; A. J. Lewis, courtesy Phil Lewis; R. C. Riley. 93 – Gordon Buck; M. Pope, courtesy R. C. Riley. 94 – Gordon Buck; Ironbridge Gorge Museum Trust: Elton Collection; H. G. W. Household; Gordon Buck. 95 – Roy Anderson collection; Jeoffry Spence collection; British Rail. 96 – British Rail; Jeoffry Spence; British Rail. 97 – Roy Anderson collection; R. J. Essery; Photo. Science Museum, London. 98 – Gordon Buck; British Rail; Gordon Buck; Gordon Buck; Gordon Buck. 99 – Ironbridge Gorge Museum Trust: Elton Collection; Lancashire & Yorkshire Railway Society collection. 100 – British Rail; Peter E. Baughan. 101 – G. Fox; courtesy of the National Railway Museum, York. 102 – Courtesy of the National Railway Museum, York; British Rail. 103 – Gordon Buck; British Rail; Peter E. Baughan. 104 – Jeoffry Spence collection; British Rail; Photo. Science Museum, London; British Rail. 105 – Gordon Buck; British Rail. 106 – British Rail; British Rail; Gordon Buck; Gordon Buck; Gordon Buck. 107 – British Rail; Lancashire & Yorkshire Railway Society collection. 108 – British Rail; Gordon Buck; British Rail. 109 – R. C. Riley; British Rail. 110 – British Rail; K. J. Norman. 111 – British Rail; Roy Anderson collection. 112 – Courtesy of the National Railway Museum, York; British Rail; Jeoffry Spence collection; Roy Anderson. 113 – Both Peter E. Baughan. 114 – British Rail; British Rail; Peter E. Baughan; Gordon Buck. 115 – K. J. Norman collection; P. W. Robinson; The Geological Society. 116 – British Rail; Peter E. Baughan; J. M. Hammond; Sankey collection, courtesy K. J. Norman. 117 – K. J. Norman; D. Jenkinson; Peter E. Baughan; Avon County Library (Bath Reference Library). 118 – K. J. Norman; British Rail; O. S. Nock. 119 – British Rail; Peter E. Baughan; British Rail.

120 – British Rail. 121 – John R. Hume. 122 – Bob Croser and Cox Cartographic Ltd. 123 – British Rail; John R. Hume; John R. Hume. 124 – John R. Hume; John R. Hume; Gordon Buck; M. W. Earley. 125 – John R. Hume; British Rail; British Rail; H. G. W. Household. 126 – John R. Hume; Jeoffry Spence; John R. Hume; John R. Hume. 127 – Both Crown Copyright, National Railway Museum, York. 128 – All Peter E. Baughan collection. 129 – Both John R. Hume. 130 – All John R. Hume. 131 – John R. Hume; Gordon Biddle; Jeoffry Spence. 132 – Ironbridge Gorge Museum Trust: Elton Collection; both John R. Hume.

ACKNOWLEDGEMENTS

133 – All John R. Hume. 134 – All John R. Hume. 135 – Gordon Buck; John R. Hume; courtesy of the National Railway Museum, York; John R. Hume. 136 – John R. Hume; H. G. W. Household; John R. Hume; British Rail. 137 – British Rail; British Rail; John R. Hume. 138 – John R. Hume; British Rail; John R. Hume; British Rail. 139 – John R. Hume; British Rail; John R. Hume. 140 – Roy Anderson collection; courtesy Great Eastern Hotel; courtesy Great Eastern Hotel; BBC Hulton Picture Library. 141 – Jeoffry Spence; British Rail; Beamish North of England Open Air Museum. 142 – All John R. Hume. 143 – Courtesy, Walton Sound & Film Services; John R. Hume. 144 – Jeoffry Spence; E. R. Wethersett, courtesy Jeoffry Spence; John R. Hume. 145 – Gordon Buck; John R. Hume; Gordon Buck; Gordon Buck; John R. Hume. 146 – British Rail; John R. Hume; John R. Hume. 147 – All John R. Hume. 148 – All John R. Hume. 149 – British Rail; John R. Hume; British Rail; John R. Hume; British Rail. 150 – All John R. Hume. 151 – All John R. Hume. 152 – All John R. Hume. 153 – Ironbridge Gorge Museum Trust: Elton Collection; Royal Holloway College, University of London, courtesy Bridgeman Art Library. 154-55 – Museum of London. 156 – Crown Copyright, National Railway Museum, York; Crown Copyright, National Railway Museum, York. 157 – John R. Hume; BBC Hulton Picture Library; Illustrated London News Picture Library; Jeoffry Spence. 158 – Both John R. Hume. 159 – All John R. Hume. 160 – John R. Hume; John R. Hume; John R. Hume; British Rail; British Rail. 161 – John R. Hume; John R. Hume; John R. Hume; British Rail; British Rail. 162 – John R. Hume; John R. Hume; Jeoffry Spence collection; John R. Hume; John R. Hume. 163 – Len's of Sutton; courtesy of the National Railway Museum, York; John R. Hume. 164 – John R. Hume; Gordon Buck; British Rail; John R. Hume. 165 – All John R. Hume. 166 – British Rail; John R. Hume; Ironbridge Gorge Museum Trust: Elton Collection; John R. Hume; John R. Hume. 167 – John R. Hume; Gordon Buck; John R. Hume; John R. Hume; John R. Hume; John R. Hume. 168 – John R. Hume; British Rail; British Rail; John R. Hume; John R. Hume. 169 – British Rail; John R. Hume. 170 – Inverness Museum and Art Gallery; Gordon Buck; British Rail; British Rail; British Rail. 171 – Courtesy of the National Railway Museum, York; John R.

Hume; British Rail; British Rail. 172 – Gordon Buck; John R. Hume; John R. Hume. 173 – All John R. Hume.

174 – R. C. Riley. 175 – BBC Hulton Picture Library. 176 – Bob Croser and Cox Cartographic Ltd.; R. C. Riley. 177 – British Rail; Peter E. Baughan; British Rail. 178 – Nicholson's Free Houses; R. C. Riley; British Rail; British Rail; Philip J. Kelley. 179 – R. C. Riley; Ironbridge Gorge Museum Trust: Elton Collection. 180 – Peter E. Baughan; Lancashire and Yorkshire Railway Society collection. 181 – R. C. Riley; R. C. Riley collection; British Rail; British Rail. 182 – Gordon Biddle; Peter E. Baughan; British Rail. 183 – British Rail; R. C. Riley; Jeoffry Spence; London Borough of Richmond upon Thames. 184 – BBC Hulton Picture Library; British Rail. 185 – Photo. Science Museum, London; B. L. Jackson; British Rail; British Rail; O. S. Nock. 186 – British Rail; Jeoffry Spence; Ironbridge Gorge Museum Trust: Elton Collection; British Rail. 187 – Both British Rail. 188 – BBC Hulton Picture Library; Jeoffry Spence; B. L. Jackson. 189 – British Rail. 190 – Gordon Buck. 191 – Peter E. Baughan; R. C. Riley; R. C. Riley. 192 – British Rail. 193 – British Rail; British Rail; Photo. Science Museum, London. 194 – Jeoffry Spence collection; British Rail; British Rail; courtesy of the National Railway Museum, York; Jeoffry Spence. 195 – Jeoffry Spence collection; British Rail; B. L. Jackson. 196 – British Rail; R. C. Riley; R. C. Riley; British Rail. 197 – British Rail; British Rail; R. C. Riley. 198 – B. L. Jackson; Jeoffry Spence; Jeoffry Spence. 199 – All British Rail. 200 – British Rail; Jeoffry Spence collection; British Rail. 201 – British Rail; British Rail; R. C. Riley. 202 – British Rail; H. G. W. Household; British Rail; British Rail. 203 – British Rail; Gordon Biddle; courtesy of the National Railway Museum, York; R. C. Riley. 204 – British Rail; British Rail; Gordon Buck. 205 – Jeoffry Spence collection; British Rail; British Rail. 206 – British Rail; Jeoffry Spence; British Rail; BBC Hulton Picture Library; British Rail. 207 – Courtesy of the National Railway Museum, York; R. C. Riley; British Rail; British Rail. 208 – Gordon Biddle; Gordon Buck; British Rail; C. L. Caddy, courtesy R. C. Riley. 209 – All British Rail.

210 – British Rail. 211 – British Rail. 212 – Bob Croser and Cox Cartographic Ltd.; British Rail. 213 – British Rail. 214 – Peter E. Baughan; British Rail. 215 – British Rail;

British Rail; H. G. W. Household collection. 216 – Adrian Vaughan; Mortimer Local History Society; British Rail. 217 – Gordon Buck; British Rail; Adrian Vaughan. 218 – Adrian Vaughan; British Rail; Gordon Buck; Peter E. Baughan. 219 – Peter E. Baughan; Peter E. Baughan; R. C. Riley collection; British Rail; R. C. Riley; R. C. Riley. 220 – R. C. Riley; Peter E. Baughan; Crown Copyright, National Railway Museum, York; Peter E. Baughan; Peter E. Baughan; R. C. Riley; Peter E. Baughan; R. C. Riley collection. 221 – Gordon Buck; courtesy of the National Railway Museum, York; Adrian Vaughan. 222 – Gordon Biddle; British Rail; R. C. Riley collection; courtesy of the National Railway Museum, York; R. C. Riley collection; R. C. Riley collection. 223 – British Rail; Adrian Vaughan. 224 – Gordon Biddle; Gordon Buck; Gordon Biddle; British Rail, courtesy R. C. Riley. 225 – British Rail; Adrian Vaughan; Adrian Vaughan. 226 – British Rail; Adrian Vaughan; British Rail. 227 – R. C. Riley; British Rail; British Rail; W. N. Lockett, courtesy R. C. Riley. 228 – Ironbridge Gorge Museum Trust: Elton Collection; Philip J. Kelley; line drawing by Alison Biddle; R. C. Riley. 229 – All British Rail. 230-31 – British Rail; Photo. Science Museum, London. 232 – All British Rail. 233 – Gordon Biddle; courtesy of the National Railway Museum, York; British Rail. 234 – British Rail; British Rail; by permission of the Institution of Civil Engineers. 235 – Gordon Buck; Adrian Vaughan; Adrian Vaughan; British Rail. 236 – R. C. Riley; R. C. Riley; R. C. Riley; Adrian Vaughan. 237 – B. L. Jackson; British Rail; Gordon Buck; Gordon Buck. 238 – British Rail; British Rail; Peter E. Baughan. 239 – Jeoffry Spence; British Rail; C. L. Caddy, courtesy B. L. Jackson. 240 – British Rail; Philip J. Kelley; British Rail; R. C. Riley; Photo. Science Museum, London. 241 – R. C. Riley; R. C. Riley; Jeoffry Spence; R. C. Riley; Jeoffry Spence collection. 242 – Ironbridge Gorge Museum Trust: Elton Collection; Gordon Biddle; Gordon Buck. 243 – Crown Copyright: National Monuments Record for Wales; Gordon Biddle; British Rail; R. C. Riley collection. 244 – Gordon Biddle; Peter E. Baughan; Gordon Buck; Peter E. Baughan; Gordon Buck. 245 – British Rail; Gordon Buck; Peter E. Baughan; Gordon Buck.

246-48 – Line drawings by Alison Biddle.

ACKNOWLEDGEMENTS

The authors and editors wish to thank all those who helped to produce this book, in particular Robert Anderson, British Rail, York; Peter E. Baughan, Burgess Hill; Gordon Buck, C.Eng.M.I.E.E., Tunbridge Wells; Valerie Chandler, London; Dr. John A. Coiley, Keeper, National Railway Museum, York; Julia Elton, London; Anne Crosby Farthing, London; John Fogg, British Rail, London; C. C. Green, Birmingham; David de Haan, Ironbridge Gorge Museum Trust; Philip Jungelson, London; Philip J. Kelley, British Rail, London; Jeremy Lawrence, London; Mike McCarthy, London; Iain McNeil, British Rail, London; Capt. Peter Manisty DSC, RN, Association of Railway Preservation Societies, Norfolk; Susan Marshall, London; R. C. Riley, Beckenham; Andrew Roberts, Northampton; Georgina Robins, London; Michael Vanns, Ironbridge Gorge Museum Trust; Nigel Wikeley, British Rail, Croydon.

Page references in bold type are to main entries. Page references in italics are to illustrations only; where relevant text is to be found on the same page as an illustration, a text reference only is given.

Railway company and Grouping names are frequently given abbreviated forms: these usually follow a standard pattern. The following are used in this index and also throughout the book:

CLC   Cheshire Lines Committee
GCR   Great Central Railway
GER   Great Eastern Railway
GNS   Great North of Scotland
GSWR Glasgow & South Western Railway
GWR   Great Western Railway
LBSCR London Brighton & South Coast Railway
LMS   London Midland & Scottish
LNER London & North Eastern Railway
LNWR London & North Western Railway
LSWR London & South Western Railway
LYR   Lancashire & Yorkshire Railway
MSLR Manchester Sheffield & Lincolnshire Railway
NER   North Eastern Railway
SECR South Eastern & Chatham Railway
SR   Southern Railway

A

Abbey Street bridge, London Bridge (earliest masonry & iron underbridge, 1836) **182**
Abbotsbury Railway *201*
Abercorn (assembly) rooms 15
Aberdalgie Viaduct **158**
Aberdeen 124, 143, 158, **164**, 171; *see also* Inverness & Aberdeen Junction Railway
Aberdeen Railway 158, 159, 164, 166
Abergavenny **242**
Aberystwyth **92**, 243
Aberystwyth & Welsh Coast Railway 92
Abingdon Road station, Oxfordshire *see* Culham
Aboyne & Braemar Railway 164
accidents 104, 244; avalanches 92-3, 150; bridges 95, 240, 244, (collapse, *or* movement) 73, 183, 216, 242, 243, *see also* Tay Bridge; collisions 15, 126; derailment 74; fire (bridges) 95, 240, (stations) 13, 181, 203, 218, 238; station roofs 35, 179; tunnels 15, 32, 33, 203, (flooding) 224, 234
Acklington **51**
acquired properties (of British Rail) 119
Adam, Matthew (arch.) 161
Adams, W. (loco. eng.) 203
Adelphi hotel, Liverpool **106**
advertising: mementos 219-20; posters and postcards 127-8, *141*
agent's house, Manchester Liverpool Road 104
Aigburth, Liverpool **106**
Aitchison, G., Snr. (arch.) 64
Albert Edward Bridge, Coalbrookdale **90**
Albrighton **90**
Alford 24
Alfreton Road bridge, Breadsall **79**
Allan Water: viaducts at Dunblane 149 (No. 4), 150 (No. 7)
Allt Slochd Mhuic viaduct, Slochd **173**
Almond River: viaduct at East Calder, 145, at Ratho 149
Alness **167**
Alnwick 43
Alton Castle 86
Alton Towers **86**
Ambergate *last endpaper*, 75
Ambergate Nottingham & Boston & Eastern Junction Railway 74
Ancient Monuments on railway land **137**; Avon Viaduct, Linlithgow 148; bridge over the River Parrett, Bridgwater 235; Deards End Bridge, Knebworth 20; Kielder Viaduct 53; Meldon Viaduct, Okehampton 239; North Road station, Darlington 42; Northampton Castle 70; Old station, Burntisland 151; refectory pulpit, Shrewsbury Abbey 91; Roman governor's palace site, Cannon Street 179; Royal Border Bridge, Berwick-on-Tweed 52; Skerne Bridge, Darlington 42-3; swing bridge over Oxford Canal 221; viaducts (4), of Settle & Carlisle line 114; Windmill Bridge, Southall 215
Ancient Monuments *not* railway property: Poundbury Camp (Iron Age hill fort) 237
Anderson, Sir Robert Rowand 131
Andover (opened 1854) 203, 204
Andover Road (*now* Micheldever, opened 1840) 203, 204
Andrew Handyside & Co., Derby 41, 99, 102
Andrews, George Townsend (arch.) 30, 31, **38**, 39, 40-1, 42, 44
Anerley **177**
Annan **124**
Annick Water Viaduct, Stewarton **138**
Appersett viaduct 114
Appleby 114
aqueducts, canal 94, 137
Arbroath **158**; Dundee & Arbroath Joint Line 158, 161
Arbroath & Forfar Railway 158, 161
arches 41, 246; Coat of Arms Bridge, Stivichall 71; Dean Street, Newcastle-upon-Tyne 50; East Green Vaults, Aberdeen 164; Euston 59, 214 *and* Birmingham Curzon Street 27, 72; Foregate Street bridge, Worcester 223; Guthrie Castle: railway underbridge 161; London & Greenwich Railway ramp 181; Maidenhead Bridge 216; Moorish Arch, Edge Hill 104; Needham Market *22*; Victory Arch, Waterloo 184; Wemyss Bay 142; Wicker Arches 32; *see also* bridges (skew arches)
Ardgay (*formerly* Bonar Bridge) 166, **167**, 169
Armathwaite *190*
Arrochar **125**
Arrochar & Tarbet 172
Arrol, Sir William (eng.) 51
art, and railways **153-6**, decoration and detail **201-2**; Britannia 59 (at Euston), 184 (at Waterloo); Brunel statues 214, 231; Eleanor Cross (at Charing Cross) 179; 'Hungerford Bridge' paintings by Monet 179; Knaresborough Viaduct, engraving by R. D. Hodgson *153*; lions on Conwy Bridge 95; Paddington 213-4, (painting by Frith) *53*; Pearson, John (statue) 106; Poole, Henry (Blackfriar Public House decorations) 178; Queen Victoria portrait, South Western House, Southampton 205; railwaymen, St. Pancras (sculptures) 63; Renton, Mr. at Rannoch (sculpture by navvies) 172; St. Pancras, painting by John O'Connor *154-5*; Stephenson, Robert, at Euston (Marochetti statue) 59; Shrub Hill faience work *81*, 223; Stockton & Darlington painting by John Dobbins 42-3; Thomas, John 59, 95, 96, 214; Tuck's 'oilettes' *128*; Tunbridge Wells Central, lithograph by J. C. Bourne 188; Waterloo, paintings by Helen McKie *156*; Wedgwood, Josiah (statue) 89
Arten Gill Viaduct 114
Ashbee, W. N. (arch.) 15, 19, 21, 22
Ashby: Burton & Ashby Light Railway 70
Ashby-de-la-Zouch **70**
Ashfield Road Viaduct, Burnley **107**
Ashford, Kent 185
Aspatria **114**
Aspinall, J. A. F. (eng.) 101
Atherstone **66**
Atholl, Dukes of, and Blair Castle 158, *159*, 160
Atkinson, F. (arch.) 106
atmospheric railway (Brunel) 238, **239**, 246
Auchterarder 149
Audley End (*formerly* Wendon) **16**
Auldgirth **125**
Aultnaslanash Viaduct, Tomatin **173**
Austin (of Paley & Austin, archs.) 118
Aviemore **167**; sheds 165, 167
Avon 227-35
Avon Viaduct, Linlithgow **148**, *121*
Avon Viaduct, Rugby **67**
Avon Viaduct, Westfield **149**
Aycliffe Lane Crossing (*now* Heighington station) 44
Aylesford **185**, 193
Ayot *191*
Ayr **125-6**, 134, 135, 136, 137

B

Baker, Sir Benjamin (eng.) 144, 185
Baker, William (eng.) 97, 105, 112
Balbirnie Viaduct, Markinch **152**
Balcombe *175*, 176, 180 **197**
Balder Viaduct, Cotherstone **37**
Ballater **164**
Ballindalloch Viaduct **164-5**
Balloch: Dumbarton & Balloch Joint

INDEX

Line Committee 130

Ballochan Linn bridge, Auldgirth **125**

Ballochmyle Viaduct, Mauchline 126, **136**

Balmoral Castle: Ballater 164

Balnagowan River bridge, Kildary **170-1**

Banavie **167**, 172

Banbury 222

Banister, Frederick Dale (eng.) 177, 195

Bank Top, Darlington 42, **43**

Barclay-Bruce, Sir George (eng.) 54

Barlow, William H. 62, 80, 231, 234; W. H. Barlow and Crawford Barlow 157

Barlow, Peter (arch.) 196

Barmouth 94, 243; Barmouth (or Mawddach) Viaduct 26, **96**

Barncluith Viaduct, Hamilton *120*, **134**

Barnes, Frederick (arch.) 20, 22

Barnes, Rev. William 237

Barnes **177**

Barnsley: Hull & Barnsley Railway 11

Barnstaple **237**

Barr, Prof. (of Glasgow University) 146

Barr, Thomas (arch.) 159

Barrhead: Glasgow Barrhead & Kilmarnock Joint Railway 138

Barrow-in-Furness 108, **114-5**

Barrow-on-Soar 70

Barry, Sir Charles 86

Barry, Charles, the younger 183; *and son* Edward 15, 16

Barry, Edward Middleton 178-9, *179*

Barry **243**

Barry Railway 243

Baschurch 90

Basingstoke lines 203, 204, 208, 216

Bath *84*, 175, **227**

Bath Road bridge, Chippenham **225**

Bath Spa 227

Bathgate: Edinburgh & Bathgate Railway 145

Bathwick Terrace tunnel, Bath 227

Battle **194**

Batty Moss (Ribblehead) Viaduct 4, 26, **114**

Battersea Park **177**; Longhedge Works 185

Battle *and* Battle Abbey **194**; first slip carriages 195

Beattie, Hamilton & George (archs.) 146

Beattock **125**; summit 8-9, 97

Beazley, Samuel (arch.) 185, 186, **187**

Beckford Road bridge and canal wall, Bath 227

Bedford 191

Bedford Railway 66

Bedfordshire 64

beer 62, 63

Beeston **73**

Belah: viaduct 157

Belfast: steamers 111

Belford **51**

Bell, David (arch.) 151, 152

Bell, William (arch.) **31**, 39, 40, 41, 43, 49, 51

bells and belfries, significant 21, 24, 170, 207

Belper **75**

bench, railway (Caledonian Railway) *124*

Benge, P.S.A. (eng.) 242

Bennerley Viaduct **80**, 239

Berkeley, George (eng./arch.) 13

Berkhamsted Castle 137

Berkshire, Southern Region 207-8; Western Region 216-7

Bervie: Montrose & Bervie Railway 162

Berwick: Newcastle & Berwick Railway 51, 53; *see also* York Newcastle & Berwick Railway

Berwick-on-Tweed **52-3**

Betts, Edward (contractor) 119

Betwys-y-Coed **96**

Beverley **30**

bicycles: ticket *219*

Bidder, G.P. (eng.) 16, 86

Biddle, C. (arch.) 69

Big Water of Fleet Viaduct, Gatehouse of Fleet *83*, **125**

Bilston Burn: viaduct at Lasswade **148**

Bintley, Job (arch.) 114

Birchill Viaduct, Bo'ness **149**

Birdsmill Viaduct, Drumshoreland **145**

Birkenhead **103**; lines 94, 96, 97, 103

Birkenhead Joint Railway 97, 222

Birkinshaw, John C. (eng.) 37

Birmingham 27, **72**, 218; *see also* London & Birmingham Railway; Manchester & Birmingham Railway; Shrewsbury & Birmingham Railway

Birmingham & Derby Junction Railway 72, 78

Birnam (Dunkeld & Birnam) **160**

Bishop Auckland 42, 44

Bishop's Road, Paddington 214

Bishopsgate Goods station (*formerly* Shoreditch) **13**

Bishopstoke (*now* Eastleigh) 203

Bishopstone Beach Halt (*originally* Bishopstone station, 1864, *later* Bishopstone Halt) **194**

Bishopstone (1938) 194

Bisset, L. (arch.) 168

Bittaford Viaduct 240

Blackburn **107**, 113; Bolton Blackburn Clitheroe & West Yorkshire Railway 112

Blackford **158**

Blackfriar Public House **178**

Blackfriars **178**, 182

Blackhall: aqueduct 137

Blackheath **178**

Blackwall: London & Blackwall Railway 13, 16

Blaikie brothers, Aberdeen: steelwork 166

Blair Atholl **158**, *159*, 165, 166

Blair Castle 158, *159*, 160

Blea Moor: signal box 191; tunnel 114

Bletchley **65**

Blomfield, A. W. (arch.) 184

Blomfield, Sir Reginald (arch.) 188

Blow, Detmar (arch.) 239

Bluebell Railway *45*, 196

Blyth, B. & E. (engs.) 126

Blyth & Tyne Railway 50

Blyth & Westland (engs.) 146, 166

Boat of Garten 164-5, 167

boat trains 12, 15, *128*, 135, 175, 207, 222, 244; *see also* ferries and steamers

Bolton **98**, 101

Bolton Blackburn Clitheroe & West Yorkshire Railway 112

Bonar Bridge (*now* Ardgay) 166, 167, 169

Bo'ness **149**; Scottish Railway Preservation Society 146, 149

Bonomi, Ignatius (arch.) 42-3

booking halls, offices: Elgin 165; Hastings 196; Heighington 44; Hull 31; in inns 42; Manchester Liverpool Road 104; Middlesbrough 41; Midland station, Nottingham *74*, 75; Monkwearmouth (replica) 50-1; Norwich *202*; Old College, Glasgow 132; St. Pancras *62*; Selby (superintendent's house) 39; Wemyss Bay 142

Bootle 117

Bo-peep Junction 196

Border Counties Railway 53

Border Union Railway 123

Borders 123-42

Borrodale Viaduct, Lochailort **171**

Boston 74, 191

Bouch, Sir Thomas 42, 144, 151, 152, **157**; *see also* Tay Bridge; Bouch & Grainger 151

Bourne, J. C. (lithographer) 9, *11*, *64*, *72*, 153, 218, 228

Bourne, John (eng.) 42, *224*

Bournemouth **208**; lines 175, 227

Box Tunnel **224-5**, 226, *232*

Boxhill & Westhumble **199**, *202*

Braddock, H. W. (arch.) 60

Bradford Forster Square **32-3**

Bradford-on-Avon **225**

Braemar 164

Braidhurst Viaduct, Motherwell **136**

brake vehicles, Cowlairs Tunnel 132

Bramhope Tunnel **33**

Brandling Junction Railway 44-5, 50

Brassey, Thomas (contractor) 20, **119**, 204

Breadsall, Alfreton Road Bridge **79**

Brechin **159**

Brechin Railway Society 159

Brecon 243

Brecon & Merthyr Railway 243

Brecon Road, Abergavenny 242

Brent Viaduct, Stonebridge Park **64**

Brentford Dock 215

Brereton, R. P. (eng.) 241

Bricklayers Arms station, Bermondsey 14

Bridge of Orchy 172

Bridge Street, Glasgow 126

Bridgehouses (*or* Spital Hill) Tunnel **32**

Bridgend 216, **243**

bridges and viaducts

    earliest *bridges* (in chronological order): earliest large metal bridge in the world, Gaunless (1825) 46, 83; earliest masonry underbridge, Skerne (1825) 42; earliest overbridge, Rainhill skew bridge (1830) 104; earliest masonry & iron underbridge, Abbey Street, London Bridge (1836) 182; earliest *surviving* iron underbridge, Gauxholme (1840) 108; earliest iron underbridge *still in use*, Windsor & Eton Central (1849) 217; earliest steel underbridge, Forth (1890) 144; earliest concrete underbridge, Morar Viaduct (1901) 171

    earliest *viaducts* (in chronological order): earliest *surviving* tramway, Laigh Milton Mill (1812) 130; earliest tramway *still in use*, Kings Mill (1819) 73; earliest

256

masonry viaduct, Sankey (1830) 104; earliest skew viaduct, Middle Gelt (1835) 54; earliest iron viaduct, Meldon (1874) 239; earliest steel viaduct, Forth Bridge (1890) 144; earliest concrete viaduct, Glenfinnan (1901) 169
other bridges and viaducts of particular importance or interest: Almond viaduct, Ratho 149; Ambergate, bridge over the River Amber, *last endpaper*; Bennerley Viaduct 80, 239; Big Water of Fleet Viaduct *83*, 125; Bilston Burn: viaduct 148; Border Viaducts 123; Bridgwater: bridge over the River Parrett 235; Chelfham Viaduct 237; Coalbrookdale: Severn bridges 90; Conisbrough Viaduct 32; Connel Ferry Bridge 126, *129*; Esk Valley bridge 39-40; Foord Viaduct 186; Forth Bridge (Bouch's suspension bridge) 144, 157; Forth Bridge (Fowler and Baker) 143, 144, *189*; Gaunless (first large metal bridge in the world (1825) 46, 83; Glenfinnan Viaduct 169, 172; Great Western through Bath: bridges 227; Guthrie Castle: railway underbridge 161; Harringworth Viaduct 68-9; Hawarden swing bridge 94; High Level bridge, Newcastle-upon-Tyne *48*, 49-50, 73; Hownes Gill Viaduct 42, 157; Lichfield Drive bridge 86-7; Linhouse Water: Locke's viaduct 148; Lockwood Viaduct 35, *37*; London & Greenwich Railway ramp 181, 182; Maidenhead Bridge (flattest brick arches in the world) 216; Menai Bridge (Britannia tubular bridge) *26*, 73, 95, *128*; Nairn Viaduct, Culloden Moor 168; Newlay Lane iron (toll) bridge, Horsforth 119; Ouse viaduct, Balcombe 197; Ouseburn Viaduct 50; Ratho: viaduct over Newbridge to Broxburn Road 149; Royal Albert Bridge, Saltash 73, *192*, 241; Royal Border Bridge, Berwick-on-Tweed 52, 73; St. Pinnock Viaduct 240; Spa Road bridge (London's oldest operational railway bridge) 182; Speymouth Viaduct 166; Stockport Viaduct 102; Tavistock Viaduct 239; Tay Bridge (Bouch's) 42, 102, 143, 144, 157; Welwyn (*or* Digswell) Viaduct 20; West Highland Railway bridges 125, 136, 172; Whalley Viaduct (blind Gothic arches) 112-3; Wharncliffe Viaduct 213; Willington Dene Viaduct 50; Windmill Bridge (Brunel's road over canal over railway) 215; Wye Bridge, Chepstow 242
other significant bridges and viaducts (by type): cast-iron 101, 102, 157, 165, 196; railway ramp 181; retractable (for passengers) 214; road *and* rail (Carron Viaduct) 165; skew arches 53, 104, 168; suspension bridges: Bouch's over the Forth 144, 157; Brunel's 241, 242, (Clifton suspension road bridge) 234, 246; swing bridges 94, over canals 167, 168, 221; timber 96, 173, (Brunel's) 240; toll-bridge 112; tubular *26*, 73, *84*, 95, *128*, 165; underbridges 137, 161
bridges and viaducts, unnamed: 96, 148,

170-1, 172, 173, 225, 235, 239, over the River Piddle, Wareham 209
bridges and viaducts: testing viaducts 118; *see also* accidents (bridges); arches; footbridges
Bridgwater **235**
'Brighton, The' *see* London Brighton & South Coast Railway
Brighton 27, **194-5**; lines 195, 200, 207; *see also* London & Brighton Railway
Brighton Lewes & Hastings Railway 195
Brighton (Locomotive) Works 207
Bristol **228-33**; Bristol Joint station (Bristol Temple Meads; earliest medium terminus station *and* earliest terminus trainshed, 1839-40) 227, 228, 232; lines 218, 221, 227; speed record, Bristol to Paddington 222
Bristol & Exeter Railway 228, 233-8 *passim*
Bristol & North Somerset Railway 234
Britannia tubular bridge (Menai Bridge) 26, 73, **95**, *128*
'British Chicago' (Barrow-in-Furness) 114-5
British Rail 18, 31, 104, 167, 181, *201*, 242; acquired properties 119; Brunel's working drawings 229; National Railway Museum, York 45-9; nationalisation 8, 90, *The Splendours and Miseries of British Rail's Architectural Heritage*, by Bernard Kaukas 25-9; *see also* Listed Buildings
British Railways Board 4, 9, 60
Broadstairs line 188
Brockenhurst line 208
Brocklesby **30**
Brora **167**
Brotherhood, Rowland (contractor) 225
Broughty Ferry 126
Browne, G. Washington 146
Brunel, Isambard Kingdom **222, 231,** 236; 'atmospheric railway' 238, **239**; bridges and viaducts *26*, *84*, 192, *211*, 213-8 *passim*, 234, 242; goods shed (*formerly* a station) 208; Great Western through Bath *84*, **227**; locomotives 246; road over canal over railway 215; stations 208, 213-25 *passim*, 235-43 *passim*; statues 214, 231; steamships 231; *and* Robert Stephenson 73, 95, 179; superintendent's house 221; Swindon, railway village 226; timber viaducts **240**; tunnels 224, 233, 237; working drawings **229-32**
Brunel, Marc 231
Brunel Engineering Centre Trust 228
Brunlees, James (eng.) 233
Buchan lines 171
Buck, G. W. (eng.) 102
Buckinghamshire 65-6; line 11
Bucknell 91
Budden, W. H. (arch.) 61
Buff, Peter (eng.) 16
bullocks, for tramroad wagons 73
Burgess Hill **198**
Burleigh, Benjamin (arch.) 43
Burleigh House 29
Burnett, Sir J. J. (arch.) 129
Burnley **107**
Burnstones Viaduct 54

Burntisland **151**; lines 144
Burrell, John and Isaac (contractors) 46
Burton & Ashby Light Railway (electric tramway) 70
Bury St. Edmunds **20**; Ipswich & Bury Railway 20, 22
buses: competition with railway 147; *see also* horse-operated road vehicles
Bute, Marquis of 243
Bute Road, Cardiff (*formerly* Cardiff Docks; earliest small terminus station still in use, c. 1840) **243**
Butlers' Stanningley Foundry, nr. Leeds 108
Butterley Company, Derbyshire 62, 63
Butterworth, Thomas (arch.) 34
Buxton **76**; *see also* Manchester Buxton Matlock & Midlands Junction Railway 77, 85

C

Caledonian Canal bridge, Banavie **167**
Caledonian Hotel, Edinburgh **146-7**
Caledonian Railway 57, 97, 121, 122, 123, **124,** 126, 129, 149, 159, 161, 162; bridges 125, 134, 147, 148, 158, 166; competition 135, 147; hotels 131, 146-7, 161; joint lines, stations 129, 133, 136, 138, 143, 162, 164; pier 134; locomotives 61, 124, *126*; signal boxes 191; stations 116, 117, 125, 130, 131, 133, 136, 142, 150, 161, 163, 164; tunnels 134
Callander 126; lines 149
Callander & Oban Railway 126, 150, 163
Calstock Viaduct **240**
Calvine Viaduct **159**
Cambrian Coast Railway 96
Cambrian Railways 92, 93, 212, **243**
Cambridge **18**
Cambridgeshire 18-19
Camden: Roundhouse **59**
Cample Water Viaduct, Closeburn **125**
canals, and railways 62, 107, 108, 115, 132, 193, **227**; aqueducts 94, 137, 147; bridges 145, 215, (swing bridges: Caledonian 167, 168, 170; Oxford 221); Brunel's road over canal over rail 215; tunnels: 57, 103 (Standedge), 117 (Hincaster), 188 (Thames & Medway) 188
Cannon Street 26, *109*, **178-9**
Canterbury & Whitstable Railway 185
Canterbury West **185**, 187
Cardiff Bute Road (*formerly* Cardiff Docks; earliest small terminus station still in use, c. 1840) **243**
Cark & Cartmel **115**
Carlisle **116**, 117; lines 69, 108, 135; Glasgow Dumfries & Carlisle Railway 124, 125; *see also* Lancaster & Carlisle Railway; Maryport & Carlisle Railway; Newcastle & Carlisle Railway; Settle & Carlisle line
Carlisle bridge, Lancaster **108**
Carnforth **108**
Carr Bridge **167**
Carron River bridge, Ardgay **167**
Carron Viaduct **165**
Carsewell, James (eng.) 132, 158
Carstairs 146, 158

INDEX

Cartmel (Cark & Cartmel) **115**
Castle Douglas: lines 135
Castle Douglas & Dumfries Railway 125
Castle station, Lancaster **108**
Castlecary **149**; line 158
castles, and railway property 137; Alton
    86; Berkhamsted 137; Berwick 53; Blair
    158, *159*, 160; Chirk 94; Conwy *84*, 95;
    Doune 149; Guthrie 161; Lancaster
    108; Lullingstone 186; Northampton
    70; Windsor 207, 217; *see also* stately
    homes
Caterham Railway 200
Cefn **94**
celebrations, commemorations: East
    Coast route, on Newcastle Central 7;
    fatal accident 104; Hawarden swing
    bridge 94; Kilsby Tunnel 69; LSWR, at
    Micheldever 204; Mark Tey 16; Mar-
    ket Harborough 71; NER 52; Rainhill
    Trials *26*, 104, *219*; Royalty and Rail-
    ways exhibition, GWR, Windsor &
    Eton Central 217; Stockton & Darling-
    ton 42; Waterloo centenary *156*; *see also*
    memorials and monuments
Central war memorials 149-50
Central stations *see* Bournemouth; Chard;
    Dumbarton; Glasgow; Leith; Lincoln;
    Liverpool; Manchester; Newcastle-
    upon-Tyne; Tunbridge Wells; War-
    rington; Windsor & Eton
Central Station Hotel, Glasgow **131**
Central Wales Extension Railway 245
Central Wales Railway 91, 244
Cethyn's Bridge (Lledr Viaduct), Betws-
    y-Coed **96**
Chadwell Heath: Coal Dues Obelisk **13**
Chalk Farm junctions 61
Challow: line 221
Chamberlain, Neville (P.M.): opened
    Welwyn Garden City 20
Channel tunnel 61, 234
Chanter, Frank W. 237
Chapel-en-le-Frith **76**
Chapel Milton Viaducts **76**
Chappel Viaduct **16**
Chard Central (*formerly* Chard Joint) **236**
Charing Cross *7*, **178-9**; 36 Craven Road
    119
Charing Cross Railway 178, 179
Charlbury 216, **218**
Charlton House 89
Chatham *see* London Chatham & Dover
    Railway; South Eastern & Chatham
    Railway
Chathill **53**
Chatsworth (Rowsley) 85
Cheddleton **86**
Chelfham Viaduct, Barnstaple **237**
Cheltenham: line 224
Cheltenham & Great Western Union
    Railway 240
Chepstow 241, **242**
Chertsey **199**, 206
Cheshire 96-8
Cheshire Lines Committee 98, 99, 105,
    106
Chester 78, 85, **96-7**; lines 90, 222; *see also*
    Shrewsbury & Chester Railway
Chester & Connahs Quay Railway 94
Chester & Holyhead Railway 57, 85, 95,

96, 118
Chesterfield **76,** 85
Chippenham 208, **225**; line to Bath 227
Chichester 191
Chipstead Valley: line 200
Chirk 90, **94**
Chislehurst 185
Cholsey **218**
Christchurch tank traps 137; Ringwood
    Christchurch & Bournemouth Railway
    238
Church, R. F. (eng.) 239, 240
Churchward, J. G. (loco. eng.) *93*
Churnet Valley Railway 86
Churston **237**
Circle Line (London Transport) 14, 185
Cirencester: line 224
Citadel station, Carlisle (earliest large
    station *still in use*, 1847) **116**, 117
City and South London Railway 185
City of Dublin Steam Packet Company 95
Clachnaharry swing bridge **168**
Clacton-on-Sea **17**
Clapham (Clapham Road & North
    Stockwell or Clapham Town) **180**;
    museum 46
Clarence Yard 203
Clark, H. Fuller 178
Clark, William Tierney (eng.) 188
Claxton, Capt. (nautical expert) 241
Clay Cross Tunnel **76**
Clayton Tunnel **198**
Cleethorpes **30-1**
Clegg Street goods warehouse, Oldham
    102
Cleveland 41-2
Clifton, Edward N. (arch.) 117, 199
Clifton Down, Bristol **233**
Clifton Extension Railway 233
Clifton suspension (road) bridge 231, 234
Clitheroe: Bolton Blackburn Clitheroe &
    West Yorkshire Railway 112
clocks and clock towers 46; Aberystwyth
    92; Barrow-in-Furness 114-5; Black-
    burn 107; Brechin 159; Brighton 194;
    Central Station Hotel, Glasgow 131;
    Cleethorpes 31; Derby *78*, *79*; East-
    bourne 195; Edge Hill, Liverpool *219*;
    Exchange, Liverpool 106; Great Mal-
    vern 222; Harrow 60; Haymarket,
    Edinburgh 146; Hull 31; Kings Cross
    14; Leicester London Road 70; Leith
    Central 147; Liverpool Street 15; Mid-
    land, Nottingham 74-5; Morecambe
    111; North British Hotel, Edinburgh
    146; Oban 126; St. Pancras 63; Scar-
    borough 38; Shrewsbury 90; Terminus,
    Southampton 205; Ulverston *25*; Vic-
    toria, London 184; Wemyss Bay 142;
    Wingfield 85
Closeburn **125**
Clumber Park 23
Clutton, Henry (arch.) 68
Clwyd 94-5
Clydebank Riverside **129**
Clydesdale Junction Railway 136
coal and steam: fireless 'Fowler's Ghost'
    185; first steam-hauled railway in south
    of England 185; mechanical coaling
    plant, Carnforth 108; Welsh economy
    243; *see also* atmospheric railway;

freight (coal); horse-operated railways
Coal Dues Obelisk, Chadwell Heath 13
coal staithes 44, 52, 151, 157
Coalbrookdale **90**
Coat of Arms Bridge, Stivichall **72**
Coatbridge 132, 136, 149
Coates village 224
Cockburnspath 123
Cockermouth Keswick & Penrith Rail-
    way *110*, 117
Colchester St. Botolphs **17**
College Burial Ground, Charing Cross
    179
College station, Glasgow **132-3**
College Wood Viaduct **240**
Colwich **86-7**
commemorations *see* celebrations and
    commemorations; memorials and
    monuments; war memorials
competition between railways: London
    Midland 57, 59, 74-5, 76, 96, 101, 113,
    114; Scottish Region 135, 147, 148, 171;
    Southern Region 175, 185, 196; West-
    ern Region 96, 212, 216, 225, 236, 237,
    240, 243
competition with other services: ferries,
    steamers 95, 103, 187, 241; Thames riv-
    er traffic 13
Congleton **97**
Conisbrough Viaduct **32**
Connahs Quay: Chester & Connahs
    Quay Railway 94
Connel Ferry Bridge **126**, *129*
Conon Bridge **168**
conservation and preservation 26-8
Consett: Hownes Gill Viaduct **42**, 157
Conwy tubular bridge, *and* Conwy Castle
    84, **95**
Cooper Bridge **34**
Copenhagen Tunnels, Kings Cross 15
Corbridge 54
Corby Viaduct 54, *55*
Cornwall 240-1
Cornwall Railway **240**, 241
Cosham: line 203
Cotherstone **37**
Coulsdon (*now* Kenley) 200
County Hotel, Carlisle 116
Coventry **72**
Cowlairs incline engine house *and* Cow-
    lairs Tunnel, Glasgow 130, 132
Cowran Hills cutting 54
Craigendoran to Fort William line 172
Creag an Arnain Viaduct, Arrochar **125**,
    172
Creagan Viaduct, **126**
Crediton **237**
Cressington **106**
Cressington Park Estate 106
Crewe: lines 90, 97; 'model' railway town
    226; railway works 36, 118
Crewkerne **236**
Crieff Junction (rebuilt as Gleneagles)
    161
Crimple Viaduct **37**
Cromford **77**
Crookston, Glasgow 130, **133**
Crosby Garrett 114
crossing-keeper's cottage, Stone 89
Crossley, John Sidney (eng.) 70, 75, 76,
    114, 115, 227

Crown Street, Carlisle 116
Crown Street, Liverpool 104
Crutched Friars warehouse, Fenchurch Street 13
Croydon: London & Croydon Railway 14, 177; Wimbledon & Croydon Railway 183
Crystal Palace 7, *109*, 193, 213, 221
Crystal Palace High Level 180
Crystal Palace Low Level *175*, **180**
Cubitt family 14, 193
Cubitt, Joseph (eng.) 14, 20, 24, 178
Cubitt, Lewis (arch.) **14**, 19, 21, 23, 24, 193
Cubitt, Thomas 14, 193
Cubitt, Sir William 14, 20, 21, 176, 186, **193**
Cubitt, William (nephew of Sir William) 186, 193
Cudworth, W. J. (arch.) 41
Culgarth 114, 191
Culham (*earlier known as* Dorchester Road *and* Abingdon Road) **218**, *229*
Culloden Moor **168**
Culrain 163, 170
Culverhouse, P. E. 228
Cumbria 114-8
Cupar 146, **151**
Curzon Street, Birmingham 27, **72**
Customs & Excise warehouse, Glasgow **133**
Customs Houses: at Grimsby **31**; at Holyhead 95
cuttings: Belper 75; Cowran Hills, How Mill 54; Olive Mount 104; Talerddig (gold found) 93; Tring *64*
Cuxton **185**
Cynghordy Viaduct **244**, 245

D

Dalguise Viaduct **160**
Dalkeith **143**; Eskbank & Dalkeith 148
Dalmally **126**
Dalmeny **144**
Dalry: line 138
Dane Viaduct, Congleton **97**
Danks, J. (arch./eng.) 217
Darley Dale **77**
Darlington **42-3**; NER headquarters 12; railway workshops 44; *see also* Stockton & Darlington Railway
Dart Valley Railway 237
Dartford 187
Dartmouth & Torbay Railway 237
Davis, Edward: statue of Josiah Wedgwood 89
Dawes, William (arch.) 100-1
Dawlish **238**
Deansgate Goods station, Manchester **99**
Dearne Valley Railway 32
Dee Viaduct, Chirk **94**
Deepdale: viaduct 157
Denbigh Hall Bridge **65**
Denmark Hill **181**
Dent Head Viaduct 114
Department of the Environment 9, 104, 239; *see also* Listed Buildings
Deptford **181**
Derby 62, 69, **78-9**; locomotive works (earliest, c. 1840) 79; Midland Hotel

78, 79, 101; Birmingham & Derby Junction Railway 72, 78
Derby Midland Railway Conservation Area 78
Derbyshire 75-85
Desford Junction *191*
destination indicators 34, 59, 131, 184
Devil's Bridge, Uphill **234**
Devon 237-9; Brunel's timber viaducts 240
Devonport 239, 240
Devonshire, Duke of 76, 77, 85, 115
Dewsbury **34**, 35
Dickens, Charles: 'Mugby Junction' 67
Didcot **218**; line 221
Didcot Railway Centre *48*, 218
Digswell (*or* Welwyn) Viaduct 20
Dingwall **168**
Dingwall & Skye Railway 168
Dinting Vale Viaduct **103**
Disley 76
Ditton Viaduct 97
Dixon, Joseph (superintendent) 42, 157
Dobbins, John: painting of Stockton & Darlington 42-3
Dobson, John (arch.) **49**, 213
Dockray, R. B. (arch.) 59
docks, and railways; Brentford 215; Bridgwater 235; Brunel 246; Cardiff 243; NER 52; Pembroke 245; Tilbury 13; Woolwich (Royal Docks) 16; *see also* ports and harbours
dogs: ticket *220*
Doncaster 21
Dorchester **208**, 209, 237; Poundbury Tunnel **237**
Dorchester Road station, Oxfordshire *see* Culham
Dorking *202*
Dorset: Southern Region 208-9; Western Region 237; Abbotsbury Railway *201*; Somerset & Dorset Joint Railway 227
Doubleday, John: statue of Brunel 214
Doune, *and* Doune Castle **149**
Dover 176, **186**; *see also* London Chatham & Dover Railway
Downham Market **22**
Drem **145**
Drigg 117
drinking fountains 112, 163
Driver, Charles H. (arch.) 68, 70, 199, 200, *202*
Druimuachdar Pass 158, 163
Drummond, Dugald (loco. eng.) **203**
Drummond, Peter (loco. eng.) 135
Drumshoreland **145**
Drury Dam Viaduct, Mansfield **73**
Drygrange (*or* Leaderfoot) Viaduct 123
Dublin: City of Dublin Steam Packet Company 95
Duffield: bridges **79**
Duke of Sutherland's Railway 167, 168, 169
Dumbarton **130**; line 129
Dumbarton & Balloch Joint Line Committee 130
Dumfries 125; lines 135; Glasgow Dumfries & Carlisle Railway 124, 125
Dumfries and Galloway 124-5
Dunbar **145**
Dunbartonshire: Lanarkshire & Dunbar-

tonshire Railway 129, 130
Dunblane 126, **149**
Dunblane & Callander Railway 126
Dunblane Doune & Callander Railway 149
Duncan, A.: drawing of Bishopsgate *13*
Dundalk Newry & Greenore Railway (LNWR in Ireland) 95
Dundee: lines 143, 151, 157, 161, 163
Dundee & Arbroath Joint Line 158, 161
Dundee & Newtyle Railway 162
Dundee & Perth Railway 161
Dunglass Viaduct, Cockburnspath 123
Dunkeld **160**
Dunrobin **168-9**
Dunston coal staithes **44**
Dunure: Maidens & Dunure Light Railway 139
Durham **42-3**
Durham Junction Railway 44
Dutton **97**
Dyfed, London Midland Region 92-4; Western Region 244-6

E

Earlestown **103**
East Calder **145**
East Green vaults, Aberdeen **164**
East Lancashire Railway 105-6, 107, 112
East Lincolnshire Railway 24, 191
East Linton **145**
East of Fife Railway 152
East station, Stamford **24-9**
East Sussex 194-7
Eastbourne **195**; lines 207
Easter Ross stations 166-7
Eastern Counties Railway 13, 16, 17-18, 22, 24, 85
Eastern Region 10-55; listed properties 249-50
Eastern Union Railway 24
Easternmost bridge, Battersea Park 177
Eastleigh (*formerly* Bishopstoke) **203**, 204; line 208
Edge Hill, Liverpool 26, 104, *219*
Edinburgh **145-7**; Princes Street 117, 145-6; Waverley 143, **145-6**; Haymarket 126, **146**
Edinburgh & Bathgate Railway 145
Edinburgh & Glasgow Railway 170; bridges 126, 148, 149; canal 145; stations 132, 143, 146, 148; wall 148
Edinburgh & Northern Railway 151, 152
Edinburgh Leith & Granton Railway 147
Edinburgh Perth & Dundee Railway 157
Edis, Col. Robert (arch.) 15, 60, *140*
Eleanor Cross, Charing Cross **179**
electric telegraph, Gosport 203
electrification: LYR 101, 103, 108; Liverpool Merseyrail 105, 106, 112; LBSCR 207; LNWR 60; NER 52; Scotland 131, 132; Southern Region 176, 183, 194, 200
electrification: overhead wires 111; for loading docks 35; signal boxes 191
Elgin **165**; line 171
Ellesmere 92; Ellesmere Port 97
Elmslie, E. W. (arch.) 222
Elsenham **17**
Ely: Lynn & Ely Railway 22

engines *and* engine sheds *see* locomotives *and* locomotive sheds
engineering and other innovations, oddities: atmospheric railway 238, **239**, 246; diesels 15, 132; electric telegraph, Gosport 203; gunpowder (18,000 lbs) electrically detonated 193; electro-pneumatic signal and point operation 52, 101, 203; lifts 178; push-and-pull trains 224; railcars 224; railway ramps 181; 'Ro-Railer' 68; rope-worked inclines 104, 132, 162; slip carriages 195; steam shovels 114; superheaters 69; Vignoles's work 65; wagon hoists 35, 240
Epsom & Leatherhead Railway 200
Epsom Downs Racecourse 200
Ericsson, John 65
Erith 187
Errington, John E. (eng.) 97, 117, 157
Errol **161**
Esk Valley (*or* Larpool) Viaduct **39-40**
Eskbank & Dalkeith (*formerly* Eskbank) **148**
Esplanade Pier *and* station, Ryde **206**
Essendine: Stamford & Essendine Railway 24, 29
Essex 16-18
Etchingham **195**
Etherow Viaduct 103
Eton *see* Windsor & Eton
Euston 35, **59**, 117; Doric Arch 59, 214; entrance lodges 59, *60*; Great Hall *46*, 59, 214
Eversholt House, Euston **59**
Evesham 218
Ewell West **199**, 204
Exchange (*or* Tithebarn Street), Liverpool **105**
Exchange, Manchester 100
Exeter 191, 236, **238**; Exeter to Newton Abbot (atmospheric) railway 239; Bristol & Exeter Railway 228, 233-8 *passim*
Exeter & Crediton Railway 237
Eynsford Viaduct **186**

F

Failford Viaduct, Tarbolton **139**
Fairbairn, Sir William (eng.) 15
Fairfields of Chepstow (contractors) 242
Falkirk Grahamston **150**
Falmouth: Brunel's viaducts 240
Far North Line (Joseph Mitchell) 166-7, 170, 173
Fareham **203**
fares: bicycles *219*; dogs *220*; Isle of Wight 206
Farnham 203
Fay, Sir Sam 61
Fearn 166
Felixstowe Town **21**
Fenchurch Street **13**, 14; steamer passengers 187
Fenny Stratford **66**
ferries and steamers; Brunel's trans-Atlantic 231; Dartmouth 237; Grainger's, to carry railway wagons 126; Hull 39; to Ireland 95, 111, 135, 138, 244, 245; Lake Windermere 57; Morecambe 111; Portsmouth 203; Scotland

122, 125, 126, 134, 135, 142, Forth and Tay 143, 144, 151, 157, 161; Tilbury to Gravesend 187; Woolwich 16
ferries and steamers, in competition with railways 13, 95, 103, 187, 241 *see also* docks; ports
Ferryport 126
Field, Horace (arch.) 41
Fife 151-7, 161
Findhorn River viaduct, Tomatin **173**
Findhorn Viaduct, Forres **165**
fire *219*; *see also* accidents (fire)
Firsby 24
Fishguard & Goodwick 244
Fishguard Harbour 222, **244**
Flanagan, Terence (eng.) 112
Folkestone **186**; Round Down Cliff 193
Foord Viaduct, Folkestone **186**
footbridges 216; Appleby 114; Dewsbury 34; Hungerford Bridge 179; Leslie Viaduct 152; New Mills Newtown 101; Redland 233; Speymouth Viaduct 166; Teviot Viaduct 123; Wall at Head of Lion Well Wynd 148
Foregate Street bridge, Worcester **223**
Forfar: line 161; Arbroath & Forfar Railway 158, 161
Forman, Charles de Neuville **136**
Forman & McCall, Glasgow **136**, 172
Forres **165**; line 158, 163
Forsinard 173
Forsyth, J. C. (eng.) 97
Fort Matilda **130**
Fort William 172; lines 136, 172
Forteviot 149
Forth Bridge (earliest steel underbridge *and* earliest steel viaduct, 1890) 143, **144**, 185, *189*
Forth Bridge begun by Bouch 144, 157
Foster, John, Jnr. (eng.) 105
Fowler, Henry (eng.) 69
Fowler, Sir John (eng.) 15, 30, 32, 90, 99, 144, 184, **185**, 216; 'Fowler's Ghost', fireless locomotive 185
Fox, Sir Douglas, and partners 39, 60, 221
Fox, Francis (arch.) 60, 228, 235, 238; with Sir Douglas 94
Foxcote Manor, at Oswestry *92*
Fox's Wood tunnel, Bristol **233**
Franklin, Benjamin: house 119
Freeman, Daniel (arch.) 241
freight 11, 48, 69, 101, 124, 244; agriculture and livestock *48*, 95, *112*, 133-4, 135, 211, 244; beer 62, 63; coal 12, 61, 73, 90, 94, 107, 124, 135, 143, 212, 221, 242, 243; cotton 102, 103-4; fish 11, 115, 164, 166, 171; gun-powder works 117; iron 117, 118, 124, 135, 243; mail 118, 164; minerals 12, 69, 145, 243, *see also* coal *above*; paper and linen 152; power station material 242; shipbuilding 124, 129; stone 95; track ballast 239; whisky 133, 146; wool 34-5; *see also* ferries; ports; warehouses
Friargate Bridge, Derby **79**
Friog Rocks **92-3**
Fripp, S. C. (arch.) 228
Frith, William (artist) 153
Frome (earliest through trainshed *still in use* – with Newcastle Central – *and* earliest wooden trainshed 1850) **236**

Furness & Midland Joint Line 108
Furness Railway *47*, 108, *110*, **114**, 116, 118

G

Galbraith, W. R. (eng.) 182, 209, 239, 240
Galloway: Dumfries and Galloway 124-5
gaol: old gaol entrance, Bristol **233**
Gardener, R.B. (arch.) 188
Gardiner, John (eng.) 242
Garelochhead 172
Garroch Viaduct, Maxwelltown **125**
Garsdale 114
Garston & Liverpool Railway 106
gas works tunnels, Kings Cross 15
Gatehead, Strathclyde **130**
Gatehouse of Fleet *83*, **125**
'Gates of Jerusalem' (entrance to Shugborough tunnel) 87
Gateshead, Tyne & Wear 12, **44-9**
gauge, gauge war 73, 231, 237, 241, 245, 246; Broad Gauge Transhipment Shed, Didcot 218
Gaunless Bridge (earliest large metal bridge in the world, 1825) 46
Gauxholme Viaduct (earliest iron underbridge, 1840) *83*, **108**
Gelt Viaduct 54
Giles, Francis (eng.) 54
Gilmour Street, Paisley **137**
Girvan: lines 135, 139
Girvan & Portpatrick Railway 138
Gladstone, William Ewart (P.M.): opened Hawarden swing bridge 94
Glasgow **130-4**; Bridge Street 126, 130; Central 124, 130, **131**, *132*, 142; St. Rollox Works 124; South Side 136; tunnel mouth, Buchanan Street 149-50; *see also* Edinburgh & Glasgow Railway
Glasgow & Paisley Joint Railway 133, 137
Glasgow & South Western Railway 57, 121, 122, 125, 132-3, **135**, 138-9; bridges **124**, 139; hotels 131, 139; stations 116, 125, 139, 142
Glasgow Barrhead & Kilmarnock Joint Railway 138
Glasgow Central Railway 130, 131, 133, 136
Glasgow City & District Railway 132
Glasgow Dumfries & Carlisle Railway 124, 125
Glasgow Museum 163, 171
Glasgow Paisley & Ardrossan Canal 137
Glasgow Paisley & Greenock Railway: underbridges 137
Glasgow Paisley Kilmarnock & Ayr Railway 134, 135, 136, 137
Gledholt (*or* Paddock) Tunnels **35**
Glen Falloch: viaduct 172
Glencorse Viaduct **148**
Glendon & Rushton **68**
Gleneagles (*formerly* Crieff Junction) **161**
Glenesk Viaduct, Dalkeith **143**
Glenfinnan Viaduct (earliest concrete viaduct, 1901) **169**, 172
Glenogle 126; viaduct **150**
glossary of terms 246-8
Glossop **79**

Gloucestershire 224; lines 234, 240
Gobowen **90**
Godalming **199**
Goddard, Henry (arch.) 19
gold: in Talerddig Cutting 93
Goldilea Viaduct, Maxwelltown **125**
Golspie **169**
Gooch, Sir Daniel 222, 231
Gooch, Thomas L. (eng.) 34, 108
goods sheds *see* warehouses
goods stations: Bishopsgate (*formerly* Shoreditch) 13; Perth 163
Goodwick (Fishguard & Goodwick) 244
Gordon, R. (eng. & contractor) 243
Gordon, Robert (squire of Kemble) 224
Gosport **203**
Govan: Polloc & Govan Railway 136
Gourock Pier 130, **134**
gradients, exceptional: atmospheric trains (Okehampton *and* Starcross pumping station) 239; Basingstoke to Winchester (Micheldever) 204; Wales 243
Graham, George (eng.) 158
Grainger, Thomas (eng.) 33, 36, 38, 42, 49; Bouch & Grainger 151; Grainger & Miller: bridges 123, 124, 125, **126**, 134, 135, 136, 137, 147, 148, 149; stations 148; wall 148; *see also* Miller, John
Grampian 164-6
Grand Junction (*later* Grand Union) Canal 215
Grand Junction Railway 72, 97, 119
Granet, Guy **69**
Grange-over-Sands **116**; Grange Hotel *110*, 116
Granton: Edinburgh Leith & Granton Railway 147
Gravesend **187**; line 188
Grayson, G. E. (arch.) 103
Great Central Railway 11, 23, 40, *45*, 60, **61**, 74, 98, 243
Great Chesterford **17**
Great Eastern Hotel, Liverpool Street 15, 140
Great Eastern Railway 11-12, 13, 15-16, 17, 19, 20, 21, 22, **24**, 140, 191
Great Haywood: bridges **87**, *88*
Great Malvern *202*, **222**
Great North of England Railway 38
Great North of Scotland Railway 121-2, 135, 164, 165, 166, **171**
Great Northern Hotel, Kings Cross 14, *140*
Great Northern Railway 11, 12, 18, **21**, 37, 40, 74, 99, *127*, *140*; bridges 20, 79, 80, 143; Cubitt's work *140*, **193**; locomotives 21, *128*, 236; signals 191; stations 14-15, 19, 20, 23, 24; warehouse 99
Great Southern & Western Railway, Ireland 244
'Great Way Round' (nickname of the GWR) 234
Great Western & Brentford Railway 215
Great Western Hotel, Taunton 236
Great Western Railway 15, *48*, **90**, 94, 96, 97, 211, 216, *219*, **222**, 233, 242, 243; bridges 90, 213, 216, 217, 218, 223, 245, (Sonning Cutting, the only timber bridge) 240; Didcot Railway Centre,

with Broad Gauge Transhipment Shed *48*, 218; harbour work 222, 233, 242, 244; hotels 140, *141*, 213-4, 236, 239, 241; locomotives *92*, 211, 222, 226, 236; railcars 224; share certificate *222*; stations 66-7, 68, 92, 97, 207, 208, 213-37 *passim*, 242, 245; subsidiary companies 97, 208, 222, 225, 234, 236, 238, 241, 245; superintendent's house 223; Swindon, railway village 212, 226; tunnels 224, 233, 234; uniform buttons *220*; war memorial 214-5
Great Western Railway Museum, Swindon 226
Great Western Royal Hotel, Paddington 140, **213-4**
Great Western through Bath **227**
Greater Manchester 98-101
Green, Benjamin (arch.) 50, 51, 53, 54
Green, John (arch.) 50
Green, W. Curtis (arch.) 36
Green Park (*formerly* Queen Square) station, Bath **227**
Greene, Richard (artist) 88
Greenesfield Station Hotel, Gateshead **44-9**
Greenloaning 149
Greenock: Fort Matilda 130; line 137
Greenodd 117
Greenwich **181**, 182
Gresley, Sir Nigel (loco. eng.) 21, *127*
Grimsby 11, **31**
Grissell, Thomas (landowner) 199, 200
Grosvenor Hotel, Victoria, London **184**
Grouping (1923) 8, 11, 57, 121-2, 175-6, 210-11; effects (companies) 13, 17, 40, 92, 118, 161, 222, 243, (stations) 184, 188
Guild Street, Aberdeen 164
Guthrie Castle **161**
Gwent 242
Gwynedd 96

H

Haddiscoe Junction, Norfolk 191
Hadfield 32, **98**
Hajwa, Marian 229
Hale **98**
Halifax 27, **34**
halts and other stopping places: Darlington (Stockton & Darlington Railway) 42; Hellifield 113; Letchworth 20; Stroud (Stonehouse to Chalford line) for railcars 224; Sugar Loaf tunnel signal box 245
Haltwhistle: signal box 191; water tower and water cranes 54, *55*
Hambledon, Viscount 239
Hamilton, Lord Claud *and* Hamilton Hall, Great Eastern Hotel, Liverpool Street 15, 16
Hamilton *120*, **134**
Hamilton Square, Birkenhead **103**
Hamlyn, William H. (arch.) 36, 59, 72
Hampshire 203-6
Hampton Court **182**
Hamworthy Junction to Dorchester line 209
Handyside (Andrew) & Co., Derby 41, 99, 102

Hannaford, J. R. (arch.) 236
Hanwell **213**, 215, 218
harbours *see* ports and harbours
Hardwick, P. C. (arch.) 213-4
Hardwick, Philip (arch.) 27, 72
Harringworth Viaduct **68-9**
Harrison, T. E. (eng.) 43, 44, 50
Harrogate **37**
Harrow & Wealdstone **60**
Hartlepool 185
Hartley, Jesse (eng.) 104
Harwich 11, 15
Haslemere 191
Hassocks 198
Hastings **196**; line 195, 196
Hatch End **60**
Hattersley, Richard (contractor) 244
Hatton incline, Newtyle 162
Haugh Head Viaduct 123
Haverthwaite **116-7**
Hawarden swing bridge **94**
Hawick: viaduct 143, 149
Hawkshaw, Sir John (eng.) 35, 95, 99, 101, 178, 179, 231, **234**
Hayle Railway 241
Haymarket, Edinburgh **126**
Haywards Heath 195, 196
Head, Sir George 107
Heal, A. V. (arch.) 59
Healey Dell Viaduct **99**
Heaton Norris goods warehouse **102-3**
Hebden Bridge **34**
Heighington (*formerly* Aycliffe Lane Crossing; earliest small station – with Stockton-on-Tees – 1825) **44**
Heiton, Andrew (arch.) 149, 150, 160
Helensburgh: line 136
Helensburgh Upper 172
Hellifield 27, *28*, **113**
Helmsdale 169
Helpston goods shed **18**
Helsby **97**
Hengoed Viaduct **243**
Hereford **222**, *223*, 242; *see also* Shrewsbury & Hereford Railway
Hereford and Worcester 222-3; lines 90
Hermitage Road Bridge and Tunnel, Dunkeld **160**
Herne Hill **182**
Hertford East **19-20**
Hertfordshire, Eastern Region 19-20; London Midland Region 64
Hewison, Charles A. (eng.) 51
Heyford **221**
High Level Bridge, Newcastle-upon-Tyne *48*, 49-50, 73
Higham Tunnel, Strood **188**
Highland 166-73
Highland Railway **163**, 170, 171; bridges 162, 173; Direct Line to Inverness 158, 163, 165, 166-7, 168, 170; engine shed, Elgin 165; signal box 191, stations 158, 163, 164-5, 167, 168, 171, 172
Hillhouse (*or* Huddersfield) Viaduct **35**
Hincaster Tunnel **117**
Hine, Thomas (arch.) 74
Historic Buildings Council 9, 27, 104; *see also* Listed Buildings
Holden, Charles (arch.) 194
Holden, James (superintendent) 24
'Holiday line' (LSWR) 203

Holker Hall, Cark 115
Holyhead **95**; Chester & Holyhead Railway 57, 85, 95, 96, 118
Holywell Junction 85, **95**
Hopkins Gilkes, Middlesbrough (bridge builders) 102
Horsburgh Viaduct, near Innerleithen 123
horses: horse-drawn railways and tramways 39, *48*, 73, 130, 164, 206; horse-drawn road vehicles 96, 107, 164, 195, 196, 221, 224; horses as freight *112*, 133-4, 211
Horseshoe Bend, Tyndrum *172*
Horsforth, Leeds 119
Horsley, Gerald (arch.) 60
Horsted Keynes **196**
Horwich 99
Hotel Curve, Kings Cross tunnel 14-15
Hotel Grand Central, Marylebone 15, 60
hotels **140-1**; Midland Hotel, Derby (earliest, 1840), 78-79; hotels of particular interest: Great Eastern Hotel, Liverpool Street 15, 140; Great Northern Hotel, Kings Cross 14, *140*; Great Western Royal Hotel, Paddington 140, 213-4; Manor House Hotel, Moretonhampstead 239; Midland Grand Hotel, St. Pancras 62-3, 140, *141*; Midland Hotel, Derby 78-9, 101; North Western Hotel, Liverpool 105; Queens Hotel, Leeds 36; Royal Station Hotel, Newcastle-on-Tyne 49, *141*; Royal Station Hotel, York 40, 140; York Old Station Hotel 40, 41
houses: acquired properties, 36 Craven Street (Benjamin Franklin's house) *and* 62 and 66 Grove Park Terrace, London 119; Aigburth 106; Burgess Hill 198; Clayton Tunnel 198; Colchester St. Botolphs 17; Corbridge 54; East Linton 145; Haverthwaite 117; Heighington 44; Manchester Liverpool Road 104; Mitcham 183; St. Germains, Longniddry 148; St. Michael's, Liverpool 106; Selby 39; Staines West 217; Steventon 221; Swindon 226; *see also* stately homes
Howard, Ebenezer: Letchworth 20
Howard, Henry: inscription 54
Hownes Gill Viaduct **42**, 157
Huddersfield *11*, **34-5**
Huddersfield & Dewsbury Railway 34
Huddersfield & Manchester Railway & Canal Company 34, 103
Hudson, George 11, 24, **38**, 39, 43, 50 (the 'Railway King'), 76, 123
Hudson House, York 41
Hughes, George (eng.) 101
Huish, Capt. Mark 76
Hull **31**, 43
Hull & Barnsley Railway 11
Hull & Selby Railway 39
Humberside 30-1
Hungerford Bridge, Charing Cross **179**
Hunt, H. A. (arch.) 89
Hunt, William (eng.) 98, 101
Huntingdon **19**
Hunts Cross 105
Hurlford Viaduct **134**
Hurst, William (arch.) 24
Huskisson Memorial, Newton-le-Willows **104**

I

Ilkeston **80**
Ilkley **35**
Immingham 61
Imperial Hotel, Great Malvern 222
Ince 97
Ingatestone **17**
Inglis, J. C. (eng.) 244
Innerleithen 123
Instow 191
Inver Viaduct, Dunkeld **160**
Invergordon: line 166-7
Inverkeithing: line 144
Inverness **170**; Direct Line 158, 163, 165, 166-7, 168, 170; Lochgorm Works 165, 170; Welsh's Bridge signal box 191
Inverness & Aberdeen Junction Railway 158, 165, 166-7, *167*, 170, 171, 173
Inverness & Nairn Railway 170, 171
Inverness & Perth Junction Railway 158, 159, 160, 161, 163, 167, 170, 171, *172*
Inverness & Ross-shire Railway 166-7, 168, 170
Invershin 163, 173; Oykel Viaduct **170**
Invertiel Viaduct, Kirkcaldy 151
Ipswich **21**
Ipswich & Bury Railway 20, 22
Ireland 6, 95; Cork 245, Rosslare 242, 244, 245
iron bridges, and change to wrought-iron 123 (Border Viaducts), 158 (Aberdalgie), 183 (Richmond), *201*; companies: Butlers' Stanningley Foundry, Leeds 108; Andrew Handyside & Co., Derby 41, 99, 102; Hopkins Gilkes, Middlesbrough 102
iron decoration and detail 201
Irvine **134**
Isle of Wight 203, 206, *219*
Isle of Wight Railway 206
Ivatt, H. A. (loco. eng.) 21, *128*
Ivybridge *240*

J

Jackson (contractor) 16
Jacomb-Hood, J. W. 183, 184
Jagger, C. S. (sculptor) 214-5
'Jazz' suburban service (GER) 12, 24
Jee, Alfred S. (eng.) 35, 103
Jesmond, Blyth & Tyne **50**; Tyne & Wear Metro 50
Jessop, Josias 73
Jessop, William (eng.) 53, 62, 94
Johnson, Richard (eng.) 80
Johnson, Thomas (arch.) 88
Johnston, R. E. (arch.) 97, 222
Jones, David (loco. eng.) 163

K

Kaukas, Bernard 4, 46; *The Splendours and Miseries of British Rail's Architectural Heritage* 25-8
Kay, Stanley R. (eng.) 32
Keith: line 171
Keithley & Worth Valley Railway *219*
Kelso: line 123

Kelvinside, Glasgow 130, **133**
Kemble **224**
Kendal 117
Kendall, H. E. (arch.) 14
Kenley (*originally* Coulsdon) **200**
Keswick *110*, **117**
Kettering **69**, 191
Kew Railway Bridge **182**
Keymer Junction 207
Kielder Viaduct **53**
Kilby Bridge 191
Kildary 166, **170-1**
Killiecrankie **161**
Kilmarnock (earliest medium station, 1843) **135**; lines 135, 138; *see also* Glasgow Paisley Kilmarnock & Ayr Railway)
Kilmarnock & Troon Railway 130
Kilmaurs 138
Kilsby Tunnel *11*, **69**, 73, 103, 224
Kincardine Glen Viaduct, Blackford **158**
Kinclair Viaduct, Pinmore **138**
King Edward Bridge, Newcastle-on-Tyne *52*
Kinghorn **151**
Kings Cross (earliest large terminus station, 1852) **14-15**, 150 (hotel only)
Kings Mill Viaduct, Mansfield **73**
Kingston (*now called* Surbiton) 183
Kingussie **171**
Kinnaber Junction 164
Kinnacher Junction 164
Kirkby Stephen: line 117
Kirkcaldy: Invertiel Viaduct **151**
Kirkintilloc 126
Kirkstall Road viaduct, Leeds **36**
Kirtlebridge: Kirtlewater viaduct **125**
Kirtley, Matthew (loco. superintendent) 79
Kirtley, William (loco. eng.) 185
Knaresborough Viaduct **38**, *153*
Knebworth **20**
Knighton **91**
Knighton Railway 91
Knowles, J. T. (arch.) 184
Knucklas Viaduct **91**
Kyle of Lochalsh: line 168

L

Ladybank **152**
Laigh Milton Mill (earliest tramway viaduct) **130**
Lairg 173
Lakeside & Haverthwaite Railway 116-7
Lambert, A. E. (arch.) 74
Lambley Viaduct *53*, 54
Lanarkshire & Dunbartonshire Railway 129, 130
Lancashire 107-13
Lancashire & Yorkshire Railway (LYR) 32, 40, 57, **101**, 113; bridges and viaducts 99, 101, 102; coat of arms *220*; stations 34-5, 37, 98, 100, 105-6, 107, 112
Lancaster **108**, 111
Lancaster & Carlisle Railway 97, 108, 116, 117, 118, 124, 157
Lancaster & Preston Junction Railway 108
Landmann, Col. George Thomas (eng.) 181

Landore: one of Brunel's timber viaducts 240
Langholm: Tarrasfoot Viaduct **125**
Larbert 149, **150**
Largo Viaduct **152**
Larpool (or Esk Valley) Viaduct **39**
Lasswade **148**
Lawley Street, Birmingham 72
'The Lawn', Paddington 214
Lawrie, see Matthews & Lawrie (archs.)
Laws, W. G. (eng.) 50
Lea Hall **72**
Leaderfoot (or Drygrange) Viaduct 123
Leadhills **136**
Leadhills & Wanlockhead Light Railway 136
Leamington Spa **66-7**
Leather, J. T. (eng.) 185
Leatherhead **200**
Leaton 90
Leeds **36**, 119; Leeds City station 36; New station 36, 43; Queens Hotel **36**; lines to Leeds **101**, 108, 135: see also Manchester & Leeds Railway
Leeds & Selby Railway 39
Leeds & Thirsk Railway 33, 36, 37, 38
Leeds Dewsbury & Manchester Railway 35
Leeds Northern Railway 42, 126
Leeming, Frank (eng.) 242
Leicester & Swannington Railway 115
Leicester London Road **70**, *201*
Leicestershire 70-1
Leighton Buzzard **64**, *65*
Leith 147
Leith Central, Edinburgh **147**
Leslie Railway: viaducts 152
Leslie Viaduct **152**
Letchworth **20**
level crossings 119; St. Germains keeper's house 148
Lewes **196**; lines 195, 196, 207
Lewes Road viaduct, Brighton **195**
Lichfield, Earl of 86-7
Lichfield **88**
Lichfield Drive bridge, Colwich **86-7**
Liddell, Charles (eng.) 115, 242, 243
Lidfort: line 239
lifts *141*, 178
lighthouse, Holyhead 95
lighting 72; gas for tunnel 198; lamp platforms 214
Lime Street, Liverpool 105, 117
Lincoln **23-4**
Lincolnshire 23-9
Linhouse Water: viaducts **148**
Linlithgow **148**, *121*
Linslade Tunnel, Leighton Buzzard **64**, *65*
Liphook **204**
Listed Buildings 9, 26-8; complete list 249-53; Grade I and Grade A (for others see individual entries): Grade I – Birmingham Curzon Street 72; Bristol Temple Meads 228; 36 Craven Street, Charing Cross 119; High Level bridge, Newcastle-on-Tyne 49-50; Huddersfield 34; Kings Cross 14-15; Liverpool Road, Manchester 104; Paddington 213-5; refectory pulpit, Shrewsbury Abbey 91; Royal Albert Bridge, Saltash

192, 241; Royal Border Bridge, Berwick-on-Tweed 52, *127*; St. Pancras (part Grade I) 62; Wharncliffe Viaduct, Hanwell 213; Grade A (Scotland) – Almond Viaduct, Ratho 149; Avon Viaduct, Linlithgow *121*, 148; Forth Bridge 144, *189*; Glenfinnan Viaduct 169; Inverness, offices 170; Ladybank (part Grade A) 152; Midcalder, viaducts over Linhouse Water 148; Nairn Viaduct, Culloden Moor 168; viaduct over Newbridge to Broxburn Road, Ratho 149
'Little' North Western Railway 111
Little Sutton 97
Littleborough **99**
Liverpool **104, 105-6**, 222; Central 99, 106; Edge Hill *26*, 104, *219*; Exchange **105-6**; Lime Street **105**, 117; lines 97, 101, 103
Liverpool & Manchester Railway 9, 57, 65, 97, 101, 103, **104**, 107, 118, 180
Liverpool Ormskirk & Preston Railway 112
Liverpool Road, Manchester (oldest station in the world; earliest small terminus station, *and* earliest goods shed, 1830) 27, 104
Liverpool Street *frontisp.*, 13, **15-16**, 140; 'Jazz' trains 12, 24
Livock, J. W. (arch.) 8, 19, 66, 86
Llandrindod Wells **244**
Llanfair 92
Llangollen: line 94
Llanidloes **92**
Lledr Viaduct (Cethyn's Bridge), Betws-y-Coed **96**
Lloyd, Henry (arch.) 238
Lochailort **171**, 172
Loch Nan Uamh Viaduct, Lochailort **171**
Lochy Viaduct, Fort William 172
Locke, Joseph 8-9, **97**, 103, 108, 119, **124**, 125, 147, 148, 149, 150, 166, 203; Locke & Errington 136, 157, 158, 204
Lockwood Tunnel, Huddersfield 35
Lockwood Viaduct, Huddersfield **35**, *37*
locomotive sheds: Derby (earliest, c. 1840) 79; Arbroath 158, 161; Aviemore 165, **167**; Blair Atholl 158, 165; Camden Roundhouse **59**; Carnforth 108; Derby Roundhouse 79; Elgin 165; St. Blazey Engine Shed, Par 240
locomotive works: Ashford 185; Battersea, Longhedge Works 185; Brighton 207; Crewe 36, 118; Doncaster Plant 21; Eastleigh 203; Swindon 212, 226
locomotives and rolling stock 9, 12, *14*, **45-8**, *52, 84, 93, 109, 113*, 135, 241; Brunel's 246; firebox reduced 243; fireless 185; Inter City 125s 15, *40*; livery (Midland Railway) 69; posters and postcards **127-8**; private trains 168-9; Pullmans 12, 113, 207; restaurants, buffets 173, 243; sleeping cars 171; slip carriages 195; span failure (two locomotives) 242; speeds (*City of Truro*) *222*; (Friog Rocks limit) 92-3, (*Mallard*) 21; 'sweedy' 11; tank *45*, 207, 243; Wansford collection of foreign steam locomotives 19; *see also* individual com-

panies
locomotives, named: *Agenoria* 180; *Blackmore Vale 45*; *Bonnie Prince Charlie 48*; *Brighton Belle* (formerly *Southern Belle*) 194, 207; *Butler Henderson* 61; *City Limited* 194, 195, 207; *City of Truro 222*; *City of Wells 40*; *Coronation* 118, *127*; *Decapod* 24; *Derwent 42*; *Earl of Berkeley 48*; *Evening Star* 212; *Foxcote Manor 92*; *Gladstone* 207; *Gordon Highlander* 171; *Hardy* 113; *Ivanhoe* 144; *Locomotion* 42, 44; *Mallard* 21; *Maude* 143; *North Star* 226; 'Old Coppernob' *47*; *Rocket* 104; *Royal Scot* 59; *Seahorse* 116; *Sultan* 153; *Whimple 109*
Logierait Viaduct **162**
London, *for* individual stations *see under* station names
London, Eastern Region 13-16
London, London Midland Region 59-64, 137
London, Southern Region 177-85
London, Western Region 213-5
London: acquired properties 119
London & Birmingham Railway 19, 59, 61, 64, 65, **66**, 69, 72, **73**, 137
London & Blackwall Railway 13, 16
London & Brighton Railway *175*, 180, 185, 194, 197, 198
London & Croydon Railway 14, 177
London & Greenwich Railway 181, 182
London & North Eastern Railway (LNER) 10, 13, 17, 20, 21, 36, 52-3, 60, 127; first railway museum at York 46; locomotives 21, 118, 127, 144; longest through service in Britain 171; uniform buttons *219*
London & North Western Railway (LNWR) 57, **90**, **91**, **96**, 97, **118**, 121, 124, 243, 244, 245; bridges 96, 97, 101, 118, 221; 'club' carriages 101; competition 61, 76, 94, 96; locomotive shed 59; mementos *127, 128, 220*; port 95; 'Premier Line' 59, 118; royal saloon *46, 47*; signal boxes 191; stations 34, 35, 36, 60, 66, 67, 72, 76, 105, 111, 117, 221, 242, 244, (joint stations) 108, 112, 116, 222; warehouse 102
London & South Western Railway (LSWR) *175*, 200, **203**, 204, 208, 239; acquired houses 119; bridges 182, 183, 203, 239; competition 216, 236; hotel (*now* South Western House) 205; pier and station 206; signal boxes 191; stations 117, 177, 182, 184, 199, 203, 204, 208, 209, 236, 237; war memorial 184
London & Southampton Railway 97, 117, 203, 206
London Bridge 178, 179, 181, **182**, 187, 195
London Brighton & South Coast Railway (LBSCR; 'The Brighton') *47*, 175, 180, 185, 196, 200, 206, **207**; bridges 177, 184, 195; luggage label 203; share certificate 207; signal boxes 191; stations 180, 181, 183, 188, 195, 196, 198, 199, 200; trainshed *128*, 194
London Chatham & Dover Railway 178, 180, 182, 184, 185
London Midland & Scottish Railway (LMS) 13, 36, 57, 59, 68, 72, 161, *219*;

locomotives *77, 78, 113*
London Midland Region 56-118; listed properties 250-1
London Road bridge, Bath 227
London Road High Level, Nottingham 74
London Road Low Level, Nottingham **74**
London Road, Brighton 195
London Road, Leicester 70, *201*
London Road viaduct, Brighton 176, **195**
London Tilbury & Southend Railway 13, 187
Longniddry **148**
Longport **88**
Longwood Viaduct, Huddersfield **35**
Lord Warden Hotel (*now* Southern House), Dover 186
Lossiemouth 171
Lothian 143-5
Lothian Bridge, Newtongrange **149**
Loughborough *45*, 61, **71**
Louth **24**
Lower Bristol Road viaduct and bridge, Bath 227
Lowestoft 11
luggage 45; Eastleigh 203; Hebden Bridge 34, luggage label tickets *203, 222*
Lullingstone Castle *and* Roman Villa 186
Lutyens, Sir Edwin 36, 41
Lyne Viaduct 123
Lynn & Ely Railway 22
Lynton 237
Lynton & Barnstaple Railway 237

M

McAlpine, Sir Robert (& Sons, engs.) 136, 171
McCall *see* Forman & McCall
McDonald, J. A. 75, 76, 103
McFarlane, G. (eng.) 164
McIntosh, John F. (loco. eng.) 124
McKay, John (builder) 54
McKie, Helen (artist) *156*
Machynlleth **93**
Madame Tussaud's Royalty and Railways Exhibition, Windsor Central 217
Maidenhead Bridge: **216**
Maidens & Dunure Light Railway 139
Makeny Road bridge, Duffield **79**
Maldon East **17-18**
Mallaig 172; line 122
Malvern *202*, 222
Manchester, Greater 98-101, 104
Manchester (and Salford) **99-101**, 104, *201, 222*; Manchester Central 99; Manchester Liverpool Road (oldest station in the world, earliest small terminus station, and earliest goods shed, 1830) 27, **104**; Manchester Victoria *26, 28*, 100-1; Huddersfield & Manchester Railway & Canal Company 34, 103; *see also* Liverpool & Manchester Railway
Manchester & Birmingham Railway 102
Manchester & Leeds Railway 34, 35, 36, 99, **108**, 234
Manchester Buxton Matlock & Midlands Junction Railway 77, 85
Manchester Sheffield & Lincolnshire Railway (MSLR) 11, 23, 30, 32, 61, 94,

99, 185; London Extension 61
Manor House Hotel, Moretonhampstead **239**
Mansfield **73**
Mansfield & Pinxton Railway 73
Manson, James (loco. eng.) 135, **171**
Manvers Street, Bath, *and* Lord Manvers 227
Margate Sands 188
Margate West 188
Margery, P. J. (eng.) 238
Marindin, Maj. (Inspector) 239
Market Harborough **71**
Markinch **152**
Marks Tey 16
Marochetti, Carlo: statue of Robert Stephenson 59
Marsh, Douglas Earle (loco. eng.) 207
Marshalls Cross Road bridge, St. Helens 107
Marykirk **166**
Marylebone 15, **60**, *61*
Maryport & Carlisle Railway 114, 116
Mathieson, Donald (eng.) 131, 142, 161
Matlock 77, 85
Matlock Bath **80**
Matthews & Lawrie (archs.) 170
Mauchline **136**
Maunsell, R. E. L. 185
Mawddach (*or* Barmouth) Viaduct 26, **96**
Maxwelltown **125**
Maze Hill: line 181
Mechanics' Institutes: at Horwich 99; at Swindon 226
Meek, Sturges (eng.) 101, 102, 112
Melbury House, Marylebone 60
Meldon Viaduct, Okehampton (earliest iron viaduct) **239**
memorials and monuments: Bramhope (Tunnel) Memorial in Otley Churchyard 33; Chadwell Heath Coal Dues Obelisk 13; Huskisson Memorial 104; *see also* Ancient Monuments; war memorials
Menai Bridge (Britannia tubular bridge) 26, 73, **95**, *128*
Mersey Railway 103
Merseyrail: Liverpool suburban system 105, 106, 112
Merseyside 28, 103-7
Merthyr Tredegar & Abergavenny Railway 242; Brecon & Merthyr Railway 243
Metropolitan Railway 15, 61, 63, 136, 214, *220*; London Transport's Circle Line 14, 185
Micheldever (*formerly* Andover Road) 203, **204**
Mid-Wales Railway 92
Midcalder: viaducts **148**
Middle Gelt Viaduct (earliest skew viaduct, 1835) 54
Middlesbrough **41**, 43; line 40
Midland Counties Railway 65, 67, 75, 78
Midland Grand Hotel, St. Pancras 62-3, 140, *141*
Midland Great Western Railway 15
Midland Hotel, Bradford Forster Square 33
Midland Hotel, Derby (earliest hotel, 1840) **78-9**, 101

Midland Hotel, Manchester **99-100**
Midland Railway 40, 57, 61, *63*, **69**, 85, 101, 125, 143, 233; bridges 70; competition 74-5, 76, 113, 114; hotel 106; locomotive works offices, Derby 79; Settle & Carlisle Line 112, **113, 114**; signal boxes 191; standard characteristics **114**; stations 18, 23, 24, *27*, 32, 62, 68-77 *passim*, 80, 99, 111, 113, 116, 227, 228; symbol, the wyvern 79, 113, *220*; tunnels 32, 75, 103; warehouse 18
Midland Railway Centre, near Ripley, Derbyshire 69
Midland station, Nottingham **74-5**
Midland station, Sheffield **32**
Milford, Salisbury 208
Milford Tunnel, Belper 75
Mill Lane bridge, Great Haywood **87,** *88*
Millbrook **66**
Miller, James (arch.) 130, **131**, 134, 137, 139, 142, 150, 161
Miller, John **126**, 143, 145, 146, 149; *see also* Grainger, Thomas
Mills, Walter (arch.) 239
Milngavie **136**
Minories (original terminus of Fenchurch Street) 13, 16
Mitcham **183**
Mitchell, Arnold (arch.) 112
Mitchell, John (eng., Joseph's father) 170
Mitchell, Joseph (eng.) 122, 158, 159, 160, 161, 162, **163**, 165, 167, 168, **170**, 172
Mocatta, David (arch.) 194, 195, 197, 198
Monkland & Kirkintilloc Railway 126
Monkwearmouth, Sunderland **50-1**
Monmouth Road (*now* Abergavenny) 242
Monsal Dale Viaduct **80-5**
Montgomerie Policies: bridge **138-9**
Montrose & Bervie Railway 162
monuments *see* memorials and monuments
Moor of Rannoch: viaduct 172
Moore, Thomas (arch.) 50
Moorgate 15
Moorsom, Capt. William S. (eng.) 209
Morar Viaduct (earliest concrete underbridge, 1901) **171**, 172
Morecambe **111**; Morecambe Bay *110*
Moretonhampstead: Manor House Hotel **239**
Morgan, Sir Charles L. (eng.) 184
Mortimer 208, **216**, 218, 225
Motherwell **136**
Moulsford Viaduct, Cholsey **218**
'Mugby Junction' (Dickens) 67
museums and exhibitions 45-8, **219-20**; Great Western Railway Museum, Swindon 226; Midland Railway Centre, near Ripley, Derbyshire 69; Monkwearmouth 51; National Railway Museum, York **45-8**, 50, 52, 180, 185, 203, 207; North Road Station Museum, Darlington 42; North West Museum of Science and Industry, Liverpool Road, Manchester 104; 'Royalty and Railways', Windsor Central 217; Science Museum, London 191; Steamtown, Carnforth 108
Myres, T. W. (arch.) 196
Mytholmroyd **36**

N

Nairn 170, 171, **172**
Nairn Viaduct, Culloden Moor **168**
naming of stations 16, 23, 177; *see also* stately homes
Nasmyth, James: steam hammer 49
National Railway Museum, York **45-8,** 50, 52, 180, 185, 203, 207, *220*
National Trust for Scotland: Hermitage, Dunkeld 160
nationalisation: effects 8, 90, 169; *see also* British Rail
'Native village', at Kings Cross 14
Neath & Brecon Railway 243
Needham Market **22**
Neidpath Viaduct 123
Neilston: line 138
Nelson 34
Nene Valley Railway 19
Netley 199
New Cross Gate, London 187
New Mills, Newtown: footbridge **101**
New Road viaduct, Chippenham **225**
New station, Leeds 36, 43
New Street bridge, St. Helens 107
New Street, Birmingham 72
Newark Castle **23**
Newbridge Road bridge, Ambergate 75
Newbridge to Broxburn Road, Ratho: viaduct 149
Newcastle & Berwick Railway 51, 53; *see also* York Newcastle & Berwick Railway
Newcastle & Carlisle Railway 12, *53,* **54-5,** 116, 191
Newcastle & North Shields Railway 50, 51
Newcastle-upon-Tyne **49-50,** 243; Central station (earliest arched and – with Frome – earliest through trainshed still in use, 1850) *first endpaper,* 11, 7, 43, 49, 213; High Level bridge *48,* 49-50, 73; Jesmond 50; Ouseburn *and* Willington Dene Viaducts 50; Railway Arch in Dean Street 50; Royal Station Hotel 49, *141*
Newhaven: line 196, 207
Newlay Lane iron bridge, Horsforth 119
Newnes, Sir George 237
Newport: one of Brunel's timber viaducts 240
Newport Abergavenny & Hereford Railway 242
Newton Abbot 191; lines 239, 240
Newtongrange **149**
Newton-le-Willows: Huskisson Memorial **104**
Newtonmore **172**
Newtown: New Mills footbridge **101**
Newtown & Machynlleth Railway 93; *see also* Oswestry & Newtown Railway 92
Newtyle Old station (earliest through trainshed, 1836) **162**
Nicholson, Peter (eng.) 53
Nine Arches Viaduct, Tredegar **242**
Nine Elms, London 117, 184, 205
Norfolk, Duke of: private line at Glossop 79
Norfolk 22-3

Norfolk Railway 22, 23, 24
North Bridge, Edinburgh 146
North British Hotel, 'The NB', Edinburgh **146**
North British Hotel, Glasgow **132**
North British Railway 121-2, 123, 124, 126, 135, 143, 150, 152, 167, 169, 172; bridges 123, 125, 143, 145, 149, 150; Headquarters 143; hotels 132, 146; level crossing keeper's house 148; signal boxes 191; stations 53, 116, 123, 132, 136, **143,** 145, 146, 147, 158, 162, 164; war memorial 146
North Dulwich **183**
North Eastern Railway 11, 31, 39, 40, 41, **43,** 44, 50, 51, **52,** 116, *141,* 243; war memorial **41**
North Kent Railway (Gravesend to Rochester) 188
North Midland Railway 75, 76, 78, 79, 85
North Pembrokeshire & Fishguard Railway 244
North Road station *and* Museum, Darlington **42**
North Shields 50, 51
North Staffordshire Hotel, Stoke-on-Trent 89
North Staffordshire Railway 86, 88, 89, 97
North Staffordshire Railway (New): preservation group 86
North (*also called* Windsor) station *at* Waterloo 184
North Street bridge, Barrow-on-Soar **70**
North Union Railway 65
North Water Bridge, Tayside **162**
North Water Viaduct, Marykirk **166**
North West Museum of Science and Industry, Liverpool Road, Manchester 104
North Western Hotel, Liverpool 105
North Western Railway, 'Little' 111
North Woolwich **16**
North Yorkshire, Eastern Region 37-41; London Midland Region 113-4
Northampton Castle **70**
Northamptonshire 68-70
Northgate, Newark 23
Northumberland 51-5
Norwich **22,** 137, *202*
Norton, John (arch.) 205
Norwood Junction: bridge collapse 183; line 180
Nottingham **74**
Nottinghamshire, Eastern Region 23; London Midland Region 73-5

O

Oban **126**; Callander & Oban Railway **126,** 150, 163
O'Connor, John: painting of St. Pancras 62, *154*
offices: Bristol (Bristol & Exeter Railway) 228; Derby 79; Dover, Southern House (SR) 186; Eversholt House (LMS) 59; Glasgow (Caledonian Railway) 131, (Glasgow & South Western Railway) 133; Glendon & Rushton, Goods Yard office (Midland Railway) *68*; Hull, Paragon House 31; Inverness (Highland Railway) 170; Marylebone, Melbury

House 60; Paddington (GWR) 213; Southampton, South Western House (LSWR) 205
Okehampton **239**
Old College, Glasgow: booking office 132
Old Cumnock **137**
Old Mill of Keir, Dunblane: tunnel mouth **149-50**
Old stations *see* Burntisland; Elgin; Lancaster; Newtyle; Selby; Tynemouth; Watford; Worthing; York
Oldfield Park 227
Oldham **102**
Olive Mount cutting 104
Orchy Viaduct, Dalmally *126*
Ordish, R. M. (eng.) 62
Ormskirk **112**
Oswestry **92**
Oswestry & Newtown Railway 92
Oswestry Ellesmere & Whitchurch Railway 92
Otley & Ilkley Joint Railway 35
Oughty Bridge **32**
Ouse Viaduct, Balcombe *175,* 176, 180, 197
Ouseburn Viaduct, Newcastle-upon-Tyne **50**
Outram, Benjamin (eng.) 62
Outwood Viaduct, Radcliffe **102**
overseas British engineering: Brassey 119; Caledonian Railway 124; Fowler 185; Hawkshaw 234; Tite 117; Vignoles 65
overseas ideas used in Britain: hotels 146; Pullmans 142
Owen, W. Lancaster (eng.) 242
Oxenhope *219*
Oxford **221**
Oxford Canal 221
Oxford Worcester & Wolverhampton Railway 15, 218
Oxfordshire 218-21
Oykel Viaduct, Invershin **170**

P

Paddington 49, *153,* **213-5,** 222; Brunel's working drawings 229; Paddington Hotel (Great Western Royal Hotel) 140, 213-4
Paddock (*or* Gledholt) Tunnels, Huddersfield 35
Paddock (*or* Gledholt) Viaduct, Huddersfield *11,* **35**
Paget, Cecil 69
Paisley **137**; Glasgow & Paisley Joint Railway 133, 137; Glasgow Paisley Kilmarnock & Ayr Railway 134, 135, 136, 137
Paley, E. G. (arch.) 116; Paley & Austin 118
Pangbourne 218
Par **240**
Paragon House, Hull 31
Park Hotel, Preston **112**, *140*
Parker, J. A. (eng.) 164
Parkside: accident 104
Parrett River bridge, Bridgwater **235**
passengers 11-12; comforts 69, 101; commuters 24, 179, 203, 207; discomforts 15, 24, 103, 104, 132, 143, 146, 164, 207;

INDEX

earliest 42, 118, 181; holiday, tourist traffic *14*, 92, 176, 182, 211-12, (Epsom Downs) 200, (Great Exhibition) 7, (Scotland) 138, 139, 149, (Southern Region, *esp.* South Coast) 16, 30, 39, 41, 101, *110*, 111, 116, 118, 124, 142, 194, 171, 194, 195, 198, 207, 208, spas 76, 80, 222, 244; mementos 219-20; one-sided stations 216; postcards 127-8; postchaise at Box Tunnel 224; public attitude to railways 25, 103, 207; 'The Shell', Glasgow 131; special trains 7, 101, 171, 194, 207; *see also* locomotives and rolling stock

Paterson, Murdoch (eng.) 167, 168, 170, 173; and William, partners to Joseph Mitchell 170

Paxton, Sir Joseph (arch.) 76, 77, 85, 213, 221

Peachey, William (arch.) 40, 41, 42, 43, 50

Pearson, John: bust 106

Pease, Alfred 42

Peddie, J. M. (arch.) 146

Peebles: line 123

Pembroke & Tenby Railway 245

Pembroke Dock **245**

Penicuick Railway 148

Penrhyndeudraeth: bridge 96

Penrith **117**; Cockermouth Keswick & Penrith Railway *110*, 117

Penrith Castle 117

Pensford Viaduct **234**

Penshurst: slip carriages 195

Penson, T. K. (arch.) 90

Penzance **241**

Perth 117, 124, 137, 149, 151, 157, 158, 161, **162-3**, 170; *see also* Inverness & Perth Junction Railway

Perth & Dunkeld Railway 160

Peterborough 24

Petersfield **204**

Peto, Sir Samuel (contractor) 119

Petre, Lord: and Ingatestone Hall 17

Pick, Frank 127

Pickering 40; Whitby & Pickering Railway 39

Pickersgill, William (loco. eng.) 124, **171**

Piddle River bridge, Wareham **209**

Piercy, Benjamin 92, 96; and Robert 93

piers: Gravesend 187; Holyhead 95; Ryde 206; *see also* ports and harbours

Pimlico, *and* Pimlico Company 184

Pinmore **138**

Pinxton 73

Pitlochry **163**, 168, 172

platforms, distinctive: Eastleigh (swivel bridge for luggage) 203; Heighington (cobbled area at rail level) 44; Kemble (platform only) 224; Manchester Victoria 100; Paddington (lamp platforms) 214; Salisbury (¼ mile apart) 207; Sugar Loaf Tunnel (request platforms) 245; York Road, Kings Cross (detached platform) 14-15

Plockton 167

Plumpton **196**

Plymouth: lines 237, 239, 240

Plymouth Devonport & South Western Railway 239, 240

Pocklington **38**

Polegate 195

Polloc & Govan Railway 136

Poole, Henry: decorations 178

Port Street viaduct, Annan **124**

Portchester Road viaduct, Fareham 203

Porthkerry Viaduct, Barry **243**

Portland Road bridge, Norwood Junction 183

Portpatrick: lines 135, 138

Portpatrick Railway 125

ports and harbours 175, 176; Broughty Ferry 126; Ferryport 126; Fishguard 222, 244; Gravesend 187; Harwich 12, 15; Holyhead 95; Immingham 61; Newhaven 196, 207; Ryde 206

Portsmouth: lines 203; Portsmouth Direct Line 199, 203, 204

Portswood (*later* St. Denys) station 206

posters and postcards 127-8

Poundbury Tunnel, Dorchester **237**

Powys 91-2

'Premier Line' 59, 118; *see also* London & North Western Railway

Preservation and conservation 26-8; *see also* Railway preservation societies

Preston **112**; Park Hotel 112, *140*; Lancaster & Preston Junction Railway 108

Prestwick 139

Primrose Hill: Camden Roundhouse **59**, 65; tunnels (first, built 1837, is the earliest tunnel) **61**

Princes Risborough: line 222

Princes Street, Edinburgh 117, 145-6

Pritchett, James Pigott (arch.) **34-5**

private railway property: Dunrobin station 168-9; Glossop private line 79; *see also* railway preservation societies

Promenade Pier, Ryde **206**

Promenade station, Morecambe **111**

Prosser, Thomas 40, 41, **43**, 49

public house: Blackfriar Public House (Poole's decorations) 178

Pugin, A. W. N. (arch.) 86

pumping station, Starcross **239**

Punch cartoon *8*

push-and-pull trains 224

Pwllheli: lines 94, 243

Q

Quainton Road Junction, Buckinghamshire 11

Quay Street viaduct, Fareham 203

Queen Alexandra Bridge, Sunderland **51**

Queen Square (*later* Green Park), Bath 227

Queen Street, Glasgow 130, **132**

Queen Victoria Street railway viaduct, Blackfriars 178

Queen's Bridge, Irvine **134**

Queen's Hotel, Leeds 36

Queen's Road bridge, Hastings **196**

quoins 248; Blackfriars *178*; Euston 59

R

Radcliffe **102**

railcars (*or* rail motors) 224

Railway Arch, Dean Street, Newcastle-upon-Tyne 50; *for others see* arches

railway bench (Caledonian Railway) *124*

Railway Clearing House, Eversholt House, Euston (*later* Headquarters of LMS) 59

railway headquarters offices 41, 59, 92

'Railway King, The' *see* Hudson, George

railway preservation societies: Bluebell Railway, Sheffield Park *45*, 196; Brechin Railway Society 159; Brunel Engineering Centre Trust 228; Dart Valley Railway 237; Denmark Hill 181; Didcot Railway Centre 218; Lakeside & Haverthwaite Railway 116-7; Monsal Dale Viaduct 85; (New) North Staffordshire Railway 86; Scottish Railway Preservation Society 146, 149; Strathspey Railway 167; Welshpool & Llanfair Railway 92; *see also* museums

railway ramps 181

railway towns 226; *see also* Crewe; Derby; Eastleigh; Swindon; Wolverton

railway village, Swindon **226**; *see also* Swindon

railway works: Gateshead 44-9; Glasgow, St. Rollox Works 124; Inverness, Lochgorm Works 165, 170; Ladybank 152

Rainhill skew bridge (earliest overbridge, 1830) **104**

Rainhill (Locomotive) Trials (1829) 180; Commemoration (1980) *26*, 104, *219*

Ramsden, Sir James (Superintendent) 114, 116

Ramsgate **188**

Ranger, W. (contractor) 229

Rannock 172

Ransomes (agricultural engs., partners of Sir William Cubitt) 193

Rastrick, John Urpeth (eng.) 176, **180**, 185, 194, 195, 197, 198

Ratho **149**

Ravenglass 117; Roman fort 137

Ravensthorpe **36-7**

Reading **216**

Redhill (*formerly* Reigate) Junction 185, 188

Redhill Tunnels, Trent **75**

Redland station footbridge, Bristol **233**

refectory pulpit, Shrewsbury 91, 137

refreshment rooms, Cleethorpes *30*; Swindon (compulsory ten-minute stop) 212

Regent's Canal 16

Reigate (*now* Redhill) Junction 185, 188

Rendel, James M. (eng.) 95

Rennie, John (eng.) 95, 137; George *and* John 65

Renton, Mr.: sculpture on Rannoch station 172

Rewley Road, Oxford *221*

Rhymney Railway *and* Rhymney Ironworks 243

Ribble Bridge, Preston **112**

Ribblehead (Batty Moss) Viaduct *4*, 26, 114

Ricardo, John L. (M.P.) 89

Richardson, Charles (eng.) 234

Richmond, North Yorkshire **38**

Richmond Bridge, London **183**

Riddings Junction *and* Viaduct **125**

Ridgmont **66**

Ringwood Christchurch & Bournemouth Railway 208

River Annan viaduct, Annan **124**

'Ro-Railers': Welcombe Hotel, Stratford-upon-Avon 68
Robert Stephenson & Co. *see* Stephenson, Robert
Roberts, Edward (arch.) 226
Roberts, William 168, 171, 172
Robertsbridge 197; line 188
Robertson, Henry (eng.) 91, 94, 244, 245
Robinson, John G. (eng.) 61
Rochester: line 188
Rogart **173**
roofs of particular interest: Bank Top, Darlington 43; Bath Spa 227; Blackburn 107; Brighton *194*; Bristol Temple Meads 228; Chard Central 236; Euston 59; Glasgow Central 131; Gosport 203; Hebden Bridge 23; North Eastern Railway 43; Paddington 213; Penzance 241; Preston 112; St. Pancras trainshed 62; Slough 217; Victoria 184; Wemyss Bay 142; York NER Headquarters Office 41
Rosendale Road bridge, Herne Hill **182**
Rossett 90
Rosslare, Ireland 242, 244, 245
Rotherham 32
Round Down Cliff, Folkestone: blasting 193
Roundhouse, Camden **59**, 65
Roundhouse, Derby 79
Rowand Anderson, Sir Robert 131
Rowland Brotherhood (contractors) 225
Rowland's Castle 204
Rowsley **85**
Roxburgh 123
Royal Albert Bridge, Saltash 26, 73, *192*, **241**
Royal Border Bridge, Berwick-on-Tweed *27*, **52**, 73
Royal Hotel, Holyhead 95
Royal Hotel (Great Western Royal Hotel), Paddington 213-4
Royal Station Hotel, Hull 31; Royal Station Hotel, Newcastle-upon-Tyne, Central station 49, *141*; Royal Station Hotel, York 40, 140
royalty and railways (ceremonies, journeys, etc.) Albert Edward Bridge 90; Ballater, for Balmoral 164; Berwick Castle 53; Blackfriar Public House 178; Brocklesby 30; Charing Cross Hotel 179; Chepstow 242; Clarence Yard, Isle of Wight 203; Cleethorpes 30; Eleanor Cross, Charing Cross 179; Holyhead 95; Immingham 61; LNWR royal saloon *46*, *47*; Newcastle Central 7, 49; Newcastle High Level Bridge 49-50; Paddington 214; Royal Albert Bridge 241; Ryde Pier (Empress Eugenie) 206; Slough 217; South Western House, Southampton 205; Victoria, London 184; Victoria bridge, Washington, Durham 44; Waterloo, London 184; Windsor Central 207, 217; Windsor & Eton Riverside 177, 203, 207; Wolferton, for Sandringham 15
Roydon **18**
Ruabon 90, **94**
Rugby **67**
Runcorn Bridge **97**
Runcorn Gap (*now* Widnes) 107

Rushton (Glendon & Rushton) 68
Russell, F. V. (draughtsman) 24
Russell, Sam: engravings 76
Rutherglen: line 136
Ryde **206**
Rye *185*, **197**

S

St. Andrews: line 152
St. Annes Park tunnel, Bristol **233**
St. Blazey engine shed, Par **240**
St. Boswells, Kelso 123
St. Botolphs, Colchester 17
St. Davids, Exeter **238**
St. Denys (*formerly* Portswood) **206**
St. Enoch, Glasgow 130, 138
St. Enoch Hotel, Glasgow 131
St. Germains Level Crossing House, Longniddry **148**
St. Germans 241; Viaduct **240**
St. Helens: bridges **107**
St. Helens & Runcorn Gap Railway 107
St. Ives: Tregenna Castle Hotel *141*, **241**
St. James's Bridge, Bath 227
St. John's Road, Ryde 206
St. Leonards Warrior Square **197**
St. Mark's Church, Swindon 226
St. Marks, Lincoln **23**
St. Michael's, Liverpool **106**
St. Pancras 14, 25-6, *28*, **62-3**, 69, 78, 140, *154-5*; counterparts in Manchester and Liverpool 99; Midland Grand Hotel 62-3, 140, *141*; tunnel 63; water tower 62, *63*
St. Pinnock Viaduct **240**
St. Rollox Works, Glasgow 124
St. Thomas's Hospital: moved 179
St. Thomas, Exeter **238**
Salford *28*, **99-101**
Salisbury **208**, 221
Salisbury & Yeovil Railway 208
Saltash 240; Royal Albert Bridge 26, 73, *192*, **241**
Saltburn **41-2**
Saltcoats **138**
Sanders, J. H. (arch.) 35, 227
Sanderson, William, and 'Anerley' 177
Sandon **88-9**
Sandon Hall 88-9
Sandown: signal box *190*
Sandringham 15
Sankey Viaduct (earliest masonry viaduct, 1830) **104**
Scarborough (earliest medium terminus station still in use, *and* earliest terminus tramshed still in use, 1845) **38**, 40
Scarborough & Whitby Railway 39
Science Museum, London: signal box 191
Scotscalder 173
Scott, Sir George Gilbert (arch.) 62-3, *141*, 226
Scott, J. R. (arch.) 184, 196
Scottish Central Railway 149, 150, 158, 160, 163, 170
Scottish Midland Junction Railway 158, 161
Scottish North Eastern Railway 160
Scottish Railway Preservation Society 146, 149
Scottish Region 120-73; listed properties

251-2
Seahorse, at Carlisle *116*
Seascale: water tower **118**
Sedbergh **118**
Selby **39**
Sellafield 117
Settle 114, 191
Settle & Carlisle Line 113, **114**, 115, *190*, 191
Sevenoaks Railway 186
Severn Tunnel **234**
Shakespeare Tunnel, Dover *176*, **186**, 193
Shankend Viaduct 123
Shap 8-9, 83, 97, 137
share certificates *222*, *243*
Shaw, Matthew T. (iron founders) 215
Shaw, Richard Norman 60, 209
Sheffield **32**; *see also* Manchester Sheffield & Lincolnshire Railway
Sheffield & Rotherham Railway 32
Sheffield Ashton-under-Lyne & Manchester Railway 32, 65, 79, 97, 98, 103, 104
Sheffield Park: Bluebell Railway *45*, 196
'The Shell', on Glasgow Central 131
Shelmerdine, Henry (arch.) 99, 105
Shillamill Viaduct **239**
Shoreditch (*later* Bishopsgate Goods station) 13
Shoreham: line 194
Shotts: line 148
Shrewsbury, 15th and 16th Earls 86
Shrewsbury **90-1**, 191, 245
Shrewsbury Abbey: refectory pulpit 91, 137
Shrewsbury & Birmingham Railway 72, 90
Shrewsbury & Chester Railway 90, 94, 96
Shrewsbury & Hereford Railway 90, 222
Shropshire **90-1**
Shropshire Union Railways 90
Shrub Hill, Worcester *81*, 223
Shugborough Park **86-7**
signals and signal boxes *190*, 191, 211, 248; electropneumatic 52 (NER), 101 (LYR), 203 (LSWR); locations: Aberdeen 164; Caledonian Canal swing bridges 167, 168; Carlisle 116; Gosport electric telegraph 203; Ladybank 152; Perth 163; Reading 216; St. Pancras 63; Shrewsbury 90, 91; Sugar Loaf Tunnel 245; Waterloo 203; Welsh queues of locomotives 243
Simpson & Wilson (engs.) 167, 169, 171
Sinclair, Robert (loco. superintendent) 15, 21
Sirhowy Valley 242
Skerne Bridge, Darlington (earliest masonry underbridge, 1825) **42-3**
Skipton *27*, 35, **113**
Skye 168
Slamannan & Bo'ness Railway 149
Slateford Viaduct, Edinburgh **147**
slip carriages: East Croydon, from Eastbourne, and at Etchingham 195
Slochd **173**
Slough **217**
Snardale Viaduct 114
Smirke, Sir Robert (arch.) 116
Smirke, Sidney (arch.) 117
Smith, George (arch.) 178, 181

Smith, Williams (eng.) 96
Somerset 235-6
Somerset & Dorset Joint Railway 227
Sonning Cutting (road) bridge 240
South Devon & Tavistock Railway **240**
South Devon Railway 238, 239, 240
South Durham & Lancashire Union Railway 157
South Eastern & Chatham Railway 175, 184, **185,** 188, 193, 200
South Eastern Railway 14, 61, 176, 178, 179, 184, **185,** 186, 187, 188, 200; bridges 179, 196; competition 185, 187; Cubitt's work 193; Southern House, Dover 186; stations 178, 179, 181, 184 (*at* Waterloo), 185, 187, 188, 194, 195, 196, 197, 200; tunnel 186
South Glamorgan 243
South Shields **50**
South Staffordshire Railway 88
South Wales Railway 240, 242, 243
South Western House (*formerly* South Western Hotel), Southampton **205**
South Yorkshire 32
Southall **215**
Southampton 176, 203, **205**; Terminus (earliest medium terminus station, 1839-40) 117, **205**; *see also* London & Southampton Railway
Southampton & Dorchester Railway 209
Southborough Viaduct (near Tonbridge) 188, *193*
Southend 13, 187
Southern House, Dover **186**
Southern Railway **175**, 183, *219*, 237; Isle of Wight fares 206; Southern House, Dover 186; stations 188, 194, 195, 196
Southern Region 174-209; listed properties 252; stations of GWR: 216 (Mortimer), 217 (Staines West)
Southsea: line 203
Spa Road bridge, London Bridge **182**
Spean Bridge 172
Spey Viaduct, Dalvey 170
Spey Viaduct, Newtonmore **172**
Speymouth Viaduct **166**
Spital Hill (*or* Bridgehouses) Tunnel 32
Springfield **152-7**
Springwood Junction 35
Sprouston **123**
Stable block, Glasgow **133-4**
staff 26, *220*; Aberdeen 164; Box Tunnel 224; Derby locomotive works 79; Friog Rocks line, watchman 92-3; Horwich Mechanics' Institute 99; Kilsby Tunnel 69; Maldon East (politics) 17-18; Midland Railway 69; Rannoch: navvies carved sculpture 172; St. Germains level crossing 148; St. Pancras (sculptures of railwaymen *and* working conditions) 63; Settle & Carlisle Line (shanty towns) 114; Sugar Loaf Tunnel (request stop) 245; Swindon and other railway towns 226; Taff Vale Case (politics) 243; Thomas Brassey, contractors 119; Winton Square 89; Woodhead Tunnel 103
Staffordshire 86-9
Staines West **217**
Stamford: East station **24-9**; Town station **24**, *29*, *219*

Stamford & Essendine Railway 24, 29
Standedge Tunnel 57, **103**
Stanley: line 160
Stansby, J. B. (arch.) 59
Starcross pumping station **239**
stately homes and railways: Audley End 16; Brocklesby Park 30; Burleigh House 29; Charlton House 89; Chatsworth (Rowsley) 85; Clumber Park 23; Cressington Park Estate 106; Holker Hall, Cark 115; Ingatestone Hall 17; Kemble (Robert Gordon) 224; Lullingstone Roman Villa 186; Manor House Hotel 239; Sandon Hall 88; Shugborough Park 86-7; Stivichall 72; Stratfield Saye 217; Trentham Hall 86; Woburn 66; *see also* castles
Station and Midland Hotel, Derby 78-9
Station Hotels at Aberdeen 164; Ayr 125-6; Inverness 170; Newcastle-upon-Tyne 49, *141*; Perth 163
stations
    earliest stations (in chronological order): earliest *surviving* small stations, Heighington 44, *and* Stockton-on-Tees 42 (both c. 1825); earliest small station *still in use*, Edge Hill (1836) 104; earliest medium station, Kilmarnock (1843) 135; earliest large stations, Carlisle Citadel 116 *and* Huddersfield 34 (both 1847); earliest *surviving* small terminus, Manchester Liverpool Road (1830) 104; earliest small terminus *still in use* Cardiff Bute Road (c. 1840) 243; earliest *surviving* medium termini, Bristol Temple Meads 228 *and* Southampton 205 (both 1839-40); earliest medium terminus *still in use*, Scarborough (1845) 38; earliest large terminus, Kings Cross (1852) 14-15
    other stations of particular importance or interest: Bolton (modernised) 98; Cark (sold cockles) 115; Clarence Yard (private) 203; Cupar 151; Earlestown (decoration) 103; Exchange, Liverpool ('joint') 105-6; Frome 236; Glasgow Central 131; GWR Brunel standard small Tudor 218; Hamilton Square (underground) 103; Heighington 44; Horsted Keynes (legal obligation, four trains a day) 196; Inverness 170; Lincoln 23; LYR Tudor 98; LSWR 205; Liverpool Road, Manchester (oldest purpose-built) 104; Victoria *and* Exchange, Manchester (connected by common platform) 100-1; Midland Railway small stations 73, 75; Mytholmroyd (narrow) 36; LNWR (Ravensthorpe, etc.) 36-7; Newcastle Central 49; North Staffordshire Tudor 86; Preston (trains altered direction without reversing) 112; Queen Street, Glasgow 132; Reading 216, *and* Slough 217 (one-sided double stations); Shrewsbury 90-1; SR 'Southern Electric' 183; Stirling (flowers) 124, 150; Victoria, London (height restricted, etc.) 184; Waterloo, London 184; Wemyss Bay 142; Wingfield 85; Wolverhampton (converted from carriage entrance of town) 73; wooden buildings, south of England

196, 218, 239; Worthing Old station 198
statues *see* art works
steam and coal *see* coal and steam
steamers *see* ferries and steamers
Steamtown 108
Stephens, John: Tregenna Castle Hotel 241
Stephenson, George (Robert's father) 46, **65,** 69, 73, 75, 76, 79, 99, 103, 108; and Locke 97; *Locomotion* 42, 44; Manchester & Leeds Railway 234; narrow gauge 246; trademark, on cornice 75, 79
Stephenson, Robert 7, 8-9, 16, 50, 69, **73,** 241; bridges 49, 52, 64, 65, 66, 69, 73, *84*, 86, (tubular bridges) **95;** LNWR 118; Roundhouse, Camden 59; stations 49, 96, 117; statue 59; tunnels 61, 64, (Kilsby Tunnel) *11*, **69,** 73, 103, 224
Stepney East viaduct **16**
Stevenson, Francis (eng.) 105
Stevenson, J. J. 209
Steventon **221**
Stewarton **138**
Stirling, James (loco. eng.) 185
Stirling, Patrick (loco. eng.) 21
Stirling 124, **150,** 191; bridges 150
Stirlingshire Midland Junction Railway 150
Stivichall, Coat of Arms Bridge **72**
Stockport Disley & Whaley Bridge Railway 76
Stockport **102-3**
Stockton & Darlington Railway 12, 41, 42-3, 44, 46, 52, 157
Stockton & Hartlepool Railway 185
Stockton-on-Tees 43; 48-56 Bridge Road (earliest small station – with Heighington, c. 1825) **42**
Stoke-on-Trent **89**
Stokes, G. H. (arch.) 77
Stone **89**
Stonebridge Park **64**
Stonegate 197
Stonehaven **166**
Stonehenge 137
Stour Valley Railway 16, 17
Stowmarket **22**
Stranraer 135
Stratfield Saye *and* Maidenhead 217
Stratford, London 16, 24
Stratford-upon-Avon **68**
Strathclyde 125-30
Strathspey Railway 164-5
Strood **188**
Stroud **224**
Stroudley, William (loco. eng.) 207
Sturrock, Archibald (eng.) 21
suburban services: electric traction 60, 101; Edinburgh 145, 146; Liverpool Merseyrail 105; Liverpool suburban stations 106; LSWR 203; Scotland 130, 131, 132, 147
subways 216; Hebden Bridge 34; Victoria, Manchester, 100; Paddington (for staff only) 214; Salisbury (between two platforms ¼ mile apart) 208
Sudbury 16
Suffolk 20-22
Sugar Loaf Tunnel 244, **245**
Sugden, William (arch.) 86

Summit Tunnel, Littleborough **99**
Sunderland 43, **50-1**
Surbiton (*formerly* Kingston) **183**
Surrey 199-200
Surrey Dining Room, Waterloo 184
Surrey Iron Railway (first public railway in the world) 183
Surtees, R. (loco. eng.) 185
Sutherland & Caithness Railway 170, 173
Sutherland Railway 169, 170, 173
Sutherland, 1st and 2nd Dukes: Duke of Sutherland's Railway 167, 168, 169; Dunrobin 168-9; 2nd Duke 169
Swanage: line 209
Swannington 115
Swansea 69, 91, 240, 244, 245
Swanwick, Frederick (eng.) 32
Swaythling **205**
Swindon 212, 222, 224, **226**, 240
Sydney Gardens, Bath *84*, 227
Sydney Road bridge, *and* retaining walls, Bath 227
Sylranger, J. W. (eng.) 239
Syston & Peterborough Railway 24
Szlumper, Alfred Weeks (eng.) 184, 188

T

Taff Vale Railway 243
Tain **173**
Talerddig Cutting **93**
tank traps, Christchurch 137
Tarbolton **138-9**
Tarrasfoot Viaduct, Langholm **125**
Tattenham Corner **200**
Taunton 191, **236**
Tavistock 239, 240; Tavistock Viaduct **239**
Tay Bridge (first, collapsed 1879) 42, 102, 143, 144, **157**; (second, opened 1887) 143, **157**
Tay viaduct, Perth 161
Taynuilt **126**
Tayside 158-63
Tees Valley Railway 37
Telford, Thomas (eng.) 73, 94, 95, 167, 168, 170
Templand Viaduct, Old Cumnock **137**
Temple Meads, Bristol (earliest medium terminus station *and* earliest terminus trainshed, 1839-40) 227, **228**, 232
Tenby **245**
Terminus, Southampton 117, **205**
Tetbury Road, Kemble 224
Teviot Viaduct, Roxburgh 123
Thames & Medway Canal (*later* South Eastern Railway) 188
Thetford **22-3**
Thirsk: *see* Leeds & Thirsk Railway
Thompson, Francis (arch.) 16, 17, 18, 57, 75, 76, 78-9, **85**, 95, 96
Thurgarton 75
Thurso **173**; lines 166-7, 169, 170
tickets *21, 24, 181*, 219, *222*; bicycle *219*; dog *220*; luggage label 203, *222*
Tilbury 13, 187
Tilt Viaduct, Blair Atholl **158**, *159*
timetables *220*
Tite, Sir William (arch.) 8, **117**, 146; hotel 105, stations 108, 116, 117, 125, 162-3, 177, 182, 199, 203-8 *passim*, 236

Tithebarn Street, Liverpool (East Lincolnshire Railway; called Exchange station by LYR) 105-6
Toad Moor Tunnel, Ambergate 75
Todmorden: Gauxholme Viaduct 83, 108
Tomatin **173**
Tonbridge (*formerly* Tunbridge): line 188
Torbay 237
Torre (*originally* Torquay) **239**
Totley Tunnel **103**
Totnes 239
town pier, Gravesend 187
Town station, Stamford 24, 29, *219*
towpath, Hincaster Tunnel 117
trainsheds 26
  earliest (in chronological order): earliest arched, *and* – with Frome – earliest through trainshed *still in use*, Newcastle Central (1850) 49; earliest *surviving* terminus trainshed, Temple Meads, Bristol (1839-40) 228; earliest terminus *still in use*, Scarborough (1845) 38; earliest *surviving* through trainshed, Newtyle Old station (1836) 162; earliest through trainshed *still in use*, Frome – with Newcastle Central – *and* earliest wooden trainshed (1850) 236
  other significant trainsheds: Brighton *27*, *128*; Haymarket, Edinburgh 146; St. Pancras *62*; Thurso *173*; Windsor & Eton Riverside 207; wooden, Brunel 231
tramways
  earliest *surviving* tramway viaduct: Laigh Milton Mill (1812) 130; earliest tramway viaduct *still in use*, Kings Mill (1819) 73; Bristol 228; canal feeder tramways, Butterley Company, Derbyshire 62; Haverthwaite 116-7; Sirhowy Valley 242
Transhipment Shed, Didcot **218**
Tredegar **242**
Tregenna Castle Hotel, St. Ives *141*, **241**
Trent **75**
Trent Lane bridge, Great Haywood 87
Trent Valley Railway 66, 86
Trentham *and* Trentham Hall 86
Tress, William 193, 194, 195, 197
'Tri-junct' station (Derby) 78-9
Tring Cutting *64*
Troon 130, **139**
Trowsdale, Jackson and Garbutt (contractors) 42
Trubshaw, Charles (arch.) 32, 69, 70, 99
Truro: lines 240, 241
Tulloch 172
Tunbridge: Tunbridge Wells Central *and* Tunbridge Wells West (*both formerly called* Tunbridge Wells) 188
tunnels: earliest, Primrose Hill (1837) 61; other significant tunnels: Box 224-5, 232; Cowlairs incline (rope-hauled trains) 130, 132; Great Western through Bath 227; Higham canal tunnel, Strood (first improvised for trains) 188; Kilsby 69, 73, 103, 224; Kemble (bribery) 224; Poundbury (avoids Iron Age fort) 237; Severn 234; Summit 99; tunnel mouths: Dunkeld 160; Hamilton 134; Killiecrankie 161; Old Mill of Keir 149-50; *see also* accidents

Turnberry hotel **139**
Turner, F. T. (eng.) 182
Tussaud's, Madame: Royalty and Railways Exhibition, Windsor Central 217
Tweedmouth: line 123
Twerton 227
Tyndrum 126, 172
Tyne & Wear 44-51, 52
Tyne & Wear Metro 50, 51
Tynemouth **51**

U

Ulverston **25**, **118**
Ulverstone & Lancaster Railway 115
underground 8, 127, 137, 185, 194; Circle Line (London Transport) 14, 185; City and South London (first tube railway) 185; Glasgow Central Railway 136; Kings Cross 14; *see also* Metropolitan Railway
Underwood, John (eng.) 68
Underwood Road bridge, Paisley 137
Uphill **234**
Urie, R. W. (loco. eng.) 203

V

Vale of Glamorgan Railway 243
viaducts *see* bridges and viaducts
Victoria, London **184**, 185
Victoria, Manchester *26*, 28, **100-1**
Victoria, Nottingham 74
Victoria Station & Pimlico Railway Co. 184
Victoria Viaduct, Carlisle **116**
Victory Arch, Waterloo 184
Vignoles, Charles Blacker (eng.) 8, **65**, 67, 75, 97, 103, 107, 115
Virginia Water: line 199

W

Wadhurst 197
wagon hoists 35, 240
Wainwright, H. S. (loco. superintendent) 185
waiting room: Battle *194*
Wakefield Kirkgate **37**
Walker, Sir Herbert 183
Walker, T. A. (contractor) 234
Walkerburn 123
Walkham Viaduct, near Tavistock 240
Wallis, H. E. (arch.) 194
walls: Conwy Castle 95; Great Western through Bath *84*, 227; at head of Lion Well Wynd, Linlithgow *148*; NER tiled wall maps 50; Swindon, Bristol Street wall *and* London Street wall 226; Windsor & Eton Riverside 207; York City walls 41
Wanlockhead Viaduct, Leadhills **136**
Wansford **19**
Wapping Tunnel 65, 104
war (World Wars 1 and 2); effect on railways 44, 61, 143, 161, 163, 184, 200; bridges 144, 157; Glasgow Central's 'The Shell', collecting place 131; horses at Ormskirk *112*; tank traps, Christchurch 137; troop movements *156*, 203
war damage: bridges 179, 195; hotels 178-

9, 205; stations 15, 41, 78, *109*, 115, 178, 179, *181*, 205
war memorials: GER, Liverpool Street 16; GWR, Paddington 214-5; Highland Railway, Inverness 170; LNWR, Euston 59; LSWR, Waterloo 184; Midland Railway, Derby 79; NER, York 41; North British, Waverley 146; North Staffordshire Railway 89; Perth General Station Joint Staff 164
Wareham **209**
Wareham Bridge 208
warehouses and goods sheds: earliest goods shed, Liverpool Road, Manchester (1830) 104; Ambergate 75; Castle station, Northampton 70; Chippenham 225; Clegg Street Goods Warehouse, Oldham 102; Crutched Friars, Fenchurch Street 13; Cupar 151; Deansgate Goods station, Manchester 99; Glasgow (GSWR) 133; Heaton Norris Goods Warehouse, Stockport 102-3; Helpston Goods Shed 18; Huddersfield Goods Yard Buildings 34-5; Manchester 99, 104; Salisbury Goods Shed 208; Selby Old station 39; Stroud Goods Shed 224; Wareham Old Goods Shed 209; Warrington Goods Warehouse 98; Wellingborough Goods Shed (hand cranes) 70; Wymondham 23
Warrington 97, **98**, lines 222
Warriston Road bridge, Edinburgh **147**
Warwickshire 66-8
Washington, Durham **44**
watchman, on Friog Rocks line 92-3
water tanks: for atmospheric railway 239; for station lifts 178
water towers: Haltwhistle 54, *55*; St. Pancras 62, *63*; Seascale 118
water troughs, in tunnels 57
Waterhouse, Alfred (arch.) 105
Wateringbury 185, **188-93**
Waterloo, Aberdeen 164
Waterloo, London *156*, **184**
Waterloo tunnel *and* dock, Liverpool 104
Waterside Viaduct, Sedbergh **118**
Watford 60, **64**
Watkin, Sir Edward 30, 61, 94
Waverley, Edinburgh 143, 145, **146**
Wealdstone 60
Wear Bridge, Sunderland **50**
weathervanes 79, 91
Weaver Viaduct, Dutton **97**
Wedgwood, Josiah: statue 89
Weightman & Hadfield (archs.) 24
Welcombe Hotel, Stratford-upon-Avon **68**
Wellingborough **70**
Wellington, Duke of 216
Wellington 90
Wellington, Leeds 36

Welsh railway companies **243**
Welsh's Bridge, Inverness 191
Welshpool **90**, 92, 243
Welshpool & Llanfair Railway 92
Welwyn Garden City **20**
Welwyn (*or* Digswell) Viaduct **20**
Wemyss Bay **142**
Wendon (*now* Audley End) 16
West Cliff, Whitby 39, 40
West Cornwall Railway **240**, 241
West Glamorgan 243
West Highland Extension Railway (North British Railway) 167, 169, 171, **172**
West Highland Railway 125, 136, **172**
West Kilbride **142**
West Midlands 72-3
West station, Dorchester 208
West Sussex 197-8
West Yorkshire 32-7, *219*
Western Region 210-45; listed properties 252-3
Westfield **149**
Westhumble (Boxhill & Westhumble) **199**, *202*
Westland: Blyth & Westland (archs.) 146, 166
Weston-super-Mare **235**
Wetheral Viaduct 54
Weybridge: line 199
Whaley Bridge 76
Whalley Viaduct **112-3**
Wharncliffe, Lord 213
Wharncliffe Viaduct, Hanwell **213**
Wheatley, Thomas (arch.) 111
whisky 133, 146
Whitby (*later* Whitby Town) **39-40**
Whitby & Pickering Railway 39
Whitchurch: line 243
Whitelegg, Robert (loco. eng.) 135
Whitland: line 245
Whitstable 185, **193**
Whittall, Richard (arch.) 200
Whittington 90
Wick: line 166-7, 169, 170
Wicker Arches, Sheffield 32
Wicker Bridge, Sheffield 32
Widnes (*formerly* Runcorn Gap) 107
Wild, C. H. (arch.) 96
Willington Dene Viaduct, Newcastle-upon-Tyne **50**
Wilmcote **68**
Wilson: Simpson & Wilson (engs.) 167, 169, 171
Wilson, Edward (eng./arch.) **15**, 223
Wilson, Sir Henry 16
Wilson, John (eng.) 15, 22
Wilts Somerset & Weymouth Railway 208, 225, 236, *237*
Wiltshire, Southern Region 208; Western Region 224-6

Wimbledon & Croydon Railway 183
Winchester to Basingstoke (LSWR) 204
Windmill Bridge, Southall **215**
Windsor & Eton Central (GWR; earliest iron underbridge *still in use*, 1849) 184, 207, *210*, 214, **217**
Windsor & Eton Riverside (LSWR) 177, 203, **207**
Windsor Castle 207, 217
Windsor (*also called* North station) *at* Waterloo, London 184
Wingfield **85**
Winton Square, Stoke-on-Trent **89**
Witley 204
Woburn 66
Woburn Sands **66**
Woking to Basingstoke: signals 203
Wolferton (royal station for Sandringham) 15
Wolverhampton 15, **72-3**, 218
Wolverton 225
Wolverton Viaduct **66**
Wood, John (arch.) 241
Wood, Nicholas (eng.) 73
Wood, Sancton (arch.) 13, 16, 18, 20, 24, 85
Woodhead Tunnel 97, **103**
Woodhouse, Thomas Jackson (eng.) 67, 75
Woolston **206**
Worcester 15, *81*, 218, 223
Worcester & Hereford Railway 222
Workington: line 117
Worksop **23**
Worth Valley *219*
Worthing **198**
Wrexham: line 94
Wyatt, Sir Matthew Digby 213, 226, 228, 232
Wye Bridge, Chepstow **242**
Wylam 54, 191
Wymondham **23**

Y

Yarm Viaduct **92**
Yatton **235**
York *11*, **40-1**, 43, 49; National Railway Museum **45-8**, 50, 52, 180, 185, 203, 207, *220*; Railway Headquarters Office 12, **41**
York & North Midland Railway 30, 31, 37, 38, 39, 40
York Newcastle & Berwick Railway 49, 50, 52, **123**
York Old Station Hotel (*now* West Offices) **40-1**
York Road: detached platform of Kings Cross 14-15
Yorkshire: *see* Lancashire & Yorkshire Railway